FIRST COLONY OMNIBUS

BOOKS 8 - 10

KEN LOZITO

ACOUSTICAL BOOKS LLC

Published by Acoustical Books, LLC

KenLozito.com

IF YOU WOULD LIKE TO BE NOTIFIED WHEN MY NEXT BOOK IS RELEASED VISIT

WWW.KENLOZITO.COM

ISBN: 978-1-945223-67-9

PROLOGUE

A n excerpt from the colonial archives: *The First Generation of the Colony:*
The *Ark* program was Earth's most ambitious effort to establish an interstellar colony in a star system twenty-five light-years away. The *Ark* was comprised of one massive ship and over a hundred automated support ships. To survive the long journey, all colonists were put into stasis and were monitored by the *Ark's* computer systems.

Communications with Earth were maintained through the deep space buoy network, which bolstered data transmissions to the *Ark*. As the *Ark* traveled through interstellar space, auto-factories built comms buoys designed to send and receive data communications from Earth.

Unbeknown to the colonists, the *Ark* received a massive update to its computer systems which overrode the core mission parameters. This included a new destination much farther away along with protocols for the automated ships to continue to gather resources on the long journey. What started out as an eighty-five-year journey, took over two hundred years to complete. The colonists woke to a star system approximately sixty light-years from Earth.

Due to limitations of the *Ark's* computer systems, detailed data received from Earth was expunged, leaving the colonists with limited insight as to what happened. Communications were limited to the speed of light, so the colonists could expect to wait a hundred and twenty years for a response from Earth. However, the *Ark's* powerful sensors monitored Earth's star system throughout its long journey. Analysis of the data revealed that some kind of calamity had befallen the Earth and the entire solar system.

Fragmented data received from Earth referred to a virus outbreak that lead to a massive war between Earth and local colonies. The virus, known as the Vemus, altered human physiology and all mammalian life on Earth. The data received from Earth included references to a massive fleet of ships. Analysis of the deep space buoy network revealed that the buoys had gone offline sequentially, beginning with those closest to Earth. It was theorized that what had happened to Earth was now in route to the colony. It was later determined that the deep space buoy network was destroyed by the Vemus fleet.

Vemus Wars: Detailed references to the Vemus Wars can be found in the colonial archives under the *Nemesis* volumes.

Colonial Defense Force: Commonly referred to as CDF, is the colonial military established to protect the colony. There were many colonists involved with the creation of the CDF, but the most influential colonist regarding its origins is General Connor Gates.

New Earth: Three hundred thousand colonists were brought out of stasis and began exploring the planet that would ultimately be named New Earth. The first generation of colonists created a home on a planet teeming with life. There was also archeological evidence of an advanced civilization similar to humans. However, since the colonists hadn't found any intelligent species currently inhabiting the planet, it was widely believed that whoever had built the cities abandoned the planet, or had wiped themselves out through multiple global wars.

Post Vemus War exploration lead to the discovery that the intelligent species, now known as Ovarrow, had not left the planet, but had gone into stasis in underground bunkers found across the main continent. Detailed references to these discoveries can be found under the *We're Not Alone: Discovery* volumes in these archives.

Ovarrow stasis technology is inferior to those used by humans. This lead to severe illness and rapid aging experienced by some Ovarrow when brought out of stasis. Colonial scientists helped the Ovarrow overcome many of these issues, but the effects of inferior stasis technology still significantly impacts their species.

It is impossible to reference the Ovarrow without also referencing a species known as the Krake. The Krake are a technologically advanced civilization who discovered the use of gateway technology that allowed them to explore the multiverse. Through the use of Spacegates and Arch Gateways (On planets), the Krake were able to explore different versions of their star system across multiple universes.

The colony strives to maintain a peaceful coexistence with all Ovarrow factions on New Earth, but as the colony grows, so do some divisions that believe the colony should limit its interactions with any Ovarrow, whether they be the Mekaal or the Konus. There are factions among the Ovarrow who promote the idea that the colonists are invaders and have no right to live on the planet.

General Connor Gates, a founding member of the CDF, was instrumental in defeating the Vemus, and has proven to be tough but fair in his dealings with Ovarrow. His actions throughout the colony's brief history are still studied by future officers in the Colonial Defense Force as well as various universities that study interspecies diplomacy.

FRACTURE

CHAPTER 1

Winter was officially over, but Connor could still feel it on the gust of wind that brushed past his face. He was farther north, well away from any colonial settlements. After hiking to the top of a hill, he turned to where the fragmented remnants of an ancient Ovarrow city disappeared into the glistening undergrowth. He wondered if any of the Ovarrow who'd been brought out of stasis remembered what the city had been like before the ice age. Probably not, and he supposed that could be a blessing, but he doubted it.

He didn't have to be there. Several teams of CDF soldiers were scouting locations for Ovarrow settlements beyond what had already been discovered, but Connor enjoyed getting away. His years on New Earth had awakened a burgeoning desire to explore every inch of it. Humanity's first interstellar colony world was a wondrous mix of mammalian life, some of which appeared familiar, while others were so strange that in light of recent events, scientists had begun to theorize whether those life-forms had evolved on this planet at all. Discovering alien technology that allowed for travel between universes tended to turn some of the mysteries of New Earth on their heads. Regardless, New Earth was humanity's only home and was as dangerous as it was awe-inspiring.

Connor activated his combat-enabled multipurpose protection suit. The MPS series twelve had recently been approved for military use as an alternative to the heavy Nexstar-powered armor. The nanosuit had several modes of operation and could double as a heavy layer of clothing. Once the nanosuit was in combat mode, the onboard AI integrated with Connor's neural implants and could operate in a variety of modes to protect him.

The helmet extended from the ring around Connor's neck, covering his head and seamlessly attaching to the front. The highly advanced suit of armor was capable of protecting him from everything but the heaviest ordnance—a long way from the prototype he'd used nearly two years earlier.

The helmet's internal heads-up display showed the location of the recon drones the survey team was using to map out the area. They were particularly interested in whether there were any hidden bunkers that might contain Ovarrow in stasis pods, but Connor already knew there was very little chance of that. He and Lenora had scouted this area over a year ago. There'd been no stasis pods then, and there probably weren't any now. However, it didn't hurt to take one last look before offering the area up as a potential Ovarrow settlement site so they could rebuild their civilization.

Connor activated the stealth field and took off at a run. Doubtless, the CDF soldier monitoring him was currently alerting his superior that General Connor Gates had suddenly disappeared from their scanners. Eventually— probably seconds from now—they'd alert Samson, who'd lead his team to track Connor down.

Connor couldn't do anything about the impact his footprints had on the low-lying shrubs he ran through. The MPS wasn't able to fly. What it *could* do was enable Connor to run as fast as a rover could cover ground at top speed. Nanorobotic actuators were specifically aligned to his body type, which allowed him to move almost effortlessly. He was required to exert minimal effort to initiate movement, but then the suit took over. The new series twelve MPSs were in short supply and were restricted to select Spec Ops platoons, but Connor planned to expand their usage.

He bolted toward a nearby grove of trees and launched himself into the air. Using his momentum to swing around near the top of the tree, he changed directions. Samson's team would have a *little* bit of difficulty tracking him, but he couldn't make it too easy for them. He kept this up until he'd left the grove behind.

An alert flashed on his internal heads-up display, and then a live video feed appeared from one of the reconnaissance drones that had been scouting the outlying areas northwest of his position. Several warning indicators appeared on the HUD, and a solitary screech pierced the air, carrying a deadly promise to anyone within earshot.

Ryklars.

Answering ryklar calls sounded from farther away. There was always more than one of them. The recon drone was just under five hundred meters away, but the ryklars were much closer.

Ryklars were New Earth predators that had been genetically enhanced by the Ovarrow. Controlled with high-frequency sound waves, they'd been used as weapons of war. They were pack hunters, and a pack could reach sizes of a hundred or more.

Connor had seen them coordinate their hunting efforts before and had even been on the receiving end. Ryklars had highly acute senses, but that wasn't what made them exemplary hunters. They were capable of running at speeds that rivaled old Earth's cheetahs, but they could sustain it for much longer. They had spotted fur on their backs and arms, which made them difficult to detect in grassland and forested areas. They also had the ability to conceal their body heat. Colonial scientists had determined that ryklars had been genetically enhanced to give them this ability. In addition, their claws were capable of tearing through battle steel. Over the years since the colonists had lived on New Earth, they'd increased the armor capability of all their vehicles with ryklars in mind.

Connor knew the MPS specs inside out. In theory, it could resist a ryklar attack, but he didn't want to test that; however, he *was* curious to see just how close he could get to the pack while avoiding detection.

He slowed his pace so he could move as quietly as possible, careful to check the area in front of him, and only the spongy crunching of dead leaves and twigs marked his passing. The closer he'd gotten to the ryklars, the louder their screeches had become. This was a big pack. He was certain he could outrun them if it came down to it, and he began to wonder what all the fuss was about. Ryklars were fairly predictable when not under Ovarrow influence, and they'd even displayed complex social structures that hinted at a species on the verge of an evolutionary leap.

Connor checked the recon drone's scan data. There were no Ovarrow signals that would activate any of the ryklars' latent protocols, some of which included the clean-sweep protocol that forced the ryklars to kill all living creatures found in Ovarrow cities. This meant that whatever was happening with the ryklars now was a natural occurrence from within the pack.

He slowed down even more and crept his way forward, using the blooming shrubbery as cover and automatically checking the holster for his weapon. The heavy-gauge pistol carried lethal darts capable of bringing down a ryklar at close range, and he also carried a combat knife. He wasn't equipped to fight hundreds of ryklars, but it was enough of a deterrence should the need arise.

With the MPS stealth mode enabled, Connor blended in with his surroundings. The MPS computer used images of the surrounding area and projected them in a holographic field around him. This technology wasn't new, but it had never been used on a weapon system that had such a small footprint. The MPS was essentially wearable armor that could double as clothing.

Connor angled his approach so he could keep the high ground, giving him the best vantage point from which to observe the ryklars. He eased his way through the shrubs, resisting the urge to crawl on the ground in order to remain hidden. He didn't have to do that, but "old habits die hard," as the saying went. Connor crouched and watched as the spotted predators gathered around a smaller group of ryklars where most of the noise was coming from.

At the center was a ryklar whose spotted golden hide showed streaks of gray and old battle scars acquired throughout its long life. It had its two front arms in front of it, and its secondary, longer, thickly muscled arms were off to the sides, but its overall countenance was as impassive as a ryklar could look. The tips of the stubby tentacles on its lower face were blood red, indicating that despite outward appearances, the ryklar was becoming agitated. Five younger ryklars were darting in toward the older one in a feigned attack and then quickly changing course at the last minute. Several others also tried to dart in.

Connor focused on the veteran, and the MPS filtered out the others. A deep growl rumbled from its chest. The gray veteran ryklar was the pack leader, and it was being challenged.

Connor spotted a large shape out of the corners of his eyes, and he went still. The breath caught in his throat, but he didn't want to risk turning his head toward it. Instead, he used the MPS cameras to show him a video feed of the area next to him and caught the faint outline of something brushing against the shrubs.

"I didn't want to startle you, General," Samson said quietly, his voice coming through the speakers in Connor's helmet.

"I have to say, you found me a lot faster than I thought you would."

"It would've taken longer if it were someone else," Samson replied without offering any further explanation.

Samson was a former Ghost, an elite special forces platoon from the old NA Alliance Military. They'd known each other for a long time and were friends, despite the falling out they'd had since they were both shanghaied to join the colony.

"Keep the rest of the team back. I want to watch this," Connor said.

Samson went quiet for a moment, and Connor knew he'd muted the comlink so he could send a broadcast to the other soldiers.

"You know what this is, right?" Samson asked.

"Looks like the pack leader is being challenged."

"So, what are you watching for? Either those younglings will work themselves up and give that veteran a real challenge, or they'll scamper out of here."

"That's not always how it happens. It's not a simple one-against-one type of fight. I would've thought you'd have seen that, given how remote you used to live."

Samson was quiet for a few moments, considering. "I didn't spend my time studying ryklars. They left me alone, and I left them alone. It was a good arrangement."

Connor watched as the five younglings, large enough and deadly enough to be considered adults, stalked closer to the pack leader. The other ryklars rocked from side to side, showing a bit of anxiousness at the display. Despite the viciousness of a ryklar attack, they were actually quite disciplined. They preferred a rigid hierarchy, and it was in times like these that the hierarchy was challenged. It wasn't simply a fight to determine who became leader, but a fight to determine the future of the pack down to its youngest member.

Two ryklars darted in toward the veteran but didn't stop this time. They collided in a furious battle—a raging inferno of vicious snarls and claws. The aged veteran hadn't attained his position and held it for so long without being among the deadliest of the pack's fighters.

Connor watched the ryklars engage. It wasn't simple, mindless fury but a delicate dance between seasoned combatants. It had taken him years to notice the subtleties of ryklar combat. There was posturing, but a veteran wouldn't seek to kill its challengers, at least not initially. The veteran would seek to disable them. When challenges for pack supremacy ended in death, it could be disastrous for the entire pack.

The two ryklars that attacked had been seriously wounded and now had dark, blood-soaked slashes in their hides. The remaining three challengers moved in closer, circling the veteran. When other ryklars started to come closer, the veteran hissed at them and they stopped. They were its loyal lieutenants, but the veteran wouldn't allow them to interfere. This was its fight, despite the five-to-one odds.

The wounded ryklars joined the others, and the five of them attacked the veteran all at once, overwhelming whatever defense it could muster. They pulled him off balance, and he went down. Screeches and snarls sounded. The grizzled veteran scrambled, throwing off some of his attackers, and Connor saw that its bearded tentacles had become even redder as it gave in to its fury. One of the ryklars went down, clutching its middle in a futile attempt to keep its life from bleeding out. Another ryklar darted in. The veteran scrambled around it, using it as a shield to block the follow-up attack by the other three. Unable to stop themselves, they collided with their ally's claws, rending through flesh. The ryklar screeched in pain as it went through its death throes.

This is it. There's no stopping it now, Connor thought grimly.

The three ryklars backed away, and the veteran pursued them. They'd crossed the line, and now the pack would pay the price. The veteran had already proven to be their better. The challengers would die.

When the battle was over, the veteran ryklar had a few new battle scars, and five attackers lay dead or dying in a quivering mess on the ground.

Connor glanced at the rest of the pack. The forest was suddenly awash in red, showing the ryklars' agitation. Scuffles broke out among them, and the pack leader roared. The nearest ryklars immediately snapped to attention, but there were others farther away that scattered, leaving the pack.

"What's the matter with them?" Samson asked.

"The pack is dead, or at least weakened," Connor said and began backing away through the shrubs.

Samson followed him, waiting a few moments for them to be well away from the area. "I don't understand. Why did the pack break apart because of a simple challenge to the pack leader?"

"The ryklars are predators, but they're more than that. They're good at killing, but when it comes to pack hierarchy, they don't handle transition of power very well. They do fight among themselves, but despite their ferociousness toward other species, a challenge to the pack leader rarely ends in death because of the risk of the pack splintering. Given the overwhelming odds, the pack leader could have abdicated his position."

"Do they do that? Stop being the pack leader so the pack stays together?"

Connor's eyebrows raised and he shrugged. "Sometimes. Depends on the leader, I guess."

Samson glanced behind them. They could still hear the ryklars screeching, though they were farther away. The once powerful pack had fragmented. "I'll never understand this planet. There are some things that remind me of Earth, but sometimes it's just so alien."

They walked in silence until they met up with several other CDF soldiers under Samson's command.

"I still don't understand why the pack split apart. If anything, wouldn't the fact that the pack leader won have solidified his hold over the pack, given that he'd been challenged and it failed?"

"You're still thinking of the ryklars as simple animals. Remember, they're genetically enhanced, which includes their brains. Look at it this way. Even though the pack leader was challenged, he allowed himself to be put in a position where he killed members of the pack. A large portion of the ryklars will likely remain, but a sizable chunk will choose to leave, having lost faith in him. This will make the pack weaker overall."

Samson eyed Connor for a minute. "You know an awful lot about these things."

"Studying them has been a hobby of mine for a while—at least until I rejoined the CDF. I've even seen the smaller factions join other packs and then exact revenge upon their old packs. Who does that remind you of?" Connor asked.

Samson thought about it for a minute. He was a soldier through and through, and one of the things he was good at was measuring the capacity of an enemy's willingness to fight. "So, we have something in common with the ryklars. Would you rather they sit down around a conference table and come to a peaceful resolution for their differences?" He paused for a moment. "Sometimes you have to be ruthless. I know you know that. Do you think the Krake will be civilized when they come here?"

"I'll be sure to share your philosophy of shooting first and asking questions later with the defense committee," Connor said.

"It does simplify things. Seriously, the committee can't really be considering how they could work with the Krake if they found a way to communicate with them. Given what they've done to the Ovarrow and the data you retrieved, I seriously doubt they're open to peace."

Connor didn't need to be reminded. He'd gone over that data many times. "It's not that simple," he said, snorting in disbelief. "Okay, from *your* perspective it's simple. I give you a weapon, I tell you to achieve an objective, and it's done. But dealing with civilians can be complicated."

Samson arched a thick eyebrow and smiled a little, but it didn't make his face look friendly. "Complicated," he repeated. "Is that what we're calling it now?"

Since Connor had invited Samson back into the CDF, he'd gotten used to some of his old friend's moods. Sometimes Samson had a simplified way of reading into a situation that was useful. This wasn't one of those times.

"I don't mean to be a hard-ass about this," Samson continued. "And I know I'm not telling you anything new."

Connor looked at him for a moment and then nodded. "I thought after the Vemus War we could leave all that behind us. I want there to be a better way, but . . ." He let the thought go unfinished.

There were a few times in a soldier's life when events would shape the kind of soldier they'd become. For Connor, the first time was when he killed an enemy combatant. He'd never forget his first kill. He'd felt numb in the beginning, and then he tried to rationalize it when he could think clearly again. He'd thought he was supposed to feel conflicted about it, but he didn't. He never did. It was then that he had to accept that fighting was something he was exceptionally good at, and possibly the *only* thing he was really good at. It didn't make him a monster, although there were some people who probably thought of him that way. He was a protector, and he would protect this colony until his dying breath.

CHAPTER 2

The CDF Hellcat set down at an impromptu landing zone out in the middle of nowhere. Connor had picked this site because it was hundreds of kilometers away from any colonial outpost and because they could control the environment.

"General Gates," Lieutenant Solari said, "General Hayes is inbound and will be here in a few minutes. The other attendees will arrive shortly."

"Thank you, Lieutenant," Connor replied and left the cockpit.

He went to the back of the Hellcat where the CDF infantry unit waited. Captain Kathy Morris came over to him.

"Have your platoon secure the area. The others will be arriving shortly."

"Yes, General," Morris replied and began issuing orders to her platoon.

Connor walked down the exit ramp and stepped onto solid ground, hearing Samson's heavy footfalls behind him. Samson was a few inches taller than Connor and outweighed him by more than sixty pounds of solid muscle.

There were vast areas of the supercontinent that were home to wide-open plains. One of the reasons Connor had selected this area was that there was very little chance anyone could spy on them.

Several reconnaissance drones flew overhead, and Connor glanced at Samson, wondering if he'd ask any of the questions that were obviously forming in his mind. Samson had only rejoined the colony in the past three months and was still prone to long bouts of silence.

"I'm glad you asked," Connor said. "The reason we're out here in the middle of nowhere is because we can secure the area and prevent anyone else from listening in."

Samson eyed him for a few moments. "I didn't ask. I'm just following orders."

"You were wondering. I could tell."

"If Wil and Kasey could see us now."

Connor sighed heavily, remembering his friends. All of them had been former members of the Ghost Platoon, but Wil and Kasey had died protecting the colony. "At least you're here."

Samson snorted, which sounded more like a bull clearing its throat. "You'll get more use out of me when the Krake actually arrive, or when we take the fight to them. I hate all the strategy stuff beforehand."

"You're only as good as the weapons you use," Connor replied.

Samson eyed him for a moment. "Unless you think some of the people coming to this meeting aren't friends."

High above, a Hellcat flew across the pale gray sky, lining up with the LZ, engines shrieking in a dopplered wail as it came in low and fast. Connor glanced at it before turning back to Samson. "If we only surround ourselves with people we trust, not much would get done."

"So, you trust me now," Samson said, which was more of a statement than a question.

"Now that you're weapons qualified again, I trust you won't shoot me in the back."

Samson's mouth split into a broad grin. "I was just keeping you on your toes."

The Hellcat landed, next in a line of several others en route to the LZ. Some of the Hellcats were smaller than the troop-carrier-sized transport, and they had different insignias for the branch of service they operated under. Two of the ships were tan and green for Field Ops, while the Hellcats from the CDF were battle-steel gray with a blue and gold stripe across the middle. They were designed for both atmospheric flight and lower orbit, but they didn't have the range of a combat shuttle.

Nathan Hayes walked down the exit ramp of the nearest CDF Hellcat and gave Connor a wave before heading in his direction.

As Nathan walked over, he looked over at the other ships landing close by. "This is something new," he said, looking around at the open grasslands surrounding them.

"It's time for it."

"I'm pretty certain we can secure our communications at any of the CDF bases," Nathan replied.

Connor nodded. "Probably, but there are other ways to listen in. It'll be a good idea for us to lay our cards out on the table before meeting with the Colonial Defense Committee."

More people disembarked from their ships, and Connor saw Damon Mills, Director of Field Ops, walking over to him. A woman in a Field Ops uniform walked at his side, and her name appeared on Connor's internal heads-up display.

Captain Leslie Tyler.

Age 51.

Senior Field Ops agent in charge of Search and Rescue at Sierra.

Captain Tyler looked barely into her twenties due to the prolonging treatments all colonists were privy to. Connor looked at her record with appreciation, glad that Search and Rescue was in such capable hands.

Damon Mills had had a career in law enforcement back on old Earth. His skin was weatherworn, and he sported an outdoorsman's deep tan. He looked to have an almost permanent scowl on his face, and he could be somewhat abrasive at times. Connor remembered getting off to a rocky start with Damon when he'd first gotten to the colony, but over the years, they'd come to a mutual respect for one another. They might never be what Connor would consider close friends, but he trusted Damon, which was why he'd invited him.

"Thanks for making time to come here," Connor said to Damon.

Damon rubbed his eyes for a moment and nodded. "Of course."

"Were you up all night?"

Damon nodded by way of tilting his head to the side once and smiling a little. "There's never a dull moment, is there? Believe me, we're all busy, and I'm happy for a little bit of a change for a few hours, at least. Lots of fresh air around here," he said while glancing around.

A text message appeared on Connor's internal heads-up display.

C. Weber: *Suppressor net ready to engage. One invitee overdue.*

C. Gates: *Acknowledged. Come on out and join us now.*

More people arrived, mostly from Field Ops, with Franklin Mallory arriving last. An older man, Franklin was taller than Connor, and the short beard he wore emphasized the long lines of his face from his high cheek-bones to the straight slash of his mouth. Fresh worry lines adorned his friend's face, and Connor's stomach knotted into a ball of acidic regret.

"Franklin, thanks for coming," Connor said.

Franklin Mallory looked as if he'd rather be somewhere else, impatient to get back to work, and Connor understood why. His son was a prominent figure associated with a rogue terrorist organization, and it tended to make for many sleepless nights.

"Connor," Franklin replied in acknowledgment.

Major Natalia Vassar joined them and gave Connor a meaningful nod. She was a short woman, and her reputation among the officers was that she was tiny but fierce.

"Gentlemen and ladies," Connor said, "this is Major Natalia Vassar, and she's with CDF Intelligence. She's activated a suppressor net, so don't be alarmed if you find yourselves suddenly cut off from all communications with the rest of the colony. There's nothing wrong with your equipment. It's just a precaution to prevent other people from listening in on this meeting."

Several people frowned, but it was Damon who voiced the unspoken objection. "Don't you think this is over the top? What if there's an emergency?"

Connor looked at Damon and smiled. "We'll be fine. We all have well-trained people in our respective organizations, and they have protocols to follow in an emergency. I promise not to keep any of you longer than absolutely necessary."

Franklin Mallory cleared his throat. "What's this about, Connor?"

"I wanted to have an open and honest conversation with all of you. You were asked to bring at least one person that you absolutely trust," Connor said and looked around at all of them. More than a few glanced at Samson, whose form towered off to Connor's right. Gesturing toward Samson, Connor continued. "This is Captain Samson. For those of you who haven't met him yet, he's a former member of the Ghost Platoon of the NA Alliance Military. He's recently rejoined the CDF and is part of Spec Ops in charge of Ranger 7th company."

Hearing that Samson was a former member of Connor's old Ghost Platoon drew a few curious looks in his direction. People like Franklin and Damon, who'd been there at the beginning of the colony, knew firsthand that not all the Ghosts had acclimated to colonial living. Samson was one of those who hadn't. He'd spent the last eight years living alone, getting as far away from colonial population centers as possible.

Samson returned their curious gazes with what he probably considered a nonthreatening look.

"I'm going to cut to the chase," Connor said. "The Krake represent a threat that's like nothing we've ever faced. All our preparation for the Vemus was designed to meet a threat coming from deep space. And though the Krake could attack us from space, they could also attack us on the ground and could already be here without our knowledge." Connor paused for a few moments to glance at the Field Ops people, who looked as if they weren't sure how to react to this news. "The purpose of the Colonial Defense Force is to protect the colony from outside threats. Given what we know about the Krake, this responsibility is going to be shared directly with Field Ops. There's a very real possibility that our conflict with them will happen on the planet, and the CDF and Field Ops need to be able to coordinate together."

Damon jutted his chin up once, indicating that he wanted to speak, and Connor nodded. "We still have the civilian readiness plans we put together in the event that the Vemus invaded us. Wouldn't that be enough?"

"That's the thing, Damon. I don't know if they are. We can plug the security holes as best we can, but the situation is different. The Krake could already be here. How would we know? How would they attack us? *Would* they attack us?"

"If you didn't believe the Krake would attack us at some point, we wouldn't be here," Franklin said.

Connor nodded. "You're right. I believe it's not a matter of *if* but *when*. The other thing that concerns me is that our best source of information is also the source of a major division between colony members. I'm talking about the Ovarrow," he said, using the NEIIS name for themselves.

"Given what the Ovarrow have done to their planet," Nathan began, "trusting them to be our allies has given me a lot of sleepless nights. I'm willing to confess to that. You and I have discussed this before, but for the rest of you, here's what I think. I do agree that the Ovarrow represent a source of the intel we need, but they're alien. They fought a war—many wars—among themselves and possibly against the Krake, and look where it left them."

Franklin Mallory crossed his arms in front of his chest and exhaled. "We still don't understand why the Krake would even come here."

"Actually," Connor said, "we've uncovered evidence from their military base that indicates they allocate a lot of resources for exploring different universes and interacting with intelligent species. I say 'interact' because the evidence we have indicates that the Krake don't simply launch an all-out campaign to conquer a target. We can talk about this for hours and days, and we already have within our various circles. What I'm looking for from all of you are ideas for how to prepare for the Krake. And I recognize that some of our ideas may not be popular with certain groups of civilians or even with each other, for that matter."

They were silent for a few moments before Franklin Mallory spoke.

"When Tobias Quinn was drafting the Colonial Charter, he had to account for the possibility that there might be factions of the colony that broke off from the main group. There are ways for them to legally do this. It's their right."

"I understand that it's their right," Connor said, "but we barely survived a war with the Vemus, and it took the effort of the entire colony to do it. The Vemus sent a fighting force across interstellar space to get us. What we're facing here has the potential to be a fighting force that doesn't have to travel so far. It's already here but in a different universe. I know it's difficult to accept, but if we make this a numbers game, then the odds are overwhelmingly in their favor."

"Excuse me," Leslie Tyler said. "How can you be so sure? We haven't even found the . . ." she paused for a moment, searching for the right words, ". . . home universe of the Krake. So, this is all speculation as to what their capabilities are."

"You're right; we haven't found it. But they're a spacefaring race, which means they must have certain technological and manufacturing capabilities that can only come from a heavily populated planet. They might even have colonies. We don't know. They could be drawing from resources that come from multiple worlds. Regardless, it will be our job to come up with a way to stop them from wiping us out."

Connor watched the others as his words were mulled over.

"So why all the secrecy?" Damon said, gesturing around them.

Connor looked at Damon, and then his gaze went to Franklin Mallory. "It's because of Lars and the rogue group he's part of."

Franklin's gaze hardened, and he glanced away.

"I know this hasn't been easy for you," Connor said, "but Lars and his group are driving a wedge into the colony."

Franklin looked at Connor. "I don't condone my son's actions, but Lars isn't forcing his ideas on anyone. They just happen to be in conflict with what your ideas for protecting the colony are."

Connor was quiet for a few moments, considering, and as each moment passed, he saw the others shift uncomfortably. Franklin was worried about his son and angry with him at the same time. Connor could tell Franklin wanted to defend his son's actions, and Connor also wanted to help protect Lars and get him to stop doing what he was doing. "All right, you have a point, but the fact of the matter is that we're putting forth a motion to have the actions of Lars and the rogue group declared illegal. Like it or not, if Lars keeps on his current path, his actions will be declared criminal."

Franklin Mallory's broad shoulders drew up tight, and a groan escaped his lips. As he lifted his eyes, the pain in his expression stabbed at Connor's chest. But Franklin quickly replaced that pain with a scowl and clenched his fists.

"I think we need a few minutes here," Nathan said, gesturing for some of the others to walk away.

Damon came to Franklin's side, trying to get him to walk away, and Franklin took a few steps. He was shaking his head, and his face had become several shades of red as he glared at Connor. "My son is not a criminal, and I don't care what motion you get passed. He is not a criminal! He's doing what *you* taught him to do. He's doing what *I* taught him to do. He's trying to protect this colony."

Connor met Franklin's gaze. He knew what it was like to grieve for a son —that gut-wrenching pain that kept stabbing until it drove you to your knees. It was a pain that Connor carried within himself, too, and it would never leave. At least Franklin's son was alive, and there was still a chance to save him from himself, but Connor wouldn't give him false hope. "Lars is treading a very thin line that he's come dangerously close to crossing. Did you forget what happened to Noah? Or the fact that he led a group that almost opened fire on a CDF squad that was protecting Dash? Lars is pulling Ovarrow from their stasis pods, questioning them, and then murdering them. In that respect, he's already crossed the line. How long do you think it will be before he does the same thing to a colonist who's standing in his way? Do you want to stand in front of another father or mother and tell *them* that Lars's actions aren't criminal? What about the Ovarrow? Don't they have a right to live just like you or me? I don't like this either. He's a good kid. They all were, but they're making grave mistakes—mistakes that are going to put them on the wrong side—"

"Stop!" Damon shouted. "Just stop."

Angry tears had gathered in Franklin's eyes. It was a gaze full of pain that touched on bitterness, and perhaps even hatred. Franklin shook his head, and his shoulders slumped. "Where did I go wrong? How could I have let this happen?"

Connor stepped closer to him. "It's not just you," he said, his voice thick with emotion.

Franklin squeezed his eyes shut for a moment, exhaling a heavy breath.

"I don't know how to protect him," he said and looked at Connor. "How can I protect him? I feel like I should've been able to stop . . . like I should've known what he was going to do."

Connor swallowed hard. "It's not your fault." Even as he spoke, he knew Franklin would never listen or accept it.

"Like hell it isn't! I raised him. I should've known."

"You didn't make Lars do what he did. Sometimes, kids start out on a path and then can't find a way out of it," Connor said as he reached out to put his hand on Franklin's shoulder. "And Lars didn't start doing this on his own. Someone else put him on this path, and that's who we need to find."

Franklin wiped away his tears and nodded, his breath coming in gasps as he struggled to control himself. Then he nodded again and allowed Damon to lead him away.

Connor watched them go. Anger like a coiled viper yearned to strike out from him. He hated this—hated whoever was corrupting young men and women to do horrible things. Yet, if he'd been desperate enough, wouldn't he have taken similarly terrible actions to protect the colony? Connor would have liked to deny such a thought. He knew he'd push himself beyond the brink to fight the Krake while keeping his integrity intact, but a more ruthless side of himself whispered that he'd sacrifice even that to save the colony. What *wouldn't* he do to ensure the colony's survival—the survival of the entire human race? These thoughts were like fire in his mind, and they burned as he realized it was those same ideas that had probably been used to corrupt Lars. Connor whispered a curse and shook his head. He'd thought he was alone, but then he saw that Samson was standing close by.

"This won't end well," Samson said and walked away.

Connor stood there for a few moments, denying what Samson had said. There had to be a way to stop Lars and the rest of the people involved, rooting out the entire terrorist organization. He had to believe there was some hope they could reach Lars and get him to stop what he was doing.

Connor couldn't imagine what Franklin was going through. He hadn't been around to raise his own son; he'd only gotten to mourn his loss. And now, his daughter was barely old enough to walk.

His thoughts traveled back to that first shuttle ride from the *Ark* down to New Earth. Lenora had been there, but so had Sean, Noah, and Lars—three young men bursting with youthful vigor and massive potential. The three of them had somehow wriggled their way into becoming family to him, and Connor wanted to protect them all, but he knew this was something he couldn't do. Noah was still in a coma and, despite their best efforts, showed no signs of waking from it. Sean was lost, trapped in another universe, and Lars was here on New Earth but beyond Connor's reach. Sometimes he felt helpless, but he had to do what he could. What good was protecting the colony when it almost seemed like everything was working against him? As deplorable as Lars's actions toward the Ovarrow had been, the fact of the matter was that in different circumstances, Connor might've been tempted to do the same if it meant saving the lives of his family. He needed to get in front of Lars so he could try to convince him that what he was doing was wrong and that there was a better way to protect the colony. He just hoped he'd get that chance before it was too late.

CHAPTER 3

Phoenix Station maintained its orbit approximately a hundred sixty million kilometers from New Earth. This put one of New Earth's main lines of defense well past Sagan's orbit but not near Gigantor's orbit. Over four thousand people resided there, and Colonel Savannah Cross was in charge of overseeing the station's activities. First and foremost, Phoenix Station was a military installation, but more than half its residents were civilians. Since there were so many civilians working there, it seemed appropriate that Savannah's counterpart was a civilian. Julius Sheppard was a good man who had a way of dealing with people.

Colonial defensive initiatives beyond Phoenix Station were comprised of missile-defense platforms stationed throughout the star system. With the advent of subspace communication, there were plans to make better use of those automated defense platforms, given the threat the Krake represented. One of the problems they'd identified from encountering the Vemus and the destruction of Titan Station was their limited communication capabilities back to New Earth.

Savannah frowned. Perhaps that assessment was a bit unfair. They were aware of the communication limitations that came with maintaining defense outposts so far from New Earth, and they'd had to account for the lag in comms as part of their strategy. It had been necessary, given the threat coming from old Earth. They also had a relay of listening outposts farther out in the system that would send an alert should any latent Vemus attack force make its way to New Earth. The chances of that happening were extremely low, but vigilance was the key to survival.

Savannah's current command, while military in nature, also had a similar job description to that of a governor on New Earth. She was responsible for the station in its entirety, including the civilians. Phoenix Station was essentially a city in its own rights—a city with heavy weaponry and a burgeoning shipbuilding capability. One day, they'd rival the shipyards at the lunar base. Savannah smiled at the thought. Her husband, Nathan, was largely responsible for everything Lunar Base had become, and perhaps there was a bit of a competitive streak in her where her husband was concerned. However, she was extremely proud of the work she'd accomplished during her tenure at Phoenix Station. It could be trying at times, given that she hadn't gotten to see Nathan very often for the past year. They essentially split their son Oliver's time between the two of them, but she knew this arrangement could only work on a temporary basis, particularly since she and Nathan wanted more children—many more children. Savannah wasn't about to let her career in the CDF stand in the way of that, but it wasn't time to go home just yet. She had important work to do. She wouldn't allow herself the luxury of returning to New Earth until they'd found Trident Battle Group.

Sean Quinn had been overdue for almost three months now. Neither Connor nor Nathan believed that Trident Battle Group had been lost to the Krake, and she shared their opinion. Despite this, their current reconnaissance efforts into the alternate universe had been severely lacking, in her opinion. The latest report was on a holoscreen in front of her, and she glared at it.

The door to her office chimed and Major Vance Peterson stuck his head through the doorway. "We have a one o'clock."

Savannah nodded and waved him inside. Peterson entered and glanced at the data on her holoscreen, seeing it through the now-translucent screen. "It doesn't inspire a lot of confidence, does it?"

"No, it does not. At this rate, it'll take us a year to recon the star system, and we don't have a year."

Peterson frowned. "I want to find them just as much as you do, but did something else happen that I'm not aware of?"

Savannah powered off her holoscreen and leaned back in her chair. "It's taking too long. The restriction of using only limited reconnaissance probes isn't going to get the job done. We thought it was the safest thing to do, but I'm not so sure anymore."

Peterson pursed his lips in thought. "Are you looking for ideas?"

Savannah shook her head and then, after a moment, shrugged. "Of course, but I already have an idea. I just need to get approval to use it."

Peterson was about to reply when the comlink she'd been waiting for chimed on the nearby wallscreen. A large image of Connor Gates' face appeared.

"General Gates," Savannah greeted.

"Colonel Cross. Major Peterson. How are things on Phoenix Station today?"

Savannah proceeded to give Connor a brief status report on current projects at Phoenix Station. "Have you had a chance to review the latest reconnaissance report from the alternate universe?" Savannah asked.

Connor shook his head. "No, I haven't, but judging by the look on your face, it isn't good."

"Sir, we've reached the limitations of what our reconnaissance drones are capable of. They're simply not up to the task. We've equipped them with high-powered telescopes and limited sensor arrays, but it's not enough. We need to send a team through."

Connor was silent while he considered.

"I'm sending you a new file, sir. The Raven class scout ship, SR-01, is ready for service."

Connor's eyebrows raised slightly. "Ready for service," he repeated. "I thought that ship was still several months from completion in favor of completing space gate components."

"Sir, we already have four completed space gates deployed in the star system. Instead of prioritizing another space gate, I allocated some resources to complete the scout ship."

"I see."

"Sir, I believe this is our best chance to find out what happened to Trident Battle Group. Sending more recon drones isn't going to give us any new data soon enough."

"Is there any supporting evidence that warrants sending another team to the alternate universe? I'm asking because that's what Governor Wolf and the rest of the defense committee will ask me."

Savannah felt the tightening in her shoulders spread down her arms and into her abdomen. She shook her head. "There's been no new evidence to support that Trident Battle Group is still there. However, I have a plan that involves the use of the scout ship in coordination with the space gates we've deployed."

"Savannah, I'm not trying to be a hard-ass about this. I want to know what happened to them as much as you do. Send your plan over. Also, what team did you have in mind for the mission?"

Savannah felt the beginnings of a smile. "I think you'll approve. Actually, I think you know him."

CHAPTER 4

Connor's Hellcat set down in the landing zone at the colonial government campus in Sierra. When Sierra had been rebuilt after the Vemus War, they'd taken the opportunity to change the design of the city. It had been rebuilt during a time of great uncertainty after they'd learned that something horrible had happened back on Earth.

The Vemus was a rare form of symbiotic viral and bacterial life form that attacked mammalian life on Earth. Earth scientists had tried to modify it to make humans immune—and Connor suspected they were trying to make all mammals immune—but there were others who saw an opportunity to acquire power. Billions of lives had been lost, and the calamity of Earth had reached out across interstellar space to invade the colony. It'd been almost three years since the end of the Vemus War, but Connor could still see the scars that impacted colonial society. Peaceful cities didn't have rail guns on their roofs or hidden missile-defense platforms buried under the ground in parks throughout the city. Peaceful cities didn't have military bases nearby with an alert force ready to defend the city should an invader appear. Perhaps one day there would be cities on New Earth that didn't require those types of defenses, but Connor suspected he'd be an old man by then.

There were multiple landing zones throughout Sierra. When the city had been redesigned, they'd taken evacuation plans into account should the residents need to flee quickly. Both New Haven and Delphi also had these accommodations in place. Sanctuary was a much smaller city in comparison. Due to its remote location and the fact there was already an underground bunker capable of withstanding an orbital bombardment, it was one of the safest cities in the event they were invaded.

Connor had to attend a Colonial Defense Force committee meeting later in the day, but he'd arrived early to meet with Governor Dana Wolf. Nathan had advised Connor to meet with various colonial leaders outside of committee meetings in order to facilitate working relationships with them. Despite his initial reluctance due to time constraints, Connor had to admit that his friend had been right. Meeting with colonial leaders *had* helped make getting things done a little bit easier. Above all, Connor wanted to avoid a situation like the one he'd faced during Stanton Parish's administration. Connor didn't think about Parish much, but since Connor had been instrumental in removing him from power with the help of Tobias Quinn, certain political leaders mistrusted him, even though Connor's actions had been necessary and legal under the Colonial Charter.

After the war, Connor had distanced himself from the Colonial Defense Force, but now that he was back in the military, he'd made an effort to "play nice," as his wife preferred to call it. Lenora had the uncanny ability to see right to the heart of matters, and Connor had come to rely on her insights, especially when dealing with civilians.

He shook his head as he walked across the campus. They were all people, but he'd always thought of himself as a soldier—a military man—even when he'd retired. Perhaps that was part of the problem. Civilians were a breed apart from soldiers. There'd been divisions among the different branches of the old NA Alliance Military, and the CDF was no different. It came from being competitive. They all had their traditions and their own ways of saber-rattling.

Connor walked into the main entrance of the administration building where the governor's office resided. He glanced up at the murals depicting scenes from Earth's history, then the *Ark*, the colonists first coming to New Earth, and the building of the cities. Across the main hall were more murals of colonists exploring New Earth, but there were two that Connor liked to take a few moments to observe. These were the murals for the Colonial Defense Force and Field Ops. They showed figures of CDF soldiers in blue and gold dress uniforms standing before a setting sun and then shifted to a scene beyond the planet showing various types of warships. The entire spacescape had been done in an outline form, depicting the heads and shoulders of the men and women who comprised the CDF.

Tobias Quinn had been an advocate of remembering where they'd come from. Without those things to remind them of who they were, they may have lost sight of their heritage. There were times when Connor and Tobias hadn't seen eye to eye on some important issues, but there'd always been mutual respect. During the time Tobias's widow, Ashley Quinn, had been acting governor, Connor had no longer been in the CDF, but they respected each other and were friends—more than friends. They were family. She was like a sister to him, but it was getting increasingly difficult to see her. The fact that her son Sean was still missing worried her beyond words, despite his assurances.

Connor acknowledged a few friendly greetings of people he passed on his way to Governor Wolf's office. When he walked in, the young secretary told him to go on inside, as the governor was expecting him.

Connor walked into the office and saw Governor Wolf standing amid a trio of holoscreens. She was reviewing various reports, and Connor noted the ever-growing list of tasks she'd noted. The amber holoscreens became translucent, giving him a clear view of her face, and she waved him over.

Connor noticed that her office had been reconfigured, looking much like his own. He didn't spend hours sitting at a desk, reviewing reports on a holoscreen. He alternated, but mostly he stood up and worked as he saw Dana Wolf working right then.

She smiled at him. "I took a page out of your book. I got tired of sitting around on my ass."

"Imitation is the sincerest form of flattery, but your secret is safe with me."

Dana grinned. "And where did *you* learn it from?"

"I didn't always have a desk at the places I was stationed, but the work still had to get done."

She nodded. She was an older woman, but Connor couldn't guess her age. She looked older than him, but with prolonging that could mean anything. The human lifespan was currently well over two hundred years.

"Did you see the new banners on your way in?"

Connor frowned and thought for a few seconds. He'd been so focused on his own thoughts that he must have missed them. "I didn't."

"It's a major milestone. The colony has doubled in size in the past twelve years. In another year, our population will be over seven hundred thousand."

She walked over to the side table and poured two glasses of dark brown liquid, added a few cubes of ice, and handed one to Connor. "Nathan Hayes gave me this, and I have to admit this latest cask of bourbon has made me a customer."

Connor took the glass and had a sip. Nathan had given him a case of it as well. "I thought you preferred wine."

She nodded. "I do, and my husband does as well, but sometimes it's nice to have something a little bit different. Don't tell my husband. He's got ideas for growing grapes and starting his own winery."

Connor took another taste, and the bourbon warmed his chest.

"Before we get started," Wolf said, "I wanted to ask how John Rollins' recovery is going."

Connor liked that she asked, although he had no doubt she'd read about Rollins' current medical status and feedback from his psychological evaluation. But there was always information that couldn't be conveyed in a report. "Physically he's doing much better. The doctors are happy that he's put on some weight, but he's still very thin."

Rollins had been held captive by the Krake, and when he'd been rescued, they'd found him starved almost to death.

"I'm sure you read that he has severe PTSD," Connor continued. "It's going to take time for him to come around, but he'll never be the same. He wasn't able to communicate with the other prisoners, and the isolation was untenable. There's some memory suppression going on, which is to be expected. What he *has* shared with us is more of a confirmation of what we already knew or suspected based on the information we'd gotten from the base and from the Ovarrow."

"I know everything that can be done is being done by the doctors, but if there's anything I can do, please don't hesitate to ask."

Connor nodded and finished his bourbon.

"Going back to the population of the colony, I've done a little bit of research. Did you know that almost ten percent of the population is serving in the CDF?"

"I wouldn't be much of a general if I didn't know the number of people in the CDF, but I don't expect that having ten percent of the population serving in the military will be something that's maintained as the colony grows."

Wolf finished her bourbon and set the glass down on the table. "I've been looking at the history of the NA Alliance, as well as the Asia Pac Alliance and the member nations that comprised them. Historically, the percentage of the population serving in the military was only that high during times of war. What we have here is something that has become ongoing. If you add Field Ops into it, the numbers reach twenty percent of the population that's devoted in some way to colonial defense. When I examined the original charters that preceded the *Ark* program, there was a much different picture being painted."

"They never expected to need a military. They believed a police force would be enough to keep the colony safe, and they might have been right in other circumstances. You seem to be preoccupied with the numbers. What are you worried about?" Connor asked.

"What do you imagine your daughter will do when she becomes an adult? I know she's just a baby, but these years will go by quickly."

At the mention of his daughter, Connor felt the edges of his lips curve upward. Diaz had called it that dopey fatherly smile that descended when a man became a father. "Whatever she wants to do," he answered.

"Fair enough, but would you want her to choose a dangerous occupation like yours? Hopefully, by the time she's an adult, colonial life will be much more settled than it is right now."

"I hope so, too. Otherwise . . . I don't want my daughter to have to do some of the things I've done, but if I'm understanding you correctly, I think you're implying that at some point you'd like to reduce the number of active military personnel."

"Eventually," she said and tilted her head to the side by way of a single nod. "We were meant to be explorers and pioneers. I understand the need for what we've done and will continue to do, but what I don't want is our legacy to be a military state that falls under a dictatorship."

There it was, Connor thought, *an acknowledgment of the fear that's been mostly unspoken.* "Let's hope we'll be smarter than that. It's not what *I* want."

Wolf smiled. It was friendly and reached her eyes. "Oh, I believe you, Connor. I have no issues trusting you, but things change. Eventually you and I won't be here, and what the people who *are* here will have is the groundwork we've laid for them. It's a concern of mine."

Connor didn't know how to respond to that. What could he say? How was he supposed to know what the next generation was going to do with the legacy they built for them?

"It's just something to think about. Anyway, it's time for us to go," Dana said. They started walking toward the door, and she stopped. "I'm glad you make an effort for us to speak outside of those meetings."

"Thank you for being open to it. I hope that whoever serves as governor in the future will have the same policy you do."

Governor Wolf still had another year left before she could be reelected, and that would be the last term she'd serve as governor. In the Colonial Charter, there was a strict two-term limit on any political office. There would be no career politicians on the colony.

This Colonial Defense Committee meeting wasn't a run-of-the-mill affair. There'd been outside agencies invited, given some of the things they were discussing. This included representatives from the legislative and judicial branches of the colonial government, along with Meredith Cain, who was the head of the Colonial Intelligence Bureau. Bob Mullins and Kurt Johnson, Dana's advisors, were also in attendance, as well as Franklin Mallory and Damon Mills. On the CDF side were Connor, Nathan, and Colonel Celeste Belonét. Celeste would be returning to her post at the lunar base, but Connor wanted representation from various CDF senior officers. If circumstances required that they interact with civilian leadership, it wouldn't be as foreign to them as it had been to Connor when he first created the CDF.

"The next order of business," Kurt Johnson said, "has to do with our state of defense readiness in the event of a threat to any of the colonial cities."

Connor noticed that Johnson hadn't mentioned the Krake and was inclined to believe Johnson would've liked to include the Ovarrow as a potential threat to the colony. He glanced at Nathan and gave him a nod.

Nathan cleared his throat. "We've established designated patrol areas in the vicinity of colonial cities that are outside those areas designated for Field Ops. We've established criteria for Field Ops to communicate with CDF alert forces that are on standby to investigate anomalies the Field Ops agents determine necessary."

"How long do you think these patrols will be necessary?" Johnson asked.

Until the Krake are no longer a threat, was the answer Connor wanted to give.

"We'll continue to reevaluate their effectiveness in the coming months and bring it up for this committee's review in six months," Nathan answered.

Johnson nodded and then looked at Governor Wolf. "There have been some concerns raised in each of our major cities about the fact that we have heavily armed ships flying overhead. People are worried that this could be an accident waiting to happen."

Connor leaned forward. "Now what would give them that impression?"

Johnson looked at Connor. "I don't understand your question, General Gates."

"There's always been a CDF base at colonial population centers. This is nothing new. Heavily armed ships coming to and from those bases aren't new, is my point. So, I'm left wondering why there's a sudden concern, unless somebody put those ideas into their heads."

"I don't know anything about a campaign to influence the hearts and minds of the colonists. But the patrols by the CDF have increased, and it's a valid concern."

"I haven't heard of any of these concerns at Sanctuary, and to the best of my knowledge, the base commanders haven't received any word of such concerns from the local colonists. There have never been any accidents involving weapons misfire. So, where did these reports come from? Why the sudden concern? These are the same ships that are there for their protection," Connor said.

There was an edge to his voice, and he knew it. The meeting had gone on pretty long, and that stretched his patience sometimes.

Johnson tapped his fingers on the table. "I'm merely voicing the concerns that have been brought to the governor's office, General Gates. I didn't make them up."

"Fair enough. I think the concerns might be a symptom of the attitude that's been growing lately regarding the Ovarrow settlement," Connor said.

Camp Alpha had been a staging area for bringing NEIIS, now known as the Ovarrow, out of stasis. In order for an alliance to work, they'd agreed to help the Ovarrow reestablish themselves in one of their abandoned cities, which was over three hundred kilometers from the nearest colonial city.

"Our office has received those concerns as well. There's a general mistrust of the Ovarrow," Johnson replied.

Connor looked at Governor Wolf. "I don't mean to circle back to what we've already covered, but I think it applies here. This is going back to the activity of the rogue group. It's the responsibility of colonial leadership to condemn their actions. The longer this doesn't happen, the more anxious people will become, and they'll start to believe we approve of such actions. I don't think anyone in this room would advocate murdering helpless victims of any race, including the Ovarrow. At least now it's been declared a war crime."

The rest of the defense committee waited for Governor Wolf to reply to Connor. "You're right, General Gates. We need to be clear on our stance regarding the Ovarrow; however, regardless of this administration's stance, people still won't trust them. Right or wrong, they have the right not to trust them."

"I understand," Connor replied. "And I'm not saying we should welcome them into our homes, but if we want an alliance with them, we need to have the right attitude about it at home. If you take my meaning."

"What do you suggest we do?" Johnson asked. "Given the current circumstances, what would you say to the average person about the Ovarrow?"

Connor took a few seconds to consider his answer. "We need an effort to demystify them. Right now, they're one of the colony's greatest mysteries—a civilization that once thrived on this planet—and now we find out they're still here. It's enough to make anyone anxious. I know one of the reasons I'm more comfortable with it is because my wife's an archaeologist. I worked with her, going to the sites to uncover their history."

Johnson nodded and tapped his chin with his fingers. "It's their history that most people find alarming."

"If someone read our history and hadn't interacted with us, they might be just as concerned about *our* intentions. Their history isn't perfect, and neither is ours. I thought one of the pillars the colony was founded on was second chances. It says it right on this building as you walk inside. This is our fresh start. A chance for new beginnings."

"I think I understand," Johnson said, and Connor doubted it. "How should the average person react if they encounter an Ovarrow? Will they be attacked? Should they attempt to communicate?" Johnson asked and then turned toward the other committee members. "Is it even possible to equip every person who leaves the city with a NEIIS . . ." he paused and frowned, then looked at Connor. "I'm sorry, old habits. An Ovarrow translator? Most people want to be reassured that it's safe to encounter them."

"This isn't just about what I want," Connor said. "This is a collective decision, and we have to live with the consequences. If you're worried about how to deal with the Ovarrow, then you need to have other experts in the room to help facilitate those questions. This committee is for the defense of the colony."

Johnson was about to reply, but Governor Wolf spoke first. "You're absolutely right, General Gates. Perhaps this is a takeaway from this meeting that we need to address outside of this committee. I can think of a few people whose opinion I would highly value on the subject."

Johnson held up his hands, letting the matter drop, and Connor nodded. "Going back to our state of readiness. We can secure our cities and keep a fairly close watch on the surrounding areas, but what we can't do is monitor activity on the entire planet. Also, there are various research efforts and exploration initiatives throughout the continent and in some of the oceans. I think we need to encourage people to report suspicious activity. And not just abroad but inside our cities as well."

Johnson's eyebrows lifted, and he looked at Governor Wolf. "Inside our own cities? Why would we do that?"

Dana gestured for Connor to continue.

"Because despite our efforts, mainly by Field Ops and Security, we haven't been able to arrest any of the rogue group. I don't want to create a society of suspicion, but we do need help. I've had quite a number of conversations with Damon Mills about this," Connor said.

Damon, who was sitting across from him, nodded. "It's true. Connor and I have spoken about this at length. I think the new laws will help. As many of you know, I come from a background in law enforcement, and we do need informers if we're going to find this rogue group."

"Also," Connor began, "we've been analyzing the data taken from the Krake military base. The Ovarrow testimonies regarding the Krake indicate that they don't simply invade a world. They study it first and then they try to influence the events that occur. I don't think the Krake's standard operating procedure really applies to us because we're different species. Presumably, we're something they've never encountered before. Regardless, we need to be informed if something doesn't look right to the average person. Then we can investigate."

"This is a good suggestion," Damon said. "I'll have my office coordinate with the other mayors, and we'll put something out for the general population."

"Excuse me, Governor Wolf," a woman said. The voice was clipped and precise. Connor turned toward it and saw that Meredith Cain had spoken. "Regarding the Krake data, my office hasn't received anything to analyze. We've sent multiple requests to the CDF for this."

Wolf looked at Connor.

"We've been holding back on it because we think the data we've retrieved might not be safe. Meaning that the data is filled with misinformation."

"That's just it, General Gates. The Colonial Intelligence Bureau is supposed to be able to dissect the information and maybe make some connections. I'm not asking the CDF to hand over the data for our exclusive use. I just want my people to have access to it, and perhaps they might offer a fresh perspective."

That wasn't all she was asking for, and Connor knew it. Meredith Cain might have been a bit on the quiet side, but when she did speak, it wasn't without purpose. He'd had his eye on her for a long time, but he couldn't connect her to the rogue group Lars Mallory was involved with.

"I think we can arrange for the data to be accessed by vetted personnel from the Intelligence Bureau," Connor said.

Meredith smiled. "That would be very much appreciated."

The meeting ended shortly after that, and Connor was walking with Nathan to the landing zone.

"I don't know about you, but I expected it," Nathan said and then added, "the request from the CIB."

"I know. Officially, there's no reason not to share the data with them."

"The older the colony gets, the more complex it is. I guess we can't expect to hold all the cards forever," Nathan replied.

"You're right, I know. It's just that the rogue group and Lars Mallory . . . They're not operating in a vacuum. They have support, and I suspect there were people in that meeting who agree with some of their efforts. There's no evidence, of course, but how else would they have evaded Field Ops for so long?"

"I know better than to question those instincts."

"What do you think, Nathan?"

"I think you're right, but I'm not sure what we can do about it without evidence. Sure, we can have our intelligence analysts watching the Colonial Intelligence Bureau, and they're likely watching us. Isn't that the name of the game? And wasn't that how things were done back on Earth?"

Connor drew in a deep breath and sighed. "Probably . . . no, not probably. More people, more complexity."

"Well, at least now we can legally pursue the rogue group, as long as they're not in any colonial city. That's a step in the right direction and will make things more difficult for them," Nathan said.

"The mandate is to capture them. They've been smart up to this point, avoiding a confrontation with the CDF and Field Ops. The closest they came to an actual conflict was with the squad we had escorting Dash to a remote Ovarrow site. I know we made progress in that meeting, but sometimes it feels like it takes so long to get anything done."

Nathan smiled. "Beats the alternative, meaning that the Krake could already be here and we'd be fighting them. I count that as a blessing."

Connor nodded. He could always count on Nathan to look at the brighter side of things. There was just so much to do and so little time. The fact was that Connor couldn't guess what the Krake would do if they ever did arrive on New Earth. He'd spent a career envisioning worst-case scenarios, but when he thought about what the Krake were capable of, he felt that his imagination might come up short. If that was the case, a lot of people would pay the price.

CHAPTER 5

Lars Mallory stood outside the exam room door. They'd been using this base of operations for almost a month. With colonial efforts focused on bringing the Ovarrow out of stasis and transporting them to their makeshift city, there were fewer resources hunting for him and the people under his command. It was almost time to move again, but Lars had decided to wait, which was a risk because the location was known and occasionally monitored by the Office of NEIIS Investigation. Lars supposed they'd have to change ONI to a more appropriate name now that the latest trend was to refer to the NEIIS as the Ovarrow. OOI didn't quite roll off the tongue like the ONI did, but Lars didn't really care what they called themselves.

The exam room door opened, and Tonya Wagner looked at him. "We're ready to begin anytime," she said and looked around. "Evans and Clark running late again?"

"They'll be here. It's not like whoever's inside is going anywhere. Did you confirm the faction before we took this pod?" Lars asked.

Tonya nodded her pretty head. She had dark brown eyes and pale skin, and her hair had a natural curl to it despite how short she kept it. She was tall and lithe, and she could run with the best of them on any survival trek.

"Of course. The three-triangle symbol, just like the other ones we've been focused on," she replied.

They'd been focused on the same Ovarrow symbol as the one on the stasis pod Connor had accidentally revived. For as long as they'd been searching, they hadn't found another Ovarrow that was anything like Siloc. That was irritating at first—that is until Lars had figured out that Siloc was way more than he appeared to be. On more than one occasion, Lars had thought about sending that information to Connor. It would have to be untraceable, of course, but Connor hadn't been wrong in killing that Ovarrow.

A message appeared on Lars's internal heads-up display. "Evans said they're about five minutes out. They're bringing some new recruits."

Tonya smiled broadly. Seeing the reaction of the new recruits to an Ovarrow was always interesting. The colonial news net did an admirable job of circulating press pieces about the Ovarrow, but it was all contrived, of course. Lars enjoyed circulating his own set of propaganda to influence the masses, a source of frustration for some.

He heard people coming down the passageway that led outside, and the muffled conversation became louder as the group got closer. He heard Evans ordering them to be quiet, and the group of recruits quieted down.

Evans came around the corner first and jutted his chin up toward Lars. "We need to talk."

"All right," Lars said and looked at the man standing behind Evans. "Justin, why don't you take the others inside? We'll be there in a minute."

"Will do, sir," Justin Clark replied.

The group quietly walked by, with some of the new recruits sneaking a glance at him. Lars was making a name for himself, at least among the people who knew better than to think they could share their planet with a species like the Ovarrow.

"We're outlaws now. Have you heard the latest?"

Lars shook his head. "No, what happened?"

"The governor's office released a statement condemning any activity that harms the Ovarrow. It does go into some specifics, and basically everything we've been doing is now illegal," Evans said and tapped a few commands on his wrist computer.

"They were bound to catch up with it sooner or later. It's a legal loophole at best, and there was a limited window of opportunity."

"Yeah, but they didn't vote on this. They just made it a law. This goes against everything else they've been telling us."

Evans was a hothead, and this was the latest thing to get his goat. It also confirmed that Evans didn't understand how laws were passed in the colony. Lars shrugged. "You can't let this get you all riled up."

"The hell I can't. Why aren't you angry? They're condemning our actions."

"They can pass all the laws they want. We have actual support outside the colonial government, and the message is getting out there. There's a growing segment of the population questioning the proposed alliance with the Ovarrow."

Evans curled his lips. "Not fast enough. We need to do more. People are still too complacent," he said and shook his head, glaring at nothing.

"Colton, you've got to calm down," Lars said and moved so he could get in front of his friend's line of sight. "You hear me? You're no good to anyone like this."

Evans shook his head and clenched his teeth. His hands were balled into fists.

"Look, why don't you take a walk? I've got this. Get some fresh air. Then we could talk more about these laws and how it affects what we need to do."

Evans regarded him for a few moments, at first looking as if he were going to protest. His left hand was in his pocket, and he seemed to be caressing something inside. Lars had a pretty good idea of what it was. And he didn't like it.

Evans bobbed his head up and down. "Okay. I'm going to go check the perimeter."

Lars watched him go. He even walked as if he had excessive energy. Too many stimulants. Lars shook his head and sighed. He needed to keep a closer eye on his friend. Evans was dedicated to what they were doing, but Lars had to redirect Evans' frantic energy at times. He had to be careful not to let it become a distraction or allow Evans to be put in a position to do something drastic.

The door to the exam room opened, and Tonya stood inside the doorway. "We're ready for you, sir."

Lars saw that the stasis pod was now open. The Ovarrow that had been inside was restrained, still looking disoriented and confused. Lars drew in a deep breath and stepped toward the door. His footsteps were heavy and carried a sense of finality with them. "All right, let's get started."

CHAPTER 6

S anctuary had begun as a forward operating research base that Lenora had gotten off the ground. For years it had been home to a small group of archaeologists, engineers, and other research scientists. As such, Field Ops had always had a presence there, and it had been a small, tightknit community. Then, when the Vemus War had finally reached them, Sanctuary had become one of the designated bunker sites to safely hold colonists.

Lenora walked through the ruins of an Ovarrow city. To her left were the geothermal power taps that had been used to provide electricity to the vault below. The Ovarrow vault was a treasure trove of recorded history. They'd made more progress translating it in the past year than they had in all the previous years combined.

Sanctuary had grown to become a city-size settlement after the Vemus War when colonial refugees had elected to stay rather than return to the other cities to rebuild. Connor's presence there had drawn no small amount of former CDF soldiers, and he'd been instrumental in getting Sanctuary the support it needed to become an actual colonial city.

She glanced wistfully up at the clear blue skies and smiled, missing him as Mayor Gates. After all those years of preparing for a war, it seemed that Connor had finally found some peace. She knew rejoining the CDF hadn't been an easy decision for him to make, but it was different this time. *He* was different. She still worried about him; that would never change. But Connor wasn't quite so consumed with preparing for the worst like he'd been after that first clash with the Vemus. The Krake certainly worried him, and if she was being honest with herself, they worried her, too.

She'd been studying archaeological records since they'd first landed on this planet, and she'd been piecing together everything she could about the Ovarrow civilization that used to live there. But she never would've expected to find stasis pods with those beings inside. Who would?

Lenora reached the interior of the abandoned city and went inside the archives, heading for the computing core. She could access all the information from her lab at the Colonial Research Institute; however, sometimes she just felt that she had a different perspective when accessing the data from its original location. Some of her students understood this. Dash certainly understood it as he trekked off to every possible Ovarrow ruin he could find.

The archives were quiet. Going down there was a reminder that a few hundred years ago, New Earth had been a much different place. Sometimes she brought Lauren with her. She tried to bring her daughter with her everywhere she went. When she did, she didn't get as much done as she would have, but she didn't mind so much. Becoming a mother had changed her perspective on work and life. But both she and Connor had demanding jobs, and given the current state of affairs, they needed to continue to work hard. Connor was focused on coming up with a way to protect them from the Krake, and Lenora believed that the answers and the insight they needed to come up with a strategy lay within the Ovarrow archives. This was how she could best contribute.

There were monitoring systems at the archives, and she'd sent her credentials through so she could just walk right in. She descended to the level where the computing core was and got to work. There were some key systems she wanted to access using the updated translator Dash had created. The new translator made some of the more obscure data repositories she'd found more accessible.

Lenora had been lost in her work for a few hours when she heard somebody walking down the corridor towards the computing core. She turned as Dash entered the room.

He smiled and waved at her. "Still prefer to work in the archives?"

Lenora stood up, stretched her arms in front of her, and rolled her shoulders. She'd been sitting a long time. "It does carry a certain amount of authenticity."

Dash nodded. "That it does."

"I was actually just giving the new translator a try on the archives."

Dash perked up. "Revision number seven, right? How'd it do?"

"It does open some doors, but it also raises more questions. At least now we can categorize more of what we *can* access. I can even task the AI at the research institute with trying to find any connections within the data that we might've missed. Some of the history makes more sense now."

"That's what I found at the capital city, but the archives there weren't as well protected as this one. Anyway, I don't get to spend much time there," Dash said.

"What brings you down here?" Lenora asked.

"I was visiting an old friend at Field Ops, and after seeing him, I thought I'd check in with you. Do you need any help with anything?"

"We still need to validate what the Ovarrow told us. The fact of the matter is that they can come out of stasis and tell us anything they want, and we wouldn't know whether it was the truth," Lenora said.

"So far, everything has checked out. I wonder how they'd react if they knew about this place."

A comlink chimed from Lenora's tablet computer, and she glanced at it for a moment before accepting the call. A small holoscreen appeared above it that showed Governor Wolf's face.

"Dr. Bishop, thank you for taking my call."

"Of course, Governor Wolf. What can I do for you?"

Dash came to her side within view of the camera. Wolf looked at him. "Mr. DeWitt, I'm glad you're there, too." She looked back at Lenora. "Dr. Bishop, I have a request. There's been a lot of debate on the proposed alliance with the Ovarrow. As someone who's studied the archaeological records, I believe you can provide a fresh perspective on the Ovarrow and possibly help improve our relations with them."

Lenora leaned toward the holoscreen. "I'm happy to give you my opinion, but I'm not a diplomat."

Governor Wolf smiled. "That's good because I don't need another diplomat. And I would value your opinion. However, it's a lot to discuss, and I was hoping you'd be open to making a short trip to Sierra."

Lenora frowned for a moment as her thoughts immediately turned to Lauren.

"We can arrange help with childcare while you're here, if that helps," Governor Wolf said and looked at Dash. "Mr. DeWitt, Darius Cohen has requested that you come as well."

Lenora glanced at Dash.

"Darius is the lead diplomatic representative for the Ovarrow," he said.

"Can I count on you to join us?" Governor Wolf asked.

Lenora considered the request for a few more moments. "I'll come. When is this meeting?"

"We're kind of in the middle of it now, but we'll also be reconvening in a few hours."

They wanted her there *now*. "I'll be there as soon as I can. I'll let your office know when I arrive."

"A C-cat is already en route to Sanctuary and will be there soon. It'll collect you and bring you straight to us."

The comlink closed and Lenora saw Dash grinning a little. "What?" she asked.

Dash shook his head and smiled. "It's not important."

Lenora narrowed her gaze. "If you were going to remark about my piloting skills, I'll have you know I've been flying ships almost as long as you've been alive."

Lenora was an excellent pilot. She just happened to make a few other pilots nervous when she flew.

"I know. I've flown with you, remember?"

She rolled her eyes. "Come on, I have some things I need to take care of."

"Yes, Dr. Bishop," Dash replied.

Lenora gave him a playful swat on the arm. "I'll give you 'Dr. Bishop.'"

CHAPTER 7

Savannah walked on the elevated pathway above the secondary hangar bay on Phoenix Station. This bay was used for ships in need of repair or for ships whose flight status hadn't yet been confirmed.

She'd risen through the ranks with the goal of commanding a warship, which she'd done for a while. Her first real ship command had been aboard the destroyer *Banshee,* which had been taken by the Vemus. Most of the crew had died, and she'd led the survivors through the enemy ship in hopes of commandeering a vessel to escape. Having survived that ordeal, she'd been put in command of Phoenix Station. At first, the station had been built from a patchwork of the battleship cruiser they'd been attempting to build. The current iteration was version two-point-zero and was designed from the beginning to be a space station capable of being among their first line of defense from an invading fleet.

It was quiet as far as hangar bays went, with the more active areas of the station being currently used. That wasn't a coincidence. Major Vance Peterson walked toward her from the opposite end of the elevated pathway. He'd just been speaking with his assistant, who had hastened in the opposite direction.

Peterson glanced down at the area below them. Several rows of Talon-V space fighters were being readied for active duty. It was impractical to bring all types of CDF ships into the hangar bay. They were simply too big, which was why most hangar bays housed the shuttles and other smaller spacecraft, while larger vessels docked with the space station itself.

She walked over to Peterson and they kept walking down a long corridor that extended out away from the station.

"I have a list of alternates in case this doesn't work out, Colonel," Peterson said.

"It's nice to have, but it won't be necessary."

Peterson pursed his lips thoughtfully. "If you say so."

"You don't know him like I do."

"I read his record. It's exemplary. He's received awards for distinguished service. Instrumental in bringing about the end of the Vemus War," Peterson said.

"Did you read down to the part where it was actually his brother he was attempting to rescue? That's when the Vemus Alpha entered the star system."

Peterson frowned as he read more of the report and then nodded. "I see."

A warning alarm sounded from the airlock on the far side of the corridor, indicating that there was a brief exposure to vacuum. A shuttle docked and then the locks switched to green. Several CDF personnel entered the station. Among them was a tall, athletic man with dark hair. He saw her and immediately headed in her direction.

He came to a stop and snapped a crisp salute. "Captain Jon Walker reporting for duty, Colonel."

Savannah returned the salute. "At ease, Captain."

Walker glanced at Peterson for a moment and then looked back at Savannah. "I didn't expect the commanding officer of Phoenix Station to meet me at the airlock."

"I wanted to show you something before your briefing, Captain," Savannah said, and without waiting for a reply, she walked to the other side of the corridor. There was a window of polarized glass that prevented anyone from seeing through it. Savannah set the window to clear, revealing the ship on the other side. Her gaze slid over the sleek lines of the vessel. It had twin engine pods near the rear, with secondary engines on top of the cigar-shaped ship.

Walker came over to her side. "It looks like a small frigate, Colonel," he said.

"It's much more than that, Captain," Savannah replied. "That's your new ship if you accept the mission we have for you."

"I wasn't under the impression that missions were optional, Colonel."

"This is a different kind of mission."

Savannah watched as Walker peered at the ship. "I know that's not a frigate. It has more sensor arrays. The hull looks different than the battle steel we use on standard CDF vessels. I'd say it's some kind of scout ship. A quick one, judging by the engines."

Savannah nodded in approval. "Very good, Captain Walker. That is the Raven class scout ship SR–01, the first of its kind. The hull is comprised of a new flexible alloy designed to thwart active scans."

Walker's thick eyebrows came together for a moment. Then he leaned toward the window, his eyes shining with desire. Savannah knew Walker's type. He was a pilot to his bones. She missed commanding a warship, but she wouldn't give up her current command to return to the gleaming decks of one. She could tell Walker wasn't done with them though.

He looked back at her and waited.

"Captain Walker, I'm sure you're aware of the disappearance of the Trident Battle Group. I want you to use this ship to find them."

Walker licked his lips for a moment and frowned.

"We've been putting together a plan to scout the alternate universe the Trident Battle Group went to, and there's a high probability of enemy forces operating in the area. We have a list of candidates selected for this mission, and you're at the top of the list. You have the most experience flying undetected among enemy forces. I believe that experience will be crucial for the success of the mission."

Walker scratched the side of his face and drew in a deep breath. Then he shook his head. "Now I understand why I would need to volunteer. This is a suicide mission. I thought the reconnaissance drones were making progress finding Trident Battle Group."

"Not quickly enough. It's been almost three months since we lost contact. We need to find out what happened to them. We already have a crew for the Raven, and all it needs is a captain. The mission is yours if you want it."

Major Peterson looked as if he was going to say something, and Savannah silenced him with a look.

Walker turned away from her for a moment, considering. "I'm sorry, Colonel. But you have the wrong man for this job."

He walked away, and Savannah could feel the proverbial door being shut in her face. She didn't like it one bit, and she didn't have time for self-absorbed antics. "Are you really content with making supply runs? Is that the extent of your legacy? You think that if you continue to make supply runs you can somehow fool yourself that you're still a pilot? That you're still capable of commanding a ship? Your record might indicate that you're a hero of the Vemus War, but your more recent record indicates a man who's barely keeping it together. I remember who you were. General Hayes and General Gates also remember, and it's with their approval that I'm extending this mission to you. Your choice is to either accept the mission to get out there and find Trident Battle Group, helping your fellow CDF soldiers in the process, or you can walk away. Scurry off this space station and crawl back to New Earth, but I guarantee you'll never fly for the CDF again. Those are your choices, Captain."

Savannah turned and walked away with Major Peterson at her side. She counted the seconds as she put more distance between herself and Jon Walker. She'd been on the receiving end of a kick in the ass once by Connor and hadn't liked it. She also didn't like having to be the one to do the kicking, but it was necessary.

"I'll call in the alternates, Colonel," Peterson said quietly.

Savannah nodded. She'd been sure that once she'd shown Walker that ship, it would spur some of that decisive gumption required by those officers who commanded ships. She might've been wrong.

"Colonel Cross," Walker called out as he hastened toward her. Savannah didn't turn around nor did she slow down. Walker repeated himself and circled in front of her. "What kind of reconnaissance do you need?"

Savannah gave him her stone-cold glare. "Time is a luxury, Captain. And I won't waste any if you're not one hundred percent committed to this."

"Understood, Colonel Cross," Walker replied. "Colonel Sean Quinn is the reason my family is still alive. I owe him, and I'll do everything I can to find him and the rest of the battle group. I promise."

Savannah regarded him for a moment. She'd already made up her mind, but she didn't want to appear to give in too quickly. She wanted Walker to believe she might not let him go. "All right then. The plan is as follows: We send the Raven through the space gate. You scout the area and come back through it at predefined times and coordinates."

Walker pressed his lips together and was silent for a few seconds. "You want to send the scout ship through the space gate here and come back through this space gate?" he said, gesturing away from him. "If we really want to scout the entire system, why not position a space gate at a predetermined set of coordinates? That way, our entry point isn't the same as our egress point. Since we have more than two gates, we could have multiple egress points should the need arise. I think it would be important to keep our options open, given the fact that there's a high probability of enemy ships in the area."

Savannah felt Peterson's gaze slip toward her and then back at Walker. She looked at her XO. "See, I told you. He's the right man for the job." She looked at Walker. "Welcome to Operation Sherlock, Captain Walker."

Walker's eyes widened for a moment. "Thank you, Colonel. I have a request."

Savannah felt her eyebrows raise. "What is it?"

"You mentioned earlier that you had a crew for the Raven. I'd like some additional crew members to be added to the roster. People I've worked with who I know are reliable."

Savannah resumed walking, and Walker and Peterson kept pace at her side. "We can discuss it, and we'll go over the specifics of the plan."

"Yes, Colonel," Walker said. "When do I leave?"

"Sooner than you'd like, but not soon enough."

Walker nodded. "Understood, Colonel."

CHAPTER 8

The CDF base at Sanctuary had grown considerably in the past eighteen months. All colonial cities had their own dedicated defensive force, but what made the base at Sanctuary different had to do with the city itself. The Colonial Research Institute drew in some of the finest minds in the colony, and this made the city a hotbed of ingenuity and technological advancement. In addition, the CDF base also had a significant section of its capacity devoted to weapons development and defense. What had begun as a stockpiling effort, with Connor doing his own weapons development, had expanded. Noah had really helped bring it along. Connor missed Noah, but he could still see his friend's contributions all around him. Civilian experts also worked at designated areas on the base.

Connor walked down the hallway, heading for an observation room with live feeds of the Ovarrow settlement. Samson caught up to him and settled into a pace matching Connor's.

"I thought you were on a training exercise," Connor said.

"This is just as important. I gave the teams their assigned tasks," Samson said. Connor raised his eyebrows and Samson continued. "This is as close as I can get to observing the enemy. I'm well aware that the Ovarrow aren't considered the enemy, but the Krake certainly are. This is as close as I can get to them until we can start using the Arch again."

"We'll get a chance, just not right now."

"I know. I know. We have a limited amount of resources and a whole lot more words to simply say we can't do it right now, but we *should* be doing it, Connor."

They reached the end of the hallway and turned down another one.

"You know how this works, Samson. We need buy-in and approval. Plus, we're still analyzing the data from the Krake base. The intelligence analysts are building profiles of the different universes. Then we have to review them to see which ones we want to recon. It's going to happen sooner than we think though."

They reached the observation room and walked inside. Carl Flint and Dr. Eric Young were already inside.

"Hello, Connor. I'm glad you're here," Eric said. "I've been meaning to talk to you, but your schedule has been pretty booked up."

Connor had first met Eric when he'd encountered Siloc, the Ovarrow they'd accidentally brought out of stasis. Dr. Eric Young was a psychologist who specialized in crisis management and coping strategies for traumatized situations. Eric had been surprisingly helpful during that time, and Connor had extended an invitation for him to advise the CDF as they learned to deal with the Ovarrow. Since the Office of NEIIS Intelligence was being absorbed into the Colonial Intelligence Bureau, Connor wanted his own intelligence assets within the CDF so they'd have reliable subject matter experts on hand. In essence, he'd done what he'd normally do in this situation and gone recruiting. Nathan often accused him of poaching the best talent, and it helped that Sanctuary held a certain amount of allure for colonists.

"It can't be helped," Connor replied.

"I understand, and I've been working with the other officers here on base, just as you asked. We're learning more about the Ovarrow each passing day. Certain behavioral patterns that were difficult to observe in a smaller group are now much easier to see as their population has grown," Eric said.

He was right about that. They'd put considerable effort into helping the Ovarrow become more independent, and that also necessitated bringing more of their people out of stasis. The Ovarrow population was over ten thousand refugees.

Connor had been part of the effort to offload over three hundred thousand colonists when they'd first arrived at New Earth. Accidentally awakened in one of the earlier groups, he'd learned that there was a balance between bringing people out of stasis and ensuring that they had adequate shelter, food, and relevant work details. What was different with the Ovarrow was that they didn't know who was in stasis. Not exactly. Having the Ovarrow involved with bringing their own species out of stasis sped up the process considerably. It made explaining things to them much easier than when it had been a purely human-based operation.

The Ovarrow city was a hundred kilometers from Camp Alpha, which was more of a forward operating base but with significant military and civilian presence.

"There are teams of scientists observing the Ovarrow and their interactions; however, I'm beginning to suspect they're aware they're being watched as closely as they were when there were only a few hundred of them at Camp Alpha," Eric said.

"Do you think it's a problem?" Connor asked.

They had stealth recon drones regularly patrolling the areas, which should have been undetected by the Ovarrow, but maybe they were wrong about that. Or the Ovarrow could simply assume they were being watched and work under that assumption.

Eric's head swayed from side to side. "It's difficult to say. Usually when people know they're being observed, they put on a performance. Given the situation the Ovarrow find themselves in, they're more anxious than they might otherwise be. It's hard to say because we still don't know when their stasis pod systems were supposed to bring them out. According to their experts, it was when the danger of the Krake had passed. How their systems were going to decide that is a bit of a mystery."

"I'm aware of this," Connor replied. "It's also important to remember that their system was flawed and breaking. Stasis pods were going offline because of a lack of resources. Their fail-safe was to eliminate the occupant rather than have them wake up earlier than intended. I believe that sheds a lot of light on how seriously they took this effort."

Samson whistled softly and shook his head. "I've witnessed the result of ruthless policies before, but this is extreme."

"The Ovarrow who got to go into a stasis pod were the lucky ones. Think about that for a little while," Connor said.

Eric nodded. "It does explain some of the violent outbursts that were observed at Camp Alpha. Having a cure for the rapid-aging illness was a big help."

That was something else that had taken them all by surprise, including the Ovarrow. They'd gone into stasis with only some of them knowing that when they woke up, they could be dead within a month. Faulty stasis tech resulted in rapid cellular degeneration, or extreme, rapid aging. They either hadn't yet perfected using stasis tech, or they just didn't understand the tech they'd stolen from the Krake.

"What else?" Connor said.

"In some respects, they're . . ." Eric said and paused for a moment, frowning in thought. "That's not right. The way they handle conflict is tied to establishing dominance. In some respects, it's like we're dealing with a primitive or immature species."

"They fought wars," Connor replied. "A lot of them. There hasn't been enough time for them to get away from that mentality. Constant war is a cycle, and it will take time for it to loosen its hold on how they deal with things."

"Except that's not what we're doing," Samson said.

"What do you mean?" Eric asked.

"We're pulling them out of stasis and telling them their worst enemy is still around and we'd like their help to fight them. How would you react?" Samson said.

"We can't keep them ignorant of the Krake. They just need some time to adapt," Connor said.

"I understand that. I've even noted it in my own observations. What's interesting is that the establishment of dominance isn't divided by males and females. They have similar stature in their society, but you're right, they've been conditioned to react to conflict in what we might consider the most brutal way possible," Eric said.

Samson cleared his throat. "Are you saying the Ovarrow are simply misguided?"

Eric nodded. "That's one way of putting it. Might be a bit oversimplistic, but it does get the point across."

Connor considered this for a few seconds. "They've been brutalized and manipulated, but on the other hand they've embraced the things they've been a victim of. I've seen that kind of behavior before."

"Where?" Eric asked.

"Back on Earth," Connor said. "My job, along with Samson's, was counterintelligence and insurgents. It was my job to deal with groups that manipulated other groups of people. There are lots of different ways to do this. Mostly it's preying on biases and prejudices. I think you see a lot of that with the Ovarrow."

"How are we supposed to deal with this?" Flint asked. He'd been listening and hadn't spoken until then.

Connor glanced at Eric and waited for him to answer. "If we interfere and force them to be civilized to each other, they'll resent it. What we need to deal with is the group mentality. Maybe focus on keeping the violence from escalating out of control."

Flint frowned and pressed his lips together. "How?"

"The Ovarrow need to feel that they can control their own destiny. Otherwise, they won't be able to help us *or* themselves," Connor replied.

"Just so I understand—we need to let them do their thing unless they're about to get out of control, at which point we step in and course correct for them?" Flint asked.

"It's a start, but again we're simplifying what's happening," Eric replied.

Samson shook his head. "This might make more sense if we were dealing with people, but they're an alien species. We can watch them all we want, but on a fundamental level, we might never understand them."

Connor looked over at the holoscreens that showed live video feeds of the Ovarrow city. The Ovarrow spent much of their time trying to provide for themselves, restoring systems in their abandoned cities. The colony provided ryklar deterrent systems so they could establish themselves without the threat of being attacked. They still had limited access to transportation beyond the city.

"I have a question for you, Connor. What do you think the Krake would do if they found this place based on what you know now? Given that this is a former world they used to control," Eric said.

"They'd probably observe us for a while. This place is one of their experiments that went wrong, and they'd likely want to understand why—how the outcome didn't match with their predictions. It also depends on how they perceive us. Are we a threat to them? I don't expect them to show up with an invasion force, at least not right away. That will come later."

"It's interesting," Eric said. "Your reply, that is. The Ovarrow seem to have a unified fear that the Krake will do just that—show up here and invade. At least, certain factions share that belief."

"That's the behavior of the Ovarrow that come out of stasis. Their soldiers come out ready to fight. I understand we're still learning more about them and observing them. We're also still analyzing the data we've taken from the Krake base. And then there's the group of Ovarrow we encountered on the other side of the continent that were guarding the Arch," Connor said.

Flint nodded. "Our recon teams couldn't find them. There were tunnels beneath the city that went on for kilometers. We had drones mapping the area, but we still couldn't find them."

"Who do you think they were?" Eric asked.

"They were different," Connor replied. "They used ryklars but in different ways. They removed the ryklars' auditory systems and relied on visual aids to control them. That kind of training doesn't happen overnight and means they must have some kind of tech base to work from. I wonder whether they were ever in stasis at all."

Eric's eyebrows lifted. "Never in stasis?" he repeated. "That means they'd have had to find a way to survive for over two hundred years in an Ice Age *and* avoid a superior enemy."

Connor shrugged. "It's not impossible. There was no power in that city, and they were keen to prevent us from using the Arch."

"I guess it shouldn't be too surprising. If the Ovarrow were strapped for resources and the stasis technology wasn't available everywhere, I guess it makes sense that there were pockets of them who tried to weather out the long winter. Why haven't we encountered them before?" Eric asked.

"We've mainly kept to our own cities and the surrounding areas. The main supercontinent is huge, so I'm not surprised we haven't come across them. We haven't been on the planet that long, and if they were hiding and had limited transportation capabilities, why would they ever need to travel across the continent?"

Eric nodded. "I guess that makes sense."

"More than that," Samson said, "we should be focused on finding them. They might be the only group of Ovarrow worth allying with. They didn't bury their heads in the sand, hoping to wake up to a better world."

"That's a bit harsh," Eric replied.

"I've been called worse."

Eric shrugged. "It's easy to judge. There's a lot of evidence out there that points to a desperate situation they were facing."

They glanced at Connor for a moment. "We still need to learn all we can about them. Then we can judge them or not—I don't care. Remember, if it comes to a fight with the Krake, we'll need more than just us to face them. The Krake could have a population that numbers in the billions and all the resources that go with that. So, whether we agree with what the Ovarrow did or not, we might still need their help."

CHAPTER 9

It was early afternoon by the time Lenora and Dash arrived at Sierra. The sky was thick with clouds, and it felt as if it was going to start raining at any moment. Sierra's proximity to a large river made for a more humid region than what they had at home. Sanctuary was closer to the foothills of an old mountain range, which generally gave them better weather, in Lenora's opinion. She found the drier region more agreeable, especially since she liked to be outside.

Dash walked beside her, and his mood seemed to have improved. She asked him about it.

"I'm happy to be working with you again, even if it's only for the next day or so," Dash replied. Then after a few moments, he added, "I do miss fieldwork. I like going into places no one's ever been before. It seems like now all I get to do are things related to the Ovarrow and translating their language."

"It's important work, Dash. You should be proud. You're becoming an authority in the area."

Dash smiled a little. "You're the real authority. You've been studying the Ovarrow since you got here."

"There's more to learn. Much more."

Dash nodded. "I know, and I'd like to get back to it."

"So, what's stopping you?"

They were walking across the garden path from the landing zone, heading into the governor's offices.

"Nothing is stopping me. There's just so much to do. I feel like I'm being pulled in a bunch of different directions, but I'm happy for all the opportunities. Mostly, I just want to help Connor as much as I can."

Lenora sensed that a "but" was implied. "I know he appreciates it."

"I even offered to join the CDF."

Lenora smiled and shook her head. "Why would you want to do that? Never mind, you don't need to join the CDF. Connor doesn't expect that from you."

Dash's face became grim.

"What happened to Noah wasn't your fault, Dash."

She understood Dash's feelings. He had a lot more in common with Connor than either of them thought. It was almost as if they were related somehow. Lenora had seen many people be drawn to Connor whether those people understood it or not. Some of those people, like Dash, were drawn toward Connor and rebelled against him at the same time. She often told Connor that he underestimated the effect he had on other people.

"I'm supposed to say that I know it's not my fault, but I was there."

"We'll find Lars and whoever he's working with. It doesn't have to be you, and it's okay if it's not you. Noah would never blame you for what happened to him. You need to let this go," she said. "Think of it like this: What if you *were* the person to catch Lars and bring him before the judiciary committee? What then? Do you think you'll feel satisfied?" Lenora asked.

Dash blew out a breath and lifted his chin. "I would. It would feel great. I'd love to see Lars get exactly what he deserves."

After years of dealing with Connor and other people from the CDF, she knew how to deal with what Dash was experiencing. "You might feel a little bit of satisfaction, but the anger would still be there. What you're really struggling with is forgiving yourself for something that isn't your fault, and that won't come from Lars Mallory at all."

Dash's eyes went cold. "What do you—"

He stopped himself from saying the rest, and his cheeks reddened a little bit.

Lenora arched an eyebrow. "What do I know about it?" she asked. "A lot. Do you know how long Connor blamed himself for not being able to help his friends Wil Reisman and Kasey Douglass? It's not just him, either. For a long time, Sean Quinn blamed himself for his father's death. It didn't matter to him that he was commanding all the ground forces engaging the Vemus. They were sacrificing entire cities to keep them from getting to us. And don't forget about Diaz. He's struggling with the same thing right now. Juan wants to do his duty, but he also wants to be there for his family. It's all different shades of guilt, and not all of it is healthy. I'm not saying you can escape feeling guilty about what happened, but you don't have to let it consume you."

Dash's eyebrows drew together, and his mouth hung open for a few moments.

"I'm also good at archaeology. Don't just stand there with your mouth hanging open. Come on, let's go," Lenora said and quickened her pace.

One of Governor Wolf's assistants met them and led them to the conference room. As they walked, Lenora glanced at Dash, and he seemed to be thinking about what she'd told him. She'd been meaning to talk to him about this for a while, but they could never quite get the chance.

Dash had the makings of a fine young man. He reminded her a little bit of Noah and Sean—probably Lars, too, if she really thought about it. She knew all three of them. They'd all been part of the early risers in the *Ark* program. Lars Mallory had always been as straight as an arrow, just like his father, and she couldn't begin to guess why he was doing the things he was. She and Connor had talked about it quite a bit, and he was less surprised than she was. At least Connor was able to rationalize it more readily than she'd been able to.

They entered the room and Governor Wolf smiled in greeting. She then introduced the other people who were in the meeting. "I'm sure there are some people here you already know and recognize."

Lenora nodded a greeting to Darius Cohen and then some of the members of his staff.

"Thank you for joining us at such short notice," Kurt Johnson said as he rose and came around the table to greet her.

Governor Wolf gestured toward a short woman with pale skin and curly brown hair. "Allow me to introduce you to Meredith Cain. She's the Director of the Colonial Intelligence Bureau."

Lenora had never met Meredith Cain before, but she'd heard of her. She gave Lenora a friendly smile.

"It's nice to finally meet you, Dr. Bishop. I've read much of your work on the Ovarrow, and I've found it very insightful," Meredith said.

"Also, we have a few of our interns sitting in on this meeting," Governor Wolf said and gestured toward the nearest young lady who had dirty blonde hair, brown eyes, and looked athletic. "This is my daughter Kayla. Next to her is Lynn Butler, and last but not least is Devon Sims."

"A pleasure to meet all of you," Lenora said.

"Dr. Bishop, it's so nice to meet you," Kayla said, and Lynn and Devon echoed the same.

Wolf smiled. "They've been excited to meet you since they first learned you were joining us. I think some of them are interested in attending the Colonial Research Institute at Sanctuary."

"It's the best place to be," Dash said and drew a few appreciative but shy glances from the two young ladies.

Lenora smiled at them and then looked at Governor Wolf. "We'd be lucky to have them."

"Thank you," Wolf said. "Back to the matter at hand. Let's bring you up to speed and we'll take it from there."

For the next half hour, Darius Cohen and Kurt Johnson went over their concerns about dealing with the Ovarrow. This was more of a strategy session for finding a way for the colony to form an alliance with them. They also highlighted the opinions of those who couldn't be at the meeting, including Connor's input. Lenora was no stranger to dealing with government officials, but it was usually over a matter of appropriating resources for her research.

"I'd like to hear your thoughts on the Ovarrow. We have the highlights from your research findings, but I'd like to hear your thoughts on how the archaeological record matches with the behavior we've seen from the Ovarrow," Wolf said.

Lenora sipped her water and then placed the glass back on the table. "For any archaeological record, we try to piece together everyday-life-type things. What makes that difficult with excavating any of the Ovarrow sites is that they've been sanitized."

Johnson frowned for a moment. "What do you mean by sanitized?"

"What I mean by that is that the sites weren't just left; they were cleaned. Evidence of the Ovarrow living in their cities was mostly erased. Some of that occurs naturally, but to the degree that we found . . ." Lenora shook her head. "There's also the purge protocol that summons the ryklars to attack and kill any living thing inside the Ovarrow cities. They could've been involved in removing all the evidence of what Ovarrow everyday life was like. I'm afraid mostly what I can speak to about this is something you already know. The wars the Ovarrow fought affected almost everywhere there was a city. We've theorized why they fought those wars, but when we introduce the outside influence that is the Krake, it just paints all their actions in a much different light. However, catastrophic events need to be taken into account. They could spur a civilization into doing the things they did—things like scrambling to get into a stasis pod. The archives that we've been able to decipher indicate there were a lot of events going on at the same time, and some of those things just spiraled out of control—a recipe for the perfect storm. I think what you're asking me is whether I think we can trust the Ovarrow. Isn't that right?"

"It wouldn't be fair to ask you that," Governor Wolf said. "Trust will be an ongoing issue until a baseline is established."

"From an archaeological perspective," Meredith interjected, "how would meeting an ancient species affect the perceptions of the archaeological record?"

Lenora thought about it for a few moments. "It would put things into context. I mean, just our interactions alone have enabled us to translate more of their archives."

Meredith pursed her lips in thought and then nodded.

"That makes sense," Governor Wolf said. "We're trying to find ways to compare the research that's been done with what we're observing now, and we're falling short. We can assign an AI to highlight some things, and it might give us some insight, but it's not the same as an expert giving us feedback, as I'm sure Mr. DeWitt can account."

Lenora glanced at Dash, and he nodded. "Being around them is different. I've observed them both in person and from video feeds from reconnaissance drones, and it's not the same. Being among them and interacting with them, seeing how they live—it just paints all the places we've explored in a new light."

"That's it exactly," Johnson said and pointed a sausage-sized finger toward Dash. "We need more of this."

Lenora frowned in thought for a few moments and then looked at Governor Wolf.

"Darius and I have spoken quite a bit about how best to deal with the Ovarrow," Wolf said. "We can try to be as diplomatic as possible, but the fact of the matter is we're still piecing this together as we go based on what we've learned. Any effort that can help this process would be a benefit to all of us."

"I understand that," Lenora replied. "I just don't know what else I can possibly say on the matter. You already have Dash working with you. I highly value his work and his observations."

"We do appreciate all of his contributions," Darius said. He gave a firm nod toward Dash and then turned back to Lenora. "I'd be curious to know whether you'd be interested in coming out to the Ovarrow city and seeing them firsthand. You've been studying them the longest of anybody in the colony."

Lenora felt as if all the eyes in the room were now focused on her. She'd been curious about Camp Alpha and everything they were doing there, but she hadn't ever been there. There was always something else getting in the way. She thought about Lauren for a moment. She loved being a mother, but it had made her change her priorities, which meant less time in the field.

"Is this something you would consider?" Governor Wolf asked.

"I hadn't thought about it, to be honest."

Wolf nodded. "One of the things Connor suggested is that we make an outward show of our support for the alliance with the Ovarrow. We rotate teams that go with the diplomatic envoys to the Ovarrow city, including interns," Wolf said and gestured toward her daughter and the other two interns. "If this is something that would interest you, then would you consider going with the next envoy? It would only be for a day or two. It could be longer if you decided you need more time, but I'd appreciate any insight you could give us. I really want the alliance with the Ovarrow to work as smoothly as possible. In a lot of ways, we're truly pioneering the effort. This is a first-contact-type scenario."

Lenora looked away from her and glanced from Wolf's daughter to Dash. His eyebrows raised, and he gave a slight nod.

"All right, I'll go."

"Excellent," Governor Wolf said.

"If you want," Darius said, "Dash and I can bring you up to speed about the Ovarrow we've been dealing with."

Lenora nodded. "That would be helpful. When do we leave?" she asked, knowing she also had to make a few calls herself before leaving.

"Not until tomorrow morning," Darius replied.

"Okay, that's fine. I'll need to make some arrangements. But right now, give me some more details about what you've learned so far," Lenora said.

This would be the first time Lenora would be away from her daughter, and she felt a slight tightening of her chest. She couldn't bring Lauren with her, but it would only be a few days, and Ashley wouldn't mind the extra time with Lauren.

They had food brought into the meeting room, which was good because Lenora was starving. She often forgot to eat when she was working. She actually didn't like being in meeting rooms all day, but they were necessary so the fieldwork could be done. It had been too long since she'd gotten into the field. This would be good.

CHAPTER 10

Lenora stifled a yawn as she sat in the diplomatic envoy's civilian air transport vehicle. There were multiple types of C-cats used throughout the colony, but this was among the biggest ones she'd been on. Since the C-cat was assigned to the colonial diplomatic effort, it also doubled as a mobile work center. She'd heard the CDF soldiers with them mistakenly refer to it as a command center.

Dash walked over carrying two cups of coffee and handed her one. Lenora thanked him.

"Are you still reeling from the crash course in Ovarrow diplomacy?" Dash asked.

Lenora blew on her coffee to cool it a little bit, then took a sip. It was delicious and not nearly as strong as Connor's experimental roasts he liked to try every now and then. "It's mostly common sense, but I don't know how they expect anyone else to remember all this. We'll have guides, of course," she said, glancing over to where she saw Kayla Wolf and Lynn Butler speaking quietly. They paused to look over at Dash. Lenora smiled and then leaned toward Dash. "I think you have a few admirers."

Dash made a point not to look over at them and shook his head. Lenora grinned. He was a handsome young man with his athletic physique, wide shoulders, and outdoorsman tan.

"That's all I need," Dash replied and sipped his own coffee.

"Mind if I join you?" Kurt Johnson said, a short man whose stomach bulged against his shirt. Without waiting for an answer, he sat across from Lenora. "Thanks again for coming along on this trip."

Lenora nodded. Johnson had sweat accumulating on his brow, and he dabbed at it with a handkerchief. His eyes were close together, which gave his face the appearance of being scrunched. She supposed it didn't help that he had one too many chins.

"Have you been to the Ovarrow city often?" Lenora asked.

"Only one time," Johnson replied and stuffed his handkerchief into his pocket. "Connor let me tag along with him a few months ago."

"He mentioned it," Lenora said.

Johnson's smile seemed more like a practiced response than one of sincerity. "We didn't always see eye to eye."

Lenora arched an eyebrow. "You think that's the case now?"

Johnson grinned a little bit. "Probably not, at least not on everything. But who does? Anyway, it gave me more insight into how the CDF operates. And more importantly, how Connor likes to work."

Lenora schooled her features. She knew Johnson was fishing for information or maybe just a reaction to his comments. "He's a tough nut to crack," she replied.

Johnson grinned, and Lenora felt that he was evaluating her. Perhaps being dreadfully obvious about it was how he disarmed a person into giving away more than they thought they were.

"What do you hope to see in the city?" Lenora asked.

Johnson pursed his lips in thought for a moment. "Their population has grown to over ten thousand, and we've expended a lot of effort helping the Ovarrow become independent. I guess you could say once the ball got rolling, we've certainly delivered on our promises to them."

"And now you're hoping they'll reciprocate."

Johnson nodded. "The Krake are as much a problem to them as they are to us. Something I'd like to get your opinion on after this trip is whether you think we can trust them."

That question had been implied multiple times by Governor Wolf. Even Darius Cohen had said they were looking for ways to better understand the Ovarrow so they could communicate in a more meaningful way. Darius was under a lot of pressure to get the Ovarrow to cooperate. Lenora understood the political bureaucrats of the colony. She had to work with them in order to get what she needed for her own work.

"Trust is a two-way street. Do they understand what we want?"

Johnson glanced at Dash. "I guess that depends on young Mr. DeWitt's translator."

Dash set his coffee cup down. "They understand."

"I hope they do because there are a growing number of people who want us to withdraw our support of the Ovarrow," Johnson said.

Lenora shook her head. "That's a bit shortsighted, isn't it? I mean, we just started helping them. That kind of thinking might make more sense a year from now if we've gotten nothing in return. My guess is that they never supported the alliance in the first place."

"Well that's another reason we're here, and we'll continue to send diplomatic envoys to the Ovarrow city. All our efforts will be in the public eye.

This is part of our new ongoing effort to demystify the Ovarrow to the colony."

It made sense to Lenora, but at the same time the whole notion to withdraw their support of the Ovarrow was borderline absurd. It was quite simply too soon for people to even form an opinion about it, much less arrive at a conclusion. "Do you know which groups have been voicing the most objections to our support of the Ovarrow?"

Johnson's shrugged. "It's nothing new. Ever since we discovered . . ." he said, pausing for a moment to look at her, ". . . *Connor* discovered that the Ovarrow were in stasis pods in secret bunkers, it's been a concern."

A concern, Lenora thought with a flash of irritation. "Were these the same people who wanted Connor to be held criminally liable for destroying the military bunker?"

She saw Dash turn toward her and then look at Johnson. The government advisor hardly reacted at all, but his dubious demeanor seemed to melt away. "I can see why you'd ask that."

"Really? The first reaction to a life-threatening situation was that Connor and the other people with him were wrong to retaliate in self-defense. I believe the term used was 'warmonger.'"

Johnson held up his hand in a placating gesture. "I understand your frustration, Dr. Bishop. But we also denounced any wrongdoing for everyone involved."

"Only because there were no actual laws that forbade what Connor had to do to survive his first encounter with the Ovarrow."

"Perhaps it's best not to dredge up something that happened so long ago," Johnson said.

"I just wanted to know whether the same people who denounced Connor's actions in the past are now opposed to helping the Ovarrow overcome the devastation that has been visited upon them from their war with the Krake," Lenora said, her voice firm and unyielding.

The conversations going on in the C-cat's cabin quieted down, but she didn't care.

"I honestly don't know, and I didn't think to check out the sources of the objections under the context of which you've just described," Johnson replied.

"Well then, perhaps you *should* check it out. In fact, I'd look forward to hearing all about it once you do," Lenora said.

Johnson looked like someone who'd gotten his hand caught in the cookie jar. He hadn't expected to be handled quite that way. Lenora was sure he'd expected the conversation to go in a completely different direction, but she didn't care. There were some things that drew her ire, and this was one of them.

An audible chime drew their attention to the small holoscreen that powered on above them. It flashed with the estimated time of arrival, and the pilot announced that they would be approaching the landing zone in a few minutes. It was probably just as well because Lenora wanted to stretch her legs. Johnson made a hasty excuse to leave and went over to speak with Darius Cohen.

Lenora finished her coffee and could feel Dash watching her.

"What?" she asked quietly.

"I just haven't seen anyone handle Johnson quite like that."

"I'm tired of all the tiptoeing and beating around the bush. We—and I mean the collective 'we'—can't go around having a knee-jerk reaction to every bit of news that sweeps across the colony. It wastes time."

Dash's smile was a borderline smirk. "You have my vote, Dr. Bishop, should you ever run for office."

Lenora glared at him for a moment and then laughed. That was the last thing she'd ever do. She loved her chosen field, and she loved teaching. She had no desire to cater to the masses and said so.

"Well, you have my vote for that, too," Dash said.

"Oh please, what's with all the flattery?"

"Nothing. You are one of my two favorite teachers."

Lenora smiled widely. Over the years that she'd lived on New Earth, she'd had many students, and very few of them had stood out as having the potential to accomplish the things Dash had achieved. He was one of the good ones, even though he'd gotten off to a rocky start. "Who's the other one? The other teacher, I mean."

Dash looked at her for a moment. "You really don't know?"

Lenora shook her head. There were a lot of teachers at the Colonial Research Institute, and as far she knew, Dash had respected most of them. He really only bumped heads with— "Connor?"

"Who else could it be?" he replied right as Darius called him over.

Lenora leaned back in her chair and closed her eyes for a moment. There was no shortage of young men who idolized Connor. He underestimated his influence sometimes. It was one of his more endearing qualities.

"Excuse me, Dr. Bishop," a high voice said.

Lenora opened her eyes to Kayla Wolf, and she gestured for the young woman to sit next to her.

"I was hoping it wouldn't be too much trouble if we stayed by you while we toured the city?" Kayla asked.

"I'm pretty sure they'll want us all to stick together, but that's fine with me."

Kayla smiled, and it made a few adorable dimples appear on her face.

"So, your internship is at the governor's office?" Lenora asked.

Kayla nodded. "Thank you for that—not calling it my mother's office. I think sometimes she just wants me to follow in her footsteps."

Lenora nodded amiably. She couldn't wait for Lauren to be old enough to come to a dig site. "What are you interested in?"

"I don't know," Kayla said, her eyes gleaming with excitement. "Everything. My last internship was at the biomedical research institute in Sierra. I helped with—well, more observed—the work done on the cure for the cellular degeneration disease that affected the Ovarrow. I loved what they were doing there. But sometimes I just want to take one of the rovers and head off in one direction and keep going."

"Well, if you're interested in leaving Sierra for a while, I'm sure you could get an internship at any of the other cities, including Sanctuary."

She watched as Kayla glanced toward Dash, her head slightly tilted, making her almost look a bit shy. She was just a girl with a crush.

"Ladies and gentlemen, we are on our final approach to the landing zone," the pilot said over the nearby speakers.

The C-cats had a soft landing that Lenora hardly felt. She supposed the large vehicle had better inertia dampeners than the smaller ones because a soft landing hardly ever happened, at least when she flew them. A flash of irritation climbed up her neck, and she scowled. She could fly a C-cat just fine and had landed them on some of the most challenging terrains on the planet.

Lenora stood up and reached behind her seat for her backpack. It contained basic survival equipment, along with a few extras she normally took with her when she went anywhere away from home. She grabbed her jacket.

Darius Cohen walked over to her and glanced at her backpack. "I'm pretty sure you won't need that while we tour the city."

"I'll bring it with me just the same. They're just some things I'd take with me to any remote site. I know there are Ovarrow living here, but this was once a site we would've excavated, so I just have some smaller handheld devices for that."

Darius nodded and walked away, heading for the nearest exit.

Dash came back over and retrieved his own backpack. He glanced at her. "How about that landing? I hardly felt it. It's almost as if that's the way they're all supposed to feel."

Lenora slipped one of her arms into her jacket and then the other, giving Dash a look of mock severity. "Is that some kind of sly comment about my flying?"

Dash smiled at Kayla and shook his head quickly. "Wouldn't dream of it. Whenever we've flown together, I'm just thankful to get on the ground safe and sound."

"I think I liked you better when you were quieter."

Dash glanced at her jacket and frowned. It was a dark brown field coat, but she wondered if he was going to notice. "Is that—"

"Yes, it is," Lenora said, cutting him off. "It's not the whole suit, just the jacket. It's a civilian version of it. Connor insists that I take it with me when I go out in the field. They're actually quite comfortable."

The material used to make her jacket was the same nanorobotic material used for the multipurpose protection suits. It could form a hood that would protect her head, but it wasn't meant for anything drastic.

"Looks good. I want one of those. My birthday is just around the corner," Dash said.

Lenora leaned toward him. "I know people, and besides, I thought you already had an actual MPS."

"I do, but sometimes it gets to be a bit much wearing that over my regular clothes."

They headed toward the door, and as soon as Lenora stepped down the loading ramp, she heard gusts of wind blowing outside. It died down after a few moments and then kicked back up again as she felt the slight tug of a few strands of her ponytail lifting off her neck. She followed the others around and got her first look at the Ovarrow city.

The midmorning sun reflected off the bronze metallic alloy the Ovarrow used in the construction of their buildings. The city had probably been home to several hundred thousand Ovarrow before the Ice Age, so the refugees had plenty of room to expand; however, there was a lot of restoration that needed to occur to make it safe. Scaffolding enveloped multiple buildings near the border. The taller buildings looked as if they'd been left alone. With only ten thousand refugees, there wouldn't be a need to expand into those areas for the time being. There were several wind turbines placed throughout the city, as well as the open field area outside the city. There was enough wind here to keep those turbines turning and charging the power station the Ovarrow used to generate electricity.

Lenora shielded her eyes from the sun and saw dark shapes moving about the city in groups. She couldn't tell what they were doing, but she assumed they must have been work crews.

A squad of CDF soldiers came over to join the diplomatic envoy. One of the soldiers glanced at her for a moment and then began speaking to the others. Several more of the soldiers looked over at her.

"Dr. Bishop, I'm Lieutenant Scott Morgan. I hadn't been informed that you were among the visitors here today."

"Is something wrong?" Lenora asked.

"Not at all. You just weren't on the visitors list. If there's anything you need, please don't hesitate to ask," Lieutenant Morgan said and left.

She saw him speaking to one of the other soldiers, nodding in Lenora's direction. She supposed she was getting her assigned escorts for this trip—one of the perks of being a general's wife, she supposed.

They waited a short distance away from the C-cats, and a large group of Ovarrow came toward them. They wore dark chest armor and carried shock lances that were capable of delivering bolts of energy. Lenora remembered Connor being quite impressed with them since they still worked after being sealed for hundreds of years.

Lenora stood next to Darius, who gave her a nod. An updated program registered itself on her wrist computer. It was the latest version of the Ovarrow translator program, so at least they wouldn't have to type in every single line of communication. Their voice-recognition software would do its best at translating human language into the Ovarrow symbols that would appear on the holoscreen. The Ovarrow would still have to type in their replies, however.

"I've just sent out the latest translator updates to everyone here," Dash said to Darius.

"Good. Let's see who they sent us."

"Do they rotate who comes out here to meet visitors?" Lenora asked.

"Yes, they do. They usually get representatives from different factions, which can be difficult sometimes, but it also allows us to interact with a variety of Ovarrow," Darius said.

Lenora watched as the Ovarrow soldiers approached them. They held their weapons with the same familiarity she'd seen among CDF soldiers. She looked for Lieutenant Morgan and saw him watching the Ovarrow approach as well. They appeared at ease, but Lenora knew that wasn't the case. If anything, the CDF soldiers were more alert than they'd been before. She couldn't blame them. There was a large contingent of Ovarrow soldiers—Mekaal— coming toward them who were heavily armed.

"Military escorts all around, I see," Lenora said.

Kurt Johnson stood next to her and watched the approaching soldiers warily. "It's one of their rules," he said.

"They'll assign escorts to guide us throughout the city. It makes them feel more secure," Darius said.

Lenora nodded. "Will they restrict us from going anywhere, or are we allowed to go wherever we want?"

Darius frowned for a moment. "You know, I'm not sure. In all my visits here, I've never been told I couldn't go somewhere, but I've always had an escort, which is fine. They don't deny us our weapons, so we do have some protection ourselves. Our presence here is hardly new, given that we brought these Ovarrow out of stasis. They've all seen humans before."

"Do they do the meet-and-greet here, or will they take us somewhere else in the city?" Johnson asked.

"They've done both in the past. Given that this is a larger group, they might want us to meet with their high commissioner, an Ovarrow named Senleon who's from the administrator faction," Darius said.

"High commissioner—administrator?" Lenora asked.

Dash nodded. "Yeah, our translators are based on the symbols we've translated from their computer networks. The translator might be off on the actual term, but it does give us the context of who we're dealing with. It beats referring to some of them as superuser or sudo. That would be awkward. Linguists are working on a better translator, but it'll take time. For now, at least, we have a foundation from which to communicate with them."

Lenora was familiar with the translation program they were using, as well as its limitations. It was all they had, and it had gotten them this far, but she hadn't realized Dash had used so much creative freedom with the Ovarrow reference. She looked at Darius Cohen. "How far is Camp Alpha from here?"

"Not that far. About fifty kilometers, but we don't have any permanent residents in their city."

"Why is that?" Johnson asked.

Darius arched an eyebrow. "Do you think Sierra is ready for an Ovarrow embassy? How about New Haven or Delphi, for that matter?"

Johnson looked at the approaching group of Ovarrow, considering. "I guess I hadn't thought of it like that."

"The Ovarrow are keen to be independent," Darius replied.

"Yes, but they do realize they need our help," Johnson pressed.

"There's a difference," Lenora interjected, "between knowing they need somebody's help and having it thrown in their collective faces. You have to remember that when they went into stasis, their world was crumbling around them. They had no idea what they were going to wake up to, and in some cases—a lot of cases—they thought they were going to die if the stasis pods didn't kill them by breaking down. Look at them," she said, and then added, "Not the soldiers, look at the city. They're working hard to get this place up and running."

Johnson frowned in thought, his expression unreadable. "Yes, I can see that they're working hard."

"You're missing the point," Lenora replied and glanced at Darius, who watched her shrewdly, waiting for her to continue. "There's probably a strong dose of survival instinct kicking in here, but we could also be dealing with psychological avoidance—meaning that if they were to slow down, they'd have to deal with the fact that the world they knew is lost to them. This is something we can all relate to, if you think about it."

Lenora looked around at the others. New Earth was a wonderful world to colonize, and even with all its dangers and nuances, it had become humanity's second home. What had haunted their proverbial footsteps was the fact that the old Earth they'd known was gone forever.

Darius nodded and smiled a little. "You make a very good point, Dr. Bishop. I think on some level I realized what you were saying just from being among the Ovarrow for months. But we've had so many other concerns that it's not something we've spoken about at Camp Alpha. We certainly haven't aligned the Ovarrow experience with what the experience of losing Earth was like for us."

"There are some similarities, I'll grant you that. Loss is a loss, I suppose," Johnson said.

"I was merely pointing out that we have some common ground. We've sent probes back to Earth that will one day give us a status," Lenora said.

Johnson shrugged. "I probably won't live to see that, given the distance to Earth. Won't it take the probe two hundred years to get there?"

"No, it won't," Dash said. "I remember this project. It's more like a probe swarm that's en route to Earth, and it can travel at near relativistic speeds. It will take them about seventy years to get there. They'll do an assessment and send the data back to us, and the fastest it can reach us is sixty years. That's how long it takes light to travel here."

Johnson gave Dash an amused expression. "Okay, fine. Not two hundred years, but a hundred and thirty years, give or take. Either way, I'll either be very old or not here at all," he said and turned back to the approaching Ovarrow.

Darius stepped in front of the others, but the CDF soldiers fanned out on either side of him, regarding the Mekaal. The Ovarrow were a tall species whose tawny skin tones were almost pebbled, like that of a reptile, but they were warm-blooded. Pointy protrusions stemmed from their shoulders and elbows. Their large, four-fingered hands were twice the size of a human's despite them being of similar size and weight. Thick brow lines framed their eyes, which were separated by a flat nasal cavity, giving their skulls a convex shape on top. Their wide mouths had frown lines that made them look aggressive.

Lenora watched as the soldiers regarded each other coolly. Darius made introductions, and she noticed that more than a few Ovarrow looked at Dash with open appreciation. Then she remembered that Dash had been instrumental in finding the medical cache they'd based the cure on for the rapid-aging problem the Ovarrow faced when coming out of stasis.

A comms drone hovered in the air, and a large holoscreen appeared above it so the Ovarrow translator could show the symbols of their language. It was a slow way to communicate.

She watched as an Ovarrow named Raylore entered his responses through the holographic interface.

"Welcome, human colonists. You are requested to see High Commissioner Senleon before any other activities in the city," Raylore said.

Lenora saw Darius hesitate for a moment and then reply. "Of course, we'd be honored to meet with the high commissioner."

Raylore turned and addressed the nearest Ovarrow soldier, and they all stepped back, making a path. The Ovarrow soldiers gave them plenty of room, but nevertheless, they surrounded the colonial diplomatic envoy.

Lenora looked at Darius. "Have you met the high commissioner before?"

"A few times. They usually have us meet with different faction leaders, but this time we're asking to have a look around. Sometimes that can put the Ovarrow on edge. This is their home, after all, and we must be respectful of that," Darius replied.

Lenora was quiet, and she noticed that one of the CDF soldiers had taken up a position to her right, matching her pace. The soldier looked at her and gave her a firm nod. His name appeared on her internal heads-up display.

"Ma'am," Sergeant Cook said.

"So, you're to be my personal escort, I take it?"

Sergeant Cook smiled. "I'm the winner."

"I'm quite certain I can look after myself, Sergeant Cook."

"Oh, I know that, Dr. Bishop; however, in the unlikely event that the shit hits"—he stopped speaking, realizing what he'd said—"uh, things go sideways, let's just say I'd rather report to General Gates that I did everything I could to help his wife."

"You do realize that the governor's daughter is several paces behind me," Lenora replied.

"Make no mistake, I'll do everything I can to ensure the envoy's protection. I'm just choosing a strategic location from which to execute my duties, Dr. Bishop."

Lenora smiled and nodded. The military had a particular way of phrasing their intentions in one of the most direct manners she'd ever encountered. She had long gotten used to it with Connor and all the soldiers she'd met over the years.

She looked around at the Ovarrow that surrounded them. These were the first she'd ever seen in person, which was much different than observing them through a live video feed from a reconnaissance drone. The way they walked seemed both familiar and foreign at the same time. She was glad Sergeant Cook was nearby, but she also knew it wouldn't make a difference with so many Ovarrow soldiers surrounding them.

Nothing is going to happen, she told herself. As they walked toward the city, she had to repeat the sentiment a few more times.

CHAPTER 11

Lenora felt as if she'd taken a trip back in time. Most of her time on New Earth had been spent exploring the alien ruins they'd found there. She'd spent countless hours trying to imagine what the previous inhabitants had looked like and how they'd lived. Now she was walking among them. Most Ovarrow they passed stopped what they were doing to watch them for a few moments. Their cinnamon-colored eyes had vertical pupils that looked more feline than reptilian. They were the eyes of a predator, and Lenora suspected that they were capable of razor-sharp focus.

As the Ovarrow watched them, Lenora wondered what they were thinking. Being around them would take some getting used to, and it was probably the same for them.

They walked down the main thoroughfare past groups of Ovarrow working to restore their living quarters. Darius continued to share what he knew as they entered the city. He was speaking in a conversational tone, and Lenora wondered if the Ovarrow thought it was rude because they couldn't understand what the colonists were saying.

"Why isn't there a team of linguists stationed here?" Lenora asked.

"They were too much of a distraction. The linguistic team is allowed to come here once every five days. They can stay for the entire day, but they have to leave in the evening," Darius said.

Lenora looked around and saw small colonial listening devices attached to the buildings, essentially hidden in plain sight. Her implants allowed her to spot them, but she wondered if the Ovarrow knew they were there.

Darius followed her gaze and then gave a slight nod in Johnson's direction. Lenora didn't think Dash approved, but perhaps the listening devices were a necessity. Improving communication capabilities with colonists was a lower priority to the Ovarrow while they started to rebuild their society.

"Do the wind turbines provide enough power to the entire city?" Johnson asked.

"No, not by a long shot, but they don't need them to power the entire city. Remember, there are relatively few of them here," Darius said.

"Yes, but at this rate of growth, won't there be a problem soon?"

"We've offered our assistance, but they haven't taken us up on it yet. They're working to restore their own reactors, but it's going to take some time. Possibly a few months to bring them back online, if they can."

"I remember working with the engineers for the geothermal taps the Ovarrow used at Sanctuary," Lenora said. "We had to replace almost all the components, but at least we had a tech base to work with."

"They're pretty good at salvage," Dash said. "I think they had a lot of practice at it before they went the stasis route. They don't appear to be surprised at the state of things," he said and shook his head. "Don't get me wrong. They're surprised when they come out of stasis, but I think they were prepared to do whatever they had to do to survive once they came out. None of them thought there wouldn't be a struggle."

Lenora glanced through the open door of one of the buildings as they walked past. There was an Ovarrow inside, attempting to use a console, and his finger had just poked through the mesh screen. The Ovarrow hastily tried to prevent it from disintegrating, but it was too late. Lenora had firsthand experience with trying to prevent the destruction of those consoles. She could help them out with that. She glanced at Dash, thinking he'd probably already offered them help, and wondered why the Ovarrow hadn't developed anything like a holoscreen but chose to instead project their interfaces onto a mesh screen. Sometimes the mesh was encased to protect it from deterioration, but all too often it wasn't. That was why Lenora had helped to develop an interface so they could access the Ovarrow consoles through their wrist computers.

A group of Ovarrow gathered off to the side of the street. They were craning their necks, trying to peer past the Mekaal as if they were looking for someone in particular. Dash stuck out his hand and waved toward them. The Ovarrow brought their left hands to one of their brow ridges and then raised them.

"What are they doing?" Lenora asked Dash.

Dash stopped waving and looked a little uncomfortable. "They're thanking me for saving them."

Johnson harrumphed. "Don't they understand that it was colonial scientists who actually synthesized the cure?"

"I've told them. Believe me, I've told them many times."

Lenora smiled. "It doesn't matter. You were the one who found it for the scientists to synthesize."

The farther they went into the city, the more attention was drawn to them.

"Darius, I haven't been able to detect any ryklar-deterrent signals here. Why is that?" Johnson asked.

"They're using their own signal, and you're scanning for a colonial one. There aren't any ryklar in the vicinity of the city. In addition, the Mekaal patrol the perimeter of the occupied sections of the city. They also assign protection details for the salvage groups that go into the city, as well as to the farmland that workgroups manage. They're having trouble with some of their equipment, but they're making it work. We're monitoring it."

Lenora hadn't looked out the window as they'd flown toward the city, so she hadn't seen any of the farmland. She wondered what they grew for food. The sites she'd excavated contained only the equivalent of colonial rations, which was a mix of dehydrated carbohydrates and proteins.

"We do bring food supplies with us. In fact, there will be a shipment here tomorrow. Apparently, the Ovarrow enjoy eating gourds. In particular, the purple variety is highly valued, so we bring crates of it as a token of good faith," Darius said.

Lenora tried not to gawk at anything, but seeing even this small section of the city filled with Ovarrow was exciting. In her experience, the only beings that had frequented an Ovarrow city besides people like her were the ryklars. They'd had more than a few terrifying encounters with ryklars until they figured out how to reproduce the ryklar-deterrent signal. However, New Earth was home to other predators—perhaps not as dangerous as the ryklars, but there was always something new to discover. She glanced at the Ovarrow and wondered who'd created the watchdogs that guarded the Mekaal bunker Siloc had taken Connor to. She found that her mind was trying to bridge who she'd imagined the Ovarrow to be with what she was seeing in front of her, and she couldn't. At least not right now.

"Where are the children?" Lenora asked.

The question drew a few raised eyebrows, but after a quick look around, they looked at Darius for the answer. All the stasis pods Lenora had ever seen were of a standard size, so it was impossible to determine who was inside.

Darius glanced around to be sure they wouldn't be overheard. "Be careful. That's a sore subject. We haven't found any yet, and when we asked, we were told that the stasis pods wouldn't work for their younglings, although a juvenile nearing the end of puberty could survive just fine."

Lenora's mouth hung open for moments. "What?"

"The stasis pods wouldn't work for their younglings."

Lenora swung her gaze toward the Ovarrow. *Younglings*, she thought. "All the Ovarrow in stasis pods are adults?"

Darius swallowed hard. "No, but most of them were. The ones with their younglings . . ." He shook his head.

"Stop calling them that! They're children, Darius," Lenora said, her voice shrill.

Darius looked away, and she inhaled sharply. She couldn't believe it. She looked around as if seeing the situation of the Ovarrow in new light as her brain raced with all the implications. The Ovarrow had to go into stasis or they were going to die, but their children . . . Her throat thickened. She was being emotional, and she knew it, but she kept thinking about Lauren. There was no way she'd ever abandon her child. She'd rather die. But it couldn't be that simple. No parent who loved their child would ever leave them to die. As she looked at the Ovarrow, she wanted so much to believe they shared that sentiment, but what if they didn't? Lenora shook her head and sighed. What had happened to their children? Had they been abandoned? Had they been slaughtered? Didn't they care about them? How could they do this?

Lenora heard Kayla whisper something to Lynn and Devon. They gasped.

"Please, could everyone just calm down a little bit? Don't jump to conclusions," Darius said. "This is an extremely sensitive subject, and I'd urge you all to be cautious about whatever assumptions you're forming in your minds right now. The fact of the matter is that we don't know the entire story."

Lenora narrowed her gaze and looked over at the Ovarrow who was leading them, the one named Raylore. She wanted to storm right up to him and demand to know what had happened, but that was foolish, and she knew it. This was grim survival at its worst.

"He's right. We can't make assumptions," Lenora said.

"We might not be able to, but when the rest of the colony learns of this, they'll make their own assumptions even if we provide the facts," Johnson said. He shook his head and folded his arms in front of his chest.

"We need to get all the facts, but people are always going to judge. There's no stopping that," Lenora said quietly. She glanced at Dash, and the forlorn look on his face indicated that he'd known about this. She felt a flash of annoyance at the fact that he hadn't warned her. Then she realized it wasn't because he was hesitant to warn her but more that she needed to experience her exposure to the Ovarrow with a fresh perspective, and that meant not tainting it at all. Academic objectivity at its best. She didn't like it, but at least she understood.

Dash mouthed the words, "I'm sorry."

Lenora nodded. The main road took them farther into the city and downward. There were bridges not far from them that connected different parts of the city. The Ovarrow architecture changed the farther they went. The buildings were taller, but they all had an overhang. It would be difficult for a ryklar to scale them onto the roof. They walked beneath footbridges that connected larger buildings to each other, and there were outdoor ramps that circled around the exterior of the buildings. The Ovarrow hadn't created stairs, which was the source of a lot of discussion among the colonists. The ramps looked to be well made, and in most cases, they were part of the actual building. The construction seemed solid enough, but she did see Ovarrow checking the supports and marking them with a black or white stripe. Lenora didn't know what that meant. She peered at the supports that had a white stripe, and they looked to have deteriorated much more than those with a black stripe.

They were led to a main square where there was a gathering of Ovarrow soldiers. Lenora glanced at Darius, who seemed surprised by the gathering.

"What's going on?" Johnson asked, his voice thick with concern.

"I'm not sure, but I believe they're taking us to the warlord and not the high commissioner," Darius replied.

Lenora looked at Dash.

"I've never met him," he said.

Lenora remembered from their conversation the previous night that the Ovarrow hierarchy was that of a shared political entity. There were faction leaders in addition to the high commissioner's office and also a warlord who was in charge of the Mekaal. Lenora glanced at the Ovarrow who were escorting them, and they didn't appear surprised at the gathering of soldiers. They were acting more like they'd expected it. The Ovarrow soldiers wore helmets, and some had a protrusion extending at the back, which Lenora supposed could be an antenna. Perhaps they had a way to communicate with each other that hadn't been in any of the sites she'd excavated. She looked at Lieutenant Morgan, who was stone-faced, but she could tell he didn't like the situation any more than they did.

Raylore led them to an armored Ovarrow who was neither heavily muscled nor extremely tall. There was no mistaking that this was the warlord because there was a general air of deference to him when he spoke.

Raylore gestured for Darius to come forward, and Lenora joined him. After a few moments, Johnson did as well. Sergeant Cook remained at her side, and Dash came forward, too.

The communications drone became active again, and a large holoscreen appeared above it. Lenora heard a banging sound from one of the tall wooden storage containers off to the side. There were Ovarrow soldiers all around them.

"Colonists, High Commissioner Senleon was unable to attend this meeting, but I present you to Warlord Vitory and the Warlord's First, Cerot," Raylore said.

Darius made the introductions, which also included a description of their roles. Lenora was introduced, and Darius described her function as someone who studied the ruins of ancient civilizations. Vitory looked at her and then stepped closer. Lenora saw the CDF soldiers become rigid next to her, but she didn't pay them any mind and kept her gaze fixed on the warlord.

"Your colony employs thieves?" Vitory asked Darius, keeping his gaze on Lenora.

"I'm not a thief," Lenora said and reminded herself that the translation might not be one hundred percent accurate, and the way the warlord was almost glaring at her led her to believe that that was the case right then.

The warlord considered her for a moment. "You raid our cities and take what doesn't belong to you. How is that anything but a thief?"

Lenora shook her head, becoming irritated. "There was no one else around. The Ovarrow weren't there."

The warlord drew his head up, and it made him look smug. "The Ovarrow never left. We were sleeping."

"Don't you mean hiding?" Lenora said. "Hiding from the Krake."

Several Ovarrow soldiers gripped their weapons tighter, and the warlord scowled.

Lenora didn't let up. She knew a bully when she saw one, and this was just for show. "If I'd found any Ovarrow, I would've been more respectful."

There was a deep rumble from the warlord's chest, and the Ovarrow soldiers immediately reacted. They gripped their weapons and slammed the ends of them into the ground. There were hundreds of them in the area, and the sound wasn't lost upon the envoy.

The CDF soldiers readied their weapons but didn't raise them all the way.

"Mr. Cohen," Lieutenant Morgan said, "this situation is getting out of control. Tell them to calm down or we will defend ourselves."

Darius spoke with Raylore and tried to reason with them. Lenora watched the warlord try to appear as if he wasn't listening, but she could tell that he was. He glanced at the holoscreen, reading every symbol that was translated. When he spoke, it was harsh, and Raylore winced. Then the Ovarrow cleared the screen and entered a few symbols.

"Visitation is over," Raylore said.

"Please forgive any offense we have mistakenly given. May we meet with the high commissioner?" Darius asked.

The translation appeared on the holoscreen. Raylore glanced at the warlord, who didn't utter a word. The answer was plain enough, but Raylore replied just the same.

"Visitation is over. You will be escorted out of the city immediately."

Darius turned toward them regretfully. "I'm afraid our visit will have to be cut short. We can try again tomorrow."

"I don't believe this," Johnson said. "How can they treat us like this? After all we've done for them," he said and then looked at the warlord. "You need to treat us better. You wouldn't be here if it weren't for us."

The warlord leaned over to speak with his second-in-command. Then he left, taking half the soldiers with him.

The warlord's first came over to them. "Please accept our sincerest apologies. The visit is over. Our projects are falling behind schedule and we cannot have a distraction at this time. That is the reason for the visit to be cut short," Cerot said. After he was sure they'd read the translation, he continued. "I will escort you back to your ship now."

Cerot took them on a different pathway out of the city, which Lenora found to be curious. As they made their way back, one of the Ovarrow came over to them. The designation on the Ovarrow shirt was for the healer's faction. The Ovarrow's skin was a bit more pebbled and had significantly more age lines than the others, but he still moved with agility.

"Jory," Dash said and walked over to meet him.

He turned on his personal holoscreen so the translation could be read.

"I'm not able to stay around today," Dash said and gestured toward the Mekaal.

Lenora watched as Jory entered his reply on the holographic interface.

"I would like to show you something," Jory said and walked over to Cerot, speaking quietly to him. The Ovarrow language still sounded so foreign to her. It was a mixture of screeches and other sounds, as if they were speaking with more than one vocal cord. Lenora didn't think they'd ever be able to replicate the sound without help.

Jory gestured toward Dash, and the warlord's first considered him for a moment. There was another exchange between the two Ovarrow, and then Jory returned.

"You are allowed to accompany me for a short time," Jory said.

Dash glanced at the others. "I'll meet you at the ship."

He looked at Lenora and then gestured toward her. "This is my teacher. Can she come with us?"

Jory took a moment to read the question and then glanced at Cerot for a moment.

"It is not permitted."

"It's fine," Lenora said. "Go on, build bridges," she said and smiled.

Dash walked away with Jory and two Mekaal escorts.

Lenora heard Johnson blow out a breath, not trying to hide his irritation at all. Lenora walked over to Cerot and brought up her own personal holoscreen.

"You mentioned that the work being done is behind schedule. Is there anything we can do to help you?" Lenora asked.

Darius and Raylore stopped speaking, waiting for Cerot's reply.

"The work will get done. Having outsiders visit so frequently disrupts things," Cerot replied. The Ovarrow's hands easily selected the symbols to craft his reply.

"Perhaps if you let us help you, we wouldn't be such a distraction," Lenora said.

"The Ovarrow must become great. This will not happen with help from outsiders."

Lenora was quiet for a few minutes as they continued walking down the street, passing under several footbridges. An Ovarrow yelled nearby, followed by a loud thud of something slamming to the ground. Lenora spun toward the sound. A group of Mekaal soldiers were dragging two prisoners toward a storage container. They unlocked it and shoved the two prisoners inside.

Lenora looked at Cerot. "What happened? What did they do?"

"Punishment," Cerot replied.

"Punishment for what?"

Cerot glared at her, and Darius came over. "I think I can help here," he said.

More Ovarrow soldiers came with citizens in custody, who were hauled to another storage crate and forced to go inside. They hardly put up a protest, seeming resigned to whatever fate had been bestowed upon them.

Lenora turned toward Darius.

"Just hold on a second," Darius said and looked at the others. "Don't jump to any conclusions. We're the visitors here."

Lenora fought to keep her voice devoid of scorn. "I understand that. I just wanted to know what happened," she said, looking at Cerot.

The Ovarrow watched them, and their escorts waited on his next command.

"It might be best if we just moved on," Lieutenant Morgan suggested.

Lenora inhaled a deep breath and nodded, and they continued onward for a few minutes. She glanced back at the storage crates as the whole event played back in her mind. The prisoners hadn't put up much of a fight, and she wondered what they could have done. Perhaps they'd stolen something. Lenora glanced around, wondering what they'd steal. Food, maybe? There were other Ovarrow going about their business, and they didn't give the storage crates anything more than a passing glance.

They continued, heading toward one of the longer footbridges that was about fifteen meters wide. There was a lot of foot traffic going to and fro. Above them was a much larger bridge, which didn't look to be in use.

"I knew it would be different coming here, but I hadn't expected all this," Johnson said to her. Beads of sweat covered his head. The wind gusts blew harder for a few moments and then subsided.

"Neither did I," Lenora admitted.

She heard Darius speaking to Raylore as they walked, and Cerot walked in front of them at a quicker pace. The ramp inclined when they were almost halfway across it. The higher elevation gave them a stunning view of a city being brought back to life.

Lenora quickened her pace, heading toward Cerot.

"Maybe it's best to leave well enough alone," Johnson called out to her as she passed him. He was breathing heavily from all the walking.

Lenora ignored him. Sergeant Cook kept pace with her and gave her a nod.

She closed the distance to the Ovarrow soldier—the warlord's first, the second-in-command, and a step away from being in charge of the Ovarrow military. Lenora just stood next to him, looking out at the city. She didn't bring up her holoscreen or engage the translator, wanting to wait and see what the Ovarrow did. Cerot seemed to regard her for a few moments and then waited.

Lenora brought up her holoscreen and thought about what she wanted to ask. There were a couple of different ways she could open this conversation. The Ovarrow were just trying to survive, but she wanted to ask them questions. She looked at Cerot, and the Ovarrow glanced at her holoscreen and then away.

"You've done a lot with the city in the short time you've been here," Lenora said.

Cerot read the message and then replied. "More work needs to be done."

There was always more to be done. Lenora could relate to that.

Another strong gust of wind blew, and Cerot turned and ran toward the edge of the ramp. A few seconds later, Lenora saw several Ovarrow gesturing toward them from a tall building down below. She could hardly hear them over the wind. Suddenly, the bridge sank, causing her to adjust her balance. She turned and saw that the bridge above them was twisting in the high wind. There was a loud crack, and the ground split apart a few meters in front of them. Lenora heard someone scream and turned to look back the way they'd come. There was another jagged split farther from them. Then the bridge collapsed under her feet, and she sank into rubble-strewn darkness.

CHAPTER 12

Connor glanced at the time and saw that it was early afternoon. His daughter, good food, and good company waited for him at the Salty Soldier. Victoria was watching Lauren, and he couldn't wait to get over there.

Major Natalia Vassar sat across from him in his office. Despite the considerable soundproofing of the walls, he could still hear the high-pitched whine of multiple Hellcats as they returned to the CDF base at Sanctuary.

"Sounds like the training exercise is over," Connor said.

Major Bethany Anders looked at her personal holoscreen and then nodded. "A bit ahead of schedule, but these are the 3rd and 7th Ranger companies."

Connor heard a bit of dismay in his operations officer's voice. The 3rd and 7th Ranger companies were led by Carl Flint and Samson.

"Is there anything I should know about the results of the exercise?" Connor asked.

"Negative, General. Efficiency scores are all at the top, as well as taking advantage of tactical awareness. However, it might be more constructive not to celebrate quite so much at the expense of the other participants in the training exercise," Anders replied crisply.

Connor smiled. At this stage in his career, he didn't have to hide it when he found the situation amusing. "Sometimes a little negative reinforcement is just what someone needs for their performance to reach new heights."

"I agree, General, but changing the names of the other units to include the word 'incompetent' in the name while they return to base might be a bit too far. In other cases, they revoked access to their designated transport vehicles, forcing the now-disgraced company to walk back to base. I had to send another team to undo the changes, and they were automatically assigned additional training—" She stopped speaking as a new message appeared on her screen.

"What kind of training?" Connor asked.

Anders looked at him squarely. "Potty training."

Samson, Connor thought and chuckled. Vassar snorted and attempted to cover it up with her hand.

Samson probably didn't have the technical know-how to accomplish all that, but he was making good use of the people under his command.

"General," Anders continued, "I think these actions are setting a bad precedent. This sort of behavior can readily get out of control."

Connor nodded. "I see your point, but at the same time, it can inspire a creative response. As long as no safety regulations were violated during the exercise, I don't see how any disciplinary action should be taken against those soldiers. What we have here is probably just a case of wounded pride. We're not in the business of coddling our soldiers."

Major Anders stiffened for a moment. "Understood, sir."

"Just to be clear," Connor began, "I'm not against retaliation, but it has to be in the right context. They have to beat them on the field. I suggest you inform their commanding officers of those options. Maybe a little reminder would go a long way in keeping things from getting out of control."

Major Anders's posture became a bit less rigid at that. "Thank you, sir. I'll make sure they know that."

"Good. Oh, you can go ahead and remove the new training item. Now, if that's it, ladies, I have another appointment that I intend to keep," Connor said and stood up.

"There's one more thing, General," Major Vassar said.

Connor remained standing and looked at her. "What is it, Natalia?"

"There's been another report from Major Alexis Brooks, the commanding officer at Camp Alpha. I think you need to see it, but in the interest of time you could probably just review the vid log," Natalia said.

Connor inhaled and rubbed his chin for a few moments. "All right, put it on the wallscreen over there and I'll take a quick look."

A few moments later, Major Alexis Brooks's head and shoulders appeared on the wallscreen in Connor's office. She was making her report from her own office.

"Major Alexis Brooks, Ovarrow report number sixteen-thirty-two. The population of the Ovarrow settlement has grown to ten thousand residents. Twenty percent of that number is from the Mekaal faction, which is the Ovarrow military designation. There have been increased instances of the Ovarrow distancing themselves from colonial support. They've also been limiting access to their city. While the Ovarrow mannerisms could be considered terse by human standards, by Ovarrow standards, it seems to be the norm. Behaviorists advised that we should not rush to judgment. However, I thought it pertinent to include more detailed findings later in this report. On the highest levels, the reports I'm seeing from visitors to the Ovarrow city are ones of increasing Ovarrow isolation—"

"Stop the video log," Connor said. He looked at Natalia.

"She appended detailed accounts from various observers. I thought this was important enough to warrant making you aware of the situation, sir," Natalia said.

Connor frowned in thought for a moment and then opened a comlink. "Dr. Young, can I see you in my office, please?"

"Yes, of course. Right away, General Gates."

A few minutes later, Dr. Eric Young walked into his office.

"Have you seen this report, Eric?"

"I was actually just reviewing it. Major Vassar sent it over to me a short while ago."

Connor looked at Natalia and she smiled a little. His intelligence officer was exceedingly efficient at managing—well, him, to be honest. Connor smiled.

"All right, do I need to be concerned about this?"

"This behavior isn't entirely unexpected. It was observed when the Ovarrow were restricted to Camp Alpha. However, it decreased when we helped them establish themselves in the city. Now we're seeing it crop up again. My opinion is that this behavior is normal. The Ovarrow need to assert some control over their own world. I mean this in the sense of their immediate vicinity."

"Wanting control over their lives doesn't equate to pushing away their support structure," Connor replied.

"Yes, it does in some instances. Asserting control over your own environment is something we see in any intelligent society. We see it among humans, especially with teens on the brink of adulthood."

Connor shook his head. "Are you kidding me? You're equating the behavior of the Ovarrow with that of a rebellious teenager?"

"Just bear with me for a second. That's an oversimplification of the situation. Think of it this way: You did the same thing when you first woke up on the *Ark*. You created a niche for yourself in the colony as a way to assert control over your own world. This is the same thing," Eric said.

"I didn't push everyone away in some silly, rebellious tactic to assert myself."

"Different circumstances. We know the Ovarrow went . . . put themselves into stasis pods as a last-ditch effort to survive. Think about the motivations behind that. There had been a definite lack of control for who knows how long before they were reduced to those options. Now, they wake up and there's this invader. I mean that loosely, but from their perspective, we are the invaders. We're a powerful group who brings them out of stasis and are inserting ourselves into their lives. It's invasive no matter our own intentions," Eric said.

"But we're trying to help them," Major Anders said.

"Yes, we are," Eric replied. "But at some point, we should stop expecting to be allowed entry into their city and start asking for permission without the expectation that they'll say yes. The Ovarrow are merely asserting their independence."

Connor was about to reply when a priority comlink registered on the wallscreen in front of him.

"General Gates, I have an alpha priority message from Major Alexis Brooks," Lieutenant Sabatino's voice said over the speaker nearby.

"Put it through," Connor replied.

A video comlink came to prominence on the wallscreen, showing Major Brooks in combat attire.

"General Gates, there's been an incident at the Ovarrow city. Reports came in a few minutes ago about a catastrophic accident. At this point, we have colonial visitors unaccounted for. The Ovarrow are highly agitated and have expelled all colonists in the city. They're barring entry. The Mekaal faction has assembled at the city perimeter and is armed," Major Brooks said.

"Who's on site now?" Connor asked.

"There's a supply team, a diplomatic envoy, and the CDF squad who were their escorts. The supply team was attempting to access the city when the incident occurred. We still don't know what happened. I'm scrambling our alert force and heading to the city now. What are your orders, General?"

"As you were, Major. Get to that site and figure out what's going on. I'll be in touch, and I'll be sending support to you ASAP. Gates, out."

The video comlink went dark. Connor turned toward Anders. "I want the 3rd and 7th Ranger companies assembled and deployed to that site in two hours. Orders will come en route. They are to be combat-ready and expect hostilities. After that, I want the First Battalion assembled and ready for deployment. Get to it."

"At once, General," Major Anders said and hastened from the office. Connor heard her shouting orders as she opened various comlinks to her command structure.

"Lieutenant Sabatino, get me Governor Wolf, now."

A few moments later Governor Wolf's face appeared on Connor's wallscreen.

"General Gates, I've just been informed about an accident at the Ovarrow city."

"That's correct, Governor. The Ovarrow are barring entry to the city. We have an unknown number of colonists unaccounted for. I know diplomatic relations are a priority, but so are colonial lives. I need authorization to engage the Ovarrow if they're uncooperative," Connor said.

"You want authorization to kill them?"

"That isn't my first choice. I want authorization to protect colonial citizens. I need to get on site to do an assessment of the situation. My first priority is to get there and gain access to the trouble area."

"I can authorize you going to the area, but I cannot authorize the use of lethal force except in self-defense at this time."

Connor strangled his frustration. "Very well. I'll keep you apprised of the situation, Governor."

"General Gates," Governor Wolf said, "my daughter is among the colonists in the city."

Connor's mouth formed a grim line. "I understand," he replied.

The comlink was severed.

"I'm here. Put me to work," Eric said.

"You're coming with me," Connor said and looked at Natalia. "I want you to stay here and figure out what the hell happened."

"Do you suspect foul play, General?"

"A diplomatic envoy just happens to be at the Ovarrow city when an accident occurs? The timing's a bit too convenient, don't you think?"

"Understood, sir. I'm on it," Natalia said and left.

Connor left his office with Eric running to catch up.

"What are you going to do?"

"It might be time to remind the Ovarrow exactly who they're dealing with. They respect a show of force, and I intend to give them one if they don't cooperate," Connor replied.

Eric looked as if he were about to say something else but didn't.

Lenora had been intrigued about seeing the Ovarrow city. She'd been studying them for such a long time. Connor had made sure she had experienced soldiers there to protect her, so she should be in good hands, even if something bad happened. She was a survivor. Connor clutched onto that hope and stormed down the hall, bellowing orders.

CHAPTER 13

Lenora woke to a muffled sound she couldn't identify. Her ears were ringing. She blinked several times, and her eyes slowly came to focus on a message in crystal-clear amber letters.

Impact detected.
Emergency protocols engaged.
MPS protection mode is active.
Power level near maximum.

Below that was a list of her vitals, which the MPS jacket was getting from her biochip. They were normal, so she cleared the message from her internal heads-up display. The MPS systems had engaged and a quick-response helmet had protected her head. She glanced around for a few moments, looking for anything that could hurt her. She was wedged between twisted metal and the construction material the Ovarrow had used for their footbridges. It was dark, but her implants adjusted her vision so she could see just fine. Lenora looked around for any sharp objects and then disengaged the helmet. She heard the faint coughing sounds of other people.

"Hello! Can anyone hear me?"

She waited a few moments. The air was thick with pulverized material, and she sneezed. She heard the deep groans of straining metallic supports, followed by clanging as some of them broke. She tried to move but was pinned where she was. A deafening rumble shook everything around her, and Lenora squeezed her eyes shut. It felt as if everything was pushing in. Lenora's lips trembled and her shoulders went rigid as she tried to worm her way free. She gritted her teeth and pushed.

"Dammit!"

The rumbling stopped, and she tried to calm down by taking several breaths. Both bridges had collapsed—the main one and the footbridge they'd been on. Her stomach attempted to slither out of her mouth when she tried to figure out how much debris was on top of her right then.

Not helping, she thought. She needed to get free.

Lenora had drawn in a breath to shout when she heard someone call out her name. "I'm here," she said.

"Dr. Bishop, it's Cookie."

Lenora was sure she hadn't heard him right. Why would someone offer her a cookie? "What?" she asked.

"It's me, Sergeant Cook . . . You know, Cookie. I'm below you. I can see your legs. Can you scoot downward? I'll catch you," he said.

Lenora tried to twist around but couldn't get enough leverage to push effectively.

"Can you work your way downward, Dr. Bishop?"

Lenora grunted, trying to move, and then cursed. "I think we can dispense with the formalities, don't you?"

"That's fine with me, Lenora. Are you able to move?"

"No, I'm wedged in pretty hard."

"Are you injured?"

"No, I'm fine. I have an MPS jacket on. It engaged and kept me from getting hurt."

"Good. That's good," he said, sounding as if he were looking around as he spoke.

Lenora grunted with effort, pushing as hard as she could to free herself. "I don't think I can do it," she said.

"Yes, you can. I'll talk you through it."

"No, I mean I don't think I can call you 'Cookie.' I can't think about cookies right now. What's your first name?"

"Benjamin, but my friends call me Ben."

"All right, Ben. I'm wedged in because my MPS is in protect mode. I think once I disable it, I'll be able to slide on down," Lenora said.

"Wait!" Ben shouted. "Make sure there's nothing around that can hurt you. The suit might be all that's supporting the pocket you're in."

Lenora glanced around and shook her head. "I think it's a little late for that."

She disabled the MPS and immediately began to slide downward. She felt something sharp scrape along her back, and she winced. The MPS had gone into passive protect mode, which prevented whatever was sticking into her back from penetrating the skin, but she'd still have a heck of a bruise. Her backpack got hung up on something and almost forced her face into a ragged wall of sharp edges. She unbuckled her backpack and felt strong hands grab hold of her feet. "Hold on," Lenora said and pulled her backpack loose.

Sergeant Cook set her on the ground, and she noticed blood from a gash on the side of his head.

"You're hurt. Let me take a look at that," Lenora said.

The CDF soldier leaned away from her and shook his head. "I'm fine. You don't need to do that."

"Don't be an idiot, Ben. You've got a head wound. Now let me see it," Lenora said and gestured for him to lean down so she could see his wound.

She took the first aid kit out of her backpack and then dabbed the wound with a piece of cloth. Next, she used medi-paste. She knew it stung, but he hardly reacted at all.

Men.

"You'll live," Lenora said. "Do you know where the others are?"

"I've only been able to find Green and Yemshi. I have them searching for other survivors. I haven't been able to reach anyone on comlink," Ben replied.

They were in a large pocket surrounded by wreckage from the bridge, clearly lucky to be alive.

Lenora glanced down. They were standing on a flat piece of the foot-bridge. Loud bangs were heard, followed by another deep rumble. They had to find the others and get out of there. She sent out a comlink broadcast but didn't get a reply, so she set the broadcast to loop while they got their bearings.

"I'm not able to reach anyone either. Not even Green or Yemshi," Lenora said and frowned for a moment. She shook her head and looked at Ben.

"That's because they must be on CDF comms channels. I'll let them know to monitor for civilian comlink chatter."

They picked a direction and headed off. As they climbed over the wreckage, the area became more cramped. Lenora could stand up straight, but Ben couldn't.

A comlink chimed, and Lenora smiled as she acknowledged it.

"Dr. Bishop, she's hurt." Lenora looked at the comlink ID and saw that it said L. Butler. "They both are. I tried to—she's hurt. There's blood. Oh God, she's bleeding so much."

Lenora shared a look with Ben. "Lynn, who's bleeding?"

"Kayla is. She had something sticking into her leg, and I pulled it out. Now I can't stop the bleeding. I need help! I need help, now! I have to help her! She's going to die!"

"Lynn, listen to me. I'm going to help you, but you have to calm down. Is there anything you can use to cover the wound? Anything at all—a jacket or a piece of your shirt? Just put something over the wound and then compress firmly with your hands. That will help staunch the bleeding. Can you do that? Find something to cover the wound and then compress it. Lean on it with everything you've got."

Lenora heard Lynn muttering half-formed thoughts to herself as she looked. "I found something. I've covered the wound. I'm pressing down, but it's soaking through. It's not stopping."

"That's okay, we just need to slow it down. Now, we're coming to you. Is your PDA working? Can you activate the emergency beacon?"

Lenora waited and then she saw the beacon on her internal heads-up display. She glanced at Ben and he nodded.

"Good. That's great. We have your signal, and we're coming to you."

"Please hurry," Lynn said, her voice sounding strained.

They hurried to the end of the pocket they were in and the path narrowed.

"I should go first," Ben said. He'd just finished bringing Green and Yemshi up to speed.

Lenora glanced back at him. "Have you had any SAR training? Have you spent years crawling around Ovarrow ruins, including tight spaces? I didn't think so. Follow me."

Ben hesitated for a moment and then gestured for her to go first. They crawled through the debris for a few minutes. Lenora checked in with Lynn to assure her that they were coming. Green and Yemshi caught up with them. On their way, they found another CDF soldier, but he was unconscious. His name was Philip Jones. Lenora checked Jones's injuries. He was just knocked out, and they were able to wake him up.

They found an open area that was an even larger pocket than the one they'd been in. Two Ovarrow soldiers were trying to rescue their comrades. The two Ovarrow were surprised to see them and didn't look too happy about it.

"This would be a good time to tell them we're here to help," Lenora said.

Ben brought up his personal holoscreen and engaged the Ovarrow translator. The two Ovarrow soldiers read the message and, after a few moments, seemed to accept that they were there to help.

"I want the three of you to stay here and help them," Ben said to the three CDF soldiers. "I'm going on ahead with Dr. Bishop."

The soldiers didn't look thrilled with their orders but walked over to the Ovarrow.

Lenora followed the emergency beacon. As they closed in on the source, they found that the area was blocked off. The beacon indicated that Lynn and Kayla were just on the other side.

"Lynn, can you hear me?" Lenora asked.

"I can hear you."

"We're just on the other side of this wall. Do you see any other way for us to reach you?"

"We're surrounded by debris. I can't look—I don't see a way."

Lenora heard a slight panic in her voice and didn't want to push her too far. "Is Devon with you?"

"Yes, he is, but he's unconscious. I haven't been able to check him."

"That's fine. It's going to be okay. We'll find a way to you."

"How? We're trapped in here. There's no way out," Lynn said, her voice rising.

"Lynn, I need you to calm down. Just give us a few minutes and we'll find a way to get to you. We made it this far," Lenora said.

While she was speaking to Lynn, Ben was looking for a way through the debris. She muted her comlink to Lynn.

Ben shook his head and stepped back. "I don't have anything that can get through this. My sidearm would just poke holes in it, and that's not going to help us. If I had some thermite, I could burn a hole through it pretty easily."

Lenora peered at the maze of twisted metal and found a flat surface that looked brittle. It must have been some kind of filler material similar to concrete. She couldn't reconcile what she was seeing in front of her with the bridge they'd been walking across. Jagged edges had burst through on the top, and she touched the flat surface. It was solid but looked brittle. She reached inside her backpack and pulled out a sonic hand blaster.

"What good is that gonna do?" Ben asked.

Lenora smiled and opened the handle. "It's been modified. I can crank up the output, but it'll deplete the power cell a lot faster. I think I can use it to shatter that wall, and we might be able to get through that way."

She raised the power output and Ben had squatted down, examining the wall she intended to use it on.

"If we're wrong, it might collapse on top of them. Maybe even us," Ben said.

Lenora nodded. "I don't think we have much choice. If we don't get in there, they'll die."

Ben turned away from her, looking for an alternative. Then he looked back at her and nodded. "Okay, let's do this. They're located over here," he said, gesturing to an area to the right of the wall. "If you angle it slightly upward, they might be able to crawl through here and then drop down."

Lenora came closer to the wall and put the end of the sonic hand blaster within centimeters of it. She adjusted some settings. Though the power output increased, it didn't unleash in one high-powered, concussive blast. This was a modified version of the sonic hand blaster Connor had used to escape when he'd been wedged in a ravine. He'd made it less dangerous.

Lenora squeezed the trigger and, at first, nothing happened. The acoustic resonance bounced off the wall, and the sonic waves increased in intensity. Dust billowed off the wall. Lenora pushed the blaster forward, and the wall shattered apart, opening a cavity inside. Lenora thrust her arm out and continued to angulate upward. She engaged her MPS jacket, and the helmet formed overhead. She peered through the dust cloud and stopped firing when she finally reached an open area.

Ben crawled up through the opening and into the cavity above, then reached his hand down and helped Lenora up. Lynn was hovering over Kayla. Both her hands were compressed over a wound in the girl's thigh. Lynn had tears streaming down her cheeks, but she wasn't injured.

Lenora went over to Kayla and took out her first aid kit. She told Lynn to take her hands away and then pulled away the blood-soaked shirt. There was a deep, inch-wide puncture in Kayla's thigh. Lenora slathered medi-paste into the wound and forced it closed with her fingers, holding steady while she waited for the medi-paste to work. A minute later, she loosened her fingers and the wound stayed closed. The bleeding had stopped. Lenora removed a syringe of medical nanites from the first aid kit and plunged it into Kayla's thigh above the wound, injecting them into her system.

"Will she be all right?" Lynn asked.

Kayla's face was pale, but at least now she had a fighting chance. "You did just fine," Lenora said.

She turned toward Devon and saw that Ben was checking his vitals. He turned toward her and shook his head. "He's gone."

Lynn gasped. "No, he was fine. I spoke to him. He said he just needed to rest for a minute," she said and began moving toward Devon. Ben blocked her path, and she struggled to get past him. "Let me see him. You have to let me see him. He was fine. He just needed to rest."

Ben remained rooted in place. "I'm sorry," he said, holding the young girl firmly. She struggled against him, and Ben leaned down so he was in front of Lynn's face. "He's dead. He had a wound on his side that he probably didn't even feel."

Lynn's face became ashen. "He couldn't have had a wound. He said he was fine. He told me . . . He told me to take care of Kayla."

Lenora's eyes tightened, but she forced her voice to remain firm. "We have to get Kayla out of here. We can't stay here. I need your help, Lynn. I need you to help me move her."

It took a little bit more coaxing, but they got Lynn to help them move Kayla out of the pocket they'd been trapped in. As Lynn and Ben worked to get Kayla out, Lenora looked down at Devon's body. Her throat thickened. He was so young, and his face looked innocent, as if he were sleeping. Her eyes became misty and she quickly wiped them, then followed the others.

They carried Kayla back to where they'd found the Ovarrow. Lynn kept talking about how she had tried to protect them both, rationalizing a desperate situation. Lenora tried to reassure her. Redirecting her attention toward Kayla helped.

When they finally reached the others, six Ovarrow had been freed. Lenora's eyes widened when she realized that the warlord's first was lying on the ground. He was conscious, but he looked as if he was in a lot of pain. The Ovarrow soldiers were agitated, and Green, Jones, and Yemshi stood off to the side.

Lenora tried to get closer to Cerot, but the Ovarrow soldiers wouldn't let her. She brought up her Ovarrow translator. "I can help him," she said and held up her medical kit. She looked at Cerot. "Let me help you."

Several Ovarrow soldiers moved to block her path. Ben was at her side, and the rest of the CDF soldiers came up behind her, ready to intervene.

Cerot growled an order, and after a few moments, the Ovarrow soldiers parted to let Lenora pass. She knelt down by Cerot and began assessing his wounds. There were more than a few of them.

"This might hurt a little," she said and waited for the translator to convey her words.

Cerot read the message and waited for her to begin.

CHAPTER 14

L ars flew the Hellcat through a narrow ravine, winding his way back to base. Newer pilots found the route to be challenging, but Lars had done it so many times he could do it with his eyes closed. The Hellcat was a highly maneuverable aircraft. It flew at high speeds and carried a respectable amount of armaments. Larger models were capable of carrying heavy loads, but this was a lightweight version, capable of transporting just one squad at a time. It was difficult to detect, which was why Lars preferred to use it when searching for Ovarrow bunkers.

Martakis closed down her personal holoscreen and stretched her arms out in front of her. "It wasn't a total waste of a trip," she said.

Lars glanced at her questioningly. "We came up empty-handed. All three sites were a bust."

Maggie Martakis had been part of Lars's team for almost a year and believed wholeheartedly in what they were doing. She had a background in Field Ops Search and Rescue and could quickly adapt to challenges. Her dark, curly hair was tied back, and she had a larger-than-normal nose.

"That's three fewer sites we have to investigate in the future. Now we can focus our efforts somewhere else," Maggie replied.

"Those sites were based on new intelligence. I would've expected to strike pay dirt on at least one of them."

"Pay dirt?"

"No appreciation for old Earth sayings?" Lars countered.

"Touché."

They'd had to change their Ovarrow bunker missions to restrict them to parts of the continent that were infrequently monitored by the CDF. This was safer for everybody.

Lars decreased the Hellcat's altitude as they approached the LZ. A large group was gathered near another Hellcat, and Lars frowned. He hadn't authorized any other missions that day.

"Looks like we missed something," Maggie said.

He initiated the power-down protocols and lowered the landing ramp. "Or we found something," he said as he unstrapped his seatbelt.

He hastened out of the Hellcat with Maggie close behind. The group of people surrounding the other Hellcat was chatting excitedly.

Lars approached them. "Did I miss something? What's going on here?"

The crowd of people quieted down and stood aside. A path opened and he saw Colton Evans grinning widely. Next to him stood Dean Morris, who gave Colton a sidelong glance.

Evans walked over to Lars. "Great, you're back. I've got good news."

The Hellcat behind them had obviously been flown, which meant someone had disobeyed his orders. Lars held up his hand and looked around at the others. "Don't the rest of you have something to do? Clear the deck. Now. Evans and Morris, follow me."

Lars didn't wait for a reply; he simply turned and led them toward the interior of the base, ignoring Morris muttering something behind them. Evans told him to be quiet.

They entered his office, and Lars nodded for Maggie to close the door.

Lars looked at Evans. "I hope you have a good explanation for disobeying orders. There were no scheduled missions today."

"A last-minute mission came in during your scouting run," Evans said.

Lars glared at the two men. "Bullshit. I would've been notified."

Evans and Morris stood motionless for a second.

"Excuse me, sir," Maggie said. "You need to see this."

She activated a nearby holoscreen, and it showed a news broadcast from Sierra. The banner at the bottom read: *Fatal accident at the Ovarrow city. Events are unfolding now. The Colonial Defense Force is on site, but the Ovarrow military is denying entry into the city.*

"That was the mission," Evans said, smiling.

Lars glanced at him and then back to the holoscreen. There was a video feed that showed that the CDF had gathered a sizable force outside the Ovarrow city walls. The video then switched to a surveillance drone feed that showed a collapsed bridge. Ovarrow were at the site, searching for survivors. Lars felt something cold sink to the bottom of his stomach, and he turned toward Evans. "What did you do?"

"The operation went off without a hitch. Now there's no way the colonial government can sit on its collective asses and do nothing about the Ovarrow. It was so easy, and we couldn't have had a better opportunity. You know who was down there—"

The rest of what Evans was about to say was cut off as Lars grabbed him by the shirt and slammed him up against the wall. "You're a god damn idiot! Who the hell authorized you to do this?" he demanded, gesturing to the holoscreen. As he did so, he was distracted by a snippet of the report.

". . . A diplomatic envoy was on scene when the accident occurred.

We've heard from Governor Wolf that her daughter, Kayla Wolf, was among the members of the envoy, as well as Dr. Lenora Bishop. The envoy is currently missing."

Lars growled and threw Evans across the room. Dean Morris attempted to intervene, and Lars twisted the man's arm behind his back and slammed his face into his desk, surprising him.

"You've put colonial lives in danger! They might be dead!" Lars bellowed. He withdrew his sidearm and pointed it at Evans.

"Wait! Wait," Evans said quickly. "We had authorization. Let me show you. I'm just going to show you the mission briefing." He activated his wrist computer and made a passing motion at the holoscreen. A second screen appeared, and Lars read the message. It had all the correct authentication codes associated with it.

Morris regained his feet.

"Get over there by Evans. Now," Lars said and looked at Maggie. "Watch them."

Maggie pulled out her own sidearm and covered the two men.

Lars initiated a secure comlink to his superiors and gave his authentication.

"Agent Mallory," a voice said through a vocalizer so he couldn't tell who he was speaking with.

"I've just read the mission briefing sent to Agent Evans. This was sent out to my team but not through me. I was kept out of the loop, and I want an explanation. This is a huge shitstorm. We've crossed the line. I have the two agents in custody now," Lars said.

"Release the agents immediately. They were following orders."

Lars clenched his teeth for a moment. "Sir, this isn't—"

"I said, release those agents now."

Lars glared at Evans and Morris, who actually seemed proud of what they'd done. He jerked his head toward the door to his office. "Get out of here. I'll find you later."

As soon as they left, he looked at Maggie. "Keep an eye on them. Make sure they stick around."

"Yes, sir."

Lars took a few breaths, trying to calm down. The comlink was still active. "Sir, I need an explanation."

"An opportunity came our way, and I chose to exploit it."

Lars frowned. He was trying to figure out which superior he was speaking with, but he knew better than to voice their actual names, even on a secure comlink channel.

"You've served the cause well, never hesitating to do what had to be done. This was the next step. We had to do this. I've initiated Operation Burrow Down."

Lars winced. "They're going to come after us," he said at last.

"That was always going to happen. You don't have time to decide how you feel about this. There's work to be done, and you have to evacuate. There are hundreds of lives at that base depending on you. Get to it."

The comlink deactivated, and Lars snarled as he shoved everything on his desk crashing to the floor. He glanced at the news broadcast again and shook his head. His thoughts raced. *Colonial lives*, he thought and clenched his teeth.

He sighed in disgust and opened a broadcast channel to the base. "Prepare for immediate evac. First alert. Wheels up in one hour."

Lars shut down the broadcast channel, his hands shaking with rage. This wasn't how it was supposed to happen. They weren't supposed to put colonial lives at risk. The Ovarrow were the enemy. Feeling bile creep up into his throat, he growled and kicked the chair, sending it to the other side of the room where it slammed into the wall.

"Dammit!"

He'd always known Evans was a hothead. Lars didn't want to believe anyone else on his team could have done what Evans had. His superiors had known just who to order to fulfill this mission. They'd also known Lars would've refused. Evans had not.

His thoughts turned toward the group of people who'd been celebrating outside Evans's Hellcat. Had he been wrong? He'd gone through great pains to instill the mission objective into his team. The Ovarrow were the enemy. Lars swallowed hard in disgust. Who was the enemy now?

The door to his office opened and Tonya Wagner stood in the doorway. "I came as soon as I heard. We're evacuating ahead of schedule. What do you want done with the prisoners?"

He frowned for a moment as images of the news broadcasts flashed his mind.

"Lars, are you okay?"

Lars gathered himself. "The prisoners?" he repeated, his voice sounding grim. "We take them with us. Prep them for transport."

CHAPTER 15

The edge of the loading ramp clanged when it hit the ground and Connor stepped off. His boots bit into the dirt and a gust of wind howled. A few thick drops of rain pelted him as he registered the faint whooshing sounds of the wind turbines the Ovarrow used to power their city.

Major Alexis Brooks stood at attention and saluted Connor.

"Sit rep, Major Brooks."

"Three hours ago, two major bridges collapsed. The diplomatic envoy was on one of the lower footbridges when it went down. We don't know how it happened, but the Ovarrow are keenly suspicious. They've locked down their city and won't let any of us inside."

"We'll see about that," Connor said.

Major Brooks led Connor to the command area.

"Have we heard from anyone inside the city?" he asked.

"Negative, sir. The Ovarrow escorted the remaining colonial visitors out of the city. They weren't mistreated. You can speak with them if you want."

Connor nodded. "Who's speaking with the Ovarrow?"

"No one right now. Our diplomatic negotiator on site is Sebastian Crosby. After initial communications ceased, he elected to wait for you to arrive before trying again," Brooks said.

Connor went into the command area where Sebastian Crosby was waiting. Connor made it a point to study the dossiers of anyone who worked in the colonial diplomatic relations office, especially those stationed at Camp Alpha.

Connor looked at Major Brooks. "Where's Darius Cohen?"

"He was on one of the bridges that collapsed, sir."

Lenora had likely been right by him, which meant she was trapped. He put a stranglehold on his fear and focused on what had to be done.

"Mr. Crosby, why won't they let us inside the city?" Connor asked.

"They said they're searching for survivors. I suspect that someone high up in the Ovarrow hierarchy must have been on the bridge when it collapsed," Sebastian said.

"We have better equipment than they do. Did you explain that to them? I have a team of engineers ready to get in there and find the survivors."

"I did try to express our interest in helping them search for survivors; however, they refused to listen."

Connor glared at the diplomat, and he flinched, but Connor resisted the urge to chew him out. It wasn't his fault. "Who were you speaking with?"

"An Ovarrow faction leader named Wigren."

Connor shook his head in disgust. "Faction leaders have limited power. We need somebody who can actually negotiate with us. I want High Commissioner Senleon, the warlord's first, or the warlord himself. Speaking to anyone else is counterproductive."

"I'll get started, but I must caution you against making demands of the Ovarrow," Sebastian warned, "if we hope to get them to cooperate with us."

Connor's muscles tensed and his tone deepened. "The window for their cooperation is closing. I'd rather have their support, but I'm prepared to do whatever I must to ensure the safety of the colonists trapped under that collapsed bridge. Convey that to them. I'll be with you shortly."

Sebastian's face went pallid, and he swallowed hard. Sensing his dismissal, the diplomat left the area.

Connor marched over to the operations center where he found Flint and Samson waiting for him. "Where are your men located?"

"About five klicks west of the city, nearest the bridge our people are trapped under," Samson replied.

"We have recon drones scouring the area," Flint said. "We don't know how those bridges collapsed, but we do have a search grid to hand off to the engineers so they can find whoever's trapped."

"Are the Ovarrow searching in the right place?" Connor asked.

"They're all over the place," Samson said. "They're trying to be as thorough as they can, but the equipment they're using to reach any survivors will take them two or three times as long as ours would. If we want to save anyone, we need to get in there and take over the search effort."

Connor's lips formed a grim line as he considered his options. First Battalion was on its way there and would arrive shortly. The Ovarrow might let them into the city after First Battalion arrived, but Connor didn't have that long to wait. Lives were on the line. Flint and Samson waited for his orders. The 3rd and 7th Ranger companies could hold their positions, but they had to choose the right bridge.

Connor looked at a holographic model of the city. "How certain are we about the target?"

"The reports I've seen show that the envoy went down the main thoroughfare," Major Brooks said, gesturing at the model. "Comlink check-in pings have them taking a different way out of the city that puts them on the path to this bridge, here. The second bridge that collapsed was farther away, and I can't think of a compelling reason why the envoy would go that way. I'm ninety-nine percent certain this is the target, General Gates."

Connor looked at the live video feed from the reconnaissance drone in the area, his mind already working on ways for the Spec Ops teams to take control of the area.

"Mission objectives, General Gates?" Samson asked.

"We need to get our engineers on site so they can use ground-penetrating scans to speed up the recovery. They also need medical teams on site. We need to rescue both the Ovarrow and the colonists," Connor said.

"They won't like us being there without their permission. This could get ugly real fast," Brooks said.

"If we can't get the Ovarrow to listen to reason, then we need to be prepared to push them back. We could focus on holding this area right here and then expand it based on what the engineers find," Connor replied, gesturing at the map of the city.

"Just give the order and we'll make it happen," Samson said.

Connor didn't doubt their capabilities, but he didn't want a confrontation with the Ovarrow. It felt like he was being backed into a corner, and his only recourse was to escalate the situation. It would be so easy for him to just give the order right then. The Ovarrow couldn't put up much of a fight, and Connor's teams could be on site and searching for survivors within fifteen minutes. Lenora would be safe if she wasn't . . . He wouldn't allow his thoughts to go there, but if she was hurt, he had to get to her as soon as possible. He could tell Governor Wolf and all the other people under his command that he was there to protect the colonists, and he was, but his wife was trapped under a bridge. He needed to find her, and he'd tear the entire city apart to do it.

They were all looking at him, waiting for him to give the order, but he still hesitated, considered the image on the holoscreen. She had to be safe. They had some time.

"Be ready to go when I give the order. First, I want to see if I can get the Ovarrow to cooperate. If not, we go in there."

"Yes, General," Flint said.

Both men saluted him and left. Connor looked at Major Brooks. "Come on, Major, let's see if we can talk some sense into the Ovarrow."

Connor headed for no man's land, which was an area just outside the Ovarrow city. CDF soldiers led the way in, but the real show of force would be there in a few minutes.

The Ovarrow had armed soldiers behind barricades at the entrance to the city, and Connor saw more soldiers on the rooftops of the nearest buildings. They had the area well covered.

Sebastian Crosby was speaking, and his words were being translated into the Ovarrow symbols that were showing on several large holoscreens. A drone within the city displayed the translation as well and was available as a user interface for the Ovarrow.

Connor walked over to Sebastian. "This is how you've been talking to them?"

"They've been on lockdown."

Connor shook his head and gestured toward the Ovarrow translator interface. He wasn't asking for Sebastian's permission to use it; he was informing him that he was going to use it. The Ovarrow knew who he was.

"This is General Connor Gates of the Colonial Defense Force. I want to speak with High Commissioner Senleon immediately."

Connor saw a brief commotion from behind the barricade.

"High Commissioner Senleon. I'd like to speak to you in person. Please meet me on neutral ground," Connor said.

The Ovarrow language was so different from anything that Connor had ever heard before that he doubted he'd ever be able to understand it. They'd always be dependent on some kind of translation device so the two species could communicate.

A message appeared on a small holoscreen in front of them, and Sebastian's eyebrows raised with surprise. "There's a group of Ovarrow coming out to meet us."

Connor walked toward the group. The Ovarrow were sensitive to certain hierarchies, and this was a meeting among leaders.

Two Ovarrow walked ahead of the Mekaal soldiers. One spoke to the other at his side, who began using the drone's holographic interface.

"I am Senleon."

"I want us to work together, High Commissioner. There are both colonists and Ovarrow trapped in the wreckage. We have the means to help rescue them quickly. Will you allow us into the city?" Connor asked.

"This is not possible. Colonial drones were spotted in the area when the bridges collapsed," Senleon replied.

Connor glanced at Major Brooks, who gave a slight shake of her head. Connor looked back at the high commissioner. "I don't know anything about that, but I assure you we'll look into it with the highest priority after we help those who are trapped."

Senleon regarded Connor for a few moments. Trying to anticipate what the Ovarrow were thinking or their intentions was extremely difficult, but Connor thought Senleon wanted to accept Connor's offer. Something was holding him back though.

"I don't know what happened here," Connor said, "but we can figure this out together. You just need to work with me. There are lives at stake."

Senleon glanced behind him at the Ovarrow soldiers for a moment and then looked back at Connor. "We are at a disadvantage. We must protect the Ovarrow."

Connor frowned in thought for a few moments. He glanced at the Ovarrow soldiers, the Mekaal. They seemed more preoccupied with watching Senleon than they were with watching Connor.

Connor narrowed his gaze. "Where are Vitory or Cerot?"

He watched for their reactions as they read the message, and the soldiers seemed to stiffen.

One of the Mekaal said something to Senleon that Connor had no hope of understanding.

Senleon looked at Connor. "We are searching for survivors and will inform you of any new developments," he replied and began to walk away.

"Senleon, do you have the authority to grant us access to the city?"

The high commissioner read the message and didn't reply. Senleon didn't have the power. The warlord and his second-in-command were nowhere to be found.

Not needing their reply, Connor used his implants to recall the communications drone from the Ovarrow. He opened a secure comlink to Samson and Flint. "You're clear to go. Surgical strike. Try to intimidate them. I don't want to take them out if I don't have to."

Connor looked at Sebastian. "We need to send a quick message, and I want as many comms drones capable of projecting holoscreens as we can deploy so the Ovarrow know exactly what's going on. We're going into that city whether they want us to or not."

CHAPTER 16

Lenora's eyebrows pulled down in concentration. The warlord's first was severely wounded. Multiple metallic shards stuck out of his body, piercing his body armor. The largest shard, over a foot long, had speared into his abdomen. The jagged edges of the fragment had mostly sealed the abdominal wound, so Lenora left that one alone while she removed the smaller shards.

"Try to lie still," Lenora said.

Cerot read the message and gave her a slight nod.

The smaller shards were in nonlethal places on his arms, with others on his legs. She even found one on top of his shoulder. As she removed them one by one, she methodically cleaned and numbed the wounds. She then applied a variant of the medi-paste they used to heal their own wounds. Medi-paste would fill up the wound and begin binding the damaged flesh back together. However, healing the damage to an internal organ required the use of medical nanites, but her emergency stock of those was for humans only.

Once she'd finished tending to the least dangerous wounds, Lenora glanced at the end of the metallic shard sticking out of Cerot's stomach. It was six inches across, and she hoped it had a pointy end like the others; otherwise, removing it might kill the Ovarrow. It still might kill him, even if the end of the shard narrowed to a point. She inhaled deeply and rolled her shoulders, stretching her neck. They couldn't move him like this or Cerot would die.

Cerot's gaze met hers. The Ovarrow's chestnut-colored eyes had bits of hazel to them that she'd never noticed before. They were two different species, but in that moment, there was understanding. She'd looked into the eyes of people who knew they were going to die many times. The last battle of the Vemus War had given her nightmares, but she had to try to save Cerot.

Lenora was no stranger to being watched while she worked. Years of teaching and fieldwork had provided an ample number of witnesses. She'd even been in quite a few survival situations. Technically, she was qualified as a field medic, but what Cerot needed was a real doctor.

The Ovarrow soldiers hovered around her, watching her with their feline eyes narrowed. It made their expressions fierce and a bit unsettling.

Cerot glanced down at the shard sticking out of his stomach and then looked at Lenora.

"It's the last one," she said.

Ben came to her side, holding a small canteen of water. He extended it and nodded toward her. Lenora sat back on her feet and gestured for him to come over. The Ovarrow soldiers allowed him to pass.

Lenora thanked him and took a long swallow from the canteen, then handed it back to him.

Ben looked down at Cerot's wound. "That could be messy."

"You've got that right. If I pull it out and it's damaged his internal organs, he could die. If we try to move him with that thing stuck inside him, he could die. If we stay here—"

"He could die. I get it. We can only do the best we can," Ben said.

Lenora sighed. "I'm sorry."

Cerot had watched their exchange and then uttered a few words. The soldier nearest her used the translator interface to input Cerot's words.

"Pull it out."

Lenora inhaled deeply and nodded. She looked at the soldier with the translator interface. "I'm going to need help. I need someone to hold down his arms, his legs, and his shoulders. He can't move at all, or it could make things worse."

Lenora knew the Ovarrow translator did the best it could with conveying the meaning of her words. Luckily for them, most computer programming languages required a subset of specific commands in order to tell the computer how to operate. So, the meaning of the message that the Ovarrow actually read might have said something like "stop motion or risk breakage." The context was conveyed through the unspoken communication of body language.

Lenora gestured the soldiers toward where she wanted them to go.

After reading the message, the Ovarrow soldiers moved into position around Cerot.

Lenora looked at Ben. "Grab his foot and hold his leg down."

She squeezed between the soldiers and peered at the shard for a moment. "Lynn, I need your help. Come over here, please."

Lynn hurried over and squatted down behind her. "What do you need me to do?"

"I need you to hand me these three things after I pull the shard out. I'll need to clean the wound with this pad. Make sure your hands are clean. Then, hand me the medi-paste, and last will be the compress to cover the wound," Lenora said.

Lynn cleaned her hands and exhaled a long breath. "Okay, I'm ready."

Lenora looked at the soldiers and gave them a nod. They put their hands on Cerot and held him in place. Cerot closed his eyes, waiting.

Lenora leaned in toward the shard. She needed to get the angle just right or she'd do more damage. She had to pull it out along the same angle it had entered Cerot's stomach. Reaching out with both hands, she took a firm grip of the end of the shard and held her breath. Then, she yanked hard.

Cerot growled in pain as the soldiers continued to hold him down. Lenora glanced at the end of the shard. It had a point. *Good*, she thought, dropping it to the ground.

Lynn already had the wad of pads ready, and Lenora began wiping around the area, careful not to press too deeply. Blood pooled out of the wound, and she couldn't see inside.

"Medi-paste," Lenora said.

Lynn handed it to her, and Lenora applied liberal amounts to the inside of the wound, as well as the outside. She squeezed the wound shut, and Cerot twisted in pain. Lenora leaned on top of him to keep him from moving. She had to give the medi-paste time to work. After a few minutes, it filled up the wound and the bleeding stopped. Lenora wiped the edges again and then covered it with the large bandage, which adhered to the skin.

She leaned back. "Okay, you can let him go."

As the soldiers removed their hands from Cerot, the lines of pain on the Ovarrow's face lessened, and he opened his eyes. He looked down at his stomach and then at Lenora. His breath came in small gasps but slowly returned to normal.

"Lie still for a few minutes and then you can move," Lenora said.

The Ovarrow soldiers watched Cerot for a moment and then looked at Lenora. One of them placed his hand on his own shoulder and pulled it across to his other shoulder. The gesture was mimicked by the other soldiers.

"It's a sign of gratitude," Cerot said.

Lenora looked back at the soldiers, and their gazes seemed less harsh. "You're welcome," she said and looked at Cerot. "How do you feel?"

Cerot sat up and winced. He slowly got to his feet, standing almost resolute and proud, if somewhat stooped all the same. He raised his large hand. The thick black nails at the ends of his long fingers touched his shoulder and gracefully glided across his chest to his other shoulder. It was a simple gesture, but it conveyed a lot.

"Good work, Dr. Bishop," Ben said.

There was plenty of light from the wrist computers the colonials wore, and the Ovarrow carried a bioluminescent stick with them. Clouds of dust swirled in the air.

"Hello?" a voice said weakly.

Lenora looked down and saw that Kayla had finally awakened. Lynn flew to her side.

"My leg hurts," Kayla said. She looked up at Lenora. "What happened?" she asked and looked around, her voice raising with alarm. "Where is everyone?"

Lynn began telling Kayla everything that had happened in a jumble of words that came out too fast to comprehend.

"Slow down, Lynn," Lenora said.

"Right. Of course, Dr. Bishop."

There was a subtle vibration that seemed to start all at once, and Lenora's eyes darted above her, afraid they were about to be crushed. She heard Jones whisper something to Ben, and the other CDF soldiers shared a look. The Ovarrow soldiers seem to mimic the gesture as well.

Lenora narrowed her gaze. "What is it?" she asked after a few moments. "Sergeant Cook?"

Ben frowned for a moment and looked away, glancing at the Ovarrow. He turned back toward her. "I don't know for sure, but it sounded like weapons fire. We felt the impact from it." He shook his head. "Again, I don't know for sure. It could be just another part of the bridge breaking apart and hitting the ground."

Lenora narrowed her gaze. "But you don't think so, do you?"

Ben met her steely gaze and swallowed hard, twitching a slight nod.

"We need to find a way out of here," Lenora said and looked at the Ovarrow. "Do you know where we are?"

They tried to review what had happened together. The way the bridge had collapsed had provided pockets, and some of them had been lucky enough to be dumped into them. Now, they needed to escape.

"I think we should pick a direction and angle upward so we're climbing out of the debris," Lenora said, gesturing toward the side.

"We can't get through. We already tried," Cerot said.

Lenora reached into her backpack and pulled out her sonic hand blaster. "I can use this to help make a hole," she said, gesturing toward part of the wall.

Cerot seemed to consider this for a moment. "How can we help?"

Lenora looked around. Nearby, several metal rods stuck out of the concrete. She pointed the sonic hand blaster near it and used the lower setting. The concrete seemed to dissipate into dust, exposing the rods. "Can we cut these into long shafts? We could use them to brace the ceiling if we need to."

She looked at Ben and the other CDF soldiers, but they didn't have anything that could cut through them. One of the Ovarrow soldiers produced a colonial-made handheld plasma torch, making quick work of the metal rods and passing them around.

Lynn helped Kayla to her feet, and she was able to stand, favoring her injured leg.

Lenora walked over to the wall. She looked around, trying to see if this was the best place to use the hand blaster. Everything looked the same, and it would be a roll of the dice.

"Here goes nothing," Lenora said and got started.

CHAPTER 17

A bruise-colored sky covered the Ovarrow city in darkness. The only light came from the sections of the city they were living in. Connor had the First Battalion divided into three companies, and the first had taken up position two hundred meters outside the official city entrance. The other two groups were stationed farther away but within view of the Ovarrow soldiers. Connor wanted them to see the CDF troops. The ground forces were a mixture of infantrymen with standard combat suits and combat-suit heavies. Falcon Fighters Series 7s performed several flybys over the city as a reminder of CDF air superiority.

Nexstar combat suits could resist a direct blast of the Ovarrow particle energy weapons, but eventually it would break through. Connor's orders were to return warning shots in the event that the Ovarrow opened fire on them. If the Ovarrow engaged them directly, they were authorized to use deadly force.

The 3rd and 7th Ranger companies were on site by the collapsed bridge and were securing the area.

"How much resistance do you think they'll get?" Colonel Jason Rhodes asked.

They were gathered around a holographic display that showed a zoomed-in portion of the city.

"They took them by surprise, so not much," Connor replied. "I'm hoping the show of force will snap them out of it."

"It could antagonize them as well."

Connor nodded. "We need to get our people in there so we can start scanning the wreckage. The Ovarrow are no strangers to posturing."

A comlink opened from Samson. "They weren't expecting us, and we've pushed them back. Zero casualties, but I think they're going to regroup and try again."

"Understood. I'm sending in the first team of engineers now," Connor replied.

Before the standoff had begun, Connor had informed them of his intentions. The Ovarrow had had plenty of warning that the CDF wasn't going to sit idly by. He'd authorized a team of engineers, along with CDF Search and Rescue, to the location.

"General Gates, I've located the warlord," Lieutenant Davis said. "He's near the first collapsed bridge."

Lieutenant Davis put the drone reconnaissance video feed on a holoscreen.

"Why would their military leader not be with his soldiers?" Rhodes asked.

Connor frowned in thought for a moment. "I need to be there."

"General Gates, I have to advise against it," Rhodes said.

"Noted, Colonel, but I'm still going. Hold the position here and continue monitoring the situation."

"Yes, sir," Rhodes said. "Governor Wolf is due to check in. What should I tell her?"

"The Ovarrow don't do anything purely by chance. The warlord is at that bridge," Connor said, gesturing toward the holoscreen, "because there's a compelling reason for him to be there. I think it has to do with the fact that his second-in-command was at the location when the bridge collapsed. Tell her that. I'll be within comms range anyway."

"Very well, sir," Colonel Rhodes said.

Connor left the command area and sent a quick message to the Search and Rescue team waiting for him. Since he was heading into a hot zone, he put the MPS he was wearing into active standby status. Once they were airborne, he'd put it in full active mode. He reached the troop carrier and climbed aboard.

"General Gates, can I interest you in a pristine AR-71 for your use?" Captain Emery offered.

Connor nodded. "Thanks. I left mine at home."

The troop carrier rose into the air and flew towards the collapsed bridge with three Hellcat escorts. Within minutes, they hovered over the LZ a short distance away from the target.

Connor engaged the MPS, and he suddenly appeared to the onlookers like he was wearing black armor with a gold stripe down the side. The helmet formed around Connor's head, and a heads-up display immediately came on.

"Nice suit. Any chance we can get some of those, General Gates?" Captain Emery asked as they walked down the loading ramp of the troop carrier.

"I'll look into that," Connor said.

Several CDF Rangers escorted Connor to the command area. Flint did a double take as Connor walked in.

"You look like you lost a bet," Connor said.

Flint nodded. "I did. Samson said you'd be coming along."

The engineers and the Search and Rescue squad immediately went to work deploying specialized drones equipped with ground-penetrating radar. They'd perform a soft-landing maneuver, scan the area, and then send the data back to the command center.

Connor heard Ovarrow weapons fire, then the CDF soldiers returning fire. The skirmish flared up in bursts of weapons discharge. Flint and the reserve platoon escorted Connor toward the fighting.

Several concussion blasts sounded, but the MPS system dampened the sound. The ground shook with each concussive blast that was used to force the Ovarrow soldiers back.

They reached the barricade and hunkered down. Samson saw Connor and grinned at Flint. "See, I told you." The grin quickly faded, and he looked at Connor. "They keep pressing forward, and we keep forcing them back. We took out a row of buildings, which convinced them to stay back, but I don't know how long that will work."

Connor nodded and opened a comlink to Captain Emery. "How much time do you need to get the scans done?"

"We've only just started. We can get the immediate area done within ten or fifteen minutes, but it's going to take awhile to do the rest of the area," Emery replied.

Connor looked at Samson. "Is there a comms drone nearby? I want to send the Ovarrow a message."

"I can get you a few. They've been shooting them down," Samson said.

"We'll group them so we can create a large holoscreen. I don't want them to miss it," Connor replied.

It took a few minutes for the comms drones to get into position above the Ovarrow soldiers where Connor expected the warlord to be. The Ovarrow were gathering to press forward between the two buildings Samson had left standing. Connor took control of the comms drones, and a large, amber-colored holoscreen appeared above them. It was a giant square approximately fifty meters across and impossible to miss.

Connor activated the Ovarrow translator and began speaking. "Warlord Vitory, we're here to rescue the people trapped in the wreckage, both Ovarrow and humans. Cease hostilities at once. We have this position, and we're not going to give it up. Further action on your part will result in more soldiers dying, and you'll be putting anyone who's trapped in that wreckage at risk."

The Ovarrow symbols took up the entirety of the space for Connor's message. They hadn't charged yet, which was a good sign, but they hadn't replied either.

Connor stood up from behind the barricade, keeping his weapon pointed down.

"Hold your position," Connor said to Samson.

Connor walked toward the kill zone. He was in plain sight of the Ovarrow soldiers, and he saw them clearly through the enhanced optical feed of his MPS. "Warlord Vitory, it's me, General Connor Gates. I think it's time for us to talk. I'm right here."

There was a bit of commotion among the Ovarrow line and then a lone Ovarrow soldier walked toward him. The others glared at Connor and the CDF. If any of them fired their weapons, the CDF would obliterate every Ovarrow soldier in the area.

Vitory carried an Ovarrow weapon, which he held loosely in his hands. Connor had one of the comms drones fly down to them so they could speak without it being written in the sky.

Vitory came to a stop three meters from Connor.

"You attack us."

"You left us no choice. Our people are trapped in there, and we have the right equipment to rescue them," Connor replied.

"Your strategy was to attack us in order to force our cooperation. This does not speak well of the proposed alliance between us," Vitory replied.

"No, it doesn't," Connor said. "But my top priority is to rescue everyone who's trapped in the wreckage. I could do that much better if you'd stop attacking us. We don't have to fight."

Vitory read the message and seemed to consider it for a few moments. "We have the right to protect our city. We were trying to rescue everyone who's trapped as well. Your attack has set us back. Leave here immediately."

Connor shook his head. "That's not going to happen. If you continue to attack, I will authorize my soldiers to use deadly force. I don't want to do this."

Vitory's body went rigid and the end of his weapon seemed to stir. "I will order my soldiers to attack if you don't leave."

"What if we worked together to rescue the people trapped in the wreckage? You come in here with a team and we work together."

Vitory regarded Connor for a moment. The Ovarrow's face was almost a sneer.

"Once we rescue everyone," Connor continued, "I promise we'll leave the city, and we won't return without your permission to enter."

The warlord glanced at the CDF soldiers behind the barricades and then looked at Connor. "We don't trust you."

Connor met his gaze and put steel into his own. "There are many of us who don't trust you either, but there are people who are important to me trapped in that wreckage. The longer I have to contend with your attack, the less time I have to spend rescuing them. And if I have to choose between this alliance and their lives, I will choose them." Connor leaned forward. "Every time." He clenched his teeth and his muscles tensed. The next few seconds would decide just how bloody this conflict with the Ovarrow was going to become.

For some reason, the warlord looked more at ease than he had before. He wasn't happy about it, but he didn't quite look so suspicious of Connor anymore.

Captain Emery sent Connor the preliminary scan results of the area. It showed open spaces where people or Ovarrow could have survived the collapse. Connor sent the image to the holoscreen, and a secondary window opened with it.

"This is what we've found so far. Do you want to stand here and fight, or do you want to go rescue our people?"

Vitory peered at the holoscreen for a few moments, and his eyes widened as he realized what he was seeing. Then he looked at Connor. "Your proposal is acceptable," he replied.

The Ovarrow went back the way he'd come, and Connor returned to the others.

"We have a deal," Connor said to Samson. "Let's give them some room. They're going to help with the rescue effort. Send an update back to the command area. We need to get to work immediately. Some of them don't have much time."

Connor brought up the scan results again on his personal holoscreen. They were going to have to dig, and they had to be careful not to trigger any more collapses as they tried to reach the people trapped underneath. This was going to be a very long night.

"I notice you didn't show him the emergency beacons from the CDF soldiers who are trapped," Samson said.

"I will because that's where the people he most cares about are as well."

Samson arched a thick eyebrow. "How do you know this?"

"If he was more concerned about making a statement by rebelling against us, he would've stayed with the troops at the entrance to the city. Instead, he's here. There's someone here he cares about."

"I never would've guessed that. I can fight them, and they wouldn't have gotten closer to this area, but I never would've figured out what motivates them. You've changed, Connor."

Had he changed? He'd been moments from committing the CDF to firing on the Ovarrow military. He wasn't going to let anyone stand in his way of rescuing Lenora and the other colonists. He might have been able to figure out what motivated Vitory, but he wouldn't have hesitated to wipe them all out, and that must have been what convinced Vitory to cooperate. The warlord seemed almost relieved to at last measure Connor's resolve. He didn't know what that meant for the future of their alliance, but the warlord had seen something that gave him pause.

Connor pushed thoughts of the warlord out of his mind and went to oversee the rescue.

CHAPTER 18

Jon Walker peered through the window at the Raven Class Scout Ship SR-01. He'd only been on Phoenix Station for seventy-two hours and was expected to depart soon, whether his crew was finalized or not. Colonel Cross had been adamant that she'd try to get his top pick for his XO but wouldn't delay the mission for it.

"You know, it's bad luck to take a ship out that doesn't have a name."

Jon snorted a little and turned around. "Lieutenant Oscar Rutland, you're late. We're shipping out, or hadn't you heard?"

Oscar glanced out the window, looking at the ship.

"Technically, I'm not late for anything. I haven't committed to going on this mission just yet," Oscar replied.

Jon rolled his eyes. "I figured this would be right up your alley—a somewhat prototype ship. It's never seen any action before and has hardly been through a shakedown cruise. And," he said, smiling wryly, "we get to take it into hostile territory."

Oscar folded his arms in front of his chest. "If you're trying to sweet-talk me into coming on this mission, you're not doing a very good job. And," he said, holding up one finger, "this mission is still voluntary. You're not going to strong-arm me into this like you did the last time."

Jon rolled his eyes. "Which time was that?"

Oscar stared at him for a moment, then turned and started to walk away.

"Hang on," Jon said quickly. "Hang on. I was kidding. Did you have a chance to look at the mission briefing?" he said in a more serious tone.

Oscar stopped walking and nodded. "Operation Sherlock. Who the hell comes up with these names?"

"That would be Colonel Cross. I think if you go far enough back in her ancestry, she's probably some kind of royalty. I do agree though. I don't know how some twentieth-century detective is going to help us with this, but I really don't care what they call this mission. They could call it Operation Finding Lost Kittens and it wouldn't matter. This is important," Jon said.

Oscar probably wouldn't believe that Jon had been just as reluctant as he was about this mission. Colonel Cross had brought him around like a bucket of ice water being poured over his head, but Jon had other ways to get Oscar on board.

"So, what can this ship do? What makes it so special?" Oscar asked.

"Well, for one, it was designed by the CDF. We didn't use any design specs from the NA Alliance Military, so you could say it's a bit of an original," Jon said, smiling. "It's designed for stealth recon; however, it can also run electronic countermeasure operations. She can jam transmissions, scramble signals of guided weapons, and assist Talon-V operations. Here, have a look at the specs."

Jon made a passing motion with his hand and sent the ship specs to Oscar's PDA. Oscar opened his personal holoscreen and began reading. "No weapons to speak of, just some countermeasures. Oh, here it is—some midrange hornet missiles."

"Our best weapons are stealth and speed. Believe it or not, that ship out there is one of the fastest ships in the CDF fleet," Jon replied.

"You do realize that the Krake ships are faster than ours. What if they detect us?"

"Impossible," Jon said, confidently. "Our cross section is much too small. If they could scan us with that much accuracy, they'd already know where we are."

"We don't even know what kind of scanners they have," Oscar countered.

Jon tilted his head toward Oscar. "Well, it's right here in the intelligence briefing summary on Krake ship capabilities," he said, sending the briefing over to Oscar. "It says 'don't get caught with your pants down or they'll eat you.'"

Another briefing appeared on Oscar's personal holoscreen. "For crying out loud, it doesn't say that," Oscar groused, peering at the holoscreen intently.

"You're right, it doesn't. It says they likely have similar scanning capabilities to ours. Their weapons are powerful, and they have faster ships, but they do have limits— What? I read the damn briefing. Don't give me that," Jon said with a bit of incredulity in his voice.

Oscar read the briefing for a few moments more and then looked at Jon. "Why did you ask for me? You could have had your pick of anyone."

Jon regarded him for a moment, allowing some of his bravado to slip. "I trust you, Oscar. We've been through a lot. And we've completed countless salvage runs on Vemus ships. Once the war was over, people seemed to forget all that wreckage in orbit nearby. We were among the crews to take care of that. I just wanted somebody with me on the bridge that I knew and could trust."

Oscar pursed his lips in thought. "Bullshit," he said with a sneer and began to walk away.

Jon's mouth hung open for a few moments. "What do you mean 'bullshit'? It's true. I meant every word," he said, catching up to him.

Oscar glared at him. "That's not the reason, and you know it."

Jon inhaled deeply and sighed. "I need a good second-in-command just in case."

"Just in case what, Jon? Ever since your brother died on that ship, you've been keen to take on the riskiest missions. The only problem is, you're reckless about it. This time there's a crew of what," he said, glancing at the ship for a moment, "forty or fifty people?"

"It's forty-nine right now. You'd make fifty," Jon said. "And I'm not like that anymore."

"I'm tired of cleaning up your messes," Oscar said and was quiet for a few moments. Jon thought it was best not to say anything. "Do they know about you? Does Colonel Cross know about your record?"

"They came to me," Jon said. A flash of irritation made heat flush his cheeks. "They recruited me for this mission. Colonel Cross said she wanted somebody in command who had experience doing reconnaissance among enemy ships. She also wanted somebody who wasn't afraid to take some risks."

Oscar licked his lips and thought about it for a few seconds. "Oh," he said quietly. "I hadn't realized that."

Jon nodded. "You should probably know that Madelyn is part of the crew."

Oscar's mouth hung open a little. Then he shook his head. "You really are something else. Just to confirm, you're talking about *my* Madelyn, right? Madelyn Kniffin."

"This isn't my doing, Oscar. I wouldn't have done that to you. She was already assigned to the crew before I took command of the mission. She's the lead engineer on the ship."

Oscar closed his eyes and shook his head. Then, he took a few steps away with his hands on his hips and looked out the window at the ship. A long airlock tube connected to it from Phoenix Station, and docking clamps secured the ship in place.

"Oh," Oscar mumbled.

"Oh, *now* it's different. *I* ask you and it's all, 'No, Jon, you're just being reckless. Do they know about your record? They can't possibly have the right man for the job.' But if it just so happens that one Sergeant Madelyn Kniffin is serving on the crew, then one Lieutenant Oscar Rutland just can't help himself," Jon said grandiosely.

"Oh, it's not like that and you know it. I made a promise that I'd watch out for her," Oscar said.

"I've seen you in a room with her. This isn't just a mere promise," Jon said and quickly added, "but anyway, that's your personal business. What I need to know is whether you're volunteering for Operation Sherlock."

Oscar looked at him like a man who'd just lost a bet. "I officially volunteer for Operation Sherlock. And try not to look so smug about it."

Jon grinned. "I knew you were going to volunteer."

"I know you're my superior officer, but don't push me."

Jon's smile turned into a grin. After a moment, Oscar joined him.

"I'm glad to have you aboard. I mean that."

They walked together in silence for a few moments.

"Hey, I'm sorry for giving you such a hard time," Oscar said.

"You weren't all wrong. Some of that stuff probably needed to be said. No worries now."

"Where are we going?" Oscar asked.

"I need to take you to see Colonel Cross. She has the final say on the crew," Jon said.

Jon led Oscar through Phoenix Station, and before long, they were sitting in Colonel Cross's office while she read through Oscar's record on her personal holoscreen. A few moments later, she made a swiping gesture and the holoscreen diminished.

"Lieutenant Rutland, I need you to confirm that you understand this mission is entirely voluntary, and that neither myself nor Captain Walker here have coerced you in any way to take this mission," Colonel Cross said.

"I understand the mission parameters, Colonel Cross. I freely volunteer and hope that my service will help achieve our objective," Oscar replied.

"Excellent. I'm glad we have that out of the way. Captain Walker will bring you up to speed en route to the space gate," Colonel Cross said.

"I thought we had another day, Colonel." Jon said.

"We're moving up the timetable. General Gates and quite a few others want this mission under way. The ship is stocked, as they say, gentlemen. Not much of a shakedown cruise, but we know it won't fall apart either." Colonel Cross paused and regarded them both. "This mission won't be by the book. It's one of the reasons I requested the crew I did. However, having said that, this is not an excuse to throw your lives away. I expect a certain amount of risk to be accepted by you and the crew, but do keep in mind that some risks are not worth taking. I'd much rather have you return with your ship intact than lose any of you to the Krake. It's not that kind of mission. Is that understood?"

"Yes, ma'am," Jon said, with Oscar echoing the same.

"Good. I'm glad we have that out of the way, too," Colonel Cross said and directed her gaze to Jon. "We have a space gate farther out in the system that you requested. At best speed, you should be able to reach that gate in a few hours. After that, we'll continue to operate the space gates at the predefined hours in the mission briefing. Make no mistake, gentlemen. We're sending you into hostile territory without a way to get home."

Jon sat up a bit straighter. "We understand the risk, Colonel. If it's all the same, I'd like to get to my ship. The sooner we can leave, the sooner we can get back."

Colonel Cross stood up and so did Jon and Oscar.

"Very well. Good luck and happy hunting. We're depending on you to get us some answers," Colonel Cross said.

They left her office, not saying anything as they walked down the corridor.

"I'll need to have my things sent aboard the ship," Oscar finally said.

Jon smiled. "I already had your stuff sent aboard."

"Is that so? Do you also offer a comfortable work environment and an afternoon turndown service? I like my morning coffee fresh."

"We can arrange all that. And you'll be bringing me *my* coffee," Jon said, arching an eyebrow. "With nothing extra, I might add. Don't need a repeat of—well, anything that might've happened before."

"I understand, Captain," Oscar replied. "If it's not too much trouble, I'd like to tour the ship once we get underway."

"That can be arranged. I think you'll find the main engineering section particularly interesting," Jon replied solemnly.

Oscar nodded. "I think you're right."

They grinned and hastened down the corridor. Jon sent a message on ahead to the tactical officer on duty to start the preflight checks before they got on board. He didn't want to waste any time now. The clock was ticking.

CHAPTER 19

The Raven class scout ship only had one command bridge located amidships. Jon sat in the commander's chair of what could scarcely be called a bridge. They weren't quite crammed on top of one another, but it also wasn't what anyone would consider overly spacious. Both the pilot's and the tactical officer's workstations were set side by side. Oscar sat at the alternate tactical workstation to Jon's right. To his left was officially the operations workstation, but it was being manned by Specialist Amber Vandercamp. Amber was the resident expert on space gates. Jon hadn't wanted somebody who knew the theoretical concepts of how space gates worked; he wanted someone who'd actually worked with them. Thankfully, Colonel Cross had agreed and approved the transfer.

They'd put Phoenix Station behind them over an hour earlier and were heading to a space gate they'd positioned out near Gigantor's orbit.

Jon glanced at Oscar, who had his lips pursed and was nodding approvingly at the data on his holoscreen.

"Our engine output is at peak performance. We won't be at the space gate for another two hours, but we could cut down that time considerably if you wanted, Captain," Oscar said.

"It's tempting, but I don't want to thread any needles before we've had a chance to begin," Jon said. His comment drew a few chuckles from the bridge crew. That was a good sign. "Maybe on the way back."

The Raven may not have packed an offensive punch, but the stealth recon ship was jam-packed with some impressive equipment. They'd had to limit the number of crew serving aboard the ship because of advanced stealth recon systems. Jon reviewed the ship's systems, deciding whether he intended to alter the plan.

Jon looked away from his holoscreen to watch his crew for a moment.

They were all quietly working, diligently going over their responsibilities, but there was very little they could do until they actually went through the space gate. The closer they came to it, the more he could feel the tension build. It could have been just him, but he doubted it. He'd never gone to another universe, but he'd led quite a few missions among hostile ships. Mostly, they'd been from combat shuttles or salvage ships with squads of heavily armed soldiers.

Jon stood up and stretched his arms overhead. He took in a deep breath and exhaled. Corporal Bruce Wente, a short man not much more than five-foot-nine, glanced at him from the pilot seat.

"It feels good," Jon said. "Go for it, Corporal."

Corporal Wente hesitated for a mere second or two and then stood up. He held his arms up over his head and stretched. Then he rolled his shoulder and stretched his neck from side to side. Jon could hear it pop and had to suppress a shudder. Hearing anything like knuckles or backs cracking had always bothered him.

"Am I right?" Jon asked and then added, "It gets the blood flowing."

"It does," Corporal Wente replied.

"Anyone else?" Jon asked, and even though he received a few speculative glances, no one else rose to their feet. "Come on Lieutenant Rutland, Lieutenant Watkins, up and at 'em," Jon said and turned toward Specialist Vandercamp, his eyebrows raised questioningly.

After a few moments, they got on their feet and did some in-place stretching.

"It's good to loosen up a little bit. I think we'll have plenty of time at our respective stations," Jon said.

"Perhaps this would be a good time to go over the mission objectives again, sir," Oscar said.

Jon nodded. "Sounds good to me. We're looking for Trident Battle Group. In the absence of any of the ships, we're supposed to figure out what happened to them. We also need to take a closer look at the NEC."

"What's the NEC, sir?" Corporal Wente asked.

"New Earth Candidate. It would be too confusing to travel to alternate universes and refer to anything like our home as New Earth. So, they'll receive designations with NEC, followed by a number that will be assigned. Since we haven't gone anywhere else yet, we're just calling this one NEC."

"Why do they want us to take a closer look? The reports from the planetary mission indicate that the Krake are no longer there, and General Gates hasn't received any signal from the Trident Battle Group," Specialist Vandercamp said.

"Therein lies the rub," Jon replied. "The drone reconnaissance from Phoenix Station through the space gates shows that the NEC doesn't match the planetary profile for the planetary missions General Gates was on. Believe me, I was just as surprised as you are. Regardless, it's our job to have a look."

Lieutenant Andy Watkins was one of his two tactical officers. His relief was currently off duty. Like most tactical officers Jon had ever worked with, Watkins had a highly analytical mind. His brows were often furrowed as if he was lost in deep thought.

"I've been going through the mission objectives, as well as the plans proposed to achieve those objectives, and there's something I'm struggling with," Watkins said. Jon nodded for him to continue. "It would take too long for us to fly and recon the whole star systems ourselves. I noticed that the briefing from CDF Intelligence wants us to assume there's some sort of Krake presence in the star system."

"That is correct. We are to operate as if there are enemy ships in the area," Jon replied.

"If we take a slow and measured approach, then we minimize the risk of being detected by the enemy, but you intend for us to move quite a bit faster than that," Watkins continued.

"I can see where you're going with this," Jon said. "We can't avoid the enemy. If they're there, as soon as we start poking around, at some point they're going to detect us—even this ship. What we *can* do is minimize the risk, and that's the plan I put forth. It's the plan we are going to execute."

There were about twenty seconds of enduring silence on the bridge and Jon continued. "The CDF spared no expense when they put this ship together. We have a lot of equipment on here that's going to be used, and much of it isn't going to come back with us. I intend to use everything at my disposal to achieve our objective. We're not going home empty-handed. One way or another, we're going to find out what happened to Trident Battle Group."

"I understand that," Watkins replied quickly. "Trident Battle Group would've gone straight to the planet once they'd gone through the space gate."

"We're going to do the same thing, but we're going to take a different route. My best guess is that they could've spent two or three days maximum before whatever happened to them happened," Jon said, enjoying the discussion. This was what got people working the problem instead of just thinking about it.

"So, the question is," Oscar said, joining the conversation, "where has Trident Battle Group been for the past three months? If they had communications capabilities, they would've responded to any one of the comms drones that've been sent through the space gate. I don't see how all communications capability across the entire battle group could malfunction at the same time, so we can rule out equipment failure."

"If they fought a battle with the Krake, we should be able to find wreckage," Watkins added.

"That's the idea. That's why we're going—" Jon began, but an alert appeared on the main holoscreen, indicating they were on their final approach to the space gate. "We'll continue this later. Right now, get back to stations."

There were three other space gates deployed throughout the star system in addition to the one at Phoenix Station. They were powered by their own reactors and had three CDF destroyer class warships along with missile-defense platforms just in case anything hostile came through the space gate while it was active.

Jon transferred his authentication to the space gate protection detail, and they activated the gate for him. Major Joseph Lovelace, commanding officer of the *Ardant*, sent them off.

Jon watched the live video feed on the main holoscreen. The space gate, even in its smallest iteration, was large enough to accommodate a CDF destroyer but could expand to accommodate a heavy cruiser. The CDF destroyer was about four times the tonnage that the Raven class scout ship was, so they had plenty of room to fly through.

Jon noted that the approach vector Corporal Wente executed would put them through dead center, and the pilot in Jon heartily approved. There was nothing quite like being dead-on balls accurate.

They transitioned through the space gate and beamed a transmission back through it. Jon switched the live video feed to the aft sensors, hoping to glimpse their home universe before the gateway was closed. He peered at the main holoscreen but couldn't find the gateway.

Jon had almost expected to feel something as he went through the space gate, but there wasn't anything. They were simply at one point in space and then were in another, much like walking through a doorway.

Jon turned his attention to the task at hand.

"Specialist Vandercamp, set Condition Two throughout the ship," Jon said.

An automated ship-wide broadcast was announced to all fifty crewmembers. Condition Two indicated that a threat was probable but not present. Although a certain amount of crew readiness was expected, it wasn't as much as full readiness in a combat situation. They would be at Condition Two until they left the star system.

"Lieutenant Watkins, I want passive scans of the system. Corporal Wente, plot a course for the NEC. Lieutenant Rutland, begin our deployment of the heavy decoys," Jon said.

The heavy decoys were equipped with a small scanner array that was capable of doing active scans. They'd been enhanced with a subspace communication module that would allow them to send and receive data in almost real time—at least within the three-to-five-minute window they had for a subspace communication channel to remain active. Jon planned to use the decoys' scanning capabilities as a way of getting an active blueprint of the star system much quicker than if he had to rely on only the ship's scanners.

Jon noticed Specialist Vandercamp watching him and bobbed his head in an unasked question.

"I finally get it, sir. The heavy decoys. You're going to use them to throw the Krake off our track," Specialist Vandercamp said.

"That's the idea," Jon replied.

"Sir, I realize my expertise is mainly around space gate operations, but would you mind if I asked another question, please?"

"No worries. Ask away."

"Our scanner array on the ship is much more powerful than on the heavy decoys. Wouldn't we just use our own scanner array and then, in the event that the Krake detect us, activate the heavy decoys' limited scanner array? With the subspace communicator, we can activate the scanners on the heavy decoys within seconds of the enemy detecting our active scan pulse."

Jon shook his head. "It would be too late by then. Even our own combat AI on any warship would advise us to focus on the first initial scan burst. I suspect the Krake would see right through it if we took that approach. What I intend to do is coordinate using the scanners in the heavy decoys. I want active data once we've deployed all of them."

Specialist Vandercamp frowned for a moment, thinking about what Jon had told her. "I see. That's much better than what I was thinking."

"Nonsense. You can't know what you haven't studied yet. Would you like to shadow Lieutenant Watkins at tactical?" Jon asked.

Her eyes widened and gleamed all at once. "I would appreciate that, sir," she replied.

"Captain," Oscar said quickly, "I'd be happy to have Specialist Vandercamp join me and go over some of the tactical approaches we've decided on for this mission."

"That's fine," Jon said, and Specialist Vandercamp scurried over to sit with Oscar.

Then, they waited.

———

They spent the next twelve hours making slow but steady progress toward the NEC. Their course wasn't a straight shot to the planet because they were deploying the heavy decoy drones. Once they were ejected, they'd travel to a predefined set of coordinates using corrective thruster capabilities and momentum from the Raven.

Jon had just gotten to the galley to have a quick bite to eat before heading to the bridge. Lieutenant Watkins and Specialist Vandercamp joined him.

"Sir, how'd you get selected for this mission?" Vandercamp asked.

Watkins closed his eyes and looked away for a moment, and Jon merely chuckled.

"Did I say something wrong?" Specialist Vandercamp asked quickly.

"Not every CO enjoys having someone ask how they got their current command posting," Jon said, smiling. "But I don't mind. I have a lot of experience."

"Salvage runs on Vemus ships," Watkins added quickly.

Vandercamp's eyes widened. Then she nodded. "Is that it? Meaning no disrespect of course, sir. But is that the only reason? I'm keenly interested in how the CDF selects people for their posts."

Jon leaned back in his chair and sipped his coffee. "Isn't that enough?" he asked and then set his coffee mug down on the table. "It wasn't just the salvage runs—at least that wasn't the only reason. Do you know how many people were assigned to the Trident Battle Group?"

Vandercamp frowned in thought. "Well, there were eleven ships—two heavy cruisers, eight destroyers, and one converted freighter that was used as a carrier. The crew was mostly CDF, but they did have civilian specialists on board." She paused for a moment and then shook her head. "A few thousand? I'm afraid I don't know."

"Two thousand, two hundred and ninety people," Jon said, and Watkins and Vandercamp went quiet. "Nearly twenty-three hundred, to make it easier. That's a lot of people. That's a lot of families and friends. Sisters," he said, his mouth going dry, "and brothers."

Jon swallowed hard. There wasn't a day that went by that he hadn't thought about his brother. If it hadn't been for Patrick, they might never have found a way to kill the Vemus. His brother had been all he had when he'd first come to the colony. He had close friends now, but he and his brother had been closer.

"I suspect Colonel Cross was aware of this when she sought me out for this mission. After my brother died on the Vemus ship, I made sure no one else was left trapped on any salvage run. Granted, this is a bit different than those missions. I want to find them because if they did make the ultimate sacrifice, their families have a right to know what happened to them. You're a part of that now," Jon said, and his two younger companions sat up a bit straighter. "It's time for us to get back to it. We'll be passing the NEC soon."

Jon stood up, and Watkins offered to clean up after them. He left the galley and headed to the bridge.

Oscar stood up from the commander's chair. "All clear, sir," Oscar said and went to his workstation.

He and Oscar were close friends, but on the bridge and while they were on duty, they followed CDF formal address.

"Thank you, Lieutenant Rutland."

The computing core on the Raven could rival that of a heavy cruiser. They had quite a bit of data storage, which would allow them to record the entire mission. The CDF had learned the value of going back over every piece of data they could collect that could potentially give them more insight into the Krake.

The image on the main holoscreen was of the NEC, and they could see the small cluster of an asteroid field that orbited the planet beyond the second moon. Jon had the high-res optics deployed so they could get detailed images of both the planet and the asteroid field. CDF intel suggested that the Krake space gate would be located near the planet.

"Anomaly detected," Lieutenant Watkins said. "The data analysis of the image shows what could be an enemy ship. It matches the profile of a Krake destroyer."

"Where?" Jon asked.

"Near the asteroid field. I'll put it on screen."

An image appeared on the main holoscreen. It was enhanced with the cyber warfare suite's AI analysis of the high-res optical feed. It could pick out the details much quicker than any of the crew could.

"Compare this image to what we have in our records and put it on screen," Jon said.

A sub-window opened on the main holoscreen showing the various profiles of a Krake destroyer. These images had been captured when the heavy cruiser *Vigilant* had engaged the enemy.

"A ninety percent match," Oscar said.

"Good enough for me. I want that ship designated as alpha," Jon said. "Has the computer detected any CDF ships?"

"Negative, Captain," Lieutenant Watkins replied.

Jon suspected as much but had to ask anyway. "Scan the data for any other ships in the area," Jon said.

"Yes, Captain," Lieutenant Watkins replied.

The two images minimized to a much smaller sub-window, and the main holoscreen went back to a star-field view with the NEC featured prominently. Jon's gaze drifted toward the current image of the enemy ship. All the reports he'd read indicated that the Krake destroyers had superior speed when compared with a CDF warship. The Raven was built for speed and stealth, but he didn't want to put it to the test against the Krake destroyer. If it came to it, the best he could hope for would be that they had enough of a head start to get away from them and escape the universe through an egress point.

Jon glanced at the others on the bridge and saw more than a few of them looking at the image of the Krake destroyer. Jon decided to remove it but left the designation and location highlighted on the main holoscreen.

For the next few hours, the Krake destroyer didn't move, remaining in orbit around the NEC. The planet was going through a severe Ice Age that reached almost to the equatorial line. Any living thing that couldn't adapt to the severe cold temperatures would likely die. Jon looked at it and shuddered. God, he hated the cold weather, but he loved working in space. He made a point to go to New Earth, but more than half his time was spent serving at the lunar base and Phoenix Station.

"Tactical, put a plot up on the main holoscreen, and I want to see the locations of the heavy decoys we've deployed," Jon said, then added, "Keep the alpha on the screen as well."

Less than a minute later, the main holoscreen showed a star map. Thirty blinking white dots appeared like a string of pearls across the star system from a distance of Gigantor's orbit, which was over seven hundred million kilometers from the star.

Jon peered at the main holoscreen. With the current deployment of the heavy decoys, they had just enough coverage for the star system's interior planets. However, if Trident Battle Group had had to retreat to the outer system of planets, they might still be able to scan them, but it would take longer and increase the risk of the Krake detecting them. If Trident Battle Group had fought the Krake here, then why would they have let the CDF retreat at all?

Jon pressed his lips together and furrowed his brow in thought. There was no sign of any CDF ships near the NEC, so he could pretty much rule out them taking any sort of refuge on the ice planet. Jon couldn't imagine Colonel Quinn abandoning all his ships without leaving any sort of comms drone out in the system. Whatever was there to find would be away from the NEC and probably wouldn't be beyond Gigantor's orbit.

Jon looked at Oscar. "I think we're ready to kick over a few stones. What do you think?"

"Agreed, Captain. We'll need just a few minutes to bring up the sub-comm network," Oscar replied.

"Very well. Do it."

Jon leaned back in the commander's chair, feeling his elbows push into the contours of the padded armrests. He opened a broadcast channel to the ship. "Crew of the *Raven*, this is the captain. Since we haven't found any sign of Trident Battle Group, we're about to execute the next part of our plan. There's one enemy ship located near the NEC. When all the scanner arrays are brought online, the active scan pulses will no doubt alert the enemy to our presence. That was always the plan. Our gamble is that the enemy will pursue the heavy decoys, giving us a chance to investigate anything we detect. If we don't find any trace of Trident Battle Group, we'll head to the nearest egress point and go home. Be ready."

He closed down the broadcast comlink and looked at Oscar.

"Ready to scan, Captain."

"Execute," Jon said.

Active scan pulses utilized a range of different detection methods by scanner array. Any intelligent species monitoring the system would be able to detect an artificial pulse such as the one occurring at that moment. What the Krake destroyer was no doubt detecting was the presence of thirty active scan pulses throughout the interior of the star system all at the same time. The Raven was the snake in the grass, slithering undercover.

"Tactical, have the new data points detected put immediately on the main holoscreen," Jon said.

"Yes, Captain," Lieutenant Watkins replied.

Jon fixed his gaze on the main holoscreen. All the while he hoped—well, he hoped they detected something, but it would be better for them if it was close to this position rather than across the star system. If they did detect something worth investigating across the star system, they'd likely have to return at another time, unless Jon was of the disposition to risk another trek across the star system, hoping the Krake would overlook them a second time. It was too soon to tell about that.

The advantage of leveraging the heavy decoys equipped with subspace comms was that it essentially gave them an entire scanner array network that delivered data in real time. This was a huge tactical advantage. With each passing second, the main holoscreen updated the star field with various detections, but they all seemed to be relegated to normal astral bodies, such as meteors with high metal content.

A second enemy ship was detected in the asteroid field near the NEC.

"Captain, we've detected another anomaly. It's a metallic mass that's not located near anything else. The AI has put together an image that looks like partial ship wreckage, but it could just be the angle," Lieutenant Watkins said.

"Does it match any of the known CDF ship signatures?"

"Negative, Captain. However, it appears to be our best lead," Lieutenant Watkins replied.

"Enemy ships are on an intercept course for two of our heavy decoys," Oscar said.

"Very well, kill the scans for now. Initiate thrust maneuver for the decoys and arm the self-destruct for the two the Krake are so keen on investigating," Jon said. His orders were confirmed. "Corporal Wente, plot a course to the anomaly. Best speed," Jon said.

"Course laid in. Thirty minutes to destination, Captain."

Jon nodded appreciatively. The Raven was fast. "Add it to the plot, Corporal."

Jon brought up the image of the metallic mass on his personal holoscreen. The AI was taking a few liberties with filling in some of the gaps, but it definitely wasn't a natural astral body. That, of course, didn't mean that it was a CDF ship either, or even the wreckage of one. They needed a closer look.

"Lieutenant Rutland, how long until the enemy ships reach the heavy decoys?" Jon asked.

"Best guess is thirty minutes. They're the closest to the NEC, Captain."

Jon nodded, doing some quick calculations in his head. "I want another active scan pulse from those two heavy decoys only. Their vicinity to the NEC should let us know if any other ships—scratch that. I want active scan pulse from every heavy decoy but not the Raven. Let's do it in fifteen minutes."

"Roger that. Active scan pulse from heavy decoys in fifteen," Oscar confirmed.

Jon had initially thought to only use the two heavy decoys with enemy ships heading toward them but decided against it. The enemy already knew they were there. He'd get a more complete picture of the current status of the enemy response if he utilized all the heavy decoys. Since the Raven was farther out in the system, he didn't need to scan in that direction anymore. There'd been no enemy detections that far out, and there was no reason to believe the Krake had stationed any warships out this far. They had the capability, but there was very little need for them to be out there.

Fifteen minutes went by in the blink of an eye. The active scans still only revealed two Krake ships, but they were closer to the heavy decoys than they'd anticipated. The Krake destroyers accelerated at speeds within the known capabilities they had on file. That was something at least. The question still remained as to whether the commanders of those Krake ships would call for backup.

They closed in on the anomaly and Jon ordered a concise scan burst, which limited the scan to ahead of the ship. Unless there was something else in that line of sight, this active scan would go undetected.

"Put the scan results on the main holoscreen. I want a good look at this thing," Jon said.

They closed in on the metallic mass. It looked to have been a part of a CDF ship, but most of it was missing.

"Captain, this is the aft section of a heavy cruiser. That's where the engine pods are, but they've taken extensive damage," Lieutenant Watkins said.

"I see that, but where the hell is the rest of the ship? What kind of weapon could do this? There's nothing else left."

"Captain, this might not be a weapon at all," Specialist Vandercamp said.

"Go ahead," Jon replied.

"This ship has been sheared off. See how it angles away at forty degrees? This is because the ship was in motion when the event horizon alignment within the space gate got distorted. Alignment must be maintained in order for a ship to transition through. When the gate machines are misaligned, everything gets severed, quite literally cutting anything and everything off. There is no fail-safe or safety mechanism for this. I think we're looking at the tail section of one of the heavy cruisers that was part of Trident Battle Group."

Jon peered at the image, thinking that everything Vandercamp had just said was making a lot of sense. "Tactical, is there any way to identify which heavy cruiser it is?"

"I'm working on it. We'll know more as we get closer," Lieutenant Watkins replied.

Jon frowned. He needed to know which ship that was. He glanced over at Specialist Vandercamp, who was smiling. "Do you have something else, Specialist?"

"This is a good thing, Captain," she replied and shook her head. "Not good for anyone left in that section of the ship, but for the rest of the battle group it means they're not here. They had a space gate with them, and they could've all gotten through except the aft section of that ship."

Jon's gaze flicked to the main holoscreen, trying to imagine what had happened there.

"I think she's right, Captain," Oscar said.

"It would explain the inability to find Trident Battle Group, but what about this ship?" Jon said, jutting his chin toward the screen. "Doesn't look like there's any power, but that wouldn't have happened right away. One of the fusion reactors is located in that part of the ship. Bulkhead doors were closed. How do we know there isn't somebody trapped in there?"

"It's been three months," Oscar replied. "Field rations and survival equipment don't account for that length of time, even on escape pods, which we haven't detected."

"Captain, that ship is the *Douglass*. The designation numbers are on the far side of the hull," Lieutenant Watkins said.

"I want to take a closer look at it," Jon said.

"Yes, Captain. I'll slow us down so we can have a closer look," Corporal Wente replied.

The hull looked as if something had scraped off the outer layer of the battle steel alloy. Jon had never seen anything like it. He turned toward Specialist Vandercamp.

"Does the damage to the ship match with a misaligned space gate?"

She frowned for a moment in thought. "I don't know for sure, Captain. I wouldn't have the data here with me, but given the evidence, what else could it be?"

"Fair enough," Jon said.

He tried to think how many of the crew would have been trapped, wondering if anyone could have survived. How had this happened? Had Trident Battle Group fought the Krake here and, while fleeing, this disaster had happened? No other ships had been detected, not even the wreckage of Krake ships. There would surely be more wreckage if an actual battle had been fought here, but it had been three months. Where had Trident Battle Group gone?

The Raven circled around the remains of the *Douglass,* scanning the remnants of the hull.

"Captain, there's something—oh my God—there's an enemy ship attached to the hull. New class, smaller than a Krake destroyer," Lieutenant Watkins said.

Jon watched the main holoscreen, and his mouth dropped open as the enemy ship came online. It was using docking clamps that were attached to the hull.

"Pilot, best speed to nearest egress point. Go emergency!"

"Nearest egress nav point entered, Captain," Corporal Wente replied.

Klaxon alarms sounded throughout the Raven, and the crew strapped themselves in. Jon felt himself pressed into his seat despite the inertia dampeners compensating for the thrust of the powerful ship engines.

"Enemy ship in pursuit," Lieutenant Watkins said. "Attack drones have been fired."

Jon's first instinct was to launch countermeasures, but he waited. "Understood, Lieutenant."

"Captain, shouldn't we—" Oscar began to say but stopped himself.

"Tactical, ready countermeasures but wait to fire them until I give the order," Jon said.

Jon watched as the enemy combat drones raced to catch up to them.

The Raven was fast, but the drones were even faster. The limiting factor of a spaceship's speed was the crew themselves. Ships without any life-forms on them didn't have to worry about keeping their crews alive. Also, the human body didn't react very well when approaching anywhere near relativistic speeds. The attack drones had no such limitations and would intercept them.

"Captain, we're not going to reach the egress point in time," Corporal Wente said.

Jon cursed and glared at the plot on the main holoscreen. His first instincts were those of a combat pilot, and that was to go as fast as he could. "Redo the calculations, Corporal, but don't slow down for the egress point."

"Captain, I don't think I can do that," Corporal Wente replied.

"Do you want me to fly the ship, Corporal?"

Corporal Wente's brows drew together and he looked to Oscar for help.

"Corporal, you can either thread the needle or you can't. If you can't, let me know so I can get someone who can, or I'll do it myself."

Corporal Wente's face went pale and he shook his head.

"Lieutenant Rutland, take control of the helm," Jon said.

"Yes, Captain, I have control of the helm," Oscar said.

A few moments passed. "It's going to be close, Captain."

The plot on the main holoscreen updated. It showed Krake attack drones gaining on them, but the time to reach the egress point had decreased significantly.

Jon looked at Specialist Vandercamp. "Is the gateway there?"

"Not yet, Captain," she replied.

Jon cursed. The space gates in the home system were scheduled to open at specific time intervals. He'd almost hoped that whoever was in charge of that space gate would open it earlier. Either they were going to overshoot the space gate, in which case the enemy drones would likely finish them off, or they could open fire while they were trying to transition, in which case they might not make it. They could end up in a worse state than that of the *Douglass*.

Close indeed.

"Captain, enemy attack drones are closing in," Lieutenant Watkins said.

"Wait," Jon replied. "A few more seconds. They've got to get closer," he said, almost to himself. He watched the main holoscreen with rigid intensity. The attack drones had just passed fifteen hundred meters. "Now! Launch all countermeasures!"

Lieutenant Watkins slammed his hand on his console. "Countermeasures launched."

Jon's gaze swooped to the space gate indicator on the main holoscreen, and it suddenly flickered to life. They raced through the gateway a half a second after it had been formed. They were going so fast that the CDF destroyers on the other side had scarcely acknowledged them.

"Fire braking thrusters. We need to slow down and report in," Jon said and transmitted his clearance to the CDF fleet so they wouldn't shoot them down. No doubt that they were targeting him, and no matter how fast he was going, he couldn't escape their missile-defense platforms.

"They've closed the space gate," Specialist Vandercamp said.

Jon blew out a long breath and laughed. "Good work, everyone," he said. Corporal Wente looked away from him. "Corporal, it's okay. You were doing what you were trained to do."

Oscar gave a nod and went over to Corporal Wente's workstation.

"Tactical, begin preparing all the data that was collected and upload to COMCENT," Jon said.

"Yes, Captain," Lieutenant Watkins said.

Oscar came over to him and Jon stood up.

"That was really close," Oscar said.

"You've got that right."

"I didn't think the gateway was going to open in time."

Jon glanced at Vandercamp. "Sometimes you just have to have a little faith. It was either that or we would've died. I'm happy with the current results."

Oscar regarded him for a few moments. "No one could have been on that ship."

Jon felt the smile drain away from his face. They'd gotten away, and that was a good thing. He met his friend's gaze. "We'll never know. They were waiting for us to come look for them."

"That may be, but they're not going to learn anything from us or from the heavy decoys we left behind. I set them all to self-destruct. There's nothing left of them."

Jon nodded and tried not to think about the CDF soldiers that had served on the *Douglass*. If any of them had survived, they were prisoners of the Krake. Who knew what was happening to them or had already happened to them? Vandercamp was right. At least they knew that Trident Battle Group had escaped the Krake. They just had no idea where they were now.

CHAPTER 20

t'd been a frustratingly long night filled with planning, then hauling out debris while trying to prevent further shifts in the wreckage. Once on task, the Ovarrow worked with dogged determination whether soldiers or laborers. Vitory, after seeing how much faster they could reach the victims with the help of the colonists, had agreed to allow the CDF Search and Rescue team to help them at the other site. But tensions between the two species were still much too high. Connor didn't need to be an expert in diplomacy to understand that. He'd been receiving steady reports of Ovarrow soldiers gathering just outside the affected areas.

Connor glanced at the people they'd been able to save, seeing Lenora bob her auburn head in response to the medic's questions. She was covered in dirt and debris, and there were shallow cuts on her hands and cheeks. Someone else's blood was on her pants. She looked at him and smiled. The Search and Rescue team had only just managed to pull them out of the wreckage. Connor watched her and tried to temper his emotions, but his throat tightened. Her gaze was a mixture of relief and shock at what she'd been through. She'd saved lives down there. That's what he'd been told, but they'd lost a lot of lives, too.

Unable to wait any longer, Connor walked over to her.

The medic looked at him. "She's fine. Just a little bruised and scraped. A little dehydrated. Keep drinking that water. You were very lucky, Dr. Bishop."

Lenora thanked him, and Connor used his implants to access the MPS jacket she wore. He quickly skimmed the log entries of the suit's activities and his brows furrowed.

"I'm fine," Lenora said.

"I know, but you almost weren't. If you hadn't been wearing the jacket—

why didn't you wear the pants?" Connor said and squeezed his eyes shut for a moment. "Never mind, I don't care. You're here. That's all that matters."

Lenora flew into his arms, and Connor gave himself this moment to forget everything that was happening around him. It didn't last long enough.

Lenora pulled away and looked around. "Who else were you able to save?"

"Darius and some of the people he was with. Not all of them. We've reached all the survivors we're going to reach. Now, we'll have to work on retrieving the people who didn't make it."

Lenora looked over at the other survivors. The Ovarrow had been taken to a separate location as soon as they were able. They'd pulled out twenty-one people, and eight more were unaccounted for.

Connor followed her line of sight. "Is that Kayla Wolf?"

Lenora nodded. "Yes, and the girl next to her is Lynn. There was another intern named Devon, but he didn't . . ." Her voice cracked.

"Hey, none of that now," Connor said soothingly. "You did everything you could and a good deal more. You saved that girl's life. You also helped the Ovarrow trapped with you. Lenora, I'm so proud of you."

Lenora's eyes became misty, and she hastily wiped away tears.

"Do you remember where Dash was when the bridge collapsed?" Connor asked.

Lenora shook her head. "He wasn't with us. He'd left the group before we even came to the bridge. He was with Jory."

Samson walked over and joined them. "The other SAR team reported in. The bridge collapse over there wasn't as bad as this one, but there were more injuries. There have been thirty-two casualties so far. The Ovarrow soldiers are insisting that the SAR team leave now."

"Understood. Did they get the scans they needed?" Connor asked.

"Affirmative."

"All right, get them out of there."

"I think someone wants to speak to you," Samson said, gesturing behind Connor.

Vitory was walking toward them, along with several soldiers. The Ovarrow looked at Connor for a moment in silent acknowledgment before looking at Lenora. A comms drone hovered near him, and he used the holo-interface.

"I've just learned that you saved the lives of my soldiers, including Cerot, my First. I was told he would've died were it not for you," Vitory said.

The Ovarrow waited for them to finish reading the message, and then all of them brought their right hands to their left shoulders and glided over their chests.

Connor had never seen the gesture before. He glanced at Lenora, who seemed to know what it meant.

"You're welcome," Lenora said.

A text message appeared on Connor's internal heads-up display.

D. DeWitt: *We need to talk.*

C. Gates: *Where are you?*

D. DeWitt: *I'm on my way to you. I don't want to send this over comlink.*

Darius joined them. Vitory and the others were watching Connor, and he looked at the translator interface.

"The rescue effort is almost finished. All of your people are accounted for. It's time for you to leave," Vitory said.

"We can help with the cleanup efforts. We will, of course, withdraw our soldiers from the city as agreed," Connor said.

"Your help will not be necessary. The terms of our agreement have been met," Vitory said.

The pre-morning gloom was giving way to a new day. There was a chill to the air, and Connor heard the wind turbines turning.

"I think we should respect their wishes, Connor," Darius advised.

Connor looked at the warlord. "We will leave now."

Orders were passed, and soon the Search and Rescue teams were being transported away. Within thirty minutes, Connor was boarding the last troop carrier to leave the city. Dash had joined them just a few minutes earlier. He hadn't said anything, and the Ovarrow had hardly reacted to Dash at all.

Connor walked to the front of the troop carrier and Dash followed him. Lenora was already on board, looking at one of the holoscreens.

Connor waved for Samson to join them, and after a few moments, asked Darius to come as well. "All right, where have you been? And tell me what you found out."

"Jory wanted to show me a new medical clinic he'd built. I was supposed to catch up with the others by the time they left the city. These bridges didn't just collapse because they were old. I went to the other site, and there were impact points indicating a sonic charge had been used, but there's also something else."

"Hold on," Darius said. "You're saying this wasn't an accident?"

Samson shook his head. "These structures have been here for hundreds of years through extreme weather. I'm surprised there aren't more accidents here."

Dash looked at Darius. "Yes, and I'll explain," he said and looked at Samson. "The materials they use in their construction are highly resistant to corrosion. The sonic charges targeted weak points in the support structure. So, someone did this, but they took advantage of someone else's work. The Ovarrow were already using their tools to weaken the support structure. I don't know why, but I've seen the results of their tools and have been in enough of their cities to know that the support structures would need some coaxing before a sonic charge would be able to finish the job."

Connor pressed his lips together for a moment, his thoughts racing. "I don't understand. Why would the Ovarrow do anything like this?"

"I don't know. Why would they send the envoy back through an alternative route rather than using the main thoroughfare?"

Darius shook his head. "This makes no sense. Cerot led us on that route. If he was involved, then why would he put his own life in danger like that?"

They were silent for a few moments. "Cerot couldn't have been involved, and Vitory seemed relieved that Cerot was okay," Connor said.

"That makes sense," Darius said. "Cerot is second-in-command of the Mekaal. Hierarchy is deeply respected among the Ovarrow."

Connor felt his mouth forming a grim line. "Unless we're dealing with someone like Siloc, a faction of Ovarrow that's loyal to the Krake. Who benefits if our alliance collapses?"

Dash nodded. "It's not just the Ovarrow. The sonic charges were colonial-made, which means—"

"That our rogue group of criminals was involved," Connor finished.

"This is something that Lars could do," Dash said.

"Yes, Lars Mallory has the skill set to do something like this, but we don't have any evidence that puts him there. I won't let this become a witch hunt, and Lars Mallory isn't working alone," Connor said, quickly quelling an accusation that could spiral out of control.

"It does mean they're changing their tactics," Samson said.

Connor shook his head in disgust, and Darius looked confused. "The rogue group's efforts hadn't put colonial lives in danger before." Dash started to say something, but Connor gestured for him to wait. "This is something different. This is more aggressive. They *wanted* a death toll with this. We need to analyze the scans and try to recreate what happened in a virtual environment. We need an official investigation, which means we need to get the colonial government involved."

Connor shared a look with Samson and Dash, but Darius frowned.

"I think I'm missing something here," Darius said.

"There are some of us who think this rogue group has been acting against our alliance with the Ovarrow, and anything related to it has support from someone high up in the colonial government."

Darius's eyes went wide. "It can't possibly be Governor Wolf."

"I agree. She's not my first choice. And the fact that her daughter was here pretty much rules her out, unless we're all underestimating her."

"Who do you think it is?" Darius asked.

"I'm not sure. I don't think it's a 'who,' but more of a 'they'— a group, a conspiracy if you will," Connor replied.

Darius sighed heavily and his shoulders slumped.

"You should go get some rest, Darius."

Darius nodded. "I will. I just can't believe this. They might've succeeded. This disaster is a major setback for the alliance."

"They still need our help. They don't have the transportation capabilities to retrieve the stasis pods to increase their population, but I agree it doesn't look good all around." Connor rolled his shoulders and stretched his neck.

Darius left them, and Samson cleared his throat.

"We should do our own investigation and then allow the data to be accessed by the governor's office," Samson said.

"Agreed, but we don't have much time," Connor replied.

"We don't need that much time—probably just a few days at the most. Mind if I borrow your protégé here?" Samson asked and nodded toward Dash.

Connor smiled a little. "Yeah, just be careful not to break him."

Dash snorted. "Protégé," he said and stood up to follow Samson.

"Hey, Dash, you did good. Keep it up."

Dash smiled and then turned around and left.

Lenora bounded over to him with a wide grin.

"Did you just see Lauren?" Connor asked. He wanted to see their daughter, too.

"I did see her, and she's fine. Ashley is with her, but I have news," Lenora said, brimming with excitement. She put her hand on Connor's arm and squeezed it. "Noah is awake."

Connor was sure he hadn't heard her right. Lenora repeated herself. Of all the things she could've told him right then, that was by far and away the least likely. He looked at her. "Awake," he said. "How?"

"She didn't say."

"Who didn't say?"

"Ashley. She was home, and she just got the call when I was speaking to her," Lenora replied.

Connor felt his lips curve upward in a genuinely heartfelt smile. Noah had awakened from his coma.

CHAPTER 21

Connor was finally home. It had taken another twelve hours to withdraw the CDF troops from outside the Ovarrow city. They'd also evacuated the camp just outside the city but left a colonial communication console for the Ovarrow to use if they wanted to contact them.

Connor heard Lenora and his daughter in the other room and resisted the urge to join them. He had a scheduled call with Darius and Governor Wolf. Listening to his daughter's squeals of delight, followed by Lenora's laugh, he knew that if he went into the room, he'd likely miss his call.

Lenora had stayed with him until he could return home, and they'd been home for less than a day, just the three of them. He kept watching Lenora, firm in the knowledge that he'd come dangerously close to losing his wife. Lauren had almost lost her mother. The thought still made him clench his teeth.

Lenora made a cooing sound, and Lauren's giggles became a full-on belly laugh. Connor stood up, thinking he'd just go in there for a minute. He had time before his meeting. He hastened over to the bedroom, but a warning chime appeared on his internal heads-up display, indicating that his call with Darius and Governor Wolf was about to begin.

Connor sighed and stepped outside his home. It was early afternoon, and thick clouds blanketed the sky with the promise of rain later on, perhaps sooner.

Connor activated his personal holoscreen and it split into two images. Darius Cohen appeared on one of the holoscreens and Dana Wolf appeared on the other.

"I wanted to make both of you aware of some of the evidence we've found," Darius said.

"Is the colonial diplomat's office involved with the investigation?" Connor asked.

"Of course we are. There's more going on here than simple relations with the Ovarrow," Darius said.

Connor glanced at Governor Wolf, who gave a firm nod. He had the CDF analyzing the scan data of the wreckage, and they were recreating a virtual model of what they thought happened with the two bridges based on empirical evidence.

"This evidence has already been shared with CDF Intelligence," Darius said, anticipating Connor's line of thinking. "We've been monitoring the Ovarrow since we helped them establish their settlement in the city. What we have is video surveillance evidence that supports Dash's theory that the Ovarrow had a hand in weakening the structural integrity of the two bridges that collapsed."

"Can you show it to us?" Governor Wolf asked.

Connor could still see the lines of worry on the governor's face. Her daughter had been there, too, and he could tell she wasn't in the mood for extending tolerance for half measures.

"Absolutely. I have three instances, but it's no—I'll let you look at it first, and then we can discuss it," Darius said.

A sub-window appeared on Connor's personal holoscreen, showing three video surveillance feeds. It looked like the stealth recon drones were making a routine patrol of the city, and the first video clip showed a group of Ovarrow gathering and working near the main support structure for the bridges.

"They could have been reinforcing it," Connor said.

"We've reviewed all the surveillance data, and this group of Ovarrow only came to these bridges in the middle of the night. And only to the two bridges that collapsed," Darius replied.

"Do we have anything better that shows exactly what they are doing?" Connor asked.

He didn't want to jump to any conclusions. It was important that the facts led to a logical conclusion free of conjecture. At least, that was what Connor wanted to have happen, but things seldom worked out that way.

"No, the physical evidence is currently cut off from us, but we should have enough scan data of the area to make an accurate theory of how the bridges collapsed."

"So, the theory is that there was a group of Ovarrow who were weakening the supports to the bridges. Then, someone else comes along and uses a sonic disrupter to finish the job?" Connor said.

"Do you think these two groups were working together? The Ovarrow" —Governor Wolf's gaze became hard—"and the rogue group of miscreants that murdered eight colonists and twenty-two Ovarrow?"

Darius hesitated for a moment and then looked at Connor.

"I don't think so," Connor said. "I think the rogue group happened upon the weak points of the main support structure for the bridge. A simple integrity scan would reveal it, even from a reconnaissance drone—well, CDF reconnaissance drones and probably Field Ops as well. A civilian monitoring drone wouldn't have that amount of sophistication."

"Unless it's for research and development," Darius replied.

"Why would the Ovarrow do this to their own people?" Governor Wolf asked.

"We can't answer that. All we can do is speculate," Connor said. "We need to share this information with High Commissioner Senleon and Warlord Vitory. They'll conduct their own investigation and let us know the results. We can at least keep the lines of communication open with them."

"This needs to be handled delicately. They've cut off communication with us, and we shouldn't force this information on them; otherwise, it will seem like an intrusion," Darius said.

"He's right," Governor Wolf said. "We can't just dump this evidence in the Ovarrow's laps right now."

"Why would we wait?" Connor asked.

"The Ovarrow are trying to sever ties with us. Their last message indicated that they were content to wait to bring their people out of stasis, but not all Ovarrow feel that way. However, they're not convinced that we can stand against the Krake," Darius said.

"They might *think* they can sever ties with us, but they need us. I think waiting to tell them what really happened is a mistake in the long run," Connor said.

"Our own investigation isn't complete, so sharing anything with them at this point would be premature," Governor Wolf said, and Connor had to agree with her.

"But you do intend to share our findings with them, right?" Connor pressed.

Governor Wolf regarded him for a moment. "That decision will be made once the investigation is complete."

Connor shook his head. She was angry with the Ovarrow, and worse than that, she was afraid. She'd almost lost her daughter. Pressing his point at this moment wouldn't be smart.

"Why don't we just give them some space for a few days? Vitory will do his own investigation," Darius said and paused for a few moments. "If anything, this experience has taught the Ovarrow that they are vastly inadequate when it comes to a conflict with the Colonial Defense Force. This is a tough lesson for them to learn because they're trying to assert their independence."

Connor agreed with Darius. Maybe they all needed to take a few days to digest what had happened. The whole situation was a mess, and his own temper flared at the thought of it. The real stink of it was the fact that all the people involved—colonists and Ovarrow—had a part in it. He clenched his teeth for a moment and then forced himself to calm down.

"I've authorized the release of all the Ovarrow from Camp Alpha, and all further Ovarrow stasis retrieval efforts have been put on hold," Governor

Wolf said. Connor looked at her sharply and she continued. "It's time the Ovarrow started holding up their end of the bargain. They need to provide credible intelligence about the Krake."

"Yes," Connor said, "but they've also awakened to a world they don't know, and the threat they'd hoped to avoid is still imminent."

"I understand that, but the Ovarrow will simply need to learn how to cope. Right now, I feel like they're taking advantage of what we have to offer —from the treatment of our diplomatic envoys to the events that took place during this disaster. They really thought they were going to keep us out of there," Governor Wolf said.

It would've been so easy for Connor to take the hard line of thinking regarding the Ovarrow's behavior, and that would have been extremely dangerous. Something he'd always known was that once they fired their weapons, they could never take it back. It was too easy to be angry with the Ovarrow.

"Are we asking so much from them that they're simply shutting down?" Darius asked and then added, "It's only been three months. We brought ten thousand of their population out of stasis. They must have had protocols for bringing their own people out, but we didn't know what they were. So, nothing about this entire situation is comfortable for the Ovarrow. Maybe 'comfortable' is the wrong word here, but everyone needs time to adapt, including the Ovarrow."

They were quiet for a few moments.

"I know firsthand what it's like to wake up and not be where I thought I was going to be," Connor said quietly.

He glanced at the others to see that his comment had had an impact on Darius and Governor Wolf. They knew what had happened to him. Connor wasn't supposed to have been on the *Ark*, but he was here—a two-hundred-year journey and sixty light-years from home. There was no going back for him. It had taken him a long time to come to terms with that.

"We'll table this discussion for the moment," Governor Wolf said and looked at Connor. "The Colonial Defense Committee will be reviewing a motion to give the CDF authorization to hunt down the rogue group responsible for the terrorist act in the Ovarrow city."

This was the first Connor had heard of this, and he said so.

"I expect the motion will pass. Nathan will attend in your stead. I thought you wanted to spend some time with your family," Governor Wolf said. "I need to thank you and Lenora. She saved my daughter's life," she said and paused for a few moments before continuing. "We need a plan to locate this rogue group as soon as possible."

"Dana," Connor said, using the Governor's first name, "we can locate their operations outside colonial cities, but I won't order anyone in the CDF to conduct an investigation inside any colonial city. That isn't the purpose of the CDF. You should also be aware that this is likely to get worse before it gets better, depending on who's involved."

Governor Wolf looked away for a moment. "They hurt my daughter," she said and looked at Connor. "They hurt her. She wasn't involved in this at all. She's innocent. There were a lot of innocent people who got hurt and others who died."

Connor met her gaze. "There were. We'll find who's responsible."

Governor Wolf leaned back from the video feed and gave a nod. Then the comlink to her office shut down.

Darius sighed. "Tempers are still pretty hot right now."

"I know, and I'm one of them. We can't keep going like this," Connor said.

"What are you going to do?" Darius asked.

Connor took a deep breath and exhaled. "I'll start doing some planning, but for the next few hours, I'm going to see a friend."

"I'd heard. Noah Barker has come out of the coma. That's amazing," Darius said.

"It is. He just started waking up on his own, is what I've been told. Darius, he always had a level head about this stuff. We need more of that right now," Connor said.

Darius gave him a long look and then nodded. The comlink closed. Connor was about to shut down the holoscreen when a new comlink registered on the screen. It was Savannah Cross.

Connor activated the comlink and took the call.

"General Gates, I'm so glad I caught you," Savannah said with a smile. "I have something to share with you that I knew you'd want to hear about right away. We found evidence that Trident Battle Group is no longer in the alternate universe. In fact, they went to a different universe altogether, which is why we haven't had any contact with them."

"Where are they?" Connor asked.

"We're not exactly sure, but we know that most of the ships made it through the space gate, which means they're still alive."

Connor had to stall his racing thoughts and process exactly what she was saying. He felt a tightening of his skin. "Okay, take me through this one step at a time."

CHAPTER 22

Connor walked to the medical center. Lenora had more or less chased him out, claiming Lauren for her own, and gone off to do her own thing. It had been a few days since the attack at the Ovarrow city, and nothing regarding that incident required immediate attention. Connor knew that their own investigation into the collapse of the two bridges was complete; however, no report had been sent to the high commissioner of the Ovarrow. If it were up to Connor, he would've sent it over immediately.

As the time went on, Connor became increasingly agitated. He could handle the pressures of command and even the standoff with the warlord, but these events had hit close to home. He wondered if it had all been orchestrated as a personal attack on him, and he also couldn't help thinking they'd been hoping to prevent an alliance with the Ovarrow. They might have delayed it, but what would they do next, and how many lives would it cost?

He could've gone to the CDF base. There was plenty of work to be done, but Nathan had insisted that he take a few days off. He'd decided to take Nathan's advice, but Lenora had her own ways of dealing with things. She was still shaken up over the whole thing. Being trapped under tons of wreckage was enough to rattle anyone's cage.

Connor walked up the large staircase that led to the Colonial Medical Center and went inside. He made his way to the long-term care wing, giving a friendly nod to the people he recognized, and went to Noah's room, but his friend wasn't there.

"Mr. Gates, if you're looking for Noah, he's out walking on the garden trails," the nurse said to him.

Connor thanked her and headed outside. There were other patients outside who were also recovering from whatever injuries they'd sustained. He spotted Noah walking in plain hospital attire, marking him as a patient. Noah saw him and waved.

Connor caught up to him. "Look who's up and about."

"That's me, making leaps and bounds. Couldn't stand being inside anymore," Noah said.

"I thought they wanted you to rest," Connor said.

"This is therapy—not physical therapy. My muscles don't need it; they didn't atrophy while I was in the coma. This is therapy for my brain," Noah said, tapping the side of his head. "They want me to get up and do things to help with my recovery."

"Makes sense, I guess," Connor said. After a few moments, he asked, "Do you remember anything that happened?"

"Bits and pieces. I remember fighting with Lars and falling off the cliff. People screaming . . . Dash. Kara filled me in on what happened after."

"We took out the archway," Connor replied.

Noah grimaced for a moment and then nodded. "I still can't believe how much time has passed. Ten months. It's hard for me to remember things, and what I do remember is fuzzy. I remember hearing your voice and Kara's. Lenora too. But it's weird—similar to a dream, or like I had something stuck in my ears. It's kinda hard to explain."

"We all came to see you. Do you remember sending me a message? A video log file before you found Lars?"

Noah frowned in thought, and then his eyes widened slightly. "I do . . . I remember making the video," he said and regarded Connor for a few moments. "It's funny because it was one of those last-minute things. I almost didn't do it." He rubbed the back of his neck and looked at Connor. "Did you do it?"

"Are you asking if I prayed for you? Yeah, Noah, I did. We thought you were dying."

Noah grinned, intrigued. "You actually prayed for me," he said, as if he couldn't quite imagine it.

Connor shook his head. "What do you take me for? A friend's last request—of course, I did."

"Yeah, but you . . . Well, you know."

It was no secret that Connor wasn't the most religious person. "I figured it couldn't hurt."

"Well, I appreciate it," Noah said.

They were quiet for a few minutes as they walked along the path. Connor noticed that Noah's shoulders were slumped just a little bit.

"Maybe we should sit down. Take a break," Connor suggested.

There were benches along the path, and they sat down on one.

"It's all right to pace yourself, you know. Three days ago, you were at death's door," Connor said.

"I feel like I've slept enough," Noah said with a bit of an edge to his voice. He looked away from Connor and shook his head. "I'm afraid to sleep. I'm worried that I won't wake up. Ashley told me that was normal—well, normal under the circumstances— but when I start to fall asleep, my mind races. What if I slip back into a coma and never wake up again?" Noah shivered at the thought.

"You've been through a lot, Noah. It's enough to shake anybody up. It'll just take time."

"And lots of rest and recovery," Noah said as if quoting the people who'd been telling him that. "Believe me, it's all I keep hearing about, but I don't want to rest. I want to do something. Go back to my work. I just want to go back to the way things were."

Noah was scared. That much was obvious, but Connor wasn't sure what to say. He decided to stay quiet and listen.

Noah arched an eyebrow. "No speeches about how I should make a full recovery or anything?"

Connor pursed his lips and bobbed his head to the side. "If there's anyone who could do it, it's you."

"That's the thing. It's like having a bunch of things at the edge of my thoughts, and I can't get to them. I want to think of them, and I feel like I should be able to do—well, anything really. What if that's the way it is now?"

"Then that's the way it is. You'll learn to live with it, but I think you're being a little too hard on yourself. You said it yourself. Your brain needs time to wake up."

Noah swallowed hard. "For me, it feels like it's only been a few days since the accident."

The muscles in Connor's shoulders went tight. "It wasn't an accident."

"Yes, it was. Lars didn't throw me off that cliff. He didn't mean to do it. We were fighting," Noah said.

"Give me a break, Noah. He may not have physically thrown you off the cliff, but he definitely created the situation where you fell."

Noah closed his eyes for a moment and looked as if he was trying to remember. He gritted his teeth and shook his head in frustration.

"Why don't we go get some food? Are you hungry?" Connor asked.

Noah opened his eyes and nodded. "I guess."

They headed back into the medical center and went to the cafeteria. As they got their food, many people greeted Noah and wished him well. Noah took it in stride. Connor thought his friend looked tired despite his assertions that he wasn't.

"Connor, can you do me a favor?"

Connor took a bite from his sandwich and put it down. "Sure. What?"

"Tell me what's been going on. Nobody really talks to me. Kara keeps telling me I need to rest and not worry about it. Ashley pretty much says the same thing. I did get to meet Lauren. She's cute. So, you're a dad now," Noah said.

Connor smiled. "Yes, I am, and dammit, Diaz was right about it."

"I hear he has a restaurant now."

Connor nodded. "The Salty Soldier. I'll take you to it when you're out of here."

Noah shook his head and smiled. "The Salty Soldier. Sounds about right for Diaz."

Connor began telling Noah what had been happening since he'd been in a coma, from reverse engineering Krake technology to what they'd learned about the Ovarrow.

"So, the NEIIS are the Ovarrow. That will take some getting used to. No one has been able to find Lars?"

"He moves around a lot, and he's actually pretty good at covering his tracks. We've come close a few times. Dash had a run-in with him about three months ago."

Connor paused, deciding whether he should keep talking.

"Don't do that," Noah said.

"Do what?"

"Treat me like a sick person."

"You almost died, Noah. You're going to have to be patient with all of us, especially Kara."

"I swear to God, if you start telling me that I need to rest, I'll start screaming and . . ." Noah clenched his teeth for a moment.

"Well, if you scream too much, they'll give you a sedative," Connor said dryly.

Noah grinned a little and then sighed. "You're right about that, but seriously, I can still do things. Can you restore my system access? Is there anything I can help with?"

"I thought you were being discharged in a day or two. You'll have access to all your things then. Your lab and all that."

Noah snorted derisively. "Like Kara is going to let me do anything. She'll no doubt have some kind of lockout in place so I can focus on recovery. But I can't just sit around. I *have* to do something."

Connor leaned back in his chair and regarded Noah for a few moments. "You want to do something?" he asked.

Noah's brow wrinkled. "Yes."

Connor gestured toward his empty cup. "I could use a little more coffee."

Noah frowned for a moment and then looked at the empty cup. He squeezed his eyes shut, shook his head, and laughed. "I think I can handle that."

Noah got them both a refill and sat back down. "I guess I walked right into that, didn't I?"

"I had to take a shot. It was a target-rich opportunity that I couldn't walk away from," Connor said.

Noah sighed and slumped back into his chair.

Connor had seen this behavior before with wounded soldiers. They wanted to get back out there and prove that they hadn't been affected by their injuries. Sometimes it was better to just let them push their limits.

"I don't think there's any harm in you reading a few reports or looking at some stuff. I'll make sure you have what you need," Connor said.

"Thank you, Connor. That means the world to me," Noah said and paused for a moment. "I haven't heard you mention Sean. What's he doing these days?"

Connor drank his coffee and told Noah about Trident Battle Group. "We just completed a reconnaissance mission, and they found part of a ship's wreckage, but it was from retreating through the space gate. We think there was a battle and they were leaving. If they'd been destroyed, there would've been more wreckage to find. So, it's safe to say there's a good chance that Sean and the rest of the battle group are still alive. We just don't understand why they haven't come home yet."

Noah looked at him with a bemused expression. "You really don't know why Sean hasn't returned?" he asked and then added. "You?"

Connor frowned for a moment and shook his head.

"The mission. Sean's objective. He won't come home until he's accomplished whatever his mission was. You guys are so much alike in that respect. That's why he hasn't come back," Noah said.

"Maybe," Connor agreed. "They were fighting a battle, and there could've been damage to the space gate. It's been ninety days though. I would've expected some kind of contact. But I understand what you're saying."

They left the cafeteria, and Connor walked Noah back to his room. Noah paused outside the doorway, looking as if he didn't want to go in.

"You know," Connor said, "I could probably get you out of here. Have someone pick us up on the roof. They'll never find out."

Noah smiled and grinned. "Kara would find out, and then I'd have hell to pay."

"Maybe they can give you a different room," Connor suggested.

Noah glared at the empty hospital room. "I have nowhere else to go," he said quietly.

"Why don't we go back outside then?"

Noah shook his head and rubbed his eyes. He walked over to the bed and more or less collapsed onto it. Rolling over to his side, he was soon asleep. Connor watched him for a few moments and then closed the door as he left the room.

CHAPTER 23

S ean entered the galley. It was midmorning, standard time, and technically they were still in the middle of the shift, so it wasn't as crowded as it would be later. Since it was between breakfast and lunchtime, there was a sandwich-making station for those who were coming in on their off-hours. Sean grabbed a couple of slices of rye bread, put some egg salad on one end, a few pieces of the lettuce, and topped it off with a few slices of bacon. He pushed the top slice down with his hand and walked over to the gleaming coffee station where he found a freshly made pot that smelled like a medium roast blend with hints of vanilla and caramel. He filled his mug and added some cream and sugar. There was no shortage of open tables, and he saw Oriana sitting by herself. Her back was to him, but there was no mistaking her long, velvety black hair. She was tall and slender, and her science team uniform hugged her subtle curves in all the right ways. He walked over. She was peering at the technical specs of the space gates.

"Want some company?" Sean asked.

Oriana looked up at him. Her face was sweetly angelic, sort of girl-next-door pretty. She smiled and gestured for him to join her.

Sean sat down. The remains of her own breakfast were evident—a healthy mix of fruits and vegetables with the remnants of eggs—and he wondered why she never finished everything on her plate. His plate would be devoid of even a crumb when he was finished.

"I didn't hear you leave this morning. Sneaking away in the middle the night?"

Oriana glanced around to see if anyone had heard. Then her gaze narrowed. "We decided to be discreet."

The words stung just a little bit, but Sean nodded. They'd been casual for almost the entire time they'd been in this universe. "Word travels fast, and we're old news."

"I doubt we're news at all. Regardless, people talk no matter what," Oriana said and tilted her head to the side. "It bothers you that I left."

Sean shook his head a little too quickly. "No, I was just surprised, is all."

"Uh huh," she said, sounding unconvinced.

"What were you working on?" Sean asked, deciding that changing the subject would be best.

"I was looking at the space gate's design spec again."

Sean took a bite of his sandwich and nodded. "I'm sure you could see it with your eyes closed."

Oriana smiled and gave a slight roll of her eyes. "Probably," she agreed. "I just don't know how the Ovarrow could reverse engineer anything like this on their own."

"We don't know how long the Krake had been around to influence them."

"No, I understand all that. But still, I think they must have had help, or maybe they found the Krake technical manual of all things related to the space gate."

Sean raised an eyebrow. "Just one volume, or the whole set?"

Oriana smiled and shook her head. "Okay, maybe not that, but I still think they had help."

"Like who?" Sean asked, finishing his sandwich.

Oriana pressed her lips together. "I don't know."

A short distance away a group of soldiers was sitting together, and their discussion was becoming heated. Sean couldn't hear the specifics of it, but the tone was enough. Fuses were running short. A few glances in his direction were enough to prompt the others into quelling the argument before it had a chance to get out of control.

"There's been a lot of that lately," Oriana said.

"Tensions are always higher before a major operation," Sean replied. But he knew it was more than that. Three months of hiding from the Krake while they repaired their ships and the space gate were taking their toll.

Oriana glanced at the soldiers for a few moments and looked back at Sean. "My brother is a bit of a hothead, always letting the pressure get to him. He wouldn't like being on a ship like this."

Sean leaned forward. "I didn't know you had a brother."

"Colton. He's my younger brother. I've never brought it up before."

"Why not?"

"You never seem to want to talk about family."

Sean frowned. "I guess I never gave it much thought." He hated how that sounded as soon as he said it. "I figured you'd bring it up if you wanted to talk about it. It's just me and my mother now."

"Do you think she'll remarry and have more children?"

Sean's mind went blank. "My mother? I have no idea." He'd never really given it much thought. It was his mother, after all. "I suppose she could if she wanted," he said and looked away from her, shaking his head.

Oriana grinned. "You do realize that your mother was a woman before she was your mother. She has a long life ahead of her. You can't expect her to be alone."

Sean reached for his coffee and almost knocked it over. "No, of course not. I just never—Do we really need to talk about my mother?"

Oriana's eyes twinkled with amusement.

Sean held up his hand. "I do acknowledge that my mother is a woman, and she certainly has the option to live her life as she wants. It's just not something I ever talk to her about."

Oriana smiled, pleased with herself, and he liked seeing it. "See? That wasn't so hard, was it?"

"Your brother," Sean began. "What does he do back at the colony?"

"He studied field biology but decided he'd rather work for Field Ops and Security."

Sean drank some coffee. "You don't approve?"

"He doesn't work well under pressure."

Sean shrugged. "Maybe he'll outgrow it."

Oriana shook her head. "He's always been that way. High strung. I don't think Field Ops is the best place for him."

Sean finished his coffee and they were both quiet for a few moments, each in their own thoughts. He didn't have any siblings. The closest people he had to brothers were Noah and Lars.

"There really isn't any other way, is there?" Oriana asked.

The operation they were about to execute was on everyone's mind. "We've done all the repairs we can do, and we've studied the Krake operation in this universe. It's strange that they had so many ships coming to where we are in this universe, but I guess since it's an industrial complex, it would make sense that there was some protection here. However, it doesn't explain why that same level of protection isn't maintained."

"Maybe they got called away to deal with something else," she said. "There's a lot we don't understand about them."

"Do you think you have the targeting figured out?" Sean said.

They hadn't been able to go back to New Earth because of the damage to their space gate and the fact that there'd been a serious flaw in how they'd targeted their home universe. Oriana and the rest of the science team had run themselves ragged trying to figure it out.

"The calculations work, but without an actual field test, we won't really know," Oriana replied.

"We talked about this before. I can't risk the Krake learning that we're here."

"I know, I know. We don't have enough space gate cubes to make a large enough gateway for the entire battle group to get through. If the Krake detected our test, then they'd come here and we'd be cornered," Oriana said.

"It's as good a tactical assessment as I've heard. I'm glad—" Sean began to say but then stopped. He'd almost said he was glad she'd been paying attention, which wouldn't have been smart. "So, the issue is with time. That's why we couldn't go back home before. Time is another layer that needs to be accounted for in the calculations used for targeting a universe."

Oriana looked at him with a dubious expression. She hadn't been fooled. She might not have known exactly what he was going to say, but she decided to let it go. "We based the new calculations off the Krake data we got from that base of operations. To put it in layman's terms, the math works. If the gate machines hadn't sustained as much damage as they did coming here, then we might've been able to get home by now."

Escaping to this universe had been a very close thing. They'd lost the *Douglass,* which was the sister ship of the *Vigilant.* Right now, only the *Vigilant* and the *Yorktown* could provide enough power to the space gate for the entire battle group to escape. Hundreds of lives had been lost, but thousands had been saved.

"I wish there was a better way," Oriana said.

"We can't minimize all risk. At least this way we won't have any surprise reserve fleets showing up," Sean replied.

"Unless they have arches on the planet."

"Even if they did, they wouldn't be big enough to accommodate ships. We'd still get the most valuable commodity, which is time—time for us to test the new targeting protocol you put together. Hopefully, we can put this place behind us."

Oriana eyed him for a moment. "You never talk about going home."

"No need to dwell on it. My time is better served by focusing on more immediate things."

"Do you *want* to go home?"

Sean frowned. "What kind of question is that? Of course I want to go home."

"You just never talk about it."

"Would it make you feel better if I did?"

Oriana's expression became one of bemusement, and Sean was pretty sure it was at his expense. He glanced around to be sure they couldn't be overheard and leaned toward her. "I don't think we have enough information to go home. We've learned a few things, which is great, but it's not enough. And we haven't learned nearly enough about the Krake to make any difference."

Oriana looked away for a few moments, considering. When she looked back, she also leaned in until they were less than a foot apart. "We don't have to do this by ourselves. You push yourself too hard."

"We're hardly alone. There're over two thousand of us here. At some point, the Krake are going to learn where we come from—our target universe, if you will. Based on our interactions with them, that wouldn't go too well for us the way things stand right now," Sean said.

"I understand what's at stake."

"You make a good point about not being in this alone, and you're not the only one who feels that way. That's why, if this operation works, we'll be returning home."

Oriana smiled and looked relieved, but then she frowned. "What happens then?"

There were a number of ways Sean could've taken that question, and he had no doubt she'd phrased it in such a way as to have multiple meanings for him.

Gabriel, the ship's AI, had just sent them both a request to come to the bridge.

"We'll finish this later," Oriana said.

They stood up and took their dirty dishes to the racks for washing, then headed to the bridge.

CHAPTER 24

Major Lester Brody stood on the bridge of the *Yorktown*, the CDF's only carrier vessel in the fleet, currently a part of Trident Battle Group. He'd just returned from an inspection tour of the ship.

The *Yorktown* had been his residence for the past three months. Since losing the *Douglass* when they'd escaped the Krake, he'd lost a third of his crew. The surviving crew of the *Douglass* had been spread out among the other ships in Trident Battle Group, with the majority of them on the *Yorktown*.

Major Christopher McKay looked over at him. "We're almost home," McKay said quietly enough that only Lester could hear.

Lester nodded and looked at the crew on the bridge. "They know it, too. All their hard work is about to pay off."

"If you'd told me we'd be launching an operation to steal Krake space gate cubes, I would've thought you were crazy," McKay said.

"It *is* crazy, and desperate, but we need them if we're going to get out of here," Lester said.

The main holoscreen showed the eight Talon-V Stormer class vessels, along with a complement of Lancer and Stinger escorts, heading to the Krake space gate. The *Yorktown* remained at a safe distance, along with two CDF destroyers. The *Babylon* and the *Acheron* were in position, with orders to decimate anything that came through the gate.

Lester looked at the tactical display on his personal holoscreen. They still had over four hours before anything was scheduled to come through the Krake space gate.

"It would be an unfortunate turn of events if the Krake decided to change their schedule today," McKay said.

Lester nodded. "Unfortunate indeed."

They had four hours to disable the space gate, and they'd achieve that by stealing eight of the space gate cubes so they could be retrofitted to their own gate. This op would allow them to hit two birds with one stone. They'd disable the Krake space gate while regaining their own mobility. They couldn't just use the gate to go home because of the risk of the Krake learning where their home universe was. Despite Dr. Evans' assertions that she'd cracked the targeting issue, they needed to test her solution. There was too much risk in testing and going home in one operation. The Krake would learn that there was a hostile force here, but their reinforcements would be delayed.

"Are you all right, Major?" McKay asked.

Lester looked over at McKay. "Yes, it's just been a . . . long deployment."

Most of the crew Lester had spoken with were eager to return home. The months they'd spent in enemy territory had been fraught with the risk of the Krake discovering them, which was enough to wear away the nerves of even the most stalwart, including the seemingly indomitable will of Colonel Sean Quinn. Even now, Lester could sense that Sean was reluctant to go home, and he agreed, in part. The more they learned about the Krake, the more they realized how much more there was to learn if they were to have any hope of engaging them from a militaristic standpoint. The Krake were a very grave threat, like a looming hurricane in the night.

It was the waiting that was the worst part. All Lester could do was to make sure the crew remained focused on the task at hand.

———

The massive space gate cube loomed in front of the Talon-V Stormer.

"Beginning final approach," Sergeant Carl Reeger said.

"Acknowledged," Harper replied and checked the progress of the other ships.

The Talon-V Stormers were designed for sending an assault force to an enemy ship; however, that wouldn't occur on this day. There was a crew of twenty aboard the ship, but they were made up of combat engineers and salvage experts. Their mission was to decouple the space gate cube and utilize the ships to tow the cubes toward the *Yorktown*.

The Krake space gate cubes each had a single flat surface area of three hundred meters. They were to try to decouple the cubes first, and if that didn't work, they were to use strategically placed explosive charges to do the job. Harper hoped they wouldn't have to use the charges because of the risk of damaging the delicate machines that allowed them to transition between universes.

"Send an update back to Major Brody," Harper said.

"Yes, Captain," Sergeant Reeger said. A few moments later, Reeger said, "Update has been sent. Now we just hope the Krake don't show up."

That was an understatement, but they had a job to do.

"Spec Ops is on it," Harper said.

Reeger nodded. "There's a whole lot of sneaking around going on."

"That's right, and the Krake won't know we're here until it's too late."

"I know I said this before, but I still can't believe the lapse in security protocols the Krake have established here," Reeger said.

Harper frowned. "Do you mean for the space gate or the industrial complex?"

"Well, both of them, to be honest. Why would they leave the space gate unguarded? It's as if they don't expect anyone to ever attack them."

"Well, why would they? They'd be cutting off their own escape as well. Plus, we haven't been to the surface of the planet, but they probably have archways there."

Reeger shook his head. "You couldn't pay me enough to go to that planet. It looks like hell. There's hardly any atmosphere and no signs of life."

"Yeah, but it's mineral-rich, which is why they have a salvage yard here, as well as a major fabrication center utilizing all the raw materials. It would be much worse for us if this was an inhabited world with a significant military presence," Harper replied.

They reached their designated landing zone and deployed the landing gear. Since the cubes didn't have any artificial gravity, they had to deploy tether hooks to secure them in place.

Harper stood up. "Time to get to work."

"This is crazy," Sergeant Benton said.

Captain Boseman smiled and shook his head, but there was no way Benton could see it. The Spec Ops platoon was wearing Nexstar combat suits, hitching a ride on an asteroid that was heading to a preprocessing area to be broken apart before going to the main Krake industrial complex.

"You said the same thing before," Boseman said.

They'd been on plenty of combat drops both in space and on New Earth. The training regimen for Spec Ops required a certain amount of crazy, and Boseman found it fun, as did most other Spec Ops team members. They trained hard to be the most physically fit and deadly of any CDF soldier. That kind of training required a certain amount of tenacity that not everyone had, plain and simple. Most of the soldiers who tried to join Spec Ops failed. They didn't have what it took. Those who made the cut were the reason Spec Ops was the best at what they did. It was why the riskiest of missions were given to them. When failure wasn't an option, they didn't. No matter the cost, the objective was everything.

"That was before I realized just how high we'd be jumping," Benton replied.

"Well, if you do it right, you'll live to talk about it. If you don't, you'll bounce off into space and we won't be able to get you back," Boseman said.

He wasn't kidding. They had no air support. They were the distraction. They were there to cause destruction and mayhem, but in such a way that they didn't impact any Krake civilians that may or may not have been working in the industrial complex.

The asteroid the Spec Ops platoon was hitching a ride on closed in on the gaping maw of an automated crusher. That's what they'd dubbed it anyway. Asteroids of a certain size went inside, and through some function they had no information about, came out the other side in smaller, bite-size pieces so the industrial complex could get at the mineral-rich ores the Krake used. This particular asteroid was composed mainly of nickel and iron.

Boseman activated the command comlink, which patched him into the entire platoon. "Max suit thrust on my mark," he said. The distance and telemetry appeared on his helmet's internal heads-up display. "Mark!"

Boseman and the rest of them engaged their suit thrusters, breaking free of the little bit of gravity the asteroid had. They then engaged secondary thrusters that would carry them over the crusher.

Boseman monitored the progress of the rest of the soldiers. All fifty of them had cleared the rim of the crusher. He looked over to the side and saw that Benton was a bit off kilter. He'd angled his jump and now was in a slow tumble that he was trying to get under control. After a few moments of using maneuvering suit thrusters, he stabilized, and their momentum carried them over the crusher.

The Krake industrial complex was a huge network of spindly arms the broken-up asteroids were fed into that then went into the main complex. It was like a giant spider in space, only this spider had hundreds of arms. The industrial complex was a vast network of these structures that spoke volumes of the Krake's salvaging efforts. Reconnaissance missions had revealed that they utilized automated processes to do the actual work, but there was still a Krake presence here. They'd selected their targets based on the minimum Krake presence they expected to find.

Boseman opened the command channel again. "Reverse thrusters on my mark. Engage."

Their Nexstar combat suits were able to use specialized attachments based on the mission. They each had an individual flight unit attached to the back. This turned upside down and, in conjunction with the maneuvering thrusters, stopped the Spec Ops soldiers from ascending and put them on an intercept trajectory with the asteroid fragments coming out the other side of the crusher.

They were breaking up into smaller teams, targeting every other shaft the asteroid chunks were heading towards. Twelve teams of four headed for their targets. Boseman had Sergeant Benton and Corporal Brentworth, as well as Private Jing on his team. Jing carried the payload.

Boseman switched to the team channel. They'd maintain comms blackout unless there was a general alert with the other teams. They had to get within close proximity to the asteroid chunks so they didn't draw notice from Krake sensors. This was a gamble because they weren't exactly sure about the capabilities of the Krake sensors. They were guessing they couldn't be that finely attuned because in all their reconnaissance, everything that was heading into the industrial complex at this point had gone inside to be processed.

"Captain, one of my main suit thrusters is faulty," Sergeant Benton said.

Boseman looked over at him and glanced down toward his feet. Given the speed they were coming in at, Benton needed both of his main thrusters in order to make a soft landing; otherwise, he'd bounce off the industrial complex.

"I'll help him with the landing, Captain," Corporal Brentworth said.

"Negative, Corporal. Stay with Jing. We need that payload. I'll take care of Benton." He switched to a private channel with Benton. "I'm going to ease over to your side."

Boseman used maneuvering thrusters to angle toward Benton. If he came in too fast, he'd knock Benton off course, so he kept his approach slow and steady.

"Dammit," Benton said. "I clipped part of the crusher on the way up. I think that's what broke it."

"I think you just couldn't stand not being close to me. Is there something you want to tell me, Sergeant?"

"Well, I've been harboring these feelings for you, sir, and I just can't keep them to myself anymore," Benton said, playing along.

Everyone knew Benton was an unabashed womanizer. It had gotten him into trouble many times, but when he was reined in, he was a good man to have in the squad.

"I knew it, but you're just not my type," Boseman said.

He slowed down and engaged his personal tether, which adhered itself to the back of Benton's combat suit.

"We're locked," Benton said, switching back to business.

"Copy that. Hold on," Boseman said.

The tether pulled them together back to back. "I'm taking over your suit functions," Boseman said.

Benton chuckled a little. "You know, if you were Delilah, I might enjoy this."

Boseman updated the calculations so the suit computer could handle the soft landing with the additional load. "Sergeant Payton? I think you're aiming too high. She's got standards."

"The higher the peak, the sweeter the reward," Benton said and laughed.

The connection points along the shaft that led to the industrial complex made it difficult to target their landing area. Boseman found an area that looked promising and had the suit computer target it.

"All right, three, two, one . . ." Boseman said.

He heard Benton grunt in anticipation. There was nothing like being in a combat suit and having no control of it, and Boseman wouldn't have liked it any more than Benton did right then. Maneuvering thrusters fired together on one side with the equivalent of a ship's braking thrusters, slowing down their approach as they angled downward toward the LZ. They were coming in fast. The main suit thrusters fired, slowing their descent, and they touched down.

Their mag boots engaged and they stopped. Boseman detached the tether, and full suit capability was returned to Benton.

"Oh God, let's not do that again," Benton said and sighed heavily.

Boseman did an internal systems check, and his combat suit was intact. He brought out his AR-71 and checked it. Benton carried a heavy plasma cannon, and he connected it to the main power source in his suit. Jing and Brentworth had landed a short distance away.

"Deal," Bosman said. "Let's catch up to the others."

Brentworth was checking the two specialized lightweight but high-yield missiles they'd been carrying.

"Both the missiles and the explosive charges check out, Captain," Corporal Brentworth said and closed the case.

"Good. We're on a tight schedule. Let's get moving," Boseman said.

Boseman and Brentworth took point while Benton and Jing stayed behind them. Their mag boots were engaged and, with the help of the Nexstar's combat suit computers, they were able to run much faster than they ever could have without a combat suit. In no time at all, they made it to the first junction that connected the shafts. It was a structural weak point that their explosive charges would do a great job of tearing apart.

It took a few minutes to set the charges and configure them for remote detonation with a fail-safe timer. Either way, these charges were going to explode on a schedule. The fail-safe only worked if comlink connectivity to Boseman's combat suit was disconnected. Then, it would do a quick calculation so the explosion happened on schedule.

They continued moving away to a minimum safe distance. Boseman sent out a signal that they were set and ready. Jing and Brentworth readied the mobile missile launcher while Benton covered them.

As far as Boseman could tell, no alarms had been raised. It was quiet right then, but in a few moments, all hell was going to break loose.

Boseman waited until all twelve teams had checked in and then sent back his authorization.

The lightweight hornet missiles raced across the span of five kilometers to the next intake shaft. The target was the end of the shaft where the asteroid chunks first went inside. They aimed for the adjacent shaft, with each team doing the same to maximize the destruction they were about to cause.

The missiles raced toward their target with rigorous fury, and twelve seemingly simultaneous explosions occurred at the end of the intake shafts. Boseman detonated the explosive charges at the first main junction. Eleven more explosions occurred, and the shaft shuddered beneath their feet. Roughly a quarter of this spider's legs had been destroyed. The crusher still spat out asteroid chunks, which continued to pelt the industrial complex, only now instead of going inside the intake shafts, they were bouncing out of control to impact other parts of the complex.

"Time to go," Boseman said.

They continued to the extraction points, and Boseman signaled for the combat shuttle to come pick them up. Six shuttles were deployed and would have to make two stops in order to extract the Spec Ops team.

"Contact!" Benton cried.

They all took cover and watched as Krake soldiers approached. Hulking figures three meters tall ran toward them.

Their extraction point had just become a hot zone.

The Krake response had been quick, and Boseman hadn't counted on that. They'd picked this target because it appeared to be lightly defended. The other CDF teams checked in. Krake soldiers were closing in on them, too.

"Let's draw them in. Wait for them to get closer," Boseman said.

They aimed their weapons at the approaching soldiers.

"Now," Boseman said.

Benton fired his plasma cannon, and a molten bolt of fury blazed into the Krake soldiers. They hadn't staggered their approach, and seven of them were blown off into space in various conditions of melted fury and pain.

Boseman configured the nanorobotic ammunition to use explosive penetrating rounds and then fired his weapon. The heavy slugs pierced the Krake armor and exploded, leaving massive holes.

The element of surprise was used up as more Krake soldiers arrived. They approached cautiously, each taking shots with their own weapons.

"Jing, keep an eye on our six," Boseman said.

The combat shuttle had picked up the other team and was heading toward them.

"Enemy contact, Captain," Private Jing said.

Dammit, Boseman thought. They were pinned down, and the enemy was closing in all around them.

The combat shuttle arrived and opened fire, first taking out the primary group and then the secondary group. The shaft rocked beneath their feet with the impact of the combat shuttle's weapons.

"Now's our chance," Boseman said as the combat shuttle swung around, presenting the loading ramp to them. They jumped and engaged their suit thrusters to clear the loading ramp.

"We're all on board. Get us out of here," Boseman ordered.

The loading ramp had just closed, and Boseman felt the shuttle lurch forward. He ran toward the cockpit.

"We're taking fire," the pilot said.

"Combat drones?" Boseman asked and peered at the shuttle's main holoscreen.

"Negative. They have automated defense turrets. Captain, you can take the aux seat behind me. Things are going to get a little rough."

Boseman sat down and auto-straps secured him in place. The tactical display showed multiple video feeds. Auto-turrets fired at them while the pilot executed evasive maneuvers. The pilot flew the combat shuttle as close to the industrial complex as he could, making it difficult for them to be targeted.

A comlink opened from another combat shuttle. "Krake ships inbound. Destroyer class vessels."

Boseman's stomach sank. "Alert the battle group. Use subspace comms."

———

"Colonel, we're getting reports of Krake automated defense turrets coming online," Specialist Irina Sansky said.

Sean swung his gaze toward the tactical workstations. "What's the status of the Spec Ops evac?"

"They're under enemy fire. The alert squadron is en route. They're ten minutes out, Colonel," Lieutenant Jane Russo said.

Jade squadron appeared on the tactical plot on the main holoscreen. Talon-V Stinger class fighters were blazing a path toward the fleeing combat shuttles.

"Very well," Sean replied.

This was only the beginning of the Krake response to their attack. The auto-turrets had been concealed within the complex. Sean had two destroyers in reserve at a midway point between the space gate and Trident Battle Group's current position. The *Vigilant,* along with three other destroyers—the *Dutchman,* the *Burroughs,* and the *Albany*—were in position where Sean had expected the Krake response to be.

"Colonel, seven Krake destroyers are coming from the planet," Lieutenant Russo said.

"On screen," Sean said.

The Krake destroyers appeared on the main holoscreen. Active scans showed a staggered deployment. "Tactical, I want a firing solution on the three destroyers on point. Designate them priority alpha."

"Yes, sir," Lieutenant Russo said.

The CDF destroyers' combat AIs were patched into the *Vigilant's* onboard systems. Gabriel, the *Vigilant's* AI, would take the data from their computing core and transmit it to the rest of the battle group. This quickened their response times in an enemy engagement.

They hadn't done any reconnaissance of the planet below. Instead, they'd focused on the Krake industrial complex and the nearby space gate activity. Sean expected that the Krake had shipbuilding facilities in this star system, but they hadn't found them. It appeared they constructed their ships planetside.

"I have a firing solution, Colonel," Russo said.

"Fire," Sean replied.

HADES Vs sped out the *Vigilant's* missile tubes, along with those of the CDF destroyers. Sean authorized five more volleys before they'd evaluate the damage they'd done to the Krake fleet.

"Helm, keep the industrial complex between us and the enemy ships,"

Sean said. Krake attack drones could fly around the industrial complex easily enough, but it would take them time.

"Third volley is away. No combat drones detected," Russo said.

HADES V missiles closed the distance to the enemy ships, and they hadn't returned fire yet.

The plot on the main holoscreen updated and showed that the first group of HADES Vs had detonated. Sean's jaw tightened in grim satisfaction.

"Krake destroyers are staggering their approach. Their course indicates they've deduced our approximate position," Lieutenant Russo said.

It was difficult not to remain in motion while ships operated in space, and a heavy cruiser was no different. The Krake might have figured out where their attack had come from, but there was still guesswork involved, and they hadn't detected any scans from Krake ships.

"Understood," Sean replied.

He glanced at the combat shuttles on the plot. They were still a few minutes out, but they were on an intercept course with the *Vigilant*.

"Ops, what's the current status of the space gate operation?" Sean asked.

"They've retrieved four of the cubes. The other teams were delayed," Lieutenant Davis Hoffman replied.

"Gabriel, how are we on time?" Sean asked.

"We're behind schedule, Colonel. Recommend holding off the Krake response here for as long as we can to give the retrieval teams enough time to secure the minimal number of cubes required," the *Vigilant's* AI replied.

Sean's gaze flicked to the tactical plot on his personal holoscreen. Another active scan pulse was about to happen. The tactical plot refreshed and showed that new Krake contacts had been detected. Two more Krake destroyers appeared on the plot. Their trajectory put them on an intercept course with the previous group of destroyers they'd already detected.

Sean frowned in thought. Why wouldn't those ships be heading toward *them?*

"Krake attack drones detected," Lieutenant Russo said.

The number of attack drones appeared on the main holoscreen, and the count quickly jumped past several hundred.

"Tactical, prepare missile-defense screen," Sean said.

During their other encounters with the Krake, they'd learned that detonating a HADES V missile blinded the attack drone's guidance systems momentarily, putting them into disarray. The missile-defense screen would coordinate the launches of HADES Vs, along with targeting the mag cannons of the *Vigilant* and the other CDF destroyers.

"Confirm, missile-defense screen protocol has designates in tubes seven and eight, Colonel," Russo said.

The Krake attack drone count on the main holoscreen climbed past three hundred, and Sean's mouth formed a grim line. That was too many drones. At the rate the Krake were launching attack drones, their defenses, even with the updated protocols, would soon be overwhelmed.

"Ops, what's the status of the combat shuttles retrieving the Spec Ops teams?" Sean asked.

"They're still a few minutes out, Colonel," Lieutenant Hoffman said.

That wasn't good enough. "Emergency landing protocols authorized. They need to get here ASAP. Helm, ready the rendezvous coordinates with the *Yorktown*."

Sean's orders were confirmed, and then the tactical plot refreshed again on the main holoscreen. Their new defensive protocols were working. The numbers of attack drones detected had ground to a halt. The Krake must have fired everything they had at them, keeping nothing in reserve.

"Colonel, recommend beginning our withdrawal," Lieutenant Russo said.

She was right and Sean knew it, but he wasn't leaving the Spec Ops team. "Helm—" Sean began to say but was interrupted by an audible chime sounding as the number of attack drones skyrocketed to over four hundred. Sean's mouth went dry, and the bridge crew seemed to hold its collective breath. The new group of attack drones had come from the Krake reinforcement ships.

"Colonel," Lieutenant Russo said, her voice a bit higher than normal, "the new detection of attack drones is on a . . . Sir, they're shooting at their own ships!"

Sean peered at the plot on the main holoscreen. It refreshed again, showing the new salvo of Krake attack drones on an intercept course with the first group of ships they'd detected.

Why would the Krake fire their weapons on one another? Scanners showed that more than half of the attack drones that had been heading toward the CDF had changed course, heading toward the two Krake destroyers.

"Colonel, combat shuttles are all aboard and accounted for," Lieutenant Hoffman said.

They couldn't afford to get caught up in whatever Krake conflict was going on here.

"Helm, get us out of here. Best speed," Sean said.

The *Vigilant* and the accompanying CDF destroyers retreated from the Krake industrial complex. Roughly a third of the complex had been impacted by the attack, and Sean hoped it had been worth it.

"Comms, open a comlink to the *Yorktown*. Get me Major Brody."

A few moments later, Major Brody appeared on Sean's personal holoscreen.

"Colonel Quinn, the Krake space gate has been disabled and we have the cubes. We're making our way to the rendezvous point, and engineering teams have already begun retrofitting the Krake space gate cubes to our existing gate."

"Excellent! Convey my congratulations to the team," Sean said and told Brody what had happened.

"They attacked each other! Are they pursuing you?" Brody asked.

"Negative. Our missile-defense screen took out the attack drones coming after us," Sean replied.

"What do you think it means?"

"Well, for one thing, the Krake aren't as unified as we'd thought."

"And this other group just happened to show up when the attack began?"

Sean nodded. "We've stumbled onto something here."

"Yeah, but now the Krake know we're here. We need to leave. We'll be ready to test the space gate in just a few hours," Brody said.

"Excuse me, Colonel Quinn," Specialist Sansky said. "We've received a data burst from the Krake."

Sean frowned and Brody went silent. "Tactical, can you detect exactly where that message came from?"

"One moment, Colonel," Russo said.

"Colonel, should I try to translate it?" Specialist Sansky asked.

"No. Standby," Sean replied.

"It's from the secondary Krake attack group, the ones that fired on their own ships," Russo said.

"Gabriel," Sean said, "I want you to seal off the Krake data in a closed system and cut it off from the rest of the ship's systems."

"Done, Colonel," Gabriel said. "Preliminary analysis indicates that there are several space gate coordinates in the data burst. I would need more time to do a full analysis."

Sean rubbed his chin for a moment.

"Colonel, did I hear that correctly? You received some kind of communication from the Krake?" Brody asked.

"It appears that way. We need time to do a thorough analysis of it though."

"I'm sure we can do that once we get back home," Brody replied.

Sean shook his head. "Hold off on testing the space gate. I'm going to send you secondary rendezvous coordinates and we'll meet up there."

"But Colonel—" Brody began and stopped himself.

"You have your orders, Major," Sean said. "*Vigilant*, out."

Sean closed the comlink. "Tactical, is there any sign of the Krake coming after us?"

"Negative, Colonel. We stopped using active scans when we began our withdrawal."

Sean nodded. "Without their space gate, we have some breathing room. Helm, update course rendezvous coordinates to bravo. We're going farther out in the system."

"Yes, Colonel. Updated our course and have sent the new coordinates to the rest of the battle group," Lieutenant Edwards replied.

The Krake were fighting among themselves, and at least some of them wanted to help the CDF.

"Colonel, our last scans indicated that almost all of the Krake ships were destroyed," Russo said.

"Understood, Lieutenant. Ops, set Condition Two," Sean said.

He opened the comlink to the secondary bridge on the *Vigilant*. "Major Shelton, I assume you've been following along?"

"Yes, Colonel," Major Shelton said.

"Excellent. Report to the bridge. We need to figure out what the hell just happened," Sean said.

They needed to go over all the data they'd collected and do a thorough analysis of the Krake message.

CHAPTER 25

Noah was in his lab at Sanctuary. A few days had passed since his release from the medical center. He didn't need to follow up with Ashley because she was tapped into his biochip, which sent her regular updates regarding his health. It had been part of his agreement for release from the hospital. Since then, Kara had been watching him like a hawk, as if he was going to suddenly disappear. To Noah, it had only been a few days with patchy memory loss, but for his wife, it had been over ten months of constant worry. Noah kept having to remind himself of that, but he was getting tired of everyone telling him what to do and being hypersensitive to the slightest mishap. Physically, he was fine, but his mind needed time to heal, and he wasn't going to get that sitting at home.

He wasn't at his main laboratory at Sanctuary. He was out along the outskirts of the city in a mobile lab he'd set up before he'd been injured. He glanced around at all the equipment and checked the logs. Dash had been in there from time to time, doing his own work. Noah hadn't seen Dash yet. The young man was working out of New Haven, but they'd had a chat via video comlink. Dash promised to come back to Sanctuary as soon as he could, but he was needed with everything that had been going on with the Ovarrow. Noah envied him. It was as if the world had kept going on just fine without him, and he didn't like how it made him feel—insignificant. There was so much more for him to see and do.

Despite the bit of isolation at his mobile lab, he did have a window to the outside. It was currently open, and a breeze was blowing in. Echoes of soothing wind chimes sounded as the breeze increased. The solitude was peaceful. It was quite a bit of work for him to be around a lot of people, and it felt almost overwhelming. Because of this, he'd taken to long periods of being alone. He couldn't escape Kara and he didn't want to, but she was being overprotective.

A live video feed came to prominence on the main holoscreen, and Noah glanced at it.

"Think of the devil, and she will appear," Noah said quietly, and then berated himself for being too harsh. Kara wasn't the devil. She was his angel.

Kara had found his little hiding spot, and he readied himself for what was sure to be an unpleasant conversation. He closed down the work he'd been doing and went to the door. It opened before he could get there, and his wife's cornflower-blue eyes narrowed suspiciously at him. She glanced behind him at the blank holoscreens for a moment.

"So, you shut down your work before I got here. How nice," Kara said.

Noah sighed. "I was just getting some fresh air, and I thought I'd come to check these things out."

Kara nodded, then walked into the work area. "How many of these things do you have?"

Noah eyed her for a moment. "You should know. You have access to all of them."

Kara crossed her arms in front of her chest, but she looked oddly vulnerable at the same time, as if her shoulders had narrowed and she was hugging herself. "Why do you keep trying to shut me out?"

Noah's eyebrows squished together, and he frowned for a moment. "I'm not . . . I'm not trying to keep anything from you. I just needed some time alone."

"I've been giving you space, but you need . . . All I can think about is how you were lying in that bed at the medical center, hooked up to all those machines that were keeping you alive. I thought you were going to die. I've been *trying* to give you space, but do you understand what this has done to me? It wasn't just a few days sitting by your bedside. It went on for months!" Her shoulders shook for a few moments and she looked away from him. "I know you didn't mean for this . . ."

"I know exactly what happened," Noah replied. He knew this whole ordeal had been rough for her. He couldn't imagine what it must have been like not knowing whether he was going to live.

Kara narrowed her gaze, her eyes glistening with anger. "Do you? Do you really? Do you know how many different methods Ashley and all the other doctors tried to bring you out of that coma? How much time and effort . . . and I needed to approve them all. Some of the things they tried hadn't been done in years, and in the end, none of it worked. You just started to slowly come out of it. First, you started breathing on your own," she said and paused, tapping her head. "But you wouldn't wake up. Your brain activity was slightly above that of a vegetable."

Noah backed away from her. He wanted to ask what she expected of him. Instead, he said, "I know. None of you let me forget everything that was done to save my life. I didn't know any of this was going to happen, and I don't know what to say. I'm sorry. Does that make it better? I'm still struggling with that and—" His thoughts scattered, and what he'd wanted to say flittered away to nothingness. He tried to recapture what he'd been thinking, but it was just gone. It was as if his mind had slammed into an invisible wall that he didn't know the limits of. Then, a sudden headache lanced across his head and went down his neck like white lightning. He swayed on his feet.

Kara rushed over to him and placed her hand on his arm. "Noah, are you okay? You look like you're in pain."

Noah squeezed his eyes shut and clenched his teeth, trying to force the pain away by sheer force of will alone. It wasn't enough.

"Here, sit down," Kara said, guiding him to a chair. "I'll get you some water."

Noah shook his head. "I don't want any water. Why does everyone keep trying to bring me water? It doesn't help. I'm not thirsty. I'm not dehydrated," he said and winced at the pain.

He felt Kara's fingers rubbing his temples. Her fingers moved behind his ears to the base of his neck and then came back again, massaging all the pressure points, relieving the tension. The pain lessened. Her fingers felt warm against his scalp, and it was heavenly.

"Thank you," Noah whispered.

"Are the headaches coming less frequently?" Kara asked.

The headaches always came. He'd been out of the hospital for barely a week and they always came. It didn't matter what he was doing. The headaches just kept coming.

"I'm not sure. You can check the logs from my biochip."

"I know I can do that, but I wanted to know if you know. Are they worse, less, or more frequent?"

"They just catch me off guard. One moment I'm fine, and the next thing, I feel like I'm spinning. The more I try to focus, the worse it gets. Then it goes away as suddenly as it came."

Kara regarded him for a moment. "All right, Noah. I won't offer you water anymore. From now on, if you're thirsty, you can get your own damn water."

Noah grinned a little. "Thanks. I didn't mean . . . I know you're trying to help."

"It's going to take a little bit of time. Maybe more than a little, but you can't expect to jump right back into things.

"Why not? Haven't I slept enough?"

Kara's gaze became unyielding. "That's enough of that right now. I'm not going to let you feel sorry for yourself. You don't have to make up for lost time. You're the victim here, and you're just going to have to learn what your limits are, Noah."

He was no stranger to his limits. He'd been pushing against them for his entire life. The thing was, it seemed like everything he was ever good at had been taken away from him.

The holoscreens came back to life, along with the information Noah had been working on. Kara swung her gaze to him. "I can't believe this. What are you doing looking at all this stuff?"

"Trying to make sense of it."

Kara scowled. "Did Connor send this to you?"

"I asked him to."

Kara made a disgusted sound. "He should know better. I'm going to send a comlink to him right now."

"No, don't do that," Noah said quickly. "I—he—he delayed sending it to me, and I kept insisting. I already have access to the data. I'm just trying to get up to speed."

Kara was quiet for a few moments. "They're still hunting down Lars."

"They're getting closer."

"I hope he gets what he deserves when they catch him."

"Don't say that. It's not right."

"Not right!" Kara cried. "Look what he's done to you. Look what he's done to the Ovarrow. He almost killed you. When are you going to admit that to yourself?"

"You make it sound like he was working by himself. He wasn't."

"He's leading them. Dash said as much and Connor confirmed," Kara replied.

Noah waited for his wife to look at him. "It's not his fault," he said and raised his hands in front of his chest. "I know what you're going to say."

"That it's bullshit," Kara said, almost snarling. "No. You wouldn't've been on that cliff if it wasn't for Lars."

"He was trying to get me to understand what he was doing," Noah said.

"Yeah, and you tried to free the Ovarrow from what he was doing to them. You knew it was the right thing to do. You decided Lars was wrong, and you needed to do something about it. Lars didn't like that. He chased you down. Your *friend* was chasing you down, and he hurt you. I know you don't like to admit it, but that's exactly what happened."

"It was an accident!" Noah shouted. "An accident," he repeated.

Kara blew out a breath in disgust. "Lars doesn't deserve you. He doesn't deserve your friendship. Don't you think he should answer for what he's done?"

Noah considered it for a few moments. "I do. I'm not condoning what he's done. He has a lot to answer for, but I just don't want to see him killed for it."

Kara stepped away from him and shook her head. "I'll never forgive him for what he's done to you. Lars has crossed the line. When are you going to understand, Noah? Some people can't be saved. Lars cannot be saved."

Noah's gut tightened. "You're wrong," he said. "You're wrong. He's walking a thin line; I'll give you that. He's done despicable things, but that's when you need your friends and your family the most. We can't just write him off. I'm not going to give up on him."

His wife's eyes watered and Noah's heart broke. There was anger and frustration in her gaze, but that wasn't what hurt the most. She pitied him, and he hated it.

"I'd like to be alone now," Noah said, his voice sounding cold.

Kara didn't say anything as she left the lab. Noah's throat became thick and he clenched his teeth as he went back over their conversation in his mind. He, Lars, and Sean had grown up together. They'd been among the first to be woken up on the *Ark*, and they'd also been among the first colonists to set foot on New Earth. What the hell had happened to all of them? All Lars had to do was come home. Why couldn't Lars just come home? He kept seeing Kara's pitying gaze, and his shoulders went rigid.

Noah felt another headache begin to come on and he snarled, looking for something to kick. There wasn't anything, and that made him angrier. He tried to calm down, but his breath was coming in gasps. Noah sank to his knees and tried to clear his mind, halt his racing thoughts, but the headache lingered on the fringe like a looming storm about to blow.

He needed to focus on something, so he brought up a new report on the space gate and glanced at the author. Dr. Oriana Evans. Noah recalled seeing that name before. He checked the space gate reports and found her name associated with many of them. Maybe she'd talk to him about her research. He looked her up and felt his shoulders drop. She was missing. She was on the mission with Sean—another thing that had happened while he wasn't around. Noah glared at the report, and the name "Evans" became bleary. He'd been at this too long, and maybe it was time he took a break. He didn't like admitting it to himself. It was okay to push against his limits and maybe even break them a little bit, but sometimes taking a little step back was what he needed in order to take a giant leap forward.

CHAPTER 26

Trident Battle Group had reached the rendezvous point, which was three hundred million kilometers away from the Krake. Sean had just left the bridge and was heading to the conference room to meet with his senior officers for the battle group. He walked into the room to find that Major Shelton was already there, as well as Oriana. Captain Chad Boseman was there to provide updates regarding what the Spec Ops team had observed during their mission. The rest of the attendees were virtual, which included all the commanding officers of the ships of the battle group. There were several holoscreens active over the main table.

Sean sat down. "I want to thank you all for coming. This is a meeting to go over what we've learned from the Krake message. But before we get into that, I need to know the status of the space gate."

"All space gate cubes are in the process of being connected. Initial diagnostics indicate that they are ready to be used. The next step is that of an actual test. I've conferred with Dr. Evans, and she's satisfied that the physical test is the next logical step," Major Brody said.

Sean glanced at Oriana, and she nodded.

"Technically, that's correct," Oriana said. "We believe the cubes will work, but there are some differences in their construction that we need to analyze. Also, we're not sure if it will alert the Krake when we use them."

"It just needs to work once," Brody said.

"At minimum, it needs to work once, but we need a reliable solution," Sean said and glanced around the room. "Let's table the space gate discussion for now. I want to go over what the science team and Gabriel came up with during their analysis of the Krake message we received. Go ahead, Gabriel."

"Thank you, Colonel Quinn," Gabriel said. "The message is a data burst that included our first contact protocols. These were the protocols that were transferred from this ship in the previous universe where we first engaged the Krake. I'd like to highlight the paramount importance of this. It indicates that the Krake have been spreading this information around."

"Why would they include our own first contact protocol?" Brody asked.

"Presumably to establish credibility that they want to communicate with us," Gabriel answered.

Sean nodded. "Makes sense. Our first contact protocols have been around for hundreds of years. We just never had to use them back on Earth. Our first contact message always included a way to talk back to us. I agree with Gabriel's assessment, and so does the science team. Gabriel, please continue."

"The other interesting part of the data is that it includes Ovarrow symbols. We also believe that whoever sent the message had knowledge of this and didn't communicate with us in their native Krake language, which we would have trouble understanding. However, we do have one advantage —the three Krake prisoners. They could provide insight into this, if we choose to share the message with them."

"I haven't made a decision on that yet," Sean replied.

"The message also contains a reference—this is a translation based on the Ovarrow language— calling themselves the overseers. They appear to be leaders in Krake society. However, there's another part of the message that indicates there's some faction, or what we'd refer to as a fifth column. At the end of the data packet is the set of space gate coordinates, along with the actual timing for using them. The time is twenty-four hours from the initial message."

"That sounds like an invitation to me. What do the rest of you think?" Sean asked.

Major Brody went first, which Sean expected since he was his second-in-command. "This is extraordinary and gives us more insight into the Krake and what their motivations are. Gabriel, you said the set of coordinates were to be used in the next twenty-four hours. Is that right?"

"That is correct, Major Brody. That means we have about twelve hours left to decide whether we follow those coordinates," Gabriel replied.

"Excuse me," Oriana said. "We've checked the data against the new calculations we've been using, and the temporal calculations do match up. This is another indicator that the next time we use the targeting coordinates to return to our home universe, they'll work. I just wanted to point that out."

Sean glanced around at the people in the room and on the holoscreens. They wanted to go home. Heck, *he* wanted to go home, but he just wasn't sure if this was the right decision.

"We have twelve hours, ladies and gentlemen," Sean said.

"This could be a trap, Colonel," Major Brody said.

"I disagree," Major Shelton said, speaking up for the first time in the meeting. Sean gestured for her to continue. "They attacked their own ships. Why would they then send us a message and invite us into a trap? I agree with Colonel Quinn that this is an invitation. The Krake had enough firepower to take us out. This other group showed up and sacrificed themselves so we could get away."

"Anything the Krake do is suspect," Major Brody replied. "There's a degree of risk with anything we do. Colonel Quinn, what do you intend to do?"

"We delay going home. We need . . ." Sean paused for a moment, noting some of the reactions, and then continued. "Our mission objective is to learn all we can about the Krake, finding their weaknesses and bringing that information back home so we can exploit it. This is worth exploring. We have twelve hours. I suggest you make all the necessary preparations."

There was a collective, "Yes, Colonel," and then the meeting ended.

"Colonel Quinn," Oriana said. They used formal address since there were others present. "I'd like to go to the *Yorktown* with my team to do our own analysis of the space gate. I just want to double-check that everything is working properly."

Sean frowned. "We have the data from the engineering team. Do you think something's wrong?"

"No, not exactly. I'd just like to double-check."

"All right, I'll have a shuttle take you guys over there, but we'll be transferring the space gate cubes over to the *Vigilant*," Sean said.

"That's why I want to run my own diagnostic before it comes here."

"Understood. Let me know the results of your analysis," Sean said.

Oriana left the room. Shelton and Boseman had stayed behind.

"Well, they weren't happy to hear about that," Major Shelton said.

"To be honest, I'm not happy about it either, but I know this is the right thing to do," Sean said and paused for a moment. "Which is another reason I told them now. Give them some time to let it settle."

There'd been a lot of tension and stress since their recent operation. While it had been a success, it could have gone terribly wrong. They needed to find a way to more effectively deal with the Krake attack drones.

"I want the simulation of our recent engagement with the Krake uploaded to the tactical computers and distributed among the fleet. Have our people go over it. See if we can improve upon our response."

"Understood, Colonel. I'll get it done."

———

Major Brody leaned back in his chair. The meeting had just ended, and only he and Major McKay were left in the room. A comlink opened, and it was Captain Ryan Ward from the *Babylon* and Captain Olaf McGee from the *Archeon*.

"Major Brody, we wanted to speak with you."

Brody narrowed his eyes and said, "What's this about?"

"We conferred with the other destroyer captains, and we were hoping you could speak to Colonel Quinn again about his decision on not going home. I'm not sure if he's fully aware of the state of the space gate. We could only have a one-time use of it."

Major Brody frowned. "You heard the colonel. We have our orders."

Captain McGee pressed his lips together and swallowed. "Permission to speak freely, Major."

Brody didn't like where this was heading, but if there was a problem, he'd rather meet it head-on than let it fester. "Okay, I'll allow it, but be careful, Captain," Brody warned.

"Thank you, Major. I'll be brief," McGee said. "I don't think chasing down this lead is worth losing the entire battle group. We've been out of touch with COMCENT for over ninety days now. We need to check in. We also need to resupply. We have ships that aren't fighting at full capacity, and we're at overcapacity for passengers. We just don't think this is the best time to chase down whatever this Krake fifth column group is," McGee said, finishing.

"I realize I gave you permission to speak freely, but what you're suggesting is—"

"Major Brody," McGee interrupted, "I just want to be clear. We request that you speak with Colonel Quinn to make him aware of the situation with the battle group. I respect the chain of command, but Colonel Quinn has a reputation of seeing nothing but the objective."

Brody had to agree with that estimate of Sean, but he wouldn't admit that to the destroyer captain. "What makes you and the other captains think he's not aware of the situation?"

"Major, we heard your comments during the meeting. This isn't just a group of captains questioning the orders of our superior officers. Certain members of our crews have voiced their concerns up the chain of command on our ships as well," Captain Ward said.

Lester inhaled and considered the two officers on the holoscreen. "Very well. I'll take your comments under advisement, and I'll let you know if anything comes from it. In the meantime, you have your orders," Brody said and killed the connection.

Major McKay sighed heavily. "This isn't good if they're coming to us. I've been hearing the same kinds of things. At some point, it's not the crew just blowing off steam. I think we need to bring this to Colonel Quinn's attention right away."

Brody felt like he'd just swallowed a mouthful of vinegar. "I'll bring it up with Sean. Better if I do it alone," Brody said.

"Are you sure, Lester? I'm here if you need me," McKay offered.

Brody thought about it for a moment and then shook his head. "It could be nothing. There's a lot of fear going on, and considering what just happened, I'm not too surprised. But we need them to focus and keep working. I've got it," Brody said.

McKay left the room and Brody sent Sean a message asking to speak to him in private. Fifteen minutes later, Sean appeared on the holoscreen in Brody's office aboard the *Yorktown*.

"I figured you'd be contacting me," Sean said.

Brody smiled a little. "To be honest, I hadn't planned on it, but some things have come up that I think you need to know."

Sean's gaze didn't quite narrow, but it definitely hardened as he braced himself for yet another thing to deal with.

"I didn't want to bring this up again, since you've already given your orders. I want you to reconsider. A couple of the . . ." Brody paused for a moment. "Never mind. We need to check in with COMCENT. I understand that this lead with the Krake is worth investigating, but we need to go back and resupply. We're at overcapacity with limited food and water. We can keep going for perhaps another sixty days, but still it's something to be aware of. I just think that if we contact COMCENT and apprise them of the situation, we could get resupplied with ammunition and go at this fresh."

"I've been hearing the complaints here too, Lester, but we can't do all that in the timeframe the Krake have given. This is a way to contact them. We have less than twelve hours."

Lester waited for Sean to continue.

"I agree in part, and you have a point. There's the risk of staying out here, and that last battle was a pretty close thing. I'd still do it again because we got the gate components, so at least somebody can go home to report back to COMCENT."

"Thank you," Lester said. "We don't know who this fifth column is, and all we do know about the Krake is that they like to manipulate an intelligent species. What if we're just next on the list?"

"We *are* next on their list," Sean said with a bit of an edge in his voice, "and we're not going to win this thing by playing it safe. We don't have any reason to trust them, but we should go out there and at least meet them. We can take the necessary precautions. They know we have a mobile space gate; otherwise, the data burst the Krake sent us doesn't make any sense. But they don't know exactly where we'll come in from. This gives us an advantage." Sean paused for a moment. "I know this isn't coming just from you."

"You're right Colonel, this—"

"Well, I don't agree with them. While they might not like my orders, they'll follow them, as you will. Is that understood, Major?"

Brody stiffened and narrowed his gaze. He'd been on the receiving end of a tongue-lashing from Colonel Quinn more than once and was getting just about tired of it.

"It's crystal clear, Colonel. Will that be all?"

"That will be all, Major. Carry on."

The comlink closed and Brody found that he was clutching the arms of his chair. His teeth were clenched, and he felt like molten fury was blazing in his gums. He needed to calm down. His thoughts were going a million kilometers an hour in the wrong direction.

Brody stood up and pounded his fist on the table, crying out in rage.

"Son of a bitch," he said between clenched teeth.

CHAPTER 27

Connor's secret office was a small combat information center isolated from access by external systems. Only one-way communications were allowed and had to be initiated from inside the room only by people with the clearance to do so. Connor had designed the system this way, hoping he'd never have to use it. The level of access he had to colonial systems would've violated even the most basic privacy restrictions.

Lars had circumvented colonial laws to achieve his goals. Connor had tried to operate within legal parameters to find him and whoever was involved with the rogue group's activities, but he'd failed. He'd also given Field Ops and Security the tools to do the job, and they'd come up short. Both Lars and whoever he was working with operated at a level above what passed for law enforcement in the colony, and this was something he couldn't allow anymore—especially now that they were willing to sacrifice colonial lives to achieve their objectives.

Few people knew about this office and what he could do there, but he was still within the secure confines of the CDF base at Sanctuary. Major Natalia Vassar stood on the other side of the room with several floating holoscreens surrounding her. She looked over at him.

"All platoons of Ranger 7th company have reported in from the three primary target zones."

"Understood," Connor replied and regarded her for a moment. Natalia had good instincts for intelligence analysis. "What is it? I can tell you want to say something."

Natalia made a swiping motion with her hand, and the holoscreens became opaque. "I was just thinking of the post-op review and the shitstorm that's going to come of this. You know it's not going to go unnoticed that we didn't have an Ops here at Sanctuary."

Connor shrugged. The trail to the rogue group hadn't implicated anyone who lived at Sanctuary. "That's just the way it happened. Anyway, are you surprised? We're going where the trail leads us."

Natalia didn't reply. Instead she re-engaged the holoscreens and frowned for a moment. "Are you aware that Captain Samson is outside the door, looking for a way in?"

Connor brought up the security video feed and saw Samson looking up at the hidden camera. Samson's position was with his back to the door, and he'd deduced where the hidden camera was. Connor chuckled a little. "No, I wasn't aware."

"I still find it odd that he doesn't use a last name."

"Oh, Samson *is* his last name. He just doesn't like to use his first name."

"I've searched the colonial records, and I can't find it. Even the records from the *Ark*," Natalia said.

"That's because he deleted them."

Samson pounded on the steel door, and Connor shook his head.

"Should I let him in?" Natalia asked.

"I've got it," Connor replied and sent his authorization for the door to open.

Samson walked in, scowling at Connor. He looked over at Natalia and tempered his scowl just a little bit. Then he looked back at Connor. "Major Vassar, I want to speak to General Gates alone," he said, his gaze never leaving Connor's. "Please," Samson tacked on at the end.

Connor looked over at Natalia and gave her a nod. She closed down her holoscreens and left the room.

"You know, if you were anyone else, no major worth his salt would've allowed you to speak to them that way, Captain."

"I think we can dispense with the ranks for a few minutes. You're so far off the map that if we were to include ranks, you'd be in a lot more trouble."

Connor regarded him for a few moments. "What is it that you think you know?"

"Where's Carl Flint and the 3rd Ranger company?"

"They're on a training mission."

"A training mission," Samson repeated. "That's bullshit and you know it. Spec Ops doesn't conduct training missions in Sierra, Delphi, or New Haven. Are you conducting an operation in colonial population centers?"

"I'm assuming you're here because you tried to access the whereabouts of Flint's company and were denied."

"Please," Samson said sharply. "It's easy to track where they went. The mission objectives might be classified, but they didn't classify the method of travel they used to get there. Nor the check-in intervals, although I doubt most people would notice that."

"Field Ops can't deal with Lars Mallory and the rogue group. They're succeeding at all their objectives, while we're being merely reactive. The status quo must change," Connor said.

"You're doing it again," Samson warned.

Connor frowned. "I'm doing what again?"

"You're playing fast and loose."

"Hardly. I've been piecing this together as we've gone along. The events at the Ovarrow city merely forced my hand."

"Is that a fact? I wasn't talking about this. You played fast and loose before, or have you forgotten? Millions of civilians paid the price."

Connor glared at Samson. He'd never forget that. "This isn't a hunt for the Syndicate."

"Call it whatever you want. This rogue group is a symptom of a larger problem. If you back them into a corner, you're risking lives," Samson said.

"Are you going to stand there and tell me you care about colonial lives now?" Connor asked.

"I didn't want to be here. I didn't ask for it. I came back to help you protect these people. Well, who's going to protect them from you?" Samson said and walked toward Connor. "It's necessary. I can already hear the argument you're about to make—'I have no choice.'"

"I don't have a choice, and you don't even know the particulars of this operation."

"You cut everyone off, and you've also failed to inform the people with the rank to stop you," Samson said, jabbing a finger toward Connor.

"No one is going to stop me from finding them. This has gone on long enough. I didn't start it, but I'm going to finish it. Are you going to stand in my way?" Connor asked.

Samson was a giant of a man, as if he'd been carved from stone, and he was much bigger than Connor. He was more heavily muscled and probably just as dangerous as Connor was, but there was no way in hell Connor was going to let anyone stand in his way.

"If I have to. You of all people should know that once you open that box . . . this operation you're doing. It will be impossible to stop what's going to happen next," Samson said.

"You don't need to lecture me about the laws of unintended consequences. I'm well aware of them. But at some point, we have to draw the line, and this is where mine is."

"You're too close to this. You've moved on with your life, started a family, and I respect that, but now this group has put your wife in danger. They hurt some of your closest friends, and you'll do whatever you have to do to stop them," Samson said.

"That's right," Connor said, not bothering to hide it anymore. "You think it was an accident that Lenora happened to be at the Ovarrow city when all that crap happened? They made this personal, and they picked the wrong person."

"You're right; this is personal, but did you ever stop and think that maybe you're playing right into their hands?"

"Did you ever stop and think that perhaps they're going to get more than they bargained for?" Connor replied.

"Give me one good reason why I shouldn't inform General Hayes and

Governor Wolf what you're up to. You're not the only one who can put in fail-safes," Samson said and held up the secure comlink.

The suppressors Connor had in the room wouldn't work against it. Connor knew that because he had several of his own.

Connor smiled a little. "Did it ever occur to you that maybe I wanted you to be here right now?"

Samson frowned. "What do you mean?"

"I need your help. I'm going to find all the hideouts. This rogue group operates away from colonial population centers, but the way to find them is by tracking the leads at our major cities. I don't have Flint's platoons conducting a clandestine operation armed to the teeth. This is an inform-and-observe operation, and they have instructions to coordinate with Field Ops and Security. So yes, I'm opening Pandora's box, but it's with limita-tions. And I know there'll be repercussions for doing this, but I'm going to do it anyway," Connor said.

Samson inhaled swiftly and sighed. "Not armed to the teeth but armed with suppressors and shock sticks. Either way, you're executing CDF opera-tions inside a population center. That isn't going to go unnoticed when this is all said and done."

"I know."

They were quiet for almost a full minute. Technically, there were legal loopholes to justify what Connor was doing, but that would only get him so far.

An alert sounded and a live video feed showed on the nearest holoscreen. Noah and Dash were standing outside. Noah was staring right into the camera feed while Dash kept a lookout.

"It looks like I'm not the only one who found your secret operations center," Samson said dryly.

Connor knew there was no way Dash could've found this place, but Noah was another matter.

"Connor, I know you're in there. We have to talk," Noah said.

CHAPTER 28

Samson arched an eyebrow toward Connor. "Is this part of the plan?"

Connor frowned and walked over to the door, then opened it.

Dash's eyes widened. "Wow, what is this place?"

"How did you get in here?" Connor asked.

Noah smiled. "I'd be happy to tell you about it once you let us inside."

Connor didn't move.

Natalia was heading down the corridor toward them. She didn't look surprised to see Noah.

"I think I figured it out," Connor said and stepped aside to allow them in.

He narrowed his eyes at Natalia as she came in.

"Leverage every asset we have," she said, reminding Connor of what he'd told her in the past.

The door closed and Connor stood next to Samson. "Plan change," he said so only Samson could hear. Samson grunted in reply.

"All right, Noah," Connor said. "You've got my attention, but before you begin, I need to ask something. Is a certain tiny but fierce blonde wife going to come hunt me down because you're here?"

The self-satisfied smile on Noah's face blanched. "I think she'll be hunting us both down. She might even recruit Lenora."

"Great," Connor said dryly. "We can get an apartment together. But I know you wouldn't be here if it wasn't important . . . Well, you wouldn't have contacted me if it wasn't important. You're here because you want to come along."

Noah met his gaze for a few moments. "I know where Lars is."

Connor tapped his fingertips against his thigh and regarded Noah for a few moments. "You have my attention, Noah."

"I know you're angry, and you have every right to be," Noah said and paused for a moment. "I'm going to tell you what you need to know. You know that, and I know that. You're right though. I want to come. I need to come with you."

Connor drew in a breath, intending to deny Noah's request.

"I was hoping I wouldn't have to say this," Noah continued, "but of everyone in this room, Lars has the most to answer for to me. I know the location, and I'm going to get there with or without you."

"It's going to be dangerous. Everything Lars has done points to a man you don't know anymore. What makes you think he won't take a shot at you while he's trying to escape?" Connor said.

Noah stared at Connor for a moment. They both knew it was dangerous to make assumptions, especially about people who'd once been close to them.

"He won't," Dash said. "As much as I hate him and blame him for what's happened, Lars stopped his men from engaging the CDF squad that was protecting me and Jory."

Connor shook his head. "That's the thing. The conflict has escalated, and that makes people reckless. Now he's backed himself into a corner, and I'm coming for him."

"He's still a colonial citizen," Noah said. "He's still subject to the law."

"They'll have a chance to surrender. If they don't take it, then one way or another, I will root them out of whatever hole they are hiding in. You can count on it," Connor said.

"Fine, and you can count on me going with you," Noah said.

Samson bellowed a hearty laugh. "Ain't it something when the kids grow up? I like this one," Samson said, gesturing toward Noah.

Noah smiled and looked back at Connor. "They made a mistake before. I don't believe what happened at the Ovarrow city was . . . had undergone much long-term planning. It would explain some of the communications channels I picked up."

"You picked up?" Connor said in disbelief. "How . . .? You were in a coma. What do you mean you picked up?"

"Before my coma, I was working on something to help track down certain network traffic patterns."

"We were already doing that, and we haven't found anything."

"This is something new. You see, what I created was something that can adapt in almost real time. It generates a lot of noise, but sometimes it can lead you right where you need to be," Noah said.

That was when Connor knew Noah had, in fact, found the rogue group.

"Let me show you what I found. They've limited themselves to three bases of operation, but the one we're most interested in . . ." Noah said and went on to tell Connor and the others exactly what he'd found.

"Ovarrow military bunkers, or at least supply caches. They'd be well hidden. I can understand why it was so difficult to find them. Their movements were covered because of all the Ovarrow bunker-hopping we've been doing," Samson said.

"They'd have more structural integrity and be better hidden than the civilian bunker sites we've found," Connor said.

"I can task some of our reconnaissance satellites to survey the area. Perhaps we can send some stealth recon drones," Natalia suggested.

Connor shook his head. "No, at least not right now. We can deploy the stealth recon drones once we get on site. I don't want to alert them that we know where they are. We need to take them by surprise."

Connor looked at Samson for a moment.

Samson drew up his chin proudly. "We lead the way."

Connor nodded. "You two," he said to Noah and Dash, "you'll need these if you're coming with us."

The two young men walked over.

"You've upgraded my MPS design," Noah said.

"I field-tested it, too," Connor said. "Come on, let's get started."

CHAPTER 29

CDF troop carriers, along with their Hellcat escorts, ripped across the pale gray sky. The engines shrieked in dopplered wails as they came in low and fast over deep canyons.

"Easy to get lost in here. This is a good spot to hide," Samson said.

Connor looked at Noah. "I hope this tracker of yours is right."

"That makes two of us," Noah said. This drew a few glances in his direction. "They're in this region. That's what I can confirm."

Connor looked at the holoscreen in front of him, which had a video feed of the landscape. Samson was right; Lars had picked a good spot to hide. Connor could've hidden several battalions here if he'd wanted.

"It's enough for us to go on," Connor said. "Once we locate them, I want one of the troop carriers held in reserve in case they try to escape."

"Understood," Samson said and then relayed the orders. He looked at Connor when he was finished. "How many people do you think are at this location?"

"Intelligence estimates anywhere from fifty to seventy-five people. Other estimates are for several hundred. We take their base of operations here and it will lead to the others as well," Connor said.

He saw Noah give them a sidelong glance.

"Only if we take their base intact," Noah said.

"Yes, and if not, we can use your tracker to find the other installations." Connor turned away. He didn't want to watch Noah's reaction. If he did, he'd say things he'd later regret.

"We're approaching the marker," Samson said.

"Send the Hellcats on ahead and do a sweep of the area," Connor said.

The Hellcats flew ahead, deploying recon drones as needed.

Interspersed between the canyons they flew over was low, level, forested

grassland. Near the marker on the HUD overlay of the video feed, a gargantuan opening appeared. A slope led to an elliptical mouth that at its widest
point was over a hundred and thirty-five meters.

"Easy enough to fly ships in there," Samson said.

A Hellcat flew down into the cave shaft and deployed reconnaissance
drones. Connor had the other troop carrier and Hellcat escorts make a grid
search of the area, looking for escape routes.

Several live video feeds from the recon drones came to prominence on
the main holoscreen. The cave bottom was over fourteen hundred feet down
and then narrowed away from the opening. They could land the troop
carrier at the bottom, but they'd have to go on foot from there.

"Power source detected, and it looks like someone's been here recently,"
Connor said.

The recon drones made slow but steady progress and showed a path that
led to a network of caves. Several shafts of sunlight were coming in through
openings above.

"That's Ovarrow-made," Dash said. "That path right there. And then it
leads to the walkway, so you don't have to climb to the bottom to make it
over there."

He was right. Connor had seen similar structures at other Ovarrow
bunkers, but they didn't have a record of this one.

"How far do you think these tunnels go?" Samson asked.

"It's hard to say," Connor said as several of the recon drones went dark.

They brought up the last images from the recon drones and tried to see
what had destroyed them. Some Ovarrow military bunkers had automated
defenses that still worked, but if the rogue group was there, then it could
have been automated defenses they'd set up.

"I can't tell what took out the recon drones," Samson said.

"We're going to have to go in there," Connor said.

The troop carrier took them down to the base of the shaft. As they were
making preparations to leave, the other teams reported in that they'd found
another cave entrance about two kilometers away.

"That's close enough to be within the same cave network," Dash
commented.

Connor nodded and looked at Noah. "Are you sure you're up for this?
You can stay behind and monitor from here."

Noah shook his head. "I'm coming."

He gave Connor a determined look, and Connor nodded. When Noah
turned to grab his backpack, Connor caught Dash's attention. He tilted his
head toward Noah and Dash nodded.

There were three platoons that made up the 7th Ranger company under
Samson's command. Lieutenant Keith Mason led the way with his platoon,
Connor and the others were in the middle, and another twenty-five soldiers
followed them.

They made their way slowly through the tunnels the Ovarrow had carved
out hundreds of years ago. Enough time had passed for moisture and sedi-

ment buildup to begin impacting what had once been a smooth path. The air was damp, but at least it was fresh. There were several smaller cave openings along the path that lit up the area and provided fresh air.

They deployed another reconnaissance drone and sent it on ahead, looking for what had taken out the others. Suddenly, several CDF automated turrets burst from the ceiling and fired their weapons at them. The soldiers on point activated portable shielding to protect them as they retreated back down the tunnel. Connor tried to send a command override, but he was locked out. Noah tried to use a back door to access them and shook his head. "They're hardened. They'll only respond to someone else's command. You'll have to take them out."

They made quick work of the automated defense turrets. There wasn't any doubt as to who was here. They'd found the rogue group, but they were going to have to take it slow, removing whatever defenses were in place. The closer they got, the more dangerous it would become.

"Alert the other platoons about the automated defenses we've encountered," Connor said.

Samson relayed the information and they continued onward.

CHAPTER 30

Lars left the Ovarrow holding cell. It had been a frustrating conversation where nothing new had been learned. Over the past year, Lars had tried a number of interrogation techniques to glean information from the Ovarrow. Some had yielded results while others hadn't at all. Actual physical torture rarely yielded any useful results, despite the preconceptions of some. They'd used psychological techniques, some of which had worked, but ultimately the Ovarrow were an alien species. However, showing them the world they'd left was an effective technique, as well as showing them an image of an active arch the Krake had used to come to this world. The Ovarrow prisoners didn't realize that it was the colonists who were using the arch, and it was enough to get them motivated to speak about what they knew. After a while, Lars had to admit that it had become more of a rinse-and-repeat-type effort. The fact was that their entire operation had been disrupted by what Evans had done—what Evans had been ordered to do, Lars amended in his mind—and it had set their entire operation back. In addition, the CDF was now looking for them in earnest.

It had been easy to avoid Field Ops and Security since they restricted their activity to colonial cities and the nearby surrounding areas. The CDF was something different altogether.

When Lars had been recruited, he'd thought he was working to protect the colony, but the Ovarrow were far from innocent victims. They'd left a minefield of horrors that colonists had stumbled into, and they couldn't be trusted. He still believed in his mission, but the rogue group's activities had become more ruthless. He'd been kept out of the loop for the mission in the Ovarrow city. His superiors had believed Lars wouldn't have carried out the operation, and they'd been right. He'd never have done it, but he did have to deal with the fallout of such activity. They'd circumvented his authority.

They'd betrayed him. The whole thing had made him watch the people around him with a fresh perspective. How much influence did his superiors have over his subordinates? There were believers in the cause just like him, but there were others who were becoming more ruthless—more like Evans.

Lars walked down the corridor toward the command center. Evans walked out of one of the adjacent rooms and looked at him. His gaze was calculating, and Lars felt his own survival instincts take over as if he were no longer looking at a friend but weighing the threat of a potential enemy. He didn't like it.

"Learn anything new?" Evans asked him.

"Just more of the same."

"Want me to dispose of them for you?"

Lars shook his head. "No. These things take time."

They were silent for a moment while they regarded one another.

"I've seen you dispose of prisoners in half the time you've spent with these. What makes them so different?" Evans asked.

"Maybe they're not different," Lars countered. "It's getting increasingly difficult to get more subjects to interrogate, and we need to make the most of what we have here now."

Evans looked away and nodded. "Have you read the latest intelligence reports? It looks like they found out some things about your friend Sean, indicating that the battle group is still around."

"I hadn't heard about that," Lars admitted. Both he and Evans had kept close watch for news about the Trident Battle Group that had gone missing months ago.

"They found a remnant, or at least a partial remnant, of one of the ships but nothing of the rest of the battle group."

"That's good. That means your sister is probably safe as well," Lars said.

Evans could be a bastard at times, but he was loyal to his family. He loved his sister, and it was hard for him to deal with the fact that she was missing.

A klaxon alarm blared in the corridor, shocking them both to silence.

"Come on," Lars said and ran toward the command center.

Less than a minute later, they ran through the doors to the command center. Tonya Wagner looked over at them. "The CDF is here. They're heading right for us."

Lars looked at her holoscreen, which showed that the CDF had found the main cave entrance to their base. Lars shook his head. He had over eighty people there, and they'd only just gotten settled in. How had the CDF found them so quickly?

"We're going to have to begin evacuation then," Lars said.

"We can't," Wagner replied. "Another CDF troop carrier just entered the cave network on the other side."

Lars looked at the video feed they'd captured before it went out. No doubt the CDF had taken it out with jamming. "Those aren't the only two ways out of here."

"We haven't fully explored that third group of tunnels," Evans replied. "We'd have to leave a lot of equipment behind if we went that way."

"I don't see that we have much choice," Lars said and looked at Wagner. "Order the evacuation."

"No," Evans said sternly. "We don't need to run from them."

Lars glared at Evans for a moment and then looked at Wagner. She hadn't followed his orders. The other agents in the room stopped what they were doing.

"The CDF is here. There's no stopping them from getting to us," Lars said.

"That's where you're wrong. My team is prepared for this," Evans said and brought up a secondary holoscreen. "While we were exploring the tunnels, we left a few surprises of our own in case the CDF found us."

Lars looked at the schematic Evans had put on the holoscreen. Explosive charges were deployed throughout the tunnel system.

"They won't detect them until it's too late. Not even their combat suits will protect them from tons of rock."

Lars's eyes widened as he realized that the CDF was already well inside the danger zone. "You can't be serious. You're going to collapse the tunnel on top of them?"

"I didn't tell them to come here."

Lars shook his head. "You're done. Shut it down, now."

Evans glared at him. "I don't think so. You see, the higher-ups thought you wouldn't have the stomach to do what needed to be done. They were right. I'm taking command."

"Like hell you are," Lars said and stomped toward Evans.

Dean Morris and Wagner pulled out their weapons and pointed them at Lars.

There was no way Lars could pull out his sidearm in time, and he didn't need to. He used his neural implants and shut down access to their computing core using his own authentication. The holoscreens around them became locked out before turning off.

Evans laughed. "That's cute, but the detonation signal can only come from me," he said, smiling wolfishly.

Lars dove toward Evans, taking him by surprise. Morris tried to fire his weapon but growled in surprise when it wouldn't respond. Lars threw Evans into Morris, and both men went down to the ground.

Wagner glanced at her weapon, which had been locked out along with the rest of the system.

"I can't believe you sided with them, Tonya," Lars said.

"Not with them. The work we've done."

"Killing colonists and CDF soldiers is not our work," Lars said. He walked over and took her sidearm from her. "Get over there with them."

His weapons worked just fine. Lars brought up one of the holoscreens and activated a camera feed, seeing a group of CDF soldiers coming toward the base. He saw Connor and his eyes widened. Then Noah walked into view. He felt a shiver run down his spine, and his mouth fell open in surprise.

Evans pushed himself to his feet, and Lars began to point his weapon at him.

"Not so fast, Lars," Evans said and glanced at the holoscreen. "Look who it is. The great Connor Gates and your friend Noah Barker. They should've joined us. Hell, Connor should've *led* us."

Lars raised his weapon.

Evans glared at him. "Are you going to kill me?"

"Are you going to kill them?" Lars countered.

Evans growled and stepped closer to Lars. "Take the shot. Take it. Take it!"

Lars hesitated. If Evans was the only one who could detonate the explosive charges, he might have a dead man's trigger set up.

Evans sneered. "That's right," he said and tapped the side of his head. "I'm the only one who can detonate them, and I'm the only one who can disable them. Do you want to say goodbye?"

Lars clenched his teeth and used his implants to increase the power output of his sidearm to maximum.

Morris regained his feet and reset his weapon's system, then pointed it at Lars.

"I'm giving you a chance to say goodbye to your friends," Evans said.

Lars regarded Evans for a moment and then squeezed the trigger. Explosive-tipped darts shrieked from his weapon, and the remains of Evans's body dropped to the ground. Lars dove to the side as Morris fired his weapon. Deep slivers of pain ran all through Lars's side as the high-velocity darts gouged through his light armor, hitting flesh. Lars swung his weapon up and shot at Morris's chest and then shot him in the head. Morris stumbled backward and went down. Dead.

Evans's dead man's trigger activated, and a new holoscreen appeared in red. Lars pushed himself up to his knees and scrambled over to the holoscreen. A countdown timer had appeared.

"You killed them!" Wagner cried out.

Lars glared at her for a moment. "Help me stop this."

Wagner looked away from Evans and Morris with a pained expression. She swallowed hard and came over next to Lars. "I can't access it. It's running on a secure subsystem. It's completely separate from our main system."

Lars tried to bypass the subsystem and shut it down, but it wouldn't work. "Dammit," he said. "They're going to die if we don't stop this. There has to be a way." He glared at Tonya. "Did you know what Evans was doing?"

"No," Tonya answered quickly. "I had no idea he did this."

Lars didn't believe her. He should have kept a better eye on Evans. The sting of betrayal felt like acid in his mouth.

"We have to warn them," Tonya said.

"They'll never believe us," Lars said. He accessed the base's computer system. Evans' secure subsystem had to be using their comms channels to trigger the signal. It was the only way for a signal to reach where he'd hidden the charges.

"Lars, we're running out of time," Tonya said.

Lars opened up a holoscreen that showed all the comlinks currently attached to their network and severed all of them, then shut the entire system down.

The countdown reached zero and they both froze for a few moments. Lars tilted his head to the side, listening for explosions, but didn't hear anything.

"Did you stop it?" Tonya asked. "You stopped it. How did you stop it?"

"I didn't stop it. I couldn't access the dead man's trigger, so I shut down the entire comms network."

Tonya's eyes went wide. "If anyone brings it back online, it will trigger the explosives."

Lars nodded. "I locked out the system. I'm going to bring up the emergency broadcast network. It's a separate system."

"You need to check—" Tonya began.

"I know," Lars said.

He brought up the emergency broadcast system one component at a time, checking that there were no latent protocols set to run by first bringing them up in a virtualized environment before bringing up the actual system. Once the system was up, he sent out a broadcast to all the people in the base.

"Stand down. Fall back to the main area. We're surrendering to the CDF," Lars said. He set the broadcast to loop three more times and then shut it down.

"We can still escape," Tonya said.

Lars shook his head. "It's over. If we try to escape, the CDF will hunt us down. The only way for us to walk out of here is if we surrender."

He dropped his weapon. It was dead anyway. The emergency broadcast he'd sent had locked out all firearms and automated defenses.

"We're just going to go out there and surrender?" Tonya asked. Then she said, "What about the Ovarrow?"

"Leave them where they are," Lars said.

"We can't just surrender."

Lars gave her a long look, and Tonya looked away. He used the emergency comms system to open a comlink to the CDF. "This is Lars Mallory. I'd like to speak to General Connor Gates."

He broadcast the channel so everyone in the base could listen.

"This is Gates," Connor said. "Lars, if this is really you, I'm giving you one chance to surrender."

Lars stood up, staggered over to a chair, and sat down. Tonya left him, saying she was going to get a medkit.

"It's me, Connor. I'm broadcasting this conversation to my people in the base," Lars said.

There were a few moments of silence. "Understood," Connor replied.

"One condition for our surrender is that I want your personal guarantee my people will be unharmed. We walk out of here in your custody. In exchange, we have fifteen Ovarrow prisoners we'll turn over to you."

Lars paused for a few moments, waiting for Connor to respond. He didn't, and Lars sighed. "I know what you want."

"You need to do better than that. We're coming for you whether you want us to or not. The moment your operations put colonial lives in jeopardy was the moment you lost all credibility for this cause you serve. I'm within my rights to blow this place sky high with all of you in it," Connor replied.

Lars winced, knowing Connor was right. "What happened at the Ovarrow city wasn't my operation. I didn't know about it until after the fact. I don't expect you to believe me."

"Your credibility isn't what it used to be."

"I can give you evidence of who was involved, including the leaders of our organization, in exchange for my people remaining unharmed. Otherwise, you'll get nothing," Lars said.

He glared at the comlink channel on the holoscreen. He'd just laid all his chips out on the table. He had nothing left to barter with. If they'd found their hideout here, then they'd no doubt be able to find the others. He glanced out the door to the command center. A crowd of people were gathered outside, waiting to hear. They looked angry and scared. They'd been backed into a corner, and they all knew it.

Lars waited for Connor to reply. "The ball is in your court. What do you say?"

"We'll talk about it. Since this is a broadcast and the rest of your people are listening in, you should all know that anyone who doesn't surrender or tries to escape will be shot on sight. You're all fugitives and enemies of the colony. If you walk out now, you'll live. This is your only offer," Connor said.

Lars stood up. Tonya had applied medi-paste and numbed his wounds, which had sealed and were no longer bleeding. He walked through the throng of people. He'd recruited most of them, and he had to be the first to walk out so they could see him surrender. Lars walked toward the main entrance, leading everyone to the CDF. What had started out as a rebellious effort to help defend the colony had morphed into something Lars hadn't anticipated. Even now at the end of it all, he couldn't pinpoint where everything had gone wrong. How had they lost their way?

He walked to the main bunker doors and entered his authorization. The large doors swung outward to grim-faced CDF soldiers. Lars held up his hands and walked toward them in defeat. Connor stood out in front, and Lars flinched from the fury he saw in Connor's gaze, but he also saw a small amount of remorse. It hit him like a punch in the gut. The only thing that would be worse was when he faced his father.

"There's someone who wants to talk to you," Connor said.

Behind Connor stood Noah.

His friend regarded him for a few moments as if he didn't know what to say. Lars thought he looked different. Noah had been in a coma, so how was he supposed to look? His throat became thick. "I'm sorry," Lars said.

Noah pressed his lips together, his mouth forming a grim line, and he shook his head. CDF soldiers surrounded Lars and bound his wrists together. Noah watched and didn't say anything. What *could* he say? Lars didn't know what was worse—the fact that after all Lars had done, Noah pitied him, or that he was starting to feel ashamed. Lars clenched his teeth and his lips trembled. He wanted to scream, revile against the shame he felt. He'd done the right thing, but the argument frayed on the edges of his thoughts.

"Take the Ovarrow to Camp Alpha," Connor said to one of the soldiers and then looked at Lars. "How deep does this go?"

Lars looked away for a moment. "It's pretty deep," he muttered and then began telling Connor everything he knew.

CHAPTER 31

Lester Brody glanced at the time in the upper right-hand corner of his internal heads-up display. No matter what, they couldn't escape the running of the clock.

He headed down the corridor toward McKay's ready room off the bridge. Lester knocked on the door, and McKay let him in.

"Is the science team still here?" McKay asked.

Lester nodded. "They've done their final diagnostics of the Krake equipment and are preparing the report."

"I can delay their shuttle departure," McKay offered.

"If we need to. It's just about time to begin," Lester said.

He activated the holoscreen above the conference table, and three destroyer captains appeared. Three of the four destroyer captains he'd reached out to had shown up. Captain Ryan Ward gave a grim nod, as well as Captain Olaf McGee. The presence of the *Diligent's* Captain, Ida Ingram surprised Lester. He hadn't expected Captain Martinez or Captain Welch to join them, so he'd kept them out of the loop, but he hadn't been sure about Captain Watkins. Three was enough.

"Thank you for coming," Lester said. "As of right now, none of us has done anything we can't walk away from. You came to me and voiced your concerns, and I took those concerns to Colonel Quinn's attention. He didn't listen, and the way he dismissed those concerns left me with little choice. I must take action."

Captain Ida Ingram raised her hand. "Major Brody, what do you intend to do?"

"I intend to use the space gate to return home and report in to COMCENT. It's my belief that when I try to do this, Colonel Quinn will attempt to take control of the space gate," Lester answered and paused for a moment. "I'm going to lay it out on the table. I'm disobeying a direct order from my commanding officer. For the record, I do believe that Colonel Quinn is unfit to command this battle group, leaving me no choice but to take command."

"But that's just it, Major," Ingram said. "We don't have the power to take control of the battle group."

"You're right," Lester said, "but we don't need to take control of the battle group. We need to control the space gate and use it to get home. Then this becomes a matter for the CDF brass to sort out, and I think they'll judge us more favorably than they'll judge Colonel Quinn."

Lester watched the other captains, trying to gauge their commitment. "I invite anyone here who has objections to voice them right now. If you're not fully committed to this, then say so, and you'll be excused from this operation, but it won't change what we're doing."

"I have no objections," Captain Ward said.

"Neither do I," Captain McGee said.

Lester turned toward McKay, who simply shook his head. Then he looked at Captain Ingram.

"We're supposed to be better than this," she said with disgust in her voice. "It shouldn't have come to this, but I don't see another way. You have my support," Ingram said and then closed her comlink.

"We will begin in fifteen minutes," Lester said.

———

Sean sat in his office alone, going over some of the latest reports. His intelligence analysts were going over the Krake message and would be providing him with another report in just under an hour. They had a little over six hours before they were due to go to the predefined set of Krake coordinates.

A comlink alert appeared on his holoscreen with Oriana's identification.

"Dr. Evans, how goes the diagnostic of the Krake equipment?"

Oriana was alone and not on the bridge of the *Yorktown*. Sean frowned for a moment. "Where are you?"

"I commandeered somebody's office. The diagnostic came back fine. I was actually done a few hours ago," Oriana said.

"This is the first I've heard of it," Sean replied.

"Our shuttle hasn't been given clearance to leave. Something about an issue with the hangar bay doors."

"I'm sure they'll get it fixed in no time."

"I checked the logs, and there's nothing in them regarding a maintenance crew dispatched to fix anything," Oriana said.

"Have you spoken with Major McKay?" Sean asked.

"He's the one who told me about the issue with the hangar bay doors. There's something strange going on here," Oriana said.

She looked away from the camera as if she'd heard something.

"What do you mean?"

"I spent enough time on the *Vigilant's* bridge to know when there's an operation going on," Oriana said.

"In a few hours' time, we're going to try to find the Krake using their own message. It's probably just that," Sean said.

"This is different," Oriana said and leaned in closer to the camera. "I feel like I'm being watched by someone from Major Brody's team. I don't know who they are, but something's not right here."

She sounded a little upset but not outright scared. And that wasn't like her at all. "There's a lot of people talking about going home."

This got Sean's attention and roused his suspicion. "I'm going to head to the bridge and see if I can get some answers. Are you safe where you are?" he asked and then felt stupid for asking the question.

They had agreed to keep things casual, but his pulse raced at the thought of something happening to her. "Stay where you are. I'll be in touch."

Sean left his office. Major Shelton glanced at him as he entered the bridge and frowned.

"What's the *Yorktown*'s status?" Sean asked.

"They're holding position," Major Shelton answered.

"Comms, get me Major McKay—" Sean began. "Forget that. Give me Major Brody."

There was a long pause while Sean waited.

"It'll be a few minutes, Colonel. Neither one of them is on the bridge," Specialist Sansky replied.

Sean narrowed his gaze and frowned. "Tactical, initiate control of the space gate."

"Initiating control, Colonel." Lieutenant Jane Russo's fingers worked furiously as she accessed the remote systems. "Colonel, I'm locked out of space gate control."

Sean clenched his teeth. He attempted to access the same system. *Denied.* "Run a diagnostic," he said.

While Sean waited for Russo to run the diagnostic, he sent Oriana a text message via comlink.

Col. S. Quinn: *Can you access space gate control systems?*

There was no reply, not even a confirmation that his message had been received by Oriana.

"Diagnostic has finished. All systems are functioning normally, Colonel," Russo said.

Major Shelton walked over to his side. "They could be having comms issues," she said, and Sean could tell she didn't believe it any more than he did.

He shook his head. "I was just speaking with Oriana," Sean said and leaned over so only Vanessa could hear. "She thought McKay was purposefully delaying her shuttle departure and that she was being watched. She finished her diagnostic of the space gate hours ago."

His XO's gaze hardened. "Colonel, are you suggesting . . ." she said and didn't include what they were both thinking.

"I don't know," Sean admitted, and then looked at the plot on the main holoscreen. "Comms, confirm communication status of the battle group. I want all of them to check in."

CHAPTER 32

"Colonel, the *Dutchman*, the *Albany*, and the *Burroughs* all report status green. Captains Martinez, Welch, and Watkins are currently on duty. I received an automated standard check-in response from the *Babylon*, the *Acheron*, and the *Diligent*," Specialist Sansky said.

"Inform the *Dutchman*, the *Albany*, and the *Burroughs* to stand by for further orders. I want a second request to the others for verbal confirmation of status," Sean said and looked at the main holoscreen, which showed the current ship positions.

"Split right down the middle," Major Shelton said.

The *Babylon* and the *Acheron* were positioned closest to the *Yorktown*. The next closest ship was the *Albany*. Captain Lori Welch had replied, so she wasn't caught up in whatever Brody was doing.

Sean looked at Vanessa. "I want you to get on a secure channel with Captains Martinez and Watkins. We have a situation, and I need them to maintain their positions near the *Diligent*."

Vanessa leaned in so only Sean could hear. "Is it a mutiny?"

"Not yet," Sean replied quietly.

Major Shelton went to the auxiliary workstation and began working.

"Colonel, I have a comlink request from the *Yorktown*. It's Major Brody," Specialist Sansky said.

Sean went to the command chair and sat down. "Put it on the main holoscreen and broadcast the feed to the bridges of the other ships."

A few moments later Major Brody's face appeared, and it looked like he was on the main bridge of the *Yorktown*. "Major Brody, we've attempted to initiate control of the space gate and appear to be locked out. Can you offer any explanation as to why that might be?"

"Colonel Quinn, you've left me no choice but to take control of the space gate. I'll utilize the gate to report in to COMCENT," Major Brody said.

Sean's tone deepened. "Doing so puts you in violation of my direct orders. You will relinquish control of the space gate at once. You are hereby relieved of duty and will surrender to Major McKay's custody," Sean said.

The video feed zoomed out, showing that Major McKay was standing next to Major Brody. Sean caught a glimpse of the back of Oriana's head on the bridge.

"I'm afraid Major McKay and I are in agreement. You are unfit to command the battle group," Major Brody said. "Major Shelton, relieve Colonel Quinn and take command of the *Vigilant*."

The bridge on the *Vigilant* went deadly quiet. "Have both of you lost your minds?" Sean said with a sneer.

"This isn't personal," Brody said. "I'm going to open the space gate now."

Sean stood up and clenched his fist. "If any part of that space gate powers up, I will use the *Vigilant's* weapons systems to take it out."

"And destroy our only means of getting home? I don't think so," Brody replied.

Sean looked at Lieutenant Russo and gave her a nod. A few moments later, there was a commotion on the bridge of the *Yorktown*. "You can't be serious—"

Sean muted communications with the *Yorktown* so they didn't have to listen to Brody.

A message appeared on Sean's internal heads-up display.

Dr. O. Evans: *I can delay him for an hour.*

Sean's gaze darted to Oriana in the background. Brody and McKay had moved over to her and pulled her away from the workstation. Sean clenched his teeth for a moment.

"I've cut off the *Yorktown*," Sean said and addressed the rest of the battle group. "For the rest of you, if you've been pulled into Brody and McKay's foolish effort, it's not too late. The chain of command exists for a reason, and you don't get to question it. My orders stand. As for Lester Brody and Christopher McKay, you have a window of opportunity to do the right thing and surrender yourselves. You have one hour to comply."

Sean cut the comlink to the rest of the battle group. "Major Shelton, you're with me. Lieutenant Russo, you have the con. I'll be in my ready room if you need me. I want to be alerted at the slightest change in the battle group."

Sean left the bridge with Major Shelton. Once they were inside with his office door closed, he looked up at the ceiling. "Gabriel, I'm enacting command protocol blackbird one-two-one-three-two-zero-nine. Ident is Colonel Sean Quinn. Please verify."

"Blackbird protocol is verified. Establishing secure communications network. Online in twenty seconds," Gabriel said.

Major Shelton frowned. "I'm not familiar with this."

"It's not official fleet standard operating procedure. I'll explain in a minute," Sean replied.

His personal holoscreen became active, and Captain Chad Boseman of Spec Ops appeared. "Blackbird status confirmed. What are your orders?"

"I need you to get to the *Yorktown*."

"Mission objective?" Boseman asked.

"There are friendlies mixed with mutineers. We need to take back control of the ship and the space gate," Sean said.

"I can get aboard that ship, no problem."

"Not so fast. They'll be on the lookout for combat shuttles leaving the *Vigilant*," Sean replied.

Boseman smiled. "Who said anything about using combat shuttles?"

Sean smiled and listened to Boseman's plan for storming the *Yorktown*.

"You have less than an hour. I want to minimize the loss of life; however, lethal use of force is authorized against any mutineers," Sean said.

"Understood, Colonel. I'll contact you directly once we're aboard the *Yorktown*," Boseman said.

The comlink went dark, and Major Shelton shot him a questioning look. "Just so I'm clear, Colonel, a secondary function of the Spec Ops platoons aboard CDF ships is to ensure command authority of the officer on board?"

"Not exactly," Sean replied. "It's for the battle group. It's one of those things you try to account for—the risk, I mean—and hope you never have to use," Sean said and shook his head.

"You didn't expect this to happen from Major Brody—Lester Brody that is," Major Shelton said, correcting herself. The moment Sean had declared Brody a mutineer, he'd lost his rank.

Sean shook his head. "I expected better from him."

"What do you need me to do?" Major Shelton asked.

They spent the next few minutes going over the strategy. Sean received check-ins from the other Spec Ops platoons on board the destroyers. The timing had to be succinct, and they needed to wait for Boseman to get aboard the *Yorktown* before they executed the operation. In spite of all their precautions, Sean had to admit that there was an extremely high risk of the situation getting out of control. The fact that Brody and McKay had delayed Oriana and her team meant that they weren't averse to taking hostages.

"What will you do if Brody decides to leverage his assets?" Major Shelton asked. She knew of his relationship with Oriana, despite the assertions that they were "just casual."

"Let's hope it doesn't come to it, but if it does . . ." Sean said and paused for a moment. "There's no negotiating with mutineers. Ever."

Casual, my ass, Sean thought and hated it.

CHAPTER 33

"Dr. Evans," Brody said, "I need to know what you did. More importantly, I need you to undo it," he said, trying to sound calm.

"It can't be undone," Dr. Evans replied.

"That's bullshit," McKay said and turned toward Kent. "Bring up her workstation session. I want to know what commands she used."

Lester noticed that Dr. Evans didn't appear concerned about that, and he was beginning to suspect she was telling the truth. "I thought you wanted to go home."

Dr. Evans regarded him for a moment. "I did, but not like this. I'd never betray Colonel Quinn or the CDF."

Lester sneered. "Don't you mean Sean?"

Dr. Evans met his gaze coolly and didn't reply.

Lester looked at McKay, who shook his head. "She put the gate control systems into a full diagnostic reset. It takes an hour to do. If we interrupt, it simply restarts, picking up right where it left off."

Lester shook his head and sighed. "A flaw in the system. So, we have to wait an hour."

Brody returned to the command chair and activated the secure comlink he'd established to Captains Ward, McGee, and Ingram. "It appears the delay wasn't a bluff."

Captain Ward nodded. "For a few moments, I thought he was really going to take out the space gate."

Lester shook his head. "That was a bluff. All of us need that gate."

"Major Brody," Captain Ida Ingram said, "are you at all worried about what Colonel Quinn will do? He seemed pretty certain he was going to take command—"

The comlink to the *Diligent* went dark. Then, the comlink to the *Babylon* and the *Acheron* went offline as well.

"Lieutenant Harish, can you get them back online?" Lester asked.

"I'm trying, Major, but they're not responding. I'll keep at it," Harish replied.

Lester's gaze swooped toward Dr. Evans, and he stomped over to her. "There has to be a way to stop the diagnostic. It's been thirty minutes. It can be cut short."

"Then by all means, cut it short," Dr. Evans replied, secure in the knowledge that she knew more about the space gate systems than he did.

She was right.

Lester clenched his teeth and growled.

"Major Brody," Lieutenant Harish said, "I have a comlink from the *Vigilant*."

———

"I thought we were done with crazy operations for at least a few days," Sergeant Benton said.

Fifty Spec Ops soldiers in full combat suits were daisy-chained to ten communications drones under Boseman's command.

"You don't like hitching a ride on a comms drone?" Boseman asked. They needed to get to the *Yorktown* as quickly as possible, and Sean had authorized him to be creative with meeting that objective.

"Oh, don't get me wrong, I like a good thrill as much as the next guy, but this is downright dangerous," Sergeant Benton said with just a hint of mock exasperation in his voice.

Boseman heard several of the other soldiers chuckle and joke in return, saying the mission was too dangerous and they wanted to go home. There was no risk of their comms being detected since they were all using line-of-sight communications. They'd been leapfrogging from ship to ship, making their way as quickly as possible to the *Yorktown*. Luckily for them, Trident Battle Group was in a tight formation—as tight a formation as any fleet maintained in space. The *Yorktown* had all its main hangars locked up tight, which Chad had expected.

"All right. Look alive, boys. We're closing in on the target," Boseman said. He marked it, and an indicator appeared on the heads-up displays of each of the soldiers' helmets. They were aiming for a maintenance hatch amidships that would put them between the primary and secondary bridges of the *Yorktown*. The carrier vessel was actually a converted freighter, which made certain construction points less secure than they would have been on a CDF warship. The comms drones slowed their approach as they reached the maintenance hatch.

"Twenty seconds," Corporal Brentworth said and brought up his wrist computer. Even though he couldn't access the main computer systems of the

Yorktown, he could override the door controls while making it appear that the door had remained shut. "We're clear, Captain."

"After you, Sergeant Benton," Boseman said.

Benton went to the hatch and opened it, and then he and five soldiers went inside. There was an empty maintenance corridor beyond. Boseman configured the comms drone they'd hitched a ride on with a quick message back to the *Vigilant.*

"All right, we're going to split up," Boseman said. "We're going to secure the ship, starting with . . ."

———

"I see you've moved on to taking hostages," Sean said.

The officers serving aboard the *Yorktown* were all armed. There was no doubt the bridge was locked down, but Sean knew it wouldn't be enough.

"Everyone here has volunteered," Brody replied.

"Is that a fact?" Sean replied. "They don't look like volunteers to me," he said and glanced pointedly at Oriana. "Some of them may have volunteered in the beginning, but much like you, they're in over their heads."

Earlier, Sean had had Gabriel attempt to gain control of the *Yorktown*'s systems, but that had been unsuccessful.

"We're about to bring the space gate online. Shall I convey anything to COMCENT on your behalf?" Brody asked.

Sean glared at the image on the holoscreen, wishing he could reach through it and choke Lester Brody.

"You're alone, Lester. Right now, my Spec Ops teams have taken control of the ringleaders of your little conspiracy. This farce of a mutiny is over. It would be better for you to surrender."

Brody glared back at him, his eyes full of contempt and hatred. "Like hell I will! You are so self-righteous, as if the great Sean Quinn couldn't be wrong. If you fire your weapons on the space gate, it'll alert the Krake, and then we'll have no choice but to go through it."

A message appeared on Sean's personal holoscreen, and he glanced at it. He typed a response but didn't send it yet, looking back at the main holoscreen on the *Vigilant*'s command bridge. "History will judge whether I'm right or wrong, but what's important right now is that I'm in command"—he sent the message—"and you're finished."

"Colonel," Lieutenant Russo said, "I'm detecting power fluctuations from the space gate. They're bringing it online."

"Acknowledged," Sean replied.

There was shouting from the bridge of the *Yorktown,* followed by several loud concussive blasts as Captain Boseman and the Spec Ops team stormed the bridge. Sean felt acid creep up into his throat, and he kept his mouth clenched shut as he looked down at the message he'd sent Boseman.

Execute the mutineers.

The first mutiny in the brief history of the Colonial Defense Force had come to a bloody end.

CHAPTER 34

Sean powered off the holoscreen at his desk and leaned back in his chair. *A mutiny,* he thought and grimaced, feeling as if the bile in the back of his throat had taken up permanent residence. The whole thing made him sick. He stood up and looked at his hands, wanting to wash them again. All he needed right then was the Krake to attack them. Considering the state of the Trident Battle Group, they'd be hard-pressed to put up a fight, considering that half the senior officers from three destroyers were on their way to the *Vigilant.*

The Spec Ops teams aboard the destroyers had successfully taken control of the bridges without any loss of life. Former CDF Captains Ryan Ward, Olaf McGee, and Ida Ingram, as well as several senior officers and security personnel on their respective ships, had surrendered in the face of heavily armed Spec Ops soldiers.

The armed mutineers on the primary bridge of the *Yorktown* had attempted to hold the bridge by use of force, hoping in vain for the space gate to activate. Lester Brody, Christopher McKay, and half a dozen other bridge officers had been killed, and Sean had just finished filing the report for his official log.

"Colonel Quinn," Gabriel said, "two combat shuttles have just arrived from the *Yorktown* with the mutineers."

"I'm on my way to the main hangar bay," Sean replied.

He walked toward the door and straightened his uniform. Major Shelton met him outside with a squad of CDF soldiers behind her. He'd gotten back control of Trident Battle Group, but the cost had been high. How could he have been so wrong about Brody? Lester had been his XO for the entire battle group.

"I want you to do a complete shakedown of the *Yorktown's* crew. We need to identify anyone else who was involved," Sean said.

"Understood, Colonel," Major Shelton said. "I just finished Captain Boseman's report. There were civilian mutineers as well who attempted to hold the bridge."

Sean couldn't keep the bitterness from his voice. "If we discover any other civilian mutineers, they'll be taken into custody and held for trial when we get back."

"Permission to speak freely, Colonel."

They walked down the quiet corridor. "Go ahead."

"For the record, I believe you did the right thing. The chain of command must be preserved; however, we now have a demoralized crew with junior officers who're going to have to function in senior posts," Major Shelton said.

"Thank you for that," Sean replied. "If I could clone you and have you command those destroyers, I would. The junior officers are simply going to have to grow up faster than we'd originally intended, but I see your point. We're going to have to do a full review and maybe shuffle some people around. If you have any recommendations, send them over to me and we can discuss it. You're now second-in-command of Trident Battle Group, and I'll be relying on you more than ever."

Major Shelton considered his words for a moment, her intelligent brown eyes appearing a shade lighter than her dark skin. "I won't let you down. We'll get them past this."

"The mutiny is finished, but as the commanding officer in charge, I need to review my actions and see if there was a way all this could've been avoided. I want you to think about that when you write your own report. The CDF brass will review the reports to look for an honest accounting of events, and I encourage you to point out any faults you see with how things were handled."

Major Shelton frowned and then straightened her shoulders. "Understood, Colonel," she said and meant it. "Brody sowed dissension in the ranks, and that's unforgivable in an officer, but this is going to take some time to overcome. Soldiers need to obey without question; however, given our circumstances, I believe they must also have hope, or they'll fail to perform their duties. I'm not saying we should share our reasons for the decisions we make, but perhaps we can do a better job of keeping the crew informed."

Sean thought he'd already been keeping the crew informed. What more did they want? The attitude of the crew was a reflection of its leadership, and Sean needed to salvage Trident Battle Group's remaining senior officers— build them up so they could keep the crew in line.

They reached the door to the main hangar and Sean stopped. "Major Shelton, I'm lucky to have you serving under my command. I can't think of a higher compliment than that."

Major Shelton stood up straight and saluted him. "Colonel Quinn, the honor is all mine."

Sean stepped through the threshold onto the main hangar bay floor where two squads of CDF soldiers surrounded the combat shuttle. He gave a curt nod to the lieutenant, and the soldiers escorted the mutineers off the shuttle. They had their hands bound in front of them, and hardly any of them dared to meet Sean's gaze. The civilians who'd participated in the mutiny had been separated from the others and stood off to the side. They would bear witness to what was about to happen. Sean spared a brief glance at Oriana as she walked off the shuttle, and his mouth went dry. He could tell there was a lot she wanted to say, but she couldn't right then.

The rest of the mutineers were lined up just outside the airlock doors. Over fifty soldiers had been implicated in the attempted mutiny, from senior bridge officers to engineering crew. Armed CDF soldiers fanned out on either side of Sean, holding their weapons at the ready but not pointing them at the mutineers. Three destroyer captains, as well as their first lieutenants, stood with slumped shoulders. Some of them glanced at him, hoping for some kind of leniency.

Sean stepped closer to them, glaring. "Mutineers," he said, "each of you has dishonored the oath you swore when you put on the uniform. That oath represents a commitment to duty and honor to the Colonial Defense Force —a cause greater than yourselves."

"Colonel Quinn," Ida Ingram cried out, "we're sorry. Please, we were coerced by Major Brody. It was Ward and McGee who came to me. I just want to go home."

The rest of what she'd been about to say died on her lips. Sean looked at Ryan Ward and Olaf McGee. They'd been good men, but now they stared defiantly back at him.

Sean looked at Ingram. "You were in command of a CDF warship. You don't get coerced into anything. You follow the orders of your commanding officer, and you execute those orders to the best of your ability—neither of which you did," Sean said, sweeping his gaze across all of them. "Do you know the difference between a mutineer and a prisoner?"

Ingram looked away from him, and Sean glared at the others. The knowledge of what was about to happen was reflected in both Ward's and McGee's pallid faces. Some of their subordinates began to shift their feet.

"A prisoner has rights," Sean said and gestured toward the CDF soldiers. A klaxon alarm blared as the airlock doors opened to the inner chamber. "Mutineers do not."

The soldiers forced the mutineers into the inner chamber of the airlock, and the door shut. Sean saw panic ensue, along with muffled cries for mercy. He walked over to the door controls and looked through the airlock window. Several of the mutineers banged on the window, begging to be let back onto the ship. But not all of them. There was a defiant few who, whether through false bravado or sheer stupidity, refused to accept the inevitable. Sean slammed his palm on the exterior airlock door controls, and the mutineers were sucked into the vacuum of space.

He stood there for a few moments, watching until the last body disappeared from view. It had been over in seconds, but he'd keep seeing their deaths for a long time.

Sean closed the exterior airlock doors and turned around. The soldiers on the hangar bay floor saluted, and he returned it, forcing his queasy stomach into submission. It wasn't the first time he'd killed, but there was a big difference between killing an enemy and executing people who'd once been comrades. He hated the coldness he felt inside.

He came to stand before the civilian mutineers, and several of them flinched at his approach. "You are all prisoners and will be held until we return to New Earth. Remember what happened to the mutineers. If any of you ever feel the urge to complain about your treatment, I want you to think about the people who were just in that airlock," Sean said, gesturing behind him.

None of the prisoners would look at him as they were escorted out of the main hangar bay to the holding cells.

Sean headed back toward the bridge. Once off the main hangar deck, he leaned against the wall and swallowed several mouthfuls of air. He wanted to scream with rage that Brody hadn't been taken into custody so Sean could deliver the justice he deserved. But it wouldn't have been justice where Brody was concerned; it would have been vengeance. Sean hated that somehow this mutiny was a reflection of his own actions, that he'd contributed to this mess and didn't know what he should change to avoid it in the future. But perhaps there was nothing he could have done to avoid it. He would never apologize or regret the orders he'd given. He believed wholeheartedly in what had to be done, but he felt a knot weighing down his stomach at the thought that this dark business had only just begun.

"Colonel Quinn," Gabriel said, the ship's AI's voice coming through the speaker in the corridor. "There are three hours remaining until the first set of Krake coordinates is to be followed."

Sean walked down the long corridor. "Understood, Gabriel."

Sean went into his office near the main bridge, intending to splash some cold water on his face, but when he walked in, he saw that Oriana was there waiting for him. He stepped inside and the door shut.

Her shoulders were drawn up tight, and she looked at him. "You killed them," she said.

"I did," Sean answered, not offering anything more than that. He hated how she was looking at him, and he felt a small urge to justify what he'd done, but it didn't last longer than a few seconds. If Oriana was going to be with him, she had to know and accept him for everything he was.

"I'm sorry you were caught up in this," Sean said.

"He tried to use me as a bargaining piece to get to you," Oriana said.

"I know," he said quietly. He wanted to reach out to her, but he didn't know how she'd react.

Oriana looked away from him. Her eyes were red. "They took us prisoner. Me and my team. Is this how it's going to be?"

Sean swallowed hard. "No, this never should have happened. Brody was desperate, but maybe it would be better if we didn't spend so much time together."

Oriana winced and looked away from him. "Our casual relationship," she said, and he abhorred how it sounded.

"It was never casual. I think we can admit that now," Sean said.

Oriana looked at him. She was angry, hurt, and scared, but she also cared about him. He could see it in her eyes, but something was holding her back. She must think he was a monster.

"I need to get to the bridge. You can stay here as long as you need to," Sean said and stepped back toward the door.

"No, don't go," Oriana said quickly and stepped closer to him. "I'm not that fragile," she said with a bit of steel in her voice. "I'm just not used to . . . this."

Sean stepped toward her. "No one should be used to this. It was a nightmare."

"It doesn't have to be," Oriana said, and reaching out, she took Sean's hand in her own. "No one should get in the way of us."

Sean pulled her into his arms, and they were quiet for a few moments. He wanted to stay there like that, but he couldn't.

He left his office, and Oriana followed him.

Sean stopped just before the bridge. "Are you sure you're all right?"

"I'm furious, but that doesn't mean I want to go somewhere and sulk," Oriana replied.

"That makes two of us," Sean said.

CHAPTER 35

The troop carrier left Camp Alpha. Connor leaned back in his chair and rubbed his hands over his face, taking a few deep breaths and sighing.

Dash cleared his throat. "I'm starting to feel a little outnumbered here. I think I'm the only civilian on this ship."

The prisoners were being taken to the CDF base at Sanctuary.

Connor shrugged and didn't say anything.

"I'm a little surprised you let me tag along," Dash said.

"You're an official witness, and Noah wanted to be alone with Lars," Connor said.

When Lars had offered a confession, Connor thought he'd had a good idea of who was involved. He'd been mostly right, but almost as surprising as who *was* involved were the people he'd suspected who *weren't* involved at all.

"So, what happens now?" Dash asked.

"That's a bit vague, don't you think?" Connor said and smiled a little. "What happens now?" he repeated. "We're going to upset the natural balance of the entire colony. Or at least its leadership."

"I understand that, but how do we do it?"

Connor chuckled. "You think I know? I wish I did. I really do," he said soberly.

Samson joined them. "We should reach Sierra soon."

Connor nodded. "I sent a message to Damon Mills. He'll be showing up with Field Ops security agents, but first I want to talk to them."

"They're too smart to confess, but I don't know so much about that stuff. I'll make sure they don't get away," Samson said and left them.

Connor had sent a message to Franklin Mallory that they had his son in custody. It was a simple and straight-to-the-point message. Mallory had sent a quick acknowledgment.

The troop carrier made a temporary stop over the colonial government building, and Connor and a squad of soldiers deplaned. Dash walked by his side.

Carl Flint, in civilian clothing, met him along the way to the offices of the Colonial Intelligence Bureau. "I'm sure glad to see you, General."

Connor arched an eyebrow at him. The entire corridor was filled with Spec Ops soldiers, but they were all dressed in civilian clothing. Officially, they weren't CDF soldiers at the moment; they were merely concerned citizens who had a right to make their voices heard to the colonial government. Connor had no doubt that Dana Wolf would see right through it, as would a lot of other people.

A few CIB agents attempted to forestall Connor's advance, but it was short-lived.

He strode to Meredith Cain's office and opened the door. Governor Wolf was inside, as well as Kurt Johnson.

"Just the people I wanted to see," Connor said and walked inside. Dash followed him in, and everyone else waited outside. "Damon Mills will be here shortly."

"Connor," Governor Wolf said, "there have been a number of alarming allegations regarding CDF special forces in Sierra."

"I don't doubt it, Governor. They're here on my orders," Connor said.

Governor Wolf glanced at the others for a few moments and then looked back at Connor. "Are you conducting a coup?"

Connor shook his head. "Never," he said. "I had to act quickly and positioned my people to prevent the escape of any of the conspirators," Connor said, glancing at Meredith Cain and Kurt Johnson.

Johnson harrumphed. "You can't be serious. There is no evidence to support this."

"Interesting you should say that because I have Lars Mallory and about seventy-five other people in custody right now. Most have given video testimony as to what they've been up to over the past year," Connor said and looked at Meredith Cain.

She smiled back at him. "Good work. You've finally found the terrorists. But all your so-called evidence is hearsay. You're not authorized by the colonial government to take anyone into custody."

Connor glanced at the governor for a moment and then looked back at Meredith Cain. "Does the governor know? Does she know you ordered the operation that put her daughter's life in jeopardy? The operations that endangered the lives of colonists, all so the alliance with the Ovarrow would fail?"

Meredith remained unperturbed by the accusation. "I'm still waiting to see evidence."

"You'll see a lot of evidence. If one thing can be said about Lars Mallory, it's that he was very well trained. He's very thorough when he puts his mind on a task. He believed in your initial cause, and he told me how you, in particular, recruited him. Protect the colony. Be able to do the things that no one else can. Does any of that sound familiar? But where you faltered was when you began seeing colonists as pawns. What was the plan? Expend a few lives here and there? Ignite fury against the Ovarrow?" Connor said.

"I believe *you* went to the Ovarrow city with a battalion of soldiers and took control of the disaster area. *You* entered into a military conflict with the very people you wanted to form an alliance with. I didn't do any of that," Meredith Cain said.

"He didn't say you did any of that," Dana said, "but you could've orchestrated events to move pieces around. Is this true?" she asked Connor.

"Lars Mallory surrendered. He told us everything. I've transferred all those files to your office so you can review them with Selena Brown and Rex Coleman for legal review," Connor said.

Meredith Cain laughed. "Now you want to use the legislative and judicial branches of our government, right after your reckless abuse of power. There've been reports in Sierra, New Haven, and Delphi of people being taken into custody."

"By Field Ops, not the CDF."

"At the behest of the CDF. They arrested Mayor Clinton Edwards in Delphi," Meredith said.

"I know, and now it's your turn."

"You can't arrest me," Meredith said. "When are you going to accept that the Ovarrow can't help us? The only thing they can tell us is how they were defeated by the Krake. Why don't you run along until I'm ready to use you and the rest of the CDF for your real purpose?"

"That's enough, Meredith," Governor Wolf said. "There's going to be an accounting here. And, in fact, I'm going to leverage the investigative arm of my office, the CDF, and Field Ops and Security to identify everyone involved in this monstrosity."

Damon Mills showed up with several Field Ops agents as Meredith Cain rose to her feet. "You can't undo what I've begun," she said, sneering at Connor. "Your precious alliance is going to fail. The Ovarrow will never trust us now, and the colony will never trust them."

Connor regarded her for a few moments. "We'll see," he said.

The security agents escorted Meredith Cain, and Kurt Johnson shouted in surprise when they took him into custody. He thought he hadn't been caught.

Connor was alone with Governor Wolf. She rubbed her eyes for a moment and then looked at Connor. "Since I'm not one of the people being arrested, I assume you found no evidence to implicate me. What about Bob Mullins?"

Bob Mullins was Dana's other advisor, and Connor didn't like the man at all. "He's clean, as far as I know. I would've let you in on the investigation, but everyone involved was part of the system, and there was no way I could communicate what needed to happen without alerting them. That's why I had Spec Ops soldiers here in plain clothes. Their orders were to provide observation and intelligence to Field Ops."

Dana regarded him for a few moments. "I know you really believe that. Your intentions were well placed, but Connor, this is a serious abuse of power. *Your* power, I might add. Regardless of your intentions, you conducted a military operation here in Sierra and the other cities. Good intentions aren't enough justification for breaking the law."

Connor had been expecting this. "I know. I knew it when I gave the orders, and I know it now."

"And you did it anyway," she said.

"It was necessary. It had to be done, regardless of what comes next."

Dana shook her head. "I don't know what's going to happen."

"Neither do I, and maybe that's a good thing," Connor replied.

Dana frowned for a moment. "Are you talking about what happened here or with the Ovarrow?"

"Both, but I'd recommend that we return the Ovarrow prisoners to the warlord and high commissioner, as well as admit our role in what's been happening. It might kill any chance of an alliance, but they also might respect honesty," Connor said.

"Perhaps, but we still don't know which of the Ovarrow we can trust. They have their own rogue groups among them."

"We do have other options. There are other avenues we can pursue, but not until all this is sorted out," Connor said.

"They might call for both our resignations," Dana said. "Right now, I'll need a replacement to take over the Colonial Intelligence Bureau. There's been abuse of power all around."

Connor didn't know what to say. She was right. He'd acted in accordance with what he thought was the best way to protect the colony. Meredith Cain had been gathering power, but she'd had the same convictions.

"I'll comply with whatever the Colonial Defense Committee deems appropriate," Connor said.

"Haven't you learned? News of this will get out, as it should, but it's the ideas that are dangerous. They'll see what you've done and what I've allowed to happen, and then plan accordingly. I really don't know where we go from here," Dana said.

"We keep things running, and we keep doing what we can to protect our homes."

"Until the next crisis, you mean," Dana said dryly. "Don't answer that, but I do have to ask. Lars Mallory, the intel he provided . . ."

"He has evidence, too. I'm not going to lie to you—this is going to hurt us. There were a lot of people involved, and a lot is going to change as a result," Connor said.

"I was afraid that was the case," Dana said and gave Meredith Cain's office a cursory glance. "I trusted Meredith. I had no idea what she and Kurt were up to," she said and looked at Connor. "I allowed this to happen."

Connor returned her gaze. He knew what it took to lead, and Dana needed time to confront the abuse of power that had occurred under her stewardship as governor. None of the evidence Lars had provided led to her, and Connor was grateful for that. Otherwise, the rift that divided the colony would be much worse.

"How would you fix this?" she asked.

"We need to figure out exactly what's broken, and we need to understand how and why their recruitment methods worked so well. I've known Lars for a long time, and I can tell you that he believed in what he was doing. The brutality of what he did to the Ovarrow is something that has changed him more than he realizes," Connor said, pausing for a moment. "I would advocate for going public with the whole thing and putting forward a strong, decisive stance. We either form an alliance with the Ovarrow or we don't, but we can't do our jobs at the whim of popular opinion."

Governor Wolf smiled a little. "Thank you for that. Sometimes I wonder what kind of governor you'd be."

Connor chuckled and shook his head. "My brief time as mayor of Sanctuary was enough."

"Who would you nominate to head the Colonial Intelligence Bureau?" she asked.

Connor frowned in thought. Dana was already looking ahead, thinking of the work that had to be done. "I'm not sure, to be honest. The people I've recruited for CDF Intel need to have an analytical mind and be capable of following the facts, but they also need to be capable of logical leaps. Whoever gets the job from here on out will require oversight from your office."

Dana nodded. "So, you're not interested in the job then."

"I have a job."

Dana gave a slight nod. "Technically, I'm your boss, and I'd just be giving you more work to do."

Connor couldn't argue with that. Instead, he said, "There would be a lot of objections if you turned the CIB over to the CDF."

"I'm not turning it over to the CDF per se. You said before that oversight is needed, and I think you're right. What I have in mind is a partnership within the CIB."

"A partnership by whom?" Connor asked. He had enough to do. Why was the governor looking at him that way?

"The CIB needs representation from the CDF, and that's where you come in, but also from Field Ops, as well as from someone appointed by the defense committee."

"The defense committee," Connor said, thinking out loud. Then he understood. "You're giving them a stake in the future of the CIB while also doling out the responsibility. I hadn't thought of that."

Dana arched an eyebrow toward him. "Are you sure you wouldn't want to be the next governor? Don't answer that. Each group would have their support staffs, but in order for the CIB to be truly effective, we'd have to mix them up a bit."

Connor was impressed by the alacrity with which the governor threw herself at solving problems. It reminded him of Lenora. He'd known there were going to be a lot of changes in the way the colony was organized, but he hadn't expected the CDF to be affected all that much. Now, he was beginning to suspect he'd been wrong about that.

CHAPTER 36

Camp Alpha was a buzz of activity. There were over fifty large storage crates full of Ovarrow equipment the CDF had brought back from the base of operations where Lars had surrendered. They'd nursed the Ovarrow prisoners back to health, and with their help, they'd identified equipment and even some vehicles the Ovarrow could restore to full operation.

Connor watched Dash and Lenora check the storage containers, along with the last Ovarrow at Camp Alpha. Trust was slow in coming, and he hoped relations with the Ovarrow would improve over time.

A C-cat landed nearby, and Franklin Mallory stepped off the loading ramp. He glanced around and walked over to Connor.

"This is quite an operation you've got going on here," Franklin said.

"It's an olive branch. We were always going to release the prisoners. Why not also deliver some of the equipment we found? It'll give the Ovarrow a little bit more independence, which I think they'll appreciate," Connor replied.

"After they accept the fact that they wouldn't have had the equipment without our help."

"Everyone needs help sometimes," Connor said.

Neither of them spoke while they watched the storage crates being loaded. Connor knew Franklin hadn't come there to discuss the Ovarrow, but what could he say to the father of the person he'd almost had to kill? Lars had saved CDF lives by stopping Colton Evans from triggering the explosives he'd hidden in the caves. There were lines that even Lars wouldn't cross. There would be some people who'd view Lars's actions as self-serving. He'd been caught, and every action he took from that point on would come under intense scrutiny. Connor wanted to believe Lars had done it because he genuinely didn't want the blood of colonists on his hands. But how Lars could brutalize the Ovarrow and yet be stalwart about protecting colonists was a sticking point. It had changed him, but it had changed people like Colton Evans even more. Objectives and beliefs had become more important than the means by which they achieved those goals. As a veteran, Connor had seen both the best and the worst in people. Some people embraced becoming a monster and the allure of power through violent means. Others glimpsed the monster in themselves and came to a breaking point where they decided who they were going to be.

"You're probably wondering why I'm here, so I'm going to cut to the chase," Franklin said. "The colony's first prison is being built in Delphi. Lars and most of the other conspirators are going to be held there until the trials start."

"I'm sorry, Franklin. I know this can't be easy."

Franklin shook his head in derision. "No, it's not, but at least I'll have access to my son. I'm going to try to help him."

Connor nodded, not knowing what to say. What could he say to someone whose child he'd almost killed? He could see it in Franklin's eyes as well, the knowledge of what had almost happened. "Noah never gave up on him."

"I know," Franklin said. "Talk about a test of friendship. Noah is something else. I know what you almost—had to do."

Connor was quiet for a few moments. "I'm glad I didn't have to."

"I'm glad you didn't either, but if it had come down to it, you would've been right. As much as I hate to admit it, you would've been right."

Connor's throat thickened. "I would've hated myself afterwards."

Franklin nodded, a hardened glint in his eyes. "I would've hated you, too." He was quiet for a few moments and then shook his head. "I had an interesting conversation with Noah's wife. She's a remarkable woman. She's a little mad at you, but . . ."

"I can hardly blame her. I almost lost Lenora, but Kara had to contend with that reality while Noah was in a coma for almost a year."

"Yeah, that must've been tough. She'll never forgive Lars, and I honestly don't blame her. But she did tell me something Noah said to her, and it's been on my mind."

Connor's eyebrows raised. "She spoke to you?"

"Not exactly. She sent me a message. She tried to stop Noah from going with you, and Noah told her something I can't get out of my head. I keep mulling it over."

Noah was still recovering from his coma. Sometimes he was like his old self, but other times he struggled. He'd lose his train of thought midsentence, seemingly at random. Connor hated watching him struggle, but there was nothing he could do about it.

"What did he say?" Connor asked.

"They were arguing about Lars, and he said that it's the times when you're alone and you've crossed the line a little bit that you need your friends and family the most." Franklin's voice sounded hoarse and his eyes welled up. He blew out a breath and wiped away the tears. "I don't know if Lars realizes how lucky he is to have a friend like that."

Connor drew in a deep breath and exhaled. "He's one of the good ones."

Franklin nodded. "You've got that right. I figure that after all he's been through, the fact that he can still find it in his heart to try and help not just my son but another human being is remarkable. You can't teach that kind of integrity. I figured if he could do that, then who am I not to do the same?" he said and extended his hand toward Connor.

Connor's eyes tightened and he shook Franklin's hand firmly. They separated and Connor swallowed hard. The tension left his shoulders and he felt a sudden lightness, as if he'd been weighed down by guilt and hadn't realized it.

"I keep wondering if I did something wrong when I raised Lars."

"You've been a father a lot longer than I have. I don't think it's anything you did or didn't do. Lars made his own choices."

"And we get to try and help them when they stumble. I get it," Franklin said.

"If you wouldn't mind, I'd like to come to Delphi and check in on Lars from time to time," Connor said.

Franklin swallowed. "I think that would be good."

———

Franklin left and Connor walked over to Lenora.

"I saw you two were talking, so I thought I'd give you some space," Lenora said.

"Thanks. I appreciate it."

Dash and Darius Cohen joined them.

"It looks like we're ready to go," Connor said.

"I think they'll appreciate the gesture," Darius said.

"I hope it does more than that," Lenora replied. "At least this way we can set the record straight. How do you think the Ovarrow will react to the evidence that some of their own people were involved in sabotaging the support structure for the bridge?"

"They won't deny it, and I think they'll work very hard to find whoever was involved," Connor said.

Lenora frowned thoughtfully. "Do you think they'll find whoever it was?"

"I don't know," Connor replied.

"Regardless," Darius said, "we'll leave them with a way to contact us if they want to, but what do you think about an invitation to some of the Ovarrow to visit Sierra?"

"It won't be easy, but it's necessary," Connor said. "I told Governor Wolf it would be in everyone's best interest if she took a firm stance on the whole thing. She took that advice and then went above and beyond it."

Over the last week, Connor had come to appreciate just how shrewd of a leader Governor Wolf actually was. She worked with renewed vigor, and Connor could do no less. He shared a look with Lenora and smiled.

They headed toward their ship, and Connor saw Samson watching them. He was grim-faced and alert, a soldier standing the watch to his core. Connor nodded toward him and Samson did the same. Their work wasn't finished yet.

HARBINGER

CHAPTER 1

Thick drops of rain pelted the rover as a sudden thunderstorm rolled in, and rivulets of water streamed across the windshield before a low-powered shield engaged. As the shield pulsed, clearing Connor's view, a notification chimed and then popped into existence on the rover's holoscreen. Connor glanced over and then quickly dismissed it.

He heard Samson clear his throat from the passenger seat. "I don't think you're going to make that Security Council meeting," Samson said.

"Nathan will be there," Connor replied.

They were driving along a rough path thirty kilometers from Sanctuary. The rover was more than up to the task of navigating the rugged terrain, but Samson was right; they weren't going to get anywhere quickly.

Samson arched a thick eyebrow and remained quiet. Connor was glad his friend had rejoined the colony, but he'd noticed that Samson was still prone to long bouts of silence. The only exception to that was when he was commanding his own Spec Ops platoon on a mission; however, when not on task, he was quietly reserved.

"This is just as important," Connor replied.

Samson made a show of glancing out the windows at the surrounding forest, looking unconvinced. "What are we doing way out here, and why take a rover?"

"I thought you of all people could appreciate a short trip away from the hustle and bustle of city life, even one like Sanctuary."

"Yeah, right," Samson said and shook his head. "Don't tell me then."

"Will anybody who's grumpy today please raise their hand? You didn't have to come, you know."

"Right now, I'm wishing I didn't," Samson said and glanced at the HUD overlay that refreshed with a flashing waypoint. "Since when is there a Recovery Institute building way out here?"

"Only the past few months. It's just one HAB unit and a bit of a work area."

"Who's it for?"

"His name is John Rollins," Connor said, and Samson frowned. "You've never met him. He was left behind in an alternate universe and became a prisoner of the Krake. When we found him, he was starving and on the verge of losing his mind."

"I've heard the name before and read the mission reports."

Connor gripped the rover steering wheel firmly. "It was bad. The atmosphere was slowly poisoning him, and I don't know how he survived. We all thought he was dead."

Samson nodded. He was a career soldier from Connor's old Ghost Platoon before they'd been shanghaied into the colony. "What's he doing way out here?"

"Hopefully, getting better."

"Are you telling me the doctors recommended seclusion as some kind of therapy to deal with what this guy went through?"

"Rollins asked for this. He had a rough time during the Vemus War and . . . let's just say he's not a people person. He's being monitored and has regular visits from the staff at the Recovery Institute, but he prefers to be alone. Part of this arrangement requires him to return to Sanctuary at least once a month."

They were both quiet for a few minutes.

"Why do you do this?" Samson asked.

"What do you mean?"

"You make it personal."

"I left him behind."

"You just said you thought he was dead."

Connor was quiet. "I'm just checking up on an old friend."

"Were you friends?"

"What's with the third degree? What's your problem?" Connor asked.

"My problem is that you're allowing yourself to be pulled in a bunch of different directions, and we can't afford that right now. This is a distraction. You brought me back to help you prepare for the Krake, and I'm just doing my job by pointing that out."

Connor kept driving. Samson could believe whatever he wanted. The truth was that Connor did sometimes make things personal, and he cared about what had happened to Rollins, but that wasn't the only reason he was there.

Connor gave Samson a flat look, and Samson blew out a breath. "You almost had me going."

"I knew you'd get there eventually. Rollins has had the most interaction with the Krake. I'm hoping he'll remember something we can use," Connor said.

He felt terrible about leaving Rollins behind, but they'd thought he was dead and hadn't had any time to do a thorough check. They'd had to flee the Krake military base and were lucky to get out alive. This was before Connor had rejoined the Colonial Defense Force, ending his early retirement.

They entered the campsite amid a few HAB units intended for long-term use away from any of the colonial cities. They were popular with the forward operating research bases that were still in use. Connor powered off the rover, and they stepped outside.

Rollins had been a combat engineer and liked to work with his hands, so Connor wasn't surprised to find a small warehouse with its doors open and lights on inside. Off to one side was a line of agricultural-type robots that were either in need of repair or just a basic maintenance cycle. Rollins had agreed to provide this service to help offset the resources required to maintain his living space way out here.

Connor called out for Rollins, and some of the machinery he could hear running from around the corner stopped. A lean man stepped out. He was wearing an apron with several tools in the pockets. His hands were dirty, and he had a few smudges on his cheeks, but Rollins looked much healthier than he used to. He'd regained some of the weight he'd lost from almost starving to death, but he was a long way from healed.

Rollins jutted his chin up once in an acknowledgment, glancing at Samson and then back at Connor. "I see you brought company this time." He turned back around the corner to the work area and put down the piece he'd been cleaning.

"I can have him wait with the rover if you want," Connor offered. The thunderstorm continued to rage outside. They were in the middle of a downpour, but it was a short walk to the rover and Connor knew the rain wouldn't bother Samson at all.

Rollins returned without the apron or the part he'd been carrying and glanced at the ground. "I know it shouldn't bother me," he said and then gritted his teeth. He looked at Connor. "He can stay."

"Thanks," Connor replied.

Rollins walked over to one of the workbenches and leaned back against it. Connor recognized that it was a strategic location that wouldn't allow anyone to approach Rollins from behind, as well as giving him a view of the entire area.

"I heard you were in trouble," Rollins said.

Connor's face reflected his surprise. "Is that so?"

"It's been all over the newsfeeds. I do check on them from time to time. The doctors are afraid I'll lose touch," Rollins said, shaking his head.

Connor glanced around the workshop. "It looks like you're keeping busy out here."

"It helps if I keep moving," Rollins replied.

"Well, you don't need to stop on my account. What are you working on?"

Rollins glanced toward his work area, and Connor followed his gaze. A standard Field Ops motion scanner was disassembled, the parts strewn across the workbench.

Rollins pressed his lips together, looking as if he was deciding whether to let Connor in on a secret he'd been keeping. Then he shrugged. "I was tweaking the detection capability of the scanner assembly."

Connor approached the workbench. "What are you trying to do with it?"

"They're preconfigured to look for things like ryklars or berwolves or any other predators we have in the area. I wanted to rotate the profiler to scan for something different. Almost like a general predator profile."

Connor pursed his lips in thought for a moment. "Easier said than done. Are you getting inundated with false-positive readings?"

"I was, but I was able to get around that by having it use a standard field survey set of protocols—you know, the ones Field Ops uses to survey the region. Instead of just flagging a species as unknown and waiting for someone to catalog it, I'm having it make a guess as to whether it's a predator or not," Rollins said.

What Rollins was describing was no easy feat. There was no way he could do this on his own, which meant he was working with somebody. This was a good thing.

"I had some help," Rollins said, rubbing at an imaginary piece of dirt on his workbench.

"Who's helping you?"

"Lockwood. He's been sending me software updates based on the changes I've been making to the drone. And don't look so surprised. The kid sent me a message a month ago asking how I was doing. He's grown up a lot," Rollins said.

Connor nodded. Rollins had an abrasive personality, and Connor remembered Rollins first meeting Lockwood almost two years ago when they'd stumbled upon the Ovarrow stasis pods. It was hard to believe it had been that long.

"He's one of the good ones," Connor agreed. "I'm glad you're keeping busy."

He could see why Rollins would take on a project like this. He'd spent months surviving, not knowing whether he was going to live or die in one of the harshest environments imaginable.

Rollins looked away from him and his shoulders rounded. "You want to know if I remember anything else."

Connor knew Rollins's recovery had been extremely difficult. The doctors had described his condition as an almost complete breakdown of conscious thought, more or less as if the man had been in a permanent mode of fight or flight. Connor had seen this behavior before in other soldiers he'd known—the ones who were broken inside but wouldn't let themselves quit.

"I wish I didn't have to," Connor said.

"You certainly gave me enough time. The Krake really didn't know what to do with me. After the bomb went off, things just fell apart. I managed to escape with the help of the other prisoners. They either let us go or they just didn't care anymore. Hell, they knew we were going to die anyway, so why waste the ammo?" Rollins said.

Connor grimaced. He planted that bomb when they'd gone back through the archway. It had been intended as a trap for the Krake.

"Now, don't go being like that. I'm glad you bombed those bastards. I would've done the same thing. They left some of their own behind."

Connor frowned. "They left other Krake behind?"

Rollins's bushy eyebrows pulled together and he nodded. "They all just killed themselves once the ships were gone. There were eight or nine of them, and they just . . ." Rollins said and squeezed his eyes shut. "They could have survived. I don't understand why they did that. Several of the Ovarrow did the same thing later on, and they might've been the lucky ones. There was a lot of fighting for resources. I stayed alive by staying away from the group and moving around at night, at least before those creatures started showing up."

Connor remembered the strange predators they'd fought. Their bioluminescent fur glowed red when they were about to attack. They were fearsome creatures whose claws could tear through CDF combat suits.

"I tried to make my way to where we'd come through the archway, but it was too dangerous. It took me . . . I don't know how long for sure. Maybe a week or two to gather the components to transmit a distress signal. I had to cannibalize my own PDA to make it work. Everything after that was just . . . surviving, scavenging for something to eat. Nothing tasted right, and the air burned my lungs. They have me sleeping with a regulator now, which is supposed to help with the pain, but it still hurts to breathe sometimes, especially if I work too hard. I wish there was more I could tell you. I wish I could tell you something so you could go hit them where they live. They knew we were alive down there, trying to survive, and they sent those creatures down. Who does that to prisoners? If I knew something that could help you hurt them, I'd tell you. Hell, I'd volunteer to help you."

"I know you would, but you've done enough, John. Let someone else do it."

Rollins inhaled deeply and sighed. "The sleep regulators are supposed to help me rest. I wish they could stop me from dreaming, but they don't make medicine for that."

"Are you sure you're all right out here? I know you want to be alone, but sometimes it might help to be around people," Connor said.

Rollins shook his head. "Based on what I'm reading in the newsfeeds, there's been quite the upheaval. Government officials are being arrested. A rogue group was torturing the Ovarrow. Then *you* are, front and center. They're claiming you abused your power as a CDF general."

"I did what had to be done. Now I'll need to answer for it," Connor replied.

Rollins snorted bitterly. "Sometimes people don't like to take their medicine. Sure, they're upset with what you did, but I bet the alternative would've been worse. I suppose you'll tell them to learn from it, but what's to stop them from making you their scapegoat?"

Connor could always count on rigid honesty from Rollins. "They need me, and they know it. At least, the right people know it."

Rollins nodded and then his eyes glittered as if he'd just remembered something. "The Krake came back to the planet two times. First, they were assessing the damage. Then the second time, they unleashed those creatures on us. After that, they never returned. The question you can ask the Security Council is: what happens if the Krake were to come here and start dumping those creatures on New Earth, wreaking havoc in the cities?"

Connor nodded grimly. "That's exactly what I intend to tell them. If you need anything at all, Rollins, you know how to contact me. If I'm not around, you can contact Diaz. He's pretty much at Sanctuary all the time."

Rollins shook his head. "That guy hated me."

"He didn't hate you. He thought you were a pain in the ass, which is the truth. You *are* a pain in the ass," Connor said, and Rollins nodded. "Seriously, he'd help you if you needed it."

Connor and Samson went back to the rover, and Samson was quiet as they drove away.

"I brought you along because you're the only one I know who's lived on his own away from everyone else for that long," Connor said.

"I lived away from the colony, but I was here on New Earth. I didn't survive on some kind of prison planet. I don't know if I could help him at all," Samson said.

Connor doubted that. Samson had lived apart from the colony for about eight years. The man had had that long to explore the continent, contending with all the creatures that called New Earth home, using only the barest survival skills. Connor knew Samson would think about Rollins and come up with some way to help the man in the future, even if he didn't think he could now. Connor couldn't do everything himself, and maybe he could hit two birds with one stone.

CHAPTER 2

Connor looked out the window of the combat shuttle as it sped across the continent. New Earth's rings stretched from horizon to horizon in pale marble ribbons. He'd gotten used to the view and sometimes had trouble remembering the view of the sky back on what was now referred to as Old Earth. The colonists kept the memory of Old Earth alive through museums and tributes to the fallen, but Connor doubted they'd ever forget the birthplace of humanity, although because the colonial population had doubled, there was a significant increase in the younger generation who would only know New Earth as their home. They'd either been born here or were brought out of stasis at such a young age that they might as well have been born here.

He remembered the first time he'd seen New Earth and its rings. He'd been aboard the *Ark* and had just been brought out of stasis. He'd thought the whole thing was an elaborate hoax, but he'd been wrong. Ending up here wasn't anything he could've imagined. The journey to New Earth had taken over two hundred years, and everything he'd known before was gone.

The combat shuttle didn't actually have any windows since they were structural weaknesses that didn't belong on a combat ship. Sensors and cameras created the images that appeared on the holoscreens. The New Earth landscape stretched out away from them, and he realized that even though he'd explored a large portion of the area they were flying over, no one had explored all of it. They'd been on the planet for almost fourteen years, but there hadn't been time to search the entire continent.

The New Earth landscape was similar to Old Earth. There were mountain ranges, vibrantly colored forests, wide-open plains, and the ruins of alien cities. Some of it reminded him of Old Earth. He'd grown up on military bases on both Earth and space stations. Most of his childhood had been spent in the heart of the North American Alliance, which was comprised of old nation-states, with its core being the United States, Canada, and Mexico, but also included Great Britain and Spain. The NA Alliance had been around for over a century before Connor was born, and most of the culture and individual societies that stemmed from the nation-states had merged by then. However, the Ark Project had been funded by more than just the NA Alliance. The Asia Pac Alliance, containing parts of Europe and individualist nation-states, had also contributed. Over three hundred thousand colonists had gone to sleep on the *Ark* and awakened two hundred years later on a planet they hadn't been heading for. And even though it hadn't been their destination, they'd made a home here.

Connor inhaled deeply and sighed. Now, they had a population of over six hundred thousand. The Vemus—believed to have wiped out all mammalian life on Earth—had followed them to New Earth. Connor and the rest of the Colonial Defense Force had been able to stop them, but it had nearly cost them everything. The Vemus was an alien symbiotic virus combined with bacterial infectious agents that had been targeted at mammalian life. The scientists who'd worked to cure it had also used it to target humans in order to consolidate power. It was that genetic modification that had made the Vemus hunt humans to the exclusion of all else and also what had driven the virus to find New Earth.

Sometimes Connor wondered what Old Earth looked like now, but maybe not knowing was a blessing. He imagined it was a place of devastation—cities destroyed and all the people gone, new animals rising up to fulfill a niche in the absence of humans. And the Vemus might still be there as well. The New Earth colony had sent probes back to Earth, but Connor would be an old man before those probes transmitted data back to them. Earth was sixty light-years away from the colony, and the probes they'd sent back, even traveling at relativistic speeds, would take at least sixty years to get there, but it was probably closer to seventy years. The probes needed time to slow down and assess the situation before moving into the system. Then, after that assessment, they'd begin transmitting data back to the colony.

Until recently, Connor had assumed that any data would take at least sixty years to reach New Earth. Given those timetables, the soonest they could learn about what had happened to the people of Earth would be about a hundred and forty years from now. He was sure the scientists could narrow it down to specifics, but his calculations were good enough for him. However, those calculations had been hypothesized before they'd been able to use subspace communication. Even in its limited form, they could potentially learn about Earth much sooner than they'd originally anticipated. The probes were not only equipped with scanners and powerful communication devices, but they also had an auto-factory with 3D printers capable of producing what the probes needed, including a subspace communication transceiver.

"Attention. We'll be approaching the landing pad in ten minutes.

General Gates, transport has been arranged to bring you straight to the Colonial Administration Building," the pilot said.

Connor switched the viewpoint on the holoscreen and could see their approach to Sierra, one of New Earth's major cities. Construction of the pylons had begun for the regional maglev trains that would connect all the cities, and one of those branches would be coming to Sanctuary. He'd been aware of the project but hadn't thought it'd gained so much traction. It had been over six months since it was first proposed. *Well, that's not exactly right,* Connor thought, silently correcting himself. It had been proposed when they'd first established colonial cities, but it had been delayed because of the imperative to reallocate resources to the Colonial Defense Force. There'd been a need for sacrifice at the time, but now, many of the projects that had been put on hold were getting the green light.

Connor understood the reasoning for this, but at the same time, they needed to prepare for the possibility of a Krake invasion. Something else they couldn't have been prepared for when the *Ark* arrived was the fact that New Earth hadn't been as unoccupied as they'd originally thought. There was an intelligent alien species living there who called themselves Ovarrow. When the colonists first started exploring New Earth, they'd found remnants of a vast civilization—abandoned cities and alien structures but also impact craters, which indicated signs of an orbital bombardment. Connor had had plenty of opportunity to study the alien ruins because his wife, Lenora, was an archaeologist.

He didn't know much about establishing a colony. He knew about space stations, military installations, and hunting shadow organizations. What he didn't know about was making a new world a home and who would be best qualified to help achieve that. There were the obvious choices of biologists, chemists, and engineers, but he'd never thought about an archaeologist. It seemed foolish to him now that this would be overlooked, and Lenora had more or less shoved him into that realization very quickly. How else would they learn about the world they were going to make a home on?

New Earth had layers upon layers of discoveries waiting to unfold—from the intelligent species like the Ovarrow to the animal life that lived here. Even the plant life was strangely familiar and yet quite exotic. Lenora had often said to Connor that they could spend the next century here and still wouldn't have unlocked all of New Earth's secrets. She liked to think of mysteries as secret stories yet to be unlocked. However, the more they learned about New Earth and the Ovarrow, the more that gave way to a general unrest that was felt by most colonists.

The Ovarrow were bipedal, with various shades of brown, pebbled skin like that of a reptile. Pointy protrusions stemmed from their shoulders and elbows. They had long arms and large hands with four long fingers, from which stubby black claws protruded. Their severe brow lines stretched to the backs of their wedge-shaped heads. They were lean and strong but had a bit of a stoop that made their heads bob when they walked.

Lenora and hordes of other scientists were working to put together the

Ovarrow's history. Connor had stumbled onto another secret of New Earth when he'd discovered that the Ovarrow had hidden in bunkers, using a primitive form of stasis. The Ovarrow had fought wars among themselves, and it was later learned that they were defending themselves against an invader they called the Krake.

Connor remembered the NA Alliance first-contact protocols that had been refined for hundreds of years in the event that aliens came to visit Old Earth. They'd never had to use them. It had always been assumed that aliens would cross vast distances between stars, but that hadn't been the case with the Krake and New Earth. The Krake were a species that lived in another universe and had the technology to cross between universes. They explored and cataloged, but at some point in their history, they'd decided to experiment on and manipulate the Ovarrow they found. Based on appearance alone, the Krake and Ovarrow seemed to share a common ancestor, or maybe they were different branches on the same evolutionary tree. The colonists lacked DNA evidence to support it, but Connor knew it was only a matter of time. The Krake were going to return to New Earth one day, and Connor was determined to find a way to stop them.

He'd found evidence of the Ovarrow's attempt to reverse-engineer the technology that allowed the Krake to traverse between universes. The Krake had built a massive arch, and even though colonial physicists and engineers hated the phrase, Connor thought of it as an "open gateway" to another universe. Colonial scientists had had even more success with making the Krake technology work for them, and that had led to discoveries Connor suspected the Krake weren't aware of, but they still didn't know much about the Krake themselves. So far, their best intelligence about the Krake was that they were a highly advanced civilization that exploited societies from alternate universes for scientific gain. They practiced a strange form of ruthless scientific pragmatism, looking to predict the outcome of everything.

Learning about the existence of the Krake had given Connor many sleepless nights. He didn't require the standard seven to eight hours of sleep civilians needed because of his specialized implants. Most nights, he only required a few hours' sleep. The only reason most colonists didn't utilize his particular type of implant was a lack of long-term studies of the effects of fooling the brain into thinking it had gotten the required amount of rest that evolution had decided the human body needed. Connor had already had the prototype implants in him when he'd gone into stasis. They'd since been studied by colonial scientists, and a variant of them had been engineered for use by select colonists, mostly those in the CDF.

The combat shuttle landed on the CDF base at Sierra, and Connor got off. He was then transferred to a civilian aerial transport vehicle, commonly referred to as a C-cat, which was smaller and meant to carry only four or five people. He was soon heading toward the Colonial Administration Building. He'd been there only a few days before and hadn't expected to be summoned back quite so soon.

The flight to the administration building only took about fifteen minutes, and after they landed, Connor walked off the landing platform and headed inside the building. The last time he'd been there was when Meredith Cain, the former head of the Colonial Intelligence Bureau, had been arrested. This was in no small part due to Connor hunting down a rogue group that was terrorizing the Ovarrow. They'd made the mistake of bringing civilians into their crosshairs, including his wife. Connor had organized operations using unarmed Spec Ops soldiers to monitor and coordinate with Field Ops, but they were also ordered to detain key suspects until Field Ops could arrive. Many government officials viewed Connor's actions as an extreme abuse of power. The result was a political crap storm, and he was still waiting to see where the pieces would fall. His actions had been necessary, but he knew there'd be a cost. There was always a cost.

Connor walked through the halls of the Colonial Administration Building. There was always an influx of people walking the halls, either going to or coming from various meetings, often speaking with people over their personal comlinks. At four inches over six feet, Connor's broad shoulders often commanded a natural pathway through groups of people. He was difficult to miss in a crowd unless Samson was with him, who was the human version of a Nexstar combat suit heavy. Connor wasn't heavily muscled, but he was extremely strong and maintained a high level of fitness. It was just a natural part of who he was and was also necessary for his overall strategy to do things like keep breathing. On more than a few occasions, he'd needed all his strength just to survive. He'd seen soldiers who let their fitness go, to their own demise. This was something the Colonial Defense Force could not afford, whereas the militaries of Old Earth could indulge when they had populations numbering over fourteen billion people to draw from. There was plenty of fat to trim with a population that large, but not on New Earth. The CDF was lean, and so were its soldiers. Most colonists were physically fit. He wondered if that would wane as the years went on and people chose to stay in the cities they'd built rather than roam the countryside.

"Excuse me, General Gates," a woman said.

Connor turned toward the woman, and she smiled. "Hi, I'm Rebecca Kent. I'm one of Governor Wolf's aides. I was sent to inform you that the meeting has been moved to her office."

Connor nodded and gestured for Rebecca to lead the way. There were clusters of people gathered outside the governor's office. A few people glanced in his direction as he approached, and conversations became hushed remnants of what they'd once been. Connor ignored them as he walked by.

Rebecca waved at the receptionist/gatekeeper to the wing of offices where the governor and her staff worked.

"Seems a bit busier than normal," Connor said.

"This is the new *normal*," Rebecca replied, voicing the first hint of weariness at all the activity.

Given the extent of how many people had been implicated in the rogue group's activities, he shouldn't have been surprised, but he was.

"I know the way from here. You can move on to whatever else you have to do," Connor offered.

Rebecca checked her wrist computer and regarded Connor for few moments. "Good luck," she said.

She turned and left, and Connor frowned. Why would she wish him luck? He strode to Dana Wolf's office and unceremoniously opened the door, walking inside.

Connor saw Nathan standing off to the side. He gave Connor a crisp nod, but his brow was furrowed in concentration. Dana Wolf stood off to the other side, speaking with Bob Mullins. Connor's neck stiffened with a flash of annoyance. Mullins's short-cropped, curly hair had an oily shine to it. He stopped speaking, and his piggish eyes narrowed a little as he looked at Connor.

Dana smiled warmly and waved him over. "Connor, thank you for coming down here again on such short notice."

"Nathan said it was important."

"He was right. We just finished meeting with the Security Council," Dana said and gestured for them all to sit on the couches on the other side of her office.

Dana and Mullins sat on one side, while Nathan sat in one of the plush chairs. He didn't look happy. Nathan was as even-tempered as they came. This was one of the reasons Connor had recruited him into the CDF and also one of the things that made him an excellent leader. He wasn't prone to impulsive actions, and it took a lot to get under his skin.

"Did I miss anything important? I know the meeting today dealt particularly with the prosecution of everyone involved in the rogue group's activities," Connor said, then sat down and waited.

"It did, and Rex Coleman and his team are working on interviewing all the detainees," Dana answered.

Connor nodded. They were detainees until they were proven guilty.

Nathan cleared his throat, and Connor glanced at him for a moment, but Nathan kept his gaze on the governor.

Connor looked back at Dana and saw that Mullins was watching him with the focused intensity of a hungry wolf.

"This is about me, isn't it?" Connor asked.

"We are implementing changes in the CDF," Dana said. "These changes will affect you specifically, Connor."

Connor had been expecting something and kept his gaze on Governor Wolf. "I understand."

"I'm not going to beat around the bush about this. We're making Nathan the head of the CDF. The Security Council has voted."

His first thought was that they were taking the CDF away from him. He glanced at Nathan, who didn't look happy about the situation.

"I didn't want this," Nathan said.

Connor softened his gaze and nodded. He'd created the Colonial Defense Force for the purpose of defending the colony from the threat of invasion. He'd been involved in every aspect from its first inception until he'd retired after the Vemus War, although "retired" was a bit of a misnomer because his exposure to the Vemus meant he might've been compromised. When he rejoined the CDF, he and Nathan had split their duties, but Connor knew there needed to be one person in charge.

"All right, what else?" Connor said.

"It's all right to take a few moments to take this in. We're all aware of the sacrifices you've made to create our defenses," Dana replied.

Connor felt a spike of irritation at feeling like he was being jerked around. "I don't need a moment. I need to know what you intend to do with me. Is my commission canceled?"

"No," Nathan said firmly.

"It's undecided at this time," Bob Mullins said.

Connor swung his gaze toward the man and then looked back at Governor Wolf.

"For the time being, you're still part of the Colonial Defense Force," Dana said.

Connor leaned back in his chair and gauged the room. He felt like he was attending the aftermath of an all-day debriefing that had probably been all about him and his actions.

"The CDF is more than just me."

Bob Mullins inhaled explosively. "You say that, but do you really mean it? We spent most of the day discussing the very actions that brought us into this situation. You treated the CDF as if it was your own personal army to do with as you saw fit without checking with colonial leadership. This makes you almost as bad as Meredith Cain. I know you think what you did was necessary, but it was no less damaging, and the repercussions will be felt for a long time."

"Bob," Connor said, "if you were any good at your job, you would've known what Meredith was doing and you would've stopped her. It's people like you who let a situation get to a point where someone like me has to do something to stop it. I don't regret anything I've done. Not one bit. I'd do it all again. You allowed that group to fester and infect the entire colony. What would you have done if I hadn't been here?"

Mullins leaned forward. "If it was up to me, you *wouldn't* be here. You'd be out of the CDF."

Connor smiled wolfishly. "At least now I know what *you* want, but you haven't answered my question. You're still looking to lay blame. You don't like how what I did made you feel. Or is it that you looked incompetent?"

"Maybe you're just too foolish to understand what your abuse of power has done," Mullins replied with a snarl.

"Bob," Dana said sternly, "you're out of line."

Mullins shook his head. "Fine."

Connor leaned forward. He was moments from springing to his feet. "No, keep going with it. Maybe there's something else you'd like to say. Take your best shot."

"Gentlemen, that's enough," Dana said. "Bob, I want you to leave, now."

Mullins glared at the governor, and she met his gaze with an unyielding one of her own. He stood up and stormed out of the room.

"Nathan," Governor Wolf said, "would you please give us a few moments? If you wouldn't mind waiting just outside."

"Very well," Nathan said and left the room.

They were quiet for a few moments while Connor slowly got his anger under control. He glanced at Dana Wolf, who was waiting for him to say something.

"I don't know why you have Mullins as one of your advisors," Connor said.

Dana smiled and grinned a little. "That's funny. Bob doesn't understand why I keep you around either. You're both very good at your jobs, even if you don't like each other."

Connor couldn't imagine what Mullins was good at other than being one giant pain in the ass, and said so.

"He gets things done. Sometimes he rubs people the wrong way, but so do a few other people I know. We're working for the same thing here, Connor."

"Really? I'm having trouble believing that. Honestly, I was shocked that Mullins wasn't implicated with Kurt Johnson or Meredith Cain."

Governor Wolf twitched one of her eyebrows. "He fits your profile of everything that's wrong, does he?"

"Yeah, sometimes."

"Do I, then?" Dana asked and immediately held up her hand. "Don't answer that. I already know the answer."

"If it's any consolation, I was glad you weren't implicated with the others," Connor said.

"I appreciate that, but it could also mean I'm just better at hiding my activity than the others were," Dana said, giving him a challenging look. "Look, we need to be honest with each other."

"I thought we already were."

"All right, then. I'm three years into my five-year term as governor. There's a significant chance that I either won't choose to run for a second term or that I might lose the election."

Connor's eyebrows knitted together into a thoughtful frown. "You wouldn't run again?"

"I haven't decided. Regardless, you need to start thinking about longevity."

"I don't understand."

"You managed to spot a massive conspiracy and root it out, but don't you realize there's a pretty significant chance that someone like Bob Mullins will be the next governor?" Dana said.

Connor shook his head. There was no way that guy could get enough votes.

"I can tell you don't believe me. Do you remember Stanton Parish? He won his election based on telling people what they wanted to hear. Like it or not, what you did is a hot topic. That's all that was really revealed in that Security Council meeting. People are afraid of you, but . . ." she said, pausing for a moment.

"They're letting it blind them to the actual problem," Connor said. "Which is the fact that I had to do what I did in order to solve the problem. I exposed the vulnerability, Dana. They don't have to like me for it, but they should damn well solve the problem so someone like me doesn't have to step in and do it next time."

Dana licked her lips and considered her next words for a few moments. "One of the things I admire about you is that when you see a problem you just go at it. You're good at working the problem, but sometimes you're a bit of a brute about it, and please know I say that with the highest affection. There's a time and a place for it, but it can also make people do foolish things. Honestly, I'm just waiting for them to start pointing fingers at me as being responsible for the entire situation."

"That's absurd."

"You're too kind."

"Fine. That's bat-shit crazy."

Dana chuckled softly. "You're a leader. It's evident in everything you do. Ultimately, we're responsible for what happens under our watches. Wouldn't you agree?"

"We are, but there are things out of our control. There's always something we can't plan for or anticipate. I think this will blow over. I knew there would be repercussions for my actions. And I knew I was risking being discharged from the CDF, but does that change what we're facing?" Connor asked.

Dana's acorn-colored eyes gleamed with amusement. "I do wonder what kind of governor *you'd* make."

Connor shook his head. "No way would I want that job. No offense."

Dana smiled. "I guess this is where I'm supposed to say you'd be perfect for the job *because* you don't want it, but I don't agree with that, at least not wholeheartedly. However, I think our motivations are quite similar. We both want what's best for the colony."

Connor nodded and was silent for a few moments. "So, you don't know what to do with me?"

"On the contrary, I know exactly what to do with you. Do you?"

Connor felt as if his thoughts had skipped a beat. Of all the responses he'd expected to hear, that wasn't one of them. "I want to—"

"Hold that thought. I'm going to get Nathan back in because I think the two of you need to talk. We're not finished, Connor, but I really do have to go," Dana said.

She left her office and Connor watched as Nathan walked back in. He walked over to Connor and watched him for a few moments.

"This is one of those moments where your old boss is now your new employee," Connor said, chuckling.

Nathan's eyes widened and then he grinned. "And here I thought this was going to be awkward."

"I've had commanding officers before, and for a lot longer than I've been the head of the CDF."

"Yeah, but did any of them recruit you and train you?"

"In that case, I can vouch for your qualifications."

Nathan smiled, and then the smile slipped away from his face. "This is serious, Connor. Mullins wasn't the only one who wanted you dishonorably discharged from the CDF."

"So, why wasn't I?"

"Because I wouldn't do it. They can make a recommendation, but that doesn't mean I have to follow through with it. So, the compromise was a demotion. A lot of bureaucracy if you ask me."

"I appreciate it."

"You'd do the same for me, and I happen to agree with everything you did. I don't know if I would've done the same thing, but I understand why it was necessary."

Connor pressed his lips together for a moment. "What would you have done differently?"

Nathan smiled wryly and pointed a finger at him. "I'm not gonna let you do that to me—make you sit there and second-guess your actions. I honestly don't know what I would've done differently. Everything happened pretty fast, and if proper channels had been used, there would've been a greater risk of losing the evidence."

Connor nodded. "What happens now, then?"

"I think they expect me to keep you in line. If I can't do that, they'll dismiss me."

Connor noted the undertones of Nathan's statement. He'd said it light-heartedly, but the CDF was just as important to Nathan as it was to Connor. "It won't come to that."

"I'm glad you didn't promise."

"You don't think I could keep that kind of promise?"

"I don't know if either one of us could keep that kind of promise."

That was a sobering thought. "So, what's next, *sir*."

Nathan shook his head. "Give me a break. Nothing's changed as far as I'm concerned. Our goal is to define the Krake threat. I want you to focus on that."

"I'm relieved. I was prepared to make a big speech about why we need to keep doing exactly that."

Nathan laughed. "You don't need to convince me, and Governor Wolf is also in agreement. As far as your status in the CDF, that could take months to work out, and I'm not going to sit by and do nothing while they figure out a way to get rid of you and me. So, what's your next move?"

"On the highest level, we need to gather more intelligence about the Krake. Right now . . ." Connor paused for a moment. "I want to find the

Ovarrow we ran into while getting components for the arch—the ones who slipped away from us."

Nathan nodded. "It makes me wonder how many Ovarrow bunkers are out there with stasis pods that we didn't find. They could have awakened earlier than the rest, or perhaps they didn't go into stasis at all."

"We're not sure. They're certainly good at hiding."

"How do you intend to find them?"

"I was planning on getting some help."

CHAPTER 3

Trident Battle Group had been conducting inner-system reconnaissance of the enemy star system for the past seventy-two hours. Colonel Sean Quinn sat in his ready room just off the *Vigilant*'s bridge, reviewing the latest status reports.

"Colonel Quinn," Gabriel, the *Vigilant*'s AI, said in a naturally modulated baritone, "there has been a reported decrease in efficiency aboard the *Babylon*, the *Acheron*, and the *Diligent*."

Sean grimaced at the mention of those ships' names. The senior officers serving aboard those ships had been part of the mutiny, and now he had junior officers filling the shoes of much more experienced officers in enemy territory.

"How bad is it?" Sean asked.

"Colonel, engineering and maintenance report standard efficiency, but it's the reaction times in combat readiness drills that have decreased seventeen percent."

Seventeen percent, Sean repeated to himself and shook his head. If the Krake were to attack them now, they might be in real trouble. "Gabriel, is that an average percentage across the combat readiness drills, or is that the most recent measure?"

"That is the most recent measure. The average—"

"Never mind the average unless it's getting worse. Can you open a comlink to Major Shelton?"

"Certainly, sir. A moment, please," Gabriel replied.

A window appeared on the personal holoscreen above his desk, and Major Vanessa Shelton greeted him. She was a dark-skinned woman who was now in command of the *Yorktown*, a carrier vessel that held Talon-V fighter groups.

"I've just been reviewing the latest reports of the combat readiness drills," Sean said.

"I have, as well. I figured we'd discuss that at our next all-hands meeting."

"Ordinarily, I'd bring down the hammer on the non-performers, but given the circumstances, I don't think that's quite fair. At the same time, I can't accept that kind of performance. Do you have any suggestions?" Sean asked.

"We knew we were going to have to change our tactics if we had to engage the Krake, and these performance scores just prove that fact. I think we should move forward with your idea, which is to pair off the less experienced commanding officers with the more experienced ones."

Sean drummed his fingers on his desk for a moment while he considered. "I know it was my suggestion, but I'm not a huge fan of it. The risk will be handicapping the more experienced warships, and the captains of those ships have enough on their plates with commanding their own ships."

They'd been in this star system for almost three days, having used the space gate and the coordinates provided by a mysterious Krake fifth column faction that had come to their aid. The Krake had transmitted a set of coordinates, which was an invitation Sean had no choice but to explore. Since arriving, they hadn't received any broadcast greeting. Trident Battle Group had transitioned into this universe at a point where their entry would be among the outer planets, which reduced the risk of them being discovered by enemy ships in case this was a trap.

"I still think this is our best option, sir. We pair them off, but we'll need to convey to the junior officers that they're still responsible for commanding their ships. We don't have time for them to spend weeks developing their tactical awareness. Most of them *were* tactical officers, after all."

"I'm going to meet with them individually to see if we can work out some of the kinks," Sean said.

"I think that would be a good idea for more than the obvious reasons," Vanessa said.

It had only been three days since Sean had executed the mutineers and ended the first-ever mutiny in Colonial Defense Force history. He knew there were several officers who felt he'd gone too far, but the majority had accepted the outcome of the mutiny. Sean had been well within his rights to execute the mutineers. He'd also required all the officers to file their own reports about those events, holding nothing back. Sean wouldn't hide from his decision. The facts were there, and they supported him. In spite of all that, he regretted that he'd had to take the action at all. He was still furious with Lester Brody for sparking the mutiny, and he was angry with himself for allowing it to happen under his watch.

"There *is* an alternative," Sean said. "We could move the XOs of the *Dutchman*, the *Albany*, and the *Burroughs* to command the other ships."

Vanessa frowned in thought. "If it was just a matter of rank, it really wouldn't make much difference. That might be a shortcoming in our overall rank structure, but the risk in doing this now is bringing our overall combat readiness down in efficiency."

"That's true, but we might not have much of a choice. If it comes to a fight, the crews of those ships deserve better," Sean said.

"Understood, sir. I do think we need to keep an eye on the *Babylon* and, in particular, Lieutenant Richard Pitts," Vanessa said.

Richard had been close friends with Ryan Ward, who'd been captain of the *Babylon*. He'd been among the mutineers and had come dangerously close to opening fire on the *Vigilant*.

"He doesn't have to like or approve of what I've done, but he's doing his job," Sean replied.

"Understood, sir," Vanessa replied.

"The *Dutchman* is due to report in soon. We'll speak again then," Sean said. "Oh, and thanks for being my sounding board."

Vanessa's lips lifted a little. "That's what I'm here for, sir."

The comlink went dark, and a short while later there was a knock at Sean's door. The door opened, and Lieutenant Jane Russo entered his office.

"You asked to see me, Colonel."

She'd been his lead technical officer on the *Vigilant*.

Sean invited her to sit down. "I need an XO on this ship, and you're my first choice."

Lieutenant Russo's eyebrows raised in surprise. "Sir?"

"I've talked about it with Major Shelton, and she has also recommended you. I realize that this is a bit of a surprise, and given the circumstances, I need you to rise to the occasion. That's why I'm going to give you a field promotion to captain, which will address any issues concerning rank when dealing with engineers and maintenance."

Russo smiled. "Thank you, Colonel. I won't let you down."

"I know you won't," Sean said. He approved of her choice of words. A lesser officer would have inserted a less direct statement along the lines of, "I'll *try* not to let you down." The way a person spoke was often indicative of their attitudes and whether or not they'd achieve their goals.

"There's more," Sean continued. He brought up a tactical recording of their last battle with Krake ships. "I know this is familiar to you, but we need to come up with a better strategy for dealing with Krake attack drones, in particular. We can't afford to keep hurling HADES V heavy missiles to blind them and then destroy them. We don't have enough missiles to sustain that level of use in an engagement."

"I understand, sir. We've been trying to think of ways to achieve more with less, but the only time we come into contact with Krake attack drones is in the middle of an actual attack."

Sean nodded. "I understand, but we'll need some out-of-the-box thinking."

Russo pursed her lips in thought for a moment. "If that's the case, then could I request clearance to show this to people who aren't in tactical, such as non-bridge crew and possibly maybe even some of the scientists? If we want out-of-the-box thinking, we might have to actually look elsewhere."

Sean smiled and twitched his head to the side with a slight nod. "Permission granted, Captain."

They both stood up and Captain Russo saluted Sean before leaving his office. Sean glanced at the holoscreen. He looked at it so much that he could see it with his eyes closed. When they'd first entered the system, he'd decided to do as much reconnaissance from the outer system as he could. But if he was going to get a good look at their target destination, which was the inner planets within the Goldilocks zone, without using any of his active scans, he needed to send a ship in.

Oliver Martinez commanded the *Dutchman*. He was an outstanding officer and a friend, but it was his affinity for playing "cat and mouse" that made him the best choice for a recon mission before Sean would commit the entire battlegroup to go to the waypoint.

They were able to use subspace communication, which allowed them to communicate instantaneously over vast distances. The theory posited that subspace communication would allow them to connect over dozens of light-years and not merely across a single star system. They hadn't tested the theory yet, for obvious reasons. Sean was grateful to be able to communicate across one star system and had utilized it in his tactics against the Krake. What they didn't know was whether the Krake were able to detect subspace comms or even use it themselves. There was so much they didn't know about the Krake, but that was why they were here. Even though there seemed to be a rebellious Krake faction that had assisted them, Sean had to be cautious, and that took time.

CHAPTER 4

A few hours later, Sean sat in the command chair amid a phalanx of workstations on the bridge of the *Vigilant*. Newly promoted, Captain Russo sat at the XO's workstation to his left, and Oriana sat at the science officer's workstation to his right.

"Colonel Quinn," Specialist Irina Sansky said, "I have a subspace communications link from Captain Martinez on the *Dutchman*."

"Good. Put him on the main holoscreen," Sean said.

A few moments later, Captain Martinez's chiseled face and powerful neck appeared on the main holoscreen.

"Right on time, Captain," Sean said.

"The *Dutchman* aims to please, Colonel. I heard that we can now talk for longer than five-minute intervals," Martinez said.

"That's the claim, although there might be a moment while we reestablish the link. What do you have to report?"

Martinez glanced at someone off-screen. "Upload the report," he said and then looked at Sean. "It looks like a dead planet, sir. Our high-res images show a landscape that is scarred by bombardment craters. There are significant particulates in the atmosphere that are indicative of either a massive asteroid impact or a super volcano, but my guess is that somebody nuked this planet. We were able to see traces of what might be orbital bombardment platforms and possibly a derelict ship. We haven't done any active scans, but passive scans don't indicate any power signatures from known Krake ship types. You should have the images now."

A series of images appeared on the main holoscreen, which showed a distant view of the planet. Either the planet had been the victim of a massive meteor shower that pelted the surface, essentially scouring it to oblivion, or Martinez's estimation was correct. But the question remained as to why the

Krake fifth column would send them here, especially given the time constraint.

"Colonel, I'd like your permission to take a closer look at those bombardment platforms and the derelict ship," Martinez said.

"Have there been any space gates detected?"

"Negative, sir."

"I want you to hold your position, Captain," Sean said. "We'll organize our timing so we arrive at the planet at the same time. That way, if we have an uninvited guest we'll be able to deal with it together."

"Understood, sir," Martinez said.

"Good work, Captain. We'll send you our intercept course in just a few minutes," Sean said, and the comlink severed. "Helm, plot a course to the NEC, best speed."

"Yes, Colonel, best speed to the NEC," Lieutenant Edwards said.

"Ops, send a briefing packet to the rest of the battle group, and I want us underway ASAP," Sean said.

"Aye, sir," Lieutenant Katherine Burrows said.

Sean looked at Russo. "Thoughts?"

"Either it's an elaborate trap for us, or they want us to find something, sir," Russo said.

Sean nodded. "That's what I was thinking."

"Sir, why didn't you have the *Dutchman* fly closer and do more reconnaissance?"

"If they'd gotten into trouble, we'd have been too far away to help. When we get closer, I'll have them move in to do more reconnaissance. We'll need to prep the away teams."

"Understood, Colonel," Russo said.

Sean brought the images up on his personal holoscreen and began swiping through them.

"Colonel," Oriana said, addressing him professionally when on the bridge, "have you thought of showing the Krake prisoners these images? Maybe they'll have something to say about it."

Sean rubbed his chin in thought for a few moments. "It's a good idea, but they haven't exactly been forthcoming with any information. They're still convinced that they should be dead," he said and shook his head. He stood up. "Do you want to observe while I ask them?"

"I'm not sure I can contribute anything," Oriana replied.

"You might see something the rest of us miss," Sean said.

"Lead the way, sir."

Sean smiled and then looked at Russo. "XO, you have the con."

Sean and Oriana left the bridge. Once they were in the corridor, she glanced at him. "Is there something else you wanted to discuss with me?"

"There's plenty I'd like to discuss with you, but none of it's relevant to what we're doing now," Sean said and then pressed the button for the elevator. "Well, there is *one* thing. Something Russo said to me earlier. We need to come up with a way to defend ourselves against the Krake attack drones."

Oriana frowned. "Again, I don't think I have much to offer there."

Sean arched an eyebrow. "For a scientist, I thought you'd be more open to tackling this particular issue."

Oriana's eyes flashed. "These are the drones that, when armed, can melt through the hull of our ship?"

"They also fly pretty fast, are extremely agile, and are resistant to direct energy countermeasures. Point defense systems with mag cannons can stop them, but they can also be overwhelmed, and we don't have an endless supply of ammunition. One of the things that's been effective is utilizing the fusion warhead of a HADES V missile. It seems to overwhelm their sensors, and they lose formation. What we've done is detonate a few missiles in their vicinity and then mop up as many drones as we can before they go active again."

They rode the elevator down several decks. Oriana was quiet for a few moments while she considered the problem.

"So, the attack drone is vulnerable to either densely solid metals or a powerful fusion warhead?"

Sean nodded. "We can slow them down, but if enough of them are fired at us, it will overwhelm our defenses. We've run the numbers, and Gabriel has done the analysis. So far, I've used clever tactics to avoid a direct confrontation, or I've at least given us an escape so we didn't end up in a shooting match. At least I tried not to."

Oriana looked as though she was about to say something a couple of times, and Sean waited her out, but she just looked at him regretfully. "I don't think this is something I can really think about while we walk down a corridor, but I'll try and work it with my team. In order to generate the heat required to quickly melt through not only the hull of the ship but the decks in between would mean . . ." she said and paused for a moment.

"They're as hot as a yellow dwarf star burning at five thousand kelvins."

"I wonder what they use to fuel those combat drones."

Sean considered it for a few moments. "That's not a bad question, and I think that given enough time, we could actually build one of these drones. The other thing is that the Krake seem to have limited themselves to combat drones as their main weapon of war, at least as far as we've seen. So, if we can come up with a way to beat their offensive, we'd gain a significant advantage over them."

"This isn't the first time we've talked about their attack drones."

"I've been banging my head against it, and so have a lot of the other senior officers. I'll make the data available to you and your team, and if you think there's anyone else who can help come up with a way to defend against them, let me know and I'll clear them as well. And if you can have that to me by tomorrow morning, that would be really great," Sean said dryly and smiled.

Oriana grinned. "No problem. I'll get right on that for you. If you want, I can also invent an instantaneous FTL engine as well."

"Teleportation would be good too."

Oriana shook her head in exasperation. "There's a reason the mysteries of the universe are mysteries. They're not so easy to solve."

"And yet we utilize the space gate to transition between universes, which makes me wonder how many of these universes there are."

"More than a little and less than too much."

"Is that an exact number?" Sean asked, feigning seriousness.

"It's not infinite," she said and paused for a moment. "Sean, I don't know if I'll be able to help with the attack drones. It's like they're flinging miniature stars at us. About the only thing they react to aside from a solid piece of metal is an even bigger, more powerful star, and then only for a little bit."

"That's because once the warhead is detonated, it quickly disperses in space," Sean said.

Oriana's brows knitted together in intense concentration, and Sean didn't want to interrupt her thoughts. After a few moments, she looked at him.

"What?" he asked.

"I'm just thinking about stars. I'm going to need time with this, but I'll let you know if I come up with something."

Sean suspected she'd just thought of something but wouldn't discuss it until she'd given it a thorough analysis. He'd worked with other scientists who were the direct opposite, sharing every single thought they had whether or not it panned out. Over time, he'd come to prefer Oriana's approach. Life didn't always give a person what they wanted, but sometimes it did give them what they had to have. He just hoped they could come up with a solution sooner rather than later.

CHAPTER 5

A pair of brilliant cerulean eyes regarded Connor from the holoscreen. Her long, auburn hair had a natural curl that seemed to complement her delicate cheekbones, although delicate was the furthest word from how Connor would describe his wife. Lenora was among the most beautiful women he'd ever seen. He hadn't sputtered incoherent sentences when they'd first met—he wasn't a foolish boy after all—but sometimes he was foolish when it came to her.

"I dare you," Lenora said.

"It's not like that at all."

"Connor," Lenora said, cramming volumes of meanings into that one word.

"You're sick, remember?"

Lenora narrowed her gaze. "I have a cold. I'm not dying."

"Colds don't normally come with nausea," Connor replied.

Lenora's slightly pink nose leaned closer to the screen. "I'm not pregnant either."

"I didn't—"

Lenora shook her head. "Ever since that whole bridge incident, you've slipped back into some old habits. I don't need your permission to see the Ovarrow."

"I never said you did."

"No, of course not. You just engineer events that make doing so incredibly inconvenient."

"Lenora, you're sick. Take a few days to get better and then go. I don't like it any more than you do."

Connor knew she wasn't really angry with him. He'd seen her angry before, and this was just mild frustration in comparison. Sometimes people just needed to rant, even if there wasn't much anyone could do about it. "I wish I could be home with you right now, but I have to do this."

Lenora inhaled deeply and sighed. "How bad is it?"

"They put Nathan in charge of the CDF."

"How does that change anything?"

"It's hard to say, really. I'm still focusing on finding out as much as I can about the Krake. And getting the Ovarrow to help is still our best shot at that."

Lenora was quiet for a few moments. "So, they demoted you and put Nathan in charge. You don't think it's going to simply stop at that, do you?"

Connor shook his head. "No," he admitted. "But Dana is still behind what we're trying to do."

"Okay, I forgive you for not being here to take care of me in my time of need. I'll just have to tough it out on my own without you," she said, her eyes narrowing playfully.

"Thanks," Connor said, smiling. "I'll make it up to you."

"Oh, I know you will. With interest," Lenora said, smiling, but then the smile seemed to disappear. "Be careful."

"I will, I promise," he answered.

Lenora looked away for a moment, pursing her lips in thought. "I know how you get. Just hurry up and get back here."

The holoscreen flickered off as she severed the connection, and Connor stared at it for a few moments. He was sitting in an isolated alcove on a troop carrier alpha. He heard the heavy stomp of footsteps approaching the area, and Samson leaned around the corner. Connor stood up.

"You sure you don't want to bring more men? The rest of the 7th will meet us at the waypoint, but we only have two squads with us here," Samson said.

"I just want to talk to them. If we bring too many soldiers with us, they probably won't talk to us at all," Connor said.

A few weeks earlier, diplomatic relations had been stretched thin between the CDF and the Ovarrow. A decisive show of force had been called for, and some lives had been lost. The Ovarrow needed to be shown that the CDF wasn't weak. Connor would've preferred a more diplomatic solution, but at the time and with colonial lives in danger, he couldn't afford it.

While in an Ovarrow city, Lenora had been trapped under the wreckage of a large bridge that had been sabotaged by a rogue colonial group. However, there was evidence showing that the support structures had already been eroded by a group of Ovarrow who lived in the city. As far as Connor knew, they hadn't received any updates about whether the Ovarrow had tracked down who the saboteurs were.

"If you say so," Samson said.

"I do."

"The Security Council is going to have kittens when they find out that you didn't bring a diplomatic envoy with you."

"We have Dash. He's done enough work with them in the past two years to fill that role for us."

Samson chuckled, and his deep voice sounded like it was coming from the base of his barrel chest. "That's thin, and you know it."

"I like to run a lean operation," Connor replied.

Dash DeWitt walked over to them. He was the only noncombatant among them, but he was in excellent shape due to the rigors of working outdoors, either exploring archaeological sites or just being active. Though he wasn't a soldier, he was weapons qualified for basic hunting rifles and powerful sidearms.

"I thought I heard someone mention my name," Dash said.

Samson merely looked at him, but Connor waved him over. A moment later, Samson left with a grunt. Connor watched Dash go a little pale as the much larger man stomped past him.

"That's one guy I don't ever want to make angry," Dash said.

"You should trust those instincts. He's a little rough around the edges, but in a fight, he'll keep you safe. I trust him."

Dash nodded. "That's good enough for me. So, what exactly do you want me to do once we get to the city?"

"I want to see if they'll help us find that other group of Ovarrow on the far side of the continent."

"I know that seems straightforward to you, but for them, it's actually quite complicated."

"I know," Connor said. "That's why you're here."

"I'll do whatever I can, but are you sure you don't want to bring in someone like Darius Cohen?"

Connor shook his head. "I can work with Darius, but for this mission, I'd much rather work with you. You know what we're up against and how important it is. You've seen it firsthand. Darius might not be any less dedicated than you are, but he hasn't seen it like you have."

"I understand. At least I think I do," Dash said with a half-smile.

The young man had certainly grown up quite a bit since he'd been Lenora's student. They'd bumped heads over the years, but growing up wasn't easy.

"Noah sent me a message saying he's been trying to get in contact with you."

Noah had been recovering from a severe head injury that left him in a coma for almost a year. Connor had previously brought him along on a short mission to deal with the rogue group, and Noah had more or less negotiated aggressively that he should also be there this time, but Connor didn't want to tempt fate twice. "Thanks for the message. I'll be in touch with Noah."

"He thinks he's been left behind," Dash said.

"He needs time to recover. I don't want to bring him on a mission like this. He still needs time to heal, regardless of what he thinks."

Dash nodded. "No, I get it. Believe me, I understand. But still, maybe you could just send him a short message just to acknowledge . . . him."

All the kids were growing up, it seemed. "I will, but after. We're almost there."

The troop carrier flew to what had been the colonial diplomatic LZ outside the Ovarrow city. The camp had been shut down, but there were still several communication terminals left for the Ovarrow to use.

The pilot flew at an altitude that didn't hide their approach while at the same time giving them a high vantage point from which to survey the Ovarrow city. Only about thirty percent of the city was occupied by the indigenous species, the ones the colonists had brought out of stasis.

Connor peered at the holoscreen image of the Ovarrow city. There was a wide expanse where the Ovarrow looked to be restoring vehicles—land crawlers. It was nothing that could be done quickly, but the Ovarrow certainly built things to last.

"We've given them time to see us. Take us to the LZ," Connor said.

The troop carrier banked into a shallow turn and landed at the abandoned camp. The loading ramp lowered to the ground, and Samson led three squads of soldiers off the aircraft. Connor and Dash followed.

Connor stepped off the ramp and circled around the troop carrier to view the city. The Ovarrow had bolstered their defenses, and he could see multiple places where Ovarrow soldiers, known as Mekaal, were patrolling. They were being watched, and Connor made no move to approach. Instead, he went to one of the consoles and Dash opened the interface.

"Send a message to both the high commissioner and the warlord that I'd like to speak with them," Connor said.

He watched Dash use the holo-interface to send the message to the terminal that was located inside the city.

"Message has been sent," Dash said.

"Excellent. Thank you. Now, we wait," Connor said.

They restricted their movements to stay near the camp, and six hours passed without any kind of reply from the Ovarrow. A few soldiers complained about the lack of acknowledgment. Connor glanced over at the diplomatic consoles and saw that there was no change. It was early in the afternoon, and he was getting a bit tired of waiting. He understood that he wasn't the Ovarrow's favorite colonist, but there was something to be said for courtesy, and the lack of it was getting on his nerves.

Connor walked out of the camp and came to a stop in plain view. They were about two hundred meters from the entrance of the city. Dash and Samson walked over to him.

"I can try sending the message again," Dash offered.

Connor shook his head. "I'm not going to play games with them," he said and looked at Dash. "Let's take a walk, you and me."

"I have to advise against that, General," Samson said.

Three squads of soldiers began standing to approach the edge of the camp.

"Understood, Captain. I'm going to try a different tactic this time around. I want you to maintain this position."

The skin around Samson's eyes tightened. "How about you take two of my men in with you? Or better yet, I'll go with you."

"Negative. If we get neck deep in it, I'll need you to come get us," Connor replied, and Dash's eyes widened.

Samson glanced at Dash. "I hope you can handle that sidearm, kid."

Connor started walking toward the city, and Dash quickly caught up with him.

"You don't really expect any trouble, do you?"

Connor wanted to dismiss Dash's concerns, but he couldn't. The last time he'd been in that city, he'd had an army with him. He'd also called the warlord's bluff and threatened him. If the Ovarrow wanted to kill him, this would be a perfect opportunity.

"I taught you better than that. Always expect trouble," Connor said.

"I'm pretty sure I'll be okay. They like me," Dash replied.

He was right, and Connor knew it. He'd sent the message and tried to be patient, but he wasn't going to wait all day. Sometimes doors needed to be knocked open.

The entry to the Ovarrow city didn't have gates per se. They were more like improvised barricades. It wasn't the only entrance into the city, but this was where the diplomatic envoys used to come, and Connor wasn't about to try and sneak into the back door for this meeting. He doubted the Ovarrow would appreciate that. It was probably too soon to even make this request, but he didn't have the luxury of time for the Ovarrow to feel ready to work with him again. The Krake could already be making their way to this planet, and they needed to be prepared. Preparedness overrode the Ovarrow's finicky feelings about the human colonists living on their planet, who, incidentally, had brought them out of stasis.

He'd seen the Ovarrow stasis pods. He'd been there when they were first discovered and accidentally triggered the "end stasis" protocols. Connor looked at the Ovarrow, who clustered together behind the barricades, watching him suspiciously as he approached. The fact that there had been a massive colonial effort to bring over ten thousand Ovarrow out of stasis couldn't be missed, given that most of the tools the Ovarrow now used had been made by the colonists. Connor had helped organize the delivery of the supply caches found in the hidden bunkers where many of the stasis pods had been found. There were still thousands of Ovarrow in stasis, and these numbers were only based on the known bunker locations that Connor and many others had mapped out.

New Earth had one massive supercontinent that was similar in size to Earth's Pangea before millions of years of continental drift had separated them. Colonial geologists had found no evidence to support the same events occurring on New Earth. The supercontinent was home to massive lakes, long, powerful rivers, and a nearly extinct species of intelligent aliens who called themselves Ovarrow.

Over the past twelve years, people like his wife had tried to piece together the history associated with the alien ruins they'd found. No one could ever think of New Earth as a dull place to live. It had taken every bit of human ingenuity to not only make a life on this planet but to learn about its history—the calamities that had occurred. There'd been an impromptu ice age that only lasted for two hundred years. They'd since learned that the ice age had been triggered by the Ovarrow in a last-ditch effort to drive the Krake away. At the time humanity loaded three hundred thousand people aboard the *Ark* and began a voyage beyond Earth's solar system, the Ovarrow had been fighting a long war both with the Krake and among themselves.

Connor had thought that all the Ovarrow had gone into stasis pods, but he'd been wrong. Only mature Ovarrow could survive going into stasis, which was why the colonists had never found Ovarrow children in the pods.

He wondered why the Ovarrow they'd discovered on the other side of the continent had never tried to contact them. They must have known the colonists were living there. They hadn't tried to hide their presence on this world. Even with colonists restricting their activities to the western side of the continent, there was no way they could have missed the Vemus War. Battles had been fought on the ground but also in low orbit and even on New Earth's moons. So, the question that tugged at Connor the most was: why wouldn't they try to contact the colonists? The colonial government had decided to keep the presence of these other Ovarrow from the ones they'd brought out of stasis, but that was about to change.

The Mekaal soldiers standing atop the barricade said something in the Ovarrow language. Dash had the translator interface ready, but Connor could guess the meaning. The soldiers' weapons were quarterstaff-sized and were able to fire powerful energy blasts. They didn't point their weapons at them, but they were held at the ready and it wouldn't take much to make use of them.

"I'm here to speak with Warlord Vitory or High Commissioner Senleon. Can you tell them we're here?" Connor asked.

Dash made his personal holoscreen spread as far as it could go so Connor could see the Ovarrow translation. The Ovarrow spoke among themselves while keeping a careful watch on Connor and Dash.

"This isn't the warmest reception I've gotten from them," Dash said quietly.

"They didn't shoot at us, so that's something," Connor replied. But he hadn't expected the Ovarrow to shoot at them. They knew who he was, and they also knew who Dash was.

Connor looked up at the Mekaal, trying to figure out which one was their leader. The Ovarrow stuck to an almost rigid form of hierarchy, and he'd have the most luck gaining entry to the city by dealing with whoever was at the top of the pecking order.

Connor raised his hand and pointed his finger at the Mekaal soldier the others seemed to defer to. "I'm General Connor Gates of the Colonial Defense Force. I know you have your orders, but if someone doesn't get here in the next few minutes, I'm going to walk into your city. Whether you shoot me or not is up to you, but I am going to speak to your leaders."

The Mekaal soldiers read the message, and the one Connor had guessed was the leader regarded him. The dark, sunken eyes with brow ridges that went to the back of his head made him look as if he were constantly glaring. After a few moments, he touched the side of his helmet, which apparently was the universal signal for speaking over the comlink. The Ovarrow communications capabilities included shortwave radio signals, which could broadcast at distances of several thousand kilometers. The Mekaal uttered a short, decisive sentence and gestured for them to follow.

"We're in," Dash said.

Connor nodded and walked toward the barricade. He only carried a sidearm, but the Mekaal hardly paid it any notice. He'd expected that they'd want him to disarm, but then he recalled that the diplomatic envoys had been allowed a squad of armed soldiers.

They weren't entirely defenseless. Both Connor and Dash wore military-grade multi-protection suits made of nanorobotic material, which mimicked the clothing the colonists wore while providing a lot of protection.

The fact that they were walking into the city was a small victory unto itself. Nathan hadn't thought he'd be able to get inside or that the Ovarrow would speak with them. But getting inside had been the easy part; convincing the Ovarrow to help them would be slightly more difficult.

Connor glanced toward a cloaked recon drone flying overhead. Samson was keeping watch, but if the Ovarrow actually intended to harm them, Connor doubted that the CDF soldiers outside the city would be able to reach them in time. Connor and Dash were on their own, but he'd faced worse odds.

Significant progress had been made with the cleanup efforts in the city, which Connor attributed to the use of the machines they'd found. This part of the city was slowly coming back to life, but Connor didn't have to look far to see the haunting remnants of a battle fought here hundreds of years ago.

He glanced down one of the side streets and stopped. A large section of the building on the corner had been torn away. Blackened, scorched remains marred what was left, with bits of jagged bronze, metallic alloy glittering in the sun. The Ovarrow preferred a rounded architecture that flared at the top, which made them defensible. There must have been an explosion. Connor glanced at the other side of the street and saw where huge chunks had lodged themselves into the nearby structures. He narrowed his gaze and peered into the building, his enhanced vision easily piercing the darkened interior.

"That was someone's home," Connor said to Dash.

"What the hell happened?"

They both looked at their Mekaal escorts, and the leader made an impatient gesture for them to follow.

Connor opened a comlink to Samson. "Scorched building southeast of us. Have the drone scout for more of the same, and look for a cause of the explosion."

"Acknowledged. Not a warm welcome, then?"

"It's too soon to tell," Connor said and closed the comlink.

As they walked farther into the city, Connor tried to get a feel for the mood of the Ovarrow they passed. Ovarrow didn't really show emotion the way humans did, or perhaps the Ovarrow were always in a near-constant state of dedicated focus on the task at hand. None of them were standing idly by. Some of them stopped for a few seconds to look at Connor and Dash as they went by, but they quickly returned to what they were doing. More than a few of them seemed to recognize them.

Dash looked at Connor. "It looks like they remember you."

"Or were warned about me," he countered, and Dash frowned. "That's just the way it is."

Connor had tried to be civil. Frowning in thought, he tried to think of the term Nathan liked to use—diplomatic. Sometimes diplomacy took too damn long, and the Ovarrow seemed to respond to the use of force. It had been a dangerous precedent to set, but lives had been on the line. In particular, Lenora's life had been on the line.

Connor had been a professional soldier for most of his life. Even when he'd awakened on the *Ark*, he'd found a niche in the colony leading Search and Rescue. His skills had been well-utilized there, but then they'd formed the CDF. In the meeting rooms with the Security Council, he'd emphasized that the primary motivating factor for the military response to the terrorist act in the Ovarrow city had been that colonial lives had been at risk. He'd sent in the CDF and threatened the warlord. If the Ovarrow had kept attacking the soldiers who were securing the collapsed bridge, he'd have hit them hard. He wouldn't have wanted to do it, but he wouldn't have hesitated either. Connor suspected that more information had been conveyed in those few moments than in most of the diplomatic envoys put together. Now Connor would learn how the warlord had internalized such a lesson. Would he and the rest of the Ovarrow resent the colonists to the point that there would be no chance of forming an alliance, or would they acknowledge the truth and accept the fact that they needed each other?

Their escorts quickened the pace, and about ten minutes later, they were brought to a large building where the thick, russet-colored walls had been drawn to the side, leaving a vast atrium opened to fresh air. Connor had been to a number of Ovarrow ruins over the years, but he hadn't known that the buildings could actually do something like this. There was some kind of mechanism on the floor and along the ceiling that allowed sections of the walls to be collapsed into each other like an accordion. Inside were several work areas where groups of Ovarrow spoke to each other.

Connor saw the warlord. He wore armor similar to the rest of the soldiers. It was deep purple and had a power cord on the back, which also was used for some of the Ovarrow's weapons. He was older, with more lines to his face, but lean and muscular. He'd been speaking with the high commissioner, as well as other faction leaders. Their conversations abruptly ceased, and they turned to look at Connor and Dash.

Their escorts came to a stop, and Connor waited for the Ovarrow leadership to acknowledge them. This was a gesture of respect, since they were guests. Off to one side, a soldier brought in the colonial translator and activated it.

The warlord regarded Connor with a hint of malice in his gaze. The Warlord's First was standing by his side, his second-in-command. Cerot watched Connor curiously. Connor looked at the high commissioner.

There seemed to be so much tension in the room that Connor began to wonder whether it was purely due to his presence, as well as the CDF soldiers outside the city. He got the feeling that there was something else going on.

Connor activated his own translator and spoke. "Thank you for seeing me, High Commissioner," he said, and his gaze flicked to the warlord. "Vitory."

The high commissioner regarded Connor for a few moments. When he spoke, another Ovarrow used the holo-interface to enter his words.

"Your presence here is surprising. It was my understanding that if the colonial government wanted to reopen communications, they'd send us a message through this console."

"You are correct, but I'm here of my own volition."

The warlord came to stand by the high commissioner's side. "Have you returned to make war?"

"No, I haven't," Connor answered.

"Then why are your soldiers outside our city walls? And there have been reports of a large force gathered some distance northeast of the city," Vitory said.

The Mekaal were scouting the area outside the city, having learned from their previous experience when they clashed with the CDF. Connor approved. "They're waiting for me. I'd like to speak with you peacefully, if you'll allow it."

Vitory glanced at High Commissioner Senleon and spoke a few words that weren't entered into the translator.

Senleon looked at Connor. "We appreciate the delicacy with which you handled coming here, but you must know we haven't changed our stance regarding an alliance with your colony."

"I understand that, and I'm not here to speak about those things," Connor said, waiting a few moments before continuing. "A short while ago, we found more Ovarrow living far away from here. We don't know much about them. Our initial contact with them was strained. It wasn't peaceful."

Connor used his neural implants to bring up a holographic map of the continent that showed their current position and then the general location of where they'd found the other Ovarrow settlement.

Vitory studied the map for a few moments. "Did you attack them?"

"No, we didn't, but we did defend ourselves."

"This place is known to us, but nobody here has ever been there. Before we slept, there were limits to where we could travel in the open. This was one of our capitals," Senleon said.

Connor wondered which faction's capital it was but was reluctant to bring the question up at this point. The Ovarrow were sensitive to accusations, and certain questions might stop them communicating altogether because it implied that they were holding back information.

"Why did you go there?" Vitory asked.

"We found records that indicated there was an arch there, and we went there to study it to help us get our own arch working. Some of my people were trapped on the other side of the gateway, and we needed our arch to work. We think they were surprised by our presence, but we never actually spoke to them. We found Ovarrow dressed in ryklar skins, and they attacked us alongside them. These ryklars were different from the others we've seen. There are auditory systems . . ." Connor paused because the translator failed at that point. Connor gestured toward his ears. "These ryklars had had their ears removed. They were controlled by spectrums of light."

The Ovarrow translator did its best to convey what Connor had said, but he wondered how much was getting lost in translation. Mention of the arch had sparked several side conversations by the Ovarrow, but Vitory studied the holoscreen for a few moments. They knew the archway was Krake technology used to traverse between universes. They also knew they were dangerous, and they were afraid.

"We've searched for the city and haven't found any stasis pods. Some of us believe that perhaps these Ovarrow didn't go into stasis. They weathered the long winter," Connor said.

"That theory may be correct. There weren't enough stasis pods for everyone," Senleon said.

A sobering silence settled on the Ovarrow. The memory of their time before stasis was still fresh in their minds. Their stasis technology had been flawed and they were lucky to be alive, but they retained their memories from before, and it had been a brutal time of survival.

"I'm here for two reasons," Connor continued. "The first is that we intend to go search for those Ovarrow, and I wanted to know if anyone here would like to come with us. I think it might help open communication between us. The reason I'm looking for them is to find out how they survived for so long. I also want to know what they know about the Krake. If they didn't go into stasis, they must've successfully hidden from the Krake. Perhaps they know something about them that will help us find where they live."

This brought another wave of scattered conversations among the Ovarrow, some of which involved both the warlord and the high commissioner, and Connor waited for them to finish.

Vitory turned to address Connor again. "You are only bringing soldiers to find them and not a diplomatic envoy?"

"That is correct. We expect there'll be significant danger, given what happened before. We've helped you, and now we seek your help in return," Connor replied.

"When do you plan to leave?" Senleon asked.

"As soon as I'm done here. We have troop carrier transports that will bring us to the city where we can begin our reconnaissance," Connor said.

Vitory stepped forward. "You expect us to send Ovarrow with you into a dangerous situation?"

"We would protect them."

"We are rebuilding and need all available Ovarrow to work toward that effort. Our answer is no," Vitory said.

Connor was about to reply when he received a comlink request from Samson.

"Go ahead," he said.

"We found four buildings in the same state. The burn marks are consistent with an overloaded Ovarrow power cell. Sergeant Ellison believes this is sabotage, and I'm inclined to agree with her."

Connor glanced at Vitory and brought up an image of the building that had been destroyed. "I've noticed that there are several buildings like this. Is there anything I can help you with?"

The warlord bared his teeth and Connor knew he'd struck a nerve. It seemed that the Ovarrow were dealing with a struggle of their own.

"We don't need your help."

"Maybe not, but you certainly didn't repay the help that's already been given to you. I think some of you would come with us, if given the chance," Connor said and glanced at the warlord's First. Cerot looked away. "We'll camp outside the city for one night and then leave in the morning. If any of your people would like to join us, they would be welcome."

Connor waited for the translator to finish and then turned and walked away. Dash quickly followed him, and after a few moments, their soldier escorts caught up to them and took up positions surrounding them.

"Dammit," Connor said. "You'd think they'd want to know about this other group. Why wouldn't they want to communicate with their own people?"

"I agree with you, but the Ovarrow are stubborn, and they're not like us. What makes sense to us is foreign to them."

Connor told Dash about the other buildings that had been destroyed. "They could be in the middle of some kind of rebellion, or perhaps the factions are striving for dominance."

"Did you notice their reaction to the mention of the Ovarrow who hadn't gone into stasis?"

Connor shook his head. "I was too busy watching them freak out about the Krake and the fact that we use an arch."

"I noticed that, too, but they looked ashamed."

Connor frowned in thought for a moment. "Why would they be ashamed?"

Dash shrugged. "Well, think about it. The world is ending around you and you have a way to weather out the storm, but not everyone can be saved. Then you wake up hundreds of years later and find out there's a group that was supposed to have died but instead they found a way to survive. Everyone who went into stasis left somebody behind. How would you feel if you woke up from all that? Maybe they just need a little bit of time."

Connor had to admit that there was some validity to Dash's argument. "I still feel like I'm wasting my time with them, and I don't know why they won't help us. Why can't they understand what's at stake?"

Dash remained quiet as they walked, and Connor sent a message to Samson that they were on their way back. Connor remembered the early days when the colonists had been building their colony, and he understood that the Ovarrow were also working hard to make this settlement work for them; but surely they could spare a few of their kind to come with them and contribute as delegates of some sort. Even if they were ashamed or were suffering from some kind of survivor's guilt, it didn't change the fact that sooner or later they'd cross paths with these other Ovarrow.

"Vitory seemed to regard that other group of Ovarrow as a threat," Connor said.

Dash pursed his lips and shrugged.

Maybe it was better that they didn't come with him. With or without the Ovarrow's help, he needed to keep pushing forward. But if all the Ovarrow reacted with an instant roadblock to any type of effort that involved learning more about the Krake, he wasn't sure how much help they were going to be. Why did it seem that the Ovarrow just wanted to pretend the Krake didn't exist, or was it that they had a different plan for dealing with the Krake when they arrived? Connor had no doubt that at some point the Krake were going to find their world. He glanced at the Ovarrow soldiers with them, and they kept their eyes forward. They were escorting them to the barricade, but he wished he could tell what they were thinking.

He felt his shoulders become tight with a very dark thought. What if when the Krake arrived, the Ovarrow chose to form an alliance with *them*? The Colonial Security Council assumed that since they'd brought them out of stasis and helped them reestablish themselves, the Ovarrow would naturally align with the colony, but could they be wrong? If the Ovarrow perceived that their survival was better served with the Krake, then they'd do what they thought was best for their people.

Connor clenched his teeth on those thoughts. He'd rather die on his feet than live on his knees, and he would've thought that anyone who'd gone to such lengths to survive would feel the same way. They couldn't form an alliance with the Krake. Connor pressed his lips together. Lars Mallory was convinced that the Ovarrow couldn't be trusted. What if Lars had been right? But he couldn't make sweeping judgments like that. If the Ovarrow chose to side with the Krake, then the colony would deal with that, too, but Connor refused to count them out until they made their intentions known.

CHAPTER 6

The Ovarrow soldiers escorted them as far as the barricades, and then Connor and Dash returned to the CDF camp.

Dash looked at Connor. "Do you mind if I write up a report to send back to Darius? I just want to tell him what we observed in the city."

"That's fine with me," Connor answered, regarding the young man for a moment. "I have nothing to hide, Dash."

"I know that, but sometimes . . ." he let the thought go unfinished for a few seconds. "I just learned that sometimes the timing of when reports are filed also has its place. It's just that this is a new development where the Ovarrow are concerned and, uh . . . Darius should know about it. I mean, they've been trying to keep tabs on them, but there's only so much you can see through the video feed from the occasional reconnaissance drone."

Dash walked away and began recording his thoughts into a log.

Samson came and found Connor. "I'd like a word in private, General."

They walked a short distance away from the others, and Connor looked at his friend. "What's on your mind?"

"Off the record?" Samson said, and Connor nodded. "You're playing this a little fast and loose, aren't you?"

"I know you didn't like that I went into the city alone, but I don't think they would've let us in otherwise."

"We could've waited for them to allow it. It was reckless, and it's my job to point that out to you."

Connor had just wanted to get to the city and speak to the Ovarrow. "I acknowledge that there was some risk involved, but that's to be expected."

"Is that so? You expected the sabotaged buildings we found in there? There's something going on with the Ovarrow. If this was some kind of stronghold, I'd say they had an insurgency problem, but this is the Ovarrow.

I know we're not supposed to associate their behaviors with ours, but I don't know what else it can be."

"You're right; I wasn't expecting that. Next time, I'll insist that a squad comes with me," Connor said.

"I'll hold you to that," Samson said. He rested his hands on his hips and arched his back in a stretch. "So, none of them are going to help us?"

Samson didn't come right out and say it, but the fact that the Ovarrow had once again refused to help them was becoming an issue.

"I know they have some very real challenges, but I'm getting kinda tired of this," Connor admitted. "But I can't do much about it unless we start abducting them."

Samson tilted his head to the side and pursed his lips as if the idea had merit. He shrugged. "If things are so bad that they can't even send a small squad with us, this might be a blessing in disguise. We have enough to worry about without bringing an Ovarrow squad to the table."

"It's not that simple," Connor said. "The Ovarrow don't rush to make decisions. That's why I told them I'd wait around until tomorrow."

Samson grunted. "Want to make a wager?"

Connor shook his head.

They made camp, posted sentries, and programmed a few recon drones to patrol the area. Connor didn't want anyone sneaking up on them. As the evening settled in, they could see lights coming from the city. Connor kept mulling over the day's events in his mind. He'd expected the Ovarrow to want to seek out others of their own kind, but that hadn't been the case. They were so guarded. Wouldn't they be interested in seeking out these others and *then* deciding whether or not they were enemies?

Frustrated with that line of thinking, he turned his attention to planning how they were going to look for the other Ovarrow. Sometime later, Private Colson came to seek him out, saying there was a group of Mekaal soldiers requesting to see him.

Connor walked to the middle of the camp where he saw six Ovarrow soldiers wearing dark armor. They were armed, but CDF soldiers nearby nullified any threat. An Ovarrow translation station was already set up, and Connor saw the warlord's First walk to the console.

Lenora had saved Cerot's life, and the Ovarrow knew that Lenora and Connor were married, which had been translated from "union" in Ovarrow nomenclature. The translators were based on the Ovarrow machine language used in their computers.

"General Gates, we would like to come with you to search for more of our people," Cerot said.

Connor read the message and regarded the young Ovarrow for a few moments. The warlord's First was related to the warlord. Connor wasn't exactly sure how the two were related, but there was definitely a family resemblance. He also understood that there was a rigid hierarchy among the Ovarrow.

"Does the warlord or high commissioner know you're here?" Connor asked.

The question appeared on the holoscreen, and all six Ovarrow glanced at each other for a brief moment before waiting for Cerot to answer.

"I am here to repay a debt. These Mekaal are here with me to also repay a debt," Cerot said.

Connor frowned in thought and gestured for Dash join him. "What do you make of this?"

"I think that at least three of them were trapped on the bridge with Lenora."

The Mekaal soldiers looked a bit on the young side, and Connor began to think this was some kind of a "rebellious youth" thing, but he needed the help. He glanced at Samson.

"You need to utilize the resources you've got. We need help, and they're here to help. Do you really want to send them back?" Samson said.

"Why the hesitation?" Dash asked.

"When someone is telling you something that's too good to be true, then it usually is," Connor said and turned back to Cerot. "I'll let you come as long as you understand that you will do exactly as I say. Is this understood?"

Cerot read the message and didn't look at the other soldiers. "We will obey your commands, General."

Connor glanced back at the city. There were some colonists who thought they were too accommodating with the Ovarrow. In this case, he doubted Cerot had gotten permission to join them, but he didn't care anymore.

He began issuing orders to break camp. They'd be leaving as soon as possible. Then he drafted a message to both the warlord and the high commissioner, informing them of the situation. He timed the message to be sent after they left the camp. They would be well away by the time it was received.

CHAPTER 7

Connor walked up the loading ramp of the troop carrier alpha, which was a beast of a ship. Calling it a mere troop carrier was a bit of a disservice. It could also haul equipment and had heavy armor but minimal weapons. It was an endurance vehicle meant to take damage. He walked over to Dash, who'd become the self-appointed liaison with the Ovarrow. Samson joined him.

"I was just trying to give them an idea about what to expect. I'm pretty sure none of the Ovarrow have flown above the atmosphere before," Dash said.

The quickest way to reach a city that was over twelve thousand kilometers away was to breach the atmosphere and then reenter. Connor also wanted to educate the Ovarrow on what their capabilities were. He expected that they'd report these events back to their leadership.

"Are these names correct?" Samson asked.

Connor frowned for a moment and then brought up his own internal heads-up display. A jumble of letters appeared next to each of the Ovarrow soldiers. Cerot was easily pronounced, but the others were a mouthful. He looked at Dash. "Is that the best we can do?"

"It's just an approximation based on the translator."

Samson shook his head. "I can't even pronounce that," he said and gave Connor a look.

"I think we can do better," Connor said and accessed the translator interface. He gestured toward the nearest Ovarrow and worked his way around, pointing at each one as he did. "Now you're Joe, Felix, Luca." He paused for a moment, frowning in thought. "Esteban."

"*Esteban*? Are you serious?" Samson asked.

Connor shrugged and turned his attention back to the Ovarrow. There was one left. "Wesley," he said. Samson gave him a monstrous glare but didn't say anything. "That should work. I updated the translator interface to associate with the new names."

One of the Ovarrow made a sound that almost sounded like "Joe," but he could have been clearing his throat.

"I should've thought of something like that. I was just trying to accurately translate what they were saying," Dash said.

Samson stormed off, muttering under his breath.

"What's wrong with him?" Dash asked.

"He doesn't approve of one of the names."

Dash glanced in the direction the big man had gone. "Why? What does he care?" Dash asked, and then his eyes widened. "One of those is *his* first name, isn't it?"

Connor feigned indifference. "I can neither confirm nor deny. I invite you to ask him, but just make sure you wait awhile. I wouldn't ask him here. Leave yourself plenty of room to run."

Dash shook his head with a bit of a nervous grin. "That's all right. I don't really want to know that badly."

Looking at Cerot and the others, Connor activated the translator. "Enjoy the ride and listen to Dash," he said, giving Dash a companionable pat on the shoulder.

Cerot gave him an awkward nod, which he must've picked up from being around humans. The Ovarrow rested his large, four-fingered hands in his lap. His forearms were heavily muscled, giving them incredibly strong grip strength.

Connor glanced at the others, who all appeared a bit nervous, except for Esteban. He seemed to be focused on taking in his surroundings. Connor walked toward the front of the troop carrier and sat down next to Samson. The Spec Ops captain didn't look up.

"You couldn't just leave well enough alone, could you?"

"Do you know what the betting pool is for your first name? I gave him a one-in-five chance of getting it right, and it's only Dash who knows."

Samson snorted.

"You could've changed it at any time. Do you know how many times I get asked about it? You should pay me a monthly stipend just for keeping it from everyone else."

"What's with the name Esteban?"

Connor smiled. "It's just something Diaz used to do. When he couldn't remember somebody's name, he just called them Esteban."

Connor missed his friend but understood why he'd chosen to step away from the CDF for a while. Diaz had come dangerously close to dying. He had five kids—four daughters and a son—and Connor knew them all. A former Marine who had worked in law enforcement back on Old Earth, Diaz had been one of Connor's first friends in the colony and was definitely someone who'd watch your back. Connor was thankful he hadn't had to inform his friend's wife that her husband wouldn't be coming home. That scared him more than he cared to admit.

Since rejoining the CDF, Connor was determined to balance his personal life with his work. It had been simpler when it was just him and Lenora, but when Lauren was born, things had changed. *He* had changed. He found that he didn't like leaving home so much because he wanted to be around his daughter. Before rejoining the CDF, he'd imagined that he'd be able to do things with whatever family he had because he wasn't a soldier anymore. Lenora had hinted at wanting to get back to fieldwork, which Connor also enjoyed. He liked exploring New Earth, but learning about the Krake had changed all that. It was something he couldn't ignore. Sometimes he thought about letting someone else take the reins and deal with the Krake. He'd trained a lot of people when they created the Colonial Defense Force. It wasn't like when they'd first arrived on this planet. The CDF had been created out of necessity by people who weren't soldiers in their previous lives back on Old Earth. They could do their jobs very well, but no one had the experience Connor had. He'd been a soldier most of his life.

"The other three troop carriers are en route," Samson said.

"The best way for us to cover the most ground is to split up into three groups. One of the groups can do aerial reconnaissance while the rest of us explore the city," Connor said.

He activated the nearest holoscreen and brought up an image of the city, highlighting the areas the previous CDF team had already explored. "They weren't able to find them after our initial encounter. We left recon drones there for a few days, which gave us a map of the city, but we need both boots on the ground and eyes in the sky if we're going to find them."

"No one has been back since?" Samson asked.

Connor shook his head. "No time. We're the first."

"All right, so how do you want to do this?"

Connor leaned back in his chair and pressed his lips together in thought. "I think we should do several flyovers of the city, looking for signs of recent use and ryklar activity. Also, see if Cerot and the others spot anything worth investigating."

"Were there a lot of ryklars the last time you went there?"

"There was a large pack, but they don't seem to stay very long. There are most likely different packs that rotate from place to place, and they vary in size. So the ryklars that were there a few months ago might not be there anymore. However, the ones that were used as watchdogs in the attack were under Ovarrow control. We don't know where those are or how many of them there are," Connor said.

Samson studied the map of the city for a few moments. "If they were breeding ryklars, we should be able to find some evidence of that. They'd have to feed them, dispose of their waste, things like that. They'd also have to go out for supplies."

The troop carrier accelerated to breakaway speeds, but the inertia dampeners prevented them from feeling the acceleration.

"I don't remember seeing anything like farmland, but you're right. We should look for evidence of someone actually living in the city. I just don't think they did," Connor said.

"Then what were they doing there?"

"We weren't even aware of them until we started salvaging parts from the arch. In fact, there were no remnant power cores in standby anywhere. That can't be a coincidence. So, the real question is: where do they live and why maintain a watch on an arch that didn't have any power anyway?"

Several of the Ovarrow made surprised noises and gestured toward a wallscreen that showed a low-orbit view of New Earth. They were beyond the atmosphere, which gleamed with a shimmering blue glow. The ring that encircled New Earth was made up of the shattered remains of a third moon and was maintained by a smaller moon orbiting closer to the planet and a larger moon farther away. The gravitational pull had spread the remains of the third moon so thin that the vertical height was typically seven meters.

The Ovarrow continued to gasp in surprise, speaking with multi-toned sounds from their intricate vocal cords. They had two distinct vocal cords, which allowed them to communicate in such a way that there was very little chance of any human being able to duplicate it.

Some of the Ovarrow looked away from the wallscreen, but Cerot and Esteban couldn't stop looking at the planet below. Connor noticed that Dash was quiet, letting the Ovarrow have this moment to themselves. Connor couldn't remember the exact date of when human beings had first left Earth, but he knew it was well over two hundred years before the *Ark* had left the Sol System. Early astronauts and engineers had pushed the boundaries, pioneering the effort for humanity's next great frontier. They hadn't been brought into it by an alien species. By the time Connor was born, going into space was commonplace. There were space stations engaged in robotic asteroid mining, as well as colonies on various moons throughout the solar system. This was a rare opportunity to witness a species' first time leaving their planet.

Several cargo ships flew within view of them on their way to the lunar base where the CDF shipyards were. The orbital defense platforms were farther away, but they wouldn't be able to see them. Connor hoped the experience would spark a flame within the Ovarrow to push past their limits.

They were able to see the reentry into the atmosphere. The video feed on the wallscreen glowed red on its edges from the heat dispersal. Connor watched as the Ovarrow winced away from it, and he heard Dash try to calm them down.

"I don't know why you put so much stock in the Ovarrow," Samson said.

"They're our link to the past and our only link to the Krake."

"I understand that. We've learned some things, but you're pushing for an alliance. There are only ten thousand of them in that city, and let's say there are two or three times that number in stasis that haven't come out yet. That's not much of an army if we're looking for an alliance."

"I see what you're saying," Connor replied. "Think of it this way: either they might never have awakened because of the faulty tech they used to go into stasis, or they might've awakened in the middle of our war with the Krake, only we didn't know as much as we needed to and the Krake surprised us by coming back here. We know they routinely check, however many worlds they keep track of."

"Yes, but the arch that they were using was under water, so it was inaccessible. I read the report."

"So, what are you saying?"

"I don't know how much help the Ovarrow can be. I mean, think about it. Their entire strategy for dealing with the Krake was to hide themselves in stasis. Are we going to do the same thing?"

Connor shook his head. "No, we're not going to hide in stasis."

"I didn't think so. So, what are you hoping to get from this other group of Ovarrow?"

"We need to find out more about them—confirm their history. If they didn't go into stasis, that puts this whole situation in a different light. They were survivors of an ice age on a planet where everyone had almost wiped themselves out fighting each other and the Krake."

"Not exactly the kind of person I want guarding my back or fighting at my side. So, the same question applies," Samson said.

"The answer doesn't change. They might know the Krake better than anyone who went into stasis. The records we were able to uncover indicate that the Ovarrow who went into stasis didn't all go at the same time. Ultimately, we need to get them to talk to us. We don't know how many there are. Maybe there are a lot of them—enough to make a difference in a war."

Samson was quiet, and Connor regarded him for a few moments. "What would you do?"

Samson frowned. "About what? There are so many moving parts to this, but I don't know if I'd go looking for the Ovarrow here. If the Krake are the real threat, then I'd want to know about them—where they live, what their capabilities are, what their weapons are, their tactics . . . probably all the things you already said in those Security Council meetings you and Nathan frequent."

Connor twitched his head to the side. "You wouldn't be wrong about that. The real question is: how long do we have before the Krake come here? And what do we do when they come?"

Samson looked at him for a few moments. "No wonder they don't want to work with you. I understand you're trying to bring awareness, but you know people don't think straight if they're scared all the time."

"Then they'll just have to learn how to cope better. I didn't create this situation, but I'm damn well going to do something about it," Connor said.

"Works for me," Samson replied. "And I'm sure they'll appreciate the hard line from you."

"They appreciate things like facts and data. We need something that's irrefutable. Otherwise . . ." Connor said, pausing for a few moments, ". . . I really am crazy to keep pursuing this."

"They thought you were crazy about a threat coming from Earth, too, but who am I to judge?"

Samson got up and walked away, and Connor shook his head. Samson had lived outside the colony on his own for years, deep in the New Earth frontier, and Connor wasn't sure if Samson was the best judge of his mental status. Samson was good with tangible threats—a combat situation or achieving an objective—but he lacked some of the finesse for intelligence gathering.

There was an open space in the middle of the troop carrier that was commonly used for briefings. Connor had Dash bring their Ovarrow guests to that space so he could watch their reactions to the city and ask them questions.

They'd come up with a way to categorize Ovarrow cities by size, and a capital was the largest. The city they were heading to covered an area of over six thousand square kilometers.

Samson brushed up against Connor's elbow as he leaned toward the holoscreen. "That's gotta be over a hundred kilometers across."

Connor nodded. "Not quite a square but close enough, even with a big river running almost through the middle."

Fragmented spires pierced the overgrowth, but they could see more of the bronze-colored buildings the closer they got to the coastal area.

"We could've used Flint and the 3rd to help recon these ruins," Samson said.

"They're on a training exercise at the lunar base," Connor replied.

"War games on the moon," Samson replied. "I'm sure that's the only reason they're not here," he added sarcastically.

"Gotta keep those skill sets sharp, and if you're implying that I deployed them in the wake of recent events, I can neither confirm nor deny any such actions."

Connor highlighted the northeastern part of the city. "Send word for Layton and the other carrier to begin scouting this area here," he said and then looked at Dash. "Do they recognize anything?"

Dash looked at Cerot and repeated the question.

"None of us have ever been here. There were pockets of fighting that divided the continent," Cerot said.

Connor took control of the city map on the holoscreen and zoomed in closer. "This is the area where we found the arch."

Cerot and the other Ovarrow peered at the map. "It looks like a Mekaal research facility," Cerot said, gesturing to the barely discernable perimeter.

Once the Ovarrow pointed it out, Connor saw it—an Ovarrow military research facility. That made a lot of sense.

"Recon drones aren't showing any ryklar activity and no deterrent signal," Dash said.

Connor nodded, brought up a recon drone feed, and put it on the holoscreen. The drone flew through the dimly lit corridors, racing to its objective.

The Ovarrow watched its progress intently. It entered a vast chamber and increased its altitude, giving them a higher vantage point.

"Where'd it go?" Dash asked.

Connor frowned and watched the video feed. Where the Ovarrow arch had once been was nothing but rubbled remains. "Someone destroyed the arch."

"Why would they do that?" Dash asked.

"They didn't want us coming back here," Connor said.

"They probably didn't want us turning it back on," Samson said.

Connor frowned in thought. "The whole city is dead. There isn't any power here. Besides, we took critical components from it, so it wouldn't have worked anyway."

"Yeah, but still," Dash said. "Why go through the trouble of destroying something that already couldn't work?"

Connor peered at the holoscreen, trying to think of a reason but couldn't.

"It's simple," Samson said, his deep voice drawing their attention. "It means 'go away.'"

Connor scratched his eyebrow. "That's not going to work. We're not leaving. Have the pilot find us a place to set down and we can begin searching for them."

CHAPTER 8

Trident Battle Group orbited around the New Earth candidate. The NEC had experienced an extinction-level event that was so catastrophic that most of the planetary surface was uninhabitable. Gabriel, the *Vigilant*'s AI, estimated that the cataclysm had occurred within the last thirty to forty standard years.

Sean had sent salvage teams over to the orbital bombardment platform where a derelict ship had been docked. He was heading toward the main hangar bay where a combat shuttle waited to take him over to the wrecked ship. Bill Halsey, the lead engineer aboard the *Vigilant*, insisted that Sean come see the Casimir power core. The man lived for ships and knew them backward and forward, particularly their power cores.

Salvage teams had been exploring every inch of the ship. Sean thought Oriana would've preferred to be on one of the away teams, but she had all but locked herself in her lab with her team. She'd review the information the salvage teams found.

Sean entered the main hangar where an eagle class combat shuttle was ready to be launched. Captain Chad Boseman stood by the loading ramp and gave him a salute as he approached.

"Are we ready to leave?" Sean asked.

"Now that you're here, we are," Boseman replied.

If any of the scientists were lagging behind or running late, they wouldn't be going. Sean kept to a tight schedule that didn't include waiting for anyone who couldn't arrive on time.

The loading ramp closed and the combat shuttle was cleared for launch. As Sean ambled up to his seat, he was greeted by the rest of Boseman's team. He recognized Sergeant Benton, who had a philandering reputation;

however, since they were about to fly over to a Krake ship, he was all business-focused, just like the rest of the Spec Ops team.

Sean could always count on Boseman to come up with creative solutions to what others would consider impossible objectives. It had been Boseman's idea to use communications drones to storm the *Yorktown* during the mutiny. When failure wasn't an option, they didn't.

Sean glanced at the Spec Ops platoon and felt a slight pang of regret. He'd led his own Spec Ops platoon for years, and they'd been a small, tight-knit, highly capable group that had been given objectives by their superior officers—mostly Connor and, later on, Nathan. But the more he thought about it, he supposed very little had changed over the years, with the exception of the resources at his disposal. He'd gone from leading a platoon to a company of soldiers, then to a brigade, and now Trident Battle Group. They represented the CDF fleet's offensive line until they could build more ships.

The combat shuttle flew toward the derelict Krake warship. It was a smaller-class vessel than the destroyers they'd encountered in previous combat engagements. The ship had no power, and there were several sections that had been impacted by Krake combat drones. They hadn't found any space gates in the area, which worried Sean. Why had they been given these coordinates if they weren't going to be contacted?

There was a significant hull breach around the middle of the ship where they'd inserted an emergency docking tube. The pilot flew the combat shuttle and docked with the tube. Sean wore a Nexstar combat suit, but he wasn't armed. He didn't expect any trouble aboard the derelict ship. Search teams hadn't found any latent systems on standby, waiting to be triggered by the next hapless visitor.

The Krake were of similar size to the Ovarrow, which made them slightly taller than the average human. The pale interior of the ship held the remnants of organic matter that had been combined with the Krake version of a nanorobotic composite. The structure seemed solid, and the floors of the corridors contained enough metal for their magboots to work.

They headed for the main reactor room. He'd been in a number of main reactor rooms aboard CDF ships and even Vemus ships that had once been part of the NA Alliance military. They were massive constructs for the larger ships, but they all had certain similarities among them. There were containment systems, coolant systems, and emergency shutoffs, but Sean didn't see any of that in the Krake power core.

Captain Halsey came over to Sean, positively bursting with excitement. "Colonel, what do you think?"

"It doesn't look like one of ours. What am I looking at here?"

"We believe this is a Casimir power core. It draws energy from a vacuum and is much more efficient than even our fusion-based reactors. Zero-point energy creation is the holy grail of power generation."

Sean wished he understood what he was looking at. "So, they can generate more power, which means everything else stems from something like this. I'm surprised the Krake don't use more energy-based weapons, given their superior power core."

Halsey bobbed his head. "Maybe they do, and we just haven't found those systems yet. But I've been over to one of the main engines, and there's evidence of overwearing. We've done some preliminary analyses of the materials they use, and with that kind of power output, these engines won't hold up for extended voyages. We've also had teams that have seen stress fractures at key load points on the hull, which we think is directly related to their powerful engines."

Sean frowned in thought for a moment. "Was this power core retrofitted to this ship?"

"I was thinking that as well. Maybe they had some kind of technical leap and started outfitting their ships with these," Halsey said, gesturing toward the power core. "We'll need more time to figure that out."

Sean nodded. "Understood. Any idea how long the ship has been here?"

Halsey shook his head. "That's outside my area of expertise. I did hear a couple of the science teams mention that the ship has been here as long as the planet's been unlivable."

Sean took another look around at the area.

"We've been scanning everything we can find in here and recording things we don't understand, but in order to really understand how this power core works, we need to bring it back with us. Take it apart," Halsey said.

"You'll have to do the best you can. I don't know if we could take the ship with us."

"I thought you'd say that, sir. But if we could bring this ship back with us and reverse-engineer some of their systems, it might make our weapons more effective against them," Halsey said.

"Do the best you can, and I'll see what kind of options we can come up with. For now, keep trying to figure out how that thing works, but don't turn it on," Sean said.

He expected Halsey knew better, but the man was excited about this find. Sean thought it better to remind him to pay attention and be careful.

"Understood, sir," Halsey said.

Sean left the main reactor area, and Boseman led him toward weapons operations.

"They didn't leave much behind," Boseman said. "I would love to have found some of those attack drones so we could figure out how they work."

"Agreed," Sean said.

They spent the next few hours going over the Krake ship. The bridge of the ship was nothing like the bridge of any CDF ship; it was a multilevel, circular room. Sean guessed the CIC was above normal ship operations.

A comlink request came from the *Vigilant*.

"Colonel," Russo said, "the *Albany* reports a ship detected on sensors."

Sean stopped what he was doing. "How many ships are there?"

"Just the one ship, sir, but it's on an intercept course. Their speed is quite slow. I think they want to be seen," Russo said.

Boseman glanced at him questioningly.

"I think we've worn out our welcome. We need to get everyone off the ship," Sean said.

Boseman nodded and opened a broadcast comlink.

"Colonel," Russo said, "at the current velocity, it'll take them several hours to reach us."

"Understood, Captain. How did they sneak up on us?"

"We're not sure, sir. We still haven't detected a space gate or a gamma burst from a gate being used. The ship is on the smaller side. There might be an arch on the planet, so they could have come from there," Russo said.

"Have they tried to communicate with us?"

"Negative, Colonel."

"I'm heading back to the *Vigilant*. Keep me apprised of any new developments," Sean said.

Using an arch on the planet made sense to Sean, unless the Krake had some sort of stealth technology that hid them from CDF scanners. Sean didn't like to think about that, but it was a possibility. However, since it was a smaller ship, it could've used an arch on the planet. They hadn't had time to thoroughly investigate. He had to get back to the *Vigilant* and hopefully find out what they wanted.

CHAPTER 9

They were able to evacuate the derelict ship relatively quickly, even with Halsey lamenting the loss of such a technological sample of superior capabilities. Sean was pleased that the teams had gotten as much information as they had in the short amount of time they were on the ship.

He wasn't taking any chances where the Krake were concerned. They'd only detected one ship, and it had a different profile than the warships they'd encountered. But the safety of the people under his command was paramount to him. He wouldn't risk their lives needlessly.

Sean staggered Trident Battle Group's formation for maximum coverage on the Krake ship as it slowly approached. The *Vigilant* was positioned to be on a direct intercept course.

"No other ships detected, Colonel," Lieutenant Scott said, giving the result of the recent active scans of the area.

"Very well," Sean replied.

"Sir," Captain Russo said, "shouldn't we try to open a communications channel with them?"

"Negative. They knew we were here, and they're coming right for us. I expect them to initiate comms."

Oriana glanced at him. She probably agreed with Russo, but he'd made his decision. The Krake rebels had initiated this first contact when they transmitted these coordinates. Sean knew they hadn't tripped any type of alarm on either the orbital bombardment platform or the derelict ship. There was absolutely no power on any of those systems, and Sean hadn't allowed any of the systems to be brought back online. They had carefully monitored for any outgoing signals and hadn't detected anything.

The Krake ship steadily approached until it fired its braking thrusters and then held its position fifty thousand kilometers from Trident Battle Group.

"Colonel, I have an incoming transmission from the Krake ship," Specialist Sansky said. "They're sending our first-contact protocols back to us."

"Acknowledged. Initiate a comlink to that ship," Sean said.

First-contact protocols included a way for an advanced civilization to be able to communicate with them. He didn't want to use subspace communications because he didn't believe the Krake had that capability. They hadn't detected anything like a subspace comlink in their previous encounter, and he didn't want to wave an advantage like that under their collective noses.

"Comlink is active, sir," Sansky replied.

"Krake ship, I am Colonel Sean Quinn of the Colonial Defense Force."

A video comlink became active on the main holoscreen and showed a Krake sitting in a command chair. The video comlink vantage was relatively close to the speaker, and Sean could see that the Krake had an elongated, wedge-shaped head with twin cranial lobes. Its azure eyes were framed under a thick brow and cheek bones. The Krake's skin had a bluish hue, and the thick flesh sprouting from its chin appeared like a beard that vibrated when he spoke.

After the Krake finished speaking, a verbal translation could be heard.

"Acknowledgment of transmission. Krake ship designate DH-Crillian. Commander designation Aurang speaking."

Sean leaned forward, and his eyes widened for a moment. "We received these coordinates from a Krake warship that had come to our aid. Are you who we're supposed to meet?"

Trident Battle Group didn't have a translator for the Krake language. They'd been using an Ovarrow translator, since that was believed to be based on the Krake language. Since the Krake had obviously analyzed colonial first-contact protocols, they should be able to understand Sean.

Almost a full minute went by without a response. "Are you receiving me?" Sean asked.

"Delayed response due to translation learning. We are not the Krake who helped you, but we are of the same group," Aurang said.

"What happened to the Krake who helped us?" Sean asked.

"Sacrificed in our war with the overseers."

"Why did they help us?"

"You fought overseer military, though you're not Ovarrow, but you've translated part of the Ovarrow language."

The Krake stopped speaking and seemed to be waiting for Sean to reply.

"We have encountered the Ovarrow. We've also encountered Krake warships. They would not communicate with us and, instead, attacked us. We defended ourselves," Sean replied.

"Are the Ovarrow with you?" Aurang asked.

Sean regarded the Krake for a few moments. "No. Are the Ovarrow with you?"

"There are no Ovarrow on the ship, but they fight the overseers as well. The overseers attacked you because they believed you were a new group of Ovarrow from an unknown beta universe," Aurang said.

The Krake was volunteering information, but Sean's gut instinct was not to trust him. It was interesting that the Krake military practiced a shoot-first methodology. "Why did you help us? What group do you represent?"

"You fought the overseers. You are aware of the Krake and what they do to other Ovarrow worlds."

"We're not the Ovarrow," Sean said.

"No, you're not."

"We are humans, and we prefer not to fight a war with anybody."

"War has already begun. We all fight it. The overseers will find your world. That is what they do."

"Is war the only option? Can't we have peace?" Sean asked.

"There has never been peace. All that matters to the overseers is dominance. They are aware of you and are searching for your world. They will search for your universe, but I can help you stop them," Aurang said.

"Why would you help us?"

"Because of your warships. You are capable. You've used clever tactics to take what you want. I represent a group that resists the overseers because we believe that the individual is as important as the whole. For that, the overseers want us annihilated."

Sean suspected there would be strings attached to whatever the Krake offered them. "What do you want from us?"

"Our operations have been compromised, and it's only a matter of time before the overseers seek retribution. We need your help to stop this from happening."

"And in exchange for our help, you promise to stop the overseers from invading our world?"

"Yes."

"You'll have to forgive me if I don't believe you. If the overseers are as powerful as you say, then how is helping you going to prevent them from invading our home?" Sean asked.

Aurang was quiet for a few moments. "We have an operation in place that is set to take out the overseers. They will be removed from power. New overseers will be appointed, and the Krake will stop. Many things will change."

Sean had seen the Ovarrow ruins on New Earth. All colonists were aware of them. The Krake manipulated the Ovarrow, and Sean felt that what he was hearing was too good to be true.

"We'll need time to consider your request. In order to do that, I need to understand exactly what you need from us."

"You have resources. Our communication network has been compromised and it's not safe for me to contact our fighters. I will transfer the data I have for you to review."

Sean glanced at Specialist Sansky.

"Data uplink has been initiated. Dumping data to secure virtual sandbox for analysis," Sansky said.

"The Krake are not all the same. There can be peace between us," Aurang said.

"We'll need time to consider your request for help," Sean said.

The comlink went dark. Sean sat back in his chair and sighed. He felt as if he'd just gone on a long-distance run and then learned that he still had miles to go.

CHAPTER 10

An hour had passed since they'd received Aurang's request for help. Sean wanted some time to analyze the data and make sure there wasn't anything hidden that could infiltrate their computer systems.

Sean and Russo left the bridge and headed for the nearby conference room. When they walked inside, Oriana was already there, along with Chad Boseman and Bill Halsey. Major Shelton, who was commanding the *Yorktown*, was online, along with the rest of the commanding officers of the battle group, half of whom were familiar. The other half were too new to know well.

"Thank you all for coming. By now, you've had time to review the data Aurang sent us. I'm going to open up the floor so you can voice your concerns, but before I do that, I want you to know that I don't have any reason to trust Aurang," Sean said.

"He's hiding something, sir," Boseman said.

"I'm sure he's hiding a lot, but he also provided some detailed information. Gabriel didn't detect any type of data tampering or latent protocols that would infiltrate our systems, so at least the data he provided is clean, but I wouldn't say it's free of risk."

"How was the data verified?" Oriana asked.

"I isolated the data on a secure system and ran it through a number of different analyses, including time acceleration that allowed the Krake data to sit there for the equivalent of ten standard years. No hidden subroutines were detected," Gabriel said.

There was silence for a few moments. Sean hadn't expected any of the junior officers to speak up.

"Sir," Major Shelton said, "they've only given us a list of targets, along with a briefing about what they need to accomplish there. This isn't enough for us to make a 'go' or 'no-go' decision."

Aurang had given them images of multiple Krake facilities, as well as star system information, including defenses and space gate and arch locations.

"Agreed, and the mission requires coordination with Aurang and whatever soldiers he has aboard his ship. Anyone else?" Sean asked.

"Sir," Lieutenant Richard Pitts of the *Babylon* said, "he's making a promise that he can stop the Krake from finding our world if we help them overthrow the current leadership. I understand he wants to protect his intelligence network, or whatever the Krake wants to call it. I think what he's promising you is something he can't deliver. It's intangible. I would call it 'pie in the sky' where they promise us the world and then ultimately can't deliver it."

"Good point, Lieutenant Pitts. How do we know this isn't a trap? How do we know we aren't being manipulated right now?" Sean said.

"Then we treat the entire operation as if it's a trap, sir," Boseman said.

Sean nodded. "That's what I'm thinking."

"Sir," Pitts said, "if we aren't going to trust the Krake or this Aurang, why would we even consider a military operation with them? Why wouldn't we decline his request and return to New Earth?"

Sean took a moment to look at the other holoscreens. Whether or not they should return home had been one of the crucial points of the entire mutiny. Pitts wasn't his staunchest supporter, but Sean could work with that. "Because of our mission out here. We've been tasked to learn all we can about the Krake and whether or not we can find a way to defeat them. We can't recon our enemy if we don't take any risks, but we can all agree that there's a high degree of risk in this undertaking; however, there's also the potential for a greater reward, meaning that we could learn something crucial about the Krake. We're all out here to protect our home, and I intend to build into our planning a way to send word back to COMCENT in the event that we fail."

There was dead silence for a few moments.

"Colonel, what about the Krake prisoners?" Major Shelton asked.

"We've questioned them before, and they've refused to communicate with us. At this time, I'm not entertaining any option to force cooperation," Sean said.

"Would they be more cooperative if they thought they were being returned to their people?" Shelton asked.

"Possibly, but I want to keep them as a bargaining piece in case we need them," Sean said.

"Sir, are you sure this is the best course of action regarding the prisoners?" Lieutenant Pitts asked.

Sean had called this all-hands meeting to keep the senior officers invested in the mission. "Do you have a suggestion, Lieutenant?"

"Just that it might be dangerous to bring them back home with us."

"I'm positive we can secure two prisoners," Sean replied. "Thank you all for your participation. I will, of course, inform you of your orders, but if you have any concerns in the meantime, raise them with your immediate superiors."

The meeting ended, and Sean returned to the bridge. He brought Chad Boseman with him so he could watch the encounter with Aurang. At the top of the hour, a comlink from the Krake ship was initiated.

Right on time, Sean thought.

"Colonel Quinn, you've had time to consider my request for aid. Have you reached a decision?" Aurang asked.

"Not yet. We need to perform our own analysis. If you want our help, you'll need to give us the coordinates of the targets and we'll have a look for ourselves."

"This is unacceptable. My people are in danger from the overseers. We must go at once."

"Then my answer is no. We will not assist you," Sean said.

"The data I provided is current. Why do you need to see these targets in order to make a decision?"

Sean leaned forward. "Because I don't trust you. You haven't given me any reason to trust you."

Sean thought he might've offended the Krake, but that wasn't the case.

"Understood, and this is to be expected. What do you want to know most about the Krake?"

Sean frowned. He hadn't been anticipating that kind of question. "I want to know how much you know about us. Is it possible to negotiate a peaceful end to hostilities?"

"No, I already told you this is impossible. The overseers will never stop searching for you because they need to substantiate how much of a threat you are. In order to achieve that, testing is required."

"That's why we must do our own reconnaissance, and then we can tell you whether or not we can help you. I want to know what communication protocols the Krake use. I want to be able to communicate with other Krake and not be reliant on you to translate for us," Sean said.

"If I provide this, will you help us?"

"No. If you provide this, then I'll consider helping you by doing our own reconnaissance of these targets."

Aurang was quiet while he considered Sean's reply.

"Giving this to us is a show of good faith. If you want to help your people, this is a small token toward building trust between us," Sean said.

"Very well, I will give you a copy of our communications protocols, as well as the translator. I would like to now discuss the use of your space gate," Aurang said.

"Continue," Sean said.

"I cannot bring this ship through the arch and go to the target universe. I will need to use your space gate."

"That is out of the question," Sean said.

There was no way he was going to allow a potential enemy ship among the battle group to watch how they used their space gate.

"Then how will we communicate?" Aurang asked.

"You can find your own way to the target universe and we'll meet you there. Give us a way to contact you. If we contact you, then you'll know our answer," Sean replied.

"What assurances do I have that you'll even honor your end of the bargain? The lives of my people are at risk if I have to wait for you and you decide not to help," Aurang said.

"You came to us for help. I want to know the coordinates of Krake outposts and the home world, or wherever it is that your overseers reside."

Aurang snarled. "I will not reveal our home world to you."

Finally, an emotional response. That was something, at least. Sean had been wondering how far he could push him before he pushed back. If Aurang had promised to give them that information, then he'd have known this entire thing was a lie.

"But I can provide you with operational data of our current outposts. That data is in the main facility that holds the operational intelligence of our group. I can give you access to it," Aurang said.

Now they were getting somewhere. "I'll be in touch after we do our own reconnaissance," Sean said.

"Sir," Boseman said, and Sean looked at him. "A quick moment, sir. This concerns the Krake."

Sean gestured for Boseman to come over. He looked at Aurang. "Give us a few moments," Sean said and muted the channel.

"Sir, that ship would fit into our main hangar, so we could bring them with us without allowing them to monitor our space gate. We could also confine them to their ship if we needed to. And if they betrayed us, we'd get one more piece of Krake tech to bring home with us," Boseman said.

Sean frowned in thought for a moment. Only the *Vigilant* or the *Yorktown* had enough room in their hangar bays to accommodate the Krake ship. He gave his friend a nod, and Boseman returned to his post.

Sean unmuted the comlink channel. "Aurang, I think we have a way to accommodate your request to come with us."

"Fortuitous! I'm eager to hear it," Aurang said.

Sean told him.

"Your caution is acceptable. We will comply," Aurang said.

"My helmsman will provide you with the coordinates," Sean said and transferred the comlink to Lieutenant Edwards.

Aurang provided the data they requested, including a translation program. Then the Krake ship was guided to the *Vigilant*'s main hangar.

"Helm, set a course for beta coordinates in the outer system," Sean said.

"Sir, I have a subspace comlink from the *Yorktown*," Sansky said.

"Send it to my personal holoscreen," Sean replied. A moment later, Major Shelton appeared on his holoscreen.

"Sir, remind me never to play poker with you," she said and grinned a little. "I know we're expecting a trap, but I find it suspicious that he expected us to up and go right now."

"Maybe the Krake are used to dealing with the Ovarrow. Either way, we'll have enough transit time to test out the Krake translator he gave us," Sean said.

Major Shelton's eyes widened. "You had already planned to ask him for that, hadn't you?"

"It was one of the things. I didn't expect he would share the location of their home world system, but his response was revealing, I think. I don't think he was expecting it."

"No, I think you're right. He wasn't expecting it."

"I'll send a copy of the data to you. If there's anyone else you want to bring in on our analysis of this, let me know. Otherwise, I'm going to keep this between us," Sean said.

"Understood, sir."

The comlink went dark and they got to work.

CHAPTER 11

Twenty-four hours had passed and Connor was no closer to finding the Ovarrow. He'd divided the 7th into ten squads and they'd spent the night among the ruins of the Ovarrow capital city. With the use of recon drones, they were covering a lot of ground, but they hadn't found any evidence of the Ovarrow they'd encountered when retrieving critical pieces of the arch. Recon drones spotted a few ryklar scouts out on the fringes of the city, but they only found older ryklar tracks inside. Mostly they saw various flying creatures, some of which might have been considered birds.

The night before, they'd seen a large group of bats take to the skies near sunset, which had startled the soldiers on guard duty. The bats that lived in this region were much larger than the similar species on Earth. Connor didn't know much about them, but Dash, ever curious about New Earth, had enlightened him about them the night before. Bats on Earth were small and harmless, and they liked to eat insects. On New Earth, they weighed six kilograms and had a wingspan of almost two meters, on average. They had a healthy set of canines, which they used to penetrate the green and yellow fruit they preferred to eat, but they also ate insects, which were quite large in this region. Connor had sampled the fruit before. It was bitter and too full of seeds to be enjoyed, so the bats could keep all that fruit they wanted. And the insects were a nonissue since humans weren't going to eat those either.

The bats had taken up residence in a few of the tall buildings that the colonists thought were monuments. They thought this because rather than being constructed from bronze, metallic-alloyed plates, these were obsidian on the outside. They were dark but shimmered when the sunlight reflected off them. When hundreds of the giant bats took to the skies at sunset, the sounds of their flapping wings ricocheted off the surrounding buildings like thunder. It was no less impressive than watching several wings of Hellcats take off and fly in formation from a CDF base.

As they explored the city, the only reports that came in indicated smaller, rodent-sized creatures scurrying throughout the city. Camping there reminded Connor of exploring other ruins with Lenora when he'd been retired from the CDF. The sleeping arrangements had been better back then, but the 7th was filled with a good group of soldiers.

New Earth was a place that explorers dreamt about. Even after living on this planet for as long as they had, the newness of it hadn't quite worn off. The planet would never be what Earth had been, but most colonists had come to love their new home as much as their old home, and Connor was no exception. Why else would he fight so hard to protect it? New Earth was a world worth protecting. This was his home.

Connor walked over to the command area where Samson was organizing troop deployments for the search grids they were going to hit that day. The group of squad leaders dispersed once they had their assignments and the comlink to the other camps flickered off.

"Layton had several squads explore some of the underground tunnels on the western side of the city, but most had cave-ins blocking them," Samson said.

The cities they'd explored had extensive sewer systems connected to dormant water treatment facilities. Now, they were little more than an underground river system that connected to major waterways.

"Were any of the cave-ins recent?" Connor asked.

"None that they could tell," Samson replied. "If I were fortifying a city against an invader, I'd block off all the underground entries," he said and glanced toward where Dash was speaking with the Ovarrow. "Especially if they were sending in their attack dogs."

Connor nodded. Ryklars could burrow and squeeze through some tight spaces when they wanted to. "It makes sense, but they wouldn't have walled themselves off completely, and we still don't know if they were just guarding the area. They might live somewhere else. I've had satellites scouring the area, but the analysts haven't found anything either."

Samson frowned, his mouth forming a grim line while he peered at the map on the holoscreen. "They could have destroyed the arch and then packed up and left."

"Maybe, but you can't cover up the movement of a big group like that. When the ryklars attacked, there were quite a few of them. I think we need to go back to the arch chamber. It might be our best lead. We know they were there and that there were tunnels in the area."

"Just say the word. I'll have the engineers bring equipment to clear a path if we need it," Samson replied.

"We'll need it," Connor said and was quiet for a few moments while he studied the map.

Samson shifted his feet. "I can hear the wheels turning."

Connor looked at him. "We assumed that they might have been living somewhere in a section of the city itself, but that could be wrong. If they've been hiding their presence for . . ." he said and paused, glancing at the Ovarrow for several seconds, ". . . a few hundred years, then maybe they abandoned living on the surface altogether. Living below ground would prevent them from being detected by the casual observer. When the Krake were cycling through different universes, their goal was to identify a place worth scouting. The Ovarrow were definitely monitoring the arch here."

Samson rubbed the stubble on the bottom of his chin in thought. "Living underground for years is a bit of a stretch."

"I don't think so. If they never went into stasis, they'd have had to survive the ice age somehow," Connor said.

"Wouldn't they have just migrated south to where it's warmer?"

"Maybe, but that would mean bringing a lot of equipment with them, which we've never found evidence of, so I'm not sure that explanation works. They could have migrated, but why come back when the ice age was over?"

"We should ask *them*," Samson said, twisting his head toward the Ovarrow.

Connor shook his head. "They wouldn't know. Maybe the warlord would but not Cerot or the others. They're young."

"So, we need a reason for them either coming back here or staying here. Maybe they were just guarding the arch?"

Connor nodded. "It's the obvious choice. I'm just not sure it's reason enough for them to stay here. They'd have to feed themselves and train future generations not to abandon their posts, but that doesn't tell us why," Connor said.

"Why do we guard anything?" Samson said. He had a point.

"They only destroyed it after they found us scavenging it for parts," Connor said. "What if they intended to use it? Or what if they'd kept it as a fail-safe in case the Krake came back through that arch we found at New Haven?"

Dash walked over and looked at them. "Am I interrupting something?"

"No," Samson said. "Connor's just trying to figure out why we haven't found them yet and why they'd stay here in the first place."

Dash's eyes flicked toward Connor. "Well, given what we've seen, I wouldn't put it past them to figure out a way to survive without giving away their presence to the Krake, or anyone else who might come looking for them."

"At some point, the Krake stopped coming here," Connor said.

Cerot and the other Ovarrow were standing nearby, and Connor considered them for a few moments. Dash looked at him questioningly and Samson merely waited. Connor scratched his eyebrow. "When we brought them out of stasis and moved them to their city, they went to work making it livable. It's what we expected them to do, but the Ovarrow here must be different."

"Should we recall the search teams then?" Samson asked.

Connor shook his head. "No, but send them an update to look for anything leading underground—hidden entrances inside buildings or anything we could potentially squeeze through."

Samson nodded and opened a broadcast comlink to the rest of the 7th.

Dash looked at Connor. "That's going to slow them down."

"I'd rather go slower and find something than move quickly and miss something important," Connor replied.

Dash smiled and nodded. "The places Cerot or others have checked don't look like they've been used in a while. Esteban and Felix found a few buildings that hadn't been opened in a long time. With no power, it's hard to get access to these places. It just makes me think that no one has lived here for a long time."

Connor powered off the holoscreen and the map of the city disappeared. "That's what they want us to think. We wouldn't have come here in the first place if it hadn't been for Raylore, but he's not the one in charge anymore."

"I'll stick with Cerot and the others."

"I want them with me, so stay close. Just remember to pay attention. They didn't want us here the first time," Connor said.

"Let's hope they'll be more willing to talk. I mean . . ." Dash said, glancing at Cerot for a moment, ". . . they should be willing to speak with their own kind, wouldn't you think?"

"I'm hoping for that."

"And if they don't?"

"I'm not leaving until I find them," Connor replied.

"Yeah, but if they—"

"It doesn't matter. They were here, so we should be able to find evidence of where they went."

They left the camp and headed for the area where they'd found the arch. Remnants of a few long spires that ended in jagged edges pierced the skyline, so it wasn't difficult to find. As they made their way closer to their destination, thick overgrowth covered most of the buildings in the area. Connor wondered whether the overgrowth in the area was a natural occurrence or something the Ovarrow had engineered. The broad leaves of eggplant-colored flora grew on thick vines that blocked much of the sunlight and created natural canopies between the buildings. The air was humid and hot, and there was a faint odor of mold that came from the moist ground. The last time Connor had been there, they'd flown over much of the city to reach their destination, so this was new to him.

He kept looking for any signs that there were Ovarrow living there, but the city looked like it had been abandoned many years ago. How had these structures survived all the wars that had been fought across the vast continent? Connor remembered seeing evidence of a bombardment at some of the other cities they'd explored but not this one. They hadn't detected any ryklar deterrent signals, but something had made the creatures abandon the city.

They finally entered a familiar, wide-open area, and Connor led them across the way. Three intertwining triangles adorned the entrance to the building they were headed for. It hadn't changed all that much—still bronze-colored and seemingly reinforced with thick plating. It was an Ovarrow military research center, but there were no latent lockdown systems waiting to ambush them. A ramp led downward. Several soldiers took point and the rest of them followed. Recon drones were already scouting ahead of them.

They headed inside and Connor used his implants to check the recon drones. They hadn't detected any energy signatures. The place was still dead.

The ramp curved around, leading them deeper into the building, and soon they were underground. There were no plants this far into the facility, and the wide doors they passed through were already open from the last time they'd been there. The first time, they'd had to force the doors open. They continued for twenty minutes until they reached a vast, open area. Their lights penetrated the darkness, but the CDF soldiers also had implants with night vision. Across the way were the remains of the arch that had been there. Connor ordered flares to be shot to the far side of the room so the Ovarrow could see better. As red flares ignited in the distance, large, intact pieces of the arch reflected the light along the ground in glistening pools.

Connor glanced to the side, scanning for the elevated platform to the right of the arch.

"Looks like they took out the command center," Dash said.

Where the elevated platform should have been there was only a heap of twisted metal blackened by scorch marks. Connor looked at Samson and gestured toward the remains of the command center. "It looks like they used some kind of explosive material. Have a team run an analysis on it."

Samson sent a team over while the rest of them made a sweep of the area.

"What are they looking for?" Dash asked.

"The type of accelerant used in the explosive. We might be able to track them with it," Connor replied.

Dash considered this for a few moments and nodded. Then his eyebrows drew up in concern. "Do you think they set traps for us?"

Connor twitched his head to the side once. "Now you're thinking like one of us."

Cerot had been watching the exchange and read the translation on the wrist computer each Ovarrow had been provided. "Mekaal tactics include the use of sabotage. We'll help watch for this."

Connor thanked him. "If you notice anything, let us know and we'll investigate it."

The rooms on the other side of the chamber were structurally intact, but the consoles had been destroyed. Dash had extracted all the data from those consoles the last time they'd been there, so there wasn't a loss. The fact that these Ovarrow were covering their tracks was indication enough as to their intentions. They must have hidden for so long that it had become part of their culture. Getting them to communicate might prove more difficult than it had been with the Ovarrow who'd slept in stasis pods for hundreds of years.

"I'll need your help when we find them," Connor said to Cerot.

"I understand, General."

Connor walked over to the remains of the arch that the CDF had taken components from for their own arch. The Ovarrow had left it intact for hundreds of years, only to destroy it now. Connor couldn't rationalize it. The components they'd taken from it would have prevented it from being used even if the Ovarrow had somehow restored power to it. Why destroy what remained? They might have anticipated that the colonists would return there, so preventing them from using the arch might have been one of the reasons. But that couldn't be the only one. Were they afraid the Krake would discover its existence and use it as a way to come to this universe?

Connor turned toward Samson and Dash. "I don't get it. Why destroy the arch?"

Samson shrugged. "They don't want us to use it."

"I thought of that, too, but that can't be the only reason." Connor looked at Dash. "Were you able to find anything in the data you got from the consoles the last time we were here?"

Dash frowned in thought for a few moments. "Just log entries—old ones —and some of the data was corrupt. We know they used the arch. I showed Cerot and the others some of that data on our way here. They said they were maintenance logs. They could have been testing it."

Connor nodded. "They spent who knows how long trying to reverse-engineer it, so that might make sense," he said and pressed his lips together in thought. "I can understand testing the arch to see if they could make it work. How much of a stretch would it be that they actually used it?"

Samson shook his head. "Not that much. They used it. They must have."

Connor gestured toward the wreckage of the arch. "Paints all this in a new light."

"How so?" Dash asked.

"Think about it. We debated whether we should use the arch, and they probably did the same. So, they could have destroyed this one to prevent us from using it and . . ." He paused for a second. "Or they did it to prevent other Ovarrow from using it—either the ones we've been bringing out of stasis or perhaps among themselves."

Samson exhaled forcefully and shook his head. "And you want to talk to them?"

"We need to."

"I'm going to see about opening a few of those hidden doors you suspected existed the last time you were here," Samson said and walked away.

Dash waited a few moments and then said, "Why is he upset?"

"Trust me, you'll know if Samson is upset. He just prefers a straight-up fight. We used to work together before . . . before the colony. Anticipating group activities was the whole intelligence-gathering part of the job."

It wasn't difficult to identify the hidden doors. They used a sonic-wave generator to cause subtle vibrations. If an echo was detected, the indication was a passageway beyond. They found five of them. Two of the passageways angled back the way they'd already come. The remaining three appeared to be intact. Recon drones flew down the passageways, scanning for ryklars, and the data they sent back was used to map the area. These tunnels connected with other tunnels.

"There's a city underneath the city. This is going to take a while to explore," Samson said.

Connor studied the holoscreen that was displaying the ever-expanding map of the underground tunnels beneath the city. "A while" was a bit of an understatement. He used his implants to update the data being shown on the holoscreen. Soon, there were paths highlighted in red. "There, that helps a little bit. The highlighted areas are where ryklar tracks were detected."

"It's broken up over here," Dash said. "Oh, I see it now. Those are probably old sewage ways, so there's water there."

"We don't know how old those tracks are, but we don't need to. They're all going in the same general direction to this area here," Connor said. He nodded to himself. "That's our target," he said and looked at Samson. "Captain, let's get everyone ready."

"Yes, sir," Samson said and began bellowing orders.

The Ovarrow had been able to conceal their presence aboveground, but underground was a different story. The tunnels underneath the city showed signs of being recently used. Even the waterways they'd crossed had reinforced bridges. They were on the right track. Some of the tunnels narrowed to barely three meters across, while others were much wider. Connor didn't want to have to fight a battle down there because of the risk of bringing the tunnel down on top of them.

Samson assigned Corporal Alanson to keep track of the recon drones and their updates to the map they were following. Connor, Dash, and the rest of the Ovarrow stayed close to the front. Connor carried an AR-71, which was standard issue for the CDF. The nanorobotic ammunition made it a versatile assault rifle.

They'd been walking up the main tunnel for the last half hour. There were offshoots, and Corporal Alanson spoke. "General, there's movement detected in some of the adjacent tunnels up ahead, sir."

Samson was about to order a scout force ahead, but Connor told him to wait. "Corporal, engage the recall signal for the ryklars," Connor said.

The tunnels lit up in a blaze of light flashing across the visual spectrum of colors. Movement in the adjacent tunnels ceased. Connor had the corporal repeat the sequence, and then they waited. The recon drone flew to one of the entrances of the adjacent tunnel and scanned inside. The ryklars had left. They were definitely on the right track.

With the presence of the ryklars confirmed, Samson had more soldiers brought to the front, armed and ready. His reasoning was that even though they were able to mimic the control signal for the ryklars, they didn't know if the Ovarrow had some way to order the ryklars to attack regardless of which light they were showing them. Connor had to agree with that. The sonic deterrent signals would work down there, but these ryklars had been mutilated by having their auditory systems removed. His mouth formed a grim line at the thought. It must've been extremely painful for those creatures. The ryklars were dangerous, but so was anything else that wanted to live. There were other predators, like berwolves, that were nearly as dangerous as ryklars, but they were nowhere near as smart. Berwolves were the size of Old Earth grizzly bears but with the agility of wolves. The ryklars were something different. They were highly intelligent. Connor had heard the term "sapient intelligence," meaning they had the potential to be almost as intelligent as human beings, but that was a bit of a stretch, even for Connor. He wasn't an expert in evolutionary science, but he'd spoken with experts in that field enough to at least appreciate that yes, there was a strong possibility that if ryklars were allowed to evolve over millions of years, they had the greatest potential of becoming an intelligent species. Right now, their intelligence was considered to equal that of an Old Earth bottlenose dolphin. They had highly complex brains and lived in a small society. It was these traits that had probably drawn the Ovarrow to utilize them the way they had. But at some point, the way the Ovarrow had used the ryklars was just cruel. Connor had never broached the subject with the Ovarrow—at least not yet.

Connor had killed hundreds of ryklars, but there had been no other choice. He'd seen potential in the ryklars when Siloc had taken him prisoner. Left to their own devices, they weren't entirely wild. That didn't mean he'd voluntarily go unarmed into a pack of them and expect not to be killed, but there was potential there. He remembered ryklars leaving him alive while killing Siloc at the Mekaal secret base. There was nothing that would convince Connor that this was because the ryklars were preoccupied with their desire to kill Siloc. They'd made a decision not to kill Connor. It was what had led him to learn as much as he could about them.

Connor heard Dash speaking in urgent tones with Cerot and the others and made his way over to them. "What's the matter?"

"They're worried about the ryklars."

"Did you explain to them how these ryklars are different?"

"Yes, but I don't know if they completely understand," Dash replied.

The ryklar tracks led to a major adjacent tunnel, and they followed them. The CDF soldiers held their weapons with practiced efficiency. These were all seasoned combat veterans.

By now, they could hear the ryklars, and it seemed that they'd gathered in a vast chamber the tunnel connected to. The entrance to the chamber was a natural cave opening. Connor heard sounds of an underground river echoing off the sides of the cave. There was moisture in the air, but there was a generally cool temperature beneath the ground. They sent the recon drones out of the tunnel and up to take a survey of the area. There were large cisterns across the chamber, and hundreds of the mutilated ryklars were gathered. Walking among them were Ovarrow soldiers, some of whom wore ryklar skins.

Two bridges crossed the wide river. The bridges were easily defendable, but it was nothing the CDF couldn't handle. However, he didn't believe it was a coincidence that the Ovarrow had taken their stand there. He wondered what was beyond this chamber that was worth defending. It could be their homes, or it could be something else.

Cerot and the other Ovarrow erupted into a quick debate. Connor glanced at Dash, who gave a slight shake of his head.

"What are your orders, General?" Samson asked.

"I'm going to try to talk to them. Let's move up to the bridge. Have the men spread out so they can cover us if we need it," Connor said.

"Understood, sir. What about our guests?" Samson said and nodded toward Cerot and the others.

Cerot gestured toward the bridge and then to the other Ovarrow.

"Let them come with us," Connor said.

They walked toward the bridge, and Connor peered at the ryklars gathered on the other side. Their bearded tentacles were gray or almost black, indicating that they were not in a highly agitated state. When ryklars were highly agitated, which occurred through the use of the control signals, their bearded tentacles became bright red. But the fact that the ryklars weren't highly agitated didn't make them any less dangerous. They drew in deep breaths and seemed to be a moment away from charging across that bridge to attack them.

Ryklars had two sets of arms. One set was directly in front of them and was a bit shorter than the heavily muscled ones on the sides. They had thick claws that could rend even the battle steel of their armored vehicles. Leopard-like spots spilled across their gray coats.

It was strange for Connor to see them waiting, and even stranger was the fact that there were definitely Ovarrow soldiers walking among them. They were easy to pick out. Standing at full height, they were head and shoulders taller than the ryklars' stooped forms. They wore dark armor, similar to what Cerot and the others wore. The reconnaissance drone detected power sources from the weapons they carried. The Ovarrow rifle could shoot a particle beam. They required recharging, but they were powerful enough to get the job done. The CDF had superior weaponry, but Connor wanted to communicate with them, not start a fight.

One of the recon drones flew up, taking a position several feet above Connor's head, and a large holoscreen appeared above them.

"Ovarrow, my name is Connor Gates, and I'd like to communicate with your leader."

The Ovarrow translator put up a series of symbols. Connor waited, but there was almost no reaction from the small army across the bridge—not exactly the warmest greeting.

"Is there a warlord among you?" Connor asked.

He noticed several Ovarrow soldiers shifting their feet. Cerot let out a harsh grunt, and Connor gestured for him to come stand next to him. Cerot came over and then spoke in rapid succession, raising his voice so the Ovarrow across the bridge could hear him. The Ovarrow had multiple vocal cords as part of their physiology and could generate sounds beyond anything the colonists could duplicate.

A loud blast of acknowledgment came from an Ovarrow across the bridge. Cerot went quiet and waited. One of the Ovarrow soldiers across the bridge strode purposefully to the entrance. He was tall, like most Ovarrow. He sported lean muscles that could be seen where the armor didn't cover, and many age lines crisscrossed his face. He uttered a short staccato series of sounds.

"What is that?" Connor asked.

"I think that's his name," Dash replied.

Cerot used the translator and a single word appeared. The name was Brashirker. Then came the title "Warlord of the Ovarrow."

Brashirker spoke again and then slammed the butt of his weapon to the ground.

"The abandoners are not welcome here," Brashirker said.

Connor frowned for a moment and then glanced at Cerot. He saw that Dash had made the connection as well. He'd brought Cerot and the others, hoping they'd be able to open the lines of communication; however, Brashirker was sending a clear message that this wasn't the case.

"How accurate is the translation?" Connor asked.

"This is accurate, Connor. It stems from the logic used in their subroutines for their programming. Some tasks are just abandoned. This isn't a mistake. He doesn't want them here," Dash said.

Connor looked across the bridge and tried to think of a way he could salvage the situation before it became untenable. Why didn't anyone want to talk to anyone else?

CHAPTER 12

onnor heard Samson provide a status to the other soldiers. Cerot and the other Ovarrow were still staring across the bridge at another member of their own species.

Brashirker made a sharp sound, and two ryklars scrambled to his side and waited.

"What's he doing?" Dash asked.

"Either he's showing off, trying to intimidate us, or he wants protection," Connor said. He took a few steps forward, leaving the others behind, and spoke to Brashirker. "I doubt anyone is welcome here, yet here we are. Your people attacked mine not that long ago. Now you've destroyed the arch. We have a common enemy, and I want to talk to you about that."

Connor sent the recon drone across the bridge and the holoscreen above it expanded to include his entire message. He wanted to be sure Brashirker could read it. He took a few more steps forward and Samson joined him, along with Lieutenant Mason. Both held their weapons loosely, but only a fool would believe they weren't moments from being at full readiness. If Brashirker or anyone else across the bridge attacked, Connor would shoot them.

Brashirker moved forward with the ryklars at his heels. Several other Ovarrow soldiers followed him, but it was only a small group. Connor did the same, and Samson called other soldiers to follow them. He heard Dash asking Cerot to wait behind.

Connor caught his first real look at Brashirker and the other Ovarrow. They looked more like aged veterans than the Ovarrow they'd rescued from stasis pods.

Brashirker began to speak, but the translator couldn't decipher the Ovarrow's spoken language. When it became apparent to him that he was to use the holographic interface and select the symbols to convey his message, he scowled and gestured for one of his soldiers to use it. The Ovarrow soldier gingerly touched a symbol and it appeared on the screen. They weren't strangers to an interface like this. It had been designed to mimic what they'd found on the Ovarrow consoles, so it seemed that the Ovarrow hadn't abandoned their technology.

"You were attacked because you were in forbidden territory. Access to the arch is prohibited," Brashirker said.

"We needed components from the arch to make ours work."

"It is forbidden."

"We've faced the Krake. It's one of the reasons we came back here," Connor said.

He'd expected more of a reaction from the Ovarrow at the mention of the Krake, but that wasn't the case. They were quiet, just waiting and listening. They acted very unlike the Ovarrow who'd come out of stasis.

"You've faced the Krake and you come here? They will follow you. They always follow you, eventually," Brashirker replied.

"Have you ever fought the Krake?"

"Our ancestors fought and died. You've seen what's left of their war."

"Did you know that we were here on this planet?" Connor asked.

"We were aware of your presence, but you kept your activities far away."

"Did your people go into stasis?" Connor asked.

His question brought an instant reaction from not only Brashirker but the Ovarrow soldiers with him—a murmuring growl that sounded like the Ovarrow were clearing their throats but with more intensity. The ryklars sat back on their haunches and merely waited.

"I meant no offense," Connor said. "I want to know more about you."

"Why?" Brashirker asked.

Connor waited a few moments before answering. "As you said, we have observed the aftermath of your wars. We know that your ancestors fought each other, as well as the Krake. But we don't know about *you*. We know that some of you—the Ovarrow—went into stasis pods. We found many of them, but some of the pods were in a state of disrepair. The Ovarrow who survived suffered from health issues that we've been able to help them with."

"That is a mistake. My ancestors never went into stasis. They didn't have the resources. They were pushed out of the strongholds that had stasis pods. We refused to sacrifice our young to live in a world without the Krake."

Samson leaned closer to Connor. "What does he mean by 'sacrifice their young'? Is the translator broken again?"

Connor shook his head. "No, the stasis tech that the Ovarrow used could only support juveniles and near adults, as well as older Ovarrow. The younger ones wouldn't survive."

"They abandoned their young so they could live?" Samson asked quietly.

"Some of them, maybe. Not all of them," Connor said. His chest tightened, and a sneer lifted his lips. It was hard for him not to judge, but he needed to keep Brashirker talking. There were so many questions he wanted to ask, but he knew this was a delicate situation. The slightest misstep would end the conversation prematurely. "How did you survive?"

"Our ancestors created strongholds of their own upon the bones of the old world. We lived underground. Some moved to the southern reaches, but none of them survived," Brashirker said.

"What happened to them?" Connor asked.

"The Krake found them. We severed all ties," Brashirker said.

Dash had come forward and was standing next to Connor. "He has to be talking about the beginning of the ice age. I wonder how long the Krake were active here."

Connor looked back at Brashirker. "How did you stop the Krake from coming here?"

Brashirker seemed to consider this for a few moments. "Many years had passed and the Krake kept coming here despite the long winter. We disabled the arch here, but there were more across the continent. We sent groups to destroy them. We knew they had succeeded when the Krake stopped coming."

Whoever had gone in search of the arches had sacrificed themselves. They must've known it would be a one-way trip. It was hard for Connor to put together a timeline without making a lot of assumptions, but at least he had a high-level overview of what had happened.

"We thought the Krake had returned when systems from the old world began to come online. If it wasn't the Krake, then it was the abandoners who were finally waking up," Brashirker said.

"It wasn't the Krake; it was us exploring your world. I can understand why your ancestors held resentment of the Ovarrow who went into stasis, but what are *your* reasons? This happened hundreds of years ago."

"We remember."

Connor's eyebrows knitted together in a frown. "I don't understand."

Brashirker took a step forward. His muscles rippled as he clenched his weapon. "Your lack of understanding is what will bring the Krake to this planet. Some of the Ovarrow who went into stasis worshipped the Krake. The Krake are their masters, and they will seek to reestablish contact with the Krake now that they've been brought out of stasis."

"How? We found one arch that was at the bottom of the lake. We've built a prototype. Are there more?"

Brashirker leaned back. "Possibly."

"Then you should work with us so we can prevent anyone else from contacting the Krake."

"It is too late for that. You've crossed paths with the Krake, and they will come back to this world."

"All the more reason to help us. Tell us what you know about the Krake. I need to find their home universe to stop them from coming here," Connor said.

He expected a similar response to the one he'd received from other

Ovarrow—something along the lines of "the Krake can't be stopped," but instead he was answered with silence.

"You will wait. Your machines will not follow us," Brashirker finally answered.

The Ovarrow warlord turned and crossed back to his side of the bridge. The others followed him. Connor recalled the recon drone and withdrew to the other side of the bridge. The Ovarrow soldiers and the ryklars withdrew into several different tunnels, leaving a small token force to stand guard at the tunnel entrances.

Connor looked at Samson. "We're going to make a camp right here. Contact the other teams and let them know our status. They are to proceed as ordered."

Samson walked away to convey Connor's orders.

"I've never seen ryklars look so calm," Dash said.

"Neither have I. What did you think about what he said?" Connor asked.

"It confirms the history we suspected. But we don't have detailed records. We don't know if this is where they live or how many of them there are."

Connor nodded and glanced at Cerot and the others. The Ovarrow were speaking to each other. "Brashirker wouldn't even speak to them."

"He thinks they're Krake sympathizers who went into stasis," Dash replied.

"It's more than that. Whatever happened to them, that dedication or commitment to those beliefs might've formed the foundation of their society. Don't look at me like that; I paid attention. What I don't know is whether I can convince them to help us."

Dash was quiet for a few moments while he considered what Connor had said. "So, you want to find the Krake's home universe and stop them there? That's the first time I've ever heard this."

"That's where we need to get to. If the Krake find us first, it'll be a lot worse for us."

"It took months to convince the Ovarrow that we were trying to help them when they came out of stasis. I think you took them by surprise. Maybe they just need some time," Dash said.

Connor's eyebrows raised. "I'm sure they didn't plan on us showing up here."

"I mean beyond that. I don't think they expected you to say the things you did. Considering that they might've been aware of our presence, they've never interacted with us. Darius often told me not to underestimate the small steps. They can add up," Dash said.

"Let's hope so," Connor said, and meant it.

CHAPTER 13

Connor had sent a few teams out to patrol the surrounding area. They were camped in the main cavern and they could see the Ovarrow soldiers across the way, but he had no intention of letting his guard down. He wasn't going to give them the opportunity to sneak around his team. Dash seemed surprised by this because he still had a certain amount of naiveté about the world. He was a very capable young man, but he was still young enough to retain some of youth's innocence.

"This has to be rough on them," Samson said and gestured toward Cerot and the other Ovarrow. "They came all this way on the hope that they were going to meet more of their own kind, only to find out that their own kind wants nothing to do with them. It's like the Ovarrow have no concept of hospitality."

Connor barked a laugh and shook his head. "Did you forget the last time Diaz and I went to your camp?"

Samson shrugged, his features impassive. "That's how I welcome everyone."

"What happened?" Dash asked.

"Let's just say that Samson has a gift for making people feel *un*welcome. His camp had a lot of traps, and Diaz got caught up in one of them," Connor said and drank some water.

Dash's gaze darted to Samson and then back at Connor. "So, that's why Diaz . . ."

Connor nodded. "Yes, that's about right."

"He's only mad," Samson said, "because he wasn't paying attention."

An image of Diaz strung up by his feet, dangling above the ground and shouting curses appeared in Connor's mind. He exhaled softly and glanced over at Cerot. He was speaking with Esteban, Joe, Felix, Luca, and Wesley.

They'd followed the conversation with Brashirker, probably better than Connor had. They understood what—

He stopped that train of thought and looked at Cerot. Dash had been watching and activated the Ovarrow translator.

"Were you able to understand what Brashirker said?" Connor asked Cerot. He knew it was an obvious question, but he couldn't afford to take too many chances on an assumption.

"I could understand him. Vitory and Senleon are aware of the Krake worshippers," Cerot said.

Connor regarded the Ovarrow for a few seconds. Cerot was the warlord's second-in-command, known as the warlord's First. Connor had no way of knowing if any of the Ovarrow he'd brought with him were Krake insurgents. Connor looked at the others. It was so hard to get an idea of what they were thinking. Cerot seemed to sense that Connor wanted more of an explanation.

"General Gates, the only thing I can tell you is that we are aware of the issue and are working to deal with it."

"Cerot, you know there was Ovarrow involvement in the bridges that collapsed in your city. You have a group that seeks to undermine the authority of your leaders. We're aware of this too, and we understand that none of this has been easy for you."

"I appreciate your understanding. Your partner saved my life. This is a debt I would like to repay, which is why I chose to come with you."

"Did you know there were Ovarrow who weren't allowed into bunkers with stasis pods?" Connor asked.

Cerot was quiet for a few long moments. Connor waited him out. "We knew. I knew about it. We didn't expect anyone to survive. The effort was to preserve our species. We knew we couldn't save everyone."

Connor considered this for a few moments, thinking about the video message recorded by his son while the Vemus were storming the bridge of the *Indianapolis*. Those brave souls on Earth had given the colonists a chance to survive the Vemus. They'd sacrificed themselves, but he did wonder whether there were pockets of humans who had somehow survived the Vemus back on Earth.

"I'm not here to judge you, Cerot, or the rest of the Ovarrow. What I'd like to do is understand. You've been given a second chance. But it may take them some time to accept the fact that you're here," Connor said, gesturing across the cavern where the descendants of the Ovarrow who hadn't gone into stasis stood guard.

"I don't think they will ever accept us," Cerot replied.

"They might not, but don't give up so easily," Connor answered.

The soldiers who were standing watch opened a comlink to report that Brashirker and the Ovarrow soldiers had returned and were waiting at the edge of the bridge. This time they didn't bring the ryklars with them. Connor and a group of soldiers walked to the middle of the bridge and waited. Brashirker met them halfway. Cerot and the other Ovarrow stayed behind so as not to stress the situation any further.

Brashirker had been gone for almost twenty hours. He couldn't have gone far to have returned so quickly. Dash activated a communications drone and sent it over to Brashirker with the Ovarrow interface engaged.

"Our ancestors have used the arch in the past. They sought, as you do, to find the Krake home world by exploring different universes. They were not successful. Eventually, they abandoned those efforts and instead disabled all the arches on this planet to prevent the Krake from coming here. They weren't able to find them all," Brashirker said.

"We've also explored other universes, both from here on this planet"—Connor gestured above him—"and from beyond." He knew the Ovarrow weren't a spacefaring race, and he wasn't sure how acquainted they were with the Krake's capabilities. "Do you have any records of when your people explored other universes that you could share with us?"

Brashirker was silent for a few moments and then looked at Connor. "We only have the historical record that our ancestors did do these things. But the specific things that you are asking for have been destroyed. Even if they hadn't, I wouldn't share them with you."

"Why not?"

"You believe you know the extent of what the Krake are capable of. You don't. They are too powerful. Our people will make preparations to find another location. We would advise you to do the same."

Connor clenched his teeth for a moment. "Hiding and hoping that the Krake won't find us isn't a long-term strategy. You were lucky the first time. There's no guarantee that will happen again."

Brashirker met his gaze. "It is the *only* strategy."

"I urge you to reconsider. We have powerful weapons. We can help each other," Connor said.

Brashirker made a show of looking at the CDF soldiers gathered on the opposite end of the bridge. "We've observed your machines, and we know their capabilities are beyond what we have. You don't take any steps to hide your presence here. This is a foolish mistake. You believe that you are powerful, but you've never fought a war with the Krake. This isn't a fight that you will face on a single battlefield. If you persist in antagonizing the Krake, this war will be fought among you, and it'll be fought among your allies," Brashirker said and gestured toward the small group of Ovarrow that waited among the CDF soldiers. "The Krake will study you—your reactions, your behaviors, your vulnerabilities. And when they're done studying you, they will crush you."

The cold words appeared completely dispassionate on the Ovarrow translator, but the look on Brashirker's face was one of absolute certainty. He believed that the best choice was to hide.

"We won't hide from the Krake. Since you're so convinced that they're coming here, aren't you concerned they'll find you? Don't you want to take steps to protect your people?" Connor asked.

"When the Krake come here, they will be preoccupied with you. They won't care about us. We'll be around to observe the aftermath," Brashirker said.

Connor inhaled explosively and then tried to clamp down on his rising temper. He'd never met a group that was so determined to hide from a problem. Some people throughout history might've endured a tyrant until such time that they could rise and overthrow him, but these were the ancestors. And they wouldn't even consider fighting the Krake.

"This is a mistake. Your ancestors made those decisions because they were probably the best decisions they could make at the time. This is different. *You* should be different."

"We *are* different, but we study our history. We learned from their mistakes. We won't repeat them. I have spoken with other leaders, and none of them will consider helping you," Brashirker said.

Connor clenched his teeth. Thoughts raced like wildfire in his mind. Brashirker had said they didn't have the records from when they used the arch. If that was true, then what history did they study? What if Brashirker was lying? Or what if someone else was lying to Brashirker?

"I have given you an answer to your question," Brashirker said.

"Well, your answer sucks," Connor said. Chances were that the Ovarrow translator didn't have a symbol that would translate his colorful metaphor of the situation, and he didn't care. Connor took a few steps toward Brashirker. "You came here with your display of force using the ryklars. You were posturing so we would know what your strength was. You haven't been to the other worlds. You think you can hide from this and you're wrong. You don't believe me because you have your precious history. But I've *seen* other worlds where the Krake have been. I've seen worlds they've destroyed. They'll come here and do the same. Then you can record your precious history of how you just hid in a cave underground while the world burned around you because that's the best your people could do. Well, that's not who we are. So hide. Stay here and hide underground like a rodent and dream of the past because you won't have a future as long as you stay here."

Connor stood for a few moments and waited for Brashirker to finish reading the message. He intended to look this bastard in the eye so Brashirker would know just what Connor thought of him. He was a coward —a coward dressed in wolf's clothing.

Connor spun on his heel and walked off the bridge. "Captain, we're leaving."

"Understood, General," Samson replied.

CHAPTER 14

Connor slipped into a cold fury as they followed the network of tunnels to return above ground. He called off all the search efforts. Samson saw to the details of organizing the withdrawal as Connor walked ahead at a brisk pace. Even Dash didn't ask him any questions.

At first, he just needed to calm down, and then he kept going over his exchange with Brashirker. Cerot and the other Ovarrow had been given a transcript of the exchange with Brashirker, but he hadn't offered to leave Brashirker a way to contact them. He supposed someone like Darius Cohen, a lead diplomat, would've handled things differently, but he was just so furious. There were so many people who questioned his objective of gaining any kind of intelligence about the Krake from the Ovarrow. It had been one of the main drivers for the effort to assist the Ovarrow in coming out of stasis, and now they'd found a completely different group of Ovarrow who'd never gone into stasis—Ovarrow who'd survived for the past two hundred years through an ice age and a superior enemy force hunting for them. But he couldn't understand how a group like that wouldn't want to defend their homes.

He heard the high-pitched whine of troop carrier engines as they flew overhead to the designated egress points. They were leaving, and he wasn't leaving anything behind except a whole lot of regret. As far as he was concerned, there was nothing left there for him or any other colonist.

He walked up the loading ramp of the troop carrier and headed for the command area so he could be alone. The soldiers aboard hushed their conversations as he stormed by. They knew things hadn't gone well, and by now the news of his failure had probably spread. He was going to have to write a report and submit it to Governor Wolf's office. Although, if he was following a strict protocol, he'd have to send it to Nathan first, who would then send it to Governor Wolf's office. The price of his previous actions had come with a demotion.

He glared at the bulkhead of the troop carrier for a few moments. He just wanted to unleash his rage, to slam his armored fists against it and obliterate it while howling in fury. The Ovarrow had been a thorn in his side ever since he'd woken one up out of a stasis pod. He lowered his chin and clenched his teeth. Why wouldn't they listen? These Ovarrow had survived for two hundred years through an ice age. They'd come up with a way to control the ryklars for protection and had made them immune to the ryklar control signals. These feats were not inconsequential, but if they weren't willing to take the next step and fight the Krake when the time came for it, what good were they? They would become fodder for the Krake or maybe even seek an alliance with them against the colony.

Lars Mallory had posited that the Ovarrow couldn't be trusted, and he'd gotten all the intelligence he could by torturing them. He'd used their fear against them. When Connor first learned about it, he'd thought it was wrong and that Lars had been severely misguided to do those things. They were better than that. But the more he thought about it, he wondered if perhaps he'd been the one who was wrong. The lives of the colony were at stake. Should *he* have been the one to lead those efforts? Would he be in a different position now if he'd done what Lars had done? Would he have the knowledge he sought from the Ovarrow if he'd been more ruthless? Connor squeezed his eyes shut, shook his head, and a soft growl escaped his lips. He could've done it. He could've ordered it and explained it in such a way as to perhaps convince someone like Governor Wolf that it was necessary. Maybe she would've even believed him.

He inhaled deeply and sighed, thinking about his home. He thought about Lenora, who was home right then with Lauren. He thought of his baby girl, staring up at him with the intensity of someone trying desperately to make sense of the world around them as quickly as possible. One day, when she became a woman, she'd judge the man he was. Could he ever explain the actions he was considering to her? Would she hate him if those horrible actions might be the only way she could live? Could he live with himself?

Connor drew in a deep breath and sighed again. He wanted to hold his daughter right then and there, feel her soft cheek up against his face and breathe in her scent. She had an easy smile, and her eyes were a deep blue like her mother's. And when she looked at him, he melted . . . The thought of her calmed him like splashing soothing, warm water on his face, and the tension evaporated. No, he wouldn't torture the Ovarrow to get the information he needed. He wouldn't become that.

Dash cleared his throat from nearby. Connor hadn't even heard him approach.

"Excuse me, Connor. I'm sorry to interrupt, but Cerot has a request I thought you'd want to hear."

Connor rubbed his brow, releasing the tension, and sat down. He leaned back in his chair and looked up at the ceiling for a few moments, then looked at Dash. "What does he want?"

"They'd like to see one of our cities. They've only seen images of them on a holoscreen. I think it might be good for them to see it, and we do have a unique opportunity since they're already here with us."

Connor frowned in thought. For a few moments, he thought about the bureaucratic red tape he'd be required to go through to facilitate Cerot's request. Then he decided he didn't care.

"We'll bring them to Sanctuary. Are you okay with babysitting them for a little while longer? I'll assign protective details to accompany you because they'll need escorts," Connor said.

Dash's eyebrows raised in surprise. "I'm fine with staying with them. I'll even show them around. Cerot, in particular, is keen to keep the lines of communications open between us."

"I appreciate that. I am . . . I can't think about this right now," Connor said and shook his head. "I don't know what time we'll reach Sanctuary, but show them around and we'll meet up after. I just need a few moments to myself."

Dash took a step back, raising his hands in front of his chest. "I understand. I'll take care of it and send you an itinerary of where we'll go. I just wanted your approval. I'll leave you alone now."

For the duration of the trip back to Sanctuary, Connor was alone. Samson hadn't come back to check on him, which probably meant that Dash had warned him to stay away unless it was absolutely necessary.

Connor drafted a few orders for the officers in the 7th to file their reports with his office within the next twenty-four hours. Then he began writing his own reports. Disclosing exactly what had happened was easy; Connor had nothing to hide. It was the parts where he included his views on what they should do next that his ideas came to a halt. He allowed his thoughts to scurry down a few proverbial rabbit holes in the hope that one of them might swing the pendulum to a way forward that he could commit to.

An alert appeared in the upper right corner of his holoscreen, informing him that they were making their final approach to the CDF base at Sanctuary. He wanted to go home and see his family, but he couldn't. It wouldn't have been fair. He'd be home, but he'd be distracted by the work that needed to be done. He didn't want to disappoint Lenora like that. She deserved better. Both his wife and daughter deserved to have his full attention when he came home.

He turned in his weapon and walked down the loading ramp. New Earth's rings were visible in the night sky, even amid the lights of the CDF base and city beyond. He hardly remembered the walk across the base to reach his office, but he soon found himself standing inside. A few holoscreens powered on when the identification from his implants authenticated his clearance. Long lists of messages from text to vid-mail came to prominence on the centermost holoscreen, and Connor gestured for the comlink system to go on standby. He didn't want to check any of his messages. Instead, he went into the bathroom in his office and took a shower. Jets of hot water pelted down on tight muscles. He rolled his shoulders and stretched his neck from side to side, staying in the shower for a long while. Then he heard someone call out to him from inside his office.

"Just a minute," Connor said and rubbed the water from his eyes.

He shut the shower off and heard someone access the door controls. Muttering a curse, he hastily grabbed a towel. "Hey, I said—"

Whatever he was about to say died on his lips as Lenora stepped boldly into the bathroom. Her long auburn hair was braided, making her delicate cheekbones more pronounced. She was a tall woman, nearly two meters, with tanned skin that sported a few freckles and soft lips the color of frozen raspberries.

"So, you don't want some company?" she asked with a wry smile.

Connor smiled back. "Your company? Always."

Lenora gave him a quick hug and a kiss. "I'm glad I'm not one of those jealous wives because I'd be wondering who else has interrupted one of your showers before."

Connor shrugged. "Anyone else would be wasting their time."

Lenora grinned. "Good answer, love," she said and locked the door.

A short while later, they both took another shower. She told him that Lauren was visiting Ashley.

Ashley Quinn was a close friend. She was one of the first people Connor had met coming out of stasis on the *Ark* all those years ago. There may have been a few incidents involving several shock-batons, something that had become a bit of a joke between them over the years, but Ashley loved to dote on his daughter.

They went into his office where a couple of trays of food were waiting, along with a pot of coffee.

Connor glanced at Lenora.

"I thought you'd be hungry, and if you weren't, I was certain we'd work up an appetite," Lenora said and sat down at the small meeting table in his office. She eyed him for a few moments. "All right, you might as well tell me what happened."

Connor sat down at the table and poured them both a cup of coffee. "You mean Dash didn't fill you in?"

"Does it matter? I want to hear it from you."

Connor told her what happened while they shared a couple of sand-wiches. The food was actually quite good, and Lenora told him she'd gotten it at the Salty Soldier on her way here.

"Diaz says hello, by the way," Lenora said and finished her coffee. "So, there's another group of Ovarrow who never went into stasis. It's amazing if you stop and think about it, given what we know about the planet."

"I thought so, and I would've thought they'd be more willing to share information with us."

Lenora pursed her full lips in thought for a moment. "Actually, it sounds like they shared quite a bit with you."

Connor shrugged. "They used the arch to try to find the Krake home world, or at least their ancestors did, but that doesn't help us."

Lenora regarded him for a few moments. "I haven't seen you like this since the Vemus War. Don't give me that look, Connor. You know what I mean. I know you know better than this. It's disappointing, and I agree with you. The Ovarrow should be falling over themselves to help us since they have a better idea of what we're facing than we do."

"You won't get any arguments from me, but the fact of the matter is that we have one group that simply won't help us, and the other group—the ones we brought out of stasis—is incapable of helping us."

"Don't you think that's a little harsh?"

"Not really, no."

Lenora gave him a level look and then nodded. "All right, what was the outcome you were hoping for?"

"Honestly, I was hoping for a lot more cooperation from them. And by 'them' I mean both of them—both groups of Ovarrow," he said and held up his hand. "I know they're worried and all that, but still, we're not the bad guys here. I really wanted to get more information from them. It's like we're going to be fighting a war with hardly any knowledge of our enemy. Back on earth, we had thousands of years of history to draw from. And despite all the efforts here to uncover the Ovarrow's history," Connor said and smiled at Lenora, "we don't know nearly as much as we need to. Everything is new, and we don't have a lot of resources to spare. And this might shape up to be a very long war. Most small wars in history were meat grinders. The conflict comes down to logistics and numbers. How many of our soldiers will it take to achieve an objective, and how much will it cost the enemy to achieve theirs? I don't want to start thinking in those terms but . . ." He let the thought go unfinished.

"It may come down to that," Lenora said, finishing for him.

Connor rubbed his fingers on the tabletop for a moment. "Honestly, Lenora, I dealt with generals in the NA Alliance, and I don't know hardly any of them who were as concerned with the lives of their soldiers as I am. And they didn't have to deal with this."

"Then I'm glad you're here and not them. Maybe we don't need any of the military leaders from your past."

"They might be able to offer something that I just can't," Connor admitted.

Lenora shook her head and steeled her gaze. "I don't believe that for a second. And neither do you, not really. Maybe you believed it at one time but not anymore, Connor. I don't care how angry you are at the Ovarrow. You're the best chance this colony has to survive. And everyone knows it, even if they won't admit it."

She reached across the table, gripping his hand for a moment.

"I appreciate the support, but I think you're just a little biased when it comes to me."

"That's funny," she said in a bit of a light tone. "I was sure you'd say I was one of your staunchest critics."

Connor grinned a little. "Brashirker doesn't understand what the CDF is capable of. Hell, even Senleon and the rest of the Ovarrow we brought out of stasis don't know what we're capable of."

"They're doing what they've always been taught to do," Lenora said.

"The Ovarrow are defeated in their hearts hundreds of years later. What can I do to show them that it can be done?"

"It might come down to that. Inspire them."

"I don't know anything about inspiring anyone. Well, if the Ovarrow aren't going to help us, we'll have to do it alone," Connor said.

"What's so bad about that?"

"It carries a heck of a lot more risk, for one. And two, I'm not sure if the Security Council will approve of scouting missions through the arch. They want credible intel for us to act on, and I can't really blame them, even though it's frustrating," Connor said.

They were both quiet for a few moments, and then Lenora spoke. "So, don't ask for approval."

"Weren't you always telling me that I should try to function within the system we have here in the colony?"

"And aren't you the person who takes action when the situation calls for it for the good of the colony?" Lenora replied.

"I'm still paying the price for the last time."

"Oh, poor me," she replied. "Stop. Nathan supports you."

"He does, and we agree that the Krake are a threat worth investigating. So that's what I'm going to do," he said and looked at Lenora for a moment. "I'm not going to just send teams of soldiers through the arch. I intend to lead them. I need to see this for myself."

Connor watched as Lenora inhaled deeply. She didn't want him to go, but she wouldn't tell him that. She didn't need to remind him of what he'd lose if he didn't come back home. That was the bedrock of their relationship, and it had taken years to build.

"Be careful," Lenora said.

"I will. You know I will," Connor replied.

Lenora looked to be on the verge of saying something else, but a comlink chimed from the wallscreen next to them. It was from Nathan.

Connor acknowledged the comlink and Nathan Hayes appeared. He smiled a greeting at Lenora and then looked at Connor. "I heard things didn't go well with the Ovarrow."

"No reason why anything should be easy where the Ovarrow are concerned, but I'm still finalizing my thoughts on it," Connor said.

"Understood. But that's not why I am contacting you. Do you remember a few years ago when we sent out probes to explore neighboring star systems?" Nathan asked.

"Of course," Connor answered. "They were sent to star systems that might have habitable planets, but we're still a few years away from hearing back from them."

"That's correct, but we heard back from one a little bit quicker than we thought we would. You see, once the scientists working on the subspace communicator got a stable working prototype, they got the idea that they could send our exploration probes instructions to build a subspace communicator of their own. Theoretically, they're well within subspace communication range. However, to make a long story short, they sent out instructions for the probes to build one, and at least one of them has gotten back to us. They found a habitable planet that's just a few light-years away from us," Nathan said.

"That's amazing," Lenora said. "Did the probe send back any scan data?"

Nathan nodded. "Some. This news is getting a lot of attention, particularly with the Security Council. I'm giving you a heads-up because we're going to have an all-hands in just a few hours."

"That quickly? Why would they do that?" Lenora asked.

"Because," Connor said dryly, "they're considering whether we should leave New Earth."

Lenora frowned and glanced at Nathan for a moment. "That's a bit premature, don't you think?"

"I agree," Nathan replied. "But as farfetched as the option is, it's still an option we need to consider."

"Is it really an option though? We have double the colonists now, and our resources are spread throughout the star system," Connor said.

"There are also the Ovarrow to consider," Lenora added, and Connor threw her a look that said he agreed.

Connor looked at Nathan. "She's right. We need to consider the Ovarrow. We brought them out of stasis. The Krake are aware of our presence and are looking for us. When they do find this planet, are we going to leave the Ovarrow at the mercy of the Krake?"

"Are you proposing to take them with us if we leave? Would they even come with us?" Nathan asked.

"I think we're getting ahead of ourselves here," Connor replied. "We'll need to work the problem through because there's a lot more to it than the three of us can think of at the moment."

Nathan nodded. "All right. I just wanted to warn you what was coming. When can you be at Sierra?"

"I'd rather stay here and attend the meeting remotely," Connor said, telling Nathan about their visit with the Ovarrow.

After some more back and forth, Nathan agreed that it was best for Connor to stay in Sanctuary. The comlink closed and both he and Lenora stood up.

"I didn't see this coming," Lenora said.

"Me either. I didn't think we'd find a habitable world so close, but there has been some discussion about whether leaving New Earth is a viable option. This discovery is going to force us to reexamine the viability of that choice."

"Do you think we should leave?" Lenora asked.

"No," Connor replied.

Lenora sighed. "I almost thought you were going to say something about weighing all our options. I don't want to leave either, but . . . well, you know."

"This is our home," Connor said. "And besides, what's to stop the Krake from following us to a neighboring star system? If we stay here, at least we can put our energy into fortifying our position. If we decide to run to another world, we'll have to not only build up our defenses, but also build new homes at the same time."

Lenora grinned, and Connor looked at her questioningly. "Your answer is purely rational, but not everything is so cut and dry. You'll see."

Connor frowned. The decision of whether they were to leave New Earth or not seemed obvious to him, but for as long as he'd known Lenora, she'd demonstrated time and time again that she was a shrewd judge of colonial politics. Her keen insight into these matters might've come from all her experience as an archaeologist, piecing together ancient civilizations, or she just had the uncanny capability of seeing right to the heart of the matter. Either way, if he were to bet on the outcome, he'd bet on Lenora's insights. She was usually right about these things, and he'd learned long ago to trust her judgment.

CHAPTER 15

The all-hands meeting was pushed back to the next day, and Connor was able to go home and spend some time with his daughter. As usual, coming home was always easy, but leaving was getting increasingly harder to do. The last time Connor had left a child of his at home was over two hundred and thirty years ago. His son had been three years old, and Connor was shipping off for a six-month assignment. That six-month assignment turned into a multiyear operation, which had broken his marriage and ultimately ended with Connor being smuggled aboard an interstellar colony ship bound for New Earth. He was a different man now. Lauren would know who her father was because he'd be there to raise her.

The personal holoscreen on his desk cycled through pictures of his family and his friends. For years, his work areas had been devoid of personal effects, but now he liked having visual reminders of the people in his life. They helped him keep things in perspective and remember what was important.

The meeting with the Security Council had begun a short while earlier, and he'd noticed that only half the participants were in Sierra to attend the meeting. It wasn't practical to have in-person meetings as often as the Security Council met. However, at least once a month, they did gather in person, and it had been agreed on by the majority that the meeting would be hosted at any one of the four colonial cities. In a few months' time, the meeting was scheduled to be at Sanctuary. Policies like this had been put forth by Dana Wolf as a way to convey to the rest of the colony that Sierra wasn't the seat of power for the entire colony. It was a unifying effort, and Connor approved.

Bob Mullins was chairing the meeting. Bob was of average height with dark, oily hair, mud-colored eyes, and a few days' worth of beard growth on his face. He had an athletic build, and his voice had a calm, soothing quality to it except when he addressed Connor. They didn't get along. In fact, Connor was of the opinion that Bob kept the stubbled growth of a beard simply because he thought it made him look more appealing to the women in the room. Diaz had often joked that there were many faces of Bob Mullins as he sought to ingratiate himself and get people to trust him. That mask was usually dropped when they were discussing anything related to CDF efforts, which was why Connor didn't like him. He didn't have to like him in order to work with him, but things would be so much easier if Mullins would simply go away.

"We pushed the schedule for this meeting back so everyone would have a chance to review the briefing about the space probe data we've received," Bob Mullins said. "We've found a viable planet that makes an ideal colonization candidate. The planet is well within the Goldilocks zone, with a chemical composition that will meet our needs. It's estimated that the gravitational field is above Earth normal but nothing we couldn't adapt to. The preliminary data provided by the probe exceeds our standard criteria for colonization candidates. It's a prime world."

A man sitting next to Governor Wolf indicated that he wanted to speak. "Dr. Trautmann, you have something to add?" Mullins asked.

Lionel Trautmann was Dana Wolf's newest scientific advisor who held specializations in multiple disciplines.

"The data from the probe is promising," Trautmann began, "but the probe is still in the system's Oort Cloud and hasn't made it to interior planets to do an adequate scan of the system."

"That is correct, but we have access to the information already gathered a lot sooner than we thought we would," Mullins said and glanced at Nathan. "Given the potential threats to the colony, there are quite a few people on this council who feel it's worth discussing whether or not we should establish a colony on that planet."

Connor reached toward the speaker button, which would indicate that he wished to contribute, and let his hand hover over it for a moment. His fingertips must've grazed it because the request was sent, and as Mullins turned toward him, his gaze narrowed.

"General Gates," Mullins said.

Connor wasn't about to admit that he'd hit the button by mistake, so he decided to go along with his initial thought. "The briefing doesn't just imply the establishment of a new colony. It implies that we need to make a decision on whether to move the entire colony to this planet."

By default, once Connor was through speaking, the floor was turned back over to Mullins.

"That is something we'll be discussing. I'd like to highlight the fact that this is just a discussion. We're not requiring decisions to be made," Mullins said.

Connor had lost count of how many items had been "just a discussion," and then, more often than not, were the precursor for an approved project. He stabbed the speaker button again, and Mullins glowered a little.

"The question is not whether or not we can colonize this other planet. We can, but the question is whether or not we should work toward that goal," Connor said.

"General Gates," Mullins said, "I will not let you domineer this discussion and rush a conclusion to these talking points. You make valid points but—"

"He has hardly begun making his point," Dr. Trautmann said, interrupting.

"Bob," Governor Wolf said. "I, for one, would like to hear what Connor has to say, and so do a lot of other people in the room. We facilitate discussions, but in order to do that, we need to listen to what people say."

The tips of Mullins's ears became red, and he nodded. "My apologies, Governor," he said and turned toward Connor. "General Gates, please proceed."

"Thank you," Connor said, directing his gaze at Governor Wolf. "I don't want to beat around the bush here. We're worried about the Krake and the threat they are to this world. That's the driver for whether or not we colonize another world in the immediate future, but I'd urge everyone here to be cautious when considering this option. We live in an established colony. We can build ships. Actually, we can build anything we could possibly need. This is a resource-rich star system. The preliminary probe data indicates that the star system in question has resources for us to use as well, but we don't know how much. However, even though it might be a safe assumption that we could colonize that world, that's not dealing with the main issue—the Krake. Let's be honest. If we leave this world, it's because we're running from the Krake."

"Excuse me, General Gates," Mullins said. "Just so I understand. You're putting forth that there are circumstances that would necessitate relocating to another world?"

"Absolutely, but only as a last resort," Connor said. "If we were to move this entire colony to a new world, it would take us years to do it right, even working at breakneck speeds, and at the end of the day, what happens if the Krake follow us?"

"The reports concerning the Krake indicate that they largely operate not only within this star system but in many different universes," Mullins replied.

"That knowledge is based on a few different scouting expeditions, one of which is overdue, as you're all aware. Our own scientists and many senior officers are divided on the capabilities the Krake have. Some of their technology seems superior to our own but not everything. It's not quite an equal playing field, but if the Krake wanted, they could follow us wherever we went."

The reactions from the people in the meeting were mostly supportive, but not all of them.

"We can't make any guarantees here," Mullins replied, "but right now, we have an option open to us, and it's something we can't afford to ignore—

that is, until we know more about the Krake, but there's also a significant risk in doing that. If we keep antagonizing the Krake, we'll give them a reason to come find us."

"The Ovarrow believe that the Krake will come here, especially now. There's no use arguing about whether or not we can put the genie back in the bottle."

Mullins shook his head. "That's just my point. Continuing to antagonize the Krake will bring them here faster."

Several speaker requests came in from the other attendees.

"Gentlemen," Governor Wolf said, "there are a lot of strong opinions here, and I don't want this meeting to descend into a theoretical debate. There are multiple issues coming to a head, and I have no choice but to address them here. Most of us would agree that we can't afford to put all our eggs in one basket, meaning that each decision we make carries with it a certain degree of risk. As Connor has highlighted, if we committed to moving the entire colony to this new star system, we'd have to start from scratch, and how much time would we really buy ourselves by doing that? Especially where the Krake are concerned. In fact, it might make it even more difficult to find a way to protect ourselves from the Krake, as General Gates has also suggested.

"However, I don't see any issue in drawing up plans on *how* we'd relocate the entire colony. We're not committing to doing anything, but colonizing this other planet is an option, and a serious one at that. It wouldn't be prudent for this council to ignore either of these options at the expense of the other. I think there are ways we can accommodate both. One"—she gestured with her index finger—"just off the top of my head is based on a discussion with Dr. Trautmann—before the discovery of this new planet, I might add—that we send a smaller colony and let them establish the planet's viability. It doesn't cost as much in resources and is certainly within our reach. There are a lot of options open since we have the capacity for subspace communication. Distance is still a factor, but a smaller colony of five thousand is something that's definitely within our reach. And an effort like that wouldn't detract from any military efforts. It could, and I stress *could*, be an avenue we might explore further."

Clinton Edwards, the Mayor of Delphi, hit his speaker button. "How would we pick the people who would go?"

"That's something we'd need to consider," Mullins replied.

"We're not going to hash out all the details here," Governor Wolf said.

"What about the Ovarrow?" Connor asked. This drew a few questioning looks in his direction. "I know we're tiptoeing around the subject, but if we do decide that leaving here is our best option, what about the Ovarrow? Do we abandon them? Do we offer to bring them with us?"

Trautmann was nodding enthusiastically. "This is an excellent question. We hadn't considered this, and it's something we should discuss."

"Yes," Mullins said in a mild tone. "There are always the Ovarrow to consider. Thank you for that, General Gates."

Connor caught the double-edged meaning of Mullins's last statement, and he wondered if anyone else did as well. It was because of Connor that they'd found the Ovarrow in the first place, and Mullins had never been an avid supporter of bringing them out of stasis. Connor was still surprised that they hadn't found any evidence to link Mullins with the rogue group activities that had been led by Meredith Cain. Either he'd covered his involvement even better than Meredith Cain, or he hadn't been involved.

"Governor Wolf," Nathan said, "this might be a good time to bring up the request for authorizing additional scouting missions to worlds potentially occupied by the Krake."

Connor noticed the hint of recognition in Dana Wolf's gaze. She'd been expecting the question.

"Indeed," Governor Wolf replied. "I see no compelling reason not to authorize more scouting missions."

"Excuse me, Governor Wolf," Mullins said quickly. "I think we should put restrictions on future CDF scouting missions."

Governor Wolf leaned back in her chair. "What kind of restrictions?"

"I agree we should go look for the Krake, but I don't think we should exhaust our resources doing so. And I don't think there should be an open policy for the CDF to conduct the scouting missions without getting any results. The purpose of these missions is to acquire intelligence about the Krake and find out what they know about us. However, every time there's been a mission to an alternate universe, it has cost a very high price in terms of lives, and it's also been a significant risk to this colony. I propose that we don't give the CDF free rein on how many operations they can conduct to scout these alternate universes. Each mission should have a clear objective and be approved by the Security Council."

Connor clenched his teeth. "Would you like a report every time we leave a room too?"

Mullins smirked. "I think you of all people should be acquainted with the concept of accountability. This ensures accountability."

Connor's response was on the tip of his tongue, but at the last second, he glanced at Nathan, who gave him a slight shake of his head. It wouldn't be the first time Connor's mouth had gotten him into trouble, so he shifted his gaze to Governor Wolf.

"The Colonial Defense Force was established based on accountability," Connor said. "We already have defined objectives of scouting alternate universes to look for the Krake."

"Yes," Mullins said, "but there's the lack of an approval step. Not all missions are the same."

"That's correct," Nathan replied. "Not all missions carry with them the same degree of risk."

Connor wanted to invite Mullins on the next mission. That way, he could leave him on an alternate world. *Accountability* . . . These were the same people who'd let someone like Meredith Cain infiltrate and manipulate the upper echelons of their government.

"I think what would help here . . ." Governor Wolf began. "A briefing should be sent out to the Security Council about specific scouting missions. That way, everyone is kept in the loop. Individual scouting missions don't require Security Council approval, but a briefing should still be sent to my office."

For a few moments, Connor thought they'd cancel all the scouting missions so they could hammer out an approval mechanism for him to operate under. Sending out a briefing about scouting missions would give Mullins part of what he asked for, but Connor knew when someone was angling to increase their influence. Mullins shouldn't have any influence on CDF affairs. He was just a governmental advisor, yet he had a satisfied expression that indicated he'd gotten exactly what he wanted.

The meeting went on for another hour as they discussed more of the specifics about the colonization of the new planet. Connor didn't pay much more attention to it. He kept thinking about the implications of what Mullins had done, and he wondered if Nathan had caught on to it. Sending out a briefing to the Security Council also gave them a window of opportunity to voice concerns, which could propel Governor Wolf to act accordingly —and not just Governor Wolf but future governors as well. Governor Wolf had another two years to serve on her term, but Mullins was playing the long game. Connor would have to keep an eye on him.

The meeting ended, and Connor received a comlink request on his private line. Only a select few people had access to that, so he answered it immediately.

"Noah, how's—how are you?" He'd almost asked how the recovery was going, but Noah was sensitive about it.

"I'm fine," Noah replied. "In fact, each day I wake up and I'm not in a coma, I call it a good day." He said it jokingly, but there was a slight edge of bitterness as well. Connor could relate. He'd been quarantined and then strictly observed at the end of the Vemus War because of his exposure.

"Excellent. What can I do for you?"

"This is more about what I can do for you," Noah replied.

"I'm going to stop you right there because Kara will kill me if I don't. No, you're not cleared to assist in the scouting missions," Connor said.

Kara had almost breathed fire when she'd learned that Connor had brought Noah along on the op to capture Lars Mallory.

"You need me for this kind of work."

"You're right; I do, but not until the doctors clear you. You spent almost a year in a coma, Noah. I'm not telling you anything you don't already know. It's just going to take some time."

Noah looked away for a moment. "I know it hasn't been that long. Honestly, the reason I contacted you is that I've been looking at the documented differences between the arch and the space gates."

"All right, I'm listening."

"The Ovarrow were attempting to reverse-engineer the arch, which is how we stumbled upon subspace communication, but I think it goes further than that," Noah said.

"Well, they *did* teleport several buildings to another planet, and we haven't been able to duplicate that. I think they were doing multiple things with technology they didn't fully understand," Connor replied.

"That's just it; the Krake never used it for that, but I'm at the point where I need some resources to conduct my own experiments."

"What are you trying to do?"

"I'm trying to overcome the five-minute window where we lose the subspace communication signal. Sometimes it's less, but it's never more, so there's got to be something we're not doing right," Noah replied.

"Have you consulted with the scientific teams already working on this?"

"I have, but there are some things I'd like to try. There are fundamental differences between the arch and the space gates, and I'm still wrapping my head around that," Noah said and paused for a moment. "Who have you been bringing with you on the scouting missions?"

"Dash," Connor answered.

Noah grimaced and looked away again.

"Noah, I promise I'll keep you in the loop. If we find anything I think you could help with, I'm not going to keep it from you. Now, can I ask how you're feeling?"

"I'm surprised you're not just looking at my medical records."

Connor shrugged. "You know I won't do that now that you're awake."

Noah sighed. "I still get painful headaches. Sometimes vertigo. The doctor believes it's temporary," Noah replied.

"Well, take it one step at a time and listen to the doctor. Send your request to my office, and I'll either make sure you have what you need or give you clearance to a place that does have it."

Noah thanked him and closed the comlink. Connor sat, staring at the empty space where the video comlink had been active. Noah had almost died. Connor could really use his help with scouting for the Krake but wouldn't involve him until he was back to normal. If Noah was never normal again, Connor would just have to find another way to solve the technical problems he faced regarding Krake technology. What he wouldn't do again is bring his friend into dangerous situations. Noah had sacrificed enough.

CHAPTER 16

Sean walked down the corridor, heading to where the Krake prisoners were being held. They'd initially captured six Krake, and three of them had committed suicide. The remaining three had attempted to end their lives, but Sean had stopped them. Using the Ovarrow translator, they'd told him they were already dead and nothing would change. Sean had found the entire exchange with them appalling. He didn't like being in the room with them, but it was necessary.

"Are the civilian mutineers being held nearby?" Boseman asked.

"Yes, they are, but I don't know how much longer I'm going to keep them here."

"Why is that? Are you getting soft in your old age?"

Chad Boseman was in the Spec Ops platoon assigned to the *Vigilant*. They had served together for years and were friends.

"Maybe." Sean said. "It's tight quarters, and I need them to work. We can't afford any freeloaders. As long as they behave themselves, I won't keep them down here, but they'll have to answer for their actions when we get home."

"Morale is a fragile thing. Who's to say that if we let them out they wouldn't cause trouble," Boseman said.

"They're scared. That's why they did what they did. And Lester used that to convince them to help him."

"That man is a disgrace. We tried to take him alive, but he already knew he was going to die."

Sean clenched his teeth a little and his mouth became a grim line. "It was either going to be you or me. The moment he put us in that situation . . ." His voice trailed off, and Boseman gave him a firm nod.

They walked to the end of the corridor toward the Krake holding cells.

The doors to the cells were translucent and the Krake prisoners could see each other. Sean wanted them to know that the others were still alive. He'd thought it would entice them to cooperate. They hadn't.

There were two CDF soldiers stationed nearby, and they saluted Sean as he went by. Sean walked to the center holding cell within full view of the others. They were under constant watch, and there was nothing in the room they could use to take their own lives. They'd had to be restrained after multiple suicide attempts.

Are all Krake as fanatical as these salvagers are? he wondered.

Sean opened the door and walked inside. Boseman followed, and the soldier outside closed the door. The prisoners had been captured from a Krake salvage ship they'd ambushed.

Sean activated a holoscreen and brought up an image of Aurang. The Krake prisoner stared at the image for a few moments.

"We've met other Krake who are willing to communicate with us. Can you understand me?" Sean asked.

The Krake prisoner winced and its eyes darted to Boseman and then to Sean.

"I'd call that a yes," Boseman said.

"Say something," Sean said.

The prisoner seemed to draw himself up to his full height. "Betrayers," he said and charged toward Sean.

Boseman stuck out the stun baton, releasing a high-powered jolt into the Krake's side and bringing the prisoner to his knees.

"If you'd just cooperate with me, I'd let you go. The same with the others. They can hear us," Sean said, gesturing toward the other holding cells where the Krake prisoners were listening. "Aurang wants us to help him against the overseers."

The Krake prisoner winced and scrambled back. "There is no outcome other than death. There is only death."

The prisoner came to his feet and charged them again. The other prisoners began banging their heads against the wall, each of them chanting that there was only death.

"Colonel," Boseman said.

Sean saw that the Krake prisoner was lying on the ground, not moving, and there was a dark ring around the side of his head. Boseman was staring at the stun baton in disbelief.

"When he charged me, he grabbed my hand and put the stun baton to his head. He held it there. I tried to pull it away, but they're strong."

Krake blood was pooling dark gray under his head. The prisoner was dead. Sean spun and hastened to the other holding cells. The two soldiers rushed inside to restrain the others.

Sean and Boseman helped get them strapped to the beds.

"You don't have to die. Stop doing this. Stop struggling," Sean said and gritted his teeth.

The prisoner struggled even more, trying to break free of his restraints. A few moments later, a medic arrived and sedated the Krake. Both the remaining prisoners were strapped to their beds, unconscious.

"They're crazy," Boseman said. "They're determined to kill themselves."

Sean looked at the unconscious Krake prisoners and shook his head. Most people had an innate drive to stay alive. It was hardwired into their DNA. Even the Ovarrow were the same. They'd fight to survive, just like most creatures of New Earth.

"It's like they've been brainwashed," Sean said.

Boseman's eyes widened for a moment. "You think this is conditioning?"

"It's not rational, unless their entire society rigidly adheres to these types of conventions. Aurang isn't like that, so there must be some kinds of established protocols for the salvagers to follow, which means we're not the first ones to capture a Krake ship," Sean said.

"They're crazy. It might be better for them if we let them die," Boseman said.

Sean was tempted to agree with this friend. The Krake prisoners were a danger to themselves and to others. He couldn't afford to set them free because of what they'd seen on the ship. "I'm not going to kill them."

"Understood, sir."

They left the area. At least they had confirmation that the Krake translator worked. Sean had strongly suspected that it would, but there was nothing like a true test. On a secure system, Sean had authorized the use of the Krake translator to interpret the data they'd taken from previous Krake places they'd been. They'd been able to cross-check the translation with the Ovarrow translator they'd used in the past. Gabriel had confirmed that the Krake translator was superior to what they were using. Sean had been concerned that there could be a subroutine hidden within the translator that would infiltrate the *Vigilant*'s computer systems, which was why he'd only authorized its use on secure systems that were isolated from everything else.

"There's something I need to ask you about," Boseman said. "A Dr. Evans requested assistance from someone under my command. Do you know anything about this?"

"Oriana is working on a lot of things, but I'm not sure why she'd need someone from your team."

"I'm not concerned about the request. I just thought it was odd. We're ready to lend a hand whenever we can, but I was surprised by who she asked for," Boseman said and paused. Sean's eyebrows raised. "Benton."

Sean frowned. Benton had a reputation for pushing the limits of acceptable behavior aboard ship. When they'd first had civilians mixed with enlisted personnel, there had been more than a few complaints about him.

"I don't know. I can check with her if you want," Sean offered.

"Negative. I already did, and she needed Benton's help. I even offered to send her someone else."

Sean shrugged a little. "You don't need to worry about Oriana. She can take care of herself."

Oriana had never been shy, but she'd gotten used to living aboard ship among the CDF. After the mutiny, she'd become more serious. They all had, but Oriana and her science team had been held captive by Brody and the other mutineers. Sean had been teaching her self-defense, including how to disarm an opponent. He rarely had occasion to utilize his training and welcomed the opportunity to revitalize his skills.

They'd had little time together after the mutiny. Each of them preferred to be as active as possible, which included downtime. Sean required very little sleep because of his military-grade implants. Oriana wanted her implants upgraded with the same capabilities, but there hadn't been enough time.

Others began to notice their workouts and asked to join them, which gave them a chance to practice against all kinds of opponents. Boseman was among the best hand-to-hand combat specialists on the ship and wasn't shy about humbling Sean when they practiced together.

They headed to the meeting room near the bridge. Dean Stonehill was already inside, along with Jane Russo, his XO. Major Shelton and Captain Martinez were on the holoscreen. Oriana should have been there, so she must have been running late for some reason.

Sean sat down at the table. "We're scheduled to meet with Aurang in a little while, but we needed to speak first."

They were in the alternate universe and had been studying their targets as best they could for the past twenty-four hours. No alarms had been raised and no Krake scout forces had been sent out, so it was safe to assume that their presence had gone unnoticed. But Sean didn't like assumptions. If this was a trap, Aurang could've arranged for the Krake defenses to simply ignore their presence for the time being.

"Gabriel, send a message to Lieutenant Pitts that I'd like him at this meeting now," Sean said.

"Message has been sent, sir," Gabriel replied.

His request drew more than a few puzzled frowns. "It's nice to know that I can still surprise all of you."

A few moments later, Lieutenant Pitts appeared on an additional holoscreen.

"Thank you for joining, Lieutenant. To bring everyone up to speed, I called this meeting with all of you because of your ability to think outside the box," Sean said.

Sean noticed that Pitts frowned for a moment and seemed to be glancing at the array of holoscreens from his ready room aboard the *Babylon*.

"So far, the Krake haven't detected our presence here. I've been able to confirm that the Krake translator does, in fact, work. Boseman and I," Sean said and twitched his head toward Boseman, "successfully communicated with our prisoners. We did get a response, but there isn't much to share on that front. Behavioral analysis indicates that these particular Krake might've been brainwashed."

"Colonel Quinn," Pitts said, and Sean gestured for him to speak. "Behavioral analysis applies to humans. While the response you received from the Krake could be conditioned, it might be premature to assign a prognosis based on limited testing."

"It's a theory, and it's supported by our senior medical doctor on board," Sean said. "We haven't detected any Krake ships at the NEC. The planet has a single moon, but there is a sizable asteroid belt relatively close to the planet. Analysis indicates that it was a dwarf-sized planet. The Krake could have an attack force hidden there."

"The lack of Krake ships in the area," Major Shelton said, "confirms what Aurang told us about how the Krake conduct operations across multiple universes."

Sean nodded. "It makes sense if you think about it. They have a ready force to deal with alerts that come in. This saves a considerable amount of resources with maintaining a fleet across multiple universes, but I don't want to get blindsided."

The door to the conference room opened and Oriana hastened to an open seat.

"There's an operational lunar base," Sean continued, "as well as an orbital defense platform. In order for this mission to work, we'll need to disable the space gate, but the timing must be in tandem with the ground force that will infiltrate a Krake military research and development complex on the surface. We'll need to hit all of these targets almost at the same time in order to prevent the Krake from mustering a response. But the attack must occur after the regular status check-in from the Krake complex. After that, disabling the space gate is key to preventing Krake warships from responding if they're able to raise an alert."

"It's the ground force operation that I am most concerned about, sir," Major Shelton said. "We're supposed to trust that Aurang will be able to infiltrate the R&D systems right before the Krake send their scheduled update to their version of COMCENT, which will then have updated orders so the fifth column will be freed or at least taken off the watch list. And in return for our help, he plans to give us operational data, particularly around the multiverses they have a presence in."

"I don't trust them either," Sean said. "That's why I'm going to equip Captain Boseman and his team with another tool for exfiltrating data from Krake systems. We refined it based on the new Krake translator interface combined with proven techniques used to remove data from Ovarrow computer systems found on New Earth."

Sean gave them a few moments to consider. "This is where I need you to raise questions if you have them."

"Ovarrow computer systems," Lieutenant Pitts said, "are a rudimentary version of Krake computer systems. How do we know that when Captain Boseman attempts to steal the data, he won't trip any of the alarms?"

"We won't know," Sean said pointedly. "There's no way around this. This mission carries a significant risk factor."

"Colonel Quinn, if I may," Boseman said, and Sean nodded. "My team is going to be thrown into the fire, but this is what we do. We'll learn something worthwhile about the Krake and their systems. There are redundancies in place that will get whatever it is that we learn out of there even if my team doesn't make it."

"Worst-case scenario, but we'll have combat shuttles on standby to extract the Spec Ops team," Sean said.

"Sir," Lieutenant Pitts said, "it just seems that you expect Aurang to betray us. So why go through with this?"

"You want to know if the risk is worth the reward. We don't have the luxury of making decisions in hindsight. We've learned a lot about the Krake these many months we've been away from home, but it's not enough. We've gathered some credible intel, but we need more if we're to begin an offensive against them. That's the purpose of our mission. Aurang could be misinformed, and we'll have to be able to adapt to that. So far, everything he's provided has been proven accurate."

"Understood, sir," Pitts replied.

"This is the first system that has a significant Krake presence, and this is what we came to find. It'll be the most complex mission we've executed to date. Let's go over the particulars of the mission," Sean said.

They discussed the plan that Sean and Vanessa had put together, even though most of the people who were at the meeting had contributed to it. Sean had decided to bring Lieutenant Pitts along because he'd been the most vocal about the state of morale after the mutiny. He asked good questions during their review of the mission, which reaffirmed Sean's decision to bring him into the meeting.

"Colonel Quinn, I have one more question," Lieutenant Pitts said.

"Go ahead."

"According to Aurang, the next window to begin this mission is in twelve hours."

"That's when Aurang wanted us to go, but we're not going to comply with that request. You see, there's a delicate balance here. If we go in twelve hours and there's an ambush waiting for us, they'll be expecting us. If we delay several cycles, they won't know when or if our mission will begin," Sean replied.

Lieutenant Pitts's eyes widened and he actually smiled. "Understood, sir, and thank you," he said.

Something in that moment changed in Lieutenant Pitts. Sean spotted it, and he supposed Vanessa had seen it too. She wouldn't be his XO for the Trident Battle Group if she couldn't identify that moment when a soldier became a believer in the mission. There was the chain of command, but there was also trust to be built.

"Aurang will be here in a few minutes. Major Shelton, I want you to brief the commanding officers of the battle group," Sean said.

The holoscreens flickered off as the comlinks to the other ships were severed.

"Colonel, I'm sorry I was running a bit late," Oriana said.

"Understood. What did you think of the way they wanted us to disable the space gate?" Sean asked.

"It should work, and we know that if there's a misalignment with the space gate cubes, you can't establish a stable gateway. I also wanted to run something else by you," Oriana began to say but stopped when the door to the conference room opened.

Captain Russo walked in with Aurang and the soldiers who were escorting him.

The chairs in the conference room couldn't accommodate Krake physiology. Their long limbs made using the chair too awkward, so Sean and the others stood up.

"Colonel," Aurang said, "you've had adequate time to consider my request for aid, and you've done your reconnaissance. What is your answer?"

"I've conferred with my senior staff and we agree this mission is possible. So far, everything aligns with the information you've given us," Sean said.

"Excellent. So, we can begin in the next cycle," Aurang said.

"That won't be possible," Sean said and began to hold up his hand so he could further explain but then realized the gesture would be lost on the Krake, who didn't understand human mannerisms. "Our teams need to train for the mission. We'll need at least twenty-four hours before they'll be ready to go."

It was a lie and everyone but Aurang knew it. Sean had no intention of telling the Krake when they would begin the mission.

"I'm very disappointed. Tell me, if I requested to leave your ship, would you let me?"

"You wouldn't make that kind of request," Sean said.

"You haven't answered my question," Aurang replied.

Sean regarded the Krake for a few moments. "If you were to make that request, I'd assume that everything else you told us was a lie. You came to us because you have nowhere else to go. That's what you told us. The overseers are about to annihilate your entire network of operations. You want to protect your people, and so do I. That means not rushing into anything. Do we understand each other?"

It was difficult trying to gauge the Krake's response. There seemed to be an exactness in how they responded to anything that was almost devoid of emotion.

"Colonel, I have teams in place that require what I have on my ship."

"And if we don't show up during this next cycle, what will they do?"

Aurang regarded Sean for a few moments. "They will wait, but time is running out for them. We have contingency plans in the event that we cannot—" Aurang stopped speaking.

"We need to go over the plan so everyone knows what's expected of them," Sean said.

Aurang glanced at the others in the room for a moment. "I will answer your questions."

CHAPTER 17

"I just heard the news," Samson said.

Connor had left the main administration building at the CDF base in Sanctuary only moments earlier. "Good. Have the 7ᵗʰ assemble so we can be underway ASAP."

"Oh, we'll be ready, but I have a couple of concerns," Samson said, matching his pace with Connor's.

Connor checked the status of the message he'd sent to Dash, and it had been received. One less thing to worry about. He looked at Samson. "We were bound to succeed, sooner or later."

Since they hadn't gotten any help from the Ovarrow, Connor was determined to get the intel he needed from the Krake by finding one of their worlds. They needed to find out more about them, but more importantly, they needed to find out what the enemy knew about the colonists. Connor had converted a CDF storage facility located over a hundred kilometers from Sanctuary into a working compound for the purpose of utilizing an archway to find a Krake world. The concept was simple. They were using the data they'd gotten from the Krake forward operating base, starting with the coordinates taken from that facility. However, the task had proven to be a lot more complicated than that.

"Since we're only bringing one platoon for the scouting mission, we shouldn't bring the Ovarrow with us," Samson said.

"Why is that?" Connor asked. He didn't want to make any assumptions.

"They're an unknown quantity. They've had some combat training, but it'll be dangerous for them. We're already bringing one civilian with us, and honestly, it's one too many," Samson said.

"Dash has a skill set that we don't have in the CDF. He's a specialist, and that's why he's coming with us. Having some of the Ovarrow will help speed the process along," Connor replied.

"Yeah, but do we need to bring all six of them? Why can't we just bring Cerot?" Samson said.

"Because Cerot is the warlord's First. He's second-in-command of their military. He'll insist that he bring some kind of protection, and he would be right to do so."

"I understand that, but this is our operation. He doesn't have to come."

"It's essential that he comes with us. We need somebody who can speak the language. And right now, Cerot and the others have agreed to help us," Connor said, silencing Samson with a gesture. "Now hold on a minute. I agree we don't need to bring all six of them. We'll probably bring only three —Cerot and whoever he chooses to bring with him. They're professional soldiers, albeit they're not us. They did fine when we went to the city."

Samson tried to think of an argument but couldn't. Things could rapidly spiral out of control, and they'd be cut off from New Earth. They'd spent the last few days strategizing on how to deal with that, which included a bunch of secondary protocols in the event that unforeseen circumstances occurred. Samson was aware of it. He was minimizing the potential impact of things outside his control, which included the Ovarrow. He was doing his job, and Connor couldn't be frustrated with that.

"To be honest, I didn't expect they'd find anything so soon," Connor said.

They made their way to the airfield where the troop carrier transports waited for them. Connor had sent the preliminary alert to Nathan to make him aware of the situation. Connor was going on-site to do a more thorough analysis and determination of whether sending a scout force to the world they'd found was required. He was due to return to the CDF compound anyway.

Dash and the Ovarrow arrived, and Connor gestured to one of the containers aboard the troop carrier as where they'd stow the Ovarrow's armor and weapons.

"Come on," Connor said. "I'll brief you on the way."

They walked up the loading ramp, and this time the Ovarrow were a lot more familiar with the troop carrier. They went to the section that was dedicated to them, and Cerot and Dash followed Connor to the front. It was always hard to gauge what the Ovarrow were thinking, but Connor speculated that Cerot looked a little excited to be on the troop carrier again. He was keenly interested in any of the vehicles the colonists used, be they for military or civilian applications. He'd even brought up the possibility of convincing the high commissioner to request a few of the rovers for their use. The Ovarrow equipment they'd found stored was several hundred years old, and anything left unused for that long wouldn't be in prime operating condition. However, there were some bunkers that'd been hermetically sealed, so they hadn't deteriorated over time. But they'd also sat unused, and there was a lengthy process to make those vehicles operational again. The

Ovarrow were primarily restricted to ground transportation, but Connor wondered how long it would be before they were able to restore more of their vehicles. They were capable of creating machines for atmospheric flight.

"Are we heading to the base at New Haven?" Dash asked.

Connor shook his head. "No, there's a compound closer to Sanctuary. We have an arch there."

Dash's expression was one of appreciation. "That was fast."

"Once we had the first one working, we built a second and then a third. We didn't want to be reliant on finding a Krake version. And I don't know how many arches they had on the planet. Anyway, it's quite a setup, and you'll get to see it," Connor said. He activated a holoscreen. "We opened the arch and sent a reconnaissance drone through. It has a look around and then comes back. This video is from a world where we believe there's a Krake city."

The others watched the holoscreen. The video had been taken from the vantage point of the drone as it ascended. In the distance, there was a distinct outline that was purely artificial. It wasn't a natural occurrence, and the recon drone attempted to zoom in on the structures in the distance. They looked to have been artificially created. It was a large series of buildings that could be the beginning of a small city. Then the video feed cut off.

"This is the first world we've seen that has any kind of structure on it," Connor said.

"How do we know this is of Krake origin?" Dash asked.

"We can't be one hundred percent sure," Connor said. "It could be an Ovarrow settlement or something else entirely. The universe coordinates were taken from the Krake forward operating base. It wasn't one they visited, so we suspected it was something they came from. That's why we think this location is associated with the Krake and not the Ovarrow. It's our best lead so far, and we're going to have another look. There's a good chance we'll be sending a scout force through."

Cerot informed them that he was going to give an update to his soldiers. Once he was gone, Connor motioned for Dash to come closer.

"I need your opinion on Cerot and the others. You've spent the past few days with them. What's your impression? Are they ready for this?" Connor asked.

Dash glanced at the other end of the troop carrier where the Ovarrow had gathered. The CDF soldiers nearby watched them. "I think it was a good idea to allow them to come to Sanctuary. That gave them more of an insight into us. Even though we still have communication barriers, I just get a sense that there's more of an understanding. There are a couple of them who . . ." Dash said and paused for a few seconds. "They're very quiet, so I don't really have an impression of them. It's Esteban and Wesley. Joe, Felix, and Luca seem more open-minded about learning new things. There's a big difference with Cerot because he seems young, but at the same time, he's . . . you can tell he's been through a lot."

Connor thanked him, and the troop carrier pilot announced that they'd be reaching their destination in a few minutes.

"Dash, I know you've agreed to come with us, and I appreciate that, but I wanted to give you the option of staying behind," Connor said, and Dash immediately protested. "No one would think less of you if you did. Exploring New Earth is one thing, but having been through this a few times, I can tell you it's quite different and very dangerous."

"I understand, Connor, and you don't have to worry about me. I'll keep my head down and do as I'm told—you know, leave the soldiering to the professionals."

Connor gave him a long look, considering. "That's just it. You're much more capable than the average citizen, but you're not a soldier. You'll be armed, and you might be called upon to do more than you ever have before."

Dash gave him a determined look. "I won't let you down."

Connor had trained a lot of soldiers throughout his career. There were some who excelled in a training environment, only to freeze up during a hostile situation. Even though Dash had never been through a CDF boot camp, much less any of the additional years of training that ranger companies went through, he'd been in some tough situations. Connor could have brought in another specialist or a soldier who knew the Ovarrow translator interface and had a basic rudimentary knowledge of it, but nothing could take the place of the years of study Dash had done at the Colonial Research Institute and in the field on New Earth. Dash knew the Ovarrow to a degree that very few had attained.

Connor had also seen it with Lenora. This was an important mission, and he needed answers as quickly as possible because lives might depend on it. And even though Dash thought he knew what it was going to be like, Connor actually had a better idea. The platoons that made up the 7th Ranger Company were all seasoned soldiers, but it was Carl Flint's men who'd actually been to another world and engaged the Krake. Connor had absolute faith in Samson, but he wouldn't have minded Flint being with them. The trouble with finding truly capable soldiers was that they tended to be put in charge, and sometimes that spread the forces pretty thin.

The troop carriers headed to the LZ inside the walls of the compound. There were habitat units on the other side where the permanent residents stayed, but the bulk of the compound was in one large warehouse capable of holding several squadrons of combat shuttles or dozens of the troop carriers they'd flown in on.

As they went inside the warehouse, Connor caught his first glimpse of the arch. It was on an elevated platform that was capable of either maintaining the arch at ground level or raising it thirty meters straight up. That had been a last-minute addition when they discovered that some of the universes they opened a gateway to had different elevations on the other side. The gateway could still be opened whether it was aboveground or beneath it. They wouldn't be able to go through if it was beneath the ground, but the goal was to explore what was on the other side. Massive power cables coiled on the ground near the platforms that raised the arch. Connor knew that a great deal of effort had gone into maintaining the alignment so they had a stable gateway. The arch itself was six meters tall and fifteen meters across at the base.

While everyone else waited below, Connor, Samson, Dash, and Cerot walked up to the command center, which maintained its elevation to be level with the arch. They used the staircase outside the command center to reach it, and even though the steps were wide enough for the average human foot, the Ovarrow's feet were both longer and wider than the average human's. But Cerot didn't hesitate to go up the stairs. Dash told Connor it was only the second time the Ovarrow had ever used stairs. In their cities, they typically built long ramps to ascend to upper levels.

Connor entered the command area and Major Kent Henderson greeted him. By his side was the familiar face of Dr. Volker, whom Connor had had transferred from the CDF base by New Haven for the purpose of this project.

"General Gates," Henderson said, "welcome to Independence Compound. We've just completed our second scouting run and have some additional intel for you."

"Show us what you have," Connor replied.

Henderson brought up several holoscreens and gestured to a particular area. These were more detailed images of the structures Connor had initially seen. Even though it was still quite distant, they were able to see large groups of figures moving in the distance. They couldn't tell whether they were Ovarrow or Krake, and he also couldn't discount the possibility that they were something else altogether. Scientists believed it was highly unlikely that they would find another completely different species. This made perfect sense to Connor because the Krake had obviously been using the multiverse for quite some time, and nothing indicated that they'd found anything but a variance of themselves in these different universes.

"General Gates," Volker said, "these images are very exciting. I was alarmed by the number of mixed results we had in the beginning."

"What were you expecting?" Connor asked.

Dr. Volker scratched his dark beard. "I was expecting more worlds like ours, but what we've been seeing is a lot of variation that goes well beyond different climates. Some of them have a completely different composition and are entirely lifeless. But not this one. There's a civilization here, but with the type of reconnaissance we're allowed to do, we're limited to a peek on the other side."

Connor nodded. "We don't want to draw attention to ourselves."

"I completely understand. I was just hoping to provide more information that you could base a decision on," Volker replied.

"I have to agree with him," Major Henderson said. "You brought a team with you, so will you be launching an operation to go through the arch?"

Connor glanced at Cerot. "Do you recognize those buildings?" he asked and gestured toward one of the images on the holoscreen.

The Ovarrow peered at the image and then opened the translator interface. "They appear to be of Krake design, at least partially."

Connor glanced at Dash.

"I see what he means," Dash said, gesturing toward a different part of the image where the buildings appeared to be rounded at the top. "These are more in line with the architecture we've found here, so they must be Ovarrow, at least at one time. But these other buildings don't match anything we've seen so far. Maybe they built something temporary," he said and asked Cerot a question.

"I've never seen these types of materials before. Therefore, they are Krake," Cerot answered.

"General, I don't think that's enough to go on," Major Henderson said.

"That's the problem," Connor replied. "We're making our best guess. I think this warrants us taking a closer look."

"We have armored rovers, but we don't have any stealth ships here," Major Henderson said.

Connor glanced at Samson for a moment, and they shared a look. "No, we need to minimize our footprint. We'll be going across in combat suits. They can keep up with any rover, and they give us more flexibility with the terrain we can cover."

Dash cleared his throat. "Excuse me, General Gates, but what about the Ovarrow? Their powered armor isn't as capable as the combat suits are."

Dash was right, and there was no way they could adapt the combat suits for Ovarrow use. He looked at Major Henderson.

"All the equipment here is designed for us," Henderson said.

"If they want to risk it," Samson said, "they could hitch a ride on the combat suit heavies if we had to move quickly."

"I'm not sure they'll like that," Dash said. "Isn't there something else they can use to keep up?"

Connor frowned for a moment and shook his head. "I'm afraid not. Everything is designed for us, and we want to reduce our presence so we're not bringing any vehicles."

"I'll go get the 7th ready, sir," Samson said and left.

Dash explained the situation to Cerot. Connor knew the Ovarrow were used to walking long distances, but if they got into a situation where they really had to move, they wouldn't be able to keep up with the soldiers in combat suits.

"What about a couple of MPSs?" Dash asked. "They're designed to be worn by—well, by anyone, and despite certain physical anomalies between humans and the Ovarrow, they're bipedal. The suit doesn't have to actually provide protection, but it could enable them to move faster than they otherwise could."

Connor shook his head. "They don't know how to use them, and there's no interface for them to utilize the features. MPSs are reliant on the standard implant interface. They wouldn't be able to turn them off and on. The MPS isn't going to help."

He tried to think of something they could bring that could help the Ovarrow, but there wasn't really anything that would fit the parameters. Most importantly, they couldn't leave anything behind. Samson was right. The Ovarrow would have to hitch a ride.

Cerot looked at Connor. "Stealth is most important for scouting missions. The Mekaal will not be a burden."

"I'm glad you understand. We're taking a small force through the archway. Therefore, I can only allow three of you to come with us. The others will have to stay behind," Connor said.

Cerot read the translation and turned to look at the arch for a few moments. Then he looked at Connor and gave him a single nod. Cerot had picked up on a few human gestures, and he'd seen Cerot and some of the other Ovarrow mimic human mannerisms when interacting with the colonists.

Connor left the command center and headed back down, Dash and Cerot following. A CDF soldier met him at the bottom of the stairs and saluted.

"General Gates, sir, I'm to escort you to your combat suit," Corporal Julia Bradley said.

"Lead the way, Corporal Bradley."

Bradley turned smartly on her heel and set a brisk pace, leading them over to the staging area. Cerot went to speak to the other Ovarrow.

Connor was already wearing an MPS that had been specifically designed for him. The suit redistributed its mass so it wouldn't weigh him down all that much, and he kept it on when he climbed into the Nexstar combat suit.

Dash gave the Nexstar an appreciative look. It added several inches onto Connor's already impressive height. "We need a civilian version of this."

"You have the MPS series 7, which is quite capable," Connor said.

Dash slipped into his MPS and it immediately adjusted to his body type. "Yeah, but the combat suit has all the extra bells and whistles. It has things like thrusters."

"I know, but don't underestimate the MPS. It can allow you to do most of the things I do from in here. But not everything. It's only a matter of time before we see more MPSs being used instead of these combat suits," Connor said.

He used implants to bring the combat suit's systems online. It went through a quick diagnostic check on startup and then showed green across the board on his internal heads-up display. The Nexstar was constructed of composite material that was quite strong without weighing the wearer down with needless bulk, which affected power consumption. The suits could operate out in the field for almost a full week before needing to recharge. All but three of the 1st Platoon in the 7th Ranger Company wore similar combat suits. Those three exceptions wore combat suit heavies. These carried heavy weapons capable of massive amounts of destruction, and they could also carry immensely heavy loads.

Corporal Bradley came back to them and handed Dash a hornet class SMG. "Mr. DeWitt, I'm told you're a capable marksman, but you're not qualified for the standard AR-71 assault rifle. This is the next best thing." She proceeded to go over the capabilities of the hornet and its operation. Connor agreed that it was the best suited for a nonmilitary person to use if they had to go into a dangerous situation. It had the option of becoming fully automatic. And even though a single dart wouldn't punch through the armor of a Nexstar combat suit, the next hundred fired inside a few seconds would chew right through it without any problem.

"I think I got it," Dash said. "I mean, I got it," he tacked on quickly.

Connor walked over to where Samson stood, and the men and women of the 1st Platoon gathered. Connor glanced at the arch behind them for a moment and then turned back to his soldiers. Dash stood with Cerot, Esteban, and Felix. The Ovarrow had put on their armor and carried their long rifles with them.

The soldiers quieted down, and Samson gave him a nod.

"In a few minutes, we'll be the first of many scout forces that will be sent through the arch. Our objective is clear. We're to scout out Krake installations for the purpose of gaining intel on our enemy. We need to know more about them so we can develop a strategy on how to beat them. This is where the groundwork gets laid—right here by all of you," Connor said, allowing his gaze to sweep across the men and women who stood before him. "We need to know what they know about us. To help speed up our intelligence gathering, we're bringing a few specialists with us," he said and gestured toward Dash and the Ovarrow. "You're here because you're among the elite. You've proven that you can adapt, and you're part of the most capable Spec Ops companies in the history of the Colonial Defense Force. Most of you have seen what the Krake are capable of. We're going in first because we do what no one else can, but remember the mission objective. We are a scout force. When it comes time for us to fight the Krake," Connor said, pausing for a moment, "we'll be able to do it more effectively because of missions like this."

Samson leaned over so only Connor could hear. "Are you planning to go on all the scouting missions?"

"I can't let you have all the fun. We'll see. You never know what we'll find," Connor said.

Samson let out a soft chuckle.

A large holoscreen came on next to the arch, and then a countdown appeared. The timer reached zero, and there was a brief shimmer in the space at the absolute center of the arch that spread to the edges. The arch was elevated about seven meters into the air, and a large loading ramp was moved into place. Two squads went up the ramp and through the arch gateway. A few moments later, they received an "all clear" message.

Connor heard Lieutenant Layton order Corporal Bradley to pick two soldiers and stay with Dash and the Ovarrow. They were behind Connor and Samson. When Corporal Bradley took up a position by Dash, Connor heard him mutter a comment about "babysitting duty." Bradley's no-nonsense look cracked into a lopsided smile for a moment, and then she was back to business.

Connor walked up the ramp and approached the edge of the gateway. For some reason, when they went through the gateway, they all leaned forward a little bit as if they expected to meet some kind of resistance. But going through the gateway didn't entail any resistance whatsoever; it was as simple as stepping through a doorway, except that when they stepped through, the ground under their feet changed to whatever was on the other side, and their view was one of emerging from the warehouse and stepping onto the plains of another universe. The gateway remained active for a few moments after the last person was through, and then it disappeared. There wasn't any flash of light; it was as if the window or doorway back to New Earth had simply ceased to exist.

They were on a schedule now. Back in the warehouse, Major Henderson would open the gateway at twelve-hour intervals. They had to adhere to the clock back on New Earth, but they also had to account for the fact that time might flow differently here. The days could be longer. They could immediately measure that the gravitational pull was three percent less than on New Earth. Initial scouting missions involving just reconnaissance probes had broken the theory that every gateway led to a world that was only slightly different from the one they called home. That wasn't the case at all, and they had to be prepared for those differences that may not be readily apparent.

Before they'd gone through the gateway, Major Henderson informed Connor that they'd moved the arch forward one hundred meters in order to allow them to emerge under cover. There were medium-sized trees about eight meters tall, with ground-sweeping branches of muted yellow and gray leaves and stout trunks with some exposed roots of dense black bark that transitioned to white in the broad, rounded crowns at the tops. The ground was covered with discarded leaves, and the air was crisp and dry.

Connor ordered stealth recon drones to be sent out. They were about a meter in length, with an elongated bulge in the middle. Reflective plates were used by a cloaking mechanism that projected the imagery of the surrounding area. The drones flew low for about half a kilometer, going in opposite directions, and then flew higher in the sky, noting significant movement toward the northwest of their position. Between the data sent back from the drones and their own observations, they were able to compile a map of the immediate area.

Connor looked at Samson. "Let's stick to the high ground on this ridge. That'll give us a better view of our approach."

They set off at a quick pace, allowing Connor to monitor the drone feeds, which were on an open channel for the officers. There was no one nearby, and they were able to move a bit quicker than he would've expected.

The drones were closing in on the small city, and he was able to make out more of the details.

"They look like Ovarrow soldiers," Samson said.

There were several hundred Ovarrow soldiers with multiple types of weapons and armored ground transportation bringing them toward the city.

Connor programmed one of the drones to speed ahead, while the others monitored it to give a better view. If the first drone was detected, they'd at least have the others in reserve.

As the drone flew overhead, Connor got more of a bird's-eye view. There was now a significant group of Ovarrow soldiers marching directly for the city.

"They have thousands of soldiers there," Connor said. "Looks like a full division, and they're storming that city."

"We just happened to pick the day that a battle is going to be fought," Samson said and shook his head in dismay.

The drone had reached the city, and Connor noted blackened craters from some kind of bombardment. "This isn't the first day of battle. There's been a lot of fighting here."

Bright flashes from particle-beam weapons came from the Ovarrow soldiers and their ground assault vehicles. Krake soldiers returned fire from the broken shells of the outer buildings. The Krake's dark gray armor had streaks of black and glowed yellow along the arms. Parts of the armor looked like they were organic, as if the armor had been grown rather than manufactured. Connor could see muscle-like tissue, even from the distance the drone flew overhead.

As the CDF soldiers made their way closer to the city, the Ovarrow began pushing toward the city that the Krake were trying to reinforce. The Ovarrow ground assault vehicles concentrated their fire, punching a hole through the Krake defense, and Ovarrow soldiers surged forward. Connor could appreciate the tactics used, but he much preferred surgical strikes rather than waging all-out war. He kept looking up in the sky, wondering why the Krake hadn't used any type of orbital bombardment, which would end this fight rather quickly. There had to be more going on here than what they were seeing.

They got within two kilometers of the city and circled around the outskirts so they could keep watching the battle. There were several bright flashes of light and thunderous sounds. Another bright flash of green lit up the sky, and a steaming swath laid waste to hundreds of Ovarrow soldiers from some kind of Krake heavy turret. Several more rose from the ruins of the city wall. There was a buildup of power as the weapon primed and then unleashed its god-awful fury onto the battlefield. The Ovarrow army scattered out of the way. Connor's enhanced vision saw that the weapon had been fired from within the city and cut through the buildings as much as it had the soldiers, as if the Krake didn't care about actually protecting the city. This was more about killing than protecting.

As the Ovarrow began to withdraw, they heard the high-pitched whine of several ships breaking the sound barrier from above. Krake combat shuttles raced down toward the battlefield and unleashed their weaponry on the retreating forces. Waves of Ovarrow soldiers came to a halt and then ran back toward the city, only to be shot at by the vicious cannon.

Samson looked at Connor. "This isn't a battle; it's a slaughter."

Connor watched as the Ovarrow soldiers tried to fire their weapons at the Krake, but they had no effect on the armored shuttles. Eventually, an estimate from the recon drones appeared on Connor's heads-up display, showing that less than fifty percent of the Ovarrow soldiers remained. He looked at Cerot and the others, who watched the carnage with grim fascination, and Connor realized that they were just as bewildered as the rest of them.

The Krake combat shuttles wheeled away and flew off, heading west. Connor sent a reconnaissance drone after them. There was a Krake military compound on the outskirts of the city that had a similar structure to what they'd found in the forward operating bases but on a much larger scale. The weapons ceased firing and the Ovarrow seemed to limp away.

"I think they're heading toward our egress point, General," Samson said.

Connor looked at the path the Ovarrow soldiers were retreating on. The area the CDF team had used for their transition into this universe had a lot of tree cover.

Dash came over to his side. "What just happened? They killed so many of them, and then they just stopped. What was the point?" Dash asked.

The second drone was making another pass over the Krake soldiers, and Connor saw that they were walking among the dead Ovarrow, killing any of the survivors. There were different groups of Krake doing the killing, and they utilized different weapons for their task.

Connor glanced at Cerot as he and the other Ovarrow watched the grisly scene, grimly acknowledging something they'd already witnessed many times before. There was no mistaking it. When a soldier had seen battle, they didn't react the same way as someone who'd never fought in one. Connor was beginning to feel that he might have been too hard on Cerot, Vitory, and the other Ovarrow.

"General, you need to see this," Samson said. He brought up the image taken from the drone video feed and made a passing motion to Connor.

Connor looked at it and saw thousands of habitation units that were cordoned off behind walls. It looked like some sort of encampment, but there were guard towers all around. Connor's mouth dropped open a little. It was a prison camp that held thousands of Ovarrow soldiers. Then he looked back at the battlefield.

"They aren't soldiers," Connor said. Dash looked at him, his mouth agape. "These are prisoners. They're being forced to fight." He looked at Cerot. He couldn't quite connect the thoughts in his mind, but he knew the brutal truth.

"This is a weapons test," Samson said. "And they are the targets."

Samson was right.

Cerot began tapping symbols urgently. "We have to help them."

Connor peered at the battlefield using his internal heads-up display. It showed different features that weren't within direct view but that his cyber-warfare suite in his combat suit knew were just beyond view based on the drone data.

"We can't help them. That's not why we're here," Connor said.

"There has to be something we can do," Dash said. "If this is a weapons test and the Krake are arming the Ovarrow, why would the Ovarrow go into that city in the first place? Why not just run away?"

Connor brought up the drone footage, looking for something he'd missed, and found a deep crater roughly in the middle of the city. There was an arch at the bottom. There were glowing lights on the outside of the arch and a slight shimmer on the inside—an active gateway. Connor looked back at the retreating Ovarrow soldiers, and it only took his brain seconds to put it together.

"You promised to help the Ovarrow," Cerot said.

Connor looked at him. "I promised to help you and your people. To prevent something like this," he said, gesturing toward the battlefield, "from happening to you on New Earth."

"They *are* us. We are the same. There are more prisoners," Cerot said.

Cerot wasn't able to see the drone video feeds, but he'd made the logical leap that there must be a place where the prisoners were kept.

A high-pitched siren sounded from the city, and the Ovarrow soldiers stopped their retreat immediately. They turned around almost as one, and Connor watched as they checked their weapons. Then, they began to march back toward the city. The siren was almost ear-piercing, and it went on for a few minutes. Several of the soldiers attempted to run the other way, only to be shot by the nearest Ovarrow soldier, who then resumed his march back toward the city. There was no retreat, and apparently there was no surren-dering either.

"What do you want to do, General?" Samson asked.

Dash had left the Ovarrow communicator on, and the words were trans-lated for Cerot and the others. They watched Connor warily.

"We have ten more hours before the gateway from New Earth is acti-vated. We need to do more reconnaissance. There's a Krake military installa-tion. I think we can circle around and have a closer look," Connor said.

Samson considered this for a few moments. "We can make it back in time if there was—if we wanted to leave at the next check-in."

"You're right, but we need to send a status report back. I don't want to leave a comms drone, so let's send a small team and then they can catch up with us," Connor said.

Lieutenant Layton, who'd been listening, ordered three soldiers to wait, and when it got closer to the time for the check-in, they'd send a comms drone directly to where the gateway from New Earth would appear.

Connor looked at Cerot. "I can't make any promises. We need to assess the situation further."

"Understood, General," Cerot replied.

They took their time circling well away from the city. Connor and Samson expected that there would be defenses in place that might even be capable of detecting them. They moved slowly and steadily, carefully navigating the battlefield and keeping as close to cover as they could. The drones continued to survey, providing valuable data on the layout of the area.

As they were circling around the city, there were two more attempted sieges by Ovarrow soldiers. Even Connor was beginning to wonder how many prisoners the Krake had there. He was impressed that they didn't run away; they threw themselves at the objective, and there was no mistaking that they were trying to reach that arch. He didn't know where the gateway went, and he wasn't about to risk sending one of the drones that close.

———

Five hours had passed since they'd observed the first grisly battle. The ground began to shake under their feet, followed by several large explosions east of their position. Connor spun around, as did Samson. Lieutenant Layton attempted to open the comlink to the soldiers they'd left behind. After a few moments, they got a reply. After a short conversation, Lieutenant Layton looked at Connor. "They're fine, but it looks like the Krake have added an orbital bombardment to their weapons testing. The area we came in through is now a massive crater a half a kilometer across and several hundred feet deep. We're not going home that way."

Connor muttered a curse. "We have contingencies for this. Tell them to leave a comms drone and schedule it to go active at the time the check-in is scheduled. Briefly update, explaining what happened. We're surveying the area to come up with another egress point, but we don't have one right now."

Lieutenant Layton relayed the orders.

Connor had been in more than a few hot spots throughout his career, but this was different. They were on someone else's battlefield, and they didn't know all the rules. More than a few soldiers glanced above them, wondering if the next orbital strike was going to be on them.

"We need to move closer to the city and head toward the Krake military compound," Connor said.

"Move closer? But won't they detect us?" Dash asked. His voice was high, but he was keeping it under control. Corporal Bradley said something to Dash, and he quickly glanced away from Connor. "I'm sorry."

"It's all right. Calm down. We're moving closer because there's less chance of the orbital strike occurring in the city. Otherwise, there'd be no city left," Connor said.

Dash nodded and pressed his lips together, determined to keep his mouth shut.

Connor looked at Samson and Lieutenant Layton. "Let's move."

CHAPTER 18

As Connor and the rest of the 7th made their way closer to the city, the reconnaissance drone flying overhead showed no sign of Krake forces being aware of their movements. The battle being fought a few kilometers away had gained in intensity, and the bombardment hadn't stopped. The Krake must've changed their tactics because they were attacking with smaller ordnance. They didn't restrict their activity to one particular area. Instead, they seemed to be blanketing the entire area, with an occasional shot that came closer to Connor and the others. As they got closer to the city, they found makeshift barriers and shallow tunnel networks from previous attempts to infiltrate the city. Also, the closer they got to the city, the ground cover lessened, leaving the area open, which would make them easy targets if the Krake were watching. There were several louder explosions that Connor equated with bunker busters, which penetrated deep into the ground.

They slipped into a pattern of evaluating the next fifty meters, then moving forward and repeating. Bright flashes made the thick cloud cover above them blaze with a blinding light. Something pierced an area over the battlefield, and then a new blossom of light appeared in rapid succession on the ground.

"Take cover!" Samson shouted as a bright flash of light appeared directly above their heads.

Connor grabbed Cerot's arm and pulled him down, shielding him. The sound of the explosion was deafening, but the combat suit dampened the sound. The ground shook, and Connor squeezed his eyes shut for a few moments, waiting for it to be over. There was nothing he could do. Cerot covered his ears, and when the roar of sound was finally over, Connor glanced around. He saw Dash a short distance from him. Corporal Bradley helped Cerot to his feet. Other CDF soldiers had protected Esteban and Felix, but the Ovarrow were disoriented and it took them a little while to regain their feet.

Connor looked up and saw that there were more bright flashes as the bombardment continued along the surrounding areas of the city. Had they been spotted? He couldn't be sure. The only time *he* would order an orbital strike that blanketed a specific area was when he couldn't find the enemy, but this was different. The Krake knew exactly where their Ovarrow prisoner army was attacking from, which meant this tactic was just as much a mental attack as it was physical.

Connor looked at Samson, who was surveying the area. "Containment strategy," he said.

"That's a bit over the top," Samson replied. "We need to find cover. We're too exposed."

The recon drone video feeds showed a large crater fifty meters from their position. Any closer and the force of the explosion would have taken lives. Those types of orbital strikes were meant to take out heavily armored units, and while the Nexstar combat suits had plenty of armor, they couldn't withstand the kinetic force of an orbital bombardment. They had to move.

The rest of the 7th sounded off, and everyone was accounted for. A short distance away, the force of the bombardment had caused the ground to cave in, exposing an underground tunnel. There was water at the bottom that must have been from an underground river system. An artificial path led inside. They couldn't see inside because of the angle of the drone cameras.

Several soldiers shouted an alarm, and Connor glanced over at them. The sky was lighting up again. This area was about to get pounded.

"Move into the tunnel!" Connor shouted.

His orders were repeated, and the 7th ran for the exposed tunnel. Once inside, they kept on going. The tunnel angled down, and they could hear the bombardment above them getting closer and closer until it sounded as if it were right on top of them. The ground shook violently, and they kept moving as fast as they could. Then the bombardment stopped. The Ovarrow coughed, clearing their throats of the dust in the air.

Connor brought up the recon drone video feed, and it showed that the area they'd been in was now a smoking ruin. Samson had one of their soldiers go back and confirm that the way back was blocked off. They weren't going to get out that way.

"Any idea what this place is?" Samson asked.

Connor glanced over the edge of the landing they were walking on and could hear the sounds of water not far away. The tunnel they were in had a rocky bottom, but it had been built by someone.

"It's gotta be a sewer system," Dash said. "I've seen something similar in the Ovarrow capital cities. We should be able to take this all the way inside. The walls are reinforced, but I don't think we want to stay here very long."

Samson raised his eyebrows and glanced at Connor.

"He's right," Connor said. "The Ovarrow built their cities by major waterways."

Samson looked at Dash. "So, anything else we should know? How bad is this place going to smell?"

"I have no idea," Dash replied. "The running water provides a natural filtration system, so hopefully it won't be too bad. The ones I saw had been abandoned for hundreds of years."

They made their way deeper into the sewer system along drainage pipes that were emptying into the area from the ceiling above. The bombardment had faded to a dull thud but was a constant reminder of the battle being fought above them.

The waterway became deeper the closer they got to the city, and the sounds of a waterfall were almost constant. They found doorways that had been blown open, so they knew they weren't the first to have come down there. They carefully scanned the area, looking for sensors that could detect their presence, but there weren't any. Given the way the Krake were conducting their war games, Connor didn't believe for a second that this was an oversight. They must have some other way to secure this entry into the city.

The drainage pipes that connected to the main waterway were about a meter and a half across, and Connor didn't relish the thought of trying to climb through one of those to reach the surface. They were dark and curved away from view. Anything could be living in there.

The soldiers ahead of him came to a stop, and Connor peered into the distance. The walkway they were on split as they reached a major filtration system where dark shadows scurried amidst the water. They looked like the glistening bodies of wet otters a meter long, and they were clamoring to climb out of the waterway. Some of them came from multiple drainage pipes, as if a clog of them had been shoved out. Dozens of dead otter-like creatures floated by. Their bloated bodies were still, their snouts frozen in agony.

Connor wanted to know what the otters were running from, but typically in nature, if rodents were running from something, it meant there was danger nearby. They reached the area where the walkway split and saw that the otters kept trying to climb up the waterfall, each using the one ahead of it to climb above. It was a savage display of determination to live. Teeth and claws were tearing into one another. Hundreds of screeches and growls pierced the sounds of the waterfalls. Beyond the water treatment center was a giant pumping station. All the waterways were filled with the scrambling otters.

Connor looked at Cerot. "What are they doing?"

"It looks like an infestation. Small numbers are used for maintaining the sewage system, clearing away debris and blockages," Cerot replied.

Across the pumping station, there were several levels above that looked clear of the rodents. Suddenly, a loud roar overwhelmed all other sounds and sent the otters into a frenzy. The soldiers at the rear began firing their weapons. The otters were storming the walkway they were on. Something large bumped into Connor's leg, and the otter flailed as Connor kicked it off over the side and into the water below.

They raced ahead, and the combat suit heavies brought up the rear, decimating the oversized otters attempting to race toward them. The heavy gauss cannons chewed away the walkway, and the otters began spilling down into the water below. But still, they came. Enough of the dead piled up to form a grisly bridge.

Several more loud roars came from the watery depths below, and the otters tried to flee in waves. There was something big down there.

Samson gestured toward the upper levels. "We can get up there," he said.

The Nexstar combat suits had grappling hooks, as well as suit jets. Connor looked over at Dash, and Corporal Bradley was already telling him to climb onto her back. Connor gestured for Cerot to grab hold of his combat suit, while Esteban and Felix grabbed onto the nearest soldiers with combat suits. Combat heavies provided covering fire while they raced to the edge of the walkway and engaged their combat suit jets. One by one, the CDF soldiers launched into the air, using the suit jets to give them a massive boost, and then fired their grappling hooks to the other side. The hooks bit into the walkways above, and the automatic retractors pulled them quickly upward.

Connor felt Cerot give a double tap, indicating he was ready. Connor raced to the edge and engaged his suit jets just as a large shadow burst from the watery depths. As he launched in the air, a gargantuan mouth with savage teeth opened, chasing him. He fired his suit jets at maximum, but the teeth were closing the distance toward him. Cerot shifted, and Connor felt his ascent slow as the suit jets tried to keep him level. They slammed against the far wall, and Connor instinctively reached out to grab hold of anything to avoid falling into the mouth of death. At the same time, the creature slammed into an area beneath them. Connor's armored fingers found purchase, and they stopped slipping. He spun around and paused, making sure Cerot still had a hold. Cerot fired his weapon at the dark beast below, and other soldiers joined him.

Connor couldn't get a good look at the creature. The way above was blocked, and he scrambled to the side. He jabbed his fingers into the rocky wall, and small bits of rock fell. The combat suit assisted his movements, and Connor was able to move faster, almost scrambling around the outcropping as the giant beast below made ready for another lunge. He saw movement above him and realized it was Dash hanging off the back of Bradley's combat suit. There were bright flashes as the CDF soldiers unleashed the fury of their weapons at the monsters below.

Connor reached for a ledge and managed to pull himself up a little bit before it started to break away. He scrambled over to another handhold and dangled, his feet unable to find purchase. He heard Cerot growling as he tried to hang on for dear life.

"General Gates," Corporal Bradley shouted, "we're dropping you a line. Take it and we'll haul you up."

Connor glanced over to the side and saw a synthetic line with a stubby end drop next to him. He reached with one hand to grab hold of it and the magnetic end attached to his suit. He let go of the wall and was quickly pulled up. Once he reached the top, they helped Cerot off Connor's back, and then Connor pulled himself up the rest of the way over the edge. There was a small group of them. Connor took a few moments to catch his breath.

"Is everyone all right?" Connor asked.

Dash nodded, and Bradley said she was all right. Private Marsters was peering over the edge of their shallow outcropping.

"There's no one else down there," Marsters said.

They had been separated from the main group. Connor opened the comlink to Samson. "What's your status?"

Most of the 7th had made it across, but they were still rescuing a few stragglers.

"What's your position? I'll send a team to get you," Samson said.

"Negative. We're down from your position, and I see a way for us to get out. We'll meet up topside," Connor said.

Samson began to protest, but several more roars rocked the cavern, rising above the pitch of the waterfall.

"You have your orders, Captain. Gates out."

Connor closed the comlink and went to the edge of the outcropping, looking up. There appeared to be a maintenance shaft not far above their position. If they could make it up there, they might be able to get away.

"General, those things aren't dead," Marsters said, looking over the edge they'd just climbed up from.

Connor went over to Marsters, and the others joined him. Down below, three of the large monsters were scaling the walls.

"Corporal, there's a maintenance shaft above us. Take Dash and go there. We'll be right behind you," Connor said. Dash hesitated for a moment, but Connor told him to go ahead. "We're going to stall them."

Connor went to the edge and Cerot stood next to him. Connor looked at Marsters. "Change your ammunition type to incendiary and check your fire so the weapon doesn't overheat."

The AR-71 utilized a nanorobotic ammunition source that was capable of becoming various types of armaments. The monsters' hides had to be thick, and the best thing to penetrate that besides firepower was firepower that was extremely hot. They leaned over the edge and fired their weapons. Incendiary darts glowed red as they streaked down into the faces of the monsters. Cerot shot a particle beam from his Ovarrow weapon, and one of the monsters screeched in pain. Connor aimed for its clawed hands as it tried to lurch upward. As the monster got closer, he saw that its face was speckled with dark liquid. They were shooting the thing up, but it wouldn't stop. Its eyes were almost black, and like a shark that had caught the smell of blood, it was beyond anything even resembling reason.

They backed away from the edge as the creature closed in on them. Connor glanced behind them and saw that there was synthetic rope hanging. He ordered Marsters to get up the rope. Cerot kept firing his weapon, keeping his focus as a giant clawed hand reached over the edge. The Ovarrow weapon wasn't strong enough to do much more than surface damage. Connor told Cerot to get back and launched a grenade.

The grenade blew chunks of the creature's flesh away and it wailed in pain. Connor gestured for Cerot to climb onto his back. Connor secured his weapon and ran for the edge just as a rescue line reappeared. As he grabbed hold of it, his momentum carried him away from the edge. He used his suit jets to angle him away from the enraged creature. Engaging the main thrusters below his feet, he surged upward with Cerot. Corporal Bradley retracted the line and brought them up out of the reach of the creatures.

They went into the maintenance shaft and ran. He wasn't sure how big that monster was, but the maintenance shaft wasn't exactly a tight squeeze. If it was determined enough, it could probably follow them.

The shaft angled upward, and they kept running. Cerot moved to climb off his back, but Connor told him to stay put. As they turned up the speed, he heard the loud roars of the creature entering the shaft. The thing wasn't going to give up. They had to get out of there.

They reached the surface and emerged into a shell of a building from which they could see the gray skies overhead. They were in the city, so at least they wouldn't have to worry about a bombardment. They walked to the edge of the building, and Connor looked down an empty street. Cerot climbed off and walked. Dash did the same. The MPS had kept him safe. Bradley and Marsters were on either side of him.

As Connor took a few steps out into the street, a small ship flew overhead. It was extremely quiet and came to a complete stop right above them. They tried to run back into the building, but the ship quickly sank down and thick, dark cords sped toward them, impossibly fast. The cords wrapped around their waists and yanked all five of them up into the air. Connor tried to force his way free, but he couldn't. The thick cord had one of his arms pinned, and he couldn't even draw his weapon. He heard the others shouting as they sped toward a larger ship. They were going so fast that Connor thought they were going to collide with the hull, but at the last second, a door opened and they were pulled inside.

CHAPTER 19

Connor's teeth rattled as he was pulled through the darkness. He slammed into the walls and flailed, trying to break free. He thought he heard someone else screaming, but his senses were jumbled with each bone-jarring slam into the walls of the tunnel. Then he was free-falling for a few moments until he hit solid ground. Between the combat suit and the MPS he wore, he was protected from the impact, but he was still disoriented.

Connor pushed himself to his feet, and the glowing lights of his suit pierced the darkness. Dash called out for him, and Connor answered but couldn't see him. He sounded as if he was speaking through a wall. Looking around, he saw that he was in a dark cell. A large shape detached itself from the wall, and Connor raised his weapon, but when the helmet's night vision adjusted he saw Cerot and lowered his weapon.

Cerot held up one hand as his other hand clutched the broken shaft of his weapon. He took a step and clutched at his side. Pieces of his armor had broken off.

"We're in some kind of a cell. Can anyone see a way out?" Connor asked.

"Same here, sir. They dumped us in a box," Bradley replied.

"We still have our weapons. Can't we just use them to get out of here?" Dash asked.

Connor was thinking the same thing, but he frowned. "I'm cut off from the others. I've got no comlink signal or anything that would reach to the reconnaissance drones. Bradley, Marsters, are you experiencing the same thing?"

"I'm cut off too, sir," Bradley confirmed, and Marsters did the same.

Connor glanced up and saw that there was light coming in from the outside. "There's a window above me. I'm going to climb up and see if I can get a look outside."

"There are no windows in here," Dash replied.

Cerot tried to get up and Connor told him to stay where he was. He walked over to the wall. It was smooth but looked as if it was made of some kind of metallic alloy. Engaging the magnetic sensors on the palms of his hands, his knees, and the tips of his feet, he climbed up the wall to the window, which wasn't a far climb and required minimal effort on his part since the suit did most of the work. He reached the top and peered out the small, round window. It was open to the outside, but there was a faint bluish force field that separated them from the outside. Connor couldn't reach it. It must've been some kind of gas that was keeping the atmosphere sealed in the ship.

The ship banked to the side, and Connor caught a glimpse of the ground below. They were being taken away from the city toward the Krake military compound. He'd wanted to infiltrate the compound, but he hadn't wanted to be a prisoner when it happened.

"What do you see?" Dash asked.

Connor climbed back down. "They're taking us to the compound."

"General," Bradley said, "I'm not detecting any other life signs. We're the only ones in here."

Connor frowned and saw that Bradley had deployed a personal recon drone, which was smaller and was able to leave the area they were in.

"We might've triggered some kind of automated escaped-prisoner retrieval protocol once we got inside the city," Connor said.

"What about the others? Won't they be captured as well?" Dash asked.

"There's no way for us to know, but they're not on this ship, so we'll just take this one step at a time," Connor said.

They checked their supplies. Marsters and Dash had dropped their weapons, so Connor and Bradley were the only ones still armed, which wasn't optimal. Connor opened the panel on the side of his combat suit and activated a personal recon drone. Flying toward the window, it approached the force field slowly. The recon drone was able to fly through the force field and get outside it, at which time Connor lost his connection to it. The video feeds cut off, and he cursed. He climbed up to see if it was just hovering along outside the force field, but it wasn't.

He dropped to the floor and helped Cerot with his wounds. They were trapped. He couldn't risk using explosives because of the close quarters they were in.

"How can we get out of here?" Dash asked.

Connor slammed his fist against the bulkhead wall. It was solid, and hardly a blemish showed from the force he'd used. "We're not getting out of here," he said.

"There has to be a way. We can't be trapped in here," Dash said.

Connor heard Bradley trying to calm Dash down, but his voice was rising in fear.

"Dash," Connor said in a firm voice, "no one is giving up. Any second now, the ship is going to land. Even if I could blow a hole in the bulkhead, we'd have to jump out. We might survive, but Cerot definitely wouldn't. We'll make our escape attempt when the ship lands. I doubt they intend to keep us in here. I need you to calm down and listen to Corporal Bradley. She'll keep you safe."

"All right, all right," Dash said. "And for the record, telling somebody to calm down doesn't make them calm down."

"Understood," Connor said. "Did anyone get a look at the ship as we were getting pulled up into it? I couldn't get a good look."

"Negative, General. It happened too fast," Bradley said.

Marsters echoed the same.

Connor peered at the ground and saw that it was smooth, with no seams, even along the wall. How were the Krake going to get them out of there? He began putting together a plan in his mind but had to do a lot more guessing than he would've liked. There were no two ways about it. They'd been captured.

"We need to keep our heads. We're going to get out of this," Connor said. Now all he needed to do was come up with a way for them to do just that. He thought about his personal recon drone and shook his head. He should've uploaded a message and set a secondary protocol to search for Samson and let him know they were alive. Once it was cut off from Connor's suit, it would just fly around uselessly until it acquired a signal. If it never reacquired a signal, it would just go into standby and be otherwise useless.

"Is your recon drone still active?" Connor asked.

"Yes, sir, it's still flying through the air ducts," Bradley answered.

Connor nodded. "Good. Let me know if it finds anything."

The only thing they could do now was wait. He hoped Samson and the others hadn't been caught in this trap. He wondered how many of the 7th had made it out of the sewers.

CHAPTER 20

Sean left the galley just after he finished his meal and was contacted by Gabriel, the *Vigilant's* AI.

"Colonel, I've noted some power fluctuations near Dr. Evans's lab. There has been a temporary loss of artificial gravity in the area," Gabriel said.

The artificial gravity on the ship was on its own separate system, just like life support. There were redundancies in place to prevent it from failing.

"Is anyone injured?" Sean asked, quickening his pace.

Oriana's work area wasn't far from the galley.

"None reported, sir."

"Thanks for letting me know, Gabriel. I'll head over there right now," Sean said.

An alert flashed on his internal heads-up display as he hastened down the corridor. It was a reminder to return to the bridge for his update with Vanessa. Sean reminded himself for the umpteenth time to thank Colonel Cross for connecting him with Major Shelton. Vanessa had become a real asset.

Sean turned down the corridor to Oriana's lab and saw her standing outside, speaking to a group of people. As he approached, they began to disperse. The door to the lab was open, and Sean leaned over so he could see inside. The place was a mess of overturned equipment and tools.

"What have you done to my ship?" Sean asked.

Oriana smiled. Her long hair was tied up, with a few strands cascading down her neck. "We'll get it cleaned up."

Sean glanced inside the lab again and saw two heavy emitters. Status windows appeared above the control console that showed a growing list of errors. Eugena Yuan was working on the consoles.

"They both redlined," Eugena said, "but I have the calculation that will prevent that. It shouldn't happen again," she said and made a passing motion, sending the data to Oriana's PDA.

Oriana opened her wrist computer and glanced at it. "This looks good. Get this to Halsey when you can," she said and looked at Sean. "I'll explain along the way."

They headed down the corridor and Sean glanced back at the lab. "Are they going to be able to clean all that up?"

"Of course. You should've seen it the first time that happened."

"First time?" Sean said and frowned.

"You asked me to come," she said and paused. "I know it looks bad, but it's actually—well, that's the result of a successful test."

If that was a success, Sean thought, he'd hate to see what failure looked like.

"Whatever you were doing affected one of the core ship systems."

"I can explain that," Oriana said.

For the next ten minutes on their way to the bridge, Oriana explained what she'd been working on. Sean felt like he had a permanent frown on his face while he tried to follow along. He thought he understood what she'd done, or at least he understood the concept.

"But as I said, the power draw will be enormous," Oriana said.

"And you consulted with Halsey on this?" Sean asked.

"Yes, of course. He even helped me get access to some of the equipment I needed, but it's not finished. I just ran out of time . . . You don't look convinced."

Sean bobbed his head to the side, his brows knitting together in thought. "I'm *not* convinced, but I don't think you wasted your time. I don't mean to take anything away from what you've accomplished."

Oriana nodded and didn't say anything. She wasn't angry or anything like that. She knew that there was still a lot more work to be done, but the source of her frustration was the lack of time, which was the source of frustration for all of them.

They walked onto the bridge and headed to the command center. Captain Russo stood up from the commander's chair and went to sit at the auxiliary workstation next to his. Sean sat down and brought up his personal holoscreen, asking Specialist Sansky to open a subspace comlink to the *Yorktown*.

Major Vanessa Shelton appeared on his screen. Sean thought he saw a hint of annoyance in her gaze. He'd decided to keep the *Yorktown* as far away from the hot zone as possible. He'd also transferred the space gate to the *Yorktown*.

"Colonel Quinn, the Talon-V squadrons have been underway for the past twenty-four hours. They reported minimal course correction and should have more than enough resources to rendezvous with Charlie team," Shelton said.

He had divided the battle group into multiple teams to achieve their mission. He'd kept the particulars of their plan from Aurang and had just given him a timeframe of when they would begin. Dividing his forces was necessary for mission success. It would enable him to hit the Krake from multiple angles of approach to their targets.

The soldiers aboard the Talon-Vs had spent the last twenty-four hours coasting through space—twenty-four hours in the same cramped space inside the same flight suits—and they had another twelve hours to go, at the very least, not to mention the time it would take after they delivered the payload to the space gate. They had one of the most crucial steps of the entire operation, and they had to send a small enough force to have the least chance of being detected by the enemy.

"Understood, Major," Sean said. "I know it's not easy staying out of the fight."

"I understand the reasoning, sir. It's the endgame that I don't particularly care for," Shelton replied.

In the event that the mission experienced complete failure, the *Yorktown* and the *Acheron* would egress through their own space gate. He couldn't leave the *Yorktown* completely defenseless, so he'd assigned the *Acheron* to stay with the *Yorktown* under the command of Lieutenant Sutton.

"I don't either, but we need to make sure we can account for anything and everything," Sean said with a lopsided smile.

"Maintenance checks on our space gate don't fill me with confidence, sir. We've been patching this together as we've gone, and some things are starting to wear out," Shelton said.

What had started out as a prototype mobile space gate had become a cobbled-together piece that contained components stolen from a Krake space gate to keep it operational. "It just needs to work one time for as long as we need it to."

"I have maintenance crews working on it now, and they'll remain working on it until the end of this mission. No matter what, that gate will be operational for you when the time comes," Shelton said.

Sean had considered moving Vanessa to one of the destroyers, but he needed her right where she was, and they both knew it.

"Aurang and our Spec Ops team have already left and are even now speeding ahead. They should reach their target three hours ahead of us," Sean said.

"The Krake are even more paranoid about their security than we initially thought. Who puts the authenticator for a secure facility on the planet on a monitoring station that orbits around the planet?"

"Don't forget the lunar base," Sean said.

Aurang had informed them that there was a mining facility on the lunar base because of the rich deposits of minerals they'd found there. "We have a good plan," Sean continued. "The Talon-Vs will disable the space gate while we disable the communication capabilities from the other Krake targets. It should keep them off balance while Aurang and our Spec Ops team reach their target."

Sean didn't trust Aurang or that part of the plan, which was why he had a few combat shuttles designated to run rescue operations should the need arise.

"I wish we had more time," Shelton began to say and then stopped. "I know I've said it before, sir. All the parts are moving. I just wish there was more I could do. The entire crew of the *Yorktown* feels the same way. You'll be in our thoughts and prayers, sir."

"Thank you for that," Sean said. "Good luck, Major."

"You as well, Colonel."

The subspace comlink went dark and Sean sat back in his chair. He glanced at Oriana for a moment, who was busy working at her console.

"Gabriel," Sean said quietly, "I need to run a few calculations by you." He didn't know why, but most people assumed—and by that he meant scientists and other specialists—that he couldn't do the same level of math they could. If anything, his parents had made sure that Sean had a good education, and the fact that he'd tested so highly in multiple fields had served him well on more than one occasion. Sean was a military man, but he could easily have been one of the specialists like Oriana.

"Okay, Gabriel. Let's begin."

CHAPTER 21

C had Boseman had been on more high-risk missions in the past eighteen months than in his entire military career. The reports they filed carried the acronym LPS, which stood for "low probability of success." Among the Spec Ops team there was a different ranking system for these types of missions, and that carried the acronym CD—certainty of death. The CD for this mission wasn't quite at the highest rank. He'd read the mission reports from when General Gates had stormed the Vemus Alpha ship and saved the entire colony. If a mission like that rated the number ten in terms of life expectancy, then this one was a solid eight in his professional opinion.

The entire Spec Ops platoon was in their Nexstar combat suits aboard a rundown Krake transport ship, which could've been a shuttle at one time but looked more like it had been converted for salvage runs. The ship's components hadn't quite vibrated when they'd done their initial burn to speed away from the *Vigilant*, but it had been a close thing. They were all on their own life support despite Aurang's assurances that the atmosphere in the ship would meet their requirements. None of them wanted to breathe the air on a Krake ship.

Aurang was the only one who communicated with them, even though there were five other Krake fifth column fighters aboard.

"I'm surprised they don't call themselves freedom fighters," Corporal Brentworth said.

They'd been aboard the ship for over twelve hours, which was long enough to become more comfortable even though they were on an enemy ship.

"So, we're helping freedom fighters," Brentworth continued.

"Are you kidding me?" Bowren said.

Bowren was in a combat suit heavy configuration and took up a lot more room than the rest of them. The man liked big guns, and it suited him.

"No, I'm not. What's wrong with calling them freedom fighters?" Brentworth asked. Then he looked at Chad.

"You need to study some history," Chad replied. "You know how many groups called themselves 'freedom fighters' who were actually little more than terrorists?" The faceplates on the combat suit were transparent because the armored cross section wasn't engaged, so he could see Brentworth's frown.

"They told us they were rebelling against those overseers," Brentworth replied.

"Yeah, and we can't trust everything they say," Bowren said.

Benton, who'd been unusually quiet, burped loudly. They were all on a shared comlink, but Benton had a habit of leaving his on, much to everyone's chagrin.

"Watch out now," Bowren said and grinned. "Sarge is going to lose it."

Benton grinned, which had started out as a groan. "Not likely."

Chad looked at Benton. "Are you sick? For real, did you catch a stomach virus or something?"

"Negative, Captain, just my insides are a bit scrambled."

Chad regarded him for a moment. Benton *had* been unusually quiet. He opened a private comlink to Benton. "What's going on?"

Benton sighed. "It's been a while since I've been in zero-G, sir."

Chad frowned. "You're telling me you're nauseous because of the zero-G we experienced for a few minutes before we did our burn?"

"No, sir. You know I can take that. It's . . . I just got a little bit of payback, that's all." He was quiet for a second. "Remember that request we got . . . well, *I* got?"

"You're telling me that Dr. Evans did this to you?"

"Not exactly. It was Eugena."

Chad remembered Eugena. Anyone who saw her wouldn't likely forget her anytime soon. She was definitely easy on the eyes. He snickered. "What did they do to you?"

"Well, they asked for my help. They said they needed a volunteer out on the flight deck—someone who could keep a clear head. So, I met them out there. They had me out on the second level. I know you told me to stay away from them, but the galley is a free area, sir. I was respectful," Benton said. "So, Eugena was standing there with a cup of coffee, and she held it out to me. When I went to grab it, she stepped back. Beneath me was the artificial gravity emitter. They reversed the field and had me dangling in the air."

Chad laughed and the others joined in. He'd opened the channel back up so everyone could hear the story.

"*Ha ha*, very funny. Yeah, I know," Benton said.

"How long did they leave you out there?" Chad asked.

"It wasn't so much the length of time but the transference to other emitter fields. They moved me in every direction possible—up, down, sideways, upside down. You name it; they did it. But I told them to. I told them I could take it, and I did," Benton said.

Chad nodded in understanding. There were certain personality traits that were almost a prerequisite for joining Spec Ops. They all rose to the challenge to prove themselves in almost everything that came across their paths.

"Was it worth it?" Brentworth asked.

Benton tilted his head to the side and swallowed a burp. "I got her to agree to meet me for a drink when we get back home. What do you think? I told you she liked me," he said and chuckled a little. "I'd do it all again."

Chad shook his head. Benton wasn't kidding. Not giving up was another character trait they looked for in recruits.

Two of the Krake fifth column soldiers ran past them toward the rear of the ship and the Spec Ops team engaged their helmet protection. They had entered the planet's atmosphere, and if everything had gone according to plan, they were over eight hundred kilometers from the south pole. Their target was in the frigid south, where the Krake ran clandestine operations on this Ovarrow world. They'd entered the atmosphere and were flying low to blend in with the frozen landscape.

"Sounds like our plan just took a turn," Bowren said.

Chad stood up and went toward the cockpit. Several violent shudders moved through the ship, and Chad had to brace himself.

"Are we under attack?" Chad asked.

They were heading toward a massive storm system, and since they were this far to the south, there were likely blizzard conditions on the ground.

Aurang was flying the ship. "No attack. The ship is breaking. We'll need to secure other options for escape."

Chad glanced at a smaller holoscreen in front of Aurang's copilot. It was showing some kind of video feed. The copilot glanced at him and quickly turned off the screen, but for a second he'd seen an arch. They weren't supposed to be anywhere near an arch on this mission.

"You should secure yourself. This landing won't be soft," Aurang said.

"I thought the arch was on the other side of the compound," Chad said.

"It is, but we also know that this is where we need to secure transport for our escape," Aurang said.

There was a loud bang from the rear of the ship, and they began to lose altitude. Chad looked at the holoscreen and saw that they were heading directly for a building near their target, but now they were veering off course. This was supposed to be a quiet operation.

Chad turned around and went back to his men. "Get ready. This is going to be a bumpy ride."

The storm was getting worse. Ice shards pelted the Krake ship. Then, large chunks of ice slammed into the side of the ship. They just had to hold on a little bit longer until they reached their destination. The storm, despite doing its utmost to bring the ship down, was a blessing because it covered their approach. They couldn't have asked for better cover than what they had.

Something large slammed into the ship, causing one side to suddenly drop downward. There was a loud tearing sound, and gusts of wind sucked out of the hole in the rear of the craft. Chad watched as the two Krake soldiers held on. The ship banked to the side and sank even farther. Then they crashed.

The Krake ship slid on its side for a few moments before the nose wedged itself into the ground, but they had too much momentum and the ship flipped into the air, snapping off the front of the vessel. But when they finally came to a stop, they were still secure in their seats.

Chad checked the combat suit statuses for his team, and they were all green. They'd survived the crash. The two Krake soldiers in the rear of the ship untangled themselves and headed outside. Aurang left the cockpit, followed by two more soldiers, and all of them left the ship. The blizzard was in full swing, blowing so hard that it was difficult to see. The combat suit systems adjusted the display, clearing the way in front of them as best they could. Chad saw that they weren't far from their destination. There was a small city laid out like a spider, with domed living spaces at the ends of long tunnels. There were no roads in. They were isolated.

Chad glanced behind him, and so did Brentworth. "Is it working?" he asked quietly.

Brentworth was carrying a modified field kit that contained a subspace communication device. It was big and bulky, and if it didn't work, it wasn't worth carrying.

"It's green across the board, Captain," Brentworth said, sounding relieved.

They went to one of the buildings on the outskirts. Aurang was able to open the door and they all went inside.

"Captain, I'll need a few moments to confirm the precise location for the uplink," Aurang said.

He was flanked by his two companions while the remaining two watched them.

"Is he serious?" Benton said. "We had a target, and they need to confirm the location?"

Chad didn't reply. Instead, he glanced over to the side where Vladek had circled around so he could have a good view of the console.

Aurang finished what he was doing and turned back toward Chad and the others. "There's been a complication. The area we need to get to has several maintenance crews nearby, along with soldiers. It's probably because of the storm, but there are a lot of defenses active."

"Did they detect us?" Chad asked.

"No, there's only a general warning about the poor weather. I'm going to need you to draw the soldiers away so we can get in to access the communications network. We don't have much time."

Chad was aware of the time constraints. There was a scheduled uplink that was to be engaged from the planet and relayed through the space gate. They had to have their dummy data uploaded by that time, because after that, the space gate would become inoperable, courtesy of the Talon-V squadrons en route to do just that.

"We can draw them off and then meet up with you," Chad said.

Aurang was quiet for a moment. Maybe he'd expected Chad to protest splitting up their forces. "Very well. We'll meet up at this location here."

This was the communication hub for the entire star system. Everything was routed through this location, but the authentication was handled through the monitoring station in orbit, which was then relayed to the space gate. Once all those things lined up, they'd proceed with an update to the Krake version of COMCENT. It was also the time they'd receive official updates from whatever command structure the Krake had.

"Captain, I cannot overstate the importance of this. You must get those soldiers out of there in order for us to access this area. Here are the schematics of this place," Aurang said. "Are you able to perform this task?"

"We'll get the job done. You just deliver on your promise to us."

"I haven't forgotten, Captain," Aurang said. Then he and the other Krake soldiers left them.

Outside, the Spec Ops team gathered.

"So now we're a diversionary force," Benton said.

"That's what *they* think," Chad said and gestured toward Vladek. "We're heading to the main complex, and once we distract those soldiers, I need you to access this specific console. There should be a linkup there."

The console was farther from the one Aurang was using, but it was their closest option. Krake communication protocols for high-level access were unique for secure systems. They hadn't had time to duplicate it, so they had to use what was already in place if they wanted to access the same uplink systems.

"I see it," Vladek replied. "I monitored how Aurang accessed the system, and I should be able to do the same."

"Remember, we need the most recent updates sent and received. We don't have time for a broad search, so we need to narrow it down to core system targets," Chad said.

"Yes, sir."

They made their way toward their target. They were moving around the outside but there weren't many windows in the complex, and Chad guessed the Krake weren't concerned with looking outside.

"Bowren, let's open some walls up. Target that building over there. It's some kind of processing center. Should be important enough for them to go and investigate," Chad said.

Bowren grinned hungrily. "My specialty, sir."

"Don't wait around for any company. Meet up with us after," Chad said.

They moved into position and then heard an explosion over the howling winds. Chad watched as Bowren sent more explosive charges inside the building, and a few seconds later those explosives detonated, causing massive destruction.

"They had to have heard that," Benton said.

Vladek got the door open and the Spec Ops team went inside. Aurang had expected them to remain outside and circle around to the rendezvous point, but Chad wasn't taking any chances. They had their own objective inside. He just hoped the schematics Aurang had given him were accurate. Otherwise, all the soldiers they'd lured away would come looking for them.

"Sir, I see Krake soldiers heading to the area. We're heading back to you," Bowren said.

They went down the corridor, and near the end was a cross section. Several Krake soldiers ran past, but the last few stopped. One of them gestured toward the Spec Ops team. Before they could raise an alarm, the CDF soldiers fired their weapons and stopped them.

They ran past the dead Krake, heading away from where the others had gone. They had a target to reach. They headed farther into the building's interior, navigating through open doors and taking out Krake along the way.

There were multiple access rooms that linked to the core comms system, and the Spec Ops team wondered if Aurang would be able to detect when they accessed the system and whether he'd try to stop them. They entered the room and took out the Krake inside.

There was a phalanx of consoles, but Vladek went to a smaller one off to the side. "I'm in, sir. I'll need some time to gather what we need."

Access to this system and the data on it would give them valuable insight into how the Krake operated across the multiverse. Hopefully, it also contained references to the Krake home system where the overseers resided. If they could learn that location, they might be able to end this war before it actually began.

"Sir, I can see what Aurang is doing. They've successfully uploaded their updates and . . ." Vladek said, pausing for a moment, ". . . authentication is complete. Scheduled uplink is about to initiate."

Chad had wanted to add a search for a reference to their home universe, but Sean had denied the request. The risk was too great because the Krake might be able to bring up Vladek's session and trace everything he'd done. They didn't need to point the Krake at New Earth by leaving a search history, despite assurances from Aurang that they could cover their tracks.

"Data transferred and received," Vladek said. A few moments later, he stepped away from the console. "We got it, sir."

"Good work. Let's head to the waypoint," Chad said.

He checked the operations schedule on his internal heads-up display. They were right on schedule. Now they just had to find a way off the planet.

CHAPTER 22

The *Vigilant* was approaching the equatorial line of the NEC. The *Dutchman* and the *Babylon* were both several thousand kilometers away on different approach vectors in the northern and southern hemispheres of the planet. The *Vigilant*'s target was the main monitoring station in low orbit on the other side of the planet, while the secondary and tertiary targets of the CDF destroyers were the Krake communication satellites that were always pointed at the space gate. According to Aurang, at least one of those satellites had a direct line to the gate, which was located on the other side of the moon.

The best approach for reaching their targets undetected was to use a gravitational assist from the actual NEC. Sean had ordered their approach vector at a specific velocity so they could also orbit the planet for several revolutions without overly taxing their inertia dampeners.

Sean sat in the commander's chair, monitoring their approach, while the crew on the bridge went about their tasks, completely focused. The best scanners in the universe couldn't penetrate through a planet. Line of sight was still a major factor in space warfare. The Ovarrow who lived on this planet were not a spacefaring race, and according to Aurang, they hadn't grown beyond an industrial age. The Krake wouldn't tell them very much, other than that this planet was a simulation where a multitude of tests were being conducted. If the Krake were running simulations on an entire planet of Ovarrow, the number of tests could be impossibly large.

So far, everything Aurang had told them about the defenses had been truthful.

"Colonel, gamma burst activity has been detected, which matches the activity of a space gate," Lieutenant Scott said.

"That will be the scheduled check-in Aurang told us about," Sean said.

He checked their velocity and time to intercept the target. If they arrived too soon, the Krake would be aware of their presence and call for reinforcements. The key to this entire operation was to strike at precise times across all the teams in order to cripple the Krake's ability to respond. Talon-V squadrons were on their final approaches to the space gate, while Charlie team was performing its own orbital assist to cripple the Krake lunar base. Sean was quite familiar with the combat tactic of hitting the enemy where they believed they were safe, and the lack of Krake ships in this system seemed to indicate that the Krake hadn't anticipated an attack here.

"Forward mag cannons locked on target," Lieutenant Scott said.

"Ops, what's the status of the space gate?" Sean asked.

"Still generating gamma waves, sir," Lieutenant Burrows replied.

Once they fired their weapons, there was no going back. They were close enough that the velocity of the slug from the mag cannon would hit the monitoring station before their target had a chance to react. If they used midrange missiles, there was a chance the Krake would detect the attack.

The forward mag cannons were built into the superstructure of the *Vigilant*. Sean had already given his authorization to fire, and Gabriel was programmed with the exact time to do so. At the same time, the *Dutchman*'s and the *Babylon*'s single forward cannons would fire their armament as well.

"Shots away," Lieutenant Scott confirmed.

Sean looked at Burrows and she shook her head. The space gate was still active. This was going to be close. Sean watched as the seconds ticked by.

"Gamma burst has ceased," Burrows said.

"Target has been hit. No alerts on any of the known Krake communication channels," Lieutenant Scott said.

"The *Dutchman* and the *Babylon* each report successfully destroying their targets," Specialist Sansky said.

"Acknowledged. Good job, people," Sean said. "Helm, adjust our heading to coordinates bravo."

"Adjusting course to coordinates bravo, sir," Edwards said.

Maneuvering thrusters became active, and the *Vigilant*'s heading began to change. They were soon flying over the southern polar region of the planet.

"Sir, I'm detecting Krake attack drones. They're hard astern of us," Lieutenant Scott said.

The plot on the main holoscreen began to populate with marks for the attack drones.

"Where are they coming from?" Sean said.

"Sir, they're coming from the planet. No Krake warships have been detected," Lieutenant Scott said.

"Ready HADES Vs. I need a firing solution on the attack drones. Ops, alert the other ships. Tell them to find alternate orbital paths," Sean said.

His orders were confirmed.

"Aurang betrayed us," Russo said.

"Maybe. Either he didn't know or he didn't tell us," Sean replied.

"Comms, open subspace comlinks to the other teams. Warn them that the Krake have other defenses in place."

HADES V missiles fired from the *Vigilant*, staggering their approaches to the oncoming swarm of attack drones. The lead missiles detonated, blinding the attack drones and temporarily disabling them, and then the second wave gouged their numbers. But more attack drones kept appearing on the scope. The *Vigilant* was too far away to take out the facility. They needed to get out of there.

Sean did a quick calculation based on the number of HADES V missiles they had and the rate the Krake were replenishing their attack drones. This was a numbers game, and the numbers weren't in favor of the *Vigilant*.

"Colonel, I have a subspace comms from Captain Boseman," Sansky said.

"Put him through to me," Sean replied. He could hear the distinct sound of weapons being fired in the background.

"Colonel, Krake forces are arriving through an arch here in the southern complex. Aurang crashed our ship and we are unable to leave," Boseman said.

"Is Aurang with you?"

"Negative, sir. We're unable to reach the rendezvous point. We need extraction."

"Acknowledged. Deploying combat shuttles to your position. Send them your beacon," Sean said.

Sean studied the main holoscreen. Krake attack drones were flying toward them, and the HADES V missile defense screen could only buy them so much time. But he wasn't going to leave those men behind. He had fifteen minutes to come up with a way to rescue the Spec Ops team on the ground and get them to their own space gate.

CHAPTER 23

The firefight had been brief but intense, and Chad ordered his men to keep moving. There were two combat shuttles on the way, and he had sent them a waypoint for extraction. The video feed from the reconnaissance drone he had hovering near the arch showed Krake soldiers coming through. Reinforcements had arrived. Chad had lost four men so far, and he'd had their combat suits self-destruct what remained of them. They couldn't leave any trace behind.

"That bastard." Benton scowled. "Looks like Aurang and his people found a way off this rock."

Aurang had avoided the Krake soldiers and made his way to one of the landing zones where he'd secured a ship. The Krake shuttlecraft looked to be powering up.

"Captain, Krake comms chatter contains references to a report that has information about Trident Battle Group," Vladek said.

"Son of a—" Chad started to say and stopped. He gritted his teeth and shook his head. They had monitored Aurang closely, but somehow the Krake rebel had deceived them. He was playing both sides of this.

"Captain, should we warn the *Vigilant*?" Vladek asked.

Chad's first instinct was to do just that. "Negative. The trap has been sprung. Brentworth, I need you to prepare the data we've gathered for a subspace comlink burst. Vladek, help him."

They were outside, sticking close to the buildings and using them for cover. The Nexstar combat suits assisted their movements with relatively low energy expenditure from the wearers. One way or another, they would get the data where it needed to go, even if they couldn't make it off this planet.

They had to move quickly, and the storm provided some cover, but the

Krake had an idea of their position. Within minutes, they were on the outskirts of the small city.

A comlink registered to his combat suit.

"Captain Boseman, this is Lieutenant Franco. I'll be at the waypoint position in under a minute. We're flying low and fast, so be ready," she said.

"We'll be here," Chad replied. The comlink closed, and he knew they wouldn't hear the combat shuttles approaching in this storm.

Suddenly, a bright flash from behind them lit up the sky. Then, a blue beam of light fired from the center of the city out toward them. It cut a swath right through the blizzard, illuminating the area above them. The beam then swept the area above them, and Chad watched helplessly as the two CDF combat shuttles exploded. As the Spec Ops platoon dove for cover, the remains of the shuttles descended over the snow-covered ground. After the beam of light stopped, Chad stood up. He scanned the area and saw a flaming wreck with the two combat shuttles raining down all around them.

"Did anyone see where that came from?" Chad asked.

"Looked like it came from the central building in city," Benton said.

Chad clenched his teeth and peered through the blizzard, trying to get a look at whatever the Krake had just fired at them. If they went back into the city, they'd have to face the Krake soldiers. They needed to find another way out.

"Brentworth, I need a subspace comlink to the *Vigilant*, now," Chad said. A few moments later, he had the link. "Colonel, both shuttles are down. The Krake have a defense weapon, and it targeted them. We didn't know it was there. Uploading a data burst of the data we extracted from the Krake's systems. Can you confirm receipt?"

"Yeah, we got it," Sean said.

Benton gestured toward the city and told him that the Krake soldiers were heading in their direction.

"Captain, can you find another ship?"

"Negative, Colonel. All ships are on the other side of the city with too many of the enemy. There's no landing zone nearby. The approach is bad, and the extraction zone is too hot," Chad said. He ordered his men to take cover and get ready to fight.

"I'm sending another shuttle down to you," Sean said.

"It's too hot. We can't reach that weapon to take it out, and Krake soldiers are closing in on us. That data is why we came here. Take it and go," Chad said.

"That's not how this works. Hold your position. That's an order, Captain. Acknowledge."

Chad gritted his teeth. "Holding position. Copy that, sir."

CHAPTER 24

"Ops, get another combat shuttle ready. I'm not abandoning those men," Sean said.

"Sir, did Captain Boseman say what kind of weapon the Krake were using?" Russo asked.

Sean glanced at his XO. "It's some kind of energy weapon. He did say it was a bright blue beam, which is probably like the Colossus cannon we use for city defenses back on New Earth. It's perfect for atmospheric defense. Probably wouldn't do anything to us up here, though. They didn't have the exact coordinates for it."

"We can't make a precision shot with the information we have, but we can create a firing solution for a bombardment run. It might give our shuttle and the Spec Ops team enough cover for an extraction," Russo said.

Sean frowned. That was a hell of a lot of guesswork, given the conditions down there. They could see the storm system. "We'll risk hitting our own men."

Russo glanced at the main holoscreen and then looked back at Sean. "Colonel, I can do this. Let me give those men one last shot."

Jane Russo had been his tactical officer for years and he knew her capabilities. If she said she could do it, then she could do it.

"Very well," Sean said.

Russo turned her attention to her personal holoscreen and got to work.

"Helm, adjust speed to allow time for a bombardment run," Sean said.

"Colonel, slowing our velocity will allow the Krake attack drones to reach the ship. A successful evacuation of the ground forces to this ship is impossible," Gabriel said.

"Acknowledged," Sean replied. "Comms, open a comlink to the *Dutchman.*"

A few moments later, Captain Oliver Martinez appeared on his personal holoscreen. "Captain, listen up. I don't have a lot of time. I have a shuttle en route to extract our Spec Ops team on the ground. It's a hot zone. We're about to blanket the area with heavy fire, but we're unable to secure the evac. Can you give our guys a window and scoop them up?"

"Receiving new mission objective, sir," Martinez said and looked away from his screen for a few moments. "I have the course. We'll pick our guys up but, sir—" he said and stopped.

"After you retrieve the Spec Ops team, head directly to the *Yorktown*. Our gate will be up for your return to New Earth," Sean said.

"Colonel, have the *Babylon* run the evac up. Let us take some of the tactical burden from the *Vigilant*," Martinez said.

"Negative, Captain. I need you on this. There are dozens of ways this could go, and I need an experienced captain to get our guys out of there. *Vigilant* out," Sean said and severed the comlink. He looked at Russo, who was still putting together a firing solution.

He opened a comlink to the *Babylon,* and Lieutenant Richard Pitts's face appeared on his personal holoscreen. "Lieutenant Pitts, you have just about enough time to use a gravitational assist to break out of the orbit and return to the *Yorktown*."

"Understood, sir." Pitts looked off-screen for a moment. "We can assist you."

Sean looked away from the holoscreen and closed his eyes for a moment. *Dammit, Ward*, Sean thought. Captain Ryan Ward had been the *Babylon*'s captain until he'd turned mutineer.

"Colonel, I know I'm not Captain Ward, but the *Babylon* is ready to assist you. Let me add our combat capabilities to your defense plans. We can increase the odds," Pitts said.

Pitts had been one of Sean's critics about how he'd handled the mutiny; now he was willing to lay down his life to make sure their mission succeeded. Sean looked at the young man. "Stand by, Lieutenant." He then looked at his XO.

"Firing solution ready, sir," Russo said.

"Execute, XO's discretion," Sean said and turned back to his holoscreen. "Lieutenant Pitts, maintain course and heading. We're coming to you."

———

Boseman finished reading the message and called the others over, then opened the comlink to the rest of the platoon. "There's another shuttle coming, but our egress point is half a klick away in an open area."

"Captain," Benton said, "Krake soldiers are already on their way here. They have our position."

"A shuttle can't get close enough to take out that Krake weapon," Vladek said.

"The *Vigilant* is going to bombard the area, and we need to get clear. In this weather, there's no way for them to make precision shots. They'll do their best to avoid us, but we have to move. Sergeant Benton, send a recon drone ahead. Maybe there's someplace we can get cover."

Boseman saw the recon drone zip away. He lost visual but could track its movement through his internal heads-up display.

———

"Krake attack drones within point defense range, Colonel," Lieutenant Scott said.

"Acknowledged," Sean said.

They had altered their course so that the bow of the ship was pointed directly down toward the planet, and the forward mag cannons sent a volley in rapid succession to the target area. The helmsman altered course and increased their velocity. Sean didn't want the *Vigilant* to break from the planet's orbit. He had to maintain the angle to utilize the gravitational assist so he could line up with the *Yorktown*. This would require them to orbit the planet one more time.

———

Above the howling winds, they heard loud pops, and streaks of red blazed down from above, heading to the city.

"Move!" Boseman shouted.

The Spec Ops platoon ran from cover and headed to the waypoint as the small Krake city felt the wrath of the *Vigilant's* weapons. Muted explosions sounded like deep impact wells in high snowdrifts. Krake soldiers fired on them as they ran. Bowren turned and returned fire from his heavy gauss cannon, causing the Krake soldiers to dive for cover, but there were more than a few who got caught in the spray.

There was an orange glow in the blizzard, and black smoke billowed in the howling winds above the city. The attack had been quick and catastrophic. A few of the Krake soldiers pursued them, but most were returning to the city.

Boseman tasked a recon drone to go behind them and make sure the Krake weren't going to follow them. Less than a minute later, the Krake soldiers had turned around and were once again heading right for them. Someone over there knew what it meant to command. Boseman would've chewed out any soldier who'd dared to let the enemy get away from a city they'd just destroyed.

"They're coming. Where's the shuttle?" Vladek said.

Boseman kept thinking he heard the high-pitched whine of a combat shuttle, but it was just the wind. They ran as best they could, but the snow was getting deeper, and he hoped they didn't accidentally fall through to a major cavern beneath them. They didn't have time to rescue anyone if that happened. As the Spec Ops team ran, the bombardment finished and

Boseman glanced off to the side, seeing deep crevices begin to form. The ground lurched beneath his feet, and he felt as if he was sliding on a board of ice and snow that was thousands of square feet.

A flash of light appeared ahead of them and a comlink connected to his suit. It was the combat shuttle. The shuttle spun around and the loading ramp lowered. The pilot couldn't land the shuttle, so it hovered in the air.

"Get on the shuttle, quickly," Boseman said.

He climbed onto the ramp and turned around. The Krake soldiers who were pursuing them fired their weapons. He and several soldiers stayed at the bottom of the ramp and returned fire while the rest of the platoon raced to get on.

"Bowren, if you don't get your ass up there, we're going to leave you here," Boseman said.

Bowren turned and leaped toward the loading ramp. Bright flashes of light came from Krake weapons as they fired on him. The combat suit heavy was pelted, and Bowren went down by the sheer force of it.

Boseman raced up the loading ramp and grabbed a metallic tether cable. In seconds, he had vaulted down to Bowren and quickly wrapped the tether cable around him. CDF soldiers returned fire from the loading ramp. The engines engaged and the combat shuttle rose into the air. They were retracted to the loading ramp and helped onboard. Bowren's suit had taken damage, but he was all right. They'd made it.

Boseman walked toward the cockpit and looked at the two shuttle pilots. "Thanks for pulling our asses out of the fire. Where's the *Vigilant*?"

"Several thousand kilometers away from here, Captain. Go strap yourself in. We're meeting up with the *Dutchman,* and then we're getting the hell out of here," the pilot said.

Boseman turned around and headed back to find a seat, ordering his men to strap themselves in. Even though they were off the ground, it sounded like things were just as hot up here as they had been below. They weren't out of this yet.

———

Sean didn't know why the Krake attack drones hadn't increased their velocity to catch up with him. Perhaps it was because there was something interfering with their navigation system or some other limitation they hadn't accounted for. He could only deal with the situation as it was, which meant that if there were any Krake attack drones left when he finally broke free of the planet's gravitational pull, they'd be able to catch up to his ship before he could reach the *Yorktown*.

"Colonel, I'm detecting a gamma burst from the Krake space gate," Lieutenant Scott said.

"Are you sure? The space gate was disabled. The Talon-V squadrons reported successfully taking out the alignment controls so the gateway couldn't form," Sean said.

"These readings are accurate. Charlie team has already picked up the Talon-Vs and they're heading back to the *Yorktown*," Lieutenant Scott said.

Sean frowned for a moment. It would take them too much time to change their course and stop whatever was happening with the space gate.

"Colonel," Specialist Sansky said, "I have a . . . It's Aurang, sir."

Sean clenched his teeth. "On my screen."

A moment later, Aurang's face appeared on his screen. "There's been a change in our plans. I congratulate you on a successful mission execution. We wouldn't have achieved our mission objective without you."

"You double-crossed us! You left my team on the planet, and you've activated the space gate that we thought had been sabotaged."

"We have fulfilled our end of the bargain. I confirmed with Captain Boseman that they had the data they sought. I'm aware of their operations. Therefore, our temporary alliance is concluded. It has been quite enlightening."

"Aurang, I'm going to hunt you down. I'll have my own update sent to your overseers," Sean said.

"Only if you manage to survive," Aurang said and severed the comlink.

Sean cursed and snarled. He looked at Lieutenant Scott.

"Krake warships are coming through the space gate, sir."

He'd covered all his bases, but once again, his plans were coming up short. There were a few moments of heavy silence on the bridge at the stark realization that they weren't going to get away this time. Sean inhaled explosively and then sighed. "Comms, open a subspace communication link to the *Yorktown*."

A few moments later, Major Shelton appeared on his personal holoscreen and he gave her a tactical update of the situation. "I'm sending a data burst to you now. This is the data we've collected from the Krake."

"Confirm receipt of the data," Major Shelton said.

"You're to open a gateway back to our universe. I want all ships to go through as soon as they reach you," Sean said.

He saw the conflicting emotions on her face, but she didn't make the protest she wanted to. She understood the tactical implications of their current position. This time, Sean had played the odds and was going to lose.

"It'll be close, but the *Dutchman* should be able to reach you."

"Colonel," Major Shelton began.

"Hold the gate open for as long as you can, but no heroics. Is that understood, Major?"

Vanessa met his gaze. "Understood, Colonel. Godspeed, sir."

The comlink severed.

Sean leaned back in his chair and tried to think of something he could do to get them out of this. He glanced at the main holoscreen and saw that the intercept course he'd laid in to meet up with the *Babylon* was only minutes away. The *Dutchman* had reported the successful pickup of the remaining Spec Ops team. This mission had cost them.

Sean stood up and walked over to the tactical workstation, and Captain

Russo joined him. He looked back up at the command area and saw Oriana staring intently at her console.

"How many HADES Vs do we have left?" he asked.

Lieutenant Scott brought it up on his screen. "Not that many, sir."

"Get them into the tubes. We can at least stall those attack drones and then make our best speed to the *Yorktown*," Sean said.

"That will get us away from the planet, but what about the Krake warships that just entered the system?" Captain Russo asked.

"It's a race. I don't know if we can win it, but I'm certainly going to try. We can have the *Babylon* fly in tight formation with us, and that might buy us a little bit of time," Sean said.

Russo looked away from him and he knew she was trying to come up with an alternative that had a higher probability of success.

Sean returned to the commander's chair. He looked around the bridge, feeling like a failure. He'd let all these people down by thinking he could achieve this mission and return home.

They completed the last leg of their orbital assist and broke away from the planet's gravitational pull. The *Vigilant* launched all its remaining HADES V missiles and the *Babylon* did the same. The two ships sped away from the planet. Active scans showed that Krake warships were trying to intercept them, but despite being faster than the CDF ships, they wouldn't be able to. They'd have to chase them, but they'd be well within the attack drones' range before they reached the *Yorktown*.

Sean looked at Oriana, and she finally looked back at him. "We have to try it," he said.

"It's not ready."

"It's our only option. The attack drones will eventually get past our point defense systems. If that happens, we won't even be able to try."

Oriana looked away for a moment. "The power requirements for sustained output will deplete the reactor cores on our ship. The *Babylon* can't even do it."

"If the *Babylon* is ahead of us, they won't have to do it."

Oriana was quiet for a moment. "I understand that, but if it doesn't work at all, then . . ."

Sean knew what she was about to say. With all the ship's power devoted to what they were about to try, they wouldn't be able to bring the point defense systems back up in time. It was all or nothing.

"Colonel, I'm not following this conversation. Can you tell me what's going on?" Russo asked.

"There might be a way to increase our defenses against the Krake attack drones, but it's never been tried and it's unconventional."

Russo's gaze flicked toward Oriana and then back at Sean. "What is it?"

"It's gravity," Oriana said. "It's the only thing I could think of that might affect the Krake attack drones. When they're active, they can generate heat equivalent to that of a G-type main sequence star. So, I realized the only thing that could withstand that kind of heat is gravity. Gravity is what keeps a star together."

Russo frowned and looked at Sean. "You want to generate an artificial gravity field that's capable of stopping the attack drones from reaching the ship?"

"Something like that, but the power requirements are enormous, and there's a bit of a debate on whether it will just stop the attack drones or cause them to be unable to reach us—almost like they're on a slippery surface," Sean said and looked at Oriana. "I understand you have reservations, but it's my call. Comms, give me a broadcast to the ship."

"Ready, sir," Specialist Sansky said.

"Crew of the *Vigilant*, this is Colonel Quinn. Everyone is to go to their emergency stations. All nonessential personnel are to secure themselves in escape pods. We're about to try something that's never been done before. If we don't do this, the Krake warships will catch up to us before we can reach our space gate. It's a numbers game, and our point defense systems cannot stop all the attack drones heading for us. Set Condition Emergency."

They were making best speed to the space gate, and Sean ordered their braking thrusters to fire, allowing the *Babylon* to move ahead of them. Lieutenant Pitts followed his orders without question.

"Emitters are charging," Gabriel said.

"I've only tried this with a single emitter in a lab on the hangar deck," Oriana said.

Sean kept his eyes on the main holoscreen. The Krake warships had launched hundreds of attack drones that were speeding toward them. He imagined they looked like a swarm of bright fireflies flying in formation, streaking toward his ship with the promise of death and destruction.

"I know that. You had a brilliant idea, but I know this ship," Sean said. "Gabriel, you'll need to update the configuration of our inertia dampeners."

Everyone on the bridge returned to their seats and strapped themselves in. Condition Emergency required everyone on board the ship to secure themselves in such a fashion and go on personal life support.

Their point defense systems stopped as the power draw was redirected to the inertia dampeners and artificial gravity emitters used on the ship. They were essentially reversing the direction and projecting it to a point beyond the ship. This meant that they would lose artificial gravity inside. They'd be in a bubble.

The power requirements were such that all non-critical power was diverted and weapons systems went on standby. The calculations for the power adjustment to their artificial gravity emitters had to be done by Gabriel. Only the ship's AI could update the calculations based on available power and prevent them from overloading. A miscalculation with the emitters would tear the ship apart.

The lighting on the bridge dimmed as they went to emergency power. Sean gripped the arms of his chair and glanced at Oriana.

"Projecting artificial gravity field around the ship, sir," Gabriel said.

Sean watched as the power spiked across all reactors aboard the ship. Sensor and video feeds didn't show them anything. Gravity was invisible, but its effects could be observed.

The nearest Krake attack drones experienced a deceleration a few kilometers from the ship. Several groups of attack drones tried to circle around the ship, but they were caught in the field and couldn't move.

"Gabriel, can you compress the field? Can you bunch them up together?"

"Calculating," Gabriel said. "Affirmative, but this will deplete our fusion reactor cores quickly."

"Understood," Sean said. "Tactical, have the point defense systems target the attack drones."

They weren't far from the space gate. However, the *Yorktown* hadn't gone through. It was maintaining the gateway. Sean frowned. "Comms, get me Major Shelton."

"Major, what are you doing?" Sean asked.

"We abandoned the ship, sir. Self-destruction has been set. I calculated your trajectory. Maintain speed and you'll get through the gateway," Major Shelton said.

Sean felt a surge of hope. "Major . . ." he began but stopped. They'd have to thread the needle one more time.

"Colonel," Lieutenant Scott said, "point defense systems are not responsive. Power draw has limited my access."

Sean opened a comlink to the *Babylon*. A moment later Lieutenant Pitts appeared on his personal holoscreen. "Lieutenant, I need you to ready a salvo of Hornet B missiles. Target coordinates incoming."

"Aye, sir," Lieutenant Pitts said.

Within the next few minutes, midrange Hornet B missiles were fired, targeted at the globular cluster of Krake attack drones. Sean watched as the power draw on their fusion reactor drained much quicker than he'd thought was possible. The Hornet missiles flew toward the Krake attack drones and came to a stop as they were caught in the artificial gravity field.

"Colonel, reactors are reaching critical levels," Gabriel said.

"Maintain speed and heading," Sean replied.

There were three fusion reactors aboard the *Vigilant*, and each operated with emergency shutdown procedures that would automatically engage. One after the other, they began to shut down, and the gravity field outside the ship began to fail. The *Babylon* transitioned through the space gate and was quickly followed by the *Vigilant*. The globular cluster of Krake attack drones followed next. Then, the *Yorktown*'s self-destruct engaged and a cataclysmic explosion destroyed both the ship and the space gate in the alternate universe. Perhaps, if they were even luckier, the explosion would take out a few Krake ships with it. In any case, there would be nothing left for the Krake warships to find.

The artificial gravity field failed when the last of the reactors aboard the *Vigilant* went into emergency shutdown and the Hornets unleashed their fury into the tightly packed Krake attack drones. But the *Vigilant* was too close. Klaxon alarms blared on the bridge as the stern of the ship was impacted by the force of the detonating Hornet missiles. Damage reports came to prominence on the main holoscreen, and the *Vigilant* switched to emergency power systems as sensor feeds went offline. They were blind to the outside, and Sean didn't know if there were any attack drones left.

An emergency comlink came from Major Shelton. "Sir, the remaining attack drones have been taken out. What's your status?"

Sean swallowed hard, trying to loosen the tightness of his shoulders. "It seems we're out of fuel. Do you think you can give us a ride?"

This drew several chuckles from people on the bridge, and Sean felt a profound sense of relief. They'd survived.

"I'll see what I can do," Major Shelton said and smiled. "Comms have lit up across the board. We're home, sir."

Sean sagged into his chair and blew out a long, slow breath. Somehow, they had done it. He looked at Oriana. "I think you've found a way to nullify the advantage of those attack drones."

"I don't know if I'd go that far. Look what it did to the ship," Oriana said.

The damage reports continued to come in. The rear of the ship had taken most of the damage, but there hadn't been any casualties. They had drilled for scenarios involving a sudden loss of power from the reactor cores, but never all three cores at once. A complete loss of all power to a CDF warship usually meant the ship was no longer operable, but the *Vigilant* wasn't dead, at least not yet. They had to examine the reactor cores and shielding. They'd probably need to be repaired or even replaced, but at least they were in the right universe to get the help they needed.

CHAPTER 25

C onnor heard the landing gear deploy and the gentle whine of the engines spinning down as the ship landed. It wasn't a large ship, and Bradley's recon drone had explored most of the ventilation shafts. The Krake ship must have been remotely piloted under the control of a sophisticated guidance system. This made sense to Connor because of the Krake's affinity for using attack drones, which were remotely controlled and somewhat autonomously guided.

"Dash, enable the privacy mode of your MPS. I don't want them to have a look at your face, no matter what happens," Connor said.

Corporal Bradley and Private Marsters wore Nexstar combat suits and would already be in combat mode. They knew better than to show their faces to the Krake, but there was very little they could do about Cerot. The Krake would be able to tell right away that he was an Ovarrow, and covering his face wouldn't change that.

Minutes went by as they waited in the holding rooms. Since Connor and Bradley were the only ones armed, he told her to wait for his signal. He would look for an opportunity for them to escape.

An interior wall slid into itself, revealing a doorway. There was a light coming from each end of the passageway. Connor stepped out of the room and glanced to his left. A short distance away was a loading ramp that had opened to the outside. He opened the comlink to the others with him, and as he suspected, the suppression field had been turned off since the ship had landed. They'd be able to speak to each other undetected by the Krake. Amber lights flared overhead, and Connor saw Ovarrow symbols appear above the exit.

Connor walked toward the exit and down the loading ramp. The others followed. They were in a hangar bay, but they were still on the planet. He glanced to the outside where a wide door was open. The ship must have flown through it in order to have landed where they had. He saw a semi-translucent shield at the edge of the door and attempted to open a comlink to Samson, but he got no reply. So, their comms must have been limited to the immediate area.

Three rows of Krake soldiers were standing near the loading ramp, and upon seeing Connor and the others, they pointed their weapons at them. They all wore that living-tissue armor that blended with powered armor. The nearest soldier spoke. Connor thought it sounded similar to the Ovarrow language, but there were differences. The Krake repeated himself, his voice sounding authoritative, but Connor had no idea what he was saying. And he didn't seem to care that Connor held a weapon.

Several Krake soldiers stomped toward them and Cerot began shouting, gesturing toward Connor and the others. Then Cerot beckoned Connor and the others to stand away from the loading ramp. The Krake soldiers seem to be waiting for someone as they kept careful watch.

"Corporal, pass control of your drone over to me," Connor said quietly.

A moment later, the drone interface appeared on Connor's internal heads-up display. He uploaded an Ovarrow interface and sent it flying off. He needed it to find the nearest terminal, which would allow the data exfil-tration software to begin copying from Krake computer systems. The small recon drone didn't have much in the way of data storage, but it could relay the information to any one of their combat suits, which had more capacity. If they needed to, they could chunk it into pieces on their individual suit computers.

Another Krake entered the hangar bay. He wore similar armor to the other soldiers, but his face was exposed. There were certain similarities to the Ovarrow, but there were also significant differences, as if they were cousins on the same evolutionary tree. There was an air of deference afforded the newcomer, which indicated to Connor that this Krake was in charge.

The Krake leader strode over to Cerot and scrutinized him closely. He noted Cerot's wounded side and then his gaze flicked toward the wrist computer that included the Ovarrow translator. The Krake spoke to Cerot, but the Ovarrow remained silent. He stared defiantly at the ground as if refusing to acknowledge the Krake's presence. Several soldiers stormed over and grabbed Cerot by his arms, pulling him away from the others. They forced him to hold out his arm, and the leader jabbed his armored hand into Cerot's wounded side. The Ovarrow let out a half-strangled cry and tried to move away, but the soldiers held him in place.

Connor glanced at the other soldiers, who watched them warily. There was no way he could take them by surprise, and as much as he hated what they were doing, he had to wait. There was a time to fight, and there was a time to wait. Connor clenched his teeth and watched. He heard Dash muttering something, but the others were silent.

The Krake leader attached a small, metallic box to Cerot's shoulder, and it shimmered as it activated. Metallic laces detached themselves from the box and plunged into Cerot's exposed neck, piercing his armor as if it provided no protection. Cerot's eyes went wide, and his body began to contort with pain.

Connor stepped forward. "Enough. It's for communications," he said and sent the signal to activate the Ovarrow translator on Cerot's wrist.

A personal holoscreen appeared over Cerot's wrist, and the Ovarrow symbols translated what Connor had said. The Krake leader peered at it and then looked at Connor. He spoke to Connor, but Connor couldn't understand him. Soldiers began stomping toward him, but before they could grab him, Connor stepped forward, moving away from the others. "I don't understand. This is how we communicate with the Ovarrow."

The Krake soldiers grabbed his arms and attempted to pull him back, but the Nexstar combat suit was capable of enormous feats of strength. Connor braced himself and refused to be moved. They struggled against his arms, trying to force him back. Power surged through his suit, and Connor tore free from their grasp. More soldiers moved forward, but the Krake leader shouted and they stopped their advance.

They hadn't fired their weapons, so it was clear that they didn't want to kill him, at least not yet. The Krake leader turned back toward Cerot and removed the colonial translator from his wrist. The interface remained active, and the Krake held a device up to it. The holoscreen began flickering as a library of Ovarrow symbols flashed across it.

"He's accessing the translator program," Dash said.

"I figured as much," Connor replied.

The Krake leader's gaze flicked toward Dash, and then, a few moments later, the Krake soldiers surrounded him and pulled him over to where Cerot was. The military-grade MPS couldn't produce the same amount of force that the Nexstar combat suit could. Connor inhaled deeply and looked at the Krake leader. Had he detected the comlink? Just then, a comlink opened from the personal recon drone and the data dump began. Connor watched the Krake for a reaction, but there wasn't any. So, he must've somehow heard the brief exchange between Connor and Dash.

The Krake leader produced another small, metallic box and placed it on Dash's shoulder. Again, the metallic laces burst forth from the box and attempted to penetrate the MPS. He heard Dash cry out in anticipation of pain, but then he suddenly stopped. The metallic laces couldn't penetrate the MPS, even though they tried several times on multiple parts of Dash's upper body.

The Krake leader held out his hand. The metallic laces lifted the box up, and it jumped like a spider into his outstretched hand. He turned toward Connor and flung the box toward him. Connor tried to swipe it away, but the metallic laces wrapped around his wrist and scurried up his arm, attempting to pierce his armor. Connor enabled his defensive countermeasures, and as power surged through his shoulder, the spider was flung off him in a charred wreck.

The holoscreen above Cerot's wrist computer went off and the Krake leader brought up several more of his own. Symbols Connor recognized from the Krake base flickered by. He must've been running some sort of analysis, and then that, too, finished.

The Krake leader gestured and one of the holoscreens flipped around. He tossed Cerot's wrist computer to the floor. The Krake soldiers let Cerot go, and he collapsed to the ground. He grabbed his wrist computer and slapped it back on. Connor's connection to Cerot's wrist computer was still active, and he noticed that there were differences now. The Krake leader spoke to Cerot again. This time, a translation appeared on Connor's internal heads-up display.

"Name of origin," the Krake leader said.

Connor's eyes widened, and he looked at the leader.

"You know better than to resist, Ovarrow. Answer me now, or you'll join the thousands of others we have participating in the trials," the Krake leader said.

Cerot regained his feet. "I'll never tell you!" he yelled and lunged for the Krake leader.

The Krake raised his hand and a burst of energy slammed into Cerot, throwing him back a dozen meters and slamming him into the wall. The Ovarrow collapsed into a heap.

Connor brought up his weapon and fired it at the Krake leader's unprotected head. Incendiary darts bounced off a personal shield, but the Krake leader flinched backward. Connor charged forward, but a soldier tried to block his path. He swung his AR-71 toward the soldier and squeezed the trigger. The incendiary darts ripped into the Krake armor and Connor updated the ammo to high-impact rounds. It would chew through his ammunition quicker, but it would also provide more of a punch.

The Krake leader sent a blast of invisible force toward Dash, catching him by surprise.

"Suppressing fire," Connor shouted.

Together, he and Bradley sprayed suppressing fire against the Krake soldiers while Marsters ran toward Dash and got him to his feet. They were close to the wide-open door, and Connor shouted for them to head toward it. He and Bradley covered their flank. Krake soldiers raced toward them. Behind them, Connor saw that they had Cerot pinned to the ground. Connor cursed as the doors began to close. There was no way he could reach Cerot. Marsters picked Dash up and slung him over his shoulder. Engaging the combat suit, he quickly made it through the door.

"I'm out of ammo," Corporal Bradley said.

Connor's ammunition was nearly empty as well. They ran through the door as the Krake soldiers fired their weapons. Bolts of energy streaked past them and into another building.

Connor and the others ran along the building until they reached the end. There was an open area beyond, where they'd be picked off when the soldiers caught up to them.

"Take Dash and rendezvous with Samson," Connor said.

"General, I can't leave you here alone. We can't even reach Captain Samson," Bradley said.

"I'm sending you the rendezvous coordinates. Make your way there, best speed. Don't look back. That's an order," Connor said.

Marsters shifted Dash's weight onto his shoulder, but he was slowly regaining consciousness and moving on his own.

"General, I can help you," Bradley said.

"No. I'm going to lead them away from you, giving you a chance to get away. The uplink is still active. Get whatever data you can back to Captain Samson, and you're ordered to go back through the gateway ASAP. I'll follow you when I have Cerot," Connor said.

The Krake soldiers were nearly upon them, and Connor didn't wait for a reply. He engaged his suit's jets and launched himself to the top of the adjacent building. Running along the roof, he fired three-round bursts at the soldiers, drawing their attention. They quickly changed course and scrambled up the side of the wall. Connor fired his remaining grenade, and it hit a Krake soldier in the chest just as he was coming over the edge. Several Krake soldiers tumbled to the ground, and Connor engaged his Nexstar combat suit and ran. Combat suits enabled him to run at ultrafast speeds. In fact, he wasn't actually running but taking super long strides.

The helmet's rear video feed showed that the Krake soldiers had climbed onto the roof, but they couldn't catch up to him. Connor dropped down off the roof of the building and headed back toward the hangar, bringing up the tracker he'd placed on Cerot's armor. They'd placed them on all the Ovarrow's armor in case they got separated.

The words "Acquiring signal" appeared, but he had to get back into the building in order for the signal to connect. At first glance there seemed to be an endless number of walls. He could create his own doorway, but that would draw a lot of attention. Connor kept running until he saw a small hatch near the ground. He grabbed the handle and pulled it, forcing the hatch to open. Slipping inside, he found himself in a different part of the hangar.

Cerot's personal locator signal went active as soon as he entered the building. He was on the other side, and Connor headed toward him.

A loud noise echoed from across the hangar. There was minimal lighting in the area, but he saw several small ships in standby mode. He ran among them, going as quickly and quietly as he could.

Connor raced to the end of the row of ships and stopped, seeing Cerot sitting on the ground. The Krake leader stood nearby, and he was speaking to another soldier on his holoscreen. Connor's Ovarrow translation program was still active, and it began putting the words on his internal heads-up display.

"Alert Skywatch Base. Have invader ships been detected in the system?"

"None have been detected, Sector Chief," came the reply.

Connor frowned for a moment. Invader ships? What were they talking about?

"Be on full alert. Invader ships utilize misdirection tactics as recorded by their assault on our processing center. Their designation is Colonial Defense Force," the sector chief said.

Trident Battle Group! They were talking about Sean! Connor felt a rush of adrenaline. They hadn't received word from Sean for months. This was the first confirmation he had that they were even alive and had attacked a Krake processing center, whatever that meant. But the moment of relief soon left him as he refocused on getting to Cerot.

He squatted down and peered across the hangar bay but couldn't tell if Cerot was awake. He wasn't moving, and Connor hoped they hadn't killed him. He needed to get a closer look, but any second now, the soldiers that were chasing him would return. Connor was on borrowed time. Thinking of a way to distract them, he hit upon the reconnaissance drone that was broadcasting from the Krake terminal. Connor accessed the drone and brought up a secondary interface to access the terminal. He ran the interface through the updated translator and was able to understand more of the layout. There were power systems, communication systems, and maintenance systems. Connor selected the maintenance systems and engaged a diagnostic. A warning appeared, indicating the recycling of some kind of shield. Connor acknowledged the warning and engaged the maintenance protocol. The semi-translucent shield on the far side of the hangar flickered off, and the sector chief, as well as several other soldiers, glanced in the direction of the door. When they approached the shield to investigate, Connor burst from cover and raced toward Cerot. As he reached the Ovarrow, a group of soldiers who'd been hiding nearby rushed him. It was an ambush. A wall of living armor tackled Connor to the ground before he could react. They slapped some kind of suppressor cuffs on his wrists and he found that he couldn't move, even though the combat suit controls still worked.

The sector chief walked back over to him and leaned down. "Now, we can begin."

The words appeared on Connor's internal heads-up display in plain English. Normally, Ovarrow symbols accompanied the English text, but there weren't any this time.

The Krake sector chief regarded him for a few moments and then spoke. "We can now communicate directly. I have questions."

The sector chief stood up and a soldier handed him a metallic rod, which the Krake held in one hand while caressing it with the other. Connor thought it looked like a stun baton. The tip glowed in pale silver, and the suppressor cuffs glowed in response. He was on his hands and knees one moment, and the next, he was being lifted off the ground by the cuffs and hung in the air several feet above the ground. He tried to yank his arms down and only succeeded in swinging his legs and feet. He could still feel his hands down to the tips of his fingers. He was able to make a fist, but he just couldn't exert any force that would free him.

"I've analyzed your translator. It's an interesting approach to communicating with the Ovarrow but still a work in progress, I think. I've augmented it to speed this interaction along. Do you understand me?" the sector chief asked.

Connor clenched his teeth for a moment. The sector chief had been manipulating them the entire time. He must have been. Why else allow your prisoners to retain their weapons and leave the hangar bay doors open with just a force field to block communications?

"I can understand you," Connor replied.

The sector chief was silent for a few moments, and Connor wondered whether he had understood him. "You returned for this Ovarrow. Why would you do that?"

"I brought him here."

"But he's Ovarrow. You are something else."

"It's called loyalty. Maybe you've heard of it."

"We are familiar with this archaic concept. We haven't seen an Ovarrow wearing armor like this for a long time. You must be from a fringe universe, but which one?" the sector chief said and watched Connor for a few moments. "We'll get back to that question. Where are your ships?"

The sector chief must have thought he was with Trident Battle Group. Whatever Sean was up to had garnered some attention. Connor considered whether Sean could actually be in this universe and decided the odds weren't in favor of that. He wouldn't wager anything, but it did give him some options.

"You don't expect me to answer that question," Connor said.

"Defiance is common in the beginning. You've traveled a long way. Why would you come here?"

The Krake was full of questions. They were exchanging blows, of a sort, and this encounter was no less dangerous than if they were firing their weapons at each other. The hangar was shielded again, and he couldn't get a signal out.

"Your reluctance to answer is anticipated, and I have you at a disadvantage—"

"I came here to learn about you," Connor said, cutting him off. Whoever steered the conversation controlled the outcome. "We're not from around here."

"That much is obvious and yet doesn't tell me anything I don't already know. This is a delaying tactic—a much different approach than brute force and too subtle for the Ovarrow, though there are some who step beyond the established confines of acceptable response."

"You're slaughtering them, manipulating them to play your game," Connor said.

The sector chief's alien gaze was filled with cold calculation and an energetic intelligence. Though the Krake held himself still, Connor wondered whether his mind was ever still or quiet.

"Why invade this planet? Your targets have had strategic importance, but I don't see the logic of the action."

"Who said anything about an invasion?" Connor replied.

"So, invasion isn't your goal?"

"Why experiment on the Ovarrow? What have they done to deserve this?"

"All external efforts are experiments. I don't need to explain this to you. The fact that you're here in this capacity indicates that you are familiar with the concept."

Connor used his implants to adjust the speed of his comlink and sent out a broadcast. The signal failed as before.

The sector chief stepped closer to Connor. The suppressor cuffs flashed, and Connor was lowered to a few inches above the ground, which put him at eye level with the Krake. The alien extended his hand toward Connor's shoulder for a moment, and Connor thought he was going to touch the armor. He had his suit's countermeasures armed, and if the sector chief touched him, the Krake would receive quite a shock.

"Interesting protection you have. Much more capable than this Ovarrow," the sector chief said, gesturing down toward Cerot.

The Ovarrow had regained consciousness and slowly rose to his feet as the Krake soldiers watched him.

"Defiant to a fault," the sector chief said and then looked back at Connor. "They are easily manipulated. Though this is our first meeting, this isn't your first encounter with my kind."

"That's obvious. I'm sure you can figure out why I'm here," Connor said.

He was able to move his feet, which meant he was only being held by his wrists.

"Won't your companions come back for you? I would expect that they would since loyalty is a behavior your species has demonstrated."

"Some things are more important," Connor replied. They'd stolen data about the Krake, and it was more important for Dash and the others to get to Samson and escape than it was to rescue him. He had no intention of dying, but he had to admit that the odds of him leaving this hangar bay alive were dwindling.

More Krake soldiers entered the hangar.

"Loyalty and sacrifice. We've seen these behaviors before—inspiration for the feebleminded. You have given me much to ponder," the sector chief said.

"I'm glad you find me so interesting. If you know so much, why do you keep experimenting on the Ovarrow?" Connor asked.

"You mistake me, or perhaps we're having an issue with the translator. It was based on inferior attempts at communication. Me saying that you've given me much to ponder doesn't mean that I find you or your species merely interesting. In fact, the knowledge I'm going to extract from you will be fascinating. Entire factions will align themselves with what I will gain here. They'll yearn for more."

"You haven't answered my question. You force the Ovarrow prisoners to fight, herding them toward an arch with a gateway to where? Their homes?"

"We do not force the Ovarrow to do anything. We simply create conditions whereby a choice must be made, and we offer them a way to salvation," the sector chief said.

He turned away from Connor and a large holoscreen appeared, showing multiple vantage points of the battlefield. Each holoscreen had a combat HUD, and Connor found that the translator was able to interpret the Krake language. The Krake had complete control over the battlefield, and Connor saw where they had their heavy cannons fortified, their soldiers deployed, and their orbital platforms locked onto the area for the next bombardment.

Connor clenched his teeth. This wasn't an elaborate experiment. He jerked his body, trying to tear free from the suppressor cuffs, but they held him firmly. The sector chief regarded him for a few moments.

"Ah, an emotional response. These images anger you, which means you're intelligent enough to realize—at least on the surface—that there is futility in fighting what is inevitable," the sector chief said and stepped closer to Connor. "But tell me, would you still fight even for the slightest chance to return to your home?"

Connor knew he was being baited, and it was working. The sector chief was putting himself within reach to try to get a response from Connor. He clenched his fists from within the armored confines of the combat suit and glanced at the dozens of Krake soldiers that stood nearby. They waited with an almost practiced patience, as if they expected him to strike the sector chief and were ready to respond once he did. He couldn't do what they expected. As much as he wanted the moment's satisfaction of kicking the crap out of the Krake sector chief, he knew it wouldn't gain him anything.

"Would you?" Connor asked.

The sector chief didn't exactly look smug, but it was as close to smug as an alien could look. Instead of answering, he engaged a holo-interface below one of the holoscreens. Connor watched as heavy cannons atop mobile platforms swung around and a bright flash of orange burst from them, scorching the ground and decimating the Ovarrow lines. They kept firing in bursts, forcing thousands of Ovarrow prisoners toward the city where Krake soldiers waited.

The sector chief's cold gaze watched the holoscreen dispassionately. This experiment wasn't about whether the Ovarrow could defeat the Krake. They couldn't. This was an experiment about what the Ovarrow would do in their last moments—how they reacted to death. Connor watched as the sector chief's gaze flicked toward the Krake soldiers. He was watching them as well. Was he measuring the reactions of the soldiers? A response to Connor's comlink broadcast appeared on his internal heads-up display. His reconnaissance drone was inside the hangar bay. It must have been close enough to detect his earlier broadcast.

The sector chief turned back toward Connor. "Are we everything you feared us to be? I know you don't like this. If we were able to measure your biometrics, then no doubt your system would be showing signs of increased stress."

"We're not afraid of you. So far, you're everything I thought you were."

The sector chief raised the rod that controlled the suppressor cuffs and thrust it above his head. Connor's body lurched into the air. Then he was flung to the side and dragged helplessly behind by the cuffs on his wrists. Connor gritted his teeth and exhaled forcefully. The cuffs changed direction and his body sped toward the floor. His armored body slammed onto the hard surface and bounced into the air. Sharp pain lanced down his back and legs, and pain suppressants and nanites entered his system. As the pain dulled, his MPS engaged from within his combat suit. Just when gravity was about to bring him down, the cuffs engaged again. Connor sent a concentrated burst of power to his wrists, intending to overload them, and as his velocity through the air slowed, he quickly sank toward the ground. He slammed his wrists together with all the force he could muster and then hit the ground, shoulder first. The combat suit absorbed most of the impact, but jarring pain still ignited down his arm. Connor regained his feet and looked down at his wrists where the suppressor cuffs were mangled and bent. He tore them off and looked around. The Krake soldiers were still gathered in an open area near the center of the hangar bay. He peered at them and saw the sector chief raise the rod into the air, making a slicing motion with it.

Connor felt his lips lift up in amusement, but then he heard the clang of something hitting the ground. He hastened to the side and saw Cerot dangling upside down. The box with metallic laces had shifted to his back, and it glowed like Connor's suppressor cuffs had.

The sector chief lifted the rod up into the air and Cerot's body rose in response. The Krake turned toward Connor. He was a hundred meters away, but the open hangar bay doors were between them. Connor could reach the door and get away if he chose. The sector chief flicked the rod and Cerot spun right-side up. The Ovarrow was bleeding from the wounds he'd sustained, but he was still conscious. He lifted his head and looked at Connor. After a few moments, he inhaled deeply and shouted.

"Leave!"

Cerot's shout was cut off by violent coughing.

The smart move was for Connor to leave, take what he'd learned about the Krake, and return to New Earth, return to his family. He closed his eyes for a moment and sneered.

"Leave!" Cerot screamed again.

Had their positions been reversed, Connor imagined that Cerot might have left, and he wouldn't have blamed him. There were so few Ovarrow on New Earth, and the intelligence gathered was worth more than one person's life. Cerot wouldn't hate Connor if he left, and Vitory probably wouldn't resent Connor when he learned of what had happened.

His personal recon drone had tapped into a Krake console, and Connor had given it more precise search parameters based on what he'd seen with the new translator program. He'd found gateway references for hundreds of universes, all accessible through the arch, but the number wasn't infinite. It wasn't even close, and Connor didn't know why that was. If he left now, he could take that knowledge with him and come up with a more effective strategy for defeating the Krake. He could make sure Cerot's sacrifice was known to everyone.

Connor watched as Cerot's body hung in the air. The Ovarrow was willing to die for this. Lenora had saved Cerot's life when they were trapped under a collapsed bridge, and Cerot must have seen this as a way to repay the debt, but that was only part of it. Cerot must've believed that Connor and the CDF were the only chance the Ovarrow had of defeating the Krake. Loyalty mixed with pragmatism.

The sector chief waited for Connor to make his choice. No matter what Connor did, the sector chief would learn something about him. He glanced at the open hangar bay doors and the path to freedom; then he looked at Cerot, waiting to die. The Ovarrow had sacrificed so much to be there. He'd been raised in a world of war, a world where sacrifice was required in order to survive. It was why the Ovarrow had gone into stasis, and it was why Cerot was willing to sacrifice himself so Connor could leave. But he wasn't going to leave. Connor decided that he was going to educate the Krake on what fighting a single human would be like. The Krake data dump would be lost, but Connor had something he wanted to teach the Krake, and Cerot.

CHAPTER 26

Connor cranked up the combat suit's power systems to maximum. Then, with a running start, he leaped into the air and engaged the suit thrusters. The Krake soldiers all seemed to move at once. Connor pulled out a massive combat knife as he closed in on the nearest Krake soldier. The soldier tried to bring his weapon up, but Connor was already on him, ramming the knife through his side. The force of the blow was augmented through his suit thrusters, and it pierced the Krake armor. The soldier let out a mournful howl, and Connor lifted him up and threw him into the nearest soldier. He leaped into the air again and stepped off the nearest Krake soldier's shoulder to jump even higher. He'd managed to get his arm wrapped around Cerot's middle when the section leader slammed his arm down, and Connor felt Cerot's body begin to plunge back to the ground. Connor jabbed the tip of his knife into the metallic box on Cerot's back and pried it loose. He then clutched Cerot to him and twisted in the air to shield the Ovarrow from harm as they landed on the ground. Pain blossomed down his side despite the pain-numbing meds already in his system. His combat suit status showed multiple damaged sections. Connor regained his feet just as another Krake soldier attacked. Connor fought him, driving him back, but more were coming. He engaged the suit thrusters near his elbow and struck a crippling blow at the oncoming soldier. Then he quickly spun around and grabbed Cerot, running toward the rows of small ships.

The Krake soldiers were quickly catching up to him. One grabbed hold of Cerot and pulled Connor off balance, so he dumped Cerot onto the ground and turned to face the soldiers. They didn't use their weapons but instead chose to fight him hand-to-hand. With the help of the combat suit, Connor was keeping his attackers at bay, but more soldiers were closing in and he was getting struck more often. If he stayed there, he'd be overwhelmed. A Krake soldier attempted to maneuver Connor toward another one who held suppression cuffs in his hand, and Connor quickly scrambled out of the way. He noticed Cerot stumbling toward some kind of small fighter that had an open seating area on top.

A Krake soldier struck Connor in the back and unleashed a burst of energy. The combat suit conducted the power as best it could, but his systems were being overloaded. Sensing he was vulnerable to the attack, the Krake soldiers banged their fists together so they were all glowing. Connor turned and ran, knocking into one of the soldiers before the rest closed in on him. He engaged the combat suit's self-destruct protocol and adjusted the timer. Then he engaged it and selected the quick-exit protocol. The combat suit split down the middle, allowing him to jump free. Connor's MPS became active and propelled him at speed away from them. He only had mere seconds before the suit exploded, and the force of it thrust him forward. He just barely kept his feet under him and stumbled into the ship Cerot was attempting to bring online. Glancing behind him, he saw that Krake bodies had been flung away from the scorched ground where his combat suit had been, but more were coming.

He hopped onto the front bench of the ship where Cerot had opened a holo-interface. Connor sat down next to him and took over. The translator enabled him to access the holo-interface, and the ship came online. It was more like a battle sled, and there was a cannon off the back. Connor activated the cannon and it swung around, priming for a few seconds before unleashing a bolt of molten fury that blasted through the hangar bay walls. There were several flashes off to the side where Krake soldiers were firing their weapons. Connor grabbed the controls and flew the Krake ship out of the hangar. He banked to the side and headed directly toward the battlefield where the battle was raging on.

"Take control of that cannon," Connor said.

Cerot brought up a secondary-weapons interface and the rear cannon responded to his commands. He looked at Connor, and Connor gestured to where the Krake weapons were herding the Ovarrow prisoners along. Cerot understood. The Ovarrow began firing on the Krake forces, taking their line of soldiers completely by surprise.

"Take out their cannons," Connor said.

Cerot began aiming for their cannons, which were unable to swing around in time to track the small ship. A proximity alert appeared on the ship's HUD, and Connor saw that there were multiple ships heading in his direction. He flew along the main thoroughfare, and Cerot was able to take out the Krake defenses there. The Ovarrow prisoners rushed down the street, heading for the arch. Connor hoped it actually led to their home world, or at least someplace that wasn't under Krake control, but he was afraid it was a lie. He couldn't be sure, but he didn't have time to worry about it because the Krake ships were firing on him.

Connor's ship dipped to the side, and Connor grabbed onto Cerot to keep them in the seat. He flew among the buildings, using them for cover, but the craft was sluggish to respond to his commands. The Krake fired on his ship again and took out his engine. They began to spin, and it took everything he had to hold on. The ship struck one of the buildings and crashed. Somehow, they landed right-side up, and Connor scrambled out of the seat, helping Cerot to his feet.

"Come on! We have to run!" Connor yelled over the din.

He engaged the comlink system of his MPS, but there was no reply and no acknowledgment of the message.

"They're going to catch us," Cerot said. "You should've left me behind."

Connor half dragged the Ovarrow down the street, hearing Krake ships flying overhead. They continued running close to the buildings, trying to stay out of sight. Cerot stumbled and nearly fell.

"Don't quit on me now," Connor said, helping him back to his feet.

Cerot held something out toward him, and he was stunned to see that it was his own personal recon drone. Connor didn't know how Cerot had gotten it, but it was the only thing that held the data they needed about the Krake.

"Hold onto it for me," Connor said. It wasn't as if he had a place to put it. The MPS didn't come with additional storage. It was his emergency protection, and he didn't have any weapons. All he had was a protective suit made of nanorobotic materials designed to protect the wearer from extreme harm.

Connor glanced at the sky, expecting more Krake ships to come flying over, but they didn't. He heard more ships nearby, and they sounded like they were hovering close, but then their engines went off. They were going to hunt them.

"Come on, we've got to move," Connor said.

Cerot clutched the recon drone to his middle and used his other hand to grab Connor's shoulder to help him stay upright. Connor glanced behind them as they made their way toward another row of buildings and saw bloody footsteps. Cerot was badly wounded. He'd have to stop soon or the Ovarrow would die.

He heard a Krake shout something in their language, and the translation appeared on Connor's internal heads-up display.

". . . trail to follow," came the partial translation.

Connor tried to hurry Cerot along and then lifted the Ovarrow over his shoulder. The MPS helped Connor bear the heavy load, but it wasn't as strong as his combat suit, and he felt the weight. Running forward, he stepped carefully so he didn't lose his balance. The dull ache in his back and legs flared intensely. Krake soldiers were closing in behind him. He reached the end of the street and hesitated for a moment, glancing back the way they'd come. Two soldiers were running toward them with their weapons, ready to shoot. Connor scrambled to the side and kept going.

Cerot's blood was dripping down his chest, and Connor realized that he was bleeding too much. Connor had to place a field dressing, but if he stopped, the Krake were going to find them. Granted, they were going to find them whether he stopped or not.

Connor saw a flash of something metallic moving among the buildings in front of him and muttered a curse. The Krake were already ahead of him. They were tightening the noose around them. Connor peered ahead and saw something out of place on top of the building. There were several shapes along the roof. Connor narrowed his gaze, seeing one of the shapes detach itself from the others. A CDF soldier waved to him and then readied his weapon. Gritting his teeth, Connor lunged forward, running as fast as he could. The Krake soldiers attempted to close in behind him, but the 7th fired their weapons, taking the Krake soldiers by surprise.

Connor ran for cover. Two CDF soldiers took Cerot from his shoulder and carried him away. He heard the CDF laying down suppressing fire, and then Samson stood in front of him.

"Your timing is almost impeccable, General," Samson said. "Come on, we only have a few minutes to reach the gateway."

Connor's breath was coming in gasps, so he didn't reply; he just followed his friend. They ran a short distance to an open part of the city. It must've been a park at some point, or perhaps a courtyard between buildings. Connor saw the semi-translucent shimmer in the air, denoting a gateway. The soldiers in front of him who were carrying Cerot ran right for it.

"Go! Don't stop!" Samson shouted.

Connor ran through the gateway and emerged into a forest glade surrounded by silence. One moment there'd been the sound of a battle being fought, and the next it was gone. Connor doubled over and rested his hands on his knees while he caught his breath. He was pulled to the side by a soldier who spoke a quick apology, but they had to keep the way clear for the rest of the 7th to come through. Samson was the last to emerge, and he ordered the gateway to shut down. The arch immediately went dead, and the platforms maintaining the alignment quickly separated.

Connor was still catching his breath when Samson walked over to him. "You crazy son of a—Did you intend to fight the Krake all by yourself? That was our final sweep. We almost left you."

Connor inhaled deeply, finally catching his breath. "I'm glad you didn't. Did you find Dash, Bradley, and Marsters?"

"Yeah, we found them. We need to talk about our secondary protocols for when our egress point is no longer a viable option," Samson said.

Connor couldn't argue with that. This whole thing had turned into something way too fast and loose for his liking. He saw Esteban and Felix kneeling by Cerot while a CDF medic tended to his wounds.

Samson glanced at all the blood covering Connor's chest. "What the hell happened over there?"

Connor looked at his friend. "We met the enemy."

———

The Krake sector chief had hunted the human. He knew what species it was, but he hadn't anticipated a connection to the Ovarrow. Some of his soldiers had been slain by this human. They weren't entirely predictable, at least not in all things. He retraced the human's path and found the Ovarrow's blood drying on the ground. Leaning down, he extracted a sample of it. It would help him identify the universe that the humans came from. It wasn't an exact measure, but it would help narrow the search. Once he reported this encounter to the overseers, things would change. The Krake had to change. The sector chief had a new project to propose to the overseers, one they couldn't afford to ignore.

A Krake soldier reported in that several hundred Ovarrow had breached the arch gateway before they'd been able to bring it down.

"Let them go. They're not important," the sector chief said.

The Krake soldier didn't question the orders he'd been given. He simply obeyed.

CHAPTER 27

Connor had sustained significant impact trauma to his back from his fight with the Krake. He hadn't realized the extent of his injuries because his system had been flooded with pain-numbing agents so he could keep moving. The Nexstar combat suit would report the injuries detected, but he'd been fighting, and the self-destruct sequence he'd used to stop the Krake soldiers from killing him had also destroyed the report of his injuries. There was no link between his combat suit and the MPS he wore, which had a limited medical interface.

The injuries did register with his biochip, however, and when the medics checked it, they discovered that he had suffered a lot more than a few bumps and bruises. He'd sustained internal bleeding that could have happened either when he was fighting multiple Krake soldiers or when he'd crashed the ship during his escape. Connor had pushed the limits of what a Nexstar combat suit was even capable of, and now he was paying the price.

He lay in the bed at the hospital on base at Sanctuary and glanced at the time on his internal heads-up display, frowning. He'd been asleep for over ten hours.

Ten hours!

He quickly brought up the status of his ZX-64c implants, which were an upgraded version of what the NA Alliance military had given him all those years ago, but the controls for the implants were grayed out. He frowned, thinking that perhaps they'd been damaged, but a quick diagnostic showed they were working fine. He'd been locked out of his own implants! He hit the call button on the panel next to the bed and attempted to sit up but winced and gasped at the sharp pain from his back and quickly lay back down.

The door to his room opened and a short, young woman with dark hair walked in. Her name and rank appeared on his internal heads-up display. At least *that* was still working.

Dr. Monica Torres smiled as she walked over to him. "General Gates, you're awake right on schedule. I'll raise the bed for you so you can sit up."

"What's going on here? Did you lock me out of my implant control systems?"

"Yes, I did. We had to, but I had permission."

Connor knitted his eyebrows together and shook his head. "I didn't give permission—"

"Your wife, General. Your wife did," Dr. Torres said, coming over to his bedside. "You broke your back. You're lucky to be alive."

Connor's mouth opened, but the words wouldn't come. He glanced down at his feet for a second. "That's crazy. I know I got hurt, but if I'd broken my back, I wouldn't have been able to walk."

"That's right, you wouldn't have been able to, but you had an MPS on. It helped you keep moving and stay alive. Had you not had the MPS on, as soon as you stepped out of your combat suit, you would've collapsed to the floor," Dr. Torres said.

Connor looked away for a moment and then back down at his feet. He wiggled his toes, relieved that he could still do so. Swallowing hard, he looked up at her, and she waited for him with a knowing look.

"How bad is it?" he asked.

"Not nearly as bad as it could have been. We've been applying treatments to you all night, and now you'll just have to take it easy for a little while. You'll also have to wear a back brace while the nanites continue to heal your spine."

Connor nodded, feeling relieved. "Why are you inhibiting my implants?"

"Because you need to slow down a little bit. The medical journals all indicate that you *can* function with a mere two hours of sleep, and you've been doing it longer than anybody else, but such little downtime does take its toll on certain cognitive functions," Dr. Torres said, leaning toward him. "Signs of this include irritation and a certain level of anxiety. In your case," she said, smiling a little in understanding, "it's to be expected, given the extreme amount of stress, but it's been ongoing for a while. You need longer blocks of rest. This will help you heal."

"I know you're looking out for me, Dr. Torres, but I've been at this for a very long time. Irritation and anxiety are part of what I do. I want full access to my implants returned to me right now. I promise to get as much rest as I can and—" Connor said, suddenly stopping when Lenora walked in the room. Lauren stood next to her with her little hand held in her mother's. She looked up and saw Connor lying there, and her eyes widened. Lauren smiled and squealed, and everything Connor had been about to say vanished as his daughter hastened over to him.

Lenora picked Lauren up and deposited her onto Connor's lap. He hugged his daughter, feeling his throat become thick, and saw Lenora share a look with Dr. Torres. Lauren wrapped her arms around Connor's neck and snuggled into him. The tension drained out of him as if the floodgates had been opened, and he squeezed his eyes shut, holding his daughter in his arms and breathing in her scent. Her silky, soft hair smelled like lavender, and he loved the feel of it against his cheek.

After a few precious moments, Lauren sat back and scrutinized Connor with a look of childlike wonder and intensity. Her gaze went to the bruise on his neck. "Ouchy," she said.

Connor smiled. "That's right. I have an ouchy, but I'll be fine."

Lenora looked at him for a moment, and Connor could tell she was reining in her emotions. Then she glanced at Dr. Torres. "Would you please give us a few minutes?"

"Take all the time you need," Dr. Torres said and left the room.

Lenora inhaled deeply and sighed. Walking over to his bed, she grasped his hand. "You know, we first met in a hospital room."

Connor chuckled a little, remembering when he'd first woken up aboard the *Ark*.

"I spoke to Samson and Dash. They told me what happened," she said.

Connor had no doubt that Lenora had pulled every ounce of information from both men. She had a way of getting what she wanted. Connor tried to think of a response that didn't make him sound foolish, but he couldn't. He'd almost died, and they both knew it.

"Connor, I know you. You did what you had to do. And I'm just so glad you're home. But we need to make some changes," Lenora said.

"All right," Connor answered.

"I just . . ." Lenora began to say and stopped. "First, the problem with the implants and . . . I've had those concerns since before you left."

"I've had them for years and have never had an issue."

"Yes, but you had check-ins, and even . . . They're not meant for long-term use."

"So what are you going to do? Lock me out of them?"

Lenora shook her head. "You know better than that. Do I need to lock you out of them? No, that's not who we are. All I'm saying is that we need more of a balance, and *you* need more of a balance. You can't be on the go for twenty-two hours a day every day for years and years and expect not to have any repercussions."

Connor was quiet for a few moments while he considered his thoughts. If there was one thing he'd learned over the years it was that there were times to think things through and then there were times to do what needed to be done. This was the latter. "All right, I'll talk to Dr. Torres and Ashley. We'll see if we can work something out."

Lenora seemed satisfied with that response. Over the years, they had learned to trust each other, but he knew she'd be watching him. He'd certainly given her enough cause to be worried about him.

They spent a few hours together, and the pain in his back lessened. He was able to sit up comfortably. Later, he received another treatment for his back, and they fitted him with a back brace to continue monitoring and administering healing nanites.

———

A few days later, Connor was in his office. Dash had come to see him.

"Cerot is asking for you," Dash said.

The Ovarrow were staying in a barracks that had been designated for them. Colonial doctors had done what they could for Cerot, but his recovery would take much longer than Connor's.

They left his office and headed over to the barracks.

"About what you did," Dash said once they were outside. Connor looked at him. "I never got a chance to thank you."

"You're welcome."

Dash eyes widened for a moment. "You make it seem like there's nothing else to say."

"What else *is* there to say?"

"It mattered to me."

"It mattered to me too. That's why I did it. And it was important to get the data we recovered."

"Do you compartmentalize everything?"

"If saving your life is going to lead to a lot of questions, I may have to rethink it in the future," Connor replied.

Dash shook his head and grinned a little.

"Look at it this way: At the rate we're going, you'll be able to return the favor by this time next week," Connor said.

"I hope not," Dash said, his voice becoming serious.

Connor nodded. "Me too."

They entered the room where Cerot was being cared for. He looked much better than the last time Connor had seen him, which was when he'd almost bled out in the middle of a battle.

Cerot spoke. "Alone," he said.

The Ovarrow soldiers left the room and Dash joined them.

"Better translator now," Cerot said.

"It's better than typing everything we want to say to each other," Connor said in agreement.

"I have to return and report to Warlord Vitory and High Commissioner Senleon."

"I understand," Connor said. He was more than a little bit curious as to what Cerot would report to his superiors.

"It may take some time, but I will gather as many Ovarrow as I can and persuade them to help you," Cerot said.

"We'll appreciate any help you have to offer," Connor said.

"My words might not be correct. What I mean to say is that I will help you in your fight against the Krake."

Connor regarded the warlord's First for a moment. He'd begun to suspect what Cerot was implying, but he wanted no misunderstandings. "You mean you'll help the colony? All of us?"

"Your colony is important to you like our city is important to us, but they are not one and the same. I meant what I said, and I will help you fight the Krake. You are beginning to understand what it means to battle them. And if our leaders are too foolish to understand that, I will help you anyway with as many soldiers as I can bring," Cerot said.

Connor inhaled deeply. "Then I hope it doesn't come to that."

Divisions among the colonists and among the Ovarrow were a danger to them all. They didn't need to agree on everything, but they did need to focus on the Krake, together.

Connor and Dash went with the Ovarrow to the hangar where a troop carrier waited to take them home. Cerot was carried onto the troop carrier first. The rest of the soldiers that they'd named Esteban, Joe, Felix, Luca, and Wesley stood before the loading ramp and faced Connor. They each placed their hand on their own shoulder and pulled it across to their other shoulder, giving Connor the Ovarrow sign for gratitude.

Connor returned their salute, and the Ovarrow soldiers walked up the loading ramp. The troop carrier doors closed, and the ship left.

"I think you made a few friends," Dash said.

"I guess I did."

"I don't know what this means for an official alliance, but the Ovarrow seem to hold actions in higher esteem than they do intentions. This is something I've noticed with them," Dash said.

Connor nodded. "It's a start, at least. We'll have to take it from there."

A short while later, Connor and Dash entered a small conference room. Nathan and Samson were speaking quietly.

Nathan looked at Connor. "You're looking surprisingly agile for someone who broke his back just a few days ago."

"You know me; I get irritated when I sit still," Connor replied and leaned in toward Nathan. "Are you trying to recruit my captain?"

Nathan grinned. Pilfering each other's soldiers had become something of a joke between them. "I'm afraid not. Captain Samson was just telling me that the Ovarrow you found have left that capital city."

Connor looked at Samson.

"The report just came in. They're gone. All traces of them, including the ryklars," Samson said.

"There isn't much we can do about that," Connor said. He'd hoped to be able to speak with Brashirker one more time with the improved translator. It might have changed the outcome.

"They worry me," Nathan said. "They don't have to work with us, but we can't let them work with the Krake."

"Agreed. We'll have to keep an eye out for them," Connor said, "but I don't think they would work with the Krake. They wouldn't have done what they've done to stay hidden for as long as they have and then decide to work with the very enemy they were hoping to avoid."

"Ordinarily I would agree with you, but I don't want to leave anything to chance. You said it before—we can't make any assumptions where the Ovarrow are concerned," Nathan said and looked at Dash. "Mr. DeWitt, I understand you had a role in all this."

"I did, sir, but I'm not sure what to do now."

"I'm sure we'll keep you busy," Connor said.

Dash looked at both Connor and Nathan. "I'm ready to help, but I have a request."

Connor arched an eyebrow. "I think you're entitled to one request."

Dash smiled a little. "I need weapons training. Things got out of control so fast, and I need to be able to do something so I'm not a liability."

"Are you saying you want to join the CDF?" Nathan asked.

Dash shook his head quickly. "No, and I don't mean any disrespect either. I'm not a soldier like all of you, but I've been working with soldiers for a long time."

Dash looked at Connor, letting the thought go unfinished.

"I'll give it some thought," Connor said.

"I'd be happy to show the kid a few things," Samson said mildly and then looked at Dash with anticipation.

Dash swallowed hard. "I'm not sure that would be such a good idea," he said.

Connor grinned and the others joined in. "We'll see. I'm sure we can come up with something, especially if we need specialists in the field with us."

"We need to start thinking about the next steps. And . . ." Nathan began to say, pausing for a moment. "Would you two excuse us for a few minutes?" he said, looking at Samson and Dash.

Samson stood up. "Come on, kid, there's something you need to see."

Dash looked only slightly worried as they left the room.

"Next steps," Connor said. "We need to analyze everything we brought back."

"You're not wrong about that, but there are a couple of things I need to discuss with you," Nathan said.

"I bet I can guess what one or two of those things might be," Connor replied.

"You've got what you wanted. You looked the enemy in the eyes."

"I've looked *an* enemy in the eyes. I still don't feel like we have a handle on them as a whole."

"Fair enough. Do you intend to lead every mission that involves a team going through a gateway, whether it be here through an arch or a space gate?" Nathan asked.

Connor shook his head. "Of course not."

Nathan smiled. "You don't know how glad I am to hear that, because it seems to me and a few other people that you excel at putting yourself right in the thick of it."

"Maybe I'm just the lucky one."

Nathan chuckled. "Or you just have a natural talent for finding trouble." He paused for a moment and regarded Connor, pressing his lips together. "We have to figure this enemy out—you and me, and a whole lot of other people. We have to be able to trust other people to get the job done. Would you agree with that?"

"I would."

"Look, Connor, I haven't been a soldier as long as you have. But I do know that not every fight has to be personal."

"You think I'm making this personal?" Connor asked.

"Aren't you?"

Connor looked away for a moment and pursed his lips in thought. "This *is* personal, Nathan. I feel like we're a heartbeat away from fighting this war in our backyards. It's worse than the Vemus. We dodged a horrible fate with that, but this is different. I know we're supposed to be diplomatic when it comes to dealing with Governor Wolf and the other Security Council members, but make no mistake—this *is* personal. The Krake are going to test us beyond anything we've ever faced before. It's like they're hyper-logical to a fault. Extremely advanced. They toy with civilizations just to see if they can influence the outcome."

"Ovarrow civilizations," Nathan said, pointedly. "They haven't encountered ours before."

"And they've been at it for who knows how long. It has to be a few hundred years at least."

"So, what are you saying?"

"What I'm saying is that I don't know how we're going to defeat the Krake. Throughout every encounter we've had, we try to be better prepared for the next encounter, and then we find that they're capable of much more than we thought. This is personal for me because that's how I can effectively do my job. Our job is to stop the Krake."

"Yes, that's our job, and we'll need to sacrifice lives in order to attain victory. That means you and I can't lead every charge."

"You've seen the Security Council. Do you think they're ready to hear about sacrifice, especially where lives are concerned?"

Nathan twitched his head to the side in a slight nod. "They might surprise you. I think you've done an excellent job of making them aware of the risk. Just because they don't like to be reminded of what could happen doesn't mean we shouldn't remind them."

"Be careful. I bet they won't like to hear that."

Nathan chuckled. "I have a few ideas of my own for how to deal with the Krake, but I don't even want to entertain the thought of fighting this war without you. This colony needs you, Connor. I know the Krake surprised you," he said and then shook his head. "I don't think I would've survived if I'd been put in the same situation. I'm not you, and there's no one else like you."

Connor shifted in his seat, feeling a little uncomfortable. "We have Sean. They thought Trident Battle Group was there. It was the first confirmation we've received that they're still around, and the fact that Sean has got the Krake worried is a win in my book."

Connor refused to even consider that Sean and the rest of Trident Battle Group had been lost. They were still out there.

"We do have Sean, and Celeste Belonét, and half a dozen other outstanding young officers, but it seems to me that we're barely staying a step ahead of the Krake. One little misstep and everything changes," said Nathan.

"We don't do this because it's easy; we do this because it's necessary," Connor said.

The conference room was profoundly quiet while the two generals regarded each other.

"I might be the head of the CDF, but you will always be its heart. I saw it on the command deck of a warship, and I've seen it in a hundred different ways ever since."

Connor felt his throat thicken for a moment. Nathan was speaking as a friend who'd watched as someone close to them almost die. Connor just wanted to focus on the next thing. This wasn't the first time he'd risked his life, or even come close to losing it. But maybe this was someone telling him to take a few moments and seriously consider what he should do next.

The door to the conference room opened and Samson stuck his head in. "You're going to want to see this. Trident Battle Group has returned home."

CHAPTER 28

The few moments of elation didn't last long after they heard the news. Connor and Nathan headed to a briefing room where Colonel Belonét gave them a brief update. The battle group had emerged in an area of space that wasn't near anything—a void between New Earth and Sagan's orbit. Phoenix Station wasn't anywhere nearby, so salvage and rescue operations had to be coordinated from the lunar base near New Earth.

The *Vigilant* was completely without power, and the CDF soldiers and civilian personnel were being transferred over to the remaining ships in operation. Trident Battle Group now consisted of only six CDF destroyers, and there wasn't enough room on the destroyers for the people currently stranded. The battle group had lost two destroyers and the converted freighter that had been serving as a carrier. In addition to smaller ships, such as combat shuttles and Talon-V troop carriers, Sean had nonessential personnel in escape pods that were running under their own power. It was a temporary solution.

"The *Vigilant* needs to be refueled," Connor said. "If we transfer the reactor core from one of the ships in the lunar shipyards, we can at least restore critical power to the *Vigilant*, and that should be enough to get them back to New Earth."

Colonel Belonét shook her head, muttering a curse. "Yes, General, you're correct. I should've thought of that. I'm sorry."

"Don't worry about it, Colonel," Nathan said. "General Gates has been doing that to me for years."

"Yes, sir. We'll get to them in time," Colonel Belonét said as a soldier called her attention off-screen. She nodded and looked back at Connor and Nathan. "I have a priority mission report that is directed to both of you, for your immediate review. It's from Colonel Quinn. I've sent it along priority channels, and you should have it now."

"Thank you," Connor said as a priority mission update appeared on the sub-window of the main holoscreen in the briefing room. "Carry on, Colonel."

The comlink from the lunar base went dark. The briefing room at Sanctuary wasn't overly large, but there were quite a few people inside. The room quickly cleared out until only Connor and Nathan remained. Priority mission reports required additional authentication, and both Connor and Nathan had to provide that in order to access the report. The minutes flew by as Connor scanned the account. As he read, he felt his brows knit together.

"Holy shit," Connor said.

"That's putting it mildly."

Connor stood up and paced for a moment. "A mutiny," he said and paced some more. "A damn mutiny!" he repeated.

Nathan looked away from the report. None of the questions that were now bursting in both of their minds were going to be answered right then. "This is going to require an extensive investigation."

Connor nodded slowly. "I know. I just don't believe it."

"Neither do I, and I don't want to jump to any conclusions. Sean was giving us both a heads-up."

Connor shook his head, still coming to grips with what he'd just learned. "What the hell happened to them?"

"That's what we need to find out."

"First things first. We need to get them to Lunar Base. Then we'll need to debrief them all," Connor said.

"The investigation will be conducted out of Sierra," Nathan said.

Connor felt a momentary territorial response, but he squelched it in an instant. He just needed to know what the hell had happened. The briefing indicated that Major Lester Brody had attempted a coup in direct opposition to Sean.

"We'll need to brief Governor Wolf," Connor said.

When word of the mutiny spread throughout the colony, things were going to get tense. They needed to conduct this investigation and get it done as quickly and as thoroughly as possible so they could be prepared to answer the tough questions.

"I'll need you in Sierra for a few weeks but not for a day or two. You're still healing, and we have a little bit of time," Nathan said.

The back brace Connor wore caused an itch that he absently scratched. He looked at Nathan.

"I want to go just as badly as you do," Nathan said, as if reading Connor's thoughts.

Hearing Nathan admit that lessened Connor's desire to get on a shuttle and order it to take him to the lunar base right then. "After they reach the lunar shipyards, we'll bring him dirtside ASAP. We need to follow the protocols for debriefing; otherwise, someone might accuse us of meddling."

"We don't want that," Nathan replied.

"The debriefings will be classified until we can present an official report to the Security Council," Connor said.

Nathan nodded and then frowned for a moment. "Have you ever had to deal with anything like this?"

"No, not like this. Mutiny is different than insubordination. This is much worse, and we could speculate on it, but I think we need to wait and get more information."

"Agreed. I'm headed back to Sierra to meet with Governor Wolf. She's going to have a lot of questions that we won't have the answers to, but at least we'll be keeping her informed," Nathan said.

Connor watched as Nathan looked at the mission report on the holoscreen for another moment and sighed, then Connor walked Nathan out of the room and headed back to his office. Debriefing soldiers who returned from a mission had well-established protocols, but what Connor needed to do was to see if they had anything on the NA Alliance military record that dealt with a mutiny. He might find some historical reference, but he doubted he'd find anything like an official report.

Connor closed his office door so he had privacy and opened a comlink to Ashley. It didn't take long for her to be reached at the medical center in Sanctuary.

"Hello, Connor."

"Sean is back," Connor said.

Ashley frowned and peered intently at him. "What?" she asked, her voice sounding slightly hushed.

"Sean is back, Ashley. Your son is home. It'll be a few days before he gets to New Earth, but I wanted you to know first, and I wanted you to hear it from me," Connor said.

Ashley's eyes welled up and she covered her mouth with her hand. She closed her eyes and he heard a half-formed moan as she smiled. "Thank you. Thank you."

Connor smiled back, happy to be the bearer of good news, at least for now. The bad news was coming, but at this moment, Connor was happy to see the relief of a mother who'd learned that her son had returned home from a very dangerous place.

CHAPTER 29

A week later, Connor was at the CDF base in Sierra. As far as weeks went, it had been long and grueling, even with the extra sleep he was getting. He still needed to wear a back brace, but the doctors were pleased with the progression of his healing spine. One of the biggest adjustments Connor was making was the additional sleep required. He was now getting six hours of sleep each night and had been given control of his implants once again. He did feel less agitated, as if the additional sleep had taken some of the edge off his mood. Connor had to grudgingly admit that perhaps the doctors had been correct.

The remaining ships of Trident Battle Group were now at the lunar shipyards. The *Vigilant* had been brought back online with emergency power, and the mission reports had been extracted from the computer core. All the ships in the battle group would be examined from top to bottom before being returned to service.

News of Trident Battle Group's return had quickly garnered the attention of the colony. What was supposed to have been an expeditionary mission had lasted almost a year, and they had the mission reports to prove it. It was going to take them a long time to go through everything. Of the 2,290 people who'd left with Trident Battle Group, 1,951 returned. There'd been 339 casualties, and among those casualties were 26 mutineers.

Both Connor and Nathan had been reviewing the mission reports from the senior officers of Trident Battle Group. Connor had a lot more to go, but he'd stopped because they were finally going to see Sean face to face. The crews of those ships had been brought back to New Earth, and the debriefing had begun.

Connor headed toward a small conference room where Sean was waiting. He had decided to head there early, and Nathan would join them later. He walked into the empty conference room and found Sean looking out the window. Upon hearing Connor enter, Sean turned around and saluted him. Connor returned the salute and took in the sight of his friend. Throughout his career, he'd seen soldiers age rapidly due to the stresses they'd been exposed to as part of the job. Sean had aged, and he had aged a lot. He was lean and his face was all sharp angles, but his dark eyes still had fight in them. They'd always had a brilliant intensity to them, even though they looked a bit strained. Connor remembered first seeing it when Sean had joined the original Search and Rescue platoon. That was when he'd seen what Sean was really made of.

Connor tried to think of the last time they'd been in each other's presence. So much had happened since then. Both men just stood there, silently regarding one another.

"Hello, Sean."

The edges of Sean's lips tugged slightly. "Sir."

"Welcome home," Connor said.

Sean's brows squished together for a moment and he sighed. "Thank you, sir."

"At ease. It's just the two of us in here. Nathan will be along shortly. You've had quite a journey," Connor said.

Sean was wound up as tight as a torsion spring.

"This isn't going to get any easier. There's a lot for us to talk about, but let's cut right to the chase. Tell me about the mutiny."

Sean did. When he first started speaking, it was only the facts—exactly what had happened and what he'd done—but the more he spoke, the more Connor could see some of the tension leaving him. Connor didn't offer any opinions or ask much in the way of questions. He just let Sean speak. Nathan had joined them part of the way through and told Sean to continue.

Sean broke down the entirety of the mission step by step from when they'd first left this universe to when they realized they had a problem with targeting and couldn't return home. The more Sean told them, the more Connor began to understand the amount of strain that had been put on the entire battle group. More than a few times, Connor and Nathan shared a glance.

"I know there will be a formal investigation," Sean said.

"You can count on it, but before we get to that, there's something I'd like to say," Connor began. "What you and your crew have gone through is beyond anything we could've imagined when you left. You've gone through hell and lived to come out the other side. I don't want you to discount the accomplishments you've achieved, especially in light of what's coming. And what's coming is going to challenge you in particular, but I want you to know that you're not alone. This is the part of the job no one likes, where every decision you made is scrutinized by people who weren't there. It's frustrating as all hell, but it makes us better. Try and remember that."

Sean gave a crisp nod. "I will, sir."

"I can only echo what Connor has said. This investigation is going to take some time to get through. It's not going to end in a few days," Nathan said.

"What happens now?" Sean asked.

"There are going to be long days ahead where you're going to be asked a lot of questions regarding your reports. This will involve all of the senior officers and probably everyone in Trident Battle Group," Connor said.

Sean swallowed and looked away for a moment.

"We need to get through this so we can continue our work building a strategy for the Krake," Nathan said.

"There's a lot you'll need to be brought up to speed on, but there will be time for all that," Connor said.

Sean's gaze hardened. "They're hunting for us. It's not a matter of *if*, it's a matter of *when*."

"Indeed," Nathan agreed. "We'll get to all that," he said and glanced at Connor. Connor wondered what Nathan had in mind but saved that question for later.

"Brody snapped," Sean said. "He snapped under my watch, and I didn't see it coming until it was too late."

Connor and Nathan were both quiet, waiting for Sean to continue.

"I've been going over everything that happened leading up to the mutiny —reviewing reports and going back through my meetings with Brody— trying to objectively look for some sign that would have given the slightest indication of where things were heading. And . . ." he said, pausing for a few seconds to collect his thoughts, ". . . now I don't know if I'm just seeing things because I know what happened. So, it's got this bias now . . . I trusted him. We had our differences, but we had an understanding. He raised good points during planning sessions. He was my XO. The mutiny shouldn't have happened," Sean said with a slight shake of his head. "I understand that there's going to be a lot of people angry about what happened to Brody and the other mutineers. There's going to be a lot of people questioning what I did. I've been questioning it myself since it all happened, and I don't know what I could've done differently to prevent the mutiny from happening in the first place."

"Maybe you couldn't have prevented it," Connor said. "Maybe in *that* situation with *those* soldiers, it was unavoidable. The purpose of the investigation is to reveal whether that was the case. The facts are pretty clear. You didn't give an unlawful command. That's not going to sit well with the civilians, but civilians aren't on the front lines. You're right, Sean. Brody cracked under the pressure. Everyone has a breaking point. We all do, but you didn't reach yours. You held everyone together, even after the mutiny, and got them home alive. Not only that, you brought home critical intel about our enemy."

Sean was quiet for a few moments and then nodded.

"Sean," Nathan said. "Why don't you get some rest and we'll continue to sort this out.

Sean left the conference room, and Connor and Nathan were alone.

"What a mess," Connor said.

"It's about to get worse. News of the mutineers' deaths has spread. We'll need to assign a protective detail to Sean for the time being. Just until we sort this out."

Connor nodded. "All right, let's get the others in here and start piecing this together."

They needed to provide an official report to Governor Wolf and then deal with the inevitable fallout from that.

CHAPTER 30

In the weeks following Sean's return, there had been long days of intensive debriefings that felt more like interrogations, like he was standing trial. Connor and Nathan weren't leaving anything to chance. Every after-action report was scrutinized closely.

Sean was prepared for news of the mutiny to make its way into the public eye. While military personnel could be instructed that events were classified, there was no such agreement with civilians. The CDF was getting pressure from the colonial government for an official report regarding its stance on Sean's actions.

Officially, he was still allowed to come and go as he pleased, but he simply hadn't had the time to leave the base. Sean was being called upon to relive some of the most intense moments of his life over and over again to be scrutinized by other people. Now that he wasn't on the *Vigilant* and in enemy territory, Sean and the other members of his team had had time to reflect on what happened. Major Vanessa Shelton had also endured grueling hours of questioning, which she'd taken in stride, and spent her evenings working out, punching a heavy bag. She'd recommended it to Sean, and he found it was a great way to blow off some steam.

It was early afternoon, and the days were starting to blur together. They were in the middle of a recess, but he knew they'd be sending somebody for him soon. Sean decided to take a walk. He needed to stretch his legs, so he left the main administration building on the CDF base. His two military escorts were an appropriate distance behind him.

The air outside was a bit humid and the skies were gray. It would probably rain later. He found that he kept looking up at the sky. He was still adjusting to not living on a ship. It was nice to be planetside again, but he'd spent too much time sitting in a chair these recent weeks, and he was becoming restless. He needed to move and be active again.

He heard someone call his name and turned to see Noah jogging toward him. Sean smiled and gave his friend a bear hug.

"I guess you hadn't heard, but I woke up," Noah said.

"They've been keeping me busy," Sean said. "It's really good to see you. I'm glad you're feeling better."

"I'm getting there. It took me a few days to even be able to get access to you. It's good to see you too."

They were both quiet for long enough that it was almost becoming an awkward silence. So much had happened to both of them.

"I'm not going to ask you about any of that stuff that's been on the news-net or anything like that."

"I heard about Lars," Sean said, switching the subject.

"Yeah, he's being detained at a facility in Delphi," Noah said. "I've been reviewing some of the research that's been done on the space gate. I'm trying to meet with the scientists involved."

"You should talk to Oriana. She came up with the foundation for the theory that we're working with. We're pretty close. I could introduce you to her. Her name is Oriana Evans," Sean said. He hadn't seen Oriana at all since they returned home. Civilians were undergoing their own debriefing, and he was getting worried.

Noah's eyes widened. "Evans? Her last name is Evans?"

Sean frowned. "Yes. Why?"

Noah looked away for a moment and then gave Sean a guilty look. "Does she have a brother?"

Sean nodded. "She does. His name is Colton—" Sean stopped at the look on Noah's face. "What's the matter?"

Noah swallowed hard. "I don't know how to tell you this. Colton Evans was working with Lars, and he was a terrorist. He's dead. Lars killed him. Colton Evans was responsible for killing both Ovarrow and colonists."

"Lars killed him?" Sean said in surprise.

"Colton almost killed Connor and a lot of soldiers, and Lars stopped him."

Sean frowned and looked away for a moment. Oriana's brother was dead. That could be why she hadn't contacted him. He needed to find her. Sean glanced back at his escorts for a moment. Then he turned back to Noah. "I need to know everything about this. And I need a ride."

Noah nodded, and at the same time, a young soldier ran over to Sean. "Colonel Quinn, they're ready for you to return."

Sean muttered a curse under his breath. "Private, tell them I had to leave. They'll need to reschedule."

The young soldier blinked rapidly. "Yes, sir," he stammered.

Sean followed Noah, and his escorts followed him. Noah glanced at the soldiers questioningly.

"They're with me," Sean said.

As they walked, Noah told Sean about what had happened with the rogue group Lars had been part of. Sean considered opening a comlink to Oriana, but if she was grieving, he needed to see her in person. She had her own apartment on the outskirts of Sierra, and it was a relatively short ride by C-cat. Noah flew them to the nearest landing area and Sean climbed out.

"Do you want me to wait for you?" Noah asked.

"No, I don't want to keep you. I'll find another way back. Thanks for coming to see me. I'll get to Sanctuary as soon as I can," Sean said.

He headed to the apartment building and was soon standing outside Oriana's door. He glanced at the two soldiers behind him.

"We'll wait outside, sir," one of the soldiers said.

Sean knocked on the door, but there was no answer. He called out for Oriana, but there still wasn't an answer. He was about to knock again when the door opened and he peered inside Oriana's apartment. She was sitting on the couch with her arms wrapped around her legs, which were pulled up to her chest. He walked inside and the door shut behind him.

She didn't look at him. She was staring at nothing in the general direction of the floor. Her eyes were puffy and red, and it was easy to see that she'd been crying.

Sean slowly walked into the room and couldn't think of anything to say to her. Maybe it would be better if he didn't say anything. He sat down next to her and rubbed her back. She squeezed her eyes shut and leaned toward him, and they sat like that for a few minutes.

"I just heard about your brother. I'm so sorry," Sean said.

Oriana lifted her head and looked at him. "I didn't . . ." she said, pausing for a moment, ". . . I didn't want to bother you."

Sean hugged her. "You . . . I'm here for you, no matter what. You know that."

Oriana nodded into his shoulder and he felt her tremble just a little bit. "I should have been here for him. I could've . . . I should have been here."

Sean didn't know what to say. What could he have said? His friend had killed her brother. They sat there together, holding each other on the couch, and eventually they fell asleep. It wasn't a fitful sleep, filled with nightmares, but a deep, dreamless sleep as if neither one of them had slept in months.

CHAPTER 31

Connor walked into the Colonial Administration Building. Both he and Nathan were meeting with the Security Council to review the official Trident Battle Group report.

They entered the meeting room that was already occupied by Dana Wolf, Jean Larson, Damon Mills, Clinton Edwards, and Connor's favorite person, Bob Mullins.

"Gentlemen," Governor Wolf said, "thank you for coming. We understand that preparing this report has required a huge effort."

Connor and Nathan sat down.

"I want to go over some of the preliminaries so we're all on the same page," Dana said. "But before I begin, is there anything either of you would like to say?"

"Just that we'll cooperate in any way that we can to put this whole thing behind us," Nathan said.

Dana looked at Connor, but he didn't have anything to say at the moment. It was probably better that he didn't say anything, at least right then.

"According to the CDF charter, Lester Brody was found guilty of sedition and mutiny. He was supported by twenty-six senior officers, which included the captains and XOs of three destroyer class vessels. No one here is going to argue that Lester Brody wasn't guilty of what he did and the situation he created. However, what we do have questions about is the handling of the mutineers who surrendered to the Spec Ops teams—those officers Colonel Sean Quinn executed by way of opening an airlock with them inside, exposing them to deep space."

Governor Wolf paused for a moment and Connor waited for her to continue.

"I think I speak for most people here by saying that these actions are highly disturbing."

"I agree," Connor said. "But Colonel Quinn did what he had to do to preserve the chain of command."

Bob Mullins leaned forward. "And this gives him the right to be judge, jury, and executioner?"

"In this case, it does," Connor said. "Without the chain of command in those conditions, you have anarchy. Colonel Quinn was establishing order."

"By murdering twenty-six people?" Mullins said.

Connor leaned forward. "Not twenty-six *people*. These were senior officers in command of military warships. They chose to disobey their commanding officer, and not only that, they tried to blockade them from the mobile space gate. They're not just twenty-six random people," Connor said, and his gaze swept across the Security Council. "These were officers who had access to the most destructive weapons in our arsenal. The equivalent would be if I were here and pointed a weapon at all of you. To go one step further, we'd be in enemy territory with the Krake breathing down our necks. So, you can try to compartmentalize what you think are the important points, but not taking the entire situation into context would be a disservice to everyone involved."

Mullins narrowed his gaze.

"Bob," Dana said.

Mullins leaned back. "I apologize, General Gates. I didn't mean to imply that the deaths of the mutineers should be considered out of context of the entire situation. However, I'd like to highlight the point that the mutineers had been taken into custody. They'd also taken the civilian mutineers, but Colonel Quinn didn't have *them* executed."

"No, he detained them."

"So detaining was an option. Why didn't Colonel Quinn choose that for those officers?" Mullins asked.

"It's in the report. We've questioned Colonel Quinn extensively on that point. In his own words, he'd decided that they were a threat. There was a significant risk that they couldn't be held in custody."

"He didn't think he could hold them, so he had them executed, and both you and General Hayes are okay with this. Do you condone these actions?" Mullins asked.

"This is pure speculation," Nathan said. "You can ask me and General Gates how we would've handled the situation, but we weren't in that situation. We might have an opinion that we can safely offer here, comfortable in this room, but would it have been the right call? We'll never know."

Mullins looked at Connor. "General Gates, I know you have strong opinions about this."

Connor clenched his teeth for a moment and inhaled deeply. "You want to know if I'd have done the same thing if I'd been in command of Trident Battle Group. Despite wearing the same uniform, we're not all the same, but I'm not afraid to answer the question. If I had been in Colonel Quinn's posi-

tion, I would've done the same damn thing. I would've executed the mutineers because it would have saved lives in the long run. Colonel Quinn was
in an extremely hostile situation with an enemy who, in a lot of ways, is
superior to our current capabilities, and that wasn't the time to allow the
chain of command to unravel. We don't make commands by popular vote,
especially not on a warship. You cannot win a war that way. And make no
mistake, this was a war scenario. Nathan is right. This is pure speculation,
but I wanted to give you an answer because I'm not afraid to give you an
answer. I'm not going to hide behind rules and regulations that I helped
create. There are reasons why a commanding officer has that kind of power. I
realize this is difficult for you to understand, and it might appear to be
brutal, but you're not out there."

"You're right. We're not," Mullins said. "What we're trying to determine
is whether or not this was a grievous abuse of power."

"You asked if I'm okay with the situation, and I want all of you to know
that I'm not," Connor said. "I want to know where we failed. You seek to
point a finger at Colonel Quinn, but I want to know how I let an officer like
Brody command a warship. Colonel Quinn's actions were within his rights
as commanding officer of Trident Battle Group."

Mullins regarded Connor for a few moments and then looked at
Governor Wolf.

"General Hayes," Dana said, "I understand your point about being speculative regarding the situation, but given your experience and the facts, how
do you think you would have handled that situation?"

"I would've reasserted control to preserve the chain of command. I
would've used deadly force, but what you really want to know is whether I
would have executed the mutineers that had been taken into custody,"
Nathan said, and paused for a few seconds. "I've tried to put myself in that
situation ever since I learned about it. What would I have done? And more
importantly, did I believe Colonel Quinn had taken appropriate action?

"First, within the letter of the CDF charter, my opinion is that Colonel
Quinn acted within his rights as a commanding officer. But to answer your
other question, I would not have executed the mutineers that I had taken
into custody. I would have detained them, and they would've been brought
back here to be dishonorably discharged and put in prison." A flurry of
comments began from Mullins and the others. "However," Nathan continued, and the room became quiet, "if detaining the mutineers became an
issue, as in they once again attempted to take control of a ship or even the
entire battle group, I would have done exactly as Colonel Quinn had done."

Connor looked at Nathan, and they regarded each other for a few
seconds. Then Connor gave him a crisp nod.

Bob Mullins appeared smug. "Thank you for your answer, General
Hayes. So, the situation we find ourselves in is that we have both of you,
who are the most senior officers in the entire CDF, and each of you would
have handled things differently."

"Congratulations," Connor said. "You just demonstrated that Nathan and I are different people who have fundamental differences in how we approach tough situations. This doesn't change anything."

"On the contrary, this could change everything."

Connor looked at Governor Wolf. "What's he talking about?"

"May I?" Mullins asked, and Governor Wolf nodded. "Our justice system doesn't have the death penalty. Those extreme measures of justice have been abolished for hundreds of years, but it still exists in the military. It's time that we put this under review."

Connor shook his head and looked at Governor Wolf. "The rules and regulations we have in the CDF charter weren't put there because we simply thought it was a good idea. These things were put there because they're built upon established military practices that have been in existence for hundreds of years. They've been proven. They work. At the end of the day, what we'll all need to accept is that this entire situation was an unfortunate consequence," he said and looked at Mullins. "You want to point a finger at Colonel Quinn, and as the commanding officer of Trident Battle Group, that might be appropriate. We, as leaders, are responsible for those under our command. But the fact of the matter is that Lester Brody created the conditions under which Colonel Quinn had to act."

"What other action could Brody have taken? He was a senior officer, and I presume he took the action he thought was necessary," Mullins replied.

"You mean what could Brody have done other than hold civilians as hostages and threaten to open fire on other CDF warships?" Connor asked, his voice like sandpaper rubbing on a bit of a snarl. "He could have recused himself from duty. That would've been a peaceful form of rebellion. Instead, he chose sedition and a grossly negligent act of mutiny," he said, his eyes glittering dangerously. He inhaled deeply and sighed. "In simple terms, he cracked under the pressure."

Governor Wolf regarded him for a few moments. Connor could tell she was conflicted. Some of these issues were hitting close to home. Meredith Cain and the rogue group's activities had occurred under her stewardship. Did this make her ultimately responsible for everything Meredith Cain had done?

"It's important that we review these things," Dana said. "It's how we improve. Maybe nothing will change, but maybe something will. We shouldn't be complacent with practices that have been around for hundreds of years. Sometimes things need to be questioned, reviewed, and considered as to whether those practices still make sense."

"I understand, Governor Wolf," Connor said.

She was doing what she felt she had to do, but what Connor knew was going to happen was that people were going to use these events to assert themselves. They were going to prop Sean up as a dark example. Sean was a war hero and deserved much better. Connor glanced at Bob Mullins and could guess where most of the mudslinging was going to come from.

As the rest of the Security Council meeting went on, Connor had to accept that there could have been no other outcome. Part of him even agreed with what Dana had said. Maybe they should review these policies, but he would never find fault with what Sean had had to do. Perhaps it was because he'd been a soldier longer than anyone here. This situation was a morally gray area, and it irritated Connor that there were going to be people who used that to gain an advantage in their political machinations. What he had to figure out now was how to prevent it from ruining Sean's life.

CHAPTER 32

Sean went with Oriana to visit her brother's grave—the place where his ashes had been buried. She wiped off the top of the headstone and placed some flowers native to the area on top. They had flaming orange petals that surrounded a purple center like a fan. He thought they looked nice.

Oriana felt extremely guilty, believing that if she'd been on New Earth she could have prevented her brother from committing his crimes. She was angry—at her brother, at herself, and even at Sean a little—but he understood. She didn't blame Sean. Not really. She was grieving. He knew what it was like to mourn the loss of someone close. Family. It'd taken him a long time to grieve the loss of his father. He'd never stopped missing his father, and there were times when he found himself wishing he could speak to his father again. How would his father have reacted to some of the things Sean had done? Would he approve? Sean didn't think his father would have, and he could live with that. It was more important that his father understood why Sean had made some of those tough decisions, even if they'd never agree. His understanding would have been enough.

He exhaled softly. Noah had been there for Sean when his father died. He was a good friend. Lars had been there for him too. They were like brothers to him. Sean winced a little.

Lars . . . what happened to you?

He shook his head slightly. He couldn't dwell on Lars right then—another time, but not now. Oriana needed him.

"He did such horrible things. That's what everyone is going to remember about him," Oriana said.

"What do *you* remember about him?"

Oriana shrugged a little. "He was my baby brother. He always had a temper, but he was sweet. He wanted to help people."

"Then remember that. Remember the good things he was and try not to hold onto the bad things he did," Sean said.

They stood there quietly. Sean would be there for as long as she needed him to be. He wished he could think of something else to say, something that would take away her pain, but he knew there wasn't anything. No one could ease her pain. She just needed time.

Later, they returned to the Colonial Administration Building where the Security Council was meeting. They had been meeting there for days, going over the Trident Battle Group report that contained the findings of the CDF investigation. Sean knew they were discussing his actions, and he felt that he should be in the room. Both Connor and Nathan agreed that he didn't need to be there, but Sean couldn't be anywhere else. If he wasn't allowed into the room to defend his actions, he could at least be nearby.

He and Oriana were sitting in the large atrium just inside the entranceway when he noticed somebody walking toward him and saw that it was his mother. She gave them both a hug.

"I'll give you two some time to talk," Oriana said and left them.

His mother looked at him with a bit of sympathy and then glanced in the direction Oriana had left. "Are you together now?"

Sean smiled. "Yes, we are, but I'm sure you don't want to talk about my love life."

"As long as she treats you right, that's all I really care about. Does she make you happy?"

Sean rolled his eyes. Of all the things that were going on right then, that question had caught him off guard. "Yes, she does. Thank you for asking."

They sat down on a nearby bench.

"You may not realize this, but I understand what you're going through," Ashley said.

Sean arched an eyebrow toward her.

"Don't give me that. You think because you're a soldier you're the only career field that deals with life-and-death decisions."

Sean considered it for a few moments. His mother was a medical doctor. "I guess I never really thought about it."

Ashley nodded. "Life-and-death decisions are my forte, and they sometimes get reviewed and scrutinized by everyone for years. So I understand what you're going through, at least in part. It's never easy."

"What I did is putting pressure on the entire CDF," Sean said.

"Sean, don't be foolish. The CDF is always under pressure. You made your decisions based on the situation. You're no stranger to making difficult choices in situations that the best of us might freeze in. Remember, the people who got to come home did so *because* of your leadership and not in spite of it. No matter what happens, never forget that."

"Do you ever second-guess yourself? I keep thinking about whether I should've handled the situation differently."

"Of course I do. It's the tough choices we have to live with that make us do so. Honestly, I'd be worried if you weren't conflicted about what happened."

Sean exhaled deeply. "I regret the lives that were lost, but I still stand by my decision. Does this make me a bad person?"

"I'm not here to judge you, Sean. You're my son, so I'm a bit biased. You have to live with the decisions you've made, and it sounds like you are. You've already answered the question. You wouldn't change anything but you don't like it, and there's nothing wrong with that."

Sean nodded. "I've been thinking about whether I should resign from the CDF."

Ashley looked at him for a few seconds and then shrugged. "That's another question I can't really answer, but I will tell you this: You don't owe anyone anything. This colony survived because of your actions during the Vemus War. Time and time again you've risked your life for this colony. You've risen so far because people trust your leadership. The question is, do you still trust yourself? I trust you. I know Connor does. And your father did. He would've understood what you did."

"But would he have been able to look me in the eye afterward without seeing all the . . ." He'd been about to say "blood on my hands," but his mother knew what he meant.

"Yes," Ashley said. She reached out and took his hands in her own. "Without question. You are our son and we love you."

Sean felt some of the weight he'd been carrying lift just a little bit. "Thank you," he said. "I guess I just need some time to think about it."

"Well, whatever you decide, I'm sure it will be the right decision."

CHAPTER 33

The early morning hours at the Colonial Administration Building were dark and quiet. Connor had gotten only a few hours of sleep, but he was restless. He could have remained at his quarters on the CDF base, but he knew he had to come here anyway for another meeting with the Security Council.

His footsteps echoed across the vast atrium just past the entrance of the building. Wallscreens were active, showing various scenes of the colony from when they'd first arrived to the sprawling cities they'd built. There were even several wallscreens showing CDF soldiers. Connor walked over to them and gazed at the various portrayals. He was about a quarter of the way around the atrium when Bob Mullins spotted him.

Connor glanced at the advisor. "I'm surprised you don't just sleep in one of the meeting rooms in the upper levels."

"It wouldn't be the first time," Mullins replied.

They were alone in the atrium and probably the whole building.

"Don't let me interrupt you, General. I'll leave you to it," Mullins said and began walking away.

Connor watched him go for a few moments. "What do you really want from me?"

Mullins stopped and turned around, frowning.

"I might be guessing, or let's call it careful speculation," Connor said. "You want to review the CDF charter. The mutiny. There isn't a legal case there. Even if something changes, it won't affect Sean. You can't change the law and then retroactively prosecute someone."

Mullins nodded. "You're right; we can't do that."

"But you can ruin Sean's reputation. What I can't figure out is why. Is it because of me?"

"What he did was reprehensible," Mullins said, but then his gaze softened. "But then again, so is war."

"I respect that you want to improve things, but do it without riling the public into a frenzy. Those kinds of decisions should be based on good judgment rather than anxiety," Connor said and closed the distance between them. "So, I figure there's something you're angling for."

"I work in the governor's office. There is always something I'm angling for. You think you're different than me, but you're not. Otherwise, you wouldn't be here."

Connor snorted bitterly. "So, we both have a healthy work ethic."

Mullins looked away, considering. "You're convinced that the Krake are going to find us. They're going to come to New Earth, and we need to be prepared."

Connor frowned and then nodded.

"Well, it just so happens that I agree with you."

Connor's eyes widened a little. "Then why are you working against me?"

Mullins shook his head. "Not necessarily against you. We just have a different opinion on how to prepare for the threat."

Connor glanced at one of the wallscreens. It showed an image of the *Ark* in orbit around New Earth. He looked back at Mullins. "This is about setting up another colony, isn't it?"

Mullins twitched his head to the side in a small nod. "A backup site. Just in case. Continuity of the species and all that."

Connor pressed his lips together slightly. "What does this have to do with me?"

Mullins let out a small chuckle. "I need your support. I won't gain any traction for establishing a new colony if I don't have your support."

It was Connor's turn to chuckle. "I don't see—"

"There it is," Mullins interrupted. "Let me put it this way. If I were to get your support, then the new colony would stand a much better chance of getting off the ground."

"Why didn't you just ask me?"

"This *is* me asking."

Connor shook his head. He was finding it hard to believe what he was hearing.

"You don't believe me, I can tell," Mullins said. "Fine. I do believe the CDF charter needs to be reviewed and challenged. This will take time, and there will be people whose performance will be highlighted as examples of our core values and of what we should strive to improve."

Connor narrowed his gaze, knowing that Mullins was referring to Sean. "You're proposing a compromise."

Mullins nodded. "Yes, neither of us gets exactly what we want, but we each get something. You get to save your protégé, and I get your support to establish a secondary colony. What do you say?"

Connor pursed his lips, thinking about all the possible outcomes of compromising with someone like Mullins. Alternatively, he could spend weeks or even months in meetings defending the CDF charter instead of devoting himself to the important task of defending the colony from the Krake. He looked at Mullins, who waited with all the patience of a spider. They clashed like water on flame. Connor thought about the work that would be involved in establishing a small colony on another world, but the request wasn't unreasonable.

"I think we can work something out," Connor said.

———

"I'm sorry for all the trouble this has caused," Sean said.

Connor and Sean were standing in Connor's office at the CDF base in Sierra. "That's the last time I want to hear that from you. Stop apologizing. I mean it."

Sean nodded. "What happens now?"

"We put all this behind us and focus on what's important. But I will say this: Over ninety percent of the soldiers that were part of Trident Battle Group would serve under you again."

Sean frowned and looked away for a moment.

"Brody was the minority, and sometimes the minority has the loudest voice. They don't represent what everyone is thinking. Remember that. You're a good soldier, a good leader. I'm proud of you. I don't think it's much of a stretch to say that one day you'll be a general."

Sean's eyes widened and he almost shook his head. "I appreciate that, but I don't know . . . if staying in the CDF is what's best for me."

"I don't care; I need you."

Now Sean did shake his head, and he smiled a little.

"You're a soldier to your bones. It's part of you just like it's part of me. So we both got beat up a little bit. We can take it because that's who we are. We can make the tough choices, but we can also evaluate our decisions to make sure we're still on the right path. Do you understand what I mean?"

"Yes."

"Good," Connor said and used his implants to activate the nearby wallscreen.

The entire wall became active. The top showed the words of the Krake hierarchy. Just below them was a label that said "Overseers?" The lights dimmed in the office, showing the full breadth of the data they'd gathered about the Krake.

"This screen just shows us what's on the surface—what we know of the Krake and how they operate. This one includes the Ovarrow and contains all the interactions we've had with them so far," Connor said and gestured toward the adjacent wall, activating a third wallscreen. "And these are things the Ovarrow believe they know about the Krake. We've been trying to analyze what's fact and what's conjecture."

"That's difficult to say because the Krake control what the Ovarrow know about them," Sean said.

Connor nodded. "That's true. There's a lot more information we have to go through, but I figured you'd want to see this."

Connor watched as Sean took a good look at both wallscreens and all the data on them.

"Somewhere, buried amid all the evidence we've gathered here on New Earth and possibly on some other world, is a way to stop the Krake. And don't doubt for a second that they can be stopped."

Sean frowned. "Aurang said the Krake had never encountered anyone like us on any of the other Ovarrow worlds. I think it's that kind of challenge that's going to draw them to us."

Connor nodded. "You're probably not wrong about that. Now, all we need to do is find out where they live and stop them from coming here."

"Just that?" Sean said. "So, you're saying this is going to take a while?"

Connor grinned. "Maybe a little."

INSURGENT

CHAPTER 1

Connor entered the command center where soldiers were actively working at their stations, their holoscreens gleaming with an amber outline in the dim light. They were comlinked to the teams out in the field, and the energy had ratcheted up with all the anticipation of a major operation about to go off the rails. He strode past the phalanx of workstations and headed directly for the holotank.

Captain O'Brien saluted him. "General Gates."

"Sitrep."

"The 7th Ranger Company has taken up support positions near the planetary arch," O'Brien said.

In the center of the holotank, an image of a Krake arch was displayed deep in the jungles of Kuret. The New Earth candidate planet, or NEC in this alternate universe, orbited closer to the star, which made for much higher planetary temperatures. The planet was nearly bursting with life—what Connor liked to think of as extreme vegetation. Almost every land surface was covered in some kind of jungle. It was sweltering and humid, and there was no shortage of rainfall. There was also no shortage of concealment on this planet, and the Colonial Defense Force would use every advantage it had.

"Good," Connor said. "The briefing said that Monin was impatient to begin."

"Yes, General, that is correct. The Gesora are anxious to take control of the Krake arch to eliminate the chance that reinforcements can be called."

Connor didn't doubt it. The CDF had been conducting clandestine operations on this planet for four months. They'd chosen it because the Ovarrow in this universe were prime candidates to rebel against the Krake.

The Krake had hidden their presence here as best they could, choosing to manipulate the Ovarrow by controlling the higher levels of government. It was a tactic that had been reported from other worlds they'd observed. However, one of the things that made moving forward with this partial coup d'état a priority was the lack of a space gate in the star system. Uncharacteristically, the Krake had restricted their activities to the planetary surface. Intelligence analysts theorized that perhaps there were limits to how many simultaneous operations the Krake could conduct across the multiple universes in which they had a presence. Regardless of the Krake reasoning for such a limited presence on this particular planet, Connor planned to exploit it and hopefully gain another ally to fight against the Krake.

The CDF wasn't limited to the single arch that was displayed in the holotank. They had multiple arches and space gates to traverse between universes, and they'd deployed a stealth satellite system that had been actively monitoring the planet for the past ninety days. The system currently had its minimum of three satellites in use, which was enough to cover the NEC. The satellites were equipped with subspace communication systems, which allowed for transmissions among them, and although line of sight was still a factor in observing the enemy, it no longer impacted their communications capabilities. For some reason, the Krake had chosen to ignore the high ground, and the war doctrine of any human military confirmed that he who controlled the high ground controlled the war.

"What is the status of the Qompiry?"

Captain O'Brien used the holotank controls to switch the view to an Ovarrow city. Dark, towering obelisks, shimmering like obsidian, were sheathed in a bronze metallic alloy at the tips. In the middle of the city were domed edifices similar in architectural design to those built by the Ovarrow they'd encountered on New Earth.

"The Qompiry's position at the capital is here," O'Brien said, and a waypoint flashed. These were the insurgency that had been rebelling against the Krake for years, which was an arduous undertaking since the Krake hid their presence on the planet. "Lieutenant Wade's platoon," he continued, "is on the north side of the city, and the Warlord's First has a platoon of Mekaal soldiers with Yerid's rebels."

The Mekaal was the military unit of the Ovarrow from New Earth. They'd been partnering with the CDF over the past year, participating in off-world operations in alternate universes.

Connor nodded. "Cerot should be able to keep Yerid in line."

The Qompiry was a rebellious group of thieves that had resisted the Krake social order almost since the beginning. They were hotheaded and immature but had conducted multiple operations, thwarting the Krake as often as they could. Connor wondered why the Krake had chosen to conceal their identity here while working out in the open on other worlds. He thought it must have something to do with the experiment they'd sanctioned for this world.

The Krake had done an excellent job of dividing the dominant nations of Ovarrow on this planet. They'd utilized virus outbreaks to cripple the Gesora's economy, and they preyed upon their religious beliefs in a way that had shaped almost all public discourse into shouting matches, fostering a culture of contempt. This had been easy to manipulate and exploit, and had later given rise to skirmish wars.

The CDF had managed to convince critical Gesora leaders from multiple provinces that the major events in their recent history were the result of Krake manipulation. These select few leaders were privy to the knowledge that the Krake were an entirely different species, but their operation today would make this knowledge open to the general public. It was an all-or-nothing effort. They had to take control of the arch, as well as the capital, where the Krake had the most influence. Hopefully, this operation would be the catalyst to free the Gesora from a Krake experiment that had been ongoing for nearly seventy years.

"Captain O'Brien," Corporal Taylor said, "I have a comlink request from Yerid."

"Engage encryption protocols and vocalizers," O'Brien said.

The Ovarrow in this universe weren't aware of humans, and it was the CDF's top priority to keep their involvement a secret. To this end, they'd used Ovarrow from New Earth to help convince others of their cause. Connor knew the Krake were hunting for humans, and if they were going to operate in alternate universes, they needed to keep their presence there a secret. As far as the Krake were concerned, this was just another rebellious Ovarrow group operating under the Krake's radar but causing trouble just the same.

O'Brien glanced at Connor, who bobbed his head once.

"Mekaal COMCENT, this is Yerid. The Qompiry are in position. How long do the Gesora intend for us to wait before they reach their target?"

"Confirm Qompiry are in position, Yerid. Hold tight. We are waiting for confirmation from the Gesora," O'Brien said.

"We can't stay here," Yerid said. "My teams will be compromised if we do. We have to go. Tell the Gesora that we're beginning our assault on the capital."

Connor heard both the commitment and the urgency in the Ovarrow's voice, even though it was coming through a translator. He could hardly blame them, but at the same time, he needed them to wait.

"Yerid," Connor said, "the only way this operation is going to work is if both you and the Gesora attack at the same time. If the Krake at the capital figure out what's going on, they'll alert the soldiers at the arch. If that happens, they'll bring the defenses online and possibly call in reinforcements."

There were a few moments of silence before Yerid replied. "Warlord Gates, I know you are aware of what the Krake have done here. Today is a day of reckoning. Today, we take back what's ours. The Qompiry will attack now. Yerid out."

The comlink severed, and O'Brien shook his head.

"Sir," Corporal Taylor said, "Lieutenant Wade has confirmed that the

Qompiry are advancing on the capital. Stealth recon drone surveillance shows thousands of Qompiry soldiers infiltrating the tunnel network under the capital."

O'Brien's lips pressed into a grim twist, and he looked at Connor. "What are your orders, General?"

Connor stared at the aerial view of the capital city in the holotank. It showed the positions of the CDF platoon, as well as the Qompiry taskforces that were moving into the capital. "Tell Lieutenant Wade that his orders are to observe and advise Yerid and the Qompiry soldiers. They'll need to assist them by disrupting all communications from the capital."

The original plan had called for Lieutenant Wade and his platoon to keep their position outside of the capital city, but in order to disable communications from the capital, they'd need to move in.

"Tell him we're sending air support," Connor said. So much for sitting this one out.

O'Brien gave Connor a sidelong glance.

"What is it, Captain?" Connor asked.

"Captain Samson said you'd find a way to see some action, General."

"He did, did he?" Connor replied. Samson had been part of the original Ghost Platoon that Connor had led before being shanghaied onto the colony ship that ended up at New Earth. "What else did he say?"

"He told us not to get too comfortable, sir. We have two Hellcats on standby. I'll see to it that they're ready to go," O'Brien said.

The young captain stepped away from the holotank and began giving orders to several soldiers nearby.

Connor opened a comlink to Samson, and the Spec Ops captain answered almost immediately. "I hear you're spreading lies about me."

Samson grinned a little. "What happened?"

"Yerid couldn't suppress his need to get his gun off, so the Qompiry have started their assault on the capital. I've ordered Wade to move in and disable communications from the capital, but it's going to be a close thing."

"Understood, General. I'll let Monin know. To be honest, I'm surprised they've worked together as long as they have. They don't trust each other at all," Samson said.

Connor took control of the holotank and switched the aerial view back to the arch. "It's not all their fault. This is what happens when you foster a culture of contempt. It's hard to trust anyone when you've been taught all your life that someone else's ideas aren't to even be considered, and anyone who thinks differently is branded a traitor."

"If you say so, sir."

"Can you reach the arch in time?"

"We can if I can get your permission to showcase some of our capabilities," Samson replied.

The CDF soldiers were all in the latest Nexstar combat suits but had slowed down to keep pace with the Gesora soldiers. The Gesora were at home in the jungle and could traverse its terrain with ease, but the Nexstar combat suit leveled the playing field considerably. The onboard combat AI assisted the wearer to efficiently handle any terrain, be it terrestrial or low-gravity situations. What Samson was requesting was permission to remove the restrictions that were in place to help them blend in.

"Understood, and permission granted, but don't get too far ahead of them. You still need the Gesora. You can't fight this war without them."

"Acknowledged, General," Samson said, and the comlink went dark.

Over the past year, they'd conducted clandestine operations, but this was the biggest. They needed a mission success for this effort; otherwise, the Colonial Security Council would order them to stop. They'd never find the Krake home world if they stopped exploring the alternate universes. And a successful mission would also mean that they didn't have to fight the Krake alone if they could find allies along the way.

Connor glanced at the holotank and rested his hands on the edge. He heard the high-pitched whine of the Hellcat's engines powering up and felt a surge of adrenaline course through him in anticipation. Breathing in deeply, he sighed and turned to O'Brien. "Captain, you're to support Lieutenant Wade with disabling communications in the capital. You're cleared for weapons-free."

For half a second, O'Brien's gaze widened. The CDF captain had expected Connor to join them. They'd all expected it, but Connor had made a promise that he wouldn't always be the one to take all the risks. The CDF soldiers were the best-trained military he'd ever seen. Connor had made them that way.

"Understood, General."

"Good hunting, Captain," Connor said.

CHAPTER 2

Lieutenant Thomas Wade of the 7th Ranger Company, 3rd Platoon Leader, alerted his unit that they'd be moving out. Yerid, the leader of the Qompiry, was moving forward with the attack. Given what the Krake had done to these Ovarrow, Wade couldn't blame them. He'd want revenge too. The Qompiry had been hunted by the very Ovarrow they hoped to save from the Krake. The group of Ovarrow that had become the Qompiry was composed of multiple factions who were considered noncompliant. They were the outliers and the rebellious few who'd chosen not to bury their heads in the sand. They'd chosen to resist, and Wade had come to respect that. He'd conducted multiple operations in alternate universes over the past year, and the one thing he'd learned about the Krake was that they were ruthlessly efficient in the way they carried out their experiments.

The fifty soldiers in his platoon were outfitted with Nexstar combat suits, with four of them configured for heavy weapons.

Wade gestured for Sergeant Mason to come over to him. "Yerid is pressing on with the attack, and we can't allow the Krake to send a warning to their base. Looks like the Gesora are running late."

"Getting into the capital won't be a problem. It's getting out that will be," Mason said.

"We've got air support, so they'll be our evacuation as well," Wade replied.

Mason grunted. "We'll need to look for a couple of alternatives in case our air support gets held up."

"Oh, ye of little faith."

"Negative, sir. I just have an aversion to getting caught with my pants down."

Wade agreed.

Gesora regulars operated security checkpoints throughout the city, and there were strongholds with a significant troop presence at each. They were strategically placed within close proximity to the capitol building, which had its own direct-action force that maintained a presence there. Across many Ovarrow cities, insurgent activity in response to the Gesora's militaristic regime had prompted the buildup of military forces.

Wade knew they'd be engaging Gesora soldiers who either were unaware or simply didn't believe their political leaders were Krake infiltrators or were being controlled by the Krake. The Ovarrow in this universe were being manipulated into fighting a civil war. The goal for the CDF was to prevent the civil war by initiating surgical strikes to change regimes and expose the Krake. Presumably, these actions would incur less loss of life than an all-out war. Wade hoped that was true. On New Earth, they'd seen the remnants of the devastation from countless wars the Ovarrow had fought among each other and eventually with the Krake. They had to stop the same from occurring here, as well as possibly gaining a powerful ally to fight the Krake.

The Ovarrow had been on a heightened state of alert for years. Skirmish wars had become the norm, and they were prepared for a frontal assault. Meanwhile, the Qompiry rebels had created a path by linking various tunnels under the city that would bring them close to the capitol building.

"We need a better vantage point," Mason said. "From there, we can put some sharpshooters up to take out whatever the Krake have on the roof."

"Agreed," Wade replied and peered at the city, looking for a good location for his snipers. "Send Dixon and his squad. I've marked a few waypoints for them."

Mason opened a comlink and relayed Wade's orders. Then he looked at Wade and nodded.

"Let's move out," Wade said.

The 3rd Platoon was stationed to the north of the capitol on the outskirts of the city. They couldn't just waltz down the street, so they'd commandeered a couple of Ovarrow ground transport vehicles, which they loaded up and set off in. They wouldn't reach the capitol, especially once the Qompiry began their assault, but at least they could penetrate some of the perimeter before they had to stop and fight.

Wade rode in the front, and Mason had control of the vehicle.

"Do we know how many Krake are in there?" Mason asked, jutting his chin up a little.

"Not exactly. Best guess is about forty of them, but they're not soldiers. They're administrators, politicians. They probably have some security details, but we need to keep them from warning their base."

"Understood," Mason said.

They headed to the interior of the city, making it through one of the security checkpoints. Wade had several reconnaissance drones patrolling and saw where the Qompiry had engaged the Gesora military that was defending the capitol. Those soldiers didn't know they were fighting for the wrong side.

The Qompiry leveraged smaller squads to distract the defenders, and then their main fighting force engaged.

The Gesora regulars reacted quickly.

"We've been made," one of the CDF soldiers said from the back of the vehicle. Wade turned around and saw that the Gesora regulars manning the security checkpoint were emphatically pointing in their direction.

"We've got incoming," Mason said.

Ovarrow howler missiles launched from the capitol and sped off in multiple directions, with several heading right for the CDF soldiers. The howlers' promise of death and destruction screeched across the sky, and the CDF soldiers abandoned their vehicles only moments before the missiles slammed into them. The platoon of armored CDF soldiers was engulfed in flame for a few moments before the explosion cleared, but they'd gotten far enough away that the Nexstar combat suits had withstood the force of the explosion.

"We've got eyes on us," Mason said.

"Stick close to the buildings," Wade said.

"It was that damn checkpoint. We should have taken them out."

Wade accessed the stealth recon drone feeds and saw that the Qompiry soldiers were emerging from the underground sewer access points. They were closer to the capitol than his platoon was.

They made their way closer to the capitol and stopped at a complex of domed buildings. Wade ordered his snipers to the tops of the buildings to survey the area. The Qompiry were now leading the ground assault on a direct path toward the capitol.

"Lieutenant, I have a target. Krake tech on the west side of the roof," Sergeant Dixon said.

Wade accessed the targeting coordinates and peered at the video feed. A metallic cylinder had emerged from one of the air conditioning units on the roof. There was a flash of purple light as something spun inside.

"Take it out, Sergeant."

The two sharpshooters opened fire with explosive rounds, and more of the metallic cylinders emerged onto the roof.

"I need heavy ordnance. We need to fire on that capitol now," Wade said. He knew the Krake would notice this attack because he was using weaponry that wasn't available to the Ovarrow.

The reconnaissance drone shrieked an alert, which appeared on Wade's internal heads-up display. He cursed, and Mason looked at him question-ingly. "Krake comm signal detected. We need to move, *now*."

———

Samson informed Monin, a warlord of the Gesora, that the Qompiry were beginning their assault on the capitol. Monin began to bellow orders to his Ovarrow soldiers, and they hastened their approach to the arch complex.

Samson had deployed multiple combat drones. It was easy for them to keep out of sight with so much vegetation in this godforsaken jungle. He couldn't wait to get back to New Earth. He never thought he'd have a thought like that, given how much he hated humanity's current home. He missed Earth, and that would never change. He was resigned to the fact that no matter how much time passed, he would always miss the home he'd lost and the people he'd never see again. They were always in the back of his mind. It had been fifteen years since he'd come out of the stasis pod aboard the *Ark*—*the* day everything changed—but Samson banished those thoughts. It was ancient history. He had a job to do, and there were Krake to kill.

The Krake didn't have a large operation on this planet, but they were always well fortified. The arch gateway was only fifty meters from end to end —medium-sized, which was good for transporting small vehicles and as many Krake soldiers as required. The Krake relied on automated defenses that could kill humans and Ovarrow alike. As tough as the Nexstar combat suits were, they couldn't withstand the high-powered particle beams from heavy defense turrets. Krake soldiers used particle beam rifles, which were precise and lethal. They could penetrate CDF combat suits in seconds; however, Krake armor was actually inferior to the CDF's, which gave them a bit of an advantage. The CDF employed a combination of kinetic weaponry, but they'd also included plasma rifles that had been reverse engineered from the Vemus weapons.

Lieutenant Layton opened a comlink to Samson. "Their defenses are coming online. I think the jig is up. They know we're coming, Captain."

"That's it," Samson said. "No more sneaking around. I want you to take out your first-priority targets, then move on to the second. We'll meet up in the middle."

He opened a comlink to Monin. "The Krake know we're here. We need to attack now."

"We are almost in position," Monin said.

Samson cut off the comlink, and Cerot came to his side. The young Ovarrow was eager to fight. Samson had been working with Mekaal soldiers in a joint task force to engage the Krake for the past year.

"The Mekaal are ready, Captain," Cerot said.

The CDF had enhanced the Mekaal's weapons and armor, which had been over two hundred years old. Even now, they weren't on the same level as the CDF, but it was much better than what they'd been using. They needed every advantage they could get.

There were several squads of Krake soldiers near the arch, which was coming online. CDF combat drones opened fire, and the Krake soldiers scattered for cover. Krake defensive turrets began firing at them, mainly targeting the Gesora. No doubt the Krake sensors were better at detecting the Ovarrow. They'd detect the CDF soldiers once they were closer.

Over one hundred and forty heavily armed CDF special forces soldiers closed in on the Krake installation from multiple directions. The Krake had chosen this location because of its isolation from the Ovarrow. That meant

Samson could fight this battle using all the weapons in his arsenal, and the Krake wouldn't know what had hit 'em.

———

Connor stood in front of the holotank, monitoring the attack on the capitol. A secondary section showed the Krake arch installation where the battle had begun in earnest. The Qompiry had successfully breached the defenses of the capitol, and the attack was proceeding just as he expected. The Hellcats were providing air support, and they were almost inside the capitol. There was a lot of confusion as the Qompiry engaged the Gesora strongholds for the purpose of keeping them distracted and out of the main battle. The CDF had sustained some losses, but so far, they'd accounted for their dead. There would be nothing left for the Ovarrow to find or the Krake to make use of. The Krake couldn't learn that humans had had a hand in this rebellion.

Connor brought up the drone video feeds of the attack on the arch gateway complex. Krake defensive towers were mainly targeting the Gesora, and Samson had abandoned any pretext of concealing their attack method. They could've destroyed the arch, but Connor had given orders that it was to be taken intact. It wasn't enough to keep the Krake from this planet. They needed the Ovarrow to be able to control that arch so it could be used in the future.

The Krake soldiers adapted quickly, considering that they'd been taken by surprise despite the warning they'd received, and they'd managed to get their defenses online. The Krake had been operating on this planet for nearly seventy years, and they'd had no indication that anyone knew the location of their base. They also hadn't expected that someone else could open a gateway to this planet. This gave Connor and the CDF a much-needed advantage, and they'd seized the opportunity to oust the Krake from power with minimal loss of life, but Connor knew this was only the beginning. They'd basically sparked civil war among the Gesora and the Qompiry. The fighting in the capital was still going on, but soon they'd call for a cease-fire. Monin had survived, and Samson had his combat engineers disabling the archway. They'd learned a lot about the arch, particularly how to disable it without destroying it. This meant the arch could be used at the behest of the Ovarrow on this planet, which was what Connor wanted. It was also what they needed to accomplish when they found the Krake home world.

CHAPTER 3

A CDF Hellcat touched down on an elevated landing platform at the Krake base of operations. The deactivated arch gateway was no more than a hundred meters away, and the dark metal glistened with moisture from a recent rainfall.

Connor and Captain O'Brien walked down the loading ramp and were greeted by Sergeant Foster, who snapped a salute at Connor. "General Gates, if you'll follow me, I'll take you to Captain Samson."

Connor returned the salute. "Lead on, Sergeant."

Troop carrier transports were landing in the area, and CDF soldiers were climbing aboard. The battle for the arch had been won, and it would now be turned over to the Gesora.

Foster led Connor and O'Brien to the Gesora encampment just outside the Krake base. Connor glanced up at the arch. The data on his helmet's heads-up display showed that the arch was sixteen meters tall. He'd seen much larger arches, as well as massive space gates. Despite the significant Krake presence on this planet, Connor believed that this was a minor effort on the Krake's part. But it was a start. They had liberated other minor systems like these in alternate universes, but Connor had to wonder how many they could free before the Krake finally caught on to what they were doing.

Gesora soldiers watched them as they walked past various staging areas where wounded soldiers were being cared for. A short distance away, the Gesora soldiers gathered their dead in preparation to return home. This battle had cost them, but it was one they'd needed to fight. At least these Ovarrow now had a chance at a future free of the Krake.

Foster led them to a command tent where Samson and Cerot were speaking with Monin. There were several Gesora soldiers nearby, listening intently. The Gesora warlord looked at Connor and noticed the deference given to him by the CDF soldiers in the area.

"Warlord Monin," Connor said, "congratulations on your victory."

The warlord from the jungle world regarded Connor with cinnamon-colored eyes. He had vertical pupils that looked more feline than reptilian, but his brown, pebbled skin was akin to that of a reptile. Pointy protrusions stemmed from his shoulders and elbows. The Ovarrow were bipedal, lean and strong, but they had a bit of a stoop that made their heads bob when they walked.

"This victory wouldn't have been possible without you and your soldiers," Monin said. "In fact, if we hadn't listened to you all those months ago, we wouldn't be here today," he said and looked at the dead soldiers being gathered before turning back to Connor. "Their sacrifice will be honored."

"Don't forget the Qompiry," Connor said.

Monin's features tightened. "Yes, of course. There's still some fighting going on at the capitol. I've sent a data burst to the Gesora regulars requesting a cease-fire. We'll be journeying there soon, and I'd like it if you'd join us there."

They'd managed to capture some of the Krake at the capitol. The CDF soldiers had already turned control of the building over to the Qompiry and the Gesora regulars they'd convinced to help them. However, there were still militant groups fighting in the city. Connor thought they were Krake sympathizers who'd been activated when the capital fell, and they couldn't rule out that some of the Krake might have escaped, but their options would be limited without access to their arch gateway. Connor expected there'd be more urban fighting the Gesora would have to contend with in the coming months before the dust settled and they could start rebuilding.

"You have all the evidence you need to convince the rest of the Gesora of what the Krake have been doing here," Connor said.

The Krake had conducted many experiments over the years, including facilitating the "discovery" of certain technology and biological weapons to manipulate powerful nations against each other. They'd also had significant control and influence over the Ovarrow economy, which seemed to the Gesora as being wielded at random, but with the help of the CDF, the Gesora had been able to identify the artificial nature of key events that the Krake were directly responsible for.

"We can't stay here any longer," Connor said. "We need to move on. There are other universes out there that need our help, and we should continue searching for the Krake home universe. You'll be able to help with that once things stabilize here," Connor said.

Monin looked at Cerot for a few seconds, considering, and the Mekaal soldier returned his gaze in kind. Then Monin looked at Connor. "He is Ovarrow, although not from this world," Monin said, gesturing toward Cerot. "But I think you are something different, despite the Warlord First's insistence that you are the same."

The CDF soldiers wore their Nexstar combat suits with the helmets fully engaged. There was no way for Monin or any other Gesora soldier to see their faces, and suspicion didn't mean confirmation as far as Connor was concerned.

"What would you like to know?" he asked.

"I want to see the faces of my allies."

"I can't do that," Connor said. "It's as much for our protection as it is for yours. We have restrictions on what we can share with you. Just accept that we're hunting for the Krake home world, and when we find it, I hope you'll remember what we've done here today. We'll need your help in the future."

Monin looked up at the arch and the equipment the CDF had installed so they could control it. "That equipment—the controller— will render the arch useless."

"It will give you control of when to use it," Connor said.

"But it won't stop the Krake from coming here."

Connor shook his head. "They could use a different arch from an alternate universe to open another gateway to this world, and you're right to be concerned about that. We have the same risk on our home world. You'll have to try to monitor for this as best you can, but you control this arch now. You'll be able to contact us through it, and eventually other Ovarrow."

Monin regarded Connor for a few moments. "What if it's decided that the arch is to be destroyed? Ever since we learned about the Krake, there are some who believe that isolation is the best defense against them. Does knowing this affect your perception of us?"

"We won't regret helping you if you decide to destroy the arch, but don't make any rash decisions. Destroying this arch would only remove your ability to engage the real enemy. As I said before, we'll need your help when it comes time to deal with the Krake where they live. That's the only way this cycle ends and all of us can be free of them. I hope you can convey that to your leaders."

Connor was silent for a few seconds. Monin was conflicted about them and Connor couldn't blame him, but they couldn't reveal themselves at this time. "And don't forget what the Qompiry have sacrificed for this. You must overcome your biases against them if you're to have a future."

Monin looked unconvinced and then seemed to reconsider. "To contact you, we must use the arch, but this gateway won't be to your home world. Is this correct?"

"Yes, that's right. The risk to our world would be too great if the information fell into the wrong hands. However, we do maintain a presence on a world you can contact through the arch. The communication protocols you've been given work both ways—for us to confirm your identity and for you to confirm ours. If we fail to meet any of the challenge protocols, it means this world has been compromised by the Krake, and I'd advise you to sever all communications from it. Eventually, we'd reestablish contact with you ourselves or through one of our other allies. I assure you that you are not alone in this fight with the Krake. Try to remember this," Connor said.

"You have given me no reason to doubt you. You've gone above and beyond what any ally to the Gesora and the Qompiry have done in the past. Our fight is not yet over. There are factions sympathetic to the Krake that need to be rooted out, but I'll do my very best to make sure all Ovarrow know we had help—*your* help," Monin said and paused for a few moments. "You said you had other allies from alternate universes. Will we be able to contact them?"

"Yes, you will, but for their protection we're not sharing their information with you today. They've faced the challenges that are ahead of you. As time goes on, we'll bring you further into our operations against the Krake, and this includes sharing other Ovarrow who have proven they will fight," Connor said. He could tell that Monin didn't appreciate being kept in the dark, but it was for the best. The Gesora had to prove themselves first.

"Perhaps we'll search for alternate universes to explore ourselves," Monin said.

"The arch belongs to all of you. I would strongly advise you to use caution if you start exploring other universes, and remember that the gateway works both ways," Connor replied.

They left the Gesora command tent and headed back toward the troop carriers. After they climbed aboard and were heading to their own egress point, Connor looked at Samson.

"You're unusually quiet."

Samson bobbed his head to the side. "The Krake had a few surprises for us, and I think there might be more. I'm just wondering if they'll still be here with Monin in command when we check in with them a month or two from now."

"It's not a perfect system, but it's what we have to work with."

Cerot nodded. The Ovarrow had been listening nearby and had adopted the human custom of nodding their heads in acknowledgment. It had become much more natural for the Ovarrow as time went on.

"Now they have a fighting chance. It was worse for us back home, especially at the end. At least the factions here are still willing to communicate with one another," Cerot said.

For as young as Cerot appeared to be, he had witnessed many horrors before going into stasis. He had seen the collapse of his civilization and the measures they'd used to survive. It was easy for some people to forget, but not Connor. He had helped study Ovarrow ruins on New Earth and was familiar with just how bad things had gotten before they'd gone into stasis. However, unearthing the archaeological record and living through it were two different things.

CHAPTER 4

Sadoon stepped off the transit platform, and the arch gateway towered above him. It had been many months since he'd been allowed to return to Quadiri. The demands on his time as sector chief were such that didn't allow for traveling beyond once a year. He glanced at the night sky overhead and saw Quadiri's sister planet Ovren. Ovren had once been a living world, but thousands of years ago, in the first wars, the Quadiri military had vanquished the Ovren invaders. Even without enhanced eyes, he could see the pale green of Ovren's poisonous atmosphere. Many Krake looked at Ovren's demise with dignified pride. And why shouldn't they? The Krake had not been the aggressor, but they had learned early on the need to be the victors.

Sadoon walked over to a waiting transport vehicle where the automated systems captured his credentials and payment. The metallic door opened with a quiet hiss, and he climbed aboard. It was empty inside. The automated systems controlled the vehicle and would take him to his destination. The transport vehicle's engines activated, and it lifted into the air, swung around, and sped in the direction of the sprawling metropolis. After many months of waiting, the overseers had finally deigned to meet with him to discuss a new research project with a primary focus on the Humans and their Colonial Defense Force. As sector chief of an R&D installation on an Ovarrow world, he had proposed to end the project he'd been working on early so he could pursue something he believed was far more important. The Humans had powerful weapons, and he later learned that their warships had engaged the Krake Space Navy on multiple occasions. Given how much destruction these Humans had caused, Sadoon thought he would've been granted a great deal of leeway when it came to finding them. The Krake were a vast empire that spanned multiple universes, and until recently, they'd encountered only Ovarrow on other planets.

Sadoon knew he wasn't the only Krake interested in being granted the rights to a research project focused on the Humans. There were multiple military leaders interested as well, particularly those of the Krake Space Navy. For months, he'd waited for a summons from the overseers in response to his numerous petitions to run the project.

Quadiri was home to vast cities that took up precisely forty percent of the continents. Any further expansion would impact the planet's climate and was therefore forbidden. Expansion onto other worlds was limited, and breeding was tightly controlled. Only Ovarrow bred uncontrolled, which was characteristic of such a juvenile species.

The transport vehicle flew over the city, and its azure glow seemed to invigorate him. Krake architecture was built not only for the purpose it was designed but also for aesthetics. Nothing Sadoon had ever seen had come close to Quadiri's splendor.

The transport vehicle landed on a designated platform, and Sadoon climbed out. He stepped onto a moving walkway, which ushered him inside the administration building where there was no shortage of Krake. The fact that the overseers had been willing to meet with him did convey a level of acknowledgment few Krake achieved.

Sadoon had studied every scrap of evidence he could find about the Humans since his own encounter with them. He remembered their remark- ably resilient mechanical armor and the Ovarrow they traveled with. Sadoon hadn't been able to identify the universe they'd come from. His scientists had been able to extract useful data from DNA samples from the Ovarrow but not the Humans. The Humans' mechanical armor self-destructed when they died, destroying all evidence of them down to the microscopic level. They were clever, worthy of the Krake's attention, and Sadoon wanted to be the Krake to win this contract.

Once he was inside the building, a message was sent to his comlink, acknowledging his arrival with instructions directing him where he needed to go. He had expected to meet with the overseers in their primary audience chamber, but that wasn't what his orders contained. He was directed to a solitary room used for secure communications. This was little more than a capsule with room enough for only him. Sadoon stepped inside as the door shut behind him. His identification was confirmed, and the room darkened. A few seconds later, the walls of the room became transparent, and he found himself standing in the middle of the audience chamber of the overseers. Sadoon knew that in the actual chamber, he appeared as a holographic image.

In front of him was a high table where seven ancient Krake overseers sat. They were many hundreds of years old. The overseers lived the longest among the Krake.

"Sector Chief Sadoon," said the Krake from the center of the table.

Their identification appeared on Sadoon's internal heads-up display, and he nearly betrayed his shock when he realized he was being addressed by Prime Overseer Ersevin. "Prime Overseer, I have come here, as you requested."

"We are here because of your request—repeated requests, I might add."

"There is sufficient evidence to support that persistence is often rewarded, Prime Overseer," Sadoon replied.

Ersevin regarded him with ancient eyes. They were piercing, and Sadoon felt his resolve being tested under their weight. "Persistence is often confused with arrogance."

Sadoon felt something cold stir inside him. He was afraid, and rightly so. With a single word, Ersevin could end Sadoon's career. His next words could forever influence the path he walked.

"In this case, my persistence is for the benefit of all Krake."

Ersevin held his gaze for a few moments. "As is every effort that comes before us," he said and gestured toward the other overseers sitting at the high table.

Sadoon's gaze swept across them. They were all old and powerful, with hundreds of years of authority and knowledge at their disposal. He bowed his head in respect.

"We are here to review your request for a new research project."

Sadoon looked back at Ersevin. "I am at your disposal, Prime Overseer."

"We have reviewed the evidence you've put together and have concluded that the Humans are a limited threat. We acknowledge that their weapons are impressive, but all predictive models indicate that the Humans are vastly outmatched by our capabilities," Ersevin said.

"Prime Overseer, are you saying we shouldn't study them?"

"I'm not saying that at all. We are in agreement that the Humans are worthy of study once we've identified which fringe universe they reside in. However, no additional resources will be allocated to that project."

"I urge you all to reconsider," Sadoon said and looked at the other overseers. "This project should have alpha resource allocation."

Ersevin's pale blue skin wrinkled along his brow ridges. "Alpha resource allocation?" he repeated. "Tell me, Sector Chief Sadoon, do you have a new predictive model we should review that supports your position?"

"Negative, Prime Overseer," Sadoon replied.

"We understand that you've had direct contact with these Humans and are intrigued by them. We commend your enthusiasm. However, we do not have infinite resources to indulge in every research priority that comes to us for our review. We have protocols in place to help us prioritize our resource allocation, as well as those for cataloging fringe universes."

Anger and frustration flooded through Sadoon's mind, but he couldn't let it show. He must appear calm, even though with one simple sentence, the Prime Overseer had dismissed his request for additional resources.

"Will you grant me clearance to pursue the Humans on my own? I'm willing to segregate my own resource allocation," Sadoon asked.

"You have a research project you're in charge of, and our records indicate that this project is not complete. Do you wish to nominate another Krake to take over your work?"

This simple question was as dangerous as an active warship combat drone. If he nominated another Krake, they could take everything he'd built and increase their own standing among the Krake hierarchy. But his research project was years from completion. Sadoon doubted he'd learn anything else that couldn't already be predicted, but if anything, the Krake were thorough in their research endeavors. He couldn't abandon years of work, not even to study the Humans.

"I do not wish to nominate another Krake. However, I would like to be granted a second research fellowship that would allow me to further gather evidence about the Humans and their Ovarrow allies," Sadoon said.

Ersevin considered it for a few moments. As the seconds went by, Sadoon suspected that the overseers were communicating with each other, although he couldn't detect any means of it. Perhaps it was being filtered out. If he'd been granted a live audience with them, he might have been able to detect additional comlink signals.

"We will consider your request at our next review of the project for which you are responsible. However, you are free to request information from the data repository to further develop a predictive model that justifies a review of resource allocation to your proposed project. I must caution you that this is secondary to your primary research project. We will not tolerate any neglect in that endeavor. Is this understood?"

"I will not neglect my current efforts in the least bit," Sadoon said.

The overseers' chambers faded, and Sadoon found himself standing inside the comlink room. The door behind him opened, indicating that his session with the overseers was over. He stood there for a few moments, reviewing the conversation in his mind. If he had gotten the overseers to escalate the priority of the Human research project, he could've changed projects without losing any standing among the oligarchy. But they wouldn't let him.

A warning appeared on the wallscreen, indicating he should leave. The room was reserved for the next occupant. Sadoon stepped out and allowed the next Krake to go inside. He was heading back to the automated walkway when he received a comlink request. He'd been so focused on reviewing his session with the overseers that he acknowledged the comlink before he realized he could not identify the sender.

"Your request was denied. Do not attempt to trace this comlink. We have been following your repeated inquiries to the overseers' office, but you had to know this was going to fail."

"You are remarkably well-informed. Why hide yourself?"

"Others may pretend we don't exist, but that doesn't change the facts."

"You are the fifth column. I will report this session immediately."

"If you'd like to wait twenty-five years to find the universe where the Humans are, then, by all means, do so. That estimate is based upon current allocated resources."

Sadoon stopped walking and frowned. He'd been about to forward the comlink session to the authorities but decided to wait. "What do I call you?"

"You can call me Aurang. You're not the only one who has intimate knowledge of the Humans and their CDF. I've been aboard one of their most powerful warships. I've seen them face-to-face, and I'm willing to share this information with you."

Sadoon couldn't be sure if Aurang was lying to him. "And what would you want in return?"

"Cooperation and help when I need it. What if I told you I could cut the timeline to find the universe where the Humans live to one to three years?"

"How?" Sadoon asked. He didn't believe it was possible.

"You've tried to go through official channels to get what you want. Have you ever considered using unofficial channels? I happen to agree with your assessment of the Human threat. They *are* a threat to us. The overseers are blinded by their own arrogance. There is much that will change."

"What exactly are you offering?"

"I'm offering a way for you to study the Humans up close and personal," Aurang said.

"These feeble acts of persuasion are not compelling."

"I believe they are. You see, we've been conducting our own research for many years. There are things many Krake realize but don't talk about."

"Such as?" Sadoon asked.

"Our biggest enemy."

"I think you might overestimate what the Humans are capable of. They are a threat, but they are not our biggest enemy. Not even close."

"You mistake me, Sector Chief. Stagnation is our biggest enemy."

Sadoon paused for a few moments, going over what Aurang was saying. One to three years was much better than languishing for the time it would ordinarily take. However, it meant working with the scourge of their society. The fifth column worked toward anarchy. They were rebels, but could they give him what he wanted? He knew the overseers wouldn't grant him another audience for at least a year, but they could delay it even longer.

He recalled the image of the CDF soldier in mechanized armor fighting his Krake soldiers. The Human was defiant, even in the face of over-whelming odds. Sadoon had seen similar behavioral traits in the Ovarrow they had studied. He wondered what else he could learn about the Humans. What were they capable of? Could he come up with a predictive model for the Humans as well?

"I'd like to hear more," Sadoon said.

"I thought you'd like to. I'm going to transfer a set of coordinates. Do not come to them from Quadiri. You'll need to use one of the tertiary worlds and a secondary arch gateway. From there, you'll receive further instructions."

He received a data packet through the comlink. Sadoon opened it up and examined it. It contained everything Aurang had said. It wasn't just a simple journey through an arch gateway; it was a complex set of instructions. All this to meet with the fifth column.

"I should also warn you," Aurang continued, "that if you attempt to involve any authority, you will never hear from us again. You'll be cut off, and instead of studying the Humans, you'll learn about them from someone else. You're not the only interested party. Is this clear to you?"

Sadoon's first thought was that Aurang had worked with other Krake before. He wasn't the first Krake Aurang had tried to win to his cause, and that was telling in and of itself. "I understand."

"Excellent. I look forward to meeting with you. And when we do meet, I'll share all the knowledge I've gathered about the Humans. I'm sure you'll find it quite insightful. And you've scratched only the surface. I look forward to working with you, Sector Chief Sadoon."

The comlink severed, and Sadoon resumed walking toward the automated walkway. He would return to his research world, gather a few things, and then meet Aurang and the fifth column. The Krake had been so confident of what he had that Sadoon didn't even doubt it. That kind of authority came with the certainty of knowledge at his disposal. Sadoon had used it himself and knew enough to recognize it in another Krake. Perhaps this trip hadn't been a waste after all.

CHAPTER 5

Connor walked into the administration wing of the governor's offices at the capitol building in Sierra. He passed the brightness of the wide corridors displaying cycled images of colonial accomplishments with little notice. He was already running late to the meeting. He gave a slight nod to people around him, those he recognized but didn't have time to talk to. Eyes forward, he walked as though he was on a dogged march toward the next objective. There was a grim set to the line of his mouth that wasn't quite a scowl, but most people got the hint and stayed away. He wasn't in the mood for talking. This day had been taxing enough already.

When Connor walked in, the strategy session was already in full swing. Twelve colonial leaders and members of their respective support staffs sat at the elongated conference table. He headed for the open seat next to Nathan, and Governor Wolf gave Connor a small nod, her aged features warming slightly.

Bob Mullins glanced in his direction with a pinched expression, then looked back at the young man who was speaking. He had a snobbish voice that sought to keep the attention of the attendees but wasn't succeeding. There was a presentation on the holodisplay showing a dashboard for various colonial project statuses. Connor looked at the young man, and a name appeared on his internal heads-up display. Brian Ramsey. His pale-skinned face had rounded cheeks that made him look more like a child than a man, and the minuscule patches of hair on his chin and jaw only contributed to the baby face he probably hoped to hide.

"General Gates," Ramsey said, making a show of looking at the clock. "I'm sorry, but you've missed the first part of the strategy session for civilian defense protocols in our cities."

"You can continue, Mr. Ramsey. General Hayes will fill me in on what I need to know," Connor replied.

"Of course, General, but with Governor Wolf in attendance, don't you think she's owed some kind of explanation for your late arrival?" Ramsey said.

Connor's gaze hardened, and Ramsey's face flushed a little bit. Assertiveness born of insecurity never quite worked, and yet so many young men and women became victims of the folly. Connor thought Ramsey was probably a smart young man, but right then, he was being foolish. And Connor didn't care.

Governor Wolf leaned forward. "That's not necessary."

Ramsey's gaze darted toward her, and he blinked rapidly. "Of course, Governor," he said meekly.

Connor glanced at the others around the table, and he could tell their curiosity was piqued. He drew himself up and leaned forward, cutting Ramsey off as he was about to speak. "If you really want to know why I was late, I was informing the families of the CDF soldiers who died in the line of duty. It's the least I can do when a soldier makes the ultimate sacrifice for the rest of the colony."

Grim, stone-faced silence lowered the atmosphere of the room by several degrees. Ramsey swallowed hard as he looked at Mullins, his gaze pleading. Bob gestured for him to sit down, and the young man beat a hasty retreat.

Mullins looked at Connor solemnly. "I think I can speak for everyone here when I express my sincerest condolences for the loss of our colonists, and we acknowledge the sacrifice of the soldiers in the Colonial Defense Force."

Connor nodded his head once. Throughout his military career, he'd seen many soldiers die. They'd lost thousands of them in their war with the Vemus alone. He didn't think he'd ever get to the point where the death of a fellow soldier was simply a number or a cost to be paid for the price of their survival. Lives mattered. They mattered to him, and they mattered to the families of the fallen. He couldn't visit every family of the soldiers who died. It wasn't practical, so the burden was spread among senior officers. He could have delegated the task, but he wouldn't. He owed his soldiers that much at least. It was a necessary duty that was never easy, but it kept him grounded, and reminding a room full of civilians—his fellow colonists—of the CDF's sacrifice helped ease the burden. It made them aware that there was a price to be paid for their survival and that it *did* affect him. He'd never be friends with Bob Mullins, but Connor had no doubt that Mullins worked on the colony's behalf. They didn't agree on a lot of things, but when it came to the importance of colonial lives, they were aligned.

"General Hayes has provided us with a briefing of the mission involving the Gesora," Governor Wolf said. "Do you have anything you'd like to add?"

Mullins had killed the slide on the holoscreen, so they were clearly going off topic from the original presentation.

"The Gesora have a long uphill battle on their hands, but this was always going to be reality for them," Connor said and paused for a moment. "Nothing the Krake do could be considered by us as minor, but on the scale of a Krake research endeavor, much of what was happening to the Gesora has been seen in various configurations before—government and economic manipulation. But in this case, they added touching upon beliefs held sacred to the Gesora."

"Religious in nature? What sort of . . ." Mullins began to say but then stopped. "I don't want to . . . Please continue."

Discussions about the Krake sometimes led down a few rabbit holes. While it was interesting to do sometimes, more often than not it ate through their meeting time.

"Not overtly religious in nature," Connor said, "but just certain beliefs or ideas that divide a society, for example. They seemed to have explored multiple ideas along these lines. They combined these efforts with what we would call biological warfare, but those closely resembled prophetic references to their ancient history."

"Biological warfare can mean a lot of different things," Nathan said. "What the Krake have been doing on some worlds is introducing certain mutations and ideas to influence the Ovarrow's reaction to them. We've been working to isolate these efforts in order to try to understand what the Krake are studying."

Governor Wolf nodded. "Natalia informed me about this."

Natalia Vassar was a trusted CDF intelligence analyst Connor had trained. Governor Wolf was looking to find a new head for the Colonial Intelligence Bureau, and Connor had recommended Major Vassar. He knew Mullins wanted to limit the influence of the Colonial Defense Force and that he likely viewed Natalia's candidacy as increasing that influence, so Mullins had put forth his own candidate.

"Not all the Krake intelligence operations are so complex," Connor said. "Some of them are pretty straightforward, but the typical trial for a Krake research project can last for years or, in some instances, hundreds of years."

"It's difficult to gauge how long the Krake conduct experiments or operations," Mullins replied. "I read the reports from Darius Cohen, and the Ovarrow history here on New Earth is spotty at best. The Ovarrow who went into stasis remember a world that had already fallen. In essence, they don't know exactly how long the Krake had maintained a presence here."

"We've been making significant gains in understanding Krake operations," Nathan said, "but of the hundreds of universes documented by the Krake, we've visited only a small percentage." He paused for a moment and added, "About fifteen percent of the total number."

Governor Wolf nodded. "Believe me, the number of universes that have been documented by the Krake has been subject to a lot of debate. The theory of a multiverse isn't new, and we've had limited proof of its existence until now. But our theories always indicated that there could be an infinite number of universes, and that's just not what we're finding, at least according to the Krake."

"And they've been at it for a lot longer than we have," Connor said.

"Does anyone have any idea how long?" Mullins asked.

"It's pure speculation," Dr. Curry said, "but based on the data we have here on New Earth and the intelligence gathered by CDF operations, it's easy to estimate that the Krake have been at this for hundreds of years. Five hundred years would be a conservative estimate, but it could also be as much as a thousand years." She paused for a few seconds before continuing. "There have been a lot of theories discussed about it in R&D, but I wouldn't say there's a consensus. What's been gaining traction among our ranks is that perhaps we're dealing with certain laws of the universe we haven't even conceptualized yet."

"What do you mean?" Mullins asked.

"Nothing is static. There is absolutely nothing here," Dr. Curry said, gesturing with her hands toward the table, "that's absolutely still. We're always in motion. And not just here. Everything is in motion—the planets, stars, and galaxies—so why not universes?"

Connor frowned in thought for a moment. "So, universes, as we know them, are in motion and . . ." He paused, and Dr. Curry smiled and nodded for him to continue. "The question becomes, What keeps them in motion?"

"That is the big question," Dr. Curry said. "The gateways we're able to open, thanks to the space gates and the arches, bend the laws of physics. At least the laws as *we* understand them. For example, we all know we can't go faster than the speed of light. We perceive that as a universal constant—gravity and mass, and that whole thing—but we've managed to bend those laws on our own. Otherwise, we wouldn't have artificial gravity. However, this is something else. So, if you can accept that multiple universes are out there and are in motion, then perhaps there's something that prevents us from accessing an infinite number of universes."

The room was silent for a few moments as everyone considered Dr. Curry's words.

Connor felt the hint of a smile tug at the edges of his lips. "You make it sound like it's a neighborhood."

Dr. Curry nodded. "You're not too far off with a simple explanation like that. Yet it means that even with a space gate, we can access only certain universes for what might be a limited amount of time, but keep in mind that 'limited' is a relative term here. In terms of space travel, the word 'limited' has a much different meaning than it does in terms of our lifespans."

"Let me see if I get this straight," Mullins said. "Are you saying that we will have access to certain universes for only a few years and then possibly never again?"

"That's just it, Mr. Mullins. We don't know. If it's relative in certain terms, it could be for as little as a few years like you said, but it could also mean thousands of years. And we think that the Krake must be aware of this theoretical universal constant we're talking about here. It would explain their reference to what they call a fringe universe. Since they have it in their terminology, the indication is that they must have knowledge that they can't always access a universe they've been to before."

Mullins's eyes widened, and Connor noticed that his weren't the only ones. Mullins looked at Governor Wolf. "So, we could wait out the Krake, in theory, and possibly they would never get to us?"

"You don't really think we'll get that lucky, do you?" Connor asked.

Mullins shrugged. "It's still something we could consider. It's an option or a scenario we should *seriously* consider. What if the threat of the Krake is something we can just endure, and it might actually just pass us by? The point I'm trying to make is that we just don't know."

Connor took a sip of his water. "It *is* interesting, and we should try to find more data to support the theory."

"That's exactly my next point," Dr. Curry said. "And again, I must emphasize that these are just theories we're considering ourselves. I don't want to inundate the CDF with requests for acquiring data that just may not be out there. I mean, what if we're wrong?"

Governor Wolf smiled. "It's discussions like these that are the reason we have these strategy sessions. It's a way for *all* of us to come together and deal with the Krake. It shouldn't fall entirely upon the shoulders of the CDF."

"I agree," Mullins said. "But given this discussion, how are we ever going to answer the question of how much time we really have before the Krake find us?"

Nathan cleared his throat. "If I could give you a definitive answer, then I would. They're looking for us. We've clashed with them enough to know that they're aware of us. The measures that the Krake have gone to in dealing with Trident Battle Group is certainly testament enough for that."

"We need to find the Krake home universe before they find us," Connor said. "If they find us first, we'll be fighting them here and looking for the Krake home universe at the same time. And that's assuming they don't bring an overwhelming fighting force here."

"And what is the strategy if we do find the Krake home universe?" Mullins asked.

"We recon the system," replied Connor. "There's no reason for us to attack as soon as we find it. But as for a strategy, it's similar to any other kind of enemy we've faced throughout history. We remove their ability to make war."

"Some of these things will have to be defined as we learn more," Nathan said. "We know the Krake have operations outside their own universe that support their industrial complex. We don't know how extensive they are, but the more we find, the better we might be able to cripple their industrial complex."

Governor Wolf nodded. "I understand the enormity of the task that the CDF is being called upon to deal with," she said. "I think what Bob is asking for, and what I think we need, is something a little bit more specific, even if it's a theoretical scenario. A 'what if,' if you will. If we find X, Y, and Z, then we do these things." Her gaze slipped to the table for a few moments as if she was lost in thought. Then she quickly shook it off.

"We'll make sure you have what you need," Nathan said.

"Thank you," she replied. "I think that wraps up this session; however, I need to keep the senior staff here for a few minutes. Everyone else can go."

The people around the conference table rose and started exiting the room. Connor stood up and walked toward Governor Wolf. "What did you think of Natalia?"

"She's everything you said she was—cunningly brilliant—and I think she'd make a fine director of the Colonial Intelligence Bureau," Wolf said.

Mullins joined them but remained quiet.

Connor arched an eyebrow. "I feel like there's a 'but' coming."

"We want to avoid what happened with Meredith Cain. Bob has made a proposal of not quite a co-leadership position but a strong second-in-command like your XOs serving on CDF warships—someone to help Natalia with the job I'm going to offer her." Connor nodded. "But there's something else I need to tell you. She'll need to resign from the CDF to take this position. Do you think she'll do that?"

Connor considered this for a few moments before replying. "I can't speak for Major Vassar. I've worked closely with her, and I think she'll be a perfect fit for the role. I assure you we'll do whatever we can to help," he said and looked at Mullins. "Who's your candidate, Bob?"

"He'll be her second if she takes the job. His name is Jerry Sherman. He's worked a lot of logistics-type projects that deal specifically with resource allocation. He's a good fit for the job too. He has a highly analytical mind," Mullins replied.

Connor glanced at Governor Wolf and thought about asking her a follow-up question but decided against it. There was something on the edge of his thoughts that he couldn't quite put into words. "I'll leave you to it," he said.

"Connor," Wolf said, "is there anything we can do for the families of the CDF soldiers?"

He looked away for a moment. "There isn't much we can do that isn't already happening. I wish there was more, but if I really had a choice, it would be that we didn't have to deal with the Krake at all."

"I understand. If there's anything you need, let me know."

Connor left the meeting and joined Nathan. "They're not going to like it," he said.

"They need to understand what we'll have to do when we find the Krake home world. They need to be prepared," replied Nathan.

"I know, but I just think they might balk at some of our ideas."

"Then it'll be our job to convince them of what's necessary. Come on, let's hammer out some of these details."

"Right," Connor said. "You be conservative, and I'll be extreme."

Nathan chuckled. "You always get to be extreme."

"Just lucky, I guess."

CHAPTER 6

While living at Sanctuary over the years, Connor had discovered that he had to travel ever farther from the growing city to reach the New Earth countryside, and he'd found that he did his best thinking when he was moving around. The trail he currently walked smelled of decaying wood, wildflowers, and moss-covered boulders. An army of croakers contested for the loudest calls over by the marshland that became part of the nearby river during the rainy season.

He'd spent a lifetime moving around from place to place, and living at Sanctuary with Lenora had been the longest he'd ever spent in a single home. Despite the extensive travel he'd done in recent years, he still had the itch to explore. He enjoyed going where no one had ever been before. There was a certain amount of satisfaction in that—a sentiment shared by most colonists. Connor may not have started out as the ideal colonist, but he'd certainly grown into one at heart.

He walked along a hiking path, easily navigating across the uneven ground, and emerged from the forested area onto a dry patch. Puffs of dirt kicked up as he strode quickly along. Connor rarely walked at a leisurely pace, except when he had Lauren with him. At those times, his two-year-old daughter set the pace.

The marked trail was easily fifteen kilometers long. It was essentially a giant loop that led to another part of Sanctuary. He remembered first exploring New Earth when people were rightly cautious about venturing beyond the fenced compounds they'd built. They'd known so little about the planet back then—a great mystery, a new world, but not the one they'd thought they were going to. Regardless, New Earth had become their home.

Connor glanced at the exotic plant life that had become the norm to him. To his right was a dazzling display of the broad multicolored leaves his wife often referred to as an artist's palette. He thought about the other worlds he'd seen through the gateway—worlds with poisonous atmospheres or frozen over because of some catastrophe—lifeless, deserted places he hoped never to see again. Things could have been much worse here on New Earth. Had the *Ark* arrived a hundred years earlier, for instance, things would have been much different. New Earth had been a frozen world because of an artificially induced Ice Age that hadn't relented until almost fifty years before their arrival.

The population of the colony had more than doubled in size and continued along a steep growing curve. Sometime within the next ten years, they'd probably have over a million colonists. Given the Vemus Wars and just the general challenges they'd faced in colonizing this planet, it was a huge accomplishment for humanity to thrive here.

Connor's memory of Old Earth was something of a dream. The people and places they'd left behind were no less important to him, but it was another life in every sense of the word. He had grown beyond the NA Alliance military officer he'd been. His enduring ache for the people he missed had become a permanent part of his existence here—friends and family, his son who'd died fighting the Vemus as part of a last-ditch effort to update the *Ark*'s destination and give the colonists a chance to survive. Connor carried so much guilt that he didn't think he'd ever be entirely free of it. There'd always be a longing for those events to have turned out differently. He wished he could have been there for his son, especially for the dark times he must have faced during the Vemus Wars of Old Earth. But an old friend had once told him that collecting a few regrets was part of living life.

Connor had purposefully taken this trail because of where it entered Sanctuary. He owed a visit to an old friend, and before too long he'd reached the edges of the city. Sanctuary wasn't the sprawling metropolis that Sierra was, but it was a city in its own right. They had room to breathe out here.

He looked at the sign above the large restaurant and smiled. It showed a cartoon rendition of a CDF soldier with furrowed brow and intense gaze. Beneath the picture was written "*I dare you not to love the food here!*"

The Salty Soldier had grown in size and popularity over the years. Connor remembered when Diaz had designed the sign that hung over the wide entrance. He remembered telling Diaz that he thought it was a little on the nose, to which Diaz had replied that this was the point. He didn't want a wishy-washy clientele coming to his restaurant.

Diaz had decided to take a page out of the history books and use hardwoods for the restaurant's construction. He'd claimed it was more inviting, and Connor agreed. The dark hardwood smelled of longevity and good times, as if the restaurant had always been there. As Connor walked toward the main doors, he caught a healthy whiff of the delicious food, and his mouth started to water. The early afternoon staff was preparing for what promised to be a busy dinner.

Connor walked through the main doors, and Victoria smiled a greeting at him. She came from around the bar to give Connor a big hug.

"You didn't bring the little peach today," Victoria said.

Connor smiled and gave her a peck on the cheek. "Not today. She's with her mother."

"Oh, I just can't get enough of her. Pretty soon, she'll have another little playmate," Victoria said and smiled with a twinkle in her eyes.

Connor frowned for a moment, and Victoria rubbed her stomach gently.

"Well, that's cause for celebration!" he said, lifting her into the air and swinging her around a few times before softly placing her back on her feet. She squealed in delight.

He heard a hearty laugh from across the room and saw Diaz walking toward him, bellowing a mock warning to stay away from his wife. He held his arms out wide and had a broad grin across his face. Diaz had a stocky build with a bit of a barrel chest. Connor noticed there was less worry around his eyes.

"Hey, hey, she must have told you about lucky number six," Diaz said.

Connor nodded. "I'd say you're trying to repopulate the human species all by yourself."

Diaz placed his arm around his wife affectionately. "Pretty soon, you'll catch up to us."

"I very much doubt it," Connor replied.

Victoria ushered them away. "Go on. I know you two have plenty to catch up on. I'll make sure you're left alone."

"Come on, I have something to show you," Diaz said.

He led Connor toward a staircase off to the side, and they climbed it. When they came to a landing, they continued climbing another set of stairs. There was a solitary door at the top. Diaz gave him a wink and opened it to reveal an outdoor terrace with a few lounge chairs and a perfect view of the landscape around Sanctuary. It was a good spot, and Connor said so.

A desk and chair were off to the side. Above it, a wallscreen cycled through a collage of pictures. Connor recognized some of them, since he was in them. A few of the pictures were from the early days of the colony when there hadn't been a CDF. They'd originally been part of Field Ops and Security. There was even a picture of Lenora speaking with Noah, who looked as if he'd just gotten out of the gawky adolescence stage. But as always, Connor's gaze was drawn immediately back to Lenora, and then he saw himself in the background, glancing in Lenora's direction.

"You never could take your eyes off her for very long," Diaz said.

Connor grinned. "Lenora had no shortage of admirers back then."

"What do you mean, back then? I still remember when the young pups all watched the young pretty doctor lady," Diaz said. "Young pretty doctor lady" was Diaz's nickname for Lenora, especially when he was speaking to somebody who had extended her some kind of favor when Field Ops wouldn't give them anywhere near that kind of cooperation.

"Would you look at us," Connor said and leaned in toward one of the pictures. He sighed and looked at Diaz. "We really had no idea what was coming."

"You're doing it again. You're sucking the joy out of the moment," Diaz said and punched him in the arm.

"I see you've adjusted to civilian life quite well. You look good," Connor said.

Diaz nodded. "I *am* good. You could adjust, too, if you wanted to."

Connor tilted his head slightly to the side and shrugged one shoulder.

"I know, I know," Diaz said. He gestured toward a couple of chairs, poured them each a glass of bourbon, and handed one to Connor.

"I see Nathan and Savannah have made customers of you too," Connor said.

"Oh yeah, this is good stuff."

Connor sipped his bourbon and then drained it. It blazed a path of warmth down his chest and into his stomach. Diaz poured him another. A few minutes later, a young man brought them a couple of sandwiches and then left them alone.

They ate and talked about little things. Diaz asked when Connor and Lenora were going to have more children. Connor had no idea. That sort of talk had a way of never coming up when he and Lenora were alone.

"I'm sure it'll happen one day. I just don't know when," Connor replied.

"Fair enough," Diaz said and took the last bite of his sandwich. "So, when are the Krake coming here?"

Connor's eyebrows raised. The question had come out of nowhere, but he had to admit that it'd been on his mind. He missed Diaz.

"That's the big question. That's what everyone wants to know."

"Well, I hope the real answer is never."

"Me too. The Security Council is pressuring Nathan and me on that very question. They want us to put a timeframe around it. They could be here now, or it could be a few years. The only way for us to find out is to keep going out there," Connor said, gesturing toward the view.

Diaz knew what he meant. He'd been through the gateway a few times as well.

"That's not even the tough question," Diaz said and poured them each some more bourbon.

Connor took the proffered glass and just held it. "They want us to revise our strategy on what we'll do after we find the Krake home universe."

Diaz snorted. "Well that's easy. We bomb them out of existence. Take them by surprise so they'll never see it coming."

"I don't know if the Security Council is quite on the same page as you."

"Well, they better get there because there's no other way for this to end. Just ask any of the Ovarrow," Diaz said.

Everything Connor had seen reaffirmed that the Krake had done truly despicable things to other intelligent species in a show of ruthless pragmatism at its worst.

"We're doing all we can to find them," he said. "We tell the Security Council that our strategy is to take away the Krake's ability to fight, but I don't know if this is good enough. The contacts we've made want revenge."

"They're entitled to it, if you ask me."

"You know the Krake have a fifth column, a group of rebels that are trying to change things."

"I don't know how much good that will do. Would you really trust the Krake to do anything but serve their own purpose?" Diaz asked.

Diaz hated the Krake, with good reason, but Connor didn't care about the Krake all that much. They were an enemy, and they needed to be stopped, but he didn't have the same hatred of them. Connor had seen it in other soldiers, both human and Ovarrow alike. It was the kind of hatred that gave rise to rogue groups doing morally gray things. His thoughts flickered to Lars Mallory. Lars had tortured Ovarrow to get information about the Krake. Connor didn't have to hate an enemy in order to defeat them, but it did raise the question of when a society is responsible for those who are in power.

"God, I can see the wheels are turning in that skull of yours," Diaz said.

"Is it that obvious?" Connor asked in mock surprise.

"I know you. You'll torture yourself about making the tough choices. But if it comes down to the Krake or us, it's going to be the Krake. You know it, and I know it. So do a lot of other people, including everyone in that Security Council."

"We just have to find them."

"How's that going?"

"We've actually made a lot of progress. We even have Ovarrow contacts in other universes that are looking for the Krake home world as well. But the real risk is that the more we bring into the fold—"

"The more it shines a light on our happy little planet here. I get it," Diaz said. "So, I guess the question is, What are you gonna do now?"

Connor feigned ignorance. "You mean after I go home?"

Diaz shook his head. "You know what I mean."

"It's the new me," Connor said. "We have multiple teams out all the time. We're going to find the Krake; it's just a matter of when. But, if you mean what am I going to do tomorrow, well, that's easy. Lenora asked me to take a short trip with her."

Diaz arched a thick eyebrow and regarded him for a few moments. "Are you two planning a weekend getaway in the middle of the week?"

Connor chuckled and shook his head. "No, it's nothing like that. She found something she wants to check out. I need some downtime, so I decided to go with her."

"Good for you, Connor. Try not to think about what the Krake are doing to find us."

"Do you have a few ideas you'd like to toss out there?"

Diaz shook his head. "I was never really the idea guy. You got Noah for that, and . . ." He paused, and his eyes widened. "What's Sean doing these days?"

"Sean is involved in building up our fleets. He and the people of Trident Battle Group have the most knowledge of Krake warship tactics. They're redesigning some of our ships with the Krake in mind. Plus they're working on a few new toys to use against them."

"That kid is pretty smart. That was a helluva thing he had to deal with."

"It was. Not everyone understands though. They think they do, but they really don't . . . never mind. He's doing fine," Connor said.

"That's good."

They both stood up.

"I'm glad we did this," Connor said.

"Anytime, Connor," Diaz said. "I mean that."

Connor breathed in and sighed. "I know you do."

CHAPTER 7

Noah engaged the autopilot mode on the civilian aerial transport vehicle—C-cat for short—that flew over thick clouds of a pretty substantial storm currently en route to Sierra. It was always serene above storm clouds, which occasionally flashed with random bolts of lightning.

He leaned back in the pilot's seat. He still got the odd severe headache from his injury, and sometimes he had trouble finding the words to convey what he was thinking. It didn't happen anywhere near as often as it had a year ago, and while Noah thought it was frequent, everyone else assured him it wasn't. He'd been convinced they were biased because they wanted him to keep a positive frame of mind. It wasn't until Kara had shown him the data from his biochip, which tracked his overall well-being, including those symptoms and behaviors related to his injury, that he believed them. His wife knew how to get him to listen. It was hard for him to argue with the data, which showed a steady decline in those symptoms. He was healing.

Years after he'd taken a swan dive off a cliff and nearly died, he'd finally recovered enough to feel almost like his old self, but not quite. Despite rapid advancements in healing the body, there were limits to what medicine could do for the mind. The human brain had a particular way of doing things, and all their medical innovation could assist with that, but they could do only so much. The damaged parts of his brain simply had to learn new pathways to reach the old information, or he had to relearn some of those things. It had been a long and frustrating journey. But he was alive, and he was thankful for it every day.

A comlink chimed, and Noah answered it. The face of Oriana Evans appeared on the holoscreen. There was a Lunar Base icon in the upper right corner, showing where the comlink had come from.

"Oriana, it's so good to hear from you. How are things on base?" Noah asked.

She had long, dark hair and almost delicate cheekbones. She was just Sean's type.

"Hi, Noah. Are you traveling alone?"

"Yes, I am. Kara will be sorry she missed your call."

"Things are great here. Lots of new discoveries being made, which is why I'm contacting you. I have an invitation I'd like to extend to both you and Kara."

"Oh, is it, uh . . ." Noah began and stopped. He'd almost asked if it was a wedding invitation, but he didn't want to add any more fuel to that particular fire. "For what?" he added hastily.

"Smooth, Noah, very smooth," Oriana said and smiled. "I want to know if you're interested in coming to the lunar base for a few months. We're doing a lot of theoretical research here, and to be honest, I could really use your help."

He had thrown himself into everything he'd missed while he'd been in a coma. He'd reviewed all the mission reports and the overviews of the R&D publications resulting from those missions. He was no stranger to Oriana's work on space gates, subspace communications, and reverse engineering the Casimir reactor.

"A few months," Noah said and leveled a look at her.

Oriana tilted her head to the side. "Okay, six months at the very least."

Noah's eyebrows raced up his forehead. He hadn't spent that kind of time at the lunar base since the Vemus War. He looked away from the holoscreen for a moment. "I'm not sure. Six months is a long time." He paused for a few moments and then looked back at Oriana. "Have you figured out how to teleport anyone yet?"

Oriana chuckled. "No. Have you?" she asked.

This had been a bit of an ongoing joke between them.

Noah shook his head. "I don't think it's true teleportation. But I keep banging my head against the wall when it comes to how the Ovarrow stumbled onto something like that. We don't even know where the other half of the town is where they conducted their original experiments. I doubt we'll ever find it."

He had other ideas, but there just hadn't been time to pursue them. He knew that if he and Kara went to the lunar base, they'd probably be up there for a lot longer than six months.

"You don't need to decide anything right now. I just wanted to ask the question."

"I'd need to talk about it with Kara."

"Of course," Oriana said. "There's been a lot of R&D in CDF warship redesign going on up here. I know a lot of that stuff is right up your alley. I've read all the work you did to prepare for the Vemus War."

Noah knew Oriana meant well. There were a lot of people, mostly scientists, who had expressed appreciation for some of the breakthroughs he'd been involved in. What none of them knew was that there were a lot of sleepless nights involved in those breakthroughs, and most of them had occurred right at the end when the Vemus had almost killed them all. He wasn't in any rush to regain that former glory. He liked where he was. He liked having a home at Sanctuary and maintaining offices in Sierra and New Haven.

"I'll give it some serious thought. I promise," Noah said.

"That's all I can ask. Will you be returning to Sanctuary soon?"

Noah was about to answer, but he stopped himself. "I'm taking a short trip to Delphi."

Oriana caught the hesitation in his tone, and her eyes tightened. Then her expression smoothed back to normal. "Oh, I see."

He had no doubt that she understood. Lars was being held in Delphi, and he had killed Oriana's brother. No amount of facts could ever outweigh the loss of family.

"I shouldn't keep you any longer then. I hope you and Kara do decide to come. I really do. We could use your help here, Noah," Oriana said.

He nodded a little. "Thanks for the invite. I'll be in touch in a few days."

"Okay. Until next time."

"Oh, and tell Sean I said not to work so hard."

"I don't think that's possible, but I'll tell him."

Noah smiled, and the comlink closed. It was more than a little tempting to relocate to the lunar base for a time, but he couldn't leave now. He had his own work to do. Besides, he could help them more from down here with access to all his resources. He'd still discuss it with Kara, but leaving New Earth right now didn't seem like the best choice for him. Over the years he'd learned to trust his instincts, and they were advising him to stay put.

CHAPTER 8

Noah landed his C-cat on the outskirts of Delphi. The incarceration center was a secure facility, established to house the colonists involved in the rogue group activities led by Meredith Cain. At one point, there had been several hundred colonists detained here as they awaited their trials. Case by case, their actions had been reviewed and justice had been served, but there were still over a hundred detainees left. And there was one person in particular he was determined to see.

He had witnessed a few of those trials and had been called upon to give a statement. He'd been there when Meredith Cain and Kurt Johnson were sentenced to exile, along with many of the other ringleaders. They'd been given survival equipment and were then flown to an isolated island surrounded by a vast ocean where they were being monitored. Once their exile was served, they'd be allowed to leave the island and return to the continent. However, this didn't guarantee them access back into any of the colonial cities.

He recalled the day Meredith Cain had been sentenced to exile. She'd glared at everyone in the courtroom, and her contemptuous gaze froze on him with searing anger. "You!" she growled. "Everyone would have been better off if you had died on those cliffs, Noah Barker. You think you've—"

Whatever else she'd been about to say had been cut off when the security agents immobilized her with stun batons.

In the days following, Noah wondered if that nutcase had set some nefarious event in motion to exact her revenge on him, but nothing ever happened. He'd taken precautions just the same.

Noah walked through the civilian entrance and told the person behind the desk whom he was there to see. About thirty minutes later, he was in one of the private visitation rooms that contained two chairs and a rectangular table. The room was located along the outer wall of the building and had a small window where sunlight shone through. The door on the opposite side of the room opened, and Lars Mallory was escorted inside. He wore a dark gray jumpsuit. Lars was a tall man like his father and could easily look eye to eye with Connor. He'd lost his outdoorsman tan, but he hadn't let his physical conditioning slip. If fact, he appeared solid, as if he had more muscle to him than was readily apparent beneath his jumpsuit.

The guard removed Lars's restraints and gave Noah a friendly nod before leaving the room.

"Hello, Noah. I figured you'd be otherwise occupied," Lars said.

"I wanted to see how you were doing."

They sat down in chairs across from each other, and Lars folded his hands in front of him, resting them on the table. He just looked at Noah for a few moments.

"I heard your trial was coming up soon," said Noah.

"It is."

"Are you worried?"

Lars leaned back in his chair and sighed. "They don't know what to do with me. I gave them all the intel I could to end it, and it all panned out for them."

"And yet you didn't try to negotiate for a lighter sentence," Noah added.

Lars frowned and shook his head. "I got what I wanted. I negotiated for the safety of my people. And in return, I gave them everything. I wasn't going to ask for leniency after we'd already made a deal."

Noah shook his head. "Aren't you worried you'll be exiled?"

Lars's gaze flicked to the window, and he breathed deeply before turning back to Noah. "I'm guilty of all their charges. I don't see how I wouldn't be exiled, to be completely honest with you."

"You were manipulated by Meredith Cain. She recruited you. She brought you into that . . . *group.*"

"She might've recruited me," Lars said, "but I did those things. I tortured the Ovarrow to get information from them. I hid data from Field Ops and Security. I leveraged their assets to give me what I needed, and I put trackers on comlink traffic, both civilian and CDF-encrypted channels. I also recruited people for Meredith."

Noah remembered trying to figure out who had been spying on them. He'd been squaring off against Lars and hadn't even known it at the time. "It's not that simple," he said. "She used your frustration to get you to do those things. That has to count for something."

Lars shook his head. "It doesn't make me innocent, Noah. Believe me, I've had this conversation with my father, my counselor, and my defense attorney. So what if I'm exiled?"

Noah pressed his lips together and looked away briefly. "Hurting the Ovarrow was wrong. If you tell them you regret doing it, they might be more lenient and allow you to stay in the colony."

Lars looked at Noah for a long moment as the seconds ticked by. His gaze became cold, almost brittle, with a hard edge. "I *don't* regret what I did to them. Don't you understand? It was necessary. You might not approve of the methods, but they did yield results. We're better prepared for the Krake because of them."

Noah clenched his teeth together. "I know you think you believe it, and you sound like you've rehearsed that little speech in your head a lot. Perhaps you even said the same thing to your father, but you're wrong. Cain got into your head."

"I do believe it. I don't regret what I did to the Ovarrow. We can't trust them."

"You're wrong."

Lars raised his chin and his lips flattened. Then he stood up. "I think maybe I should leave," he said, then walked over to the door and banged on it a few times.

Noah stood up and accessed his wrist computer. The guard appeared at the door but was unable to open it.

"You don't get to leave that easily," Noah said and opened a comlink to the guard. "We'll need a few more minutes. It's fine."

The guard looked at him through the window, and Noah held up his wrist, showing he had the room locked down. Then the guard left, and Noah had no doubt that in a few minutes, they'd cancel his override.

Lars leaned back against the wall and looked up at the ceiling. "What are you doing, Noah?" he asked tiredly.

"You've built this wall around you, Lars. The person I know—the friend I grew up with—wasn't okay with hurting anybody. I know you hurt the Ovarrow. And I know you work hard convincing yourself it was necessary and that you were working to protect all of us. But don't stand there and tell me you don't regret it—that you looked into the eyes of intelligent beings, knowing you were causing them pain, and you have no regrets. It's a shield, Lars. Because if you admitted regret for what you did, that would call into question *all* the things you did, and you'd have to realize that maybe you went too far."

Lars's mouth formed a grim line, and he regarded Noah coldly.

"Exiling you to some island isn't going to help you."

Lars shook his head slightly. "It's not about helping me. It's about justice."

"What if they don't exile you? What if you're allowed to stay under some kind of probation?"

Lars considered it for a few moments. "It doesn't matter. I'll never have security clearance again."

"You don't need security clearance to help protect the colony. But before any of that, you have to admit the truth to yourself."

Lars looked away from him and glared toward the window.

"Admit it. Just admit it to yourself at least. It's not going to hurt you to admit you regret what you did," Noah said and stepped toward Lars.

"It doesn't matter," Lars said, his voice sounding raspy.

The locking mechanism of the door opened, and the guard came in.

"It *does* matter. It's the only thing that does, Lars."

The guard took Lars into custody and escorted him out of the room, but Noah remained. For a few seconds there he'd thought he was beginning to reach him. Noah wanted to help his friend see reason, but he wasn't sure if he could.

He sighed.

It didn't mean he'd stop trying. He looked down at the chair. Suddenly irritated, he shoved it toward the table and left the room.

CHAPTER 9

onnor walked into the Colonial Research Institute at Sanctuary. The institute had expanded over the years as more specializations were added. It now rivaled other more well-established schools on New Earth and was still a popular choice among new students, despite its unfortunate acronym. Connor had seen more than a few students cry at some point, but he was also sure it had nothing to do with the name "CRI."

The recovery institute Connor had helped establish here at Sanctuary had a close partnership with the CRI. Connor still remembered when he'd proposed the project to Ashley Quinn while she'd been governor of the colony. He'd done it to help veterans of the CDF, which was later expanded to include Field Ops and Security. A few years later, there was another expansion to include civilians who suffered from PTSD. The model for the Sanctuary Recovery Institute had been copied and implemented at other colonial cities. Connor's involvement was minimal these days, especially since he'd rejoined the CDF. Diaz volunteered there on a regular basis and was involved with organizing events for veterans.

Connor walked through the halls of the CRI and heard a heated discussion coming from one of the laboratories. The young researcher who was standing in the doorway turned, and her eyes widened at seeing Connor.

"I'm sorry about that," she said and gestured toward the room.

He waved it off. "No worries."

She walked back into the room, and Connor heard her urge the others to calm down, then suggested they all go get some coffee.

He kept going, and he wasn't sure if it was because he'd heard coffee mentioned that he began to smell it. He rounded the corner and headed to the end of the corridor where Lenora's office was located. Someone was brewing a medium roast blend. It wasn't the dark and bitter Colonial Death Wish he'd taken a liking to, but it could do in a pinch.

A short distance ahead was an open door, and the sweet scent of freshly baked pastries wafted into the hall, making his stomach growl. Ian must have baked this morning and brought his wares in. Ian Malone was a field researcher specializing in seismology. They had teamed up for a few field missions, exploring various regions of the continent. It would be good to catch up with him.

He was almost to Ian's office door when he heard Lenora's voice echoing down the hall.

"What do you mean the transport has been canceled?" Lenora asked with a slight rise in volume and a tone of irritation.

Connor quickened his pace, bypassing Ian's office, and headed straight to Lenora. "That was me," he said. "Don't bite their heads off. I've arranged for our transport."

Lenora gave him a slightly exasperated look. He should've told her, but he'd forgotten. He looked at her, offering a one-sided smile as an apology. She answered it.

"Never mind then," she said and closed the comlink. She arched an eyebrow. "When I invited you to come with me, I figured we'd use a standard Field Ops escort."

Connor nodded. "Yeah, I know that, but I have a squad with me. The Hellcat will get us there faster."

Lenora's full lips lifted, and her gaze narrowed playfully. "So, you'd like this to be a fast trip is what you're telling me?"

Connor grinned and shook his head slowly. "Yeah, sometimes when we're out there for a few days, you get kind of whiny and needy, and I just can't take it anymore."

"Is that so? I guess this is a good time to bring up what the sleeping arrangements will be on this trip. Separate tents," she said as if she was checking a box, turning her back to him to pick up a tablet computer from her desk.

Connor seized the moment to grab her from behind and swing her around. Lenora erupted into a gale of laughter. "I know exactly where I'm going to be sleeping," he said and set her down. She turned around and put her hands on his shoulders, smiling. Her eyes gleamed. When he was with Lenora, he was home.

She stepped away from him and walked around her desk, putting things into her backpack. "Is Nathan still insisting that you travel with a protective detail?"

"What can I say? I'm essential to the CDF. It's one of the perks that come with the job," Connor replied.

Lenora glanced away from him for a moment and powered off her holoscreen. "It's probably a good idea that they come."

"Why is that?"

"You never know what we'll run into out there."

"All right, now you've piqued my interest. What are we looking for?" he asked.

"Since we have better Ovarrow translators, we've been going back through the archives we found here," Lenora said, fastening her backpack. "Well, not just here—every site we've ever cataloged, but nothing really rivals or has the most intact systems as what we've found here at Sanctuary."

There was no one who knew the Ovarrow data archives better than Lenora. She had spent years here, and even though she'd collaborated on other research efforts outside Sanctuary, this was where it had all started.

Something in her tone gave him a mental jolt of excitement. "Wait a minute. Are you saying you found something?"

"Not exactly," she said.

"I thought the data analysts had done an exhaustive search on everything we collected so far after we brought home the new translators we got from the Krake," Connor said.

As they walked out of Lenora's office, he glanced toward Ian's door, but it was closed. He must have left.

"They did," Lenora said. "They've categorized things, and that data is still being analyzed. What did you expect them to find—something in big bold lettering that says 'The key to defeating the Krake is here'?"

He gave her a look and shook his head. Then he pretended to consider it for a moment and shrugged. "I would accept that. It would make things a lot easier. Could you make that happen?"

"Aren't you the one who says that if it's too easy, it probably means we missed something."

"Yeah," Connor said. "We need a breakthrough."

"Don't I know it, but no, we haven't found anything like that yet. In my experience, at least with any archaeological records, the recorded history isn't something that points a big sign at the data we're most interested in. No treasure maps here, but I found clues and some rumors about what the Ovarrow were doing in the final days of their war with the Krake. I can show it to you when we're en route, but it's . . ." Lenora paused for a moment, gathering her thoughts. "You have to understand—and you do better than most—but there was limited communication among the Ovarrow at the end of their war. There was a whole lot of mistrust, so what I have is just clues that the Ovarrow might have been holding Krake prisoners."

Connor did a double take and his eyes widened. "I love how you just casually throw that out there. This could be huge, Lenora."

She bit her lower lip a little and chose her words carefully. "I know it can have a major impact, but it also might be nothing. We might not find anything. I've chased a lot of red herrings over the years."

Connor nodded in understanding. "Why didn't the Ovarrow just send the data here?"

"Communications were spotty, and this place was a secret. The estimated timestamps for the entries were well after the Ice Age had already begun in earnest. I think we're lucky to have any references at all. Most of our searches into the Ovarrow data we've gathered focus on events that led up to the war they fought, but little focus has been on what came after. We know they went into the stasis pods—the ones that could anyway—and you found a group that didn't, but *they* don't want anything to do with us."

"Brashirker," Connor said and pressed his lips together for a few seconds. "He did tell me that his ancestors had a working arch gateway. They tried to find the Krake home world but failed."

She nodded and tucked her long auburn hair behind her ears. "It was that report that got me thinking about this and looking in other places. The Ovarrow essentially staged a rebellion in the midst of their own catastrophic war. They destroyed gateways while attempting to reverse engineer Krake technology. I don't think it's that far of a stretch to consider that they had taken Krake prisoners and were attempting to glean some intelligence from them."

"Maybe we should bring a few of Senleon's people with us to help with the search," Connor said.

Lenora was quiet for a few moments as they walked. "I thought about it, but I think we shouldn't for right now. Sometimes it's difficult for the Ovarrow to revisit some of the old sites and not have a certain bias about them. The Ovarrow who went into stasis still remember the world they left behind. I'm not saying we should keep it a secret from them, but maybe we should bring them in after we do our own analysis."

"This is your project; I'm just here to help. We'll do this your way," Connor said.

The Ovarrow had soldiers who were working with the CDF for off-world missions. There was even cooperative military training occurring now for joint task forces. The Ovarrow population had nearly doubled in the past year as they built up their city to be able to accommodate those recovered from stasis pods. It was good that they'd managed to bring more Ovarrow out of stasis, but it took time for them to acclimate to an unfamiliar world. It also took time to build trust. Lenora, and especially Dash, had worked with the Ovarrow, but they weren't the only ones. Relationships were being built, and ever since Cerot had returned with Connor from their mission on the Krake world, the Ovarrow's attitude toward the colonists had begun to change for the better. There was more cooperation, and the Ovarrow had come to respect the colonists and the CDF. More and more Ovarrow were starting to believe that their best chance of surviving another war with the Krake was to work with the colonists. Their help had been instrumental to successful off-world missions, such as what they'd done with the Gesora.

"So how many sites are we going to then?" Connor asked.

"At least six to start with, and their locations aren't as far as you might've expected. We don't have to go to the other side of the continent where you encountered Brashirker, although it *is* several thousand kilometers from here."

"A more central region. Vitory told me those places were among the last to hold out. There had been a strong military presence there," Connor said and pursed his lips in thought. "I wonder if we'll find any equipment they could use."

"You never know. They were good at salvaging old equipment and making something new out of it."

They left the Colonial Research Institute's main building and headed across the campus toward the nearest landing platform.

"I haven't heard from Dash in a while," Lenora said.

"He's been assisting the CDF with off-world missions. He's rather unique in that he has the expertise from all his Ovarrow research and he's also able to keep up with the physical rigors involved with those missions. He's not the only one. There have been others, and I think that's due in large part to him."

Lenora smiled. "So, you've got him recruiting for you."

"I can't do all the work now, can I?"

"I'd hate to see anything happen to him."

"You say that about all your former students."

Lenora grinned a little. "Not all students are the same, but there are a few of the good ones that kinda stick with you. Like how you feel about some of the soldiers you've trained. Do you remember what Sean was like in the beginning?"

"I'll never forget, but try not to worry. I have good people keeping an eye on Dash, and he can take care of himself."

"I know you do. I . . . It's a shame we can open a gateway between universes, and the only thing we seem to do is use it for war. There are, what, hundreds of worlds we intend to explore, but the primary objective is the Krake. And I get how important that is. I just wish it was different. I wish we could . . . I wish we didn't have to worry about the Krake anymore."

"Me too, Lenora."

Over the years he'd been with her, Connor had watched her come to understand some of the dangers that came along with his line of work, but that didn't make worrying about them any easier for her. Sometimes it came to the surface in a conversation, and he felt a slight pang of regret about it. It was an irrational thing, but he felt it anyway. He wanted to make Lenora happy, and he wanted them all to be safe. She wanted *him* to be safe. Connor knew he wasn't the only person to ever want to change things so the woman he loved wouldn't have to worry. She felt the same too. The best thing for him to do was to let her vent her feelings, even if there wasn't anything he could do about it.

He was glad he'd decided to take some time off to travel with her. In the years preceding the Vemus War, Connor had run himself ragged preparing their defenses and essentially creating the CDF. He'd alienated Lenora and his friends during that time, and it had nearly cost him everything. He wouldn't do that again. These precious moments were just as important as all the other efforts he was a part of to help defend the colony. Sometimes when Connor thought about the person he'd been during those times, he became more aware of just how far he'd come. He supposed he took a certain comfort in it. There were too many people who would never get that kind of chance, and now even more people were going to die in this war with the Krake. Maybe it would even cost him his life. If this happened, Connor wouldn't hesitate. If he could trade his life to prevent the Krake from attacking New Earth, he'd do it, but that didn't mean he'd throw his life away; it was just that he was willing to make the sacrifice. He wasn't the only one. Every soldier who put on the CDF uniform was willing to do the same.

The colonists were a lot different from the people he'd known back on Old Earth, and there were now generations of them here. They'd claimed a home on this planet, made their lives here, started families here. Connor had kept himself apart from all that for years, but not anymore. There'd been many reasons for this separation throughout his military career, whether it was duty and honor or necessity. But none of those reasons could hold a candle to the one that eclipsed them all—his family and his friends. New Earth was his home. It was the place where he'd truly started to live. That was why Connor was willing to take time to accompany Lenora on this trip. These were the moments that made all the work worthwhile.

He reached out and took Lenora's hand. Her eyes widened for a moment, and she smiled. She gave his hand a gentle squeeze, and they headed to the landing platform.

CHAPTER 10

Over the next few days, they searched for hidden Ovarrow sites within the borders of one of their most powerful nation-states. The sparse landscape hardly indicated that this had all once been densely populated.

"I thought the places we'd be looking for would be easier to find, sir," Sergeant Benjamin Cook said.

Connor glanced at Cookie. He'd first met the young sergeant after the bridge collapsed in the Ovarrow city. Lenora had helped save his life.

"Are they that good at hiding things, sir?" Corporal Dugan asked.

"Sometimes," Connor replied. "Also, this entire landscape has been altered by glaciers."

They were finishing up another day of fruitless searching and had made camp for the evening. He glanced over to where Lenora stood, studying a map on a holoscreen. She was discussing something with Keras. On a secondary screen, they were reviewing the references that Lenora had found in the Ovarrow archives.

They'd just finished eating dinner, and they'd split up into clusters, talking around the two campfires. Connor loved camping, and it was also a popular pastime for colonists. They had recon drones patrolling the area, which were being monitored by the soldiers on watch.

"Yeah, but could the glaciers really change the landscape that much? To the point where we wouldn't be able to tell if we were standing on top of some kind of Ovarrow facility?" Lieutenant Doug Garfield asked. The CDF pilot was tall and lanky, with narrow shoulders.

"It depends," Connor replied. "The way it was explained to me was that it had to do with the geology of the surrounding area. If this place had been mainly bedrock, then when the glaciers traveled, they would've just formed over the top of it, but this area here would be considered soft. The soil underneath is quite deep. That's why the trees in this area are so tall. So, when the glaciers came through here, they literally pushed everything out of their path, and when they retreated, the same thing happened."

"How do you know so much about this, sir?" Cookie asked.

"We needed to learn it, or *I* needed to learn it when we were searching for Ovarrow bunkers. They were hidden and not always easy to find."

They had spent the last few days flying and surveying regions of the continent. They'd also explored select areas on foot but hadn't really found anything all that encouraging. Lenora was attempting to find places that were secret when the Ovarrow built them. They'd been built away from population centers like cities, so she was trying to triangulate the location based on rumors from a few hundred years ago. So much time had passed that most travel routes or anything resembling roads were gone. They had tasked a few satellites in the area to perform another topographical analysis of the region they were searching to help narrow down their search grid.

Lenora powered off the holoscreen and joined them.

"Dr. Bishop, are we there yet?" Cookie asked, drawling out the question with a grin. Several of the other soldiers joined in.

Lenora smiled. "Very funny," she said and sat down across from Connor. "We have a new site to go to tomorrow, and it looks promising."

"I hope so. Right now, we're striking out. We're oh for three," Connor said.

Lenora drank out of her canteen and then glanced at the group of men around the campfire. "I know you guys like a contest. I'll tell you what. If we don't find anything by lunchtime tomorrow, I'll let General Gates here pick the next destination, and you can vote on it."

Cookie and Dugan looked at Connor for a moment and then nodded.

"Ready, willing, and always able," Connor said.

Lenora gave him a knowing smile.

Keras closed her tablet computer and looked at Connor. She seemed to be considering whether or not to ask him a question. He waited her out.

"General Gates," Keras said formally, "with everything we've built here on New Earth, all our defenses that we have in place, if the Krake came here . . . I guess I'm just trying to understand how bad it would be. I know that when the Vemus attacked us, it was . . ." she paused for a moment before continuing. "I understand that they overwhelmed our defenses. So, what I'm trying to ask is that with what you and the rest of the CDF have built up in our defense, do we even need to worry about the Krake?"

The other soldiers around the campfire glanced at Connor and then focused their attention on the flames. Valerie Keras was an Ovarrow technical expert from the research institute.

"You're asking me whether you should be worried about the Krake. The answer is yes. The Krake concern all of us. But you're right. We *have* been building up our defenses, and we're doing everything we can to keep everyone safe," Connor said.

"Some people I know are worried that if the Krake find our world, they could wipe us out. I just don't know what to think about it," she said.

Connor looked at her for a few moments. He knew people were talking about it, as well they should, but he didn't want to scare the young woman. However, he didn't want to lie to her either. "We've been asked to consider contingency plans if things get really bad. You've heard of the new colony that's going to be set up on Alpha-Zeta-Seventy-Four?"

"I've heard of it. There are going to be only five thousand colonists selected to go though."

Connor nodded. "That's right, and part of the parameters are for them to get the colony up and running as quickly as possible but also to prepare for the possibility of more colonists arriving. They'll have years to prepare and advance warning thanks to recent breakthroughs in communication. Would you consider applying to be a colonial candidate for the new colony?"

Keras frowned in thought for a few seconds. "I don't know. I like New Earth, and my family is here."

He glanced around at the others. "Anyone else considering volunteering?"

There was a small chorus of noncommittal "maybes" interspersed among acknowledgments that they hadn't even considered it.

"What about you, sir, and ma'am?" Cookie asked Connor and then looked at Lenora.

Connor glanced at Lenora for a moment, and she gave him a slight shake of her head. She wouldn't leave New Earth. "We're not volunteering to go. Don't get me wrong. I think it's a tremendous opportunity, but I like it here too much."

Corporal Dugan sighed heavily. "I think I speak for most of us here, sir, and ma'am, but that makes us feel a lot better."

"Why is that?" Connor asked.

Dugan looked at him with an unwavering, determined gaze. "We need you, General."

The sentiment was echoed by the other soldiers, and Connor gave them a nod. They were part of the reason he'd returned to the CDF.

Connor stood up. "I think I'll take a short walk," he said and looked at Lenora with an unspoken invitation to join him.

She got to her feet. When they were far enough away from the others, she spoke. "You were never really comfortable with that sort of thing."

Connor raised his eyebrows questioningly.

"People admire you."

"Not all of them."

"Not everyone's perfect, love," Lenora said. "Tomorrow we'll have to get up early because there's a lot of ground to cover. This one is by what used to be a major city in the area."

"Has anyone been there before?"

"They've done preliminary scouting but nothing substantial. We had probes search the area years ago, and it looked like remnant ruins, but back then, we stuck mainly to settlements that were more easily accessible. What we're looking for is military in nature."

"All right, sounds good to me," Connor said and then added, "Did you know Keras was going to ask me those questions?"

"Yes, she asked me if it was all right if she asked a few questions about the CDF. I told her it was fine."

"Diaz said we should start having more kids."

Lenora snorted and gave him a playful sideways look. "Well, since Diaz wants it, that settles it."

Connor chuckled. "We haven't talked about it."

"I figured you had enough on your mind, and I'm pacing you," Lenora said. He arched an eyebrow toward her. "I'm not in any rush, Connor, and neither are you. I'm afraid Diaz is just going to have to wait."

"I'll let him know," he replied with mock severity.

"Do you think he'll be all right with our decision?"

"He'll just need time. He really had his heart set on it."

———

The next day, a few hours after sunrise, they'd found something. From overhead, the area had looked like a shallow forest, but they were able to see to the ground with relative ease. What they'd discovered was a network of paths that could only be artificial. Straight edges and ninety-degree angles only occurred when people made them that way—or, in this case, the Ovarrow.

They'd found a safe place for Lieutenant Garfield to land the Hellcat and set off on foot. The winding path angled downward before opening up and becoming straight. The wind whistled through trees. Normally, descending pathways led to a river or stream, but not here. The path led downward because there had once been some kind of Ovarrow facility here. Collapsed rooftops packed tightly from sediment and overgrowth could be seen like the bones of a buried skeleton.

"I never expected it to look like this," Cookie said.

The path was gritty and coarse, as if the dirt was composed of more rock than actual soil. They reached the bottom, and the path leveled off. Deep tree roots were intertwined among the remnant Ovarrow buildings on either side of them. Connor glanced upward, and the gray skies looked to be a long way above them.

"Sanctuary was like this when we first discovered it," Connor replied.

They had six reconnaissance drones mapping the area, and it was proving to be extensive. He looked at Lenora. "I think we're going to need to split into two teams."

"Yeah, we'll be able to cover more ground that way. We may even want to camp down here tonight," Lenora said.

Connor heard a couple of the soldiers ask if she was serious, and they were quickly hushed. Lenora looked over at the soldiers.

"I have allergies, ma'am," Murray said and sniffled.

"So do I," Lenora replied, knowing that Murray was joking.

"Did someone say they have allergies?" Corporal Dugan said, looking at Murray. "I've got the perfect cure for that. Come with me," he said, and the two jogged ahead, scouting the area.

Connor heard Dugan tell Murray about how exercise was a cure for allergies. They eventually reached an area where there were quite a few paths branching off from the one they were walking on.

"All right, everyone, gather around," Connor said. When they did, he continued. "We're going to split up into two groups. Sergeant Cook, I want you to escort Ms. Keras here and take Green, Jones, and Yemshi," he said, bringing up a partial map based on the recon drone feeds. "Looks like there's a central area here where we can meet. Everyone else is with me." He glanced at Lenora. "Lead the way, Dr. Bishop."

Keras came over to Lenora. They exchanged a few words, and then she rejoined the second group.

As they continued, they noticed that many of the buildings they passed had collapsed and were so overgrown with thick, thorny vines that anything inside had long since been destroyed.

"We need to look for access below ground. Anything that's been on the surface here isn't going to be salvageable," Lenora said.

Connor nodded. "It looks like there's a bigger building not far from here. One of the drones tagged it."

She had cross-referenced the location of this site against any of the known Ovarrow cities they'd found in the records, and there wasn't any record of the site on any map they'd found so far.

"The Ovarrow wouldn't have marked military sites," Connor said as they came to a stop in front of a large building. The walls looked like they'd been reinforced with thick plating that could only be used for armor. Whoever built this place had wanted it to be protected.

He watched as Corporal Dugan set thermite charges to burn through the lock on the door. Connor sent one recon drone to patrol the area around them while tasking the remaining two to help them explore inside.

As they went through the door, the corridors beyond reminded him of that first bunker where they'd encountered Syloc such a long time ago. So much had changed since then.

The musky scent of stagnant water mixed with rotting vegetation quickly gave way to stale air. Dark mold covered the walls in a porous buildup over small puddles of water that dripped down from cracks in the roof. They worked their way through the facility, but Connor didn't think they'd actually reached it yet. They were still walking down one of several interconnecting corridors.

"What do we expect to find down here?" Murray asked Lenora.

"I'm hoping we'll find some data repositories for what happened here," she replied.

"And in them, you're looking for a reference to the Krake?" Murray asked.

"I hope so. Don't worry, I'm not going to do the analysis here. We'll take a copy of the data we find, and I'll do the analysis back at Sanctuary."

They were all quiet after that. They found rooms, but they were empty, and no one could begin to guess what they'd been used for. The facility didn't have power in any of the rooms they found, but they'd brought portable power generators with them to open the doors. Lenora had the latest translator software on her PDA and had distributed it to their group. Connor had his on as well, and the translation of the Ovarrow language automatically showed on his internal heads-up display.

"It's this way," Lenora said.

"How can you be sure?" he asked.

"Because I recognize the layout. I think the archives at Sanctuary were modeled after this place."

Connor had one of the drones fly ahead of them to scout the area and then launched another one to scout a different path just in case they found something else. So far, the drones had found various storage rooms filled with Ovarrow weapons that probably wouldn't work anymore. All their power sources were depleted. He began to wonder if any of the Ovarrow had ever planned on coming back to this place.

"General, I'm getting a power reading up ahead," Dugan said.

Connor gave them a nod, and Corporal Dugan gestured for Murray to follow him. Connor glanced at Lenora. He could remember a time when she'd been impatient with efforts to secure the area, but now she knew the value of a little extra precautionary effort. She wore a sonic hand blaster on her belt, but the rest of them were armed with AR-71s, which were standard issue for the CDF.

A little farther on, they found a room with multiple consoles inside. Most of the consoles in the room were dead and beyond repair, but there was a central console that had a small power supply still available to it. The Ovarrow mesh screen had deteriorated and was unusable. Connor squatted down in front of the control panel and used his combat knife to pry it open. Lenora squatted next to him and connected a data relay device.

"I have an active connection. Downloading the data to my PDA," Lenora said.

Dugan and Murray joined them. "How can anything be stored on that console? It looks like it's falling apart," Murray said.

"That's because the data isn't actually stored in the console. It's linked to another area," Connor said.

Lenora monitored the download on her PDA and then glanced up at Connor. "We should look for the data storage archive too. There might be repositories that this console doesn't have access to but that we could bring back with us. If they're too fragile, I can try a few things to get the data we need."

Connor nodded. "Is there any way to tell whether the data is different from what we already have?"

Lenora had begun to reply when two of their drone video feeds suddenly went dark. Both Dugan and Murray turned and faced the door.

"Sir?" Dugan said, looking at Connor.

"The feed is gone, Corporal. Something took out the drones."

"Yes, sir."

The two CDF soldiers went to the door and checked the corridor just outside.

Connor looked down at Lenora. "How much longer?"

"It's almost finished," she replied without looking up. "What happened?"

"We had two recon drones go down at the same time."

"I guess that rules out a malfunction."

Connor nodded. He brought up each of the drones' video feeds before they'd gone off-line but couldn't see anything. He had maintained a comlink connection to the recon drone that was patrolling outside the building, and that one was still working.

"The one outside is still functioning . . ." he began to say and then stopped. "Scratch that. It's down as well. We have to go."

Lenora took her backpack off and pulled out a small comlink. She attached it to the Ovarrow console, checked her PDA, and stood to put her backpack on. "We can go. I've connected the comlink to the PDA to get the rest of the data."

Connor checked his AR-71 and put his MPS into protect mode. Lenora did the same with her suit.

He walked toward the door. "Have you been able to contact the others?"

"Negative, sir," Dugan replied.

"All right, let's get out of here. You two are on point," Connor said.

The two CDF soldiers led the way, and Connor gestured for Lenora to walk ahead of him so he could bring up the rear. They hadn't detected any ryklars in the area or any Ovarrow, for that matter. Ryklars sometimes hunted the recon drones when they weren't in stealth mode, and they hadn't put the drones in stealth mode. But the drones were able to project the ryklar deterrent signal, so that should've taken care of any predators lurking in the area. He didn't think there were ryklars down here. It was too quiet.

"What do you think took out the drones?" Lenora asked.

"I don't know. Maybe this place had some kind of countermeasure set up . . . you know, some kind of defense," Connor said. He didn't like that they weren't able to reach the others. The colonists needed to develop and distribute handheld subspace communicators. Right now, they had them only on ships and vehicles.

They were all quiet as they made their way back to the main corridor. Connor saw Lenora check her PDA a few times, monitoring the progress of the data dump.

CHAPTER 11

Something else was in the corridors with them. Connor and the others heard movement through the tunnels—just snippets of sound but something they couldn't ignore. Even with enhanced vision in the dim light, none of them had actually seen whatever it was.

Lenora put her PDA into her pocket and pulled out her sonic hand blaster. They hurried down the corridor, pausing at each intersection. Murray and Dugan cleared the corners and then gestured for the rest of them to follow.

They repeated this four more times, and then Murray came to a halt. "Gah!" he said, peering down one of the adjacent corridors.

Dugan turned toward him and aimed his weapon. "What is it?"

"I don't know. I thought I saw something moving down that way."

Connor joined them and looked down the long, dark passageway. It was clear. "What did you see?"

Murray looked at him. "That's just it, sir. I saw it for only a second. It was toward the ceiling."

"There's a corridor that runs parallel over there," Lenora said quietly.

Connor brought up the partially finished map from the recon drones' scouting. "Looks like there are multiple corridors all around here."

Dugan glanced at Connor. "Ryklars?"

It was a good guess. Ryklars could mask their body heat from thermal imagers and were known to stalk their prey.

"Stay sharp," Connor said and looked at Murray. "Cover our six."

The CDF private took up a position at the rear, and they continued onward, moving slow and steady. If there really were ryklars here, they could be circling, waiting to ambush.

They approached the next intersection, and Connor slowed down. He glanced at Dugan, who shook his head. Connor didn't hear anything either. They cleared the corners and moved on. Just one more section of intersecting corridors before they reached the long corridor that led to the exit.

"Be ready," he whispered, and Dugan nodded.

He had observed ryklars in the wild for years, and he'd witnessed the hunting tactics that the deadly creatures executed with cunning efficiency. Connor had seen ryklar packs teach young hunters to stalk prey. They preferred to attack when least expected. Just when their unsuspecting quarry thought they were safe, the ryklars would attack with sudden ferocity, blind-siding their prey.

Nearing the corridor that led to the exit, both Connor and Dugan slowed down, then stopped and waited. Murray moved up behind Dugan on the opposite side of the corridor, hugging the wall, while Connor and Lenora were on the other side. Connor glanced back at her. She looked at him and bobbed her head in a small movement.

They crept to the edge of the corridor. Once they were in position, Connor and Dugan spun around the corner, weapons held ready.

Nothing.

The corridor was empty. They didn't linger for more than a few seconds before heading toward the exit. It was a straight shot right to the outside. Connor saw the open doorway up ahead and slowed down. There was no need to rush outside. Whatever had been stalking them hadn't come any closer. They waited there for a few moments.

"I'm not able to establish a link to any of the recon drones," Murray said.

They stepped outside, keeping their weapons ready, and made a quick sweep of the area.

"Clear," Dugan said, and Murray echoed the same.

Connor opened a comlink to the other team, and Sergeant Cook answered.

"What's your status, Sergeant?"

They began walking down the pathway, and Connor looked at Dugan. "Get a lock on their position," he told the corporal.

"General," Sergeant Cook said, "we were exploring the area when some flying creatures attacked our recon drones. They were large enough to take them out. They swarmed them, forcing them to land, and pounded on them until they stopped working. I don't think we should camp here tonight. There's been a group of those things following us, and more are gathering. Have you seen them?"

"Negative. We were inside one of the buildings when our drones were taken out. We didn't get a good look at what did it," Connor replied and scanned the upper levels of the buildings nearby. In the shadows, there was a flutter of movement. "Hold, Corporal," he said and gestured toward where he'd seen the movement.

"I see them, sir."

"We have company too," Connor said to Sergeant Cook on the comlink. "We're trying to get a better look at them."

They were reptilian in appearance, with wedge-shaped heads and large mouths, which probably had rows of razor-sharp teeth. Connor's internal heads-up display showed infrared on one half. Their bodies glowed with the orange glow of their body heat. One of the creatures walked on bent wings, which looked awkward. These creatures didn't spend much time on the ground. Their rib cages expanded deep in their chests, and there was a grouping of flutters from gill-like slits on their necks. They looked to be about a meter from head to hind quarters. Then Connor caught sight of their long tails that more than doubled the creatures' body lengths.

One of the creatures saw them and grunted a warning to the others. The group swung their heads toward Connor and the others. Their forward-facing eyes glared at them, and the grim set of their mouths appeared moments from shrieking.

"There are more behind us," Lenora said.

Connor turned and saw that twelve of the flying creatures had flown out of the building they'd just come from. Their leathery skin displayed a wide range of complex, earth-toned color schemes. They hovered in the air for a moment and then flew toward them, roaring as they came.

Connor and the others scattered to the side.

"Yemshi, get that deterrent signal up now," Sergeant Cook said, his voice coming over the comlink. "General, we have ryklars in the area," he said and paused for a moment. "What do you mean it's not working?"

Connor couldn't hear the other end of the conversation and waited. He mouthed the word "ryklars" to the others. The flying creatures swooped past them and circled around.

"Sir, the ryklars are not responding to the deterrent signal."

"Are they closing in on you?" Connor asked.

"Negative. They don't seem agitated . . . uh, they aren't red-faced. There are eight of them just a hundred meters away."

A few moments later, Sergeant Cook marked the location of the ryklars on the map, and Connor was able to see it. He looked at Dugan. "Check to the west."

Dugan and Murray went a short distance away from them to the nearest adjacent path.

Dugan opened a comlink to Connor. "No contact," he whispered.

Connor highlighted a waypoint on the map for Sergeant Cook. "Can you reach that location?"

"I think so, sir."

"All right, we'll meet you there."

"Sir, what should we do about the ryklars?" Sergeant Cook asked.

Ryklars could cover a hundred meters in a few seconds in an open area.

"If they don't attack, then don't engage them. We don't know how many of them are here," Connor replied.

"Understood, sir," Sergeant Cook said.

The comlink severed. Connor sent their coordinates to Lieutenant Garfield, who had waited with the Hellcat. After Connor received confirmation from Lieutenant Garfield, they began heading toward the waypoint. They stayed close to the walls of the pathway, and the flying creatures followed overhead. The narrow pathway prevented the creatures from dive-bombing them.

Connor glanced at Lenora. She held her weapon ready and stayed close by. "Never a dull moment, is there?" he said.

"Only if our luck changes," she replied. "Seriously, this stuff only happens to you." Lenora smiled at him.

The pathway ended, and they had to move along a wider thoroughfare. The flying creatures shrieked and dove closer and closer. Their high-pitched screams echoed all around them.

"They sound like damn banshees," Murray shouted.

"Watch out," Lenora said.

Connor spun around and brought his weapon up. There was a trio of the creatures flying right toward them, their claws extended. Connor aimed and fired. Three controlled bursts of hypervelocity darts tore into the creatures, and they crashed, tumbling to the ground. Dugan and Murray fired their weapons. The banshees flailed for a few moments and then became still.

Ahead of them, six ryklars stood in a phalanx formation. The spotted predators squatted down and watched them intently, their chests heaving as they drew breath. They had a set of smaller arms toward the front and much longer arms behind those. Thick, stubby tentacles hung down, making their hideous faces long and menacing. At least the tentacles were a deep gray like the fur of their spotted hides.

They were nearly two hundred meters away from them.

"They don't look agitated," Lenora said.

If their bearded tentacles had been red, the ryklars would have been in a highly agitated state, and they'd attack anything that moved.

"They're agitating me," Dugan said.

"Hold your fire," Connor said. "Someone is controlling them."

He peered at them, and his neural implants enhanced his vision. Connor looked at the ryklars' ears, almost expecting that they would be mutilated like the ones they'd found before under Brashirker's control. But these ryklars weren't mutilated. One of the ryklars cocked its head to the side, and Connor saw a shiny piece of metal.

"They've got a transmitter on the sides of their heads," Connor said.

They backed away and went down a side street. On each adjacent path they passed, they saw more ryklars. They were being herded.

They kept moving and heard sounds of weapons-fire nearby. They started running, and Connor heard someone scream in the distance. They rounded the corner and saw several dead ryklars lying on the path. Sergeant Cook and Keras were lending a hand to Private Yemshi, pulling him back to cover. Connor and the others joined them.

"They attacked us from above," Sergeant Cook said. "They seem to be coordinating with those flying creatures."

"Is anyone else hurt?" Connor asked.

"Negative, sir."

Connor opened a comlink to the Hellcat. "What's your ETA?"

"ETA is eight minutes, sir," Garfield replied.

"Understood. Be advised the area is hot," Connor said.

He looked at the others. "The Hellcat is on its way. We need to hold out here. Dugan, take Green and Murray and hold that position across the street."

They were at a major intersection. The paths had opened pretty wide, and there was more than enough room for the Hellcat to set down when it arrived. Connor told Lenora to stay back while he and Cookie went to the corner.

Without recon drones, he couldn't get a bird's-eye view of the area. Overhead, the flying creatures circled in an ever-expanding group. There were dozens of them now, with more on the way. Two separate groups of ryklars were also on approach, using the buildings for cover and preventing them from getting a clear shot.

"Conserve your ammunition. Controlled bursts only," Connor said.

More ryklars arrived.

"General," Sergeant Cook said, "are those Ovarrow moving with the ryklars?"

Connor looked where Cookie had gestured with the end of his rifle. The Ovarrow had a distinctive profile. They were tall, with long limbs and pointy protrusions on their shoulders and elbows. These were covered in a pale green metallic armor. They carried long rifles, similar to what the Mekaal used.

The Ovarrow soldiers sprinted in the midst of the ryklars, completely at ease among the deadly creatures. They moved with precision and a soldier's discipline, and they had Connor and the others surrounded.

Connor activated the Ovarrow translator and stepped out from cover until he stood in the middle of the intersection.

"We are not your enemy. We didn't realize this was your territory," Connor said.

The Ovarrow soldiers went quiet, and then there was a burst of sound from their ranks.

"My name is Connor Gates. You're not the first Ovarrow we've met. Which one of you is the warlord?"

One of the groups of Ovarrow soldiers spoke quietly among themselves for a few moments. Then one of them came forward. He removed his helmet and his jade, feline-like eyes narrowed. "How do you speak our words?"

"We use a translator interface," Connor replied, staying where he was.

"Where did you get the translator?"

"From the Krake."

The Ovarrow soldier went rigid. "The Krake are here?"

The soldiers began focusing their attention on the skies overhead, attempting to peer through the tangle of trees above them.

"They're not here," Connor said quickly. "They don't know about this world."

The warlord studied him. "They once knew this world. They will be back."

Connor regarded the Ovarrow. "Yes, they will."

"I am called Kasmon, and we are the Konus." He looked from Connor to the others for a few moments. "Why have you come here?"

"We came here looking for information about the Krake."

The Konus soldiers still had their weapons pointed at Connor and the others.

"How did you find this place?" Kasmon asked.

"Tell your soldiers to lower their weapons, and we'll do the same," Connor replied.

Kasmon regarded him with a hard glare. Then he turned away and gestured for the soldiers to stand down. Connor followed suit. He also sent a message to Lieutenant Garfield, ordering him to stay back. He'd call in the Hellcat if they needed it.

"I've done as you asked," Kasmon said.

Connor first explained how they arrived on the planet almost fifteen years ago, how they'd explored the ruins, found arch gateways, and encountered the Krake. Then, he told the Ovarrow how they'd found references to this place with indications they might have had Krake prisoners during the war.

Kasmon didn't look like he believed Connor, who then showed him the translator interface. The Ovarrow studied it for a few seconds and then gestured for one of his soldiers to come over. They both examined the interface.

"You might have encountered the Krake, but you could also have found their tech," Kasmon said. "We recognize their technological footprint from our own archives. What I'd like to know now is whether or not you are allied with the Krake."

"We're not," Connor replied. "We've fought them. We've used the arch gateway and constructed our own space gates based on what we found. I can share this information with you. We're not here to fight with you. We're trying to find the Krake home universe. We've encountered other Ovarrow who are helping us."

"The gateways were destroyed."

"They weren't. We found one at the bottom of a lake and the remnants of the space gate elsewhere," Connor said and paused for a moment. "Far away from here."

Kasmon seemed to consider this.

"We've been on this planet for over fifteen years. We've never seen you before," Connor said.

"We work to keep our presence a secret, preparing for when the Krake return. You said you've encountered other Ovarrow. That means you must have found our stasis pods."

"Yes, we have. We've helped other Ovarrow come out of stasis."

"You've brought Ovarrow out of stasis? Where are they?"

"They are living in their own settlement. Their own city," Connor replied.

"How many of them are there?" asked Kasmon. Ovarrow had different ways of showing excitement, and having worked closely with them for the past year, Connor could tell Kasmon was keenly interested in this.

"Over sixty thousand have been brought out of stasis. How many Konus are there?"

Several of the Konus soldiers had joined them and were listening to the conversation. Lenora and the others had also joined, standing by Connor. The Konus soldiers gave a startled reaction to the number of Ovarrow Connor had mentioned.

Kasmon turned back to Connor. "There are many of us. We've brought Ovarrow out of stasis as well. The number of Konus is over one million citizens."

Connor's eyes widened. One million Ovarrow. Could Kasmon be lying? Where could they hide that many?

As if sensing his doubt, Kasmon continued. "We live underneath where it's safe. We have entire cities and a network of tunnels throughout this entire region. We are highly interested in meeting the Mekaal. They are a faction of Ovarrow we've heard of. Soldiers. They can help with the fight against the Krake."

Connor used his PDA to create a holographic screen that showed the continent. He then highlighted the region they were in and then the general region of where the colony was located. "This is where we live, and the Ovarrow city is within that region."

Kasmon studied the map.

"Why did you attack us? Why didn't you just try to contact us?" Connor asked.

"We didn't know who you were. We knew you used technology similar to the Krake and could be allied with them. If you are open to this, I would like to show you our city. You said you were seeking allies to fight the Krake."

Connor didn't like the flimsy excuse, but he did want to see their city. They might have just gotten off on the wrong foot. "I'd like that very much," he replied.

Kasmon shared the coordinates of where they were heading, and Connor forwarded that to Garfield. The Hellcat flew overhead, and Kasmon watched it with a bit of awe. There were over a hundred Konus soldiers escorting them. The ryklars and the flying creatures had left the area.

Kasmon told Connor how a group of them had emerged from their stasis pods over forty years ago. The stasis pods suffered some damage, and many Ovarrow had died. Connor knew this had to do with the faulty stasis technology the Ovarrow had used. Kasmon also told him about how some Ovarrow had rapidly aged after coming out of stasis. However, the survivors continued to rebuild. They sought out other bunker sites, and over the years, many Ovarrow had joined them.

Connor glanced at Lenora more than once. She listened to the conversation, as did Keras. The CDF soldiers were quiet and kept watch over the Konus soldiers. Connor was more comfortable being around so many Ovarrow soldiers since he had done so on many off-world missions. He knew Sergeant Cook was an excellent soldier and would keep a level head. Corporal Dugan would keep an eye on the other soldiers as well.

Throughout Connor's encounters with Ovarrow, they had been curious about human technology, but Kasmon was more interested in learning about the Mekaal. The Konus had mainly explored bunkers to the east.

"We've encountered Ovarrow far away on the eastern side of the continent, thousands of kilometers away from here," Connor said. He told Kasmon about Brashirker and the claim that they represented a group of Ovarrow who hadn't gone to stasis. They'd weathered the Ice Age.

"We've always wondered about that. There were rumors of groups of Ovarrow who banded together. We will try to find them as well," Kasmon said.

"We haven't been able to find them since the initial encounter. When they learned that we had encountered the Krake, they didn't want to get involved. I don't know how many of them are alive. They had adapted ryklars to be controlled like you did but using a different method."

"Different? How so?" Kasmon asked.

"We've encountered the ryklars before and are aware of the control signals used to command them. However, this group of Ovarrow didn't use implants like you do," Connor said and explained how the ryklars' heads had been mutilated so they couldn't hear the high frequency sound waves. Instead, they used flashes of different colored lights to control them.

"We began using implants on the ryklars after the great migration. Old city sites were coming online, and defense protocols were commanding the ryklars to . . ." Kasmon paused for a moment and looked at Connor. "Ryklars were used to help fight our wars."

They continued onward, and Kasmon led them to a plain building that never would've been spotted from above. Inside, a massive opening led to a dark tunnel.

Lieutenant Garfield initiated a comlink, and Connor answered. "General Gates, there has been an emergency call for you to return to Sierra. It's from General Hayes."

Garfield sent the official orders, and Connor viewed them on his internal heads-up display. He had stopped walking, and Kasmon watched him.

"I'm afraid I must apologize. I can't go with you. I've been recalled," Connor said.

Kasmon frowned for a moment. The other Konus soldiers had paused and waited for Kasmon to give them an order.

"Once I tell my government about you," Connor said, "they'll want to send an official diplomatic envoy to meet you. I'm sure they'll get out here as soon as possible. Meanwhile, I can leave you with a way to communicate with us," Connor said.

"I don't understand what can be so important that you need to leave right away, but I do understand that orders are orders. We take them just as seriously as you do. I look forward to our next meeting," Kasmon said.

Connor had Lieutenant Garfield fly the Hellcat nearby and land. He then left a long-range comlink system with a standard Ovarrow interface they'd used with the Mekaal in the past.

"I'll need to discuss it with our own leadership, but in this instance, I'm confident about what they would say," said Kasmon. "We have a common enemy in the Krake. And since we share this planet, we need to work together to defeat them."

After his experiences with all the Ovarrow he'd met on New Earth, Connor almost didn't know how to react to such a show of cooperation and an acknowledgment that the Krake were not only a threat, but something that could be overcome. Perhaps it was because the Konus had had over forty years to come to grips with their new lives. They had built themselves up in anticipation of continuing a fight with the Krake. It was almost refreshing.

"Until our next meeting," Connor said.

They returned to the Hellcat and walked up the loading ramp. Once they were airborne, he heard Murray talking to some of the other soldiers.

"I'm so glad we made it out of there. I wasn't sure if they were going to let us leave," Murray said.

"Did you see their reaction when General Gates told him we had to go?" Yemshi asked.

Connor glanced at Dugan and Cookie, and they both gave him a nod. "I think they were just as surprised to see us as we were to see them."

"It's probably that, sir," Cookie said.

Connor sat next to Lenora. "Were you able to get all the data off that console?"

"Yes. It must've finished sometime between when those flying creatures showed up and when the ryklars chased us into the Konus ambush," she said.

Connor's eyebrows raised. He knew that tone. Now that the danger had passed, she was allowing herself to digest what had happened. "You noticed that too."

Lenora nodded.

"I know what you mean, but the Ovarrow are aggressive when it comes to securing their territory. I've read reports of it from other world missions, and I've seen it myself."

She swallowed hard and then shook her head. "I'm just glad you were with us."

"Me too," Connor replied.

"I've been to countless Ovarrow ruins. Some of those expeditions had several hundred people, Field Ops included. Then I've been on others where it's just a handful of us. I figured with a CDF squad we'd be relatively safe," Lenora said, venting her frustration and fear.

"I thought we'd only find some abandoned ruins too. I don't know what to say, Lenora. No one can be prepared for everything."

She sighed. "I know, and you're right. I just haven't been in a situation like that since . . . it's been a while. I kept thinking about Lauren. You know."

Connor wrapped his arm around her shoulders in a hug.

"What's wrong with me? When did I become such an emotional mess?"

"You're not a mess. We have a family now. You're a mother. I feel the same way. There's nothing wrong with it, Lenora. It's natural. Hey," he said, "do you understand what I'm saying?"

Lenora nodded and then took a steadying breath. "I'm fine now," she said. "Do you know what the emergency recall was for?"

"It was just a recall. Nathan would have included more information if he needed to. I'm sure it's important but not . . . life-threatening."

"Okay. I'm not going to be able to do much in the way of analyzing this data until I get back to Sanctuary."

"Really? You're not going to dive right in here and now?"

Lenora chuckled. "No, and you can blame Noah for that. I get much better results when I upload the data to our systems back home. Much more processing and computational power. And, honestly, I'm fine with waiting until we get home."

Connor pursed his lips. "Wow, I mean, I never thought I'd see the day where you'd show that kind of patience."

She elbowed him in the side. "Jerk."

He grinned, but after a few moments, he started to think about their encounter with the Konus. He would have liked to have seen where they lived. Over a million Ovarrow here on New Earth! He didn't believe Kasmon was lying. All his encounters with the Ovarrow had allowed him to develop a keen sense of how they conducted themselves. Kasmon wasn't lying about how many Konus there were, but Connor did wonder whether Kasmon would've tried to stop them from leaving if the Hellcat hadn't shown up. There had been a moment where the soldiers had been poised to take action. He hadn't missed it, and neither had the others. But the fact that Kasmon had all but promised an alliance with the colony to unite against the Krake made Connor pause his suspicions.

He wondered how Senleon and Vitory would react when they learned that so many of their people were alive and thriving. What would this mean for them? Would they seek to join the Konus, or would they want to remain independent? Connor really didn't know and couldn't guess. Too many of the Ovarrow that had come out of stasis carried with them the nightmares of a collapsing civilization. It would take them time to move on and rebuild. Perhaps working with the Konus would help the Mekaal adjust to life after the stasis pods.

CHAPTER 12

onnor managed to snatch a little bit of sleep on the Hellcat as it flew them to the CDF base at Sierra, and after it landed, he and Lenora went to their on-base apartment. He had some time before he had to report to the Security Council meeting—time enough to take a shower and put on a clean uniform. By the time he was out of the shower, he found Lenora asleep in their bed. Connor quietly left their apartment and headed to the roof, where an aircar waited for him.

It was just after nine in the evening by the time he arrived at the capitol, where they were meeting in the main congressional chambers near Governor Wolf's office. He could hear the low buzz of multiple conversations before he even walked into the room.

He saw Bob Mullins speaking quietly with Selena Brown and Rex Coleman, and Connor frowned. The legislative and judicial branches of the colonial government usually didn't attend Security Council meetings. He spotted Nathan and went over to him. He didn't see Governor Wolf at all.

"Sorry I had to cut the holiday short," Nathan said.

"What's going on?" Connor asked.

"All I know right now is that Governor Wolf collapsed yesterday. She's been at the intensive care unit at Sierra Medical Center."

Connor's eyes widened. "Is she all right?"

"I don't know."

Dana Wolf was an older woman, but she was in excellent health. Connor couldn't think of anything that would knock her off her feet for long. She worked hard and was remarkably resilient. She reminded Connor of Tobias Quinn and was a worthy successor.

"Can everyone please quiet down," Mullins said. "We're going to start the emergency session now."

The people in the room found their way to their seats, and those who were in attendance from afar quieted down.

Mullins sat in the centermost chair where Dana Wolf usually sat. "Yesterday, while visiting New Haven, Governor Wolf collapsed from an unknown illness. This morning she was moved to the medical center here at Sierra. Earlier today, I was informed that Governor Wolf has suffered a massive coronary episode her doctors believe was caused by a rare virus found here on New Earth. The virus attacks the heart muscle, causing inflammation that prevents the heart from working properly. I've just been informed that the virus has spread to her other internal organs. At this time, the doctors are doing everything they can to save Dana Wolf's life."

Connor raised his hand.

Mullins looked at Connor. "Yes, General Gates."

"Has her family been informed?"

Mullins nodded. "Her husband, David, was at Phoenix Station and is currently en route back to New Earth. Her daughter is at the medical center, along with Dana's sister Beverly."

Connor had met Kayla Wolf on multiple occasions, but Lenora had had more contact with her after their harrowing experience together on the bridge that had been sabotaged at the Ovarrow city.

"In the interim," Mullins continued, "and in accordance with our laws, I will take over the governor's duties as the deputy governor until such time that Dana Wolf can resume her duties."

Bob Mullins was Dana Wolf's chief of staff and could be named the deputy governor. However, if he received a vote of no confidence by the other colonial leaders, then that office could be rescinded. Despite their differences, Connor knew Mullins could do the job. He had been suspicious of Mullins for years, especially when he was trying to find the rogue group that had implicated Kurt Johnson and Meredith Cain, and he felt a little of that old suspicion return. Sudden illnesses did occur randomly, and he couldn't entirely discount that fact, but he was still suspicious of the timing.

"I realize this comes as a shock and will be difficult," Mullins said. "I'll be releasing a statement to the colony in the morning. I don't want to keep this emergency session any longer than necessary. Anyone who is not on the Security Council will need to leave or disconnect. My office will be in touch with each of you tomorrow."

It took a few minutes for people to file out of the room, leaving a much smaller group. Connor saw a few new faces in the room—Major Natalia Vassar and a civilian named Jerry Sherman, both of whom were the lead candidates to become director of the Colonial Intelligence Bureau.

The meeting resumed.

"I realize that this news has come as a shock to most of you. I learned of it only this afternoon, and to be honest, I'm troubled by the whole thing," Mullins said.

Connor didn't doubt the sincerity in Mullins's voice.

"Our thoughts and prayers will be with Dana, but she would want us to keep the wheels turning," Mullins said and looked at Major Vassar. "As many of you are aware, the director of the Colonial Intelligence Bureau has not been named. Major Natalia Vassar was Governor Wolf's first choice for that position. In fact, if none of this had happened, she would have been offering you the position tomorrow . . . today that is," Mullins said, looking at Natalia. "Major Vassar, before you decide, I want to make sure you're aware that if you accept this position, you'll be resigning your commission to the Colonial Defense Force."

Natalia always sat ramrod straight, and she looked at Mullins with an unwavering gaze. "I understand, Mr. Mullins. I do accept the position as director of the Colonial Intelligence Bureau."

Connor felt a sense of relief knowing that the CIB would be in such good hands. He'd also need to find a replacement for her in the CDF.

"On behalf of all of us," Mullins said, "we thank you for your service in the CDF and look forward to your contributions leading the CIB," he said and looked at the man sitting next to Natalia. "Jerry Sherman, the position of deputy director of the CIB is offered to you if you will accept."

"I do accept," Jerry said.

Connor couldn't help but think that these were the strings attached to Natalia's new position as director of the CIB.

"Thank you," Mullins said. "There will be an investigation into Governor Wolf's illness. I don't think this comes as a surprise to any of you," he said and glanced at Connor. "There has been no indication of foul play, but we cannot afford to take something like this at face value. Dana Wolf was and is our leader, and given some of the current challenges, I don't want to rule out repercussions from the takedown of the rogue group led by Meredith Cain."

"This investigation will be my top priority," Natalia said firmly.

"How could Meredith Cain be involved?" Mayor Larson asked. "She's been banished and is living at a currently undisclosed location along with the other ringleaders of the rogue group."

"Meredith Cain was highly manipulative, and this is something she could have planned for. But this is why I want the investigation done," Mullins said.

The meeting continued for a little while longer, discussing status updates and next steps to allay the concerns that would be raised tomorrow when the rest of the colony learned what had happened to Dana Wolf.

"I realize it's getting late, but I have news that can't wait," Connor said and proceeded to give a high-level debriefing about his encounter with the Konus.

"This is very important news, and I appreciate your sharing it with us even though you haven't had time to put an official report together," Mullins said.

For years, Connor and Mullins had clashed over various issues concerning the colony, but he was sure Mullins was feeling emotional over what had happened to Governor Wolf. Maybe a little solidarity would go a long way.

The meeting ended, and after a short conversation with Nathan, Connor went to the medical center. He found Dana Wolf's room and stood outside it for a few minutes. He wanted to go inside, but he wasn't sure if it was appropriate.

"General Gates?"

Connor turned and saw Kayla Wolf walking up the corridor. Her face looked a bit strained, and she held a cup of coffee in her hand.

"Hello, Kayla. I came as soon as I could. I just heard about what happened to your mother, and I'm so sorry."

She nodded and smiled sadly. "The doctors are still identifying the virus," she said and looked at the door, her eyebrows pulling together into a frown.

Connor wanted to ask her if she was all right, but he already knew the answer to that, so he just waited.

Kayla glanced at him. "I know I'm supposed to be strong and sit by my mother's side." Her face crumpled slightly and her voice cracked. "It's just that seeing her like this . . . It's just so . . . It's just so hard."

He put his hand on her shoulder. "I know. I really do," he said, and she looked up at him. "You have to believe that your mother is strong. She's one of the strongest people I know."

Kayla nodded and sighed. "She likes you. A lot. I think you're one of her favorite people."

Connor smiled a little, and his throat became thick. "Do you mind if I wait here with you?" he asked and gestured toward the chairs outside the hospital room.

"I'd like that," Kayla replied.

CHAPTER 13

Connor walked with Nathan across the well-manicured courtyard broken up by islands of brightly colored flowers. One side of the wide path displayed hybrid plants brought from Old Earth, none of which Connor knew the names of beyond a few varieties of roses. He was more familiar with the side that had plants from New Earth. The gardens were well kept since some of the New Earth variety of plants would aggressively wreak havoc on the surrounding plants if left unattended for long periods of time.

They climbed up the steps to enter the colonial administration building in Sierra.

"What is it?" Nathan asked.

Connor finished reading the message he'd just received. "Governor Wolf's condition has taken a turn for the worse. They're putting her into stasis so the doctors have more time to research the virus."

"Oh my God, that's awful," Nathan said.

Two days had passed since Bob Mullins had become the deputy governor of the colony. If the doctors had decided to put Dana Wolf into stasis, it meant they were running out of options for treatment. They were scrambling.

"Who sent you the message?" Nathan asked.

"It came from Lenora. She's been in contact with Kayla Wolf."

Nathan frowned and shook his head. "Have there been any other cases of the virus?"

"I asked Ashley about that last night, and she said it was rare. They've seen some of the symptoms before, but none of those other cases took a turn for the worse like this. Dana Wolf is dying."

Nathan was quiet for a moment. "I still can't believe we don't know how she got the virus."

"Natalia is looking into it. If there's foul play, she'll find it, but—" Just then, Connor received another message from Lenora. "There've been five more cases of the virus in New Haven, but they're milder."

There was an audible chime on Nathan's PDA. "Looks like the news net has gotten a hold of this. We're going to need a way to test whether somebody has the virus or not."

They continued on their way, heading up to the governor's office where they found Bob Mullins sitting at Dana's desk. It felt wrong, and Connor wished Dana would be joining them at any moment.

Mullins was reading his holoscreen and waved for them to come in. "They've put Dana into a stasis pod."

"We just heard," Connor said.

If Mullins was surprised by this, he didn't give any indication. Connor and Nathan sat down in the chairs on the opposite side of the desk.

"I read your updates about the defensive strategy for colonial cities, but I want to better understand what our offensive doctrine is going to be where the Krake are concerned," Mullins said. He paused while he regarded both of them for a few moments. Then he sighed. "I feel awkward sitting at Dana's desk. It's a bit strange given what's happened."

"I can sympathize," Nathan said. "At the end of the Vemus War . . ." he said and glanced at Connor. "Let's just say the circumstances are somewhat familiar to me."

Mullins pressed his lips together and nodded once. "You've stated that the goal would be to remove the Krake's ability to wage war."

"That is correct," Nathan replied. "Once we find the Krake home world, we look for strategic targets and take out the infrastructure the Krake use to build their ships, weapons, and even the gateways."

"What about after that?" Mullins asked.

"What do you mean?" replied Connor.

"Assuming we succeed, how do we make sure the Krake don't simply rebuild and come after us?"

"We'll need to monitor the situation. We don't have the resources to leave an occupying force. That's not something we should even consider," Connor said.

Mullins nodded and then frowned. "This might never end. This conflict with the Krake could just keep going."

"It's difficult to say, really. When we fought the Vemus, we wiped them out. The Krake are spread out, and there are civilians to consider," Connor said.

"Krake civilians." Mullins sounded as if he hadn't considered the concept before. "And we don't have any evidence that the Krake are any closer to finding New Earth."

"That is also correct," said Nathan.

"But we can't let that lull us into a false sense of confidence," Connor said.

"I understand that. I'm just merely stating a fact."

"In any war, there are calms between storms. But we can't lose faith."

"I agree with you, Connor," Mullins said. "I'm going to propose that we increase the priority of the new colony. We've received continued updates from the probe we sent to the planet. I have agreements from other colonial leaders that five thousand colonists is the number we're going to move forward with. We haven't elected a project leader yet, but we have a few candidates we're considering. The drone data looks favorable. Actually, there might've been a recent extinction event that the ecosystem is recovering from. The best estimate is that it will take ten years for the colony ship to make the journey there. I wanted you both to know we're going to be calling for representatives from Field Ops and the CDF to go with the colony. Approximately ten percent of the candidates will be from those two organizations."

The last thing Connor had heard was a much lower number. Something must have changed. "I think that's a good start," Connor said.

"It was based on your recommendation," Mullins replied.

"The main goal for the colony is what exactly?" asked Nathan.

"Well, the establishment of the colony is their first priority. Their second priority is . . . Well, it will depend on what happens here. We'll send constant updates to their ship and to the probe. But if things get really bad here, I want plans in place to get as many of our people off this world as we possibly can."

Connor glanced at Nathan for a moment. "Are you proposing we build more colony ships?"

Mullins pressed his lips together. "I had seriously considered it, and I still might want to do that. However, I know there are options to convert our existing fleets into transport ships, where we could save as many people as possible."

Connor was becoming increasingly concerned with how alarmed Mullins was behaving. "So, if not building ships specifically, then you're proposing to at least build stasis pods."

Mullins nodded. "Not here on New Earth. I want them built at the lunar base facilities. A stockpile, if you will. However, I don't want it to detract from the ongoing building efforts there."

"I don't see how that's possible. It's a matter of allocating resources. We can't have our cake and eat it too. If we're going to devote resources to building stasis pods, then it's going to affect something else," Connor said.

"I was afraid you'd say that, and you're right. The other thing is that I want the effort to be kept secret."

"You don't want us to tell anyone?" Nathan asked.

"Since this effort will be confidential, it must be contained within the CDF. I'm sure you guys can guess why this needs to be secret."

The colony was already worried about the threat of invasion from the

Krake. If it became common knowledge they were building and stockpiling stasis pods in case they had to flee the planet, then it would negatively affect the colony as a whole.

"Bob," Connor said, "Nathan and I can give you numbers and a projection of what we can do over the course of twenty-four months. But you must understand that if the Krake come here with a significant fleet, there'll be a lot of fighting, and there's a good chance no one will get to use the stasis pods."

Mullins considered this for a few moments. "Do you think it's not worth the effort?"

"No, but I think I need to set expectations. We're talking about stockpiling over six hundred thousand stasis pods on the lunar base. And that's just for the colonists. What about the Ovarrow?" Connor said.

"Our first priority has to be the colony. I realize this might sound kind of sudden, but it's been on my mind, especially since what happened to Dana."

Connor regarded Mullins. He was beginning to accept that the job of being governor was tougher than he had probably imagined.

"I just want us to do everything we can to protect everyone," Mullins said. "If the lunar base is too close to home, what about building a secret storage facility somewhere else in the star system?"

"We'll look into it," Nathan said.

Mullins nodded again. "I read your report on the Konus. We'll be sending a diplomatic envoy to them. It looks like you met one of their military leaders."

"His name is Kasmon. They said they've been preparing for another conflict with the Krake since they came out of stasis," Connor said.

"They've had forty years to prepare. It would be great if *we* had forty years to prepare," Mullins said.

Connor exchanged a look with Nathan. He agreed with Mullins's comment, but the deputy governor needed to adjust to his new role quickly.

"All right, what's next?" Mullins asked.

CHAPTER 14

So much had changed in the colony that Noah felt he'd never catch up. Ever since he'd awakened from the coma, he'd felt that things had been out of his control, and he was out of step with everything. He sometimes tried to remember what life had been like before he'd gotten hurt, but it was a distant memory that was sometimes fragmented. He had strong inclinations of the person he'd been, but he wasn't quite the same, and he might never get back to being that person. For the past year, he'd thrown himself into his work, believing that if he could catch up on all the new developments, he'd somehow be made whole again. He'd been playing catch-up ever since, and some days it felt like he hadn't made any progress.

He was walking on a hiking trail near Sanctuary. Towering trees of white hardwood that were highly resistant to moisture stood like an army of sentries in the crisp winter air. They were similar to the birch trees of Old Earth, but near the treetops, branches latched onto neighboring trees, forming an intricate canopy. Colonial scientists had observed that this strange behavior didn't occur until the tree reached maturity. Each new connection reinforced its neighbor until the entire region was united. In recent years, some of Sanctuary's younger residents had climbed to the top and raced along the canopy.

The rustling of fallen leaves brought Noah's attention back to the ground. He watched with a smile as a large chocolate Lab zoomed among the trees. Amos sometimes just had to run. He'd pause for a moment, chest down and hindquarters raised in a play stance. Then, he'd let out a high-pitched playful bark and sprint off again. He went on like that for a few more minutes before coming back to Noah and leaning his body against Noah's legs, waiting to be scratched.

"Hey, buddy," Noah said while giving him a vigorous scratching that sent tufts of fur into the air. Amos raised his head and looked back at him. His mouth hung open, and a thick pink tongue hung off to the side in a derpy canine smile.

Amos was among the first litter of puppies ever to be born on New Earth. They had been genetically enhanced for greater size and slightly higher intelligence than the true-blooded Labrador retrievers of Old Earth. The genetic enhancements had been necessary for the dogs to adapt to New Earth.

Noah heard someone else walking up the path, and Amos began wagging his tail vigorously. He charged forward, and Noah heard his wife greet the Lab. He began walking down the path to meet her.

"I thought I might find you out here," Kara said. Her lips curved upward into a smile that exposed an adorable dimple on the side of her cheek. Her shoulder-length chestnut hair curled at the ends, which bounced a little as she walked.

Noah smiled. "I'm glad you did."

"It's almost decision day," Kara said.

Tomorrow Noah needed to let Oriana know whether they'd be going to the lunar base. He'd asked for a few weeks to consider it.

"Do you still want to go?"

Kara was leaning down to give Amos another rubdown. The Lab couldn't get enough of that sort of thing. "I don't know if I can part with my little man here."

If they went to the lunar base, they'd be up there for six months at least. Amos and his sister Maggie would be put into pet stasis. Noah wouldn't want to burden anyone with caring for his dogs for that long, and it wasn't fair to them either. He couldn't take them to the lunar base, and even if he could, it still wouldn't be right. Oriana was one of the lead scientists working to develop and reverse engineer cutting-edge technology in preparation for their war with the Krake. At least, that was what they told everyone, but he knew better. They were already at war. Even though there hadn't been a full-scale battle, it was obvious.

"We don't have to go," Kara said. Noah arched an eyebrow. "We can have the same access to the data and work on it in our own labs here on New Earth."

"But that's not what you want."

"I worry about you, Noah. You try so hard to save everyone. It's one of the things I love about you. But eventually, you need to let go," she said.

He knew she still blamed Lars for what had happened to him. But she had come to respect—if grudgingly so—Noah's desire to help his friend.

"I know," he said. "Sometimes I really want to go to the lunar base and spend some time away from here, but part of me thinks I'm just running away from something."

"Or you could be running toward something. It's okay to get away for a while."

"I've already missed so much."

"What do you think you'll miss if we go to the lunar base? We'll still be in contact, and we can still come back to the surface if we need to."

Noah smiled a little. "I know. I didn't say it was smart. It's just how I feel. The two aren't mutually exclusive."

Kara circled in front of him and gently grabbed his hands. "You know it'll be fun up there."

She gave him a knowing glance with a slightly arched eyebrow. They had met on a space station on the edges of the star system. It had been one of the happiest times of his life—and one of the most terrifying. That was when the Vemus War had begun.

"Okay, let's do it," Noah said.

Kara's eyes gleamed, and she hugged him tightly. He felt a bit elated at making his wife happy but still felt a pang of guilt for leaving. It didn't make any sense, but the feeling was still there. Maybe she was right that he needed a change of scenery.

A comlink chimed, and Noah checked to see who was calling before he acknowledged it.

"Hi, Noah," Ryan Lynch said.

"One second, Ryan. My wife is here, and I'm going to transfer this to my PDA so she can join us," Noah said.

He put the comlink on hold and transferred it to his PDA, which projected a holographic image of Ryan Lynch's head and shoulders into the air.

Kara looked at him curiously.

"This is Ryan. He's Lars's lawyer," Noah said.

Kara greeted the lawyer, but Noah thought she stiffened a little. Perhaps he was just sensitive to it.

"It's a pleasure to meet you," Ryan said. Then he looked at Noah. "Normally I can't discuss the details about my client's case, but Lars has given me permission to speak to you about it."

Both Noah and Kara sat down at a nearby bench, and Amos lay down at their feet.

"I'm surprised it's taken this long to get Lars's case into the courts," Noah said.

"These things take time, and it's actually to his advantage. The precedent has already been set with the sentencing of people like Meredith Cain, Kurt Johnson, and several others."

"Lars has cooperated. Do you think they'll exile him to that island like they did the others?" Noah asked.

"It's difficult to say. Yes, Lars did cooperate and was instrumental in exposing the extent of the rogue group's activities; however, he didn't bargain for leniency when he cooperated. Therefore, there's no reason for them to be lenient with him."

"I was there," Noah said. "He was concerned with the lives of the people serving under him. He actually saved the lives of the CDF soldiers that day."

Kara reached over to hold his hand.

Ryan gave them an understanding nod. "I'm not judging him, Noah," he said gently. "I know you're his friend, but I'm just stating the facts. The courts have no reason to be lenient when it comes to Lars Mallory. In fact, there will be many people who would protest if they gave Lars leniency because of his family connections. They'd view it as Franklin Mallory trying to save his son."

"That shouldn't matter. I know it does, but it shouldn't."

"You're right. It shouldn't, and it might not, but I'm trying to be as completely transparent as I can with you. I had a similar conversation with Franklin Mallory. The facts of the case are what Lars will be measured by."

Noah looked away from the holoscreen for a moment. "Is there anything I can do? Would it help if I made a statement? You know, come down and testify or something like that."

"I already have your statement, and there's no need for you to come down."

"There has to be something I can do," Noah said.

"You've done enough," Kara said tenderly.

He glanced at her and saw nothing but love and concern in her gaze.

"His case is special," Ryan said, "but he hasn't done the one thing the courts will look for. He needs to express regret for the actions he's taken. Even then, there's no guarantee he'll get leniency and be allowed to stay in the colony. I've done an exhaustive search throughout our data repositories for war crimes. That's essentially what this is, even though we weren't officially at war with the Ovarrow. It's a gray area. I think the best thing Lars can do for his own defense is to express regret for the actions he's taken. I wish I had something more to offer, but that's where we're at right now."

Noah sighed. He licked his lips and then replied. "Thank you. I know you're doing everything you can."

The comlink closed, and Noah and Kara sat there quietly. He wanted to speak to Ryan more, trying to reason with him, but he'd just be making excuses, which would never outweigh the facts.

"I'm sorry this has happened," Kara said. He looked at her but didn't say anything. "Go talk to him one more time. I know it's what you want to do. It's really all you *can* do. His fate is in his own hands."

Noah had already talked to Lars about this, and he really didn't think speaking to him again would change anything. However, believing that wouldn't stop him from trying one more time.

He kissed his wife. "You're the best."

Kara smiled. "You can never say that too much," she said and stroked his hand. "So are you."

They stood up and walked back to their house, where they began planning to go to the lunar base. She would contact Oriana to let her know the good news. Maybe it would be nice to get away from New Earth for a little while.

CHAPTER 15

Noah walked down the echoing hallway of the detention center, his shoes squeaking on the smooth floors, and he looked up to see Franklin Mallory walking toward him. Noah still had the urge to call him Mr. Mallory, as was the habit he'd formed when he'd been a lot younger, but Lars's father wouldn't hear of it.

Franklin Mallory was six foot five and broad-shouldered, with a long, thick beard. The older man's eyes widened, and then he smiled, giving Noah a nod as he walked over. Electronic security doors buzzed at the end of the long hallway.

Noah noticed the worry lines that creased the older man's forehead, and his eyes were a bit strained around the edges.

"Noah, it's so good to see you. I just wish we didn't keep bumping into each other here," Franklin said.

There was something about standing in front of the tall man that made Noah stand a bit straighter. It was much like being near Connor. They both commanded respect.

"It's good to see you too, sir."

Franklin eyed him for a moment. "Sir? You're thirty-two years old now and a veteran of the CDF. You've more than earned the right to call me by my first name."

Noah smiled, and remnants of old feelings crept to the surface. "It's a habit. I'll work on it."

They stepped to the side of the corridor to allow other people to walk by them.

"Lars's trial begins tomorrow," Franklin said somberly.

"I know, and it's one of the reasons I'm here to see him."

Franklin put his hand on Noah's shoulder and looked at him sternly.

"Noah, Lars is my son, and I love him very much. I feel the same way about you, and not just because of everything you've done. I appreciate that you come here to see Lars, but he can be extremely stubborn. You don't owe him anything."

Noah's throat became thick and his eyes tightened. He had been selected for the original *Ark* mission based on his aptitude test scores, but in many ways, he was an orphan here. Franklin, Connor, Lenora, and others had become his adoptive family. "I know that, but I have to try. He's my friend."

Franklin's gaze softened. "No, you don't. You've done enough. More than enough, to be honest. You should move on with your life."

"I am. Trust me, I am. I just want to . . ." His voice trailed off. He wanted to help Lars, as if the decisions Lars had made could've been prevented somehow.

Franklin breathed in deeply and sighed. "I know you do," he said and looked away for a moment. "I'm very proud of you, Noah. And I want you to know it's okay for you to move on with your life. Lars will be fine."

Noah didn't know what to say. Franklin released his shoulder and gave a firm nod, then continued down the corridor. Noah watched him go for a few seconds before resuming his own route.

He walked through the corridors almost on autopilot, knowing the way to the visiting rooms without thinking about it. A few of the people he passed greeted him by name, mainly the security personnel who worked at the detention center.

He stood outside the door to the visitor room and paused. Why couldn't he let this go? He'd already said everything he was about to say to Lars before. Why couldn't he just leave it at that? Noah rubbed his forehead and breathed in deeply.

One more time, he thought to himself. Then he placed his palm on the identification pad, and the door buzzed before opening.

Lars sat at the table in the middle of the room. His hands were folded in front of him, and he glanced up. Without saying anything, Noah sat down across from him.

"No snarky greeting?" Noah asked.

Lars frowned and then shook his head. "My trial is tomorrow."

"I know. I won't be there though."

Lars looked at him and then nodded. "I understand. You don't need to be there."

"Kara and I are going to the lunar base for the next six months. We're working on a couple of projects with Sean," Noah said.

"I'm happy for you. Didn't you guys meet on a space station?"

Noah smiled and then nodded. "Titus Space Station."

Lars smiled a little. "You know, at one point I wanted to join the Colonial Defense Force like you and Sean."

"Why didn't you?"

Lars shrugged one shoulder. "I was heavily involved with Field Ops, and I thought the best way to help the colony was to do it from there."

"And now?" Noah asked.

"Now, what?"

Noah met his friend's gaze. "Now what do you want to do?"

Lars shook his head. "This again. I don't know. I guess it depends on what they decide to do with me."

"That's not entirely out of your hands, Lars. But what if they let you go?" Noah said and raised a hand when Lars began to voice a protest. "Just for the sake of argument. You stand your trial, and tomorrow or the next day you become a free man. What would you do?"

Lars looked away, and his gaze swept the room, looking anywhere else but back at Noah. He shifted in his seat and finally glanced back to Noah. "It really depends on what they would let me do."

Noah tilted his head to the side. It wasn't enough, but he was glad Lars hadn't dismissed the notion all together.

"You could work for me," he said. "I realize it's not Field Ops or that kind of stuff, but it's honest, and it does contribute to the colony. You have a technical background with a specialization in security systems."

Lars was quiet as the seconds ticked by. "You'd do that? I know you've offered before, but I just feel like this would put a strain on you and Kara."

"To answer your first question, yes, I would do that. As for the second, that's between me and Kara. You guys wouldn't need to work together. I have a pretty sizable operation, with research labs in all the colonial cities, and they're all working on different things. Some of those R&D projects are backed by the colonial government, and others are things I'm working on. It's an option is all I'm saying. What do you think?"

Lars swallowed hard and avoided his gaze. He then reached out and drank from his cup. When he set it down, he looked at Noah again and shook his head.

"I'm serious, Lars. You don't have to rot in a cell or be banished to an island with just enough supplies to survive."

Lars pressed his lips together and looked like he was actually considering it, which gave Noah some hope.

"I heard there are multiple islands," Lars said. Noah frowned in confusion. "Where they're banishing people. There are three islands, to be exact."

"Oh, I had no idea."

"Anyone living on the island will be monitored, and a review will be conducted at the end of their term on whether they can return to the colony or be allowed to leave the island."

Lars had spent a lifetime in Field Ops. He was no stranger to surviving outside the cities. If he were banished to the island, he would survive just fine, but at the same time, Noah thought it would be a waste.

"It doesn't sound that terrible when you put it like that, but you and I both know there's a real possibility the Krake will find this world. Where do you want to be when they come here?"

"It's not that simple."

"Yes, it is," Noah said. "It's *that* simple. Why don't you see that?"

"But it's not up to me. I have to take responsibility for all of my actions."

"Yes, but taking responsibility doesn't mean you have to sacrifice your future."

Lars considered what Noah said for a few moments.

"I can send my proposal to the courts. It doesn't mean they'll listen to me, but it's an option, and you'd have to make a statement about how you regret your actions," Noah said.

Lars winced and then shook his head. "That's like taking the easy way out. No one would believe me."

"No, it's not. You've had time to reflect on everything that's happened from the start when Meredith Cain recruited you and convinced you those actions were necessary. It's okay to admit you've been manipulated. It doesn't make you any less responsible, but if they take that into account along with your cooperation, it might just convince them that you're worth keeping around. But you have to give them a reason. You have to fight for this."

Lars stood up and walked away from the table. His head was bowed, and his hands were thrust into his pockets.

Noah stood up. "It's not taking the easy way out, Lars. It proves that you're actually willing to take steps to atone for what you've done. You made a mistake. You're human."

Lars turned toward him, his face a mask of concentration. He then extended his hand, and Noah shook it. "Thank you. Thank you for not giving up on me," he said and paused for a second. "I don't know what I'm going to do. I need time to think about it."

Noah had hoped for more, but he supposed it would have to be enough. Lars had been adamant he didn't regret what he'd done to the Ovarrow. Noah didn't believe that was because Lars was without emotion; he believed it was because Lars would have to come to terms with the darkness inside him. He believed his friend could be redeemed, that he was worth fighting for.

"Good luck," Noah said.

Lars shook his hand again, and for a brief moment, he looked like Noah's childhood friend. It was as if a spark had been lit, and he could see it in his eyes. He hoped Lars could fan it into a flame, but that would be up to him. There was nothing else Noah could do. He had to move on, and so did Lars.

CHAPTER 16

There was a secret CDF base on New Earth that was well away from any colonial city, located over six thousand feet beneath the surface of the planet. The CDF soldiers who were stationed there were committed to spending six months on base without access to the world above. The base was known among the senior officers of the CDF as Hammerholde, but it had a much more well-known name.

COMCENT.

CDF Command Central had multiple key components that were grouped under the umbrella of COMCENT, consisting of Hammerholde and the lunar base. There were secondary and tertiary installations that could be tasked with the duties of COMCENT, but they were maintained in a semi-permanent state of standby. Those installations would be used under only the direst of circumstances. These efforts were an improvement in the CDF post Vemus War, during which they'd lost strategic command due to the overwhelming forces of the Vemus. And now the Krake had the ability to conduct hostile operations both on New Earth and in its star system. They needed a unified command center that had the ability to fully function even in a fragmented state of operations.

Colonel John Randall was in command of Hammerholde and was on duty in the main headquarters. They had access to every satellite in orbit around New Earth and city defenses. They were even tied into Lunar Base and Phoenix Station. Eventually, all CDF communications routed their way through COMCENT. The CDF base was equipped with state-of-the-art technology that was constantly evolving, and they also had one of the most complex computing cores ever created. Randall had served multiple rotations in command of COMCENT. Standing watch over the colony was a duty he took seriously.

It was the middle of the afternoon, not that anyone could tell when they lived one and a half kilometers beneath the ground. The command center was a vast chamber where CDF operations and defenses were monitored on an ongoing basis.

The filtered air was cool and carried just a kiss of spicy evergreen-like scent to it. Randall had experienced most of the variations of Hammerholde's atmospheric support systems, which had been developed to help alleviate the stress of a long duty rotation underground. They were well stocked with supplies they could stretch to a full year if they needed to. Hydroponic gardens could extend that timeline even further. They weren't lacking room to expand, even with the recreational areas built for the enjoyment of base personnel. As far as CDF assignments went, Randall preferred it to most others.

The command center was host to multiple teams sitting behind long desks with both personal holoscreens used for specific duties and a main holoscreen that showed the prioritized projects. They coordinated with other CDF teams, as well as colonial government agencies, including Field Ops and Security.

Randall noticed one of his tactical officers, Lieutenant Amber Wong, sit up and lean forward, peering at something on her holoscreen. Wong was one of the good ones. She was highly intelligent, able to sift through many different data feeds to get at crucial, if obscure, data points of reference.

Their mission was to monitor New Earth against the threat of invasion, be that an invasion begun on the surface of the planet or utilizing their extensive monitoring network throughout the star system. Their network was almost constantly being improved upon and had been completely overhauled in the past year to include secondary subspace communication systems. Never before had they had near real-time monitoring of almost the entire star system. It was the kind of advancement that led some officers into a false sense of overconfidence. Not Randall though, and he made sure the people under his command didn't become overconfident either.

"Colonel Randall, I have an anomalous activity report I'm sending to you," Lieutenant Wong said. Several satellite images showing a specific region of the continent appeared on Randall's holoscreen. "Sir, this area is within two hundred kilometers of the known location of the Konus city."

Randall peered at the images. West of a nameless river was a region of grasslands near low-lying mountains that snaked along the continent. A buildup of clouds was beginning to cover the area of the Konus city. He looked closely at the open area Lieutenant Wong had highlighted. The image showed globular clusters that, when the image was zoomed, became digitally enhanced, and he saw that it was a long caravan of Ovarrow vehicles. They ranged in various sizes, but some were massive ground transportation vehicles, the likes of which he'd never seen the Ovarrow use before. The only parallel he could draw on from his own experience was similar images when the CDF had conducted training drills with their ground forces, except that the Konus had fielded a much larger army. They must have been hauling equipment as well, but he had no idea what they were carrying.

"How far back in time does the image history go, Lieutenant?" Randall asked.

"Approximately four hours, sir."

"Where are they going if they continue to follow this heading?"

A map of the region of New Earth appeared on the main holoscreen. Hammerholde was home to one of the most robust AI systems on the planet. It plotted multiple routes based on satellite imagery and quickly provided a probability rating for each destination. Lieutenant Wong highlighted her best guess in accordance with what the AI had provided. One destination brought them close to New Haven, but the highest probability rating had the Konus on a direct—or as near direct possible—path for the Ovarrow city that the colony had helped establish for the Mekaal.

"Tactical, reorient our satellite coverage of the area so we have eyes above them at all times," Randall said. "Ops, work on getting some flight plans ready so we can take a closer look at whatever it is they're doing."

"Stealth protocols, sir?" Lieutenant Zima asked.

"Authorized," Randall said. "Comms, I need General Gates immediately."

"Yes, sir. I'll track him down," Sergeant Terrence Brooks said.

Randall studied the satellite images for a few moments longer. He'd read the briefing that had come out a few weeks ago after first contact had been established with the Konus. It had been disconcerting to learn that there were over a million Ovarrow living undetected on New Earth. And given those numbers, they very well could field an army the size he was seeing on the images. They didn't know how many Ovarrow were traveling inside the large ground transport vehicles, and upon closer inspection, there were ground forces traveling outside the vehicles as well. He couldn't tell from the images what they were. They could be small vehicles, or they could be something else. They had a lot of intelligence to gather, and he knew General Gates would have many questions.

"Comms, put us at Condition Two," Randall said.

For the first time since the Vemus War, the CDF ground forces on New Earth had raised their combat readiness status to a severity just below that of an actual attack. His orders had brought about a sobering silence in the command center, but only for a moment. Then his soldiers went to work.

———

Connor had been living at the CDF base at Sierra while Nathan was traveling to Phoenix Station with Savannah. Nathan was long overdue for an inspection of Phoenix Station operations. At this stage of his military career, Connor wouldn't have chosen a long deployment away from Lenora like what Savannah had done for the past two years. Though the work done at Phoenix Station was extremely important, Savannah was due to return to New Earth, and command of the station would be turned over to someone else. Nathan was the pinnacle professional when it came to running the CDF, but Connor knew his friend was excited that his wife was finally returning home.

For the next six weeks, Connor would be spending the bulk of his time at the CDF base at Sierra, becoming the point of contact for the Colonial Security Council. He'd expected his six-week rotation at the CDF base in Sierra to be a quiet affair. He was always busy, be it reviewing the various developments the CDF was involved in from off-world missions, trying to find the Krake, or building up their fleets and combat capabilities. What he couldn't have expected was the Konus fielding what could only be an army, which was even now making its way to the Ovarrow city that was home to the Mekaal.

He stood in his office, looking at the intelligence reports that had come from COMCENT. Colonel Thomas Beckly was at his side.

"They really could go to either New Haven or the Ovarrow city," Beckly said.

"There's no reason for them to go to New Haven. The diplomatic envoy reports from their meetings with the Konus indicate that they had a significant interest in the Ovarrow we brought out of stasis."

"It makes sense they'd be interested in them."

Connor gestured toward the satellite image on the main holoscreen in his office. "That looks like a little more than interest to me."

Before Beckly could reply, a comlink from Deputy Governor Bob Mullins came to the forefront on the main holoscreen. Connor acknowledged it, and the connection established.

Mullins was in his office, surrounded by his staff and advisors. "General Gates, patching you into a conference call with High Commissioner Senleon and Warlord Vitory."

"Understood," Connor replied. He had been due to meet with the Colonial Security Council in a few hours, but Mullins must have decided to inform the Ovarrow about the Konus.

A few seconds later, the comlink on the holoscreen changed to show Senleon and Vitory from someplace in the Ovarrow city.

Mullins began speaking. "High Commissioner, I invite you and Warlord Vitory to join us here at Sierra so we can discuss the Konus."

"Deputy Governor Mullins, we must respectfully decline the invitation, given this news."

"If Sierra is unacceptable, then we would be willing to meet with you at New Haven or any of the other colonial cities."

Senleon declined again and looked at Connor. "General Gates, in your meeting with the Konus, did they indicate they would send an army to us?"

"No," Connor said. "They were highly interested to learn we'd been bringing Ovarrow out of stasis. They expressed an interest only in learning more about you." He had told Kasmon about the Ovarrow they'd rescued from stasis. Had this been a mistake?

"We don't know what their intentions are," Mullins said. "We haven't initiated contact with them since our initial envoy left several days ago."

"I request that you do not contact them," Senleon said.

"Why not? We could learn what their intentions are if we initiate communication," Mullins replied.

"They don't understand," Vitory said to Senleon.

"Then help us understand," Mullins said.

"Before the Ovarrow went into stasis, there was war," explained Vitory. "This war was fought until the ice and cold made it impossible to survive. Smaller groups were conscripted into the larger groups. Whoever had the dominant army would swallow up everyone else."

"This is why it's important that we establish communication with the Konus. We're making assumptions. They could be sending supplies and a force to help you rebuild," Mullins replied.

The two Ovarrow leaders were quiet for a few moments, and then Senleon spoke. "Throughout our interactions, we have come to appreciate your desire to communicate. This helps to avoid misunderstandings, but in this . . . Given a choice, we will fight for our independence."

"We respect your independence," Mullins said.

"General Gates," said Vitory, "what do you think the Konus intend, given the images you've shown us?"

Mullins turned toward Connor. His gaze was expectant, and the room became quiet. Connor knew Mullins would look for him to defuse the situation, but he couldn't. He'd been heavily exposed to the way the Ovarrow handled things on New Earth and on other planets. The intention was clear to him.

"I think your concerns are right on the mark," Connor said. "The Konus could have requested to communicate with you through our comlink. Instead, they chose to send a sizable force we believe is heading toward your city. In this situation, you'd be better able to estimate what they intend than we would."

"This is why it's important that we open a line of communication to the Konus," Mullins repeated.

"Again, we request that you don't do that," Vitory said.

"Why not?" asked Mullins.

"The Konus are unaware that we know they're heading for us," Vitory said. "If you established communications with them, this would give them an advance warning of our knowledge. They could change their tactics. The speed at which they're moving gives us time to prepare for them; however, if you inform them, they could move much faster. This would impact our preparations in defense of our homes."

Mullins considered this for a few moments and then turned toward Connor. "General Gates, what do you think?"

"I think Vitory is correct that we should be cautious with how to proceed. The Konus are largely unaware of what our capabilities are."

"They must have some idea. They know we're looking for the Krake, and they expressed interest in an alliance with us against them," Mullins said.

Connor shook his head a little. Governor Wolf never would've made such a misstep. "I think we should keep the two issues separate for now."

Mullins frowned and then glanced at someone off-screen. "High Commissioner Senleon and Warlord Vitory, we will not contact the Konus. We need time to consider our options, but I want you to know that we respect your desire for independence."

"Thank you," Senleon replied. "We need time to consider how best to proceed as well."

The conference call ended, and Mullins requested that Connor come to the emergency Security Council meeting.

"Sir," Beckly said after the comlink closed, "do you have any orders for me?"

"Continue to monitor the Konus. We're not authorized to make any other preparations unless they decide to head for one of our cities. For the moment, our hands are tied."

"Understood, General. I'll update you immediately if anything new develops."

CHAPTER 17

A CDF transport skimmer flew away from the main CDF base in Sierra. The aircraft could carry a number of human passengers, as well as cargo containers. Connor sat in the copilot's seat, and the pilot was quiet. Sometimes pilots liked to fill the time with idle chatting, but Sergeant Miller had taken one look at Connor and remained all business. Connor had flown with Miller a few times before, and he knew that if he initiated a conversation, Miller would be more than happy to oblige. Today wasn't one of those days.

If the army traveling across the continent had been of Krake origin, the CDF response would have been swift. Both Senleon and Vitory were certain of what the Konus intended. Connor had told Kasmon about the Ovarrow they'd rescued from stasis, and he'd shown them the general location of the Ovarrow city. He'd even given Kasmon specific numbers. He'd done it because it seemed like the best way to ingratiate the colony with the Konus. Now, hindsight was giving him the proverbial kick in the ass.

Connor was busy reviewing the day he'd met Kasmon, trying to recall the entire conversation, looking for some indication of what he'd missed— anything that would've indicated the response they were seeing on the satellite images. Mullins had been happy with the results of the diplomatic meeting with the Konus, and Connor was sure Dana Wolf would've had the same reaction. So, where had he gone wrong with his estimate of them? What hadn't he seen? He'd become accustomed to dealing with the Ovarrow in alternate universes, where they had multiple layers of security between them and the colony. Forward operating bases were established on other worlds. Some of them were automated listening posts, but they also had some that were operated by CDF personnel.

He couldn't have known. He brought up the satellite images of the

Konus and tried to think of a legitimate reason for them to commit so many of their population to this. Despite all his experience with the Ovarrow, they were still alien in many ways. They had different motivations and could be brutal when dealing with nonconformity among their peers.

The transport skimmer drew in its small wings as it hovered above the landing pad at the capitol, and Miller guided them down for a perfect landing. Connor thanked him, opened the hatch, and climbed out. He walked across the landing pad and through the transparent entryway doors. The building's security systems registered his ID transmitted via his neural implants, and he strode down the glossy floors to a staircase that would let out near the meeting room where the Colonial Security Council was convening.

The halls echoed with the conversations and goings-on of the people who worked there. Connor walked into the meeting room, one of the last people to arrive, and bit back a grimace. He really hated being late or close to late, but it couldn't be helped sometimes. The doors shut behind him, and he headed for his seat.

Natalia Vassar sat across from him in civilian attire, and it took him a second to reconcile that she was no longer with the CDF. They both shared a knowing look, and Connor gave her a slight nod.

Mullins cleared his throat. "Let's get started," he said. "A reminder to all of you that the discussions at this meeting are considered confidential and should not be disclosed to anyone who doesn't have the necessary security clearance."

Connor arched an eyebrow at Natalia, and his former lead intelligence officer's lips lifted a little.

"First up," Mullins continued, "is whether we should initiate communication with the Konus. I'm aware that this action goes against what High Commissioner Senleon and Warlord Vitory want, but our highest priority is the welfare of the colony. We should seek to defuse the situation."

"This action seems premature," Jean Larson, the mayor of New Haven, said and looked at Connor.

"I agree," Luther Rosenbaum said.

Mullins frowned in thought. He'd probably expected Connor to voice the initial protest, but instead it had come from the mayors of New Haven and Delphi.

Mullins looked at the holo-image of Sanctuary's mayor. "Bernard, do you agree?"

Bernard Shaw had first come to Sanctuary to help establish it as a city when Connor had been mayor. A few years ago, the residents had petitioned for Bernard to serve as mayor when Connor had rejoined the CDF.

"I'm conflicted about it, to be honest," Bernard began. "I think it's a forgone conclusion that we will at some point initiate communication with the Konus. What we need to decide is when and where we do so."

Unable to wait any longer, Mullins turned toward Connor. "General Gates," he said.

"Their actions are highly suspicious. We left the Konus a way to communicate with us, but they haven't done so. From the Konus perspective, they may believe they don't need to contact us. Our estimates put their numbers in excess of over two hundred thousand soldiers," Connor said.

"Has it been confirmed that they're soldiers?" Mullins asked, looking at Natalia and Connor.

"We're still gathering intelligence, and several stealth reconnaissance missions are scheduled. We'll share our findings with the CIB for their review," Connor said.

Mullins nodded.

"There's more we need to think about," Connor said, and Mullins gestured for him to continue. "If their intentions are hostile toward the Mekaal, is the CDF authorized to aid the Mekaal's defenses?"

Mullins frowned, his forehead wrinkling. "I don't know if this is appropriate."

"How is this not appropriate?" Larson asked.

"The CDF conducts off-world missions with the Mekaal, but we've never had a formal alliance with them that specifically states we will come to their defense for circumstances beyond a Krake invasion," Mullins said.

Connor's thoughts raced. Their treaty with the Mekaal stated they would join forces against the Krake. Mullins was right. There was nothing specifically stating that their alliance applied to what would be considered a domestic conflict.

"Considering our extensive interactions, I can't believe we're going to stand by and let the Konus come in and do whatever they want," Connor said.

"I think General Gates makes an excellent point," Darius Cohen said. "After all the time and resources we've spent on helping the Ovarrow reestablish themselves, and assuming that the Konus intend to harm the Mekaal, are we just going to allow that? On the other hand, while the Konus' actions appear to be hostile to us, this might just be how their society operates."

"Senleon and Vitory will never go along with the Konus," Connor said. "They already stated they would defend their homes."

Darius raised a hand in front of his chest. "I'm not condoning what the Konus are doing. I'm merely speculating that from their point of view, they're doing something they've always done. Granted, this must be on a much larger scale, and there's also the complication that we represent."

"Agreed. This is a complicated situation," Mullins said. "The Ovarrow would be stronger overall if they were united."

"That's easy for us to say," replied Connor. "We're not the ones being forced from our homes. Conscription is a short-term solution that leads to more problems. We wouldn't tolerate it. Why should the Mekaal?"

Mullins pressed his lips together and glanced at the others in the room. "If we send a delegation to find out what the Konus' intentions are, it would mean taking an intermediary role."

"If we did that at the outset, we'd run the risk of sending the Konus mixed messages," Darius said. "We can't be intermediaries and then take a side later. That might guarantee that any conflict would be resolved only through the use of force."

"We want to avoid that," Mullins said and looked at Connor. "We need allies against the Krake. That's one of the prevailing reasons for our off-world missions and for bringing the Ovarrow out of stasis."

Connor's eyebrows pulled together, and heat gathered around his neck. "I think we should inform Senleon and Vitory that we intend to stand with them if the Konus prove to be hostile. To do anything else would be viewed by them as a betrayal, and they'd be right. Then, we either communicate with the Konus ourselves or jointly with Senleon and Vitory."

The room went silent. He'd just taken the moral high ground away from Mullins's objective approach, and irritation was evident in the deputy governor's gaze and rigid posture. The entire discussion had left a bad taste in Connor's mouth.

"We can't let an oversight in our alliance dictate whether or not we take action right now," Connor said.

Mullins regarded him for a moment. "Even if the Konus would make for stronger allies? Tip the balance against the Krake?"

Connor's shoulders stiffened, and his moral-high-ground response stalled in the back of his throat. He wanted to help the Mekaal. "We're not there yet."

Mullins inhaled deeply and sighed. "You're right. We might be getting ahead of ourselves. We need to wait and see how Senleon wants to deal with it."

There was a general murmur of agreement throughout the room that Connor didn't like. Senleon might base his actions on whether the colony would support him.

"To be clear, diplomatic channels will remain open to the Mekaal," Mullins said, and his gaze came to rest on Connor. "But at this time, there will be no authorization given for any direct action against the Konus. This includes advising and providing intelligence to the Mekaal about the Konus."

Connor clenched his jaw, and his eyes flicked to the table for a second. Now was not the time to become a stick-in-the-mud. "Understood," he said.

Mullins appeared surprised by his response but didn't belabor the point. They had to work together.

"We should give Senleon some time to confer with his own advisors," Darius said, and Mullins agreed.

The meeting ended, and Darius asked to speak with Connor. The head diplomat waited until they were well away from the meeting room before speaking.

"That was difficult," Darius said.

"Which part?" Connor replied. "The part where we considered abandoning the Mekaal, or the part where we decided not to take an active role where the Ovarrow are concerned."

Darius smiled. "That's one of the things I've always liked about you, Connor. You're straight to the point. Not quite black and white, but in this situation, your mind is already made up."

"You're damn right, it is. The Mekaal have come a long way. The more we work together, the stronger we both become. That's what's going to help us against the Krake. The Konus haven't earned that."

"I understand what you're saying, and I agree with you, but even you have to acknowledge that in some respects, this is a numbers game. There are more Konus than there are Mekaal," Darius said and raised his hand again in a placating gesture. "I'm just stating facts. If the Konus intend to bring the Mekaal into the fold—absorb them, if you will—then they'd be stronger for it, and we'd have a sizable group who are already familiar with working with us. I'm just saying that there isn't an entire downside to what the Konus might do. And I stress the word *might*."

"No," Connor said and shook his head. "How would you react if you were taken from your homes and forced to live by someone else's rules? I know what I'd do. It's easy for us to rationalize it so we feel better about making a bad decision."

"It's all bad, then?"

"Yes, it is, because the Konus won't stop, and they haven't proven that they'll back up their offer to help us against the Krake. The Mekaal have already done so, and that has to count for something," Connor said.

Darius scratched his eyebrow for a few seconds and then nodded. "You make a good point, Connor. I think of all the people in that meeting, you're the closest to really understanding the Ovarrow."

"A lot of good it did back there. I didn't see the Konus doing something like this."

"It just takes time. My advice would be to keep making the arguments," Darius said.

"Thanks," Connor said and meant it, but he couldn't help thinking about how much time they actually had. He wanted to help the Mekaal, and he needed to find some way to do that.

CHAPTER 18

T he next day, Connor was in his office at the CDF base in Sierra. Preferring to stand up while he worked, he faced a grouping of holoscreens. Colonel John Randall, the commanding officer at Hammerholde, was on one of them, while Nathan and Savannah were on the others.

"Thank you, John, for giving us this update," Nathan said.

If there'd been any doubts that the Konus had fielded an army, they had just been debunked. At least now they had evidence to support the claim. Increasing cloud cover was impacting satellite surveillance, which had been taken over by stealth recon drones.

"Continue to keep us updated at the predefined schedule," Nathan said.

"Yes, General," Randall said, and the comlink to Hammerholde went dark.

Nathan was still at Phoenix Station. He looked at Connor. "We'll need to present these findings to the Security Council."

"Do you think it'll sway them one way or the other?" Connor asked.

Nathan had more experience dealing with the Security Council in recent years, and Connor had to acknowledge that Nathan was better at it.

"Mullins isn't entirely wrong in deciding to wait."

"Oh really? Ever since he became deputy governor, he seems to be more . . ." Connor paused, trying to think of the right word. "Erratic."

"I think it's just Mullins coming to terms with the pressures of the office. It's one thing to be at the right hand of our governor as an advisor, but it's quite another to fill her shoes."

Connor couldn't think of an immediate argument that wasn't sarcastic. He had learned to work well with Dana Wolf over the years, but Mullins . . . "Dana wouldn't have let us pressure her into making a decision early, but I can't see her abandoning Senleon. She just wouldn't do it."

"Mullins hasn't abandoned Senleon."

"You know what I mean. Mullins is in the hot seat now, and he seems as likely to make a rash decision as he is to make a logical one."

Nathan glanced at Savannah. "He's right, Nathan," she said.

The door chime for Connor's office sounded, and a small holoscreen appeared, showing that Lenora was standing outside. He authorized the door to open, and she walked in.

"I'm sorry," Lenora said. "Am I interrupting something? Should I come back?"

"Nonsense," Nathan said. "We could use a fresh perspective."

She walked in and stood next to Connor.

"We're trying to find a way to help Senleon and the rest of the Mekaal," Connor said.

She nodded. "Mullins still won't commit to helping them?"

"No—well, not exactly. He's waiting to hear what Senleon wants to do, but I think he's just delaying making a decision," Connor said.

"Well, I can't see Senleon or any of the Mekaal wanting to join the Konus," Lenora said. "At least, not this way, not with an army coming to their city. It seems like the Konus are skipping a few steps in their plans to bring the Mekaal into the fold."

Nathan arched an eyebrow. "You think the Mekaal would be more inclined to accept an invitation to join the Konus if they'd sent a small envoy?"

Lenora considered it for a few moments and then shook her head. "Point taken. I suppose not. We'll never know now. However, the issue is that we have two major, competing Ovarrow factions, and the colonial government is reluctant to come between them because of certain political pressures."

"I think that about sums it up," Connor said.

Lenora looked at some of the other holoscreens showing the Konus army. She'd done her fair share of satellite image analysis to scout out potential archaeological sites worth investigating. Her head was slightly tilted to the side, and Connor could tell she was thinking. Then she turned toward him. "What if we weren't dealing with two Ovarrow factions? What if the Mekaal became colonial citizens? If the Konus were heading toward one of our cities, then dealing with this situation would be a lot more straightforward."

Connor's eyebrows pulled together, and his mouth opened a little. Then he chuckled and looked at Nathan. "You wanted a fresh perspective. I hadn't considered that at all."

Nathan exchanged a glance with Savannah. "I suppose I did. This feels like it's too simple a solution."

"Simple isn't always easy," Connor replied. "I don't know how Senleon would react to that."

"They might not be as closed off about it as you think," Lenora said. "You've been working together on off-world missions. There's more of an alliance with them now than there ever has been before."

"Yeah, but becoming citizens. That's a whole new direction," Nathan said.

Connor pursed his lips in thought, then tilted his head in a small nod as he considered it. "We have received requests for safe harbor from the Ovarrow in other universes. I know this isn't the same thing, but I do wonder how everyone would react to this kind of proposal."

"I don't know if it would work," Nathan said. "Would they be willing to live under colonial law? They'd need representation. Senleon would effectively become a mayor, of sorts. Colonial laws are more individualistic than the Ovarrow's, which are way more militaristic."

"We're not going to figure all this out here," Lenora said. "It's certainly controversial, especially among our own people. Possibly even for the Mekaal as well."

"The Mekaal have a lot of pride. I don't know how . . . They've changed in recent months, but I don't know if they're willing to take a step like this," Connor said.

Lenora gestured toward the holoscreen showing the Konus army. "Given what's heading for them, what choice do they have?"

"If given enough time, perhaps they might've approached us," Savannah said. "However, if they do approach the colonial government with a proposal like this, it would be looked at with bias, as if they were trying to avoid the lesser of two evils."

"To get a better understanding of just whether or not this is an actual option, we should talk about it with both parties," Nathan said.

Connor shook his head. "You want to add this as a line item to a Security Council meeting? Mullins would never go for it that way."

"You're right. He probably wouldn't. But if it's just a discussion in his office, he might be more open to it," Nathan said.

"Subtle," Connor said slowly and smiled. "There's just one problem. We're not authorized to even speak to Senleon about this. If we go through the diplomatic channels, they'll likely take their direction from Mullins, and we'll have the same problem we have right now."

"Not necessarily," Lenora said. All eyes looked at her, and she smiled. "I'm not in the CDF, and I'm not in the colonial government. I'm just a concerned citizen who happens to have regular communications with the Ovarrow. I can talk to them about this, and there isn't anything anyone can do about it."

This time Connor's mouth did hang open.

"Don't look so surprised," Lenora chided him.

"I'm not," he began. He'd almost said he wasn't surprised, but he was. "I don't like the idea of you going out there with everything that's going on."

"Connor is right, Lenora. There's potential for the situation to become dangerous," Nathan said.

"Oh please," Savannah said. "The Konus are still several days away at their current pace. Lenora can be in and out of there in that time."

Connor watched as the two women smiled at each other. "Mullins isn't stupid. He's going to see right through this."

Lenora shrugged. "So what?"

"All right," Connor said. "But we'll give you a ride, at least to New Haven. We have several troop carrier transfers bringing troops there. You can catch a ride on one of those."

Lenora gave him a look indicating he wasn't going to like what she was about to say. "That's not going to work."

"Why not?"

"If I catch a ride on the CDF troop carrier, someone will say you sent me to Senleon, and I don't want to give them any more ammunition to use against you. I need to get there on my own."

"They're going to say whatever they want, regardless."

"It's better this way. We want to rock the boat only a little bit," Lenora said.

She was right, but Connor still didn't like it at all. The Mekaal would be preparing their defenses, which wasn't exactly the safest situation he could send his wife into. But he wasn't sending his wife there. She was going to go whether he wanted her to or not. He'd seen that look in her eyes before, and there would be no talking her out of this.

"Be careful," Connor said.

Lenora smiled at him. "I'll be back before you know it."

He watched as she left his office and then turned back to the holo-screens. Nathan gave Connor an understanding look.

"I married a strong woman too," Nathan said, and Savannah grinned.

"Lenora can take care of herself, but I'm going to let Major Brooks at Camp Alpha know, and she'll send an escort with her anyway. She can come up with some excuse for being there," Connor said.

Nathan grinned.

"All right, I'll head over to Mullins's office tomorrow," Connor said and looked at Nathan, "unless you want to cut your trip to Phoenix Station off sooner."

"The thought did cross my mind, but you can't give Lenora a twenty-four-hour head start. It's better that Mullins hears it coming from you. We'll be waiting for the call."

Connor shut down the holoscreens. It hadn't taken them long to get used to subspace communications. They never could've had a conversation like that before. There would've been a fifteen-minute lag between responses.

A little over half an hour later, Connor was sitting in Bob Mullins's office. Connor looked around and saw that Mullins had kept all the furnishings Dana Wolf had placed in her office, treating it as if he was simply working there for a few days. Connor's opinion of Mullins ticked up a few notches.

"I can't move her things out of this office," Mullins said.

Connor nodded slowly. "Have there been any updates about her condition?"

Mullins shook his head.

"I wanted to talk to you before our next Colonial Security Council meeting. This really couldn't wait. Nathan wants to join us too," Connor said.

"Of course."

Connor opened a subspace comlink to Phoenix Station, and Nathan appeared on the holoscreen.

Connor proceeded to explain their discussion about the possibility of Senleon and the other Ovarrow becoming colonial citizens. Mullins's initial reaction was pretty much what Connor expected—complete and utter shock —but after that, he seemed to really consider the idea.

Mullins stood up and paced back and forth. "Let me get this straight. You're proposing that we give the Mekaal the option to become colonial citizens, and then we commit resources to protecting them?"

"Only if the Konus push our hand."

"Are the Konus a threat to us?" Mullins asked.

"They've been actively preparing for conflict with the Krake," Connor said. "Their weapons are superior to what we've seen come out of storage caches, which means their army must be well-equipped. It really depends on if it comes down to how we wage the battle. They have a lot more troops than we do, but we have superior weaponry and firepower."

Mullins looked out the window and shook his head. "We didn't expect to find a large group of Ovarrow. They outnumber us by more than double our current population. If they are as militaristic as you think they are, then they have more Ovarrow trained to fight. But on the other hand, we have the Mekaal, who we've already been working with—and successfully, I might add. If they became citizens, would we allow them to travel through colonial cities? Would we allow them to live here? When we take those things into account, it becomes a more complicated discussion. I think it's more complicated than anyone realizes, and the impact to the colony would be significant."

"What if the colonists choose to support the Ovarrow of their own volition?" Connor asked.

Mullins frowned and arched an eyebrow. "Are you saying that we should put this up for a vote?"

"It might make it easier, but I don't know if we have enough time. If the issue of whether or not we allow the Ovarrow to become colonial citizens becomes a talking point or debate, then we run the risk of not making any decision at all, at least not in time to help them."

"I'm not going to promise anything," Mullins said. "I think this is worth an open discussion inside the Security Council and in other offices. I think there are actually some policies already drafted in the event we encountered an alien species."

Connor's eyebrows raised. "You mean as part of the *Ark* program?"

Mullins nodded. "I think so. They tried to account for different scenarios and provided articles to help guide us along. But I doubt any of them could've imagined the situation we find ourselves in." He was quiet for a few moments, then looked at Connor. "I know you think we should just help them."

"You're right; I do. I don't think we should stand by while their freedoms are taken away from them. If they choose to join the Konus, that's one thing, but that's not what's going to happen."

Mullins regarded Connor and then glanced at Nathan. "Well, I think we should examine this in more detail sooner rather than later. I'll be in touch with you."

Connor suspected that Mullins wondered whether he would simply command the CDF to defend the Mekaal. Connor had bucked the system once, and he felt that if he did it again, the repercussions would be even more severe. He had no plans to do any such thing. He wouldn't order any CDF soldier into that kind of situation. As much as he wanted to, he understood he had to work within the current system whether he agreed with it or not.

Connor left Mullins's office and headed back up to the landing pad. A comlink registered on his internal heads-up display, and he saw that it was from Dr. Eric Young.

"Dr. Young," Connor said, "what can I do for you?"

"I need your help, Connor," Dr. Young said. "Do you have a few minutes to talk?"

"What's this about?"

"It's about our Krake prisoner."

CHAPTER 19

A year ago, when Trident Battle Group returned to New Earth, they'd brought a Krake prisoner with them. The prisoner had been taken to a secret facility near Sanctuary, and Connor had taken every opportunity to observe and, on occasion, interact with him over the past year. It was a rare opportunity to associate with a Krake who wasn't trying to kill him. Many scientists were fascinated by Krake physiology, and there was sufficient evidence of genetic modification. They had highly advanced brains, with large portions devoted to complex thinking and critical reasoning. Connor had seen the brain scans, and even he could see they were vastly different than the human brain. There were similarities to the Ovarrow brain, however, which supported the theory that the Ovarrow and the Krake shared a common ancestor.

In under forty minutes, the S7 Falcon Fighter had gotten Connor to the remote location where the Krake prisoner was kept. Dr. Eric Young met him on the landing platform.

"Connor, thank you for coming so quickly."

They went through the double doors and passed through a security checkpoint before being allowed into the secure wing where the prisoner was kept.

"You said we were at a crossroads."

Eric nodded. "Yes, we are. We've run all the biological tests we can run, and we've moved on to behavioral modification."

Connor knew that on multiple occasions, the Krake prisoner, known as Eyman, had tried to commit suicide. Eyman asserted he was already dead. Connor had seen the video recordings of when Sean had first interrogated the Krake prisoners aboard the *Vigilant*, and he'd never witnessed behavior that showcased such fanaticism before. The prisoners had maintained their stark belief that their lives were forfeit because they'd been captured. The CDF hadn't been able to capture any Krake from other missions to decide whether Eyman was a member of an outlier group or if he represented what counted as "normal" among them.

"I read the reports, and the latest ones indicated that some progress was being made," Connor said.

"It was, and then it all stopped. Eyman refuses to cooperate or even acknowledge when we try to speak to him."

"And you think he'll interact with me?" Connor asked.

"Yes, I do. I've checked the logs, and each time Eyman was conscious, he seemed most responsive to you," Eric said.

"I guess that makes me the lucky one, but I don't understand why."

"I discussed this with several colleagues, and we think it's because you've interacted with the Krake before. I think he senses a certain command authority with you. That's something he's familiar with. Many of his responses to our questions are conditioned. I'm hoping we'll get more when you speak with him."

Connor glanced at Eric for a moment, then gave him a long look. "This is your area of expertise."

Eric nodded. "And I'm making an educated guess. If I'm wrong, then I'm right back where I started, but if I'm right, then maybe we can get a little more cooperation from him."

Connor had first met Eric years ago when he'd encountered an Ovarrow out of stasis. Since then, they'd kept in touch. Eric had been on the team that helped develop communications with the Ovarrow, a job that had gotten significantly easier with the Krake translators they were now able to use.

"I'll do the best I can, but what is it you want me to do?"

"I'd be happy if he just reacts to you. If you can get him to talk, that would be good as well."

"Talk about what?"

"Anything, as long as he's participating."

They walked into an observation room, and Connor saw a walled-off cell in the center of the room where Eyman was kept. From the control room, they could make all the walls translucent, but currently they resembled the sparse walls of an ordinary habitation unit.

Connor approached the room with Eric right behind him. The metallic gray doors opened to Eyman strapped to a chair in a reclined position. The Krake had pale blue skin. His brow ridges extended on either side of his head, similar to the Ovarrow, but there was a third brow ridge over the center of his forehead that was more pronounced. His eyes were closed.

Connor glanced at the Krake's wrists and could see scarring from his struggles against the restraints.

"We've had him sedated. I'll bring him out of it," Eric said.

Connor walked over to Eyman, and the Krake prisoner began to stir. After only a few minutes, he was fully awake. Multiple straps secured him to the chair. The Krake watched Connor through alien eyes revealing vertical pupils, like those of a feline, and jade-colored irises.

Connor looked over to the side where there was a holoscreen showing a scene of the landscape outside. Fallen trees leaned drunkenly against one another, and animal burrows were hidden beneath the tree roots. Fresh sprouts grew from a dead stump, and a puddle of sunlight warmed a patch of earth nearby. He looked at Eyman, who was only partially watching the holoscreen.

Connor took control of the screen and brought up an image of the ship Eyman had been captured on. The Krake looked at it for a moment and then simply stared at him.

"This was your ship. Did you live there?" Connor asked.

Eyman tried adjusting his position, but the straps kept him firmly in place. He looked away.

"Do you want to go back to your ship?" Connor asked.

Eyman turned back toward Connor. "The ship is destroyed."

Connor heard Eric shift his feet but ignored him. "What if there was another ship?"

"No," Eyman said and looked away again.

Connor circled around the chair and stopped when he was in Eyman's direct line of sight. "What did you do on the ship?"

"I worked. We searched for materials to reuse."

"A salvage ship," Connor said. "You were able to travel through space gates."

Eyman was quiet.

"You think you're already dead. And yet you're not."

"I am."

"If you know you're already dead, then what's the harm in speaking to my friend or me," Connor said and gestured toward Eric, who came to stand at his side.

Eyman looked away and closed his eyes. Connor tried asking him more questions, but the Krake wouldn't respond.

"This is what happened before," Eric explained. "He'll answer a few questions, and then he just shuts down."

"How can you be sure it's not an act? Maybe it's his way of showing defiance," Connor said.

"It's not, because we monitor his vital signs, and they are relaxed. When any test subject is being defiant, their heart rate increases. In men, testosterone is released, along with stress hormones."

Connor walked to the other side of the bed and leaned in toward Eyman. The Krake hardly moved or gave any indication that he knew Connor was mere inches from him. He stood back up and regarded the Krake prisoner for a few moments. Then he accessed the controls for the chair and all the restraints released.

"What are you doing?" Eric asked.

"If you want more interaction from him, we need to give him a little bit of freedom."

"But he'll hurt himself. Have you seen the video logs of the others when they were held captive on the *Vigilant*?" Eric asked.

Eyman opened his eyes and sat up. He flexed his hands and looked at Connor suspiciously. Then he stood up.

"Would you like to go outside?" Connor asked.

Eyman's gaze darted between Connor and Eric.

"I don't think this is a good idea," Eric said.

"You said we're at a crossroads with him. Let's see what he does," Connor said, walking toward the door and opening it. He stepped through the doorway and looked back at the Krake prisoner. "You can stay in here, or you can follow me. It's your choice," he said and gestured for Eric to leave the cell.

Eric walked out the door, his eyes wide. Connor stepped away from the doorway, and they walked toward the command center. CDF soldiers were heading toward them with stun batons ready.

"Stand down," Connor said.

The soldiers hesitated for a few seconds and then did as Connor ordered.

"Get us a clear path to the outside," he said and glanced behind him at the cell door. Eyman hadn't come out yet.

Connor walked back toward the cell and heard Eyman scramble back to the far side. His gaze was wild and uncertain, his breathing rapid.

"You're not aboard a ship anymore. You're on a planet. I know you said you're already dead, but maybe you could hang on for a little bit longer."

Eyman looked away from Connor, his shoulders slumped. "Why would you do this?"

"I don't want to help you. I don't feel sympathetic to you at all."

Eyman looked at Connor, and then his gaze quickly darted away. "What do you want?"

"You know you're never going back home, and they're never coming to rescue you. And why would they? You're just a salvager," Connor said and stepped into the room. He used his implants to put an image of Mekaal soldiers on the screen.

"The enemy," Eyman hissed.

"Why? Why are they the enemy?"

"They are . . ." Eyman began and stopped.

A comlink opened on Connor's personal heads-up display, and he heard Eric's voice. "Connor, you're a genius. Keep him talking."

"Do you know why they're the enemy, or were you just told they're the enemy? What did they do to you?"

"They are the enemy of all."

"Is that why you salvage from star systems? You search for things to be used against the enemy?"

Eyman turned toward Connor. One of his hands came to rest on the back of the chair, as if he was using it to hold him up.

Connor put another image up that showed Ovarrow soldiers with CDF soldiers. "They're not *our* enemies."

Eyman glared at him.

"We don't have to be enemies. I would prefer not to be enemies."

"What do you want from me? What do you want to take from me?"

Connor leveled his gaze at the Krake prisoner. Eyman was more than a prisoner of this cell. He was a prisoner of his own mind, conditioned by his own species.

"I want you to tell me where the Krake home system is. I want the space gate coordinates that will take me there. I want to know the name of the Krake home world."

Eyman looked as if he was on the verge of speaking a couple times but clamped his mouth shut.

"What do you know about the overseers?"

Eyman flinched, showing more of a reaction at the mention of the overseers than he had to the image of the Ovarrow.

"Since you don't want to tell me about the overseers, how about you tell me where you would take your salvage."

Connor used his implants to put a holographic interface in the center of the room that had the coordinate interface for using a space gate. He did a quick search for the coordinates of the universe where Eyman had been captured and put them on the holo-interface.

"This was where you were when you were captured. Where were you going from here?"

Eyman brought his other hand to the back of the chair and braced himself.

"Careful, Connor," Eric said. "One of the prisoners ended his life by slamming his throat into the back of a chair."

Connor regarded Eyman for a moment. The Krake was rigid, his muscles shaking. "I already told you that I'm not going to stop you if you want to kill yourself. You don't have to cooperate with me. Your life is in your own hands. Has that ever happened to you before?"

The muscles in Eyman's arms became even more rigid, and his grip hardened on the chair backrest. Then, the last of the translation played back for him, and the strength seemed to drain out of the prisoner.

That's it, Connor thought. He knew Eyman wasn't going to kill himself. Perhaps at one time he would have, but not now.

Eyman backed away from the chair and sat on the floor. "Shipyards," he said quietly. "We bring our salvage to shipyards."

Connor blinked several times, unsure he had heard it correctly. "Do you like the shipyards?"

"I like ships," Eyman said. His gaze seemed to take in the room.

"I like ships too," Connor replied.

He considered asking Eyman about the Krake home system again, but he was beginning to think Eyman didn't know where it was, that he was from a different universe than the Krake home star system. How many alternate universes had the Krake spread to?

Eyman lay on his side on the floor and brought his knees up to his chest.

Connor heard somebody walking over to the cell and saw Eric standing in the doorway. "I wouldn't put him back in the restraints. Get him a bed."

"What if he tries to hurt himself?"

Connor looked back at Eyman for a few seconds. "Let him."

"Are you sure?"

"No, I'm not, but I can't think of anything better. I think if we give him some freedom, he might be more cooperative. If he'd wanted to kill himself right now, I would've let him," Connor said as he watched the Krake prisoner on the floor. "He didn't. It might be the first decision he's made in a long time."

They walked out of the cell and closed the door. Eric looked at Connor with a wide-eyed gaze. "I never would've thought to ask him those questions."

"He knows he's a prisoner. Going in there and pretending to be his friend wasn't going to work. He would've seen right through it."

Eric nodded. "That was a hell of a gamble."

"I don't think he knows where the Krake home system is."

"Why do you think that?"

"A couple of reasons, really," Connor replied. "His response to an image of the Ovarrow was conditioned. I don't think he's ever had any interaction with one before."

"The lack of a personalized nature to his assertion that they were the enemy. That's what you mean, isn't it?"

"I think that's fair to say."

"Do you think he'll share anything else with us?"

"I think so," Connor said, after considering it for a few moments.

"I think I'll try your approach from now on, but if he reverts to how he used to be . . ." Eric said, leaving the rest unfinished.

"If he *is* brainwashed, then this moment right now is the first time he's exerted control over his own world. He defied the conditioning that he should end his life," Connor said.

"Yeah, but what will come next? We can't base it on our own psychology."

"You know more about that than I would. I don't think he'll ever really be free."

"But what do we do with him? Just keep him captive for the rest of his life?"

Connor breathed in deeply and sighed. "I don't know, and it's not up to you or me. If we can get usable intelligence out of him that will help us against the Krake, then this will have been worth it."

"I see your point. Do you have any other suggestions for me?"

"Do you want me to do your job for you?" Connor asked him and grinned. Eric laughed. "I would suggest getting rid of that chair and putting a bed in there. Allow Eyman to start caring for himself. Give him a taste of what a little bit of freedom could feel like. I think if he embraces that at all, he might open up more."

"I was thinking along those lines myself. We'll review this session and come up with another plan. I know you're really busy, and I just want you to know I really appreciate you taking the time to come here and help me with this," Eric said.

Connor smiled. "I owed you."

Eric frowned in thought. "Are you talking about Syloc?"

"He was the first, but with all the Ovarrow coming out of stasis, your contribution has had an impact. Keep it up."

Eric said he would, and Connor headed back out to the landing pad.

CHAPTER 20

The CDF troop carrier transport was completely full. Connor stood up, rolled his shoulders, and stretched his neck. He looked behind him and saw a few pockets of men from the 7th Ranger Company speaking to one another, but the vast majority of them were taking a nap. He glanced off to the side at the wallscreen that showed the flight status of the other transports carrying a mix of cargo and the rest of the 7th. They would reach the Mekaal city within the next twenty minutes.

Connor needed to stretch his legs and walked toward the front of the aircraft. There was an alcove off to the side, and Samson was sitting there with a holoscreen in front of him. The big man was reading so intently that he hadn't heard Connor walk up to him.

"Who is Saul Ashworth?" Connor asked.

Samson minimized the message on his holoscreen a little too quickly, and then it flicked off. He glanced up at Connor. "No one."

"That's a pretty long message from a person who doesn't exist."

Samson shrugged thick shoulders, and the muscles in his neck rolled. "He's just some scientist or project lead asking about my time away from the colony. I think they're looking to update some of the survival guides."

Connor nodded. Samson had lived apart from the colony on his own for years. He'd actually explored a pretty large portion of the continent, and he'd done it all on foot.

"Are our hands still tied?" Samson asked.

"We have no official role here. This is a training exercise for the 7th Ranger Company. I'm here to meet with Darius Cohen from the diplomatic envoy," Connor replied.

Samson arched a thick, dark eyebrow toward him. "Right," he said, drawing the word out for a few seconds.

"This is a good time for a field survey around the city."

"And?" Samson prodded.

"You're to discuss defense options and potential ambush sites. Maybe a few choke points. And if any of the Mekaal soldiers happen to be around during those discussions, it'll be fine. It's not confidential," Connor said.

Samson looked at him doubtfully. "I follow orders, sir. But you know that anyone who looks at this is going to see through that flimsy excuse."

"I'll worry about that. This comes under the heading of peaceful cooperation for our off-world initiatives."

Samson grinned. "Now you almost sound like Wil."

Connor smiled with one side of his mouth. "Reisman always had a knack for finding his way around certain regulations. It was part of what made him so good at breaking into secure systems."

Samson nodded, and his eyes became distant. They didn't often speak about the Ghost Platoon. "He had a story for every occasion. I wonder how he slept at night," he said, and Connor grinned. "Seriously, sometimes we couldn't get him to shut up. He kept telling that story about the bucket of frogs."

Connor chuckled, and for a few moments, he recalled the day Wil Reisman died aboard a Vemus ship. He'd become trapped in Vemus exoskeletal material while accessing their systems. There was no way to free him, and Reisman knew it, but he'd never lost focus, even when Connor had wanted to give up. Reisman had been a good friend.

Both of the former Ghosts had become uncomfortably silent. Samson had had the most difficulty adjusting to life in the colony. He'd left behind a lot of people he cared about on Old Earth. They didn't speak about it. There was no need.

Connor glanced at Samson and could see a hardened edge to his gaze. Samson blamed him for being shanghaied onto the *Ark*. Samson looked away and shook his head.

"Not today," Samson said quietly. This was something he said from time to time. It was his way of focusing his thoughts away from painful memories.

There was an audible chime above them, and the pilot announced, "We'll be hitting the landing zone in five minutes."

Someone cried out in mock terror that they hoped the pilot would simply land them safely rather than "hit the landing zone." This drew more than a few jeers from the others. Connor looked back at them and smiled. He remembered a much smaller platoon doing something similar. They'd been hidden in a shipping container bound for a civilian space station. These were different men, but they demonstrated the same camaraderie. It had been such a long time since he'd led the Ghosts, but sometimes when he least expected it, memories of them amplified, reminding him of a past life he no longer wanted but sometimes longed for in a rare moment of nostalgia. He went back to his seat and gathered up his things.

The troop carrier landed, and Connor exited the side hatch, along with a squad of CDF regulars. Once they were off, the aircraft departed and headed toward the next destination.

The main entrance to the Ovarrow city was just under two hundred meters away. Located in the foothills of a vast mountain range that stretched over four thousand kilometers beginning far to the north, the city was nestled just past the midpoint. The rounded architecture combined the bronze metallic alloy that was extremely resistant to oxidation and a polished form of ebony concrete. Ivory accents along the edges of the buildings had faded to a dull ashen color, and the Mekaal hadn't addressed that yet while they made the city livable. Taller buildings near the southern parts of the city had defense towers in place. Only sixty thousand Ovarrow made their home in a city meant to house millions. Most of it remained untouched, and there were remnants of collapsed buildings that Connor suspected were from the previous war the Ovarrow had fought before they'd gone into stasis.

Connor hadn't been to the Ovarrow city in over six months, and the population over the past year had doubled in size, the result of a joint effort between the colony and the Ovarrow to find the remaining stasis pods in the region and give those Ovarrow a chance at life. Many of the bunker sites that contained stasis pods would have remained in stasis until one of the specialized groups brought the Ovarrow out. He had learned that different Ovarrow factions had reconfigured their stasis pods to reanimate after a certain number of years had passed. It was a heck of a gamble because the technology—at least for the Ovarrow—hadn't been proven, and they didn't know if the equipment would function properly for the length of time required to endure the Ice Age. There had been no shortage of casualties for the Ovarrow in stasis pods, ranging from mechanical failure to power depletion. And if they survived all that, there was a chance they would suffer from cellular degeneration after they awakened.

Near the city entrance, the colonial diplomatic envoy waited for him. Darius Cohen waved as they approached, and Connor walked over.

Darius glanced at the people he was with. "Would you please give me and General Gates a few minutes to talk?"

The twelve people in the diplomatic envoy moved away from them, giving them some space.

Darius smiled and looked at Connor. "I guess you're not violating any orders if you're invited to come here. I have to say that Mullins wasn't pleased about Senleon's request for you to come in person."

"He couldn't have been *that* upset because he didn't forbid me from coming," Connor replied.

"Would you have listened?"

"Yes, but if Senleon really wanted to speak to me, there's very little Mullins can do to stop it. He probably decided it wasn't worth the effort of keeping us apart."

"I suppose you're right about that, and regardless, you're here, so let's make the most of it," Darius said.

The Ovarrow were hardly ever idle. They had a strong work ethic, much like most human colonists. There was also never a shortage of important tasks to be done. But as Connor looked around while they walked through the city, he saw that many of the Ovarrow moved with even more of a sense of urgency than was normal. There was general unrest in the air, and more than a few of them looked his way.

They made their way to a pavilion where High Commissioner Senleon and Warlord Vitory were speaking with faction leaders. When they saw Connor, they quickly ended their meeting and invited him up. There was a show of respect and deference given to Connor as the faction leaders dispersed.

"General Gates, thank you for coming here so quickly," Senleon said.

"You're welcome, High Commissioner. I hope you don't mind, but I brought some soldiers to help with a field exercise," Connor said.

"What is the nature of the field exercise?" Senleon asked.

Connor looked at Vitory for a moment. "They are to evaluate the area, looking for defensive positions and other things that might be of relevance to anyone with similar interests."

Senleon looked at Vitory, who said, "I'll inform Cerot that we have a contest."

Darius cleared his throat. "I don't understand. What contest?"

Vitory looked at Darius. "Cerot is leading Mekaal soldiers in performing a similar function. It will be interesting to see how our two militaries develop solutions based on the field exercise."

Vitory walked away from them and opened a comlink to Cerot.

"I told you *they* wouldn't mind," Connor said when Darius glanced at him. He looked at Senleon. "How are your people holding up?"

"There is much uncertainty," Senleon said. "It is our way that stronger factions absorb the weaker ones as a matter of course, especially at the end of the war with the Krake. We knew when we came out of stasis that this practice would resume."

"But this isn't your practice anymore?" Darius asked.

"The Ovarrow here are free to leave if they choose, but it wasn't always this way," Senleon replied.

"What changed?" asked Connor.

"It surprises me you need to ask that," Senleon said.

"Please, High Commissioner," Darius said. "We don't want to make any assumptions where the Ovarrow are concerned."

Vitory rejoined them.

"We changed," Senleon said and looked out into the city. Groups of Ovarrow were working to set up a gun nest on the rooftops of nearby buildings. "*You* do not force your citizens to remain with you, and yet there is loyalty among you. Our soldiers who work with the Colonial Defense Force return with stories. We encourage our soldiers to share their experiences, and this has triggered a departure from what we've done in the past."

Connor and Darius shared a glance. So much had changed over the past year, but it wasn't so long ago that Connor couldn't remember being extremely frustrated with the lack of cooperation.

"Darius has advised us to contact the Konus," Senleon said.

"Yes, it's important to open the lines of communication," Darius said.

Senleon and Vitory looked at Connor expectantly. They wanted his opinion.

"I agree with Darius," Connor said. "I also think it's important that you make your intentions clear."

"What intentions are you referring to?" Senleon asked.

"Do you want to join the Konus?" Connor asked.

"We desire to keep our independence."

Connor looked at Vitory and saw grim-faced determination.

"Are you open to communicating with the Konus?" asked Darius.

"Not if they come here with their army."

"Then you need to define that for them. In essence, you're claiming a territory," Connor said.

"If the Konus were heading to a colonial city, what would be your response?" Senleon asked.

"First, we would attempt to communicate with them to establish their intentions," Darius began.

"Darius is right," Connor said. "We'd try to communicate with them, but the CDF would make preparations in case diplomacy failed. We'd request their intentions, and if they violated our space, we'd put it in no uncertain terms that there would be consequences and retaliation."

Senleon was quiet for a few moments while he considered what Connor had just said. "Do you believe we could defend the city from the Konus if it came to a military confrontation?"

Connor looked away. The pavilion was at a higher elevation, which gave him a view of the city. Then he looked back at the Ovarrow. "It's possible. It would be better if you had help. It would be bad if you were boxed in here."

Again, Senleon was quiet, and Connor waited him out.

"We cannot ask that you fight on our behalf."

Connor frowned. That was exactly what he'd been expecting them to ask.

"Just to be clear," Darius said, "we're not authorized to engage the Konus here."

Connor stepped toward Senleon. "Why wouldn't you ask for our help? You'd have a much better chance with us."

When he'd spoken to Lenora, she had informed him that Senleon and the other faction leaders were open to the idea of joining the colony. He wondered what had changed. Maybe they'd just been open to considering the idea.

"This is not your fight," Vitory said, and Senleon nodded.

"What if we wanted to show our support to you? Would you allow us to facilitate a meeting with the Konus using our comms drones?" Darius asked.

Connor knew it was just a symbolic gesture. Senleon and Vitory would know it, too, but it couldn't hurt to remind the Konus that the Mekaal had allies.

Senleon told them they would need a few minutes to discuss this, so Connor and Darius gave them some space, walking to the edge of the pavilion that overlooked the city.

"Do you really think the city can be defended?" Darius asked.

"It's not that simple," Connor said. "If I were in their shoes, I wouldn't give the Konus an inch without making them pay for it. And by that, I mean I wouldn't wait for the Konus to arrive at the city to start defending it. I think Vitory understands that."

Darius glanced at Senleon and Vitory, who were still speaking quietly. "But Connor, they're so outnumbered."

"I know," Connor said grimly. "How do you think Mullins would react if we relocated sixty thousand Ovarrow to New Haven? Do you think he'd turn them away, or would he authorize the CDF to stop the Konus?"

Darius's eyes widened. This was the first time Connor had directly voiced one of his ideas about how to help the Ovarrow here. "Is that what you're really considering? Moving them wouldn't be easy, and that's even if they'd want to leave here. Technically or legally speaking, it's not up to Mullins. It's up to Mayor Larson whether she would allow the Ovarrow to take refuge in New Haven, but I see where you're going with this. You could bypass Mullins altogether, but I think there would be long-term consequences if you did that."

Connor nodded. "Me too, and I don't want to do that. I don't want to play politics with the politicians. The Ovarrow are the ones who need our help," he said and gestured toward the cityscape.

Senleon and Vitory walked over to them.

"We accept your offer to use your communications drone to initiate contact with the Konus," Senleon said.

"That's good," Connor said. "We can have a drone intercept the Konus within the next two hours."

Senleon looked surprised, but Vitory did not. He was familiar with how fast the CDF could move when it had to.

"I shall recall the faction leaders, and we will confer until the comms drone is ready for us," Senleon said.

Connor nodded and began opening a few comlinks of his own to get things moving.

CHAPTER 21

The CDF comms drone hovered in the air above the pavilion of the Mekaal city. Over seven hundred kilometers away, there was another CDF comms drone near the Konus army. Connor had deployed stealth recon drones along with the comms drone. The stealth drones broke away on approach and were collecting data about the Konus.

The Konus had brought equipment Connor couldn't identify. Large haulers were carrying giant metallic spirals that could have any number of uses, from drilling into the ground, which didn't make sense to him, to some kind of communications tower. He'd have to show the images to Vitory and get his opinion.

The large holoscreen in the pavilion showed Kasmon, along with what Connor assumed were senior officers in the Konus army. Connor and Darius stood off to the side, and the discussion was led by Senleon and Vitory.

"I have already told you," Senleon said. "We are an independent city. We've been rescuing Ovarrow from stasis pods and administering a cure for the illness caused by stasis."

"There is no such cure," Kasmon said.

"The cure was developed by the humans. They are sincere in their desire to help us," Senleon said.

"That is possible, but they've also made you dependent upon them."

"We needed their help in the beginning but not now."

"And yet I can see them there beside you," Kasmon said, and his gaze slid toward Connor and Darius.

"We are here because they asked us to be here," Darius said.

"This is a matter for the Ovarrow," Kasmon said, and looked at Senleon. "Why do you fear our approach?"

"Because I know what you'll do when you come here," Vitory said.

"Warlord Vitory," Kasmon said, "this is the way the Ovarrow become strong again. You knew there was a chance when and if you came out of stasis that factions would be forced together for the good of the whole."

"We are not a threat to you, and we are open to working with you. However, we cannot allow such a large military force to come to our city," Senleon said.

Kasmon waited for the length of a pregnant pause. Then he looked at Vitory. "Warlord, does the High Commissioner speak for you?"

Connor kept a careful watch on the exchange. Kasmon had changed since he'd first met him. He'd become more aggressive, but that wasn't what worried him. Kasmon was a believer, and he'd spent decades with the belief that the Ovarrow were stronger together. The Konus were a militaristic society. Kasmon knew the answer to the question before he asked it. It was a slight on Vitory because according to whatever plan the Ovarrow had had for when they awakened from stasis, it wasn't to have a democratic society.

Vitory regarded Kasmon for a few moments. "The High Commissioner and I work together to rebuild. The plans of old needed to change. The Ovarrow who made them are gone."

"Needed to change, or were you forced to change because of the humans?" Kasmon asked. There was no mistaking the vehemence in his voice.

Vitory stepped toward the holoscreen. "We are not under their dominion, and we will never be under yours."

"You are puppets for them, and you don't even realize it. If this is what they made you, then they are no better than the Krake," Kasmon said.

"What would it take to convince you that they are not puppets?" Connor asked. It was the first time he'd spoken up, and Kasmon's harsh gaze swooped toward him.

"I acknowledge that you have assisted my people. Now that we are aware of them, they will not need your assistance anymore. I advise you to stay out of Ovarrow affairs," Kasmon said, and he glanced at Darius. "That is, of course, if you wish to remain allies against the Krake."

Connor knew there was no way Kasmon was going to let this go. They were going to come here no matter what they said.

"Then you give us very little choice," Senleon said.

"Please," Darius said, "there must be a peaceful resolution to these issues. What if High Commissioner Senleon and Warlord Vitory allowed you to send a delegation here?"

Connor's gaze darted toward Senleon and Vitory, but their facial expressions gave nothing away. It was difficult to read the mood of any Ovarrow. Oftentimes, their mood was shown through actions rather than facial expressions. This had taken some getting used to for joint CDF missions.

"Peacekeeper," Kasmon said to Darius, "yours is a world that has not experienced what we have. If this is how you would engage the Krake, then you will lose everything. Delegations accomplish nothing except delaying the inevitable."

"That's just it. We're not Krake," Darius replied.

Kasmon didn't reply. Instead, the comlink severed.

Darius watched the holoscreen for a few moments, and Connor thought the diplomat hoped the comlink would reconnect.

"The comms drone is off-line. They destroyed it," Connor said.

"We can send them another comms drone," Darius said and looked at Senleon and Vitory. "We don't have to close the lines of communications. We should keep trying to speak to them. Perhaps there is someone else we can talk to—someone who can get Kasmon under control."

"Darius, why don't we give them a few minutes to talk," Connor said with a small tilt of his head toward the Ovarrow.

Darius looked at Senleon and Vitory. "Of course," he said.

As they walked away, Connor could hear Senleon and Vitory speaking with the faction leaders.

"The Konus aren't going to stop," Connor said to Darius.

"What makes you so sure?"

"Kasmon isn't interested in working with the Ovarrow here. He sees them as a way of building up his own strength."

"But why bring an army that large?"

"Intimidation for both the Ovarrow here and for us."

Darius's brow furrowed, and he blinked rapidly before his face went slack. "Do you think he'll attack *us*—*uh*, one of our cities, I mean?"

"I don't think he wants to attack us. The closest city to here is New Haven, and we've been building up CDF forces there. But if we're here when the fighting starts, I don't think he'll hesitate to attack us here."

Darius shook his head. "If Kasmon wants to make the Ovarrow here join the Konus and they refuse, how many soldiers will he have to lose before the cost is too high, even for him?"

"Darius," Connor began.

Darius inhaled explosively and shook his head. "It's such a waste of time and resources. Why do you look like you've been expecting something like this to happen?"

"I know you were hoping for a peaceful resolution."

"I still hope for it," Darius said.

Both men regarded each other for a few moments. "We need to inform the Security Council," Connor said.

Darius looked away and nodded slowly. They both went back to the comms drone and opened a comlink to Sierra. Darius proceeded to give a report on what had occurred. Connor answered a few questions but otherwise let Darius take the lead.

Senleon walked over to them while the faction leaders left the pavilion. Vitory joined after speaking to a few Mekaal soldiers.

"High Commissioner Senleon and Warlord Vitory," Mullins said, "I think I can speak for everyone in this room by saying you have our deepest sympathies for the situation you're in."

Senleon briefly looked over at Connor, who couldn't hazard a guess as to what the Ovarrow was thinking. Then, he turned back to Mullins and the rest of the Security Council on the holoscreen. "We have many difficult decisions to make. We are at"—he paused and again looked at Connor—"a crossroads. Many things are going to change for us, and I suspect these changes might affect you as well."

"I think you're right about that," Mullins replied.

"We've discussed multiple options with the faction leaders," Senleon continued. "The Konus want to absorb us into their population, and they're willing to exert force to achieve this. Warlord Vitory intends to defend us, but I'm not sure it will be enough." He looked at Vitory, who wore a mask of grim determination. "Another option we were asked to consider was to petition you for help. We've been allies for off-world missions, and perhaps we could negotiate support to help us keep our independence from the Konus. You've expressed resistance to this option in the past, and we understand why. Another option has come to my attention and was something we'd considered even before the Konus were encountered. The option I'm talking about is to join your colony and become citizens." Senleon looked directly at Connor. "General Gates seeks to find a way to help us. If we were to become colonial citizens, then we would have the support of the Colonial Defense Force. Right, General Gates?"

The Security Council looked at Connor, and he cleared his throat. "That is correct. I do want to help you, and there are many others who would like to help you as well."

Senleon turned back to the holoscreen. "The timing for this type of request isn't appropriate, even though it could be perceived as necessary. The perception is that we would request to become colonial citizens only in order to get your protection and not because we choose to merge our two societies."

"The situation is very complicated," Mullins said in agreement.

"Is it?" Connor said before he could think better of it.

"Yes, it is, and Senleon understands this," Mullins said. He looked at the High Commissioner. "We need time to consider the best way we can help you. An armed conflict with the Konus will guarantee the loss of life—both for you and for them."

"We have many of our own preparations to make," Senleon said.

"High Commissioner Senleon, we will be in touch with you," Mullins said.

Senleon and Vitory left the pavilion. Connor and Darius stayed behind at Mullins's request.

Heat gathered in Connor's chest, and he felt his blood near boiling. "'We need time'?" he said, glaring at Mullins. "They will never survive without our help. You can see it in their faces."

"I understand your tactical assessment of the situation," Mullins replied with an edge in his voice, "but I cannot simply make them colonial citizens. We could never force this through without it being challenged. I'm afraid the path to colonial citizenship will not be resolved in the next few days."

"Then authorize me to help them," Connor said.

Mullins was quiet for a few moments, and Connor could tell he was trying to control his own frustration. "Connor, ever since we learned about the Krake, you and Nathan have advised that we need as many allies as we can get to fight them. The reality is we need the support of the Konus, especially if the Krake discover New Earth. I'm not trying to be obtuse; I'm just trying to be realistic."

Connor clenched his teeth for a few tight moments, then breathed in deeply and sighed. Mullins was right that they needed all the allies they could get, but this was too much. "I don't trust Kasmon. I trust Vitory and Senleon."

"If the Council decides to commit the CDF against the Konus, they might never help us in the future," Mullins said.

"What if . . ." Darius began to say and paused. "What if we helped evacuate the Ovarrow here?"

"To where?" Mullins asked.

"The closest city that could take them in is New Haven," Darius said.

There was a commotion among the Security Council, and Mullins called for quiet. "Doing so would put colonial citizens in harm's way. We need to defuse the situation without adding fuel to the fire."

Connor could hear Nathan's warning in his head—the warning that said not to buck the system. So, he didn't. "Well then, let's vote on it right now. The Security Council can vote on whether to allow the CDF to help the Mekaal defend their city."

"We would need more information," Mullins said.

"They're gathering ryklars as they come," Connor said. "Kasmon was always coming to fight, regardless of what we said. I have the video feeds to prove it, and I can further confirm it based on the stealth recon data we've gathered."

"General Gates," Mayor Jean Larson said, "I agree with Bob in that we shouldn't evacuate the Ovarrow to New Haven unless there was no other choice, but that's an entirely different conversation. What we would like to know is the potential impact on CDF soldiers."

"I can't guarantee there will be no losses. Nathan and I have worked on certain tactical scenarios since we first learned that the Konus were heading toward the city. These include the use of our ground forces, as well as our orbital defensive installations."

"You would seek to wipe them out, eliminate all of them?" Mullins asked.

"It could come to that, but no, that wouldn't be our first-strike scenario," said Connor. "Senleon and Vitory are sincere that they do not want to fight the Konus. They want to defend their homes. They are willing to fight for that, but I think they want to convince the Konus that it's not worth the fight to come here. We can help them do that. Do you now have enough information to put it to a vote?"

There was a short discussion among the Security Council members. After a few minutes, they quieted down, and Mullins turned to address Connor. "We need to confer with General Hayes about the specifics of these plans you have. Then, we'll put it to a vote. However," Mullins said before Connor could interject, "we recognize that time is of the essence, and you are given clearance to help the Ovarrow prepare defenses and tactics for defending their city and their territory. You are cleared to defend yourself, but I want you to keep one thing in mind, General Gates. If the Security Council decides to withdraw from this conflict, then you will quit the field. Is this understood?"

"I understand," Connor said.

"Very well."

The holoscreen powered off, and Connor turned to Darius.

"Well, it looks like you got what you wanted," Darius said.

"Provisionally, at least," Connor replied. "I need to make every minute count."

"I understand. Is there anything I can do to help?"

"Stick around and help Senleon. We might need an evacuation plan for Ovarrow civilians," Connor said.

Darius nodded. They left the pavilion, and each of them headed off in different directions. There was work to be done and troops to deploy.

Connor opened a comlink to Samson. "I have a job for you, Captain."

"Finally," Samson replied.

"Get a command center up. I'm coming to you."

CHAPTER 22

The CDF mobile command center was designed for quick deployments in the field, containing all the necessary equipment for conducting military operations. Connor stood at a large holotank that showed a three-dimensional image of the region surrounding the Ovarrow city. They were connected to COMCENT, which was the hub for all CDF activities on New Earth.

The mobile command center and equipment shared many of the same functions as the bridge of a warship. Connor had designed their functions this way to streamline how military operations were conducted. The rudimentary functions of the command center formed the foundation for the officers and soldiers who used them. The bedrock was the same, regardless of whether the CDF required the soldiers to serve aboard warships, space stations, lunar bases, or terrestrial bases. They all required specialized training for the purpose-built application, but Connor had designed the CDF to be as agile a military as possible.

Over the past year, the Mekaal had worked closely with the CDF and had been equipped with certain advancements that had been unavailable to them before—things like comlinks and better weapons. Although they still preferred their energy-based weaponry, they'd come to appreciate the CDF armament for use among their infantry.

The Mekaal didn't have neural implants, and Connor didn't believe they would be getting them anytime soon since that would require further study and experimentation. They were, however, equipped with PDAs in the form of wrist computers designed with an Ovarrow interface. Imitating the basic colonial interface for PDAs had been surprisingly easy with the Krake translator. It hadn't been seamless, and there was still a learning curve, but it had become an essential tool for basic communication. The Mekaal had eagerly seized these advantages, which enticed them to want to learn more ways to use the tools on hand.

A comlink appeared at Connor's personal workstation at the holotank. He acknowledged it, and Samson appeared on the video feed. Thunder rumbled overhead, and Connor heard it echoed from Samson's location. The 7th Ranger Company was deployed near the forward position where defensive installations had been established to deter the Konus from going any farther.

Samson proceeded to give Connor an update. "I don't see how the Mekaal can win against the Konus. Sheer numbers were bad enough, but they're gathering ryklars along the way."

"The numbers are growing, but we've increased the range of the ryklar deterrent signal, which should help with that," Connor said.

"That deterrent signal won't work if they're able to put implants on the newer ryklars. Maybe we should use the ryklar signal to have them attack the Konus."

"I spoke to Vitory about that. What we have is a purge protocol that essentially forces the ryklars to attack anything that moves. We wouldn't be able to tell them not to attack the Mekaal, or you for that matter, and that's not the kind of chaos we want on a battlefield," Connor said.

Lightning flashed behind Samson's head, and he glanced up for a moment. "I've deployed additional reconnaissance drones to help with our field coverage. The Konus haven't deviated from their present course."

"Understood," Connor said.

"We're authorized to engage the Konus, but why aren't we using the orbital defense platforms for a strike before they even reach our area?" Samson asked.

"For one, we're losing visibility, so we'll be more reliant on you to provide a targeting area. The additional recon drones will help with that. For two, they haven't actually engaged us," Connor said.

Samson gave him a calculated look. "I see."

Connor knew that Samson understood. They were authorized to use force on the ground, but until the Konus reached an area and engaged in hostilities against the Mekaal, the CDF wasn't authorized to use the defense platforms.

"We don't want to annihilate them."

Samson arched an eyebrow. "So, we have a few hundred thousand Konus just out and about, looking for trouble."

Connor tilted his head to the side in a small nod. "We need to convince the Konus that having us as their enemy isn't in their best interest."

"Roger that, sir."

The wind was beginning to gust strongly. "I want you to send Lieutenant Layton to these coordinates to help with the reconnaissance."

Samson nodded. "I'll have him cherry-pick a few targets for you."

"Sounds good," Connor said, and the comlink severed.

Samson had no illusions about the Konus, unlike the Security Council, which seemed to think that after a small display of force, they could be persuaded to see reason. It was a nice sentiment, and Connor hoped it would happen, but he just didn't believe it was going to. He'd looked Kasmon in the eye, and he knew the Konus warlord wouldn't deviate from his chosen path. He meant to absorb the Mekaal into the Konus, and he had committed a massive force to accomplish the task. Connor believed Kasmon had a two-pronged approach to this. The first was teaching the Mekaal that they couldn't maintain their independence, and the second was convincing the colonists they should defer to the Konus in their war against the Krake. Connor, of course, couldn't agree with that.

An official comlink appeared at Connor's workstation, bearing the seal of the Colonial Security Council. Mullins's face appeared.

"I've just spoken with Senleon," Mullins said. "I wanted you to know that we are postponing the proposal for the Mekaal to become colonial citizens."

Connor frowned. Why would Mullins tell them this now when the CDF was essentially committed to helping the Mekaal defend themselves against the Konus?

"We both decided it was best that we table the discussion until after the Konus have been dealt with," Mullins said.

Connor nodded slowly. "For a moment there, I thought you were going to order me to withdraw."

Mullins shook his head. "No, never."

"Good."

"Inviting the Mekaal to become colonial citizens will be an uphill battle. Regardless of how that turns out, I want you to know you have the full support of the Security Council," Mullins said.

For years Connor had butted heads with Mullins over a variety of issues, mainly surrounding the CDF. Something had changed in the past year. They would never be friends, but they shared common goals for the colony, even though they approached solutions to those goals from very different perspectives. For years, Connor had questioned Governor Wolf's decision to keep Mullins on as an advisor. When she'd become ill, some of those old feelings resurfaced—feelings that Mullins would work to thwart Connor's efforts to defend the colony against the Krake. Although Connor could now see this wasn't the case, Mullins was still adjusting to his role of acting governor, and that was causing a few challenges as he became more adept at leading.

"Thank you," Connor said. "I appreciate it."

"We appreciate you, Connor. I know we haven't always seen eye to eye, but I'm actually glad we can work together with or without General Hayes," Mullins said with a hint of a smile lifting the edges of his lips.

"Nathan is on his way back from Phoenix Station, but he won't be here for another twelve hours."

Mullins nodded. "I spoke to Nathan a short while ago. The subspace communicators are quite an achievement. But in the end, I agreed with Nathan that he should return to New Earth," he said and paused for a moment. "I'll let you get back to it. If there's anything you need, I hope you'll contact me."

Connor regarded him for a few moments. "I will."

The comlink went dark, and Connor went back to reviewing the latest intelligence data from the recon drones.

CHAPTER 23

Samson had never been what anyone would call a people person, and certainly not any of the colonists. The people who'd known him best were long gone, dead for hundreds of years. They'd either become victims of the plague that had almost consumed all of mankind or fought and died in the ensuing wars after the collapse of Old Earth. Like most colonists, he'd left people behind, but unlike most colonists, he'd never had a choice or a chance to say goodbye. As far as those he'd left behind knew, he'd simply disappeared. It was possible he'd been reported as killed in action, which didn't matter because the end result was still the same.

Gone.

Thunder rumbled powerfully overhead, as if the sky itself were clearing its throat to bellow. A sudden gust of wind howled as it shoved against the trees, causing them to sway violently. Brittle branches from winter snapped and plummeted to the ground like flailing missiles. The powerful winds slammed uselessly against the Nexstar combat suit, and Samson paid them no more notice than he would a summer breeze.

This wasn't a time to think about the family he'd left, but sometimes the echoes of the past forced themselves into the forefront of his thoughts, triggered by seemingly nothing. A snippet of some conversation that pulled him into a memory of his sisters, who'd banded together to protect their baby brother; some intonation of a laugh by someone; or a subtle blend of seemingly unrelated, almost random things could suddenly remind him of home. Coming from a family of nine siblings, they'd had to look after one another. He wasn't like Connor. He'd never made peace with the life he'd left behind. Samson ground his teeth at the thought. No, Connor may have moved on with his life, but Samson doubted he'd ever be at peace with what had happened. None of the Ghosts were, and if they said they were, then they were fooling themselves. The former Ghosts had done as they'd always done. Adapted. They gritted their teeth, buried their pain, and picked up the pieces to carve out a life on this planet. Except him.

He sucked a deep breath in through his nose, his lips lifting into a sneer that threatened to blossom on his face. He'd never liked New Earth, and he'd never quite fit in with the colonists. No matter how long he lived, New Earth would never be his home. Living alone for years while he explored only a portion of the vast continent had imparted harsh lessons about this godforsaken planet. New Earth wasn't for the weak. If they ever left their cities, this world would chew them up and be done with them. That was what he'd expected to happen to him when he left the colony all those years ago. Instead, he'd survived. For years he was alone, walking endlessly across a continent among the graveyards of the Ovarrow. He'd braved everything this planet had to offer and survived, but returning to the colony had allowed him to do what he was best at. His blood still boiled, and he'd found that if he didn't focus those instincts, he'd be washed out in a sea of molten fury.

Rejoining the CDF had allowed him to channel that energy into something worthwhile. But what he lived for was to fight, and he only felt truly alive when facing his own mortality. The only other thing that made him feel human was the people under his command. The 7th had become his surrogate—not quite family but pretty damn close. Connor had probably orchestrated that. Stubborn, that one. There were few men Samson had ever known who were as tenacious as one Connor Gates. This commanded his respect, even when he blamed him for what happened to the Ghosts, but that didn't prevent him from making Connor work for it. How he'd wanted to vilify Connor, make him the reason for everything wrong, but Samson was the one who'd been wrong. Connor wasn't any more to blame than the damn howling wind flinging the rain in a liquid assault.

He'd heard a few of his soldiers complain about the weather, but it was half-hearted. Samson was used to it. The Konus thought they could do whatever they wanted, but they'd picked the wrong fight. If he couldn't fight the Krake, then they'd become the next best thing against which he could use his God-given talent for mayhem and destruction.

Samson opened a comlink to Layton. "What's your status, Lieutenant?"

"Almost to the coordinates, Captain. Had a few issues with the terrain, and the Mekaal don't move as fast as we can," Layton replied.

The Mekaal had a basic version of powered armor, but they were simply outclassed by the CDF combat suits. Even with inferior equipment, the Mekaal, for the most part, were able to keep up. He'd challenge any other CDF soldier to do the same. It wasn't easy. They were a tough act to follow.

"Slow is fast," Samson said.

"Yes, sir. They haven't noticed us. We've engaged stealth protocols, and with this weather, we should be able to flank them easily enough."

"Understood. Let me know when you're in position."

"Will do, Captain," Layton said.

Samson closed the comlink. Layton was leading the 3rd Platoon on a scouting mission and also had an equal number of Mekaal lending support. The Mekaal knew the stakes. They were defending their homes. They'd been given a second chance, and they weren't going to let anyone take that away from them.

Cerot, the Warlord's First, walked over to him. All the Mekaal outside the city were under his command, and the off-world missions they'd been on for the past year had made them familiar with each other. Despite the different species and uniforms, there were some things that transcended life-forms that, for lack of similar appearances, were alike in so many other ways. Cerot exhibited a strong sense of honor and was a good leader. His loyalty to Warlord Vitory, who Samson suspected was some kind of relative, was rivaled by Samson's own loyalty to Connor. And that was something else Connor excelled at. Most people either loved him or hated him. There were very few who walked the middle ground with their opinion of him.

"Our soldiers are in position. The Konus will come down these paths," Cerot said and gestured toward the holoscreen.

"Possibly," Samson replied. "That's what they'd like us to think."

"With such a large force, why would they need to deviate?"

"Just because we can't think of a reason doesn't mean they don't have one. We'll need to pay attention and watch out for any surprise tactics. Kasmon seems craftier than the other Konus," Samson said.

Cerot considered this for a few moments and said, "He has the bearing of having been in command for a long time."

Samson nodded in agreement. "And he's used to getting what he wants."

"Precisely."

The holoscreen showed the deployment of the CDF and Mekaal soldiers. Combat suit heavies and armored rovers were deployed among their ranks. Hellcats weren't far off and would be on hand when the fighting began. Samson felt a spike of energy in anticipation. On the off-world missions, they'd had to work with rebel Ovarrow groups to help overthrow the Krake. Most weren't anyone Samson would want as neighbors, but they were necessary for their war with the Krake. He didn't like that the Konus had proven to be nothing more than a domestic bully who believed might would always be right. Well, today they'd be wrong, and Samson couldn't wait to teach them his part of that lesson.

CHAPTER 24

Colonel John Randall stood in the command center at Hammerholde. They'd been fully staffed and on high alert since they first detected the Konus army moving across the continent. General Gates was about to begin his operations at the Mekaal city. They'd deployed troops composed of CDF infantry divisions, along with Spec Ops companies. Air support had been withheld for the time being, and they'd covered the area with reconnaissance drones. Satellite feeds were off-line now because of the storm that had quickly developed, blanketing the region. The orbital defense platform was in position above the target, online and waiting for General Gates to command its use.

The sounds of people talking either to each other or on comlinks to the outside world could be heard throughout the command center. The conversations were even in tone with a slightly heightened energy but with none of the desperation Randall could recall from the Vemus War.

A sudden flashing on the main holoscreen at the tactical and operations work area snatched his attention. Alerts appeared, and then a klaxon alarm sounded.

"Colonel," Lieutenant Wong said, "reconnaissance drones over the Konus have all gone off-line."

Randall frowned and checked the feed on the main holoscreen. Then the defense platform status changed to gray. "We just lost our defense platform."

"Yes, Colonel, checking right now." Lieutenant Wong's hands flew through the holo-interface.

"Ops, confirm the most recent commands to the defense platform. Orbital, has anything been detected on our sensors?" Randall asked, needing to know whether a Krake attack force had suddenly emerged through a gateway.

"Colonel, last orders to the defense platform were from General Gates with targeting updates for the mag-cannons. He wanted them fired."

Randall's shoulder went tight. General Gates wouldn't have ordered those cannons to fire if he hadn't been committed to engaging the Konus. "Comms, we need to deploy reconnaissance drones and combat drones to that area. Send out a general alert to the CDF base at New Haven."

Sergeant Brooks confirmed and began opening comlinks to those places.

"No ships have been detected on any scanners in the star system," Lieutenant Mitchell said.

"Colonel, I've deployed a repair drone task force, and they're heading to the defense platform now. ETA is at least forty-five minutes."

Randall ground his teeth in frustration. "Understood. Keep me updated."

CDF and Mekaal forces began engaging the Konus in a ground battle. The CDF had lost their eyes and ears over the Konus. Randall tried to think of something else he could do. The CDF was mobilizing. How had they underestimated the Konus so completely?

"Colonel, repair drones are making their final approach to the defense platform. It's still not responding to any of our commands. It seems to be in a state of unresponsiveness but not fully off-line."

"Put it on screen," Randall said.

A new window appeared on the main holoscreen, showing the video feed from the lead repair drone on its way to the defense platform. The video feed suddenly cut off and went off-line.

"Ops, what the hell happened to our repair drones?"

"We've lost communications with them, sir. They're off-line. Something . . ." Lieutenant Zima said and paused for a moment. "Sir, the defense platform's countermeasures engaged and took out the repair drones."

Active sensors around New Earth still hadn't detected any enemy ships in the area. At least this wasn't an invasion force, but how the hell had the Konus taken out his defense platform? "Ops, can you access the most recent transmission logs to the defense platform? Timeframe to fifteen minutes before it went off-line."

"I'll try and get them, sir. It's going to take me a few moments."

Randall waited, and then Lieutenant Zima spoke again. "Sir, there was a tight-beam transmission that came from the Konus position."

"That's impossible," Randall said. "Even if they could figure out where our defense platform was, that doesn't . . . Find out what they did."

"Sir, they were using a CDF broadcast comlink to the platform. They had credentials, and then they uploaded the data package. After that, the targeting computer began spewing errors in its FOH systems. The onboard computer automatically launched diagnostics and then the system froze in a partial system reset, but the targeting system is having trouble determining friendlies from hostiles."

Randall's stomach attempted to slither out of his mouth. A highly capable defense platform meant to protect New Earth was malfunctioning, and now it was at the mercy of whatever the hell the Konus had done to it.

"Sir, I can send more repair drones, but the countermeasures are going to take them out."

"Understood," Randall said. "I need options. Is it responsive at all? Can we bring it down? I need that platform down. I can't have a rogue targeting computer on a defense platform that's capable of bombarding colonial cities."

"I'm trying to gain control of the system," Lieutenant Zima said.

"Tactical, I want a firing solution on that defense platform right now. If we can't regain control of it, I want it taken down ASAP."

"Understood, sir, creating the firing solution now," Lieutenant Wong said.

"Colonel," Lieutenant Zima said, "I'm able to put the defense platform into standby diagnostic for a time."

"What does that get us?" Randall asked.

"It gives us a window to get somebody out there to reset the computer systems on the platform. I can't do it remotely because it's hardened against communications in the mode it's in right now."

Randall considered this and then looked at Lieutenant Wong. "Tactical, what have you got for me?"

"It's difficult, sir. The defense platform will treat any approaching vessel as hostile, which would include any missiles we send up to it. If we attempt to take it out, it may unleash its arsenal against us. I advise sending a team up there to fix it."

Randall shook his head. He should have anticipated this. The defense platforms had been designed to engage an enemy from space. In the event it was about to be taken out, it would unleash everything it had, essentially going out in a blaze of glory while attempting mutually assured destruction. Only this time, the receiving end of all that armament was the region of New Earth where the colonists were.

"Understood," Randall said, his voice sounding strained. "Do we have any ships in the area? Who's closest? Get me somebody who can help."

"Scanning now, sir," Lieutenant Wong said.

Randall cursed inwardly. A standard op, even one with combat, shouldn't have gone to shit so fast, but he'd be damned if he'd worsen the situation by making rash decisions. There had to be somebody who could help.

———

Noah looked out the floor-to-ceiling windows at the back of his house. They had an elevated view of the natural landscape away from Sanctuary's interior. To his left was the forest, filled with the towering trees Kara informed him had been likened to Old Earth sequoias. The view was both serene and peaceful, and despite it, Noah still felt a building of anticipation. They were leaving. They'd had to secure the house because they wouldn't be back for over six months. During all his time here, he hadn't spent much of it enjoying the view from his house. To his right, he could see a few other residences before the small city that was Sanctuary began in earnest. It probably wouldn't be long before the borders of the city expanded beyond where he was.

Noah had built an impressive laboratory beneath his house. He wasn't sure where he fit with the saying that one lived to work or one worked to live. Was it really work if he loved what he was doing? Both he and Kara had their own pet projects they liked to tinker with, and they collaborated on some of them.

The front door opened, and Noah turned to the sound of Maggie and Amos running toward him. The clickety-clack of their paws on the smooth floor echoed as they raced over, their tails windmilling excitedly. Noah squatted down and gave them a quick, vigorous scratch along their backs, which they loved.

He looked up at Kara. "I guess it's about that time."

She smiled and then nodded once. She walked over to him and bent over to pat Maggie's haunches. "I wish we could take them with us," she said.

"Me too. Can you imagine them running on the lunar surface? Even if we had a spacesuit for them, they'd probably love it."

"They'd probably build up so much momentum they'd launch clear off into space."

Noah stood up, and Kara did as well. Over by the wall were two specialized stasis pods that had been designed for Maggie and Amos. He'd already put their beds inside so they would smell familiar. The stasis pods were patched into the power in the house but also had redundancies in place should there be any kind of disruption. In addition, the pods would be monitored by their veterinarian. The dogs' vital signs and all other states of being would be monitored as if they were staying in a medical center. Any deviation would trigger an alarm, and someone would be able to address the problem. The alarm would also send a message to both Noah and Kara. Additionally, he could access a video surveillance system and look in on them at any time. The floor-to-ceiling windows would remain clear so the sunlight could reach the stasis pods. It wasn't a requirement, but Noah knew what it was like to be shut away from the outside world.

His time in a coma had brought forth some strange memories that were difficult to place. He remembered hearing voices and snippets of conversation, but it was almost as if he'd been in a great motionless fog. He also had memories of feeling warmth on his face, and he'd awakened to see windows in his hospital room. Kara had told him that when she would visit him, which had been daily for almost a year, she'd open the windows to allow fresh air in. She read to him and told him about what she was working on. Noah shuddered to think of what that must've been like for her.

They walked over to the stasis pods, and both Amos and Maggie approached warily, but after taking a few tentative sniffs, they walked inside fearlessly. They circled around, pawing at the cushions of their beds, and then settled down. Noah activated the door control, and it slid silently shut. A warm amber light came from the back of the pod, and soon both his dogs stopped moving altogether. He frowned with concentration as he tried to see them breathe. The only confirmation of life was on the holoscreen that showed the vitals of his two dogs.

Noah rubbed the top of the stasis pod where Amos slept. "Sleep well, buddy. We'll be home before you know it."

Kara said her own goodbyes, and she turned toward him misty-eyed. They hugged for a few moments. "It's silly," she said. "We'll be back in six months, but this is so much harder than I thought it was going to be."

"Not to them, it won't be. To them, only a short time will pass," Noah said.

Kara wiped away a tear and nodded. They both took one last glance at their babies and left the house.

They'd just closed the door and put the house on lockdown when a comlink registered on Noah's PDA. It was from Sean.

"Are you all packed up and ready to go?" Sean asked.

"Yes, we are," Noah said. "And I expect the white-glove treatment when we get there."

Sean arched an eyebrow. "Of course. I have you down for a room with a view, and I might even throw in a few sandwiches."

Noah grinned, and Kara looked at him questioningly. "We'd gone on a camping trip and left our food back at the base, so I appropriated a recon drone to retrieve them for us."

"Yep, and Field Ops thought they had a drone that had gone rogue," Sean said. "There's been a change in your travel plans. I sent a shuttle to your location, and it should be arriving there shortly."

Noah's eyebrows raised. "Door-to-door service."

"Nothing but the best. But seriously, thanks for agreeing to come up to the lunar base. I think you're gonna love some of the things we're doing here," Sean said.

"There's no doubt about that," Noah said. He'd spent the last two days reading the briefings from Oriana. "I'll see you in about twelve hours."

"Looking forward to it," Sean said, and the comlink closed.

Noah glanced at Kara, and she was positively beaming. He might've underestimated her desire to go.

High above, a shuttle flew across the pale gray sky, lining up with an open area a short distance from the house. The engines shrieked in a dopplered wail as it came in low and fast. A loading ramp opened at the rear of the Valkyrie class combat shuttle, and standing just inside was a young pilot with brown hair and a dimple on his chin.

"Hey there, I'm Lieutenant Owen Sykes. I'm here to give you a lift to the lunar base."

Lieutenant Sykes stepped off the ramp and helped them load their belongings. They secured their equipment in the rear storage compartment.

Noah looked at the young man. "So, did you draw the short straw or lose a bet?" Shuttle duty could be tedious for pilots.

Owen smiled and shook his head. "Negative, sir. I just happened to be in the neighborhood."

Kara arched an eyebrow toward him. "Or Colonel Quinn orchestrated events so you'd be nearby."

"I can neither confirm nor deny that, ma'am," Owen said. He had an authenticity about him that Noah liked immediately.

"All right, flyboy. Just get us there in one piece," Kara said.

Owen grinned. "Yes, ma'am."

The loading ramp retracted into the shuttle, and they closed the hatch. Owen headed toward the cockpit, leaving Noah and Kara to sit wherever they wanted. The combat shuttle wasn't especially large, and it was meant for quick transport.

Noah sat and opened a holoscreen. Kara took a seat next to him. "What should we do first?" she asked.

"Oriana sent me some updates regarding the subspace theory. She thinks we're only scratching the surface of what it's capable of. I agree. I think there's a lot more we can do with this," Noah said.

"Well, we have a lot of time. Let's get started," Kara said.

As the combat shuttle rose into the air and flew away, Noah and Kara hardly noticed. They were completely focused, with multiple holoscreens up in front of them. Noah knew they'd go on for hours like this. He'd been very lucky to find someone who was a kindred spirit. There was no better woman for him than Kara.

She paused when she noticed him looking at her. "What?" she asked.

Noah shook his head. "It's nothing. I'm just glad you're here."

She smiled and leaned toward him. Her eyes twinkled affectionately. "Same here."

He leaned back in his chair and thought about Lars. He'd done everything he could, and now it was up to him. He hoped . . . Noah frowned, choosing not to allow his thoughts to run down familiar worries and fears.

He just hoped, and that was all.

CHAPTER 25

T he CDF mobile command center, located along the northeast region of the Ovarrow city, had become a hotbed of activity. Connor stood at the holotank and studied the aerial layout as the Konus drew steadily closer. The storm had picked up in earnest, and he couldn't remember if it had even been on the latest weather reports. But it didn't matter because the storm was here, and they had to deal with it.

At the top of the holotank range was the designation for the orbital defense platform DPO-47, but the icon for the defense platform was grayed out. It had been grayed out for over twenty-five minutes. They had to wait several hours to get the defense platform in place above this particular region of the continent. The platform was armed with HADES V missiles, which they wouldn't be using, two heavy mag-cannons capable of dispensing extreme destruction that could turn entire cities into slag, and two medium mag-cannons capable of firing smaller, solid projectiles at a rapid rate.

If Connor had wanted to wipe out the entire Konus army, he could've done it with a single HADES V missile and not even with a max load for the fusion warhead. At this instance, he had chosen to use the medium mag-cannons to pepper the Konus army. They were capable of launching projectiles with incredible accuracy, speed, and power. They could also be used for long-range targets, but that wasn't the case for using the weapons to fire down at the planet. For that, they'd have to adjust the mass drivers to a speed that wouldn't pierce the crust of the planet. They'd been experiencing delays in recalibrating the targeting computer on the defense platform.

Connor looked at Major Alexis Brooks and raised his eyebrows.

"Not yet, General. We're almost there," Brooks said.

They had a firing solution and no shortage of targets. Connor wanted to conduct this operation with a minimal loss of lives. He wanted to teach the

Konus a lesson, and that was all. They had air support on standby, with squadrons of Hellcats and Talon-V Stinger class vessels waiting to make runs on the Konus lines if they needed them. They had combat drones in the air, deployed along with the reconnaissance drones, and they had more than enough firepower to drive the point home. Kasmon didn't know what was coming for him. There was no way he could know.

They had waited for the Konus to reach a position where they'd be bottled up across a few kilometers, leaving them vulnerable. They knew exactly where the CDF troops were, and the Konus front lines would be within effective combat range.

The heavy defense platform was meant for engaging a target invading them from outer space. When it had become apparent that the Krake could very well invade them by opening a gateway on New Earth, they'd had to upgrade the cyber warfare suite on the defense platforms so they could target enemies on the surface of New Earth. It wasn't as simple as swinging the defense platform around so its armament faced the planet. These were highly sophisticated war machines that required precision. If the targeting was off even just a little bit, it could be disastrous for them.

Major Brooks looked over at Connor. "It's coming online now, General."

"Understood," Connor said. "Lieutenant Morgan, have your team double check the firing solution."

"Yes, General," Lieutenant Morgan said.

The defense platform icon depicted on, or in, the holotank had become green. The systems were online and in sync with the mobile command center. The work area where the tactical team was assembled showed a wall of holoscreens displaying multiple feeds from the reconnaissance drones and CDF troop deployments.

"General Gates," Lieutenant Morgan said, "the firing solution checks out, but the Konus are starting to split their forces. They've increased their speed and—" The tactical officer stopped speaking. Connor's eyes flicked to the holoscreens that had begun flashing—first one, then a couple, and then more spread across the board. "General, our recon drones are going off-line. They're being taken out."

Connor watched the feed in shock as nearly every one of the reconnaissance drones went off-line, seemingly all at once. He'd never seen such a thing before. They had thousands of drones covering the region.

"Run a diagnostic, Lieutenant," Connor said.

"System checks out, General. They're taking out our drones."

"Order the combat drones to fire on their targets."

There was a flurry of activity at the tactical work area. Connor shifted his feet, a sinking feeling dragging at his core, and he felt like he was the one being ambushed instead of the Konus. His orders should only have needed to be confirmed, and then the combat drones would engage, but Major Brooks began conferring with Lieutenant Abernathy at operations.

Connor walked over to Lieutenant Morgan.

"General, I can't get any confirmation from our combat drones. One moment they were all there, and the next . . ." Morgan said and shook his head.

"If they were being destroyed, at least some of them would have registered the attack," Connor said.

Lieutenant Morgan nodded. "The last activity logged was a strange power surge. It affected them all at once."

Connor gritted his teeth. The Konus must have had some kind of weapon they hadn't encountered that enabled them to destroy all the CDF drones. With the intense storm, they could have hidden the attack.

"Does the defense platform firing solution still check out?" Connor asked.

"Yes, General."

"Fire. Authorization given."

"Confirmed. Sending the clearance code for the firing solution to the defense platform," Lieutenant Morgan said.

Connor turned back to the holotank and waited. What the hell could have taken out the combat drones and the reconnaissance drones? That they hadn't even detected? Their eyes, ears, and first-strike weapons had been snuffed out. His mind reeled with the knowledge that the Konus must've been able to track the CDF drones this entire time. They'd just *let* the CDF watch them. He furrowed his brow in concentration. He'd underestimated Kasmon.

"That can't be right," Lieutenant Morgan said in a harsh tone. He looked over at Connor as if fearing to give him a status update that was the precursor to the shit hitting the fan. "The defense platform is not responding."

Connor blinked his eyes for several moments, and Lieutenant Morgan flinched. "Say that again, Lieutenant."

"I sent the command authorization for the firing solution and received no acknowledgment. The system is not responding," Lieutenant Morgan said.

Connor swung his gaze back to the holotank, and he opened a comlink to Hammerholde. Colonel John Randall appeared on a holoscreen. "Colonel Randall, I have a defense platform I can't communicate with."

"We're seeing the same thing, General. We've deployed repair drones that are en route to the defense platform. ETA is thirty-seven minutes."

Connor clenched his teeth and shook his head. Then he looked back at Randall. "Keep me apprised, Colonel."

He severed the comlink.

"Ops, send an emergency broadcast to all forward forces. They are cleared to engage the enemy. Attack orders Bravo."

"Yes, General. Relaying orders now," Lieutenant Abernathy said.

"Major Brooks, we are going to need air support," Connor said.

"Understood, General. How many, sir?" Brooks asked.

Connor swallowed hard. "All of them."

"I'm on it, sir," Brooks replied.

Connor turned back to the holotank, glaring at the lack of information he had on there now. The Konus were on the move, and with each passing moment, the data he did have on hand became less and less accurate. They'd been blinded. Hell, they'd been knocked back on their asses before the battle had even begun. The operation had gone sideways, and now they were scrambling to catch up.

In the distance, Connor heard the shrieking engines of the Hellcats rising into the air. They flew overhead, speeding toward a battle that was about to begin. Connor balled his hands into fists, wanting to lash out. The plan had just gone out the window, and he needed a new one. And something told him deep in his gut that the Konus weren't finished with their surprises. He looked over at Vitory.

"The Konus are coming, and we need to be on high alert. Make sure the soldiers at the defense installations around the city are ready," Connor said.

Vitory leveled a look at him. "They are ready."

Connor wondered if the Ovarrow had suspected the Konus could do something like this, but there was no way they could've known. If Vitory had suspected such a thing, he would've told Connor. They were both veterans enough to understand that the events of a battlefield changed quickly, and now they needed to adapt. Now, they needed to fight.

CHAPTER 26

amson deployed the 7th along the ridgeline of a string of deep forested valleys. Mekaal infantry units were spread throughout the area for half a kilometer. Sheets of rain pelted down in thick volleys, thwacking the CDF soldiers who lay in wait. The muddy ground had become saturated, and Samson expected that mudslides could occur at any moment.

The CDF soldiers hid, using makeshift cover to blend in with the landscape. The storm blowing through the area made it extraordinarily dark, which wasn't so much an obstacle for CDF soldiers, but a darkness this profound, broken by random lightning in combination with an intense storm and a rapidly approaching enemy army, was a potent hurdle to overcome.

Samson knelt behind the corpse of a massive fallen tree that hadn't quite succumbed to its untimely demise. It lay against its neighbors in a tangle of brush that stubbornly kept it from dropping completely to the ground. The highly dense wood could absorb even the most powerful plasma bolts from Ovarrow weapons. He could exhaust his entire supply of nanorobotic ammunition to chew through the compact hardwoods, but it would take time. He'd take any additional protection to the battle-steel of his combat suit armor, so this was a good location from which to engage the enemy.

The rangers were quiet as they peered into the gloomy veil of darkness. Enhanced night vision through the Nexstar combat suit was as close as they were going to get to seeing clearly this night. The heads-up display of the combat suit helmet filtered out the things they didn't need to see in order to help them identify the targets they were most interested in. The falling rain appeared as a semitranslucent silhouette of oblong drops splattering as they hit the ground. They had infrared for detecting heat signatures, but everyone knew that ryklars could conceal their body heat. Samson wouldn't allow any of his soldiers to assume anything about the enemy. Whether the Konus soldiers could hide themselves as well as the CDF Rangers remained to be seen. They'd deployed acoustic sensors with which their combat suit computers filtered out sounds they'd already accounted for, so their suit computers focused on the anomalies. CDF training included using these tactics as part of their scout training and also for points of engagement at ambush sites.

The Konus had superior numbers, making them able to field more soldiers. They had more weapons, whose abilities the CDF had yet to really see in action, and then there were the ryklars. Samson had hunted the ryklars before and had been hunted by them during his long years of isolation. High frequency sound waves wouldn't send the ryklars with Konus implants running, which made them all the more dangerous. Ryklars were powerful and quick, and when in a pack, they'd coordinate their attacks.

The heavily forested region would slow the bulk of Konus ground transportation vehicles, forcing them to circumvent the area entirely. They'd either have to come through on foot with smaller vehicles or slow their progress to a crawl, which made for easier targets. But the loss of the forward reconnaissance drones had plunged their bird's-eye view of the enemy into complete and total darkness. Samson had recalled their platoon-specific drones. No use leaving them out there for the Konus to use for target practice. If they could detect and eliminate stealth recon drones, then they could very well see in the dark. The Konus had been preparing for war for years, and Samson had no illusions they weren't well-practiced in armed conflict.

"Look alive. A scouting force is trying to sneak in here," Sergeant Dixon said on an open broadcast comlink to the 7th. The CDF sniper had set up a perch above their position. Armed with an M-Viper rifle, he was among the deadliest sharpshooters in the entire company. "Painting the targets," he said.

The M-Viper had a highly specialized scope that linked to Dixon's Nexstar combat suit. Once he identified hostile forces, the data was uploaded to Samson and the squad leaders in the area. In the absence of recon drones, it was the next best thing.

"I have them on my scope too," Mason said. His squad's position was on another ridge at the adjacent valley.

Chatter began to pick up as more and more of them detected the Konus.

"Hold your fire," Samson ordered. "This is a scout force. Let them come in farther."

They'd know soon enough if the Konus could detect them. The comms chatter ceased. Sound-dampening tech from the combat suits would prevent the CDF soldiers from being overheard, but the Mekaal didn't have that kind of advantage. They relied on gestures to communicate. They wouldn't break the silence until the first shots were fired.

Samson felt cold anticipation gather inside him that he felt in his gut, and it traveled along his muscled arms to his fingertips as he caught his first glimpse of the Konus soldiers. They moved in small groups, carrying long staff-type energy weapons that Samson had seen in Ovarrow military bunkers. They advanced with efficiency and precision that was almost surgical, as one group moved up about ten meters, checked the area, and gestured for the next group to move forward. They spread into the deep valley, and Samson spotted other groups higher up.

Diversion force, Samson thought. They were the bait. They certainly had enough soldiers to spare. He sent a tactical update to his squad leaders that would be trickled down to the men.

Samson opened a comlink to Matheson. "I've got a special target for you, Sergeant."

Matheson's loadout was a combat suit heavy equipped with a quad-barrel M547 gauss cannon, which could mow down forests. It drew its ammunition from multiple nanorobotic blocks that, when activated, could form a number of specialized ammunitions. It could alternate between generic high-density projectiles, incendiary rounds, and explosive rounds, or a combination of all three. This allowed them to conserve ammunition and make it stretch for longer bursts.

"Yes, Captain, just point me in the direction you want gone," Matheson said.

"Coordinates on the way, and wait for it," Samson said.

"Understood, sir."

The Konus continued to delve deeper into the valley, and Samson spotted more units cresting the ridge across the valley. Something caught his eye, and he peered into the darkened sky. Thunder rumbled, and lightning lit up the area. Then he saw it. Large winged vehicles were flying directly to his position, riding on the wind. Their metallic wings glinted in the flashes of light.

The passing moments built up in a pregnant pause, preceded by a shallow gasp.

"Light them up," Samson bellowed.

Next came the unleashing of CDF weaponry, followed by that of the Mekaal. The deep valley blazed into light, and the basin walls reverberated with the concussive blasts of the CDF armament tearing into the Konus scout force. The sudden chaotic cadence of AR-71s and Ovarrow rifles was drowned out by the CDF heavies firing their quad-barrel M547s. Streaks of red burned into the Konus forces, tearing through their armored soldiers, followed by blasts from explosive rounds.

Pop.

Pop.

Pop.

Boom!

The diversionary force was taken completely by surprise, as well as the main attack force that attempted to flank the defensive positions maintained by the CDF and Mekaal protectors.

More Konus soldiers pressed forward into the valley, but they made it

INSURGENT **539**

only a short distance. Samson heard Dixon's M-Viper sniper rifle hiss into the storm, and Konus soldiers fell one after another.

"Ruo, plug that valley entrance," Samson said.

Specialist Ruo brought up his missile launcher and launched twin scorpion missiles that blazed a path toward the Konus. The explosion engulfed the Konus in molten flame, and the percussive force shoved the downpour of rain back in vengeful defiance as it consumed its victims.

Samson and the rest of the 7th pushed forward. They had to move. The Konus had been marking the CDF positions and would be calling in heavy ordnance of their own. They had ground assault vehicles and the aerial fighter he'd glimpsed before. Samson needed the Konus to think they were committed to seizing the opportunity of their surprise attack and blindly charging forward.

They moved forward fifty meters. Samson had been right. The scouting force had been detached from the Konus' main fighting force. The soldiers painted targets via an infrared laser, and a few moments later, scorpion missiles destroyed the targets.

Samson called for a halt. This had been the easy part. The 7th Ranger Company and the Mekaal soldiers were no strangers to armed conflict. They'd worked together off-world against the Krake and Ovarrow alike. The fog of war would settle in as they engaged the Konus, and then the grind would begin. There was no way they could halt the army indefinitely. They needed the orbital defense platform strikes. In the absence of that, multiple squadrons of Hellcats would make short work of the Konus front lines.

Samson heard Dixon's sniper rifle take out Konus targets. Each platoon had several snipers. The M-Vipers could be heard among the sounds of the other weaponsfire. Samson and the other CDF soldiers fired their AR-71s in controlled bursts of hypersonic darts.

The combat suit heavies held their fire, waiting for Samson's command. Their weapons could unleash holy hell on a battlefield, but there was always a cost. Heat built up, and those heavy weapons needed strict pacing if they were to stay operational for the duration of the battle.

Konus ground assault vehicles barreled toward them. Bright particle beams fired from the mounted weapons atop. The beams blazed through the forests, sizzling through the dense trees in great bursts.

The Mekaal returned fire from their own particle rifles, which heated the metallic alloyed armor plating of the Konus assault vehicles but didn't burn through it. Samson fired incendiary rounds at the base of a vehicle. The high heat burned through the alloyed mesh that composed the vehicle's tires, and it wobbled. Other CDF soldiers followed his example and focused their fire on the other wheels.

The Konus heavy cannon swung toward them, the interior glowing molten yellow.

"Fall back," Samson bellowed. "Get to cover."

They scrambled back, and a thick, deadly particle beam blazed like the sun, so hot it ignited the damp ground as it raced toward them.

He broadcast the mine activation signals. They'd peppered the Konus-occupied region with Ovarrow defense mines, and the CDF enhancement made it possible to detonate them remotely. They didn't need to wait to be triggered by some unsuspecting enemy. The ground roared up, sending bright, explosive blasts that illuminated the area amid the chaotic lightning splitting the sky overhead.

Samson heard the hearty grinning of the CDF soldiers, and he felt a few moments of grim satisfaction, but he wouldn't allow himself to be distracted. He opened a broadcast channel. "All right, let's fall back to the second position."

The Konus would be cautious as they came forward after regrouping. The CDF and Mekaal special forces had just killed thousands of them, but there were many more. This was where the grind would begin. They'd lure the Konus forward, and just when the army became emboldened, they'd strike. The attacks would seem random to them. Samson would keep the Konus off balance as much as possible, and the storm would impact them as much as it had the CDF.

"Corporal Bradley," Samson said, "let's send up a few of our reserve recon drones. I want a quick survey of the damage."

"On it, Captain," Corporal Bradley said and set about to deploy the recon drones she carried.

Despite the success of the engagement, Samson knew it was only the beginning. Now the Konus were aware of them. They'd adapt their tactics, and the real work would begin. This night would be a long endurance run for both sides.

CHAPTER 27

"Maybe we need to think about this another way," Noah said.

They had a cluster of holoscreens around them now with different reports and engineering specs for the subspace communication transceiver.

Kara rubbed her eyes and gave her forehead a gentle massage. Then she rolled her shoulders and sighed. "You want to go back to the space gates again, don't you?"

Noah nodded enthusiastically. "Yes, because it's tied into subspace communications. I know it's tied into that town."

She pressed her lips together in thought. Twin blonde eyebrows pulled together, and then she nodded once. "You mean the Ovarrow town that somehow arrived on Sagan."

"It wasn't an accident. And it wasn't teleported there," Noah said.

"What makes you so sure?"

"I'd tell you that teleportation is impossible, but in light of the other things we've seen, I'm not entirely sure I could rule it out. But I really don't think that applies here. The Ovarrow were attempting to reverse engineer space gates and stumbled upon subspace communication. Those two things have to be related. So, if the space gates are used for transitioning between universes, then before that actual transition takes place, there must be a way to send the matter to subspace."

"So, you think that somehow the Ovarrow stumbled upon sending part of their research installation with multiple buildings across a massive expanse of space nearly instantaneously, and this isn't teleportation," Kara said.

Noah frowned as he tried to follow her logic. Then his eyes widened, and he shook his head. "No, because in order to teleport, you have to disassemble the object being teleported on a molecular level, and that didn't happen. Also, how would it reassemble on the other side? You can't take that step out of it," he said and tapped the tips of his fingers on his thigh. "What I think the Ovarrow stumbled onto was using the space gate as a receiver of sorts. They were conducting the experiment using an arch gateway. For some reason we haven't figured out yet, the Krake had a space gate by planet Sagan."

Kara shook her head. "You're reaching, Noah."

His gaze went skyward for a moment while he gathered his patience. "Yeah, that's kind of the point of out-of-the-box thinking, love. Okay, let's think this through," Noah said, continuing with his line of reasoning. "They send a group of buildings, and it emerges somehow between an arch gateway and a space gateway. Then it winds up on the planet surface completely unscathed—maybe. At least the reports say it was relatively intact. And that's the problem right there. That's the gotcha. The rub. At least one of them anyway. If it had come out of the space gate and headed down to the planet, it would've disintegrated on impact. There would've been nothing left at all —nothing but an impact crater among all the other impact craters. Sagan doesn't even have an atmosphere to speak of."

He minimized all the holoscreens. "I have to show you," he said and drew two circles separated by a short distance. "We have New Earth here and Sagan over here." He then drew a small circle and labeled it as the space gate. "Now keep in mind that this is pure theory, but what if they didn't know they'd actually done this? When they engaged the arch, it simultaneously was connected to the space gate at Sagan. We don't know how that works, but we know that it did work. Sean found that out the hard way, if you remember." Kara nodded, and Noah continued. "So, if the two gateways were joined, then there's a transitioning over vast distances quickly. And if you want to take it one step further, they could've projected whatever came through down to the surface of Sagan."

She sucked in her bottom lip and let it slide back through the top of her teeth. She peered at Noah's childlike drawings with the rigid intensity of an engineer seeing things conceptually. "Okay, if we put all the assumptions aside, there should be evidence of it besides the town that was no longer there."

He nodded slowly. "I'm not sure what evidence would be there. The arch was at the bottom of a great lake. If water were to suddenly appear on the surface of the planet, then it would have evaporated."

"Yeah, but if it periodically happened over several hundred years, then there should be some kind of . . ." she said and paused for a moment, searching for the right word. "I don't want to say 'residue' because that's not right. It's almost like looking for evidence of impact craters from a meteor shower. But what we're looking for . . ." she paused again, and this time she smiled. "Almost like a comet hit the planet. It does interact with the surface of the planet, but we'd probably need some help with that."

"We need to speak to an astrophysicist, and we'd need to convince the powers that be that this is worth sending a science vessel to investigate," Noah said.

"Are they still salvaging wreckage from the Vemus War on the planet?"

He shrugged. "I don't know. I don't think so. Why would I know this?"

"So, that's one thing we'll need to find out."

"If we do find evidence, we'll have physical evidence to support my theory."

"Let's not get ahead of ourselves," Kara said. "If it all proves true, what exactly is your theory?"

"Just that the technology for subspace communications has more applications than mere communications. We might possibly be able to use it to travel vast distances, but if we can somehow figure out how to link space gates across multiple—"

"Excuse me," Lieutenant Sykes said, "would both of you join me in the cockpit please."

"We'll be right there," Noah said and killed all the holoscreens. He glanced at the time and realized that they'd been at it for almost six hours. That's how it was when they started working on problems. It was as if they'd entered a time machine, and it flowed by at breakneck speeds.

They walked over to the cockpit and saw that Lieutenant Sykes was speaking to another man on the holoscreen.

Years of training kicked in, and Noah stood up straighter. "Colonel," he said.

"Mr. Barker," the colonel said. He looked at Kara. "Mrs. Barker, I'm John Randall, the CO of COMCENT. I need your help."

Noah shared a glance with his wife, then looked back at Colonel Randall. "Our help? What do you need?"

"Less than an hour ago, one of our defense platforms became nonresponsive. We dispatched repair drones to assess the problem, and the automated defensive measures activated and destroyed the repair drones while on approach to the platform."

Noah frowned. "That shouldn't be possible," he said. He had done extensive work with the defense platforms, particularly those of the missile defense platforms that were deployed throughout the star system. They'd been instrumental in defeating the Vemus fleet.

"Be that as it may, it's what happened."

"Yeah, but that would mean the targeting protocols . . ." Noah's eyes widened.

Colonel Randall nodded. "That was our assessment as well."

Kara looked at him. "I don't understand."

"Are the Krake here? Have any ships been detected?" Noah asked.

"Negative. We have no enemy ships near New Earth or in the star system. We believe that a group of Ovarrow called the Konus used some piece of technology we aren't aware of that impacted the defense platform's ability to target properly," Randall said.

Noah felt his stomach flip, and his mouth hung open a little.

"I see that you understand the ramifications of this technology," Randall said. "I need to send a team to the defense platform."

Noah breathed in deeply. "We're the closest ones, aren't we?"

Colonel Randall nodded. "I know you're not officially with the Colonial Defense Force anymore, and I have no authority to ask you to do this."

None of that mattered to Noah. There were lives on the line. If these Konus had used some kind of tech to neutralize the CDF defense platform, there was a lot more going on than he'd realized. "You don't have to ask," he said. "Just tell me what you need."

He glanced at Kara, and she nodded once, watching Colonel Randall expectantly.

"We can create a window of time for you to reach the platform by triggering a diagnostic shutdown of the system. But you'll have a limited amount of time to figure out the problem before the automated defenses come back up, and we have no way of knowing whether it will perceive you as hostile."

"So, we have a time crunch. How close can we get to the platform in the shuttle before the automated defenses open fire on us?" Noah asked. If the targeting systems had been completely compromised, the defense platform could open fire, using its vast armament against a whole host of targets— from CDF or civilian ships to colonial cities. Right now, it sounded like the defense platform's targeting systems were only partially compromised. This didn't mean they were in any less danger than they'd been before, but it did mean the systems could become completely compromised at some point, and disaster could strike at any moment.

"I'll send you the information right now," Colonel Randall said. "And thank you. You don't have to do this."

Noah felt the edges of his lips lift into a small smile. "Yes, we do."

He didn't know why, but despite the danger they were heading toward, he felt more alive than he had in months. He looked at Kara and saw the same determination in her eyes. They'd both served in the CDF, and the years of service had instilled in them a no-nonsense attitude toward protecting the colony. It was time for them to step off the sidelines and help.

CHAPTER 28

"General Gates, SRD groups are flying over the Konus army now," Lieutenant Morgan said.

The stealth recon drones were grouped together with combat drone escorts in an effort to cover the area where the Konus army was supposed to be.

"Acknowledged," Connor replied.

The Konus wouldn't have been idle since their surprise attack had taken out the SRDs they'd had monitoring them for days. The new SRDs were making high-speed passes overhead, and their data feeds were constantly being fed back to COMCENT.

Connor ground his teeth. He'd become too complacent with the advantages they'd had over the other Ovarrow they'd encountered, not only on New Earth but on other worlds as well.

He peered into the holotank, attempting to glean some more useful information from it, but the data they had was a few hours old now. Multiple infantry divisions were fighting the Konus, along with Spec Ops companies. His gaze drifted toward the casualty count. The small amber font showed a number in the hundreds. Each one of them was a life, and this didn't account for the Mekaal losses.

"Ops, we need better coordination with our air support. There are still too many gaps. Concentrate deployment where the fighting is heaviest," Connor said.

Hellcat squadrons were lending support where they could to relieve the pressure on the ground forces. The Konus were paying a heavy price for every meter of ground they took, but the numbers were in their favor. If this conflict remained purely ground-based, when would the Konus decide that the price of taking the Mekaal city was too much? Use of the orbital defense platform would have made a much more compelling argument for the Konus to rethink their strategy.

Connor flicked his gaze back to the holotank and frowned. He'd been focusing the image where the fighting was occurring, but he decided to push it back out to a higher level where he could take in the entire theater of battle. The Konus wanted to get to the city, and they were prepared to fight for it, but that didn't necessarily mean they simply intended to match their army against the combined forces of the CDF and the Mekaal.

His eyes drifted toward an area thirty kilometers away from the city where the fighting was the worst. The storm was impacting the way this battle was being fought, but Connor couldn't afford to dwell on what he couldn't control. He needed to put the shoe on the other foot, so to speak, and get into Kasmon's head to figure out what he really intended to do. Kasmon had allowed the CDF stealth recon drones to observe him, only to take them out when it really mattered. That would level the engagement to some degree, but it couldn't be all there was to it. The Konus were on the move. His gaze returned to the far side of the holotank, which showed the city. That was the end goal. That's what they wanted.

If Connor had wanted to take control of the city before the battle really got out of hand . . . His eyes widened, and he knew exactly what he would have done. He zoomed in closer to the Mekaal city. The sixty thousand inhabitants occupied only a small portion because much of the city was uninhabitable.

"Ops," he said, "how many reserve forces do we have in the city?"

Lieutenant Abernathy double-checked her holoscreen. "CDF forces, or do you want numbers from the Mekaal as well?"

"Just CDF."

"We have the 3rd Brigade located in the LZ. Four thousand soldiers. We also have troop transports in the area that are waiting to bring them where they need to go. Do you want to send them somewhere?" she asked.

"Yeah, I want five platoons to make a sweep of the uninhabited parts of the city."

"Understood, General Gates. Deploying now," Lieutenant Abernathy said.

He'd been too reliant on stealth recon drones and wanted actual soldiers sweeping the area. If they found the Konus, they would engage.

"Tactical, I want a general advisement sent out to our forces in the city, including the Mekaal. They are to report in on anything that looks suspicious. The Konus might be trying to sneak into the city," Connor said.

A few moments later, Lieutenant Scott Morgan replied. "The update has been sent out, General."

"Major Brooks, what is the status of the orbital defense platform?"

"They're sending in a team to investigate. The initial repair drone group was destroyed by the defense platform's point defense systems," Major Brooks said.

Connor hoped whomever they had going in could get the defense platforms back up quickly. And he wanted to know how they'd been neutralized. Had the Konus done it? He didn't believe in giving the enemy capabilities they hadn't proven they had, but the evidence was clear. He'd underestimated the Konus, and now they were paying the price.

An information alert appeared on his personal holoscreen. Class III Hellcat squadrons had finally left the base at Sierra. They were armed with heavy ordnance, and Connor nodded grimly. The bombing runs would start.

Being part of the reserve forces really sucked. Sergeant Hunter Riley had been keen to see some action, and he wasn't the only one. Platoons that had been assigned to the reserve force hated the wait while other soldiers were doing the fighting. They were eager to do their part.

"Finally," Corporal Blackman said, "we get to get off our sorry asses and do something."

They'd just received the call a few moments ago.

"Don't get too excited," Lieutenant Thomas Wade said. "We're doing a patrol run."

"Where to, sir?" Blackman asked.

The rest of the men had gathered around.

"They want us to make a sweep of the unoccupied parts of the city," Wade said.

Hunter pressed his lips together for a moment. "They think the Konus are sneaking in? If that's the case, why don't they send more of us over there?"

Thomas gave him a look, and Hunter realized the answer.

"Understood, sir. That's what we're going to find out," Hunter said.

"All right, let's saddle up. Sergeant Riley, you and your squad are on point," Wade said.

"Yes, sir. Roger that, sir. The tip of the spear," Hunter said, and this drew a few hearty grins.

They left the occupied city and headed out into the dark wasteland of another world from another time. The storm raged above them, but inside their Nexstar combat suits, it had very little impact on them.

Hunter was on point, along with Blackman, Dunning, Morrison, Trevor, Bowden, and Gorman. Gorman was their heavy hitter, so he brought up the rear.

The city still had main thoroughfares that they could use to make a sweep out toward the edge. They took it slow and steady, checking the buildings as they went. The rain was still coming down in buckets, but the wind only howled some of the time.

The farther they got from the base, the more desolate and silent things became, and the more isolated they felt. Lightning flashed overhead, and a few of the men jumped at shadows. There were other platoons patrolling the other side of the city. The plan was for them to meet up in the middle and then make their way back.

The Ovarrow city had been constructed with that bizarre rounded architecture Hunter had never really cared for. Someone had told him it was to help with defenses, particularly against the ryklars—as if they couldn't climb up the walls even with the severe overhang these buildings had. They gave a cursory glance at the buildings they were able to access as they moved through the area.

A comlink registered on Hunter's heads-up display.

"Riley, take your squad in toward the outer thoroughfare," Lieutenant Wade said.

"Understood, sir," Hunter replied, accessing the broadcast channel to his squad. "Change of plans. We're heading toward the outskirts."

They broke away from the others and began their patrol, making their way along the outskirts of the city and stopping to do a scan of the immediate area outside the city. They encountered a station broadcasting the ryklar deterrent signal, which was fully operational. Smaller creatures scurried through the area.

They came to a taller building, and Hunter had no idea what its original use had been, but he knew it would give them the bird's-eye view he wanted. He left Gorman, Trevor, and Morrison on the ground while the rest of them climbed to the top using the climbing configuration in their combat suits.

Hunter scaled the wall, along with Blackman, Dunning, and Bowden. When they reached the top, they began to look around. Lightning flashed overhead, but the onboard computer of their combat suits filtered out the flashes of light so they wouldn't be blinded. Hunter caught sight of something moving in the distance. He was on the outskirts of the city, and he wasn't sure if it was actually a trick of the light due to the storm. Now *he* was jumping at shadows, but they had to check it out.

"Blackman," Hunter said, "do me a favor and look out over there. Do you see anything out of place?"

Corporal Blackman came to his side and peered in the direction Hunter had indicated. He waited a few moments. "I don't see anything, sir."

"Did you see something, Sergeant?" Bowden asked.

"I thought I saw something. We need to check it out. Let's climb back down and head over," Hunter said.

They climbed down to the ground and informed the others. Hunter didn't make a straight line toward the waypoint. He preferred to take a different route that would lead to the same area. The squad settled into a quiet routine, moving slow and steady. The main part of the platoon was now half a kilometer away.

They soon made it to the area, and there was nothing there. Hunter wanted to take a closer look, so they moved in cautiously.

"What do you think you saw?" Blackman asked.

"Movement. Just something moving in the distance. I didn't get a good look." Hunter glanced back the way they'd come and could see the tall building they'd climbed. He was in the right area. When he returned his gaze to the ground, he saw a set of tracks and frowned. A vehicle had been through there. He gestured down, and the others saw it too. They immediately began scanning in all directions, looking for the Konus.

Hunter opened a comlink to Lieutenant Wade. "Sir, I have a set of tracks here that aren't from any of our vehicles. They appear to have come from outside the city, and they're heading around toward the other platoon."

"Understood, Sergeant. Keep tracking them, and we'll make our way to you. Sending rendezvous coordinates to you now," Lieutenant Wade said.

A waypoint appeared on Hunter's internal heads-up display. He marked it and distributed the data to the rest of the squad. This time, they set a quicker pace. They were playing catch-up now, and they had to move faster in order to find and stalk their prey. It must've been some kind of Konus ground transport vehicle, and given the number of tracks, there must've been a lot of them. It looked like they were trying to get through the area as quickly as possible.

Hunter peered ahead of them using all the available spectrums the combat suits had to offer. Nothing appeared on infrared, and the only evidence of the Konus being there was the tracks in the muddy ground. They came to an area where they were the farthest away from the CDF base at the occupied section of the city.

"Sir, you're going to want to see this," Corporal Blackman said. Hunter joined them, and Blackman gestured toward the ground. He saw dozens of clawed footprints that seemed to have sprung up from out of nowhere.

"What the hell is this?" Morrison asked.

Hunter squatted down and took a closer look. Then he quickly stood up. "They're ryklar tracks," he said, continuing to study them. "Looks like they're mixed with Ovarrow tracks as well. The Konus are in the city."

"Hold on. The deterrent signal is on. How can ryklars be in the city?" Blackman asked.

Hunter pressed his lips together in a frown. Blackman was right, but . . . He brought up the latest intelligence about the Konus. "The Konus have ryklars with implants that make the deterrent signal ineffective."

"Holy shit," Morrison said.

Gorman swung his quad-barrel around, pointing it toward the city, looking for any excuse to unleash hell.

"Stay frosty," Hunter said. He opened a comlink to Lieutenant Wade. The lieutenant answered, and Hunter could hear fighting and weaponsfire in the background. "Let's move. They're under attack."

As the squad began to run, Hunter sent an alert to COMCENT, which would make its way to General Gates. Given the number of tracks he'd seen and the fact that they hadn't found the Konus ground transport, the Konus were probably deploying groups at different points of entrance to the city. They were here, and they were going to attack at any moment. Right now, everyone in the city was completely unaware and would be caught by surprise.

The Nexstar combat suits were capable of moving at high speeds, but they couldn't move as fast as Hunter would have preferred since Gorman was equipped as a heavy. However, they could still move at a pretty good clip. Hopefully, they'd be able to take the Konus by surprise.

CHAPTER 29

The combat shuttle flew toward the heavy defense platform. It had been constructed of fourth generation battle-steel alloy with a silicon-based, artificial bacteria that not only helped maintain the hull but also regenerated lightly damaged sections. The defense platform had a thick cross section in the middle where the large missile tube was located, with two sections on either side that held the two classes of mag-cannons. It was an automated space station that carried a tremendous destructive capability to engage fleets of enemy ships.

Noah watched as Lieutenant Sykes kept the tiny combat shuttle on a straight approach vector to the sleeping leviathan in geostationary orbit around New Earth, noting that Sykes and Kara were both tensed as they watched the main holoscreen. They'd changed into individual life-support suits in case they experienced a sudden loss of atmospheric pressure in the combat shuttle.

Noah cleared his throat. "If the automated defenses decide we're a threat, we won't even see a flash of light before it takes out the shuttle," he said.

Kara glanced at him in exasperation. "Not helping," she said.

"I'm just saying that we wouldn't feel a thing." He couldn't help that a small smile lifted his lips despite the danger.

"He's right, ma'am," Lieutenant Sykes said.

"Not you too," Kara said. "I already know that." She glared at Noah for a moment, then her gaze softened. "*Jerk.*"

He grinned. He'd known his comment would work to defuse the tension. "It's off-line. Look, the orbit is deteriorating. The systems are down and so are the maneuvering thrusters that maintain its orbit."

Lieutenant Sykes nodded. "All right, making the final approach now."

Noah and Kara left the cockpit and went to their own life support, after which Lieutenant Sykes vented the atmosphere in the combat shuttle. A few minutes later, they docked near the maintenance hatch and walked to the rear of the shuttle. Two automatic tethers extended from a port on the wall and connected to the rear of their space suits.

Noah saw Kara lick her lips and sigh. "You know, I can go out there and take care of this myself," he said.

"Don't be silly. I'm not letting you go out there alone," she replied.

"It's just that I know you're not a big fan of space walks."

"Will you stop? It's been just as long for you since we've been on a space walk. Let's go see if we can fix this thing and get out of here," Kara said.

"Yes, ma'am," Noah replied and gave her salute.

They engaged their magboots and opened the rear hatch. Then, they stepped onto the defense platform's outer hull.

"Who designed the system this way?" she asked.

"It's designed to be secure. It's supposed to be tamperproof."

They walked along the outer hull near the base of the enormous mag-cannons that loomed above them. New Earth filled the view below them with an azure glow that was offset by the planetary rings. It'd been years since Noah had left New Earth, and he'd almost forgotten how beautiful it was from up here. But he didn't have time to admire the view. He needed to keep moving, promising himself that he'd make time to take in the view soon.

"Once we're inside the maintenance hatch, we should be fine," he said.

He heard Kara let out a startled gasp and turned to find her slightly off balance. One foot was in the air, and she seemed to be leaning too far to the side. Noah walked back toward her and helped her regain her balance. Her other foot hit the metallic alloy of the defense platform, and she righted herself.

"Are you all right?" he asked.

Kara nodded and let out a huge breath. "I'm fine. It's just . . . It's been a while. I'll be fine. Keep going."

"I know you will be. And if we're not, the tether still works. We're not going anywhere," Noah said and smiled.

"How do you do it? How can you be so calm?"

He hadn't realized it, but he was calm. He just focused on the problem. "Later. Now I'm just fine. Let's get this over with."

There was a countdown timer in the upper right corner of his heads-up display. They had plenty of time to diagnose the problem, but he was most worried about how long the CDF ground forces would be exposed to the massive Konus army they were fighting.

Noah turned around and walked toward the maintenance hatch thirty meters away. Using the space suit's comms system, he was able to authenti-cate and open it. He carefully moved the hatch away and gestured for Kara to go in first. He wouldn't have been able to lift the armored hatch on New Earth, even with the assistance of an exoskeleton. Zero-G did have its advan-tages sometimes. He followed Kara inside and closed the hatch.

"Lieutenant Sykes, we're in," Noah said.

"Good," Sykes said. "There should be a console just beyond that access corridor."

They headed away from the maintenance hatch and rounded the corner. "Found it."

The defense platform computer systems were essentially paused at the start-up. No systems had come online; the whole thing was in a holding state, which allowed him to bring the systems up one at a time so he could check that they were working properly.

First, he had it perform a diagnostic of the weapon systems, and they were unaffected. According to the diagnostic, they all worked properly. It was the targeting subsystem that controlled the weapon systems operations that had been impacted.

"This is a mess," Kara said. "Are they sure that a single tight-beam data upload broke the system?"

"I don't know," Noah said. "Lieutenant Sykes, initiating a dump of the defense platform's system. Are you ready for it?"

"Yes, sir," Sykes said.

Noah initiated a dump of the entire system to a special storage matrix on the combat shuttle. They'd use that later to figure out how the Konus had broken the targeting systems, which would presumably enable them to prevent the same thing from happening in the future.

Kara walked over and brought up a secondary holoscreen. "I have the backup system online. Are you ready for me to initiate a restore?"

"Wait a second," he said. He was navigating the interface and checking the logs around the time the event had taken place. "Damn."

She turned to look at him. "What is it?"

"There's a firing solution in here that has Connor's authorization."

"We should be able to port that over and make it part of the restore," Kara replied.

"I know that, but it's old now. They'll need to reconfirm the targets before they can be allowed to open fire. Plus, we don't want to be anywhere near here when this thing starts going off."

"Okay, so we restore the firing solution and put it in standby for confirmation, then alert COMCENT. They can coordinate with Connor and take it from there," Kara said.

Noah considered this for a few moments and then began poring over the firing solution. "I knew there was a reason I kept you around."

Kara smiled at him. "You're not so bad yourself. Let's wrap this up."

He checked the start-up scripts, wanting to make sure everything was set up right. It was worth a second look because he didn't want to have to come back here. He found an alternate subsystem to the communications link that contained remnant code from the update. He deleted the code and then initiated a full system reset.

Noah closed his session on the defense platform's systems. "All right, that should do it."

"Looks good on my end too," Kara said.

He activated the comlink to the shuttle. "Lieutenant Sykes, I'm going to enable the point defense systems on the opposite side of the platform. Can you launch a decoy with a CDF ship signature?"

"Will do," Lieutenant Sykes said. "Launching now."

Noah waited a minute for the decoy to pass in front of the point defense systems and brought them online. He tried not to hold his breath as he watched the onboard computer systems do a quick threat assessment. A few seconds later, the point defense systems stopped tracking the decoy.

"Successful test," Lieutenant Sykes said.

"Good," Noah replied.

They headed back to the hatch and were soon walking to the combat shuttle. Noah turned toward the view of New Earth. The rings around the planet were actually quite far away from the atmosphere, maintained by two small moons, but that wasn't what had his attention.

"What are you looking at?" Kara asked.

"That must be the storm," he said. The massive storm front was stretched out, entirely covering the region of the continent where the battle was being fought.

"You're right. It's a storm. Now let's get the hell out of here," Kara said and ushered him along.

They made it to the combat shuttle and stepped inside. She closed the rear hatch while Noah headed to the cockpit. Once they were aboard, Lieutenant Sykes restored the life-support system inside the combat shuttle, and Noah removed his helmet.

Lieutenant Sykes released the docking clamps, and they flew away from the defense platform.

"Can you take us over there?" Noah said, gesturing northwest of the storm.

The CDF pilot frowned for a moment. "No problem."

Noah brought up a secondary holoscreen and zoomed in on the part of the continent where the storm was concentrated. "It doesn't look right."

"What do you mean?" Lieutenant Sykes asked.

"Something about that storm doesn't look right at all. Can you open a comlink to COMCENT?"

A few moments later, Colonel John Randall appeared on the holoscreen. "My tactical officers just informed me that the defense platform is coming back online. We now have full access. Thank you so much for doing that."

"You're welcome, Colonel," Noah said. "Do you have anyone available who can validate the storm system where General Gates is?"

Colonel Randall frowned. "I can get someone."

"I think you should. There's something about the storm that doesn't seem right. Normally a storm system develops and can be tracked through barometric pressure, but what I see down there looks like the storm has an epicenter stemming from a specific area."

Colonel Randall considered this for several seconds and then gestured toward someone off-screen. "We'll chase this down. Stand by."

The comlink went to standby mode, and Noah glanced at Kara.

"Oh my God," she said. "I would've missed it completely."

"We don't know if it's anything yet."

"I think you're right, sir," Lieutenant Sykes said. "Now that you pointed that out, I can't *not* see it."

Kara shook her head. "We need to pull up the history of this region. If the Konus have some kind of technology that allows them to manipulate the weather like this, then . . ." She let the thought go unfinished.

"It might not be their technology," Noah said, his eyebrows raised.

Kara's mouth hung open. "You think this could be Krake technology?"

"That's what we need to find out, and we need to stop it," Noah said and looked at Sykes. "Are the weapons systems on the shuttle operational?"

Sykes nodded. "Always."

CHAPTER 30

Connor heard the faint sounds of weaponsfire in the distance, even above the unrelenting storm. He rested his hands on the edge of the holotank and then gripped it firmly, squeezing it. He wanted to be out there in the fight, but he also needed to be right where he was, coordinating the defenses.

They'd received an alert from Sergeant Riley about Konus soldiers and ryklars found trying to infiltrate the far end of the city, and he'd dispatched his reserve forces over to that area. Warlord Vitory informed him that they had additional defenders Connor considered Ovarrow militia. They weren't professional soldiers, but all Ovarrow who came out of stasis were qualified in the basic use of their weapons. They were no strangers to fighting, and Connor knew he shouldn't hesitate to use them. He had Vitory put them on defensive lines in different areas of the city to provide a much-needed function without calling upon them to achieve mission objectives. What he didn't like about it was that he now had to worry about friendly fire. Any type of untrained soldier, and even some of the greener recruits, would be likely to shoot first rather than check their fire to make sure there was, in fact, an enemy on the other end.

"We've increased the high frequency sound waves for the ryklar deterrent signal, but it's not having an effect on them," Lieutenant Scott Morgan said. He stood at the tactical workstation near the holotank in the mobile command center.

"That's because the Konus use an implant to ensure they follow orders," Connor replied.

"How does it work? Is it something we can initiate a remote override on?" Major Alexis Brooks asked.

Connor shook his head. "We don't know how it works."

"They have to give them instructions somehow, which means there's gotta be some kind of broadcast," Lieutenant Morgan said.

"Send an SRD over the area to see if it can detect any frequencies we can't account for," said Connor. "It'll take time because the drones don't have that kind of computing power, but you can route the data back to COMCENT, where they can isolate the signal."

"Yes, General," Lieutenant Morgan said.

They still didn't have an accurate count of how many Konus soldiers and ryklars had slipped past their defensive lines to breach the city. There couldn't have been thousands of troops, so Connor felt safe in assuming that there were probably hundreds of them, no more than a thousand.

"How did they slip past our defensive lines and all the sensor nets we had out there?" Major Brooks asked, looking at Connor from across the holotank.

"Given the chaos that's going on, it could be any number of things, all of which we'll have to revisit when we—"

"General, reports across all fronts indicate that the Konus are making a massive push," Lieutenant Abernathy said.

The images on the holotank switched to the front lines. The data was piecemeal as the reconnaissance drones made high-speed passes overhead. A few were taken out by Konus weaponsfire, but at least now they had some eyes in the sky to give them insight into their enemy's movements.

"They need to make it to the city," Connor said.

Major Brooks frowned, and she studied the holotank. Then her eyes widened. "They're trying to overwhelm us."

"If they reach us and break through the lines, it makes fighting this battle that much harder. It would limit our air support and anything from our orbital defense platform," Connor said and gritted his teeth. He glanced at the status of the defense platform, and it was still off-line.

"I'll get another status update," Major Brooks said.

Connor nodded. There was a CDF heavy cruiser on the way from the home fleet, but it was still several hours out.

"General Gates," Morgan said, "I have an idea about the ryklars."

The young man's eyes were wide with anticipation. Connor glanced at the SRD they had tasked to fly over the city, but it hadn't even gotten there yet.

"What have you got?"

———

The ryklars moved so damn fast that Hunter could hardly keep a good bead on them, even with the help of the combat suit systems. The creatures didn't attack head-on but preferred misdirection and blindsiding their prey. Hunter and his team had tracked dozens of them heading toward the rest of the platoon.

Lieutenant Wade's group had taken cover in one of the buildings and were making their way to the roof. Hunter and the rest of the squad had slowed down so as not to draw the ryklars' attention. They hadn't seen any Konus soldiers, but there were reports that the other platoons were engaging them in the city.

Hunter saw the CDF soldiers fire their weapons, and a group of ryklars went down, quivering bodies of torn flesh and blood staining the streets. He'd never had an up-close-and-personal encounter with ryklars, but they seemed bigger in the flesh, or maybe it was just that they seemed more real now. They weren't just some animal that was given to attacking because of a predatory instinct. There was intelligence and purpose behind their movements.

"What are we gonna do, Sergeant?" Corporal Blackman asked.

"We can circle around and try to get to the rooftops of one of the other buildings nearby. Then we can create a kill zone," Hunter said.

"That'll take the pressure off the others, but what happens when the ryklars regroup, sir?"

"I don't know. Look, they need our help, and we're going to give it to them." None of the soldiers said anything, but Hunter could sense some hesitation. "They'd do the same for any of us. Now let's go."

With the storm raging on around them, it was a lot easier to stay relatively quiet while moving quickly. Even the ryklars had limits, it seemed. They headed down a narrow pathway and climbed about seven meters to the rooftop of the building, a feat easily achieved by a combination of raw power from their combat suits and the brittle outer layer of concrete on the buildings. Once on top, they raced to the edge and leaped across to the next rooftop. It sloped up at an incline, and gushing water sloshed past them, splattering onto the ground below. They halted a few feet from the edge of the roof. The rest of the platoon was seventy meters away, but they didn't have a clear view of them.

"Sergeant, we've got eyes on us," Gorman said.

Several dark shapes skittered onto the roof a few buildings across from their location. Hunter brought up his AR-71 just as the ryklars realized they'd been seen and started charging forward. Hunter and the rest of the CDF squad squeezed off several bursts of fire. The kinetic force of the weaponsfire slammed into the ryklars, causing them to stumble. A few ryklars dropped off the roof, disappearing from view.

Hunter ordered them to the next rooftop, and they continued onward. CDF weaponsfire intensified from the location of the rest of the platoon. The ryklars were making a push toward the taller buildings.

"Gorman, unleash the heavy," Hunter said.

The combat suit heavy stepped toward the edge of the roof, bringing up the quad-barrel M547, dealer of death. The heavy weapon wound up and began firing at the ryklars, sputtering so loudly that the ryklars perked up at the noise, only to be cut down. The rest of the squad joined in, firing their weapons and taking the ryklars by surprise.

Hunter opened a comlink to Lieutenant Wade. "Sir, we're southeast of your position."

"Thanks for the help, Sergeant, but I'm ordering you to head back. There are hundreds of ryklars heading toward us. You can't see them from your position," Wade said.

"I'm not leaving you, Lieutenant," Hunter said.

"I know you're not. See if you can get them to chase you."

Hunter looked around, searching for the best path, but ryklars were converging on their location. Everywhere he looked, he saw movement heading toward them. They were on the adjacent rooftops, and he knew they were down on the ground as well.

"Oh shit! We're surrounded," Morrison yelled.

"Well then, give it all you got, soldier," Corporal Blackman bellowed.

"None of us are getting out of here, Lieutenant," Hunter said over the din of weapons fire.

Between the slight pauses of controlled weaponsfire, the screech of the ryklars could be heard above the rolling thunder overhead. Lightning split the sky in bright, flickering flashes, and all they could see was the threat of a deep, deadly menace that was coming to kill them all.

"Understood," Wade said. "I'll see you after."

The comlink went dark, and the CDF soldiers prepared to make their final stand.

The ten-man squad coordinated their attack so they had a coverage area of both their immediate surroundings and those far away. But the ryklars moved fast, and it took a lot to bring them down. They were most vulnerable in the face and neck, which were difficult to shoot once they were on the move.

A combat drone flew overhead, and Hunter happened to look up to see it approach. As it flew over their area, he saw something drop from it. When the object hit the ground, a deafening blast of energy left all the ryklars in the area stunned. They simply stopped moving. The CDF soldiers kept firing their weapons, seizing the opportunity to bring down more of the predators.

The ryklars stopped trying to reach the soldiers, appearing confused, as if taking in their surroundings. Many were shaking their heads, moving erratically and flailing about.

"What the hell did that drone do?" Corporal Blackman asked.

Hunter shook his head. He had no idea. The ryklars scrambled back, fleeing the area. It was as if some unseen force was compelling them to leave. He opened a comlink to Lieutenant Wade. "They're leaving. I don't believe it. What the hell did that combat drone drop?"

"No idea," Wade said. "We'll hold position here for a few more minutes, and then we'll meet up."

Hunter and the rest of the squad watched as small groups of ryklars fled from the city. Comlinks from other CDF platoons were reporting the same thing. The combat drones had dropped EMP grenades, which interfered with the ryklars' implants. With the implants off-line, the ryklar deterrent signal had begun to do its job.

Hunter had no idea who'd come up with using EMP grenades against the ryklars, but whomever it was, he was going to buy them a round of drinks whenever he saw them, for the rest of his life.

———

Reports had been coming in that the ryklars were fleeing the area, and Connor broadcast a flash report to the CDF soldiers out in the field. EMP grenades weren't part of the standard kit for combat operations, so they'd loaded up combat drones and were sending them out as fast as they could. CDF soldiers were now sweeping the area, taking out Konus infiltrators as they went, and the Konus sneak attack was in disarray.

Connor looked at Lieutenant Scott Morgan. "Good work, Lieutenant. You saved a lot of lives today."

The young lieutenant beamed at this recognition from his superior officer. "Thank you, sir."

Connor glanced at Major Brooks, who was speaking to COMCENT. She looked at him and shook her head. The Konus were still making a heavy push toward the city, and the CDF and Mekaal forces were steadily moving back to the city, trying to stall the Konus and buy all the time they could. Connor needed the defense platform operational, and he needed it now.

CHAPTER 31

Orders appeared in the upper right corner of Samson's heads-up display. They'd received an ammo drop not too long before, but they'd been fighting the Konus for hours and were running low again. CDF regulars were slowly retreating, and the Konus pushed toward them in a hail of fire. The Spec Ops platoons and companies were mainly in the forward and flanking positions.

"They're sending a troop carrier transport, Captain," Sergeant Matheson said.

They had climbed up the last ridgeline of the fingers, and there were several kilometers of forest between them and the Ovarrow city.

Samson glanced at Matheson. "Say again?"

"Troop carrier transports are incoming, Captain. We are to hold position and wait for extraction."

They couldn't hold the position. They had to keep moving. The Konus ground assault vehicles carried high-powered particle beam cannons that could melt through even the battle-steel armor of the combat suit in seconds. The Konus assault vehicles had such an impact on the CDF that they'd become high priority targets, but they were protected with uncompromising determination.

"Specialist Ruo, the SRD on our six. What's it seeing?" Samson asked.

Specialist Ruo checked the SRD data feeds. "Konus soldiers. A lot of them. We can try to outrun them and circle back to the city."

"Negative," Samson said. "But we can't stay here."

"But Captain, our orders," Sergeant Matheson said.

"I know what the orders are, Sergeant. If we stay here, we'll be overwhelmed."

He was sure the troop transport would make its way to them eventually, but he'd been in too many situations where there was simply so much going on that it was easy to get overlooked. The fact that the troop transports were even making these high-risk runs to extract them meant the Konus must be making a major push toward the city. This was Connor's response, which meant they still didn't have that damn defense platform ready.

Samson opened a broadcast comlink. "Listen up. We're heading east—"

Several Konus ground assault vehicles drove over the ridge at high speed and headed straight toward them. The CDF soldiers dove for cover and began firing their weapons at the assault vehicles. The particle beam cannons on the vehicles had to be cycled; otherwise, they'd overheat. After they were fired, there was a rise of intensity as power built up, but that couldn't be sustained for long periods of time.

"Hold your position," Samson said. "When they cycle the cannons down, then we can take them out."

They returned fire, and Samson, along with a few others, began circling around, moving to flank the assault vehicles. He ordered a group of soldiers to draw their fire, keeping the Konus' attention where he wanted it while the rest of them closed in.

Several squads of Konus soldiers spotted their approach, so Samson and the CDF soldiers fired explosive rounds that tore through them. They reached the first assault vehicle, and Matheson attached an explosive charge to it. They moved on to the next one and set another charge.

Samson activated the charges, and the Konus assault vehicles blew apart.

There were two more vehicles nearby.

"I'm out of explosives," Matheson said.

"Hold on," Samson said and gestured for Cerot to come up. When the Ovarrow came over, he asked, "Do you think you can get them to open the hatch? I want to take a vehicle intact."

Cerot nodded once and gestured for the other Mekaal soldiers to follow. They weaved their way through the trees, cautiously approaching the assault vehicle, but Samson couldn't hear what they were saying. Loud thunder rumbled overhead, drowning the Ovarrow out. The particle cannon locked onto the Mekaal soldiers.

Samson and the others hastened over, using the trees to cover their approach. Whatever Cerot said had worked. Konus soldiers opened the rear hatch, and the CDF soldiers made quick work of them. They never even fired the particle cannon.

Samson went over to Cerot. "Can you drive these things?"

Cerot looked inside the assault vehicle for a few moments, exchanging a few quick words with the other Mekaal soldiers. Then he looked at Samson. "We can operate them."

"Good. Go on inside and get someone on that cannon," Samson said.

The Mekaal soldiers climbed inside. After a few moments, the particle cannon swung to the side, and the vehicle lurched forward around a tree. They targeted the other assault vehicle, firing the particle cannon. A thick molten yellow beam burst from the barrel, mowing down Konus soldiers. Cerot concentrated fire on the assault vehicle, destroying its particle cannon.

Konus soldiers fled the vehicle, and the CDF shot them. Samson sent a group of Mekaal to the damaged assault vehicle to see if they could still use it, when a distress beacon broadcast alert appeared on his heads-up display. It had Layton's identification. Layton had taken a platoon and was scouting Konus heavy targets for their Hellcat squadrons to take out.

A few moments later, other distress beacons came from more members of the 3rd Platoon. They were in trouble. Samson gestured for Matheson. "Where's the troop carrier?"

"ETA is fifteen minutes, Captain," Sergeant Matheson said.

Samson glanced at the Konus assault vehicles, an idea forming in his mind. "Send them these updated coordinates," he said.

Matheson glanced at the coordinates. They were well within enemy territory, but he didn't question it. There was no need to. The 7th Ranger Company wouldn't abandon their own men. Matheson moved away and opened a comlink to the troop carrier.

Samson quickly relayed his plan and made sure Cerot and the other Mekaal soldiers understood. They'd be leading the charge in the assault vehicles. Samson was gambling that when the Konus saw their own vehicles heading toward them, they'd hold their fire long enough for the CDF soldiers to wreak havoc.

Matheson rejoined him. "Captain, I've been informed by the troop carriers and their Hellcat escorts that they're going to be making an extraction in a hot zone," he said, tilting his head to the side in a slight nod. "Well, *more* of a hot zone. I'd say it's like a cauldron of fury. You know, like bathing in liquid hot magma."

Samson arched an eyebrow toward him. "You're a poet," he said and looked at the others. "I want my combat suit heavies leading the charge just behind the Konus assault vehicles."

Sergeant Dixon gave the assault vehicle an appraising look and then shook his head. There wasn't enough room for him on the back. The sharpshooter would have to stay on the ground just like the rest of them.

Samson opened a comlink to Cerot. "As fast as you can. Let's move it."

The Mekaal soldiers swung the assault vehicles around and began driving back over the ridge, heading toward the enemy soldiers on the other side. The Konus soldiers hesitated, and Samson thought he heard Cerot speaking. He must be using the Konus comms from within the vehicle, but Samson had no idea what he was saying. It didn't matter. Their hesitation was his advantage, and the mighty 7th Ranger Company punched a hole through the enemy lines. The fighting was intense and quick. They charged forward, cutting through the enemy as fast as they could. As the minutes flew by, the distress beacons began going off-line. They were dying.

The 3rd Platoon wasn't so far into the fold of the Konus that it was impossible to reach. This hadn't been a suicidal charge. As they got closer to the distress beacons, they were able to better pinpoint their locations and saw that they were surrounded by the enemy. The lightning seemed to come less frequently, and they thought that perhaps this damn storm was finally starting to relent. Bright flashes came from the particle beam cannons mounted atop the Konus assault vehicles, and the CDF combat suit heavies fanned out, firing their weapons.

The Konus returned fire in a blazing retaliation of defiance before they were overwhelmed. Samson checked the status of the troop carriers, and they were still minutes out. They made it to where the bulk of the 3ʳᵈ Platoon soldiers were holding out, and the first person Samson spotted was Private First Class Fletcher.

"Where's Lieutenant Layton?"

"I don't know, Captain. We lost him hours ago," Fletcher said.

Samson frowned and scanned for someone else. "Sergeant Schultz, give me a sitrep."

The rest of the 7ᵗʰ Ranger Company formed a perimeter around the exhausted and battered 3ʳᵈ Platoon.

"They surprised us, sir. Lieutenant Layton went with Herrera and his squad to check on something, and then the Konus arrived. There aren't many of us left, sir," Schultz said.

"They're making another push, Captain," Sergeant Matheson said.

"We're not out of this yet," said Samson.

Layton was gone, and Samson suspected the worst. He reached the perimeter and saw thousands of Konus troops heading toward them. Ground assault vehicles stretched back as far as his enhanced vision could see. He swallowed hard. The Konus charged, and Samson ordered his soldiers to fall back. They needed every second.

Matheson yelled and gestured overhead. Samson heard the familiar high-pitched scream of Hellcat engines barreling toward them, and the troop carriers weren't far behind. The Hellcats flew toward the enemy weapons hot and stalled the Konus advance. Samson saw them circle around, giving the troop carrier transports time to land. Particle beam weapons lit up the sky, and one of the Hellcats crashed in a fiery explosion.

The sky had become brighter, and Samson could tell that the rain was definitely slowing down. Amid a torrent of particle beam weapons being fired at the CDF soldiers, there was a powerful sonic boom, louder than anything the storm had given them. Then there was another. Something punched through the clouds, blazing into the Konus army. The ground shook beneath Samson's feet, and there was a bright flash of light that was immediately cleared out by the smart filter of his combat suit's helmet.

"Take cover!" Samson shouted. "Orbital strike inbound. Take cover!"

The skies above opened up as hulking projectiles pierced the atmosphere in a deluge. He had never been near an orbital strike in his entire military career. He'd witnessed them only from afar during practice sessions. The ground assault from the orbital defense platform sent waves of kinetic energy, and it was all they could do to endure. They took cover as best they could, waiting for it to be finished. Then, after an indeterminate amount of time, there was silence. He climbed to his feet and looked at the havoc wreaked by the CDF weapons. The devastation had occurred downrange from them, decimating the Konus in the area.

Samson led a group to where Lieutenant Layton's beacon had last been active. He was dead. The Konus had connected something to his suit that looked like it was part of a comms broadcast. They disconnected it, and Samson ordered his men to bring the entire setup with them on the troop carrier. He looked down at his friend and gritted his teeth. He knelt down, picked up Layton's body, and carried it back to the troop carrier transport. Then they retrieved the bodies of the other fallen 3rd Platoon members. They would be brought back home and buried with the honor of those who'd sacrificed themselves. Sorrow attempted to close Samson's throat, but he refused to let it. Instead, he grabbed his rifle as an urge to keep fighting hit him. He glanced up at the sky, willing the orbital defense platforms to keep firing. He didn't care if every Konus died on this battlefield. If he could've killed them all, he would have without hesitation—the Krake be damned.

CHAPTER 32

The Konus had gambled and lost. The orbital strikes had brought their massive army to a halt. In the hours that followed, they began to accept the fact that their army was facing annihilation.

Connor had extracted all CDF and Mekaal soldiers caught behind enemy lines. Next, he allowed the Konus soldiers to return to the bulk of their army in a show of cooperation, but that was about as much cooperation as Connor was willing to give. Lives had been lost on both sides of the conflict, and it had all been a pointless waste.

He had communicated to the Konus that Kasmon must surrender himself to the CDF. This was nonnegotiable. Any delay in response or compliance and the CDF orbital defense platform would annihilate the remaining Konus army. Connor had suspected that the Konus would resist, that their most powerful military leader would never surrender and would need to be taken by force. But that hadn't happened, and Kasmon was on his way there now.

Connor rubbed his eyes and sighed. The sky was clearing, and it was already morning.

Noah cleared his throat, and Connor looked back at the video comlink feed. "Sorry. It's been a hell of a day."

"I was saying that we disabled the device the Konus were using to create that storm. We weren't able to stick around and do a thorough analysis because they started firing at us," Noah said.

Connor looked at his friend. "We'll get it sorted out," he said and regarded him for a second. "I don't know if you realize what you've done."

Noah looked away and scratched the back of his head. "Now don't give me that. We were just the closest ones available."

Connor shook his head. "It doesn't matter. You were the ones who got it done, and you spotted something no one else had anticipated."

Noah lifted his eyebrows, smiling a little. "No one can think of every-thing, Connor. Not even you. Why would they even have that tech anyway?"

"I don't know. It's probably not their tech, which means we'll have to find out what else they have and where they got it from."

"Did you figure out how they disabled the defense platform?"

Connor nodded. "They captured one of our officers and used his comlink to infiltrate the network."

Noah whistled softly. "One officer and all that happened."

"The officer was on a mission to identify targets for us to hit with the defense platform, and that's why he had the access he did, but I hear you. We might need to reconsider some of those things we take for granted," Connor said.

Noah was quiet for a few moments and then said, "Yeah. I know there've been suggestions of using subspace comms to replace all our comms capabili-ties, but I don't think we should."

"Why not?"

"We're still learning how it works. We can use it, but that doesn't mean we actually understand everything about it."

"I see what you're saying," Connor said. "I won't keep you any longer, and thank you for everything."

"You don't need to thank me. I'm just glad I could be there for you for a change," Noah said and smiled, reminiscent of the young man Connor had met when he'd first come to the colony. "What I don't understand is why the Konus did this in the first place. They lost a third of their troops at least."

Connor shook his head. "I don't know. We know the Ovarrow are terri-torial, but this was something else."

"It's crazy, is what it is," Noah said. "You still want them as allies against the Krake?"

"Wanting and needing are two different things, Noah."

"You can't be serious."

"I am, but we'll need to figure out what to do with them," Connor said and couldn't keep the edge from his voice. "I have to go. I've got a million other things to do. Good luck at Lunar Base. Make sure Sean gives you a VIP room."

Noah grinned. "Heck, if he doesn't, I'll start calling him 'cadet bling.'"

Connor chuckled and closed the comlink. *Cadet bling,* he thought, shaking his head in amusement.

He received a notification from Vitory that Kasmon was now in their custody. He headed toward the Mekaal pavilion where High Commissioner Senleon and Vitory were, along with the other faction leaders. Connor brought some of the other senior officers with him, and Darius Cohen was there.

Kasmon glared at Connor, still managing to look smug even in defeat. He knew his gamble had almost worked.

Connor walked over and stood in front of Kasmon.

"You need us," Kasmon said.

"I don't think we do," Connor said. "In fact, I'm inclined to turn you over to the very people you sought to enslave," he said and gestured toward Senleon and the others.

Kasmon looked at them for a moment, and there was a darkly gritty intent in his eyes. "They wouldn't have been enslaved. They would've become part of the Konus, and we would've been stronger for it. They would've been stronger as well."

"Do you expect me to believe your intentions were so ethical? There was more to it than that," Connor said and leveled his gaze at the Konus military commander. "Did we pass *your* test?"

Kasmon regarded him. "A demonstration was required."

Connor's fist flew through the air. The MPS he wore became an armored gauntlet that struck Kasmon in the face. The Konus soldier fell backward and sprawled on the floor. He shook his head to clear it and regained his feet. Blood trickled from one side of his wide mouth.

"Strength isn't something you can communicate through anything but conflict. You will need all of yours if you hope to defeat the Krake," Kasmon said.

"You wasted lives and resources for a damn contest," Connor snarled. "We could've been working together against the Krake."

"You still need our help."

Connor's knuckles burned to strike again, but he didn't. "The remainder of your army will go back to your city. They will know that both day and night, our defense platform will be right above that city. If a large group that looks anything like an armed fighting force gathers outside your territory again, I'll order that platform to strike, and we won't stop until every one of you is gone. I'll raze that entire region," he said and leaned closer. "Now do you have the measure of our resolve?"

Kasmon's flinty glare became cold and hard, and Connor felt a modicum of grim satisfaction in that. "You'll be held by the Mekaal until we decide what to do with you," Connor said.

Kasmon swung his gaze toward Senleon and Vitory and then turned back to Connor. "Your faithful servants."

Connor shook his head. "No, not servants," he said, looking at Senleon and the others. "Allies—and one day, fellow citizens."

Mekaal soldiers took Kasmon away. Connor had already assigned soldiers to interrogate him. It would be a joint effort between the Mekaal and the CDF. They would learn everything there was to know about the Konus, especially the Krake tech they'd adapted for their use. But like it or not, Kasmon might be right. They might need the Konus, and he hated that thought.

Senleon walked over to Connor. "There isn't enough gratitude we can show to you and the Colonial Defense Force."

Connor gave him a long look and then nodded slowly. "We're in this together."

"Yes, we are," Senleon said.

If someone had come up to Connor a year ago and told him what was going to happen, he'd never have believed them—the discovery of the Konus, the Mekaal and the other factions petitioning the colonial government to become citizens, none of it. He had underestimated the Konus. They'd had over forty years to prepare for a war with the Krake. They'd used tactics against an enemy that outmatched them technologically, and those tactics had almost worked against the CDF. The last twenty-four hours had reinforced one thing in Connor's mind. They weren't ready for a war with the Krake. They just weren't. Despite all the preparation, there was still so much to do. While this battle with the Konus had cost colonial lives, a colder, more ruthless part of Connor's brain started to believe that this experience would end up saving more lives in the long run. Time would be the judge of that, but they'd be better prepared. He would have to use everything the colony was capable of giving if they were going to survive.

Vitory walked over to him, looking even more exhausted than Connor felt. The Warlord carried the weight of protecting his people on his shoulders. It was a common burden between them. They shared a look that seemed to confirm what the other was thinking. They needed to adapt quicker. They couldn't afford to slow down their efforts on any front, and they'd even have to increase their off-world missions to find more allies against the Krake. And, above all, they must find the Krake home world. There was no way to survive if they couldn't do that.

CHAPTER 33

The combat shuttle flew toward Lunar Base, and a video feed from the forward cameras showed on the main holoscreen. It'd been years since Noah had been here. He glanced at Kara, whose gaze seemed to drink up the view of the vast metropolis on the lunar surface. There were shipyards in orbit around the moon where massive 3D printers worked.

Noah squinted and could just barely make out the space dock for the CDF fleet. He knew that if they were closer, he'd be awestruck at the sheer size of the heavy cruisers being constructed.

"How long has it been since you've been here?" Lieutenant Sykes asked.

Noah cleared his throat. "It's been a while. A few years. They've expanded a lot."

"Eighteen months for me," Kara said. "This is just the surface stuff. There are extensive installations underground."

Noah looked at the view of the lunar base appreciatively. They'd put so much into building the initial base, and it had provided a crucial function to their overall defensive readiness.

"There's a significant civilian presence here now, particularly in the R&D sections," Lieutenant Sykes said. "There's also a lot more entertainment than there used to be. Can't be all work and no play."

Noah smiled a little and then shook his head. "I can remember when they were scouting for sites to build the lunar base."

Kara nodded. "That was three years after the *Ark* first arrived here."

Lieutenant Sykes's eyes widened. "That was the year they officially created the Colonial Defense Force."

"That's when it was officially recognized, but Connor had been working toward building a military long before that," Noah said.

Lieutenant Sykes glanced away for a moment, looking somewhat uncomfortable. "He might be Connor to you, but he's General Gates to everyone else up here."

Sometimes Noah forgot that the early risers on the *Ark* had lived and worked together for most of a year in preparation for bringing everyone else out of stasis. Friendships had been forged that were still strong to this day.

He watched as Lieutenant Sykes confirmed the landing pad with Lunar Base Control. There was no shortage of space traffic going to and from the base proper. The combat shuttle flew away from the main base facility, and Lieutenant Sykes told them they'd been directed to a secondary location.

"You must have a higher security clearance than I do. I've never been over here," Lieutenant Sykes said and raised an eyebrow toward them. "Are you sure they're not recommissioning you back into the CDF?"

"No, they're not," Noah said.

"We're consulting," Kara said.

The CDF combat shuttle flew over an immense crater that was nearly three thousand kilometers in diameter and fourteen kilometers deep. The waypoint indicating on their main holoscreen showed that their destination along the walls of the crater was three hundred kilometers away.

Eventually, the waypoint highlighted a cave entrance in the distance. Noah peered at it, and as they came closer, he saw massive metallic gray doors that had begun to separate in the middle. He could almost make out the semitranslucent shield that kept the atmosphere contained. As they got closer, Noah saw that the large doors had a sheen that reminded him of the battle-steel bulkheads used on CDF warships. The thick doors could take a pounding and had been built with defense in mind. There were mag-cannons on either side of the doors, as well as some secreted farther away. He wondered what other defenses had been hidden that could be readily brought online.

A comlink registered on the combat shuttle's systems.

"This is Lieutenant Sykes, and I have Noah Barker and Kara Robertson onboard."

"Confirmed identity of Lieutenant Sykes," the flight officer replied. "Please have your passengers forward their identifications via their neural implants."

Noah and Kara sent their identifiers, a combination of a unique ID and their DNA, through the comlink.

"Identities confirmed. Please proceed to docking bay thirty-three. Your escort will meet you there," the flight officer said.

The comlink severed, and Noah glanced at Lieutenant Sykes. "I guess they don't want you to disembark beyond the docking bay."

Lieutenant Sykes shrugged a shoulder. "I'll try not to take it personally."

"Where do you go from here?" Kara asked.

Lieutenant Sykes smiled. "Wherever they tell me to."

The combat shuttle flew through the massive doors and landed at the designated docking bay area. Noah and Kara went to the back of the shuttle to collect their belongings, and Lieutenant Sykes opened the rear hatch. The loading ramp extended to the ground.

"Thanks for getting us here safely," Noah said.

"A pleasure," Lieutenant Sykes replied.

They walked down the loading ramp, and Lieutenant Sykes went to speak with the deck officer. A CDF soldier checked his tablet computer and then looked at them as if confirming their identities. "Hello, and welcome to Osiris. I'm Corporal Yelland. I'll have your belongings moved to your quarters. You can just leave them there. I'm to escort you to Colonel Quinn."

Noah shared a glance with Kara and then looked at Yelland. "Lead the way."

Corporal Yelland led them away from the docking bay and took them straight to a security processing center where both Noah and Kara registered with the CDF base. Their clearance levels were confirmed, and their identities were officially imported into the system.

They left the processing center and walked down a few corridors to an elevator, which they took down several levels. The elevator doors opened to a train station that had multiple tracks going to and coming from various dark tunnels. They climbed aboard a maglev train, and it accelerated into the tunnel.

"How far away is our destination?" Noah asked.

Corporal Yelland smiled. "It's not far. Just under a kilometer."

Noah pressed his lips together. "I wonder how long it took them to tunnel all this out."

"This part of the base is actually pretty new. Only about . . ." Corporal Yelland frowned in thought for a moment. "It's under two years. And they didn't have to tunnel all this out. They did a seismic survey and found an open cavern under here, so they utilized the space that had already been created."

The dark tunnel began to brighten, and they emerged onto an elevated platform. There was a vast cavern underneath, and Noah's mouth hung open. There had to be thousands of people working here. The vast open chamber was divvied up into sections, and he had no idea what they were meant for.

"Would you look at that," he said with appreciation.

Kara smiled and nodded. "It's amazing."

The chamber was so big that Noah actually had trouble seeing to the other side, and it didn't look like the CDF had used up all the space. There was a network of maglev train tracks that wasn't only at the upper levels where they were but also at the lower levels they could just now see.

The train came to a stop at a platform, and the doors opened. Noah walked out and breathed deeply through his nose. The air smelled clean, with a hint of pine. He'd expected the air to be cool and humid since they were so far underground, but it wasn't.

Corporal Yelland led them away from the train station through a series of white corridors. There were wallscreens spaced out along it that showed images of New Earth landscapes, along with several deep-space images of the star system.

They eventually came to a series of offices, and Corporal Yelland left them in a waiting area. Noah and Kara didn't have to wait long before Sean came out to greet them.

Sean Quinn was of average size and still retained an athletic physique. The skin around his eyes was tight, and Noah saw a much harder glint to his friend's gaze than what used to be there. They'd all been through a lot, but Sean's smile lit up his whole face.

"I heard about what happened," Sean said. "You two couldn't just come up to the lunar base. You had to repair a defense platform and save a lot of lives in the process."

Noah shrugged a shoulder. "Some of us are just lucky, I guess. Luck and timing, my friend. Luck and timing."

Sean gestured for them to follow him through the doors. "I'm really glad you're here."

"Will Oriana be joining us?" Kara asked.

Sean nodded. "Yeah, she'll be along. I figured I'd show you guys around first," he said and looked at them for a moment, "but you've had a helluva day. If you'd like to rest, we can postpone all this. Maybe get something to eat," he said and shrugged. "You know, have some food?"

Noah shook his head, and Kara did the same. "We just spent almost an entire day on a combat shuttle. I don't want to sit around anymore," she said.

"Well, we did get to stretch our legs on the defense platform," Noah replied.

"That's not my idea of fun," Kara said.

They continued, and Sean began showing them around.

"There's a lot of security here, a lot more than I would've expected," Noah said.

Sean led them to his office, where food had been set out for them. Noah's stomach growled and saliva flooded his mouth in anticipation. He hadn't realized how hungry he was.

"Yeah, it was decided that we needed additional layers of security because of the work we're doing here," Sean said and looked at Noah. "I knew you'd both be hungry, so let's just eat. Oriana will join us in a little bit, and then we'll continue the tour."

They sat down and ate a home-cooked meal that tasted delicious. Oriana joined them before too long, and she and Kara began talking in earnest.

Sean raised his eyebrows in mock frustration. "Pretty soon the three of you will start talking, and I won't be able to understand what you're saying."

"I doubt that," Noah said. He studied Sean for a few moments. "Any chance they'll recall you back to New Earth, given what just happened?"

Sean shook his head. "No, this work is too important, and they've got things in hand there. The report I read stated that it escalated quite quickly, but it's settled down now."

"I'm sure you know more than I do at this point."

Sean's gaze took on a somber expression. "Just when you think you have a handle on a situation, that's when the ground falls out from under you," he said and sighed.

Noah sipped his water and set the cup down. "What do you think will happen with the Konus?"

"I don't know. I guess it's pretty much up to them, but you can bet your ass we're going to be keeping a closer eye on them for sure."

"Yeah, I don't get it. They offer to become our allies against the Krake, and then all this happens. It makes you think you really don't know whom you can trust," Noah said.

Sean arched an eyebrow and a bit of mirth crept into his gaze. "I thought brooding was my thing."

Noah chuckled and grinned. "I guess you're rubbing off on me. Or I'm just a little tired. No, not so much that I . . . You look like you have a big secret you want to show me."

Sean laughed, and this drew Oriana's and Kara's attention, Oriana's expression asking a silent question.

"Noah wants to know our secret."

Oriana looked at Noah. "Then I think it's time we show you."

They stood up and left Sean's office, walking down a short corridor to enter a large conference room. Sean led them over to the far wall. He looked at them for a few moments and then tilted his head toward the wall. It sank down into the floor, and they saw a wide-open cavern that was separate from the one they'd seen earlier.

Noah's eyes widened as he looked at Sean. "I thought you were just refitting the fleet, reverse engineering the Krake tech you found," he said and glanced at Oriana.

Sean nodded slowly. "We're doing that, but we also quickly arrived at one conclusion."

"What's that?" Noah asked.

"We don't have enough ships. You're right; we're building up our fleet, but it won't be enough. So, we had to think up other ways to engage the Krake. This is what we came up with," Sean said and gestured toward the cavernous chamber.

Noah observed the vast assembly line. His mind computed a quick production schedule, but he didn't want to go into full engineering mode yet. He looked at Sean. "What else have you got?"

Sean smiled. "There's a lot more to see. We'll bring you up to speed."

Noah smiled and swallowed hard. There was no way he was going to be here for only six months. He stepped toward the open window to gaze out onto a massive assembly line of equipment. Most were implements of war. The CDF and the colony as a whole had already increased its production of the equipment they thought they needed to fight the Krake.

He breathed in deeply and knew this was exactly where he needed to be. "All right, let's get started."

CHAPTER 34

The Colonial Security Council listened as Connor gave his report. The battle with the Konus had been only the week before, and it still seemed like they were putting the pieces back together.

"The Konus army has returned to their city, and as of right now, they are in compliance with our demands that they stay in their own territory," Connor said.

"How long can this go on?" Mullins asked.

"It's difficult to say for sure. They'll want Kasmon released."

The leader of the Konus army was currently being held prisoner by the Mekaal. Connor was in regular discussions with Senleon and Vitory, who had assured him that their treatment of Kasmon would be fair and much better than they would have received if Kasmon's plan had actually worked.

"They can come to us with a request. They still have a comlink available to them," Mullins said.

Nathan cleared his throat. He'd returned from Phoenix Station shortly after the battle ended. "I don't see how an alliance with the Konus will work, at least for the immediate future."

"I'm inclined to agree with you," Mullins said. He looked around at the others in the room. "Does anyone have an objection to rescinding our offer of an alliance with the Konus?"

Stoic silence was the only reply. Connor hadn't expected anyone to be in favor of an alliance.

"I just don't understand their motivation," Mullins said and looked at Connor.

"According to the Ovarrow, the stronger nations absorbed the weaker ones," Darius Cohen said. The diplomatic leader for the colony normally didn't attend Security Council meetings, but given that he'd been at the

Ovarrow city when the battle had taken place, he had valuable insight into what was going on.

"That was part of it," Connor said, and Mullins waited for him to continue. "They wanted to see what we were capable of, and I think they also wanted to know how effective their tactics would be against someone with similar capabilities as the Krake."

Mullins shook his head.

"It doesn't make any sense to me either. I would have preferred to work with them, but Vitory didn't seem surprised."

"That brings us to our next order of business," Mullins said. "High Commissioner Senleon and Warlord Vitory have indicated that they still desire to join the colony in a more official capacity."

"I thought we weren't considering it at this time," Jean Larson said.

"They're not expecting a decision anytime soon. I assured them that our mutual defense pact would still apply whether they joined the colony or not," Mullins replied.

Larson frowned in thought. "I guess I just find it surprising since our alliance with the Mekaal already gives them the protection they need."

"I think it's encouraging," Darius Cohen said, "and I think they're sincere in their desire to become colonial citizens. We've been working together closely, especially with the CDF."

"So, you think we should just welcome them with open arms. Make them colonial citizens and call it a day?" Larson asked.

"No, I wouldn't. This isn't something we would decide on a whim," Darius replied.

"You're right about that," Mullins said. "And I would add that this decision isn't up to just us. We'll need to involve the colony. They should have a say in whether or not we move forward with this. Perhaps we'll be only allies with the Ovarrow."

"There was a project proposal to connect the Ovarrow city via a maglev train. That would enable them to travel to other colonial cities," Darius said.

"That's true," Mullins said. "We would have to make the translator available to all colonial citizens. And again, this is something each of us should discuss with the colonial citizens in our cities."

"Why not let the Ovarrow speak for themselves?" Connor asked.

Mullins paused in thought for a few moments. "I'm afraid I don't understand."

Connor leaned forward. "Let them petition the colonial government and let everyone see them doing it. Broadcast it. Let Senleon and Vitory and their faction leaders make the case on why this is good for everyone."

He glanced around at the others in the room, and there were a few different reactions. What surprised him was that none of them had seemed to consider this before.

"I think this is a good idea," Darius said. "It would allow the colonial citizens to actually see who the Ovarrow are. Maybe we could organize some events where colonists could ask them questions."

"You're not proposing that we just turn them loose in the colony?" Mullins said.

Darius shook his head. "Of course not. But doing this might alleviate certain prejudices against the Ovarrow."

"I'm curious," Mullins said. "Given what we know right now, how would you vote on extending colonial citizenship to the Ovarrow if they wanted it? And this is hypothetical and noncommittal. Feel free to abstain from it. I'm just curious."

They went around the room, and the discussion continued. There were a few well-thought-out concerns, but at least half of them were in favor of coming up with a plan to allow the Ovarrow to become colonial citizens.

Mullins's gaze rested on Connor. "Yes, we should," Connor said. "I know there will be challenges with this—growing pains, if you will. Regardless of what the colony votes for, CDF soldiers have trusted the Ovarrow with their own lives. The joint off-world missions require it. So, there might be more support than you think there is, at least from members of the CDF."

"This will be a controversial topic. It needs to be handled delicately but honestly," Mullins said.

Connor cleared his throat, and Mullins looked at him. "You didn't say how you would vote."

His comment drew a few chuckles from the others in the room, and Mullins smiled. "I share the same concerns that have already been mentioned, but I think this is something we should consider. I think Dana would have been open to this."

The meeting soon ended, and Connor and Nathan walked together as they headed to the rooftop landing pad.

"Are you heading back to Sanctuary?" Nathan asked.

Connor shook his head. "I'm going to Delphi," he said.

Nathan's eyebrows raised. "Delphi? What for?"

"Lars Mallory's trial is ending, and I promised Franklin I'd be there for him."

Nathan's mouth became a grim line. "What do you think will happen to him?"

"I honestly don't know."

"Are they going to ask you to make a statement?"

"I don't think so. I doubt it would change anything. Lars is guilty."

"So, he'll be banished then," Nathan said.

"There are worse things, but I might have a few ideas about that," Connor said.

Nathan lifted an eyebrow. "I'm sure you do."

Connor smiled. "Doesn't Savannah come back today?"

Nathan smiled. "Very soon. That's where I'm going right now. Her ship reached the space dock, and the shuttles will start coming down to the planet soon."

"Well, tell her I said welcome home."

"I will," Nathan said and headed toward his transport ship.

CHAPTER 35

The courthouse in Delphi was part of the city's government complex where the mayor worked. Connor didn't often travel there. As he walked into the building, he recalled the last time he'd been there, trying to convince Mayor Edwards to help him with an investigation concerning the Ovarrow.

The government complex was similar in layout to Sierra. Wallscreens lining the corridors displayed various images that were agrarian in nature. Delphi could be considered the colony's breadbasket. The vatteries were located here that produced what Diaz liked to call "the most succulent meats available."

Diaz had sent him a message asking when he was going to return to Sanctuary. He wanted to try a new recipe out on Connor, but mostly it was Diaz's way of checking to see if he was all right.

It was half past one, and the afternoon sessions at the courthouse would begin shortly. The corridors revealed the regular foot traffic of the people who worked there. Connor spotted Franklin Mallory sitting outside one of the courtroom doors. He saw Connor and waved.

Connor walked over to him. "I'm here for Lars."

"I appreciate it," Franklin said, shaking his hand. He glanced at the polished wood doors and then back at Connor. "This isn't going to end well."

"Lars is still alive, Franklin. That's gotta count for something."

Franklin nodded. "Yes, but if he gets banished, I won't have access to him beyond restricted messages and maybe the occasional comlink."

There wasn't much Connor could say. Banishment from the colony also included restricted communications.

There was an audible chime from the speakers in the corridor, indicating that the sessions were about to begin again, and Connor followed Franklin into the courtroom. There was space on the bench behind the defendant's table on the left. The jurors were escorted to two rows of seats in a cordoned-off area to the right. A nearby door opened, and Lars Mallory was brought in. He looked at Connor, and his eyes widened for a moment. Then he gave Connor a grim nod in greeting. Connor returned the nod in kind.

The court resumed its session with the Honorable Vivian Kennedy presiding. Connor didn't know her at all, but her eyes came to rest on him after she sat down.

Lars Mallory's defense attorney stood up. The name Ryan Lynch appeared on Connor's internal heads-up display.

"Your Honor, Lars Mallory would like to address the court before sentencing, if you will allow it?" Ryan asked.

Vivian Kennedy's shrewd gaze flicked to Lars. "I will allow it, Mr. Mallory."

Ryan gestured for Lars to stand up.

"Thank you, Your Honor," Lars said. "I've had a lot of time to think about my actions. I'm guilty of all the charges. I also understand that this is a very difficult decision to make, for this case in particular. I've always wanted to protect the colony," he said and paused for a few seconds. "My friend, Noah, kept coming to see me these past few months. He was trying to help me. I know there are psychological evaluations out there that say I was manipulated by Meredith Cain, and I suppose I was. I allowed her to convince me to join her, but that doesn't excuse my actions. I'm prepared to take full responsibility, but I wanted the court to know that I regret the things I did. I regret hurting the Ovarrow. I wish I could change what I did, but I can't. That's all I wanted to say."

Lars remained standing, and the court officer called for all of them to rise.

"Mr. Mallory," Vivian Kennedy said, "your case *is* challenging because while you yourself weren't guilty of directly injuring or killing a colonial citizen, it was your actions that helped build an organization that *did* do those things. So, some of that responsibility does fall on your shoulders. Your actions directly influenced those events. You have served this colony with distinction in Field Ops and Security for a long time. In essence, you were trusted to perform a particular function in society, and the fact of the matter is that you abused that trust. You abused your power within the colony, and it is for our actions that we are judged. I recognize that your assistance helped root out the corruption among our leaders. However, in response to your actions, I have no choice but to sentence you to twenty years banishment from this colony, after which time you can petition to return. This sentence will be upheld immediately."

Court was dismissed. Lars looked up at the ceiling and then turned to look at his father, but he had trouble lifting his gaze. After a few seconds, he exhaled softly and raised his eyes. The only thing Connor could see in Lars's affect was resignation. Lars had to have expected this. He'd known that this court case could have no other outcome.

Connor took a few steps away so Franklin and Lars could speak quietly for several moments before Lars was taken away. More than once, Lars glanced in Connor's direction. He looked as if he had something to say but decided against it.

Connor wanted to say something to Lars too—some kind of platitude about staying strong—but he couldn't. Connor wished things could have been different. He shook the thought from his head, and Lars gave him a small nod.

Connor made a mental note to tell Noah what had happened here. He wanted Noah to hear what Lars had had to say—that he'd finally come to regret his actions against the Ovarrow. Noah had been successful in reaching his friend and had perhaps saved the parts of him that really mattered.

"I have to go," Lars said to his father.

Franklin's hand was on his son's shoulder. "I know," he said, reluctant to let go.

Lars reached up to grip his father's hand. "I'm sorry," he whispered in a voice that was little more than a rasp. "I'm sorry I put you through this, Dad."

The security agents shifted their feet. It was time for Lars to go.

Franklin's eyes became misty. "It's all right. It'll work out. You take care of yourself. You hear me? *You* take care of yourself, son."

Connor's throat became thick, and his eyes tightened as they escorted Lars away. The courtroom emptied, and Connor looked away as Franklin wiped the tears from his eyes.

Together they walked out of the courtroom and into the corridors beyond. More than a few people glanced in their direction, but no one said anything. They walked outside. The air was humid, if a little bit cool, but the skies were clear.

Franklin came to a stop and looked at Connor. "Thanks for coming today, Connor."

"Of course."

Franklin glanced back at the courthouse and grimaced. "I wish there was something I could do. I knew this was going to happen, but part of me also can't believe it's happening. Do you know what I mean?"

Connor nodded. He licked his lips and regarded Franklin for a few moments. "I know. I feel the same way. Are you going to be okay?"

"No," Franklin replied. "But I'll live."

———

Colonial news feeds circulated the outcome of Lars Mallory's trial, and banishment from the colony was met with general approval among the citizens.

There were colonists who still viewed the Ovarrow as something to be feared, while others sympathized with the trials they'd had to endure. Connor had his own biases where the Ovarrow were concerned, though his opinion of them had changed over the years, and he supposed that most colonists would just have to get used to the idea that they were here to stay. They would be part of New Earth's future, whether the colonists wanted it or not.

"Are we going to get into trouble?" Lenora asked.

"Are you scared?"

She snorted. "No . . . well, it has been a while since you've flown. I'd hate for us to have to test the escape system."

"You mean the ejector seat?" Connor asked dryly.

Lenora chuckled. "No, I believe it's called the egress system."

Connor laughed. "Now you're just showing off."

"What's this button do?"

He glanced at her in the seat next to him as she reached for the flight controls that would switch over to her.

"No—" Connor began, and she snatched her hand back into her lap, giggling.

They were in a CDF S7 Falcon Fighter. Designed only for atmospheric flight, the ship had a dark, sleek body with stub wings. They were part of the quick-response teams and provided air support for CDF ground forces.

"You should see the look on your face," Lenora said.

Connor's lips curled upward, and he banked hard to the right and then back to the left, straining the inertia compensators. He then executed an aileron roll maneuver, and the S7 spun. The landscape blurred with the open sky around them as pressure built up, and Lenora grunted. He eased up.

"Is that all you got?" she said.

He chuckled and effected another aerobatic maneuver. Lenora squealed in delight.

They were rapidly approaching Sierra, and Connor leveled off. They both were laughing, and she sighed. He'd sent his flight plan to the CDF base ahead of time.

Lenora checked their heading and looked at Connor. "What are you doing? The base is over there," she said, gesturing toward the left.

"I know," he replied and kept flying in the opposite direction.

They were flying over the main part of the city, and Connor activated the egress system. The canopy split down the middle, opening up, and the wind came rushing in. Then, the thrusters hidden in their seats activated, and they burst from the S7.

Lenora screamed for a few seconds, and he laughed. The thrusters continued to fire, leveling them off as they began to descend.

She glared at him. "You!" she said. Her eyes were wide as she looked up at the S7, which was flying away.

"Relax. It's on autopilot. It'll reach the LZ probably at the same time we'll be landing," Connor said and arched an eyebrow toward her. "You said you wanted to have some fun."

Lenora elbowed him hard. "Next time, *I'll* fly us to Sierra."

They touched down on one of the landing pads at Sierra Medical Center. Connor stood up and helped Lenora get to her feet. She began getting her windswept hair under control.

"I like the new look," Connor teased.

"Maybe I'll cut it all off and go high and tight like your haircut."

He tried to imagine it. For as long as he'd known her, she'd always had long hair that went down past her shoulders.

"Fine, then I'll grow a beard," he replied.

One of Lenora's pet peeves was that the stubble around his lips was too rough. Connor had jokingly told her that it was what made him irresistible, and she'd rolled her eyes.

They'd received notification yesterday that Dana Wolf had woken up, and the doctors had made a breakthrough in combating the virus she was afflicted with.

As they were about to enter the medical center, Lenora gestured behind them. The S7 seats were sitting on the landing pad. "Don't you need to do something about that?"

"Already done. There's a delivery drone coming to pick them up," Connor replied.

They entered the medical center and went to the level where Dana Wolf's room was.

Kayla Wolf spotted them and walked over.

"Dr. Bishop, it's so good to see you," Kayla said.

"Please, call me Lenora," she said and gave Kayla a hug.

"How's your mom doing?" Connor asked.

"The doctors think she's through the worst of it, but her recovery is going to be a long one," Kayla said.

Connor was a bit surprised to hear that. He'd thought that since they'd had a breakthrough for the virus, Dana Wolf's recovery would have been relatively quick. It must have been much worse than he'd originally thought.

"She'd love to see you," she said to Connor. Then she looked at Lenora. "Can I speak with you for a minute?"

"Of course," Lenora said. "Why don't we go grab a cup of coffee."

Connor watched them go for a few seconds, then knocked on the door to Dana's room and walked in. The head of the bed was raised, and she was almost in a sitting position. To say that she looked tired would have been an understatement. She looked bone-weary and weak, like she hadn't slept for months.

Dana smiled tiredly when she saw him. "Connor," she said. "Please, have a seat." Her eyes flicked toward the seat next to the bed.

He walked over and sat down. "How are you feeling?"

"Like I've been trampled by berwolves," Dana said and gave him a long look. "I suppose this is how you feel after one of those missions of yours."

Connor grinned. "Sometimes."

She smiled.

"Do you need anything? Can I get you some water?" he asked, gesturing toward the empty cup on the bedside table.

"No, thank you."

"Do the doctors have any idea where you contracted the virus?" Connor asked.

Dana blinked slowly and shook her head. "They don't know. They said it could have been dormant in my system for years."

He nodded. "I'm surprised Bob's not here giving you an update on what's been going on."

She looked at him, and Connor saw some of the strength she'd once had in her gaze. She was tired and maybe a bit beaten up, but it was still there. She was a strong woman. "Not this time."

He frowned. "What do you mean?"

"What I mean is that I won't be able to serve as governor anymore."

His mouth hung open, and his eyes widened. "What?" he asked, stunned.

Dana smiled a little. "You're stuck working with Bob Mullins, and I expect you two to behave yourselves."

Connor felt the edges of his lips curve upward and he chuckled. "No, it's not that. I just can't believe you're not coming back."

"I'm not dying, Connor. I just won't have the strength to . . . well, you know."

He did know. Being the governor of the colony required a high level of endurance and a great deal of patience. He had plenty of endurance, but it was the patience that ran in short supply sometimes.

"I'm sorry," he said. "I know what it meant to you."

Dana blinked her eyes slowly. She was likely getting tired again. "Thank you for coming to see me. But I need to sleep now."

Connor stood up. "Of course. I'm just a comlink away if you need anything."

"What I need is for you to continue to work with Bob. I know you two don't always see eye to eye, but it's important you get past that. The colony is depending on you both," she said and settled back onto her pillow, closing her eyes.

He walked out of the room, making as little noise as possible. Once he was outside, he inhaled deeply and sighed. The virus had been one of those random things, and he supposed it could have happened to any of them. He didn't think someone had made an attempt on Dana's life. He'd been suspicious at first, but sometimes events were a little too random to be suspicious. As much as he wasn't a fan of Mullins, the man was loyal to her and had been genuinely concerned when she'd become ill. Also, there had been an investigation, which had turned up nothing.

Connor glanced back at the door to Dana's room. Something like that could easily have happened to Lenora, and he was thankful it hadn't.

Lenora and Kayla walked up the corridor toward him.

"She's resting," Connor said. His gaze lingered on Lenora for a moment, his eyes tightening with concern. He didn't know why, but he just felt lucky —fortunate to be alive and lucky that the people he loved were healthy. He supposed that when it came right down to it, that was most important of all.

CHAPTER 36

As the months passed, Sadoon had been in regular contact with Aurang and his fifth column network. He'd been doubtful of the promises made by Aurang but was curious enough to meet with him after his failure to secure a project from the overseers. In that time, Sadoon had done some recruiting of his own, particularly from among the soldiers who had encountered the Humans. The soldiers that proved loyal would remain useful, and the ones that leaned toward the status quo had been eliminated. His Ovarrow test subjects seemed to become emboldened whenever they managed to catch a squad of Krake soldiers. It renewed their efforts to try to breach the arch gateway.

Hope among the Ovarrow was an interesting field of study that he had devoted nearly fifty years of his life to. A belief in hope was easy to manipulate. It had taken many years of fine-tuning to draw a belief in hope from even the most conditioned subjects, be they Ovarrow or Krake. Even now, Sadoon could feel it inside his own deepest desires.

Sadoon knew that Aurang was familiar with the use of hope as a primary motivator in getting what he needed. Sadoon had tried to find records about Aurang, but there was nothing—no record at all of his existence. He'd even gotten DNA samples to use as a search in their primary data repositories. Aurang was a ghost. He might have never existed until the moment he'd contacted Sadoon. Then, everything changed.

Evening had settled on this world, and the mock wars he'd orchestrated for testing the Ovarrow were eerily quiet. Sadoon didn't want to be here anymore. In his mind, he had already moved on, and he'd delegated a large portion of his work under the guise of giving other Krake a chance to prove themselves.

He accessed a secure messaging system, looking for a reply from Aurang.

The fifth column leader was due to contact him, and Sadoon had been growing anxious.

He stood up from his desk and walked toward the balcony. The doors were open, and an evening breeze blew in, but Sadoon hated the smells of this world. Of all the tactics the Ovarrow employed when fighting their wars, one of the most effective was that when they thought they were defeated, they'd inflict their wrath on the habitable world, making it as unlivable as possible. The Krake also employed such tactics, but Sadoon would need to research whether they had been the first. Were the Ovarrow merely copying what they'd learned from the Krake? Sadoon was almost sure of it. Their behavior was controlled and easy to manipulate—predictable, some Krake would say, and Sadoon had to agree.

He had a clear view of the landscape, but he knew he wasn't alone. "How did you get here?"

Aurang came out of his stealth field, seeming to materialize in front of him. "It's not as difficult as you think it is."

Sadoon considered this for a few moments. "I trust the resources I made available to you have been put to good use?"

"Indeed, they have, and I have news to share with you," Aurang said. "The Humans are moving much quicker than even I thought they would."

Sadoon frowned. "They're an active species, but what do you mean by moving? What have they done?"

"There's been a trend of experiments that are experiencing outlier events."

"Where?"

"Dozens of worlds," Aurang said and paused for a moment. "Well, potentially dozens of worlds. It depends on where we draw the line for qualifying a statistical anomaly."

"Can I see the data?"

"Of course," Aurang said. "I don't want there to be any secrets between us."

Sadoon didn't believe him. A data upload registered on his personal systems, and he opened a holoscreen and began peering through the data. "There are no clusters."

Aurang nodded in agreement. "It almost looks random, doesn't it?"

Sadoon's gaze flicked back toward the holoscreen for a moment. "They're probing."

"They're searching for Quadiri."

The fact that the Humans were searching for the Krake home world made perfect sense to Sadoon.

"But they're doing something else I hadn't anticipated," Aurang said. "They're recruiting allies. Wherever they are, their outlier behaviors have been affecting the predictive models, and we've seen an uptick in rebellious activity—almost as if they were being provided knowledge about us."

Sadoon considered this. "I know you don't want to hear this, but we must inform the overseers. They can't ignore this now."

Aurang looked away from him and took a few steps, seemingly to examine the room. "Not yet. There isn't enough information to garner the support of the overseers."

"Yes, there is. If they continue, they'll gain more allies against us."

Aurang shrugged as if it didn't matter. "The Ovarrow aren't a threat to us. They're tools we can use, and they're tools that the Humans *are* using. The more active the Humans are, the quicker we can identify their home system."

Sadoon began calculating probabilities in his mind. Data models and theorems were what he lived and breathed. But something he kept coming back to distracted him. "The risk—"

"It is necessary," Aurang said, cutting him off. "Remember, stagnation is our biggest enemy. And we've been stagnant long enough. The goal hasn't changed. Allow yourself to imagine, if you can . . ." he said, pausing for a moment, and Sadoon waited, ". . . a world without Prime Overseer Ersevin. Without any overseer, allowing the factions to pursue what they want."

Sadoon shook his head. "You speak of anarchy."

"I speak of freedom."

"Freedom is an idealistic ploy. We need structure. Otherwise, we're no better than the Ovarrow."

Aurang regarded him for a few moments, considering. "Then we're both right, and together we can find a solution that's better than what we have today. The Humans are key to this. Stagnation is the enemy."

Sadoon looked back at the reports on the holoscreen. If the Humans were instrumental in influencing the outliers they'd observed, then they were a shrewd species. He looked back at Aurang. "We need allies ourselves."

Aurang's feline eyes narrowed contentedly. "Now, you finally understand."

CHAPTER 37

When Lars left the courtroom, he'd thought he would immediately be brought to the transport ship to begin his banishment. Instead, he was taken back to his cell. No one had contacted him, and he wasn't allowed to contact anyone. He had more restrictions now than when he'd first arrived. After two days, someone had finally come for him.

"Mr. Mallory," the prison guard said, "your transport has arrived. I need you to turn around and put your hands on the wall."

Lars stood up and did as requested. He felt a device attach itself to his back, and he knew what it was. If he made any sudden movements, it would activate and release a shock, rendering him immobile. It was akin to the shock sticks used to enforce compliance.

"All right, follow me," the guard said.

Lars turned around and followed the guard. This was it. His banishment would begin today, and for the next twenty years, he'd be shut away on some island without the means to escape. He walked by the other cells, and their occupants stared at him as he passed.

Lars had heard the other prisoners talk about banishment and where they were heading. Some of them even thought they could build a craft that would take them away. He had no such illusions. Even if they somehow managed to escape the island and, even more unlikely, return to a colonial city, they'd be caught well before then. Each of them wore a personal tracker that was broadcasting their position at all times. Even if they could escape, there'd be no disabling the tracker. The other prisoners didn't like it when he told them that, but Lars didn't care. It was the truth, and sometimes the truth sucked.

Over the past two days, he'd gone over his court case in his mind, particularly Judge Vivian Kennedy's comments about him. She'd been right, and so had Noah. Lars had been stubborn. Noah had to all but push the truth in front of him, and even then, Lars had refused to acknowledge it for such a long time.

He walked down the long corridor, each step bringing him closer to the new life he sure as hell didn't want but probably deserved. He shook his head. No, he *did* deserve it. Noah and his father had questioned him thoroughly about how Meredith Cain had recruited him. They'd been looking for a way to bolster his defense, but there wasn't any *one* thing Meredith had done or said; it had been lots of little things that just seemed to feed off his own frustration and fear—fear of what the Krake would do when they came here. Lars had risked everything to try to find a way to prevent that from happening.

He had to push those thoughts from his mind. Sometimes it did no good to dwell on his regrets. That's what he'd been told anyway. He'd have plenty of time to think about them later.

He was brought to a holding area where other prisoners were joining them. He recognized most of them because he'd recruited many of them, but not all. There were more than thirty prisoners in the holding area, and they were instructed to go through an outside door where a Field Ops and Security troop carrier waited for them. They climbed aboard and sat down. There were six security agents in the passenger area, armed with suppressors and shock sticks. The suppressor could release a field of energy that would immobilize anyone who was stupid enough to attack them. Lars glanced around at the others, and all he saw was mostly resignation. None of them looked like they wanted to attack the security agents.

There were several wallscreens that showed a video of the outside, but once they took off, the wallscreens powered down. The pilot accessed the intercom and informed them that they had a six-hour flight ahead of them. That was all the information they were given. Lars knew there had been several sites selected for banishment. They'd be given tools to use for their survival and some supplies. After that, they were expected to provide for themselves—grow their own food and build their own shelters. They'd be monitored from afar. If they wanted to live, they'd do the work. It had been made apparent to the prisoners in no uncertain terms that no type of colonial aid would come for them should they neglect to care for themselves.

Lars leaned back in his chair, closed his eyes, and went to sleep. The slight rocking of the transport carrier settled into a familiar rhythm, and then it was gone altogether while he slumbered.

The hours went by as he dozed somewhere between sleep and awareness of his surroundings. He heard snippets of hushed conversations, but mostly everyone was quiet. Eventually, he felt the troop carrier change its altitude. Wherever they were being taken, they'd be arriving soon.

Lars sat up, rubbing the sleep from his eyes and stretching a little bit. He heard the landing gear deploy, and soon the troop carrier landed. An alarm blared for a moment, and then the rear loading ramp opened.

He peered outside. There was a rolling tundra that was almost blinding in the middle of the day.

"This is your stop. Get up and exit out the back," one of the security agents said.

A few of the other guards repeated the same message, and Lars stood up. He walked to the loading ramp and descended, stepping onto the ground. Over to his right were twenty CDF soldiers.

He heard the dopplered wail of another troop carrier approaching, and it came to a landing nearby. Lars and the others looked over and saw that there were more prisoners being off-loaded.

"Eyes front," the security agent said.

Lars looked over at him and saw a tall man with a few days' worth of stubble on his chin. There was a hardened glint to his gaze—the glint of someone who'd been in the thick of it. He had CDF captain's bars on his shoulders.

The CDF captain gestured toward the other carrier. "Sergeant, bring those prisoners over here."

A group of CDF soldiers went to the other troop carrier and began yelling for the prisoners to come over to them. Less than a minute later, nearly a hundred prisoners were clustered in a group.

"Prisoners, I'm Captain Flint, the CO of the 3rd Ranger Company of the Colonial Defense Force. I've been ordered to see whether any of you are worth redemption," he said, and his steely-eyed gaze settled on Lars momentarily before moving on. He was quiet for several seconds, and Lars heard a few of the other prisoners begin speaking.

"First off," Captain Flint said, and the prisoners became quiet, "any one of you who wants to climb back aboard this troop carrier can do so right here, right now, and you'll be taken to your designated banishment site to serve out your term."

Lars watched some of the prisoners glance at the troop carriers with interest, but most waited for Captain Flint to continue.

"That's right. No one is forcing you to do a damn thing. You can be equally as useless in your banishment. I'm told that many of you joined your misguided group because you thought you could do a better job protecting the colony than the CDF. Better than me," Captain Flint said with bitter amusement. "I recognize some of you who used to be in the CDF. What the hell happened to you?" he asked. Then, holding up one of his hands, he said, "Never mind, I don't care. This isn't about your feelings. What I'm offering you is a chance at redemption—not because I think you deserve it, but because I've been ordered to do so. I'm to evaluate the lot of you. Some of you, maybe most of you, are wondering why you should consider this. You've received your sentencing, and you've been convicted. However, if you make the cut and serve your term of enlistment, the CDF will petition on your behalf for a pardon of your past crimes."

Lars's eyes widened, and he felt his pulse quicken in his chest.

"I personally guarantee that this will not be easy or safe," Captain Flint continued. "Many of you will fail. If you're former CDF, I'm going to be twice as hard on you as everyone else because you should have known better. It's my job to pick the best from you. If you make it through, you'll get to experience the most dangerous missions, the ones with the lowest probability of success. Chances are you won't survive, even if you make the cut." He paused for a moment. "You guys wanted to 'protect the colony.' That was your reason for joining the rogue group. Well, here's your chance to make good on that promise. If you agree to this, just walk right over to the CDF troop carrier behind me, and you'll be taken to a particular training ground that has been established just for this mission."

"Where?" someone asked.

Captain Flint smiled widely, showing a healthy set of pearly white teeth standing in stark contrast to his rugged exterior. "Oh, it's nowhere around here. I guarantee it's not anyplace you've ever seen."

Lars believed him. He exhaled explosively and marched toward the CDF troop carrier. He didn't even look back, and the CDF soldiers he passed along his trek scowled in his direction. He ignored them. He didn't want to waste away banished to some island. He'd always only wanted to protect the colony. He still did, and maybe, just maybe, redemption could be his.

A CDF sergeant waited inside the troop carrier. He eyed Lars, seemingly impassive but calculating just the same. He jerked his chin to the side, and Lars sat down in an open seat. More prisoners climbed aboard, but not all of them. Lars glanced toward the loading ramp, expecting to see more people. He scanned the others and guessed that about half of the prisoners had decided to come, perhaps fifty of them. He'd expected more, and he gritted his teeth a little. Did the others hate the colony now?

He heard the Field Ops prisoner transport ships engage their engines. That was it. The rest of the prisoners had made their choice. They'd rather rot away on an island, bitter at the fact that they couldn't return to the colony. How did they think they'd feel after the terms of their banishment had been served? Would they choose to return, or would they be so far gone that rejoining the colony would never happen?

"Idiots," a man grumbled next to him and shifted in his seat.

Lars didn't recognize him.

"We're heading to the shit now."

"It beats fishing and gardening on an island," Lars replied.

The man grinned a little. "Maybe," he said.

"If you think that, then why did you come?"

"Because I didn't travel sixty light-years to sit on my ass doing nothing."

"We'll get it shot off instead," said another man sitting across from them. He was younger, but not so young as to not know any better. "Derrik," he said and looked at them expectantly.

"Lars."

"Oh boy," the first man said and shook his head. "I thought I recognized you."

"That's me. I'm famous," Lars said, deadpanning.

The loading ramp retracted into the carrier, and the rear doors closed.

Derrik cleared his throat. "If you don't tell us your name, I'll just make one up for you."

"You could try it, but you wouldn't like it. Orin Toshi."

Lars remembered the name from various reports but had never met him. The CDF troop carrier lifted off.

"Where do you think they're taking us?" Derrik asked.

"Does it really matter?" Orin replied.

Derrik leaned back and shook his head. "I was just wondering is all."

Any reply Orin might have made fell silent as Captain Flint walked toward them.

"You're a chatty bunch," Flint said.

They were silent for a few moments, and Flint stood rooted in place.

"I was just wondering where we were going, sir," Derrik said.

Flint nodded and then turned toward Orin. "Toshi, I'm surprised you didn't scurry off to that island with the rest of the deviants."

Orin clenched his teeth and looked away. Flint waited briefly and grunted. Then he turned toward Lars.

"Mallory," Flint said.

Lars expected the CDF captain to make a snide comment or otherwise assert himself, but he didn't. He didn't need to, just like Lars chose not to present a false sense of bravado. He was here, and that's all there was to it.

An hour later, Lars felt himself lift upward as the CDF troop carrier performed a rapid descent. He looked at Captain Flint, who smirked at them. "Time to find out what you're worth," he said.

Lars felt his cheeks burn. The CDF captain's words bit into his chest and sank heavily to his gut. The words stung, and he hated how he'd let it show. He looked at Captain Flint, but the contest was over. He'd blinked first, and the CDF captain knew it.

The landing gear deployed, and the troop carrier touched down. After the rear doors opened, they were ushered off.

Derrik craned his neck, trying to peer past the others to the outside. Orin growled a few incoherent words and glared at Lars for a moment before walking ahead.

Lars walked down the loading ramp and slowed. Twenty meters away was an arch gateway. The metallic alloy gleamed in the afternoon sunlight, but in the middle of the gateway was a deep, dark, gray nothingness. The prisoners had stopped just a short distance away from the troop carrier.

Lars saw Captain Flint off to the side. He watched them all with a tight mouth while he waited. Lars strode through the throng of prisoners.

"I told you that you've never been where we're taking you," Flint said.

The center of the arch gateway shimmered, and Lars could see a hazy view of the other side. It was like trying to peer through ripples of water streaming over a window. He couldn't be sure what was on the other side of the gateway, and it didn't matter. Lars strode toward it. He was either going to appear the fool, or his next steps would carry him away—away from his past and the things he'd done. He'd never be entirely free of either. That wasn't how it worked. But as he closed in on the threshold of the gateway, he quickened his pace to a run, eager to get on with it, eager to matter. But above all else, he wanted to be away from here.

AUTHOR NOTE

Thank you for reading this First Colony Omnibus for Books 8 - 10. I genuinely hope you enjoyed it and the rest of the books in the series. Telling Connor's story has been a privilege, along with all the other characters in this series. Do you have a favorite character? I'd love to hear who it is.

These days it seems like everyone is asking for a review for anything and everything. I get review requests when I go to stores, visit the doctor's office, and even the dentist. Enter for your chance to win...I bet you can guess what's coming next. I'd like for you to leave a review for this book. I know. *Not another one!* I get it, but they are essential to help spread the word about the book to other readers. Your reviews also help Amazon decide whether to show my books to other readers. I also read all my reviews. Every single one of them. I don't respond to them, but I definitely read them all. If you've reviewed my other books, please accept my thanks and consider writing another one. If you don't want to leave a review, then don't worry about it. I get it. Telling a friend who might like the book also helps a lot.

Again, thank you for reading one of my books. I'm so grateful that I get to write these stories.

ABOUT THE AUTHOR

I've written multiple science fiction and fantasy series. Books have been my way to escape everyday life since I was a teenager to my current ripe old(?) age. What started out as a love of stories has turned into a full-blown passion for writing them.

Overall, I'm just a fan of really good stories regardless of genre. I love the heroic tales, redemption stories, the last stand, or just a good old fashion adventure. Those are the types of stories I like to write. Stories with rich and interesting characters and then I put them into dangerous and sometimes morally gray situations.

My ultimate intent for writing stories is to provide fun escapism for readers. I write stories that I would like to read, and I hope you enjoy them as well.

If you have questions or comments about any of my works I would love to hear from you, even if it's only to drop by to say hello at KenLozito.com

Thanks again for reading.

Don't be shy about emails, I love getting them, and try to respond to everyone.

www.ingramcontent.com/pod-product-compliance
Lightning Source LLC
Chambersburg PA
CBHW030920020726
47498CB00001B/47